P9-CDN-693

Hearken unto the Voice

Other Works by Franz Werfel

THE ETERNAL ROAD

THE FORTY DAYS OF MUSA DAGH

THE PASCARELLA FAMILY

THE PURE IN HEART

TWILIGHT OF A WORLD

VERDI: A NOVEL OF THE OPERA

Hearken unto the Voice

FRANZ WERFEL

TRANSLATED BY MORAY FIRTH

THE VIKING PRESS · NEW YORK

1938

PUBLISHED IN FEBRUARY 1938

PRINTED IN U. S. A. BY THE HADDON CRAFTSMEN, INC.

Contents

CONTENTS

Hearken unto the Voice

1

Conversation by the Dead Sea

CLAYTON REEVES was silent, tensely and obstinately silent, as he listened to the others talking in a light tone of a weighty theme.

In the limp and pensive ease of early afternoon, they were sitting on the terrace of an inn drinking their coffee. The terrace was built far out over the water, if the blackish, viscous, unbreathing liquid could be called water. The indeterminate element of the Dead Sea—no longer wholly liquid and not yet solid—spread out sluggishly to where the easterly rays of a weak sun presented a varying spectacle as they struggled to pierce their vaporous envelope. Towards the south the distance seemed illimitable and hurt the eyes, but to the east and west the gaze could linger on the mountain ranges that hemmed in the asphalt lake. Were they actually mountains or were they petrified clouds, crystallized vapour from the boiling streams that poured into the basin of Sodom and Gomorrah? The hills in the foreground did possess a certain reality and seemed to be anchored in this earth which was so different from the earth elsewhere, a difference and uniqueness that oppressed the five people on the terrace and inevitably coloured their conversation. As the rocks of Moab receded farther and farther into the intangible distance, however, they were divested more and more of their mountainous quality. Translucent fortresses of smoky topaz, jewelled towers, crowned the eastern shore—ghostly formations of glass flux, salt, and unknown substances, shining in tones of bottle-green, violet, and light aquamarine. It was as though the mountains were endowed with all these enchanting colours through some process other than the refraction of light, as if their inmost nature consisted of jewel and crystal.

To travelled Englishmen who had experienced a variety of climates besides this, which played at being tropical but lacked the fierceness of the real thing, the mild warmth was very pleasant. It was delightful to sit here for an hour on the terrace after lunch, enjoying the open air and giving no thought to the future. Behind them stretched the narrow level plain of the Dead Sea with its stunted, thorny shrubs and low *sidr*-trees, covered with a thick rime of gypsum and gleaming crystals of salt, and immediately beyond this desiccated frill were the fertile meadows of Jordan, the luxuriant estuary of the sacred stream, a friendly wilderness of green-scummed swamp and pool, filled with reeds and osier thickets and clouded with shining poplars round which birds continually circled. Here they had visited, a short time before, the celebrated ford at which Jesus is said to have been baptized by John the Baptist. A number of Greek pilgrims, garbed in white shrouds, had just arrived in an omnibus for the purpose of immersing themselves according to consecrated custom in the swiftly flowing Jordan. The women, with serious and apprehensive gaze, knelt down by the bank and filled with the yellowish water of baptism the tin receptacles they had brought. Burton, an archæologist engaged on the excavations at Jericho, had pointed silently to the tin cans, which all bore the inscription "Vacuum Oil." Dorothy Cowell had acknowledged the tremendous antithesis, which linked and divorced the ages, by a fleeting smile.

The conversation was broken intermittently by sudden pauses. A perceptible silence, resembling no other silence in the world, closed over the discussion as it died away, like water over a sinking stone. Surrounded as it was by transparent, spectral mountains, the place seemed to be shut out from the eternal tidal roar of the universe, listening for the voice which is elsewhere submerged. The workmen at the asphalt lake were taking their noonday rest. When a throaty human voice penetrated from the distance, it was as if the heavy, expectant surface of the Dead Sea shuddered beneath its apparent indifference. Some leagues away lay the beautiful oasis of Jericho with its groves of lemons, oranges, and grapefruit, its life-giving springs, its accumulation of shards from the remote past (which Burton was engaged in excavating), its Arab huts of clay, and its hotels with their high-sounding names. The sweet enveloping fragrance of flowers that was exhaled by the oasis was wafted even as far as this. From time to time, however, the air grew noticeably heavier, as though it were coagulating into a jelly-like substance which had to be bitten off rather than breathed. This sudden heaviness of the air was all that reminded them that they were sitting in one of the deepest hollows of the earth, more than thirteen hundred feet below the level of the sea.

". . . The centre of the world . . ."

The five companions—four men and a woman—detached their gaze in surprise from the jewelled mountains of the Dead Sea and looked at one another as though the words had been spoken not by one of themselves, but by a tranquil and solemn voice from outside their circle. Dorothy Cowell lay in a deckchair, a little to the side. The men had pushed their chairs away from the table, which was covered with half-emptied carafes, glasses, and cups. They were all wearing smoked spectacles with the exception of Clayton Reeves, who was very near-sighted and wore thick lenses to aid his long-lashed eyes. He sat in stubborn silence, and this together with his myopia set him apart from the others and made him seem shy. Neither Cartwright nor Burton nor Major Shepston broke in upon his silence in any way. Only Dorothy Cowell looked across at him from time to time. She probably felt a sense of responsibility, having introduced the young writer to the three other men some days before, and it was at her suggestion in the lounge of the King David Hotel that they had made this excursion together to the Dead Sea. Perhaps she had thought that Reeves might be taken out of himself by a trip in the company of these unusual men. The day had turned out well. They were now resting amid this almost unearthly landscape as if they were enchanted in the depths of a mysterious crater, and the feeling that overwhelmed them had found its groping expression in the words, "the centre of the world." Professor Cartwright, who was the oldest of them, pushed back from his forehead the sun-helmet which he wore because of his complete baldness, then he said:

"Wherever true religion has its cradle, there you will find a centre of the world. In Benares, for example, one has a similar feeling. . . ."

Cartwright broke off abruptly, and a shadow passed over his colourless face as he sought for a more apposite explanation. He, more than anyone else, possessed the right to talk about such matters. He was returning to London from India after years of research at various institutes of Sanskrit studies.

"My comparison is not quite accurate," he amended. "Cults and philosophies, pandemonia of all kinds, have originated everywhere. But religion in the most exact sense arose only here, in this small country . . . and that is why it is most probably the divinely ordained centre of the world. . . ."

Major Shepston, the lean little man who was sitting next to Cartwright, crinkled his tanned face into a hundred lines. "One thing is certain, at any rate," he suggested thoughtfully. "The biblical God of this little country was victorious over all the other gods in the world . . . in Christendom and Islam . . . for the time being, at least. . . ."

"There's no need to worry," laughed Burton. "No unknown God is lying dormant, of that I am sure, either in this enlightened generation or in the next three. . . ."

Major Shepston suddenly looked very embarrassed, as if he had been disagreeably affected by his own comment, into which he had been betrayed by the remark concerning the centre of the world. After a time he added, as though in excuse:

"When a man has lived in this country as long as I have, you know . . ." Shepston had been living and working in Palestine for more than ten years. He was attached in an official capacity to the High Commissioner, knew every corner between Hermon and the Sinai Desert, and loved it all so much that he had already twice refused to leave it to accept promotion. His tanned face, with its dried-up skin and clipped grey moustache, made him look older than he was. The archæologist Burton, on the other hand, looked far younger than his years. His powerful body was topped by a round baby face which wore a perpetual look of surprise and whose only sign of anything like the weathering of age was a multitude of bleached freckles that resembled pock-marks. His high-pitched voice was inclined to be slightly solemn.

"It is true," he admitted, "that I have not yet spent ten years in this country, but at any rate I have been here for over ten months. And I still feel the same about it as I did on the first day. When one sees these ancient places, with their familiar, sacred names . . . it gives one an incomparable thrill. . . . I'm not a novice and I've been digging for years in Greece and Egypt. . . . The earth here is not so luxuriant, so communicative, as it is there. It is taciturn, almost dumb; it preserves its secrets. The smallest discovery sets one's heart beating . . . perhaps that is where the difference lies. It is the difference between Homer and the Bible . . ." And he concluded with a boyish dreaminess: "Or, if you like, the difference between one's schooldays and one's childhood."

"Homer and the Bible, schooldays and childhood! You don't put it at all badly, you treasure-hunter," growled Shepston amiably. "If a boy in this enlightened age can still identify the Bible with his childhood, what must be the emotions inspired in those of more advanced years who were brought up in the Puritan tradition? There's a good story I could tell you in that connexion. But it's about the War, and when other people tell stories about the War I generally get up and go. . . ."

Professor Cartwright quietly encouraged him. When he spoke his thin lips scarcely moved:

"None of us imagines that you are going to recount an heroic adventure, Shepston. . . ."

"It is not even a story," the major declared disparagingly, "but only a bare relation of fact, and there's no particular point to it. Yet it made a certain impression on me. It concerns General Allenby. I was here in Palestine during the War, and when our army made its big advance I was attached to Headquarters as aide-de-camp. The Fourth Turkish Army had taken up strong positions in the Plain of Jezreel on the

Megiddo-Affule line, and the night before our big attack we were billeted in the hamlet of Jenin. I think you all saw the place on your journey to Nazareth. About two o'clock in the morning the general sent to have me wakened. It was a weakness of his to like chatting to me now and then. This time, of course, I thought that he wished to give me official instructions—zero hour was fixed for five a.m.—and I got into field kit. . . ."

Dorothy Cowell's laughing voice echoed across from her deckchair:

"So it is at least a gallant ride that you are going to tell us about, after all!"

"Quite to the contrary, Miss Cowell," Shepston assured her brusquely. "It is true that the general was sitting bent over a map, but it was not the big General Staff map on which our positions were marked. It was an atlas of biblical Palestine. And the only things on his large table which he appeared to have been consulting were two copies of the Holy Scriptures. Allenby sat alone in a bare and wretched room in an Arab house. He asked me to keep him company for a little while, since he could not sleep with all the thoughts that were going round in his head, and I waited expectantly to hear something of the worries which were torturing the mind of the general in command during the night before the decisive action. The situation was not very encouraging. We had a march through the desert behind us, weeks of privation and heavy losses. Our artillery was alarmingly weak, and during the previous months that of the enemy had been considerably reinforced by German and Austrian batteries. On the following day the Suez Canal would be at stake, perhaps the whole Empire. But of all these burning questions on the eve of the great decision not a word passed the lips of General Allenby. He began instead to interrogate me in his slow, severe way. 'Tell me, my dear fellow, how often do Megiddo and the Plain of Jezreel occur in the wars of the Bible? What do you know about it?' My knowledge of the subject was nil, and I reported in that sense to the general with the requisite appearance of contrition, thus giving the old man the opportunity he was looking for to start a lecture. If I am not mistaken, the Old Testament tells of five or six battles that took place on the very plain where we were about to begin our attack, and it was of these biblical encounters only that Allenby spoke. He did not even mention Napoleon's victory on Mount Tabor, though that is used as a notable strategic model in all the military academies. One individual and one battle in particular seemed to exercise a special fascination for him on that memorable night, perhaps for the very reason that the issue of the battle was disastrous. You are an historian, Burton, so perhaps you can help me! What was the name of that biblical king who launched his little army against the mighty hosts of Egypt at Megiddo?"

"King Josiah," replied the archæologist indulgently. "He was the one in whose reign the prophet Jeremiah began his activities."

"Yes, that's right, King Josiah!" Shepston had worked himself into a state of impatience. "You see, it really is only a bare relation of fact without any particular point. It is only that the general in command of a British army, shortly before one of the most important actions of the Great War, turned his thoughts not to the hazards of the morrow but to the Bible. Perhaps he was only seeking distraction by this means, or he might have been hiding the predominating thoughts on which his mind was still intent. It is more probable, however, that Allenby was seeking in the Bible, which for him was the Word of God and whose history was sacred history, for a situation similar to his own from which to draw fortitude and consolation whatever might betide."

Burton smiled with all the freckles of his baby face.

"So after more than three thousand years Great Britain won the eighth or ninth battle of Megiddo. A pretty respectable tradition!"

"One might draw further conclusions from Shepston's pointless story," interjected Cartwright in his deliberate way, without moving his lips. "General Allenby, with his faith in the Bible, achieved a very legitimate purpose by conquering Palestine, since the English people, as you know, trace their mythical descent from the ten lost tribes of Israel."

At these words Dorothy Cowell rose from her chair. She was a young woman, not yet thirty, and in spite of her disillusioning profession as a journalist—she was very well known in the corridors of the League of Nations at Geneva—she was remarkably handsome. Her black hair, which had a narrow grey streak in it, formed an attractive contrast to the large blue eyes that could light up on occasion with fiery animation. These eyes rested for a second with concealed anxiety on Clayton Reeves, whose short-sighted countenance was turned towards the speakers as he listened to the conversation in which he took no part. His tense and stiff attitude had lost nothing of its absorption, yet he seemed suddenly to have given way to an inward despair which he was struggling to overcome. Dorothy noticed this, and she thought that she knew the reason for the abrupt change in him. The thought of the tragedy that he had experienced a few months before had probably got the better of him again.

She stepped between him and Burton, presumably to help

her protégé and encourage him to join in the discussion.

"The lost tribes . . ." she repeated in her melodious voice, and then paused for a moment. "If you would like accurate information about the various Committees of Eighteen, Committees of Twelve, or Committees of Five in Geneva, I shall not disappoint you. But so far as ancient history is concerned I am much less at home. Mr. Reeves here, who is intolerably learned, will confirm my words."

Reeves did not even raise his eyes to Dorothy, whose somewhat exaggerated cheerfulness had not driven away the shadows from his mind. Burton, however, stood up, took her by the arm, escorted her two or three paces away from the shore, and pointed in the direction of the Jordan meadows, which were enveloped in a delicate and hazy radiance:

"Look there! Do you remember the place of baptism, where we met the Greek pilgrims?"

"I can still see those dreadful modern petrol tins," said Dorothy, blinking, "which they were filling with holy water."

Burton continued, his voice high-pitched and solemn:

"A hopeful symbol for us, who are all dreadful modern receptacles and yet capable of being filled with that which is holy. . . ." The zealous historian was now in full swing. The baby face on the gigantic body began to glow. His hand pointed in the direction of Jericho, where, more than thirty-three centuries before, a number of insignificant nomad tribes had crossed the Jordan to take possession of their promised land. Dorothy Cowell suddenly found herself listening to an enthusiastic lecture, depicting the way in which Palestine had presumably been conquered by that strange nomad race. Poor and ill-armed hordes had succeeded in overcoming and assimilating a native population which in every way was superior to them a hundredfold. True, they had brought with them something so tremendous that human history has known nothing like it either before or since—a unique God of Creation, who had created them and was Himself created by them. Burton's narrative was adorned with quotations from the Old Testament and Egyptian inscriptions, but before he could finish, Dorothy gave vent to a sigh of irritation:

"Historians look down on us journalists with contempt. But I can tell you, Burton, if any of us were to send in a report about a contemporary event packed with such detail as you've been giving me, there isn't a newspaper that would print it."

"You forget," Burton retorted, "that we have less right to lie than you have."

"Yet science has the inestimable advantage of being able to tell lies that are not subject to control and cannot be disproved."

The victory was with Dorothy Cowell and she had the last word, but with the obstinacy of all independent and rather domineering women she stuck to her point:

"Well, that's that. But I still don't know why the Anglo-Saxons trace their descent back to the lost tribes."

Professor Cartwright intervened with a weighing of arguments:

"The Romans derived their origin from the Trojans on grounds that were no more justifiable. It is a myth like many others, but behind every myth there is something. . . ."

"Of course there is something," complained Dorothy. "We have been sitting now for several hours on the shores of this magnificent Dead Sea and we are still talking about the same things, as though our own bitter problems did not exist. And my day's work is not yet over, for Clayton Reeves has invited me to inspect the site of the Temple under his guidance. . . .

It seems to me that you are all obsessed by this Holy Land!"

"That's true! Dorothy is right," said the archæologist, as he dropped heavily into his chair. "It is often a veritable case of *déjà vu.*"

A sudden thudding noise interrupted him, and they all looked round to see where it came from. It was the silent listener, Reeves, knocking out his pipe, and he answered the questioning gaze of Dorothy with a slight smile that seemed to mean: "Please don't take any notice. It's nothing!" His forehead shone damply and his black hair, which grew low down in front in a queer triangle, had become untidy. In contrast to the other men, who were dressed in light suits, he wore dark blue, with a mourning band on his left sleeve which had slipped down over the elbow, making him look awkward but at the same time pathetic. The attention which he had attracted to himself seemed to increase his uneasiness still further, and as he lowered his head a little his eyebrows formed a straight ridge.

"You used the expression *déjà vu,*" said Cartwright, bringing the short silence to an end. At last he took off the sun-helmet which had been bothering him for some time and placed it on his knee, and it could then be seen that his skull really was completely hairless from the forehead to the back of the neck. His eyebrows, which existed only as bare welts, had been painted in with two finely drawn lines, and he resembled certain statues of Egyptian priests.

"My dear Burton," he continued, his lips moving almost imperceptibly, "you were speaking of the mysterious but short-lived sensation which comes over us now and then when a particular moment or a particular situation appears to be a repetition of something that has already happened to us in the past. For a moment time is eliminated, the chronology of the world destroyed, and therein lies the confusing, even frightening aspect of the experience which has been designated by the unsympathetic term *déjà vu.* There are numerous so-called psychological explanations for this phenomenon, but I have enjoyed the distinction of being permitted to discuss it with a very wise man of the East. I wonder if you have ever come across the word *akâsha*?"

Burton pushed his spectacles onto his brow and screwed up his eyes in deprecation.

"*Akâsha*? That smacks strongly of theosophy!"

"Quite correct, Mr. Burton. The theosophists have a special preference for the Vedic writings. And *akâsha* is an almost untranslatable term which appears in the Vedas. My very wise friend, during our unforgettable discussion, defined it as a mind-stuff, as an expansion of the primal emanation, which issues directly from the creative godhead and condenses in accordance with cosmic law into more and more compressed states—from a ray of light, for instance, to a hydrogen atom, and then to a solid. Tradition tells us that it is a suprasensual substance which is uncounted æons earlier, older, and nearer to God than light. My friend, who has had by the way a thorough scientific training, employed the term 'picture-ether' or 'phenomenon-ether.' "

Here Cartwright hesitated. The eyes of the others were fixed intently on the bald head with the painted eyebrows. The objective, almost mathematical calm with which he spoke acted like a spell. Only Clayton Reeves kept his face averted, with a tormented twist of the neck—the first time since they had begun to talk. Perhaps Cartwright wished to rebuke him for his resistance, for he added:

"You will soon see what I am driving at!"

" 'Picture-ether,' " Major Shepston repeated, almost with

a groan. The term seemed to cause him some difficulty and to fill him with unease.

"All these words," Cartwright admitted, "are of course only inadequate circumlocutions whose purpose is to bring the inconceivable within the scope of the imagination. For example, we can quite easily imagine that a ray of light, on its precipitous journey from star to star, immortalizes or renders timeless the pictures and happenings which it carries with it. We cannot, however, imagine the suprasensual substance *akâsha*, since *akâsha* is Pre-Light, Primal Light. According to my friend's teaching, in some incomprehensible way, *akâsha* contains in each of its particles, simultaneously and pervading the whole of space, all the phenomena and happenings of the cosmos. If one could make up one's mind to employ lame comparisons, one might speak of a mysterious film archive or a complete photographic montage, of an all-embracing chronicle, a cosmic protocol, of the universal mind projecting its memories into the present. Since *akâsha* pervades everything far more even than light can do, it pervades us too. Even our personal memories exist only by virtue of *akâsha*. Without *âkasha* there would be no urge to write history. That which you call *déjà vu*, my dear Burton, is explained by my friend in the East as a sudden condensation of *akâsha*, which is trying in vain to come to consciousness within our minds."

"I once read a book," said Dorothy Cowell with half-closed eyes, "that was called *An Adventure.*" She paused for a moment, but as no one seemed to have heard of the book she mentioned, she ventured to continue: "It was written by two Englishwomen. One of them was a certain Anne Moberley. The name of the other I have forgotten. I imagine them as being two elderly ladies of strict upbringing, prosaic, energetic, beyond any suspicion of hysteria or vague mysticism. In a dry and documentary style they describe a walk they once took through the park of Versailles when, without any warning, they suddenly came upon a group of courtiers playing at being shepherds and shepherdesses. The incident occurred, I believe, on a spring day in the year 1905. The company of courtiers, dressed like rococo shepherds, seemed thoroughly substantial; there was nothing ghostly about the way they behaved; on the contrary, they chatted and joked with liveliness and unconcern. There was nothing to indicate that the whole thing was a phantom, although undoubtedly it could have been nothing else, and everything was clear to the smallest detail. The two estimable ladies saw every button, every clasp, every buckle in the commonplace light of day; they distinguished individual faces, they described the appearance and position of buildings which had long since vanished and had suddenly become visible again; for example, the famous cowshed of Marie Antoinette. The details of their story were investigated by experts. Everything was correct to the yard and to the inch. And, strange to say, the astounding adventure was repeated when the Englishwomen next visited the park. The book attracted considerable attention. I don't know whether you think, Mr. Cartwright, that this true ghost story has any bearing on what you have been telling us. . . ."

"The name of the other author was Eleanor Jourdain," Professor Cartwright informed her in a gentle voice. "Thank you, Miss Cowell. Your ghost story is very apt. You must know that there are places which are saturated with history, which are centres of the world. In these places *akâsha* collects, the mysterious 'picture-ether' which retains the chronicle of what has happened. That which has been pervades that which is and unites with it, ready to emerge into consciousness again at a given moment. Perhaps that is the explanation of our conversation today by the Dead Sea, for nowhere is the present so profoundly pervaded by the past as here."

Major Shepston cupped his tanned face gloomily in both hands, as he said:

"Then this world must be full of its dead. To think that by abusing this chronicle of yours man might one day be able systematically to conjure up the dead! . . . Dreadful! . . . Dreadful! . . ."

Burton suddenly broke in with a high-pitched cry:

"I say, just look over there!"

He had jumped up, had swivelled round, and was pointing into the distance with outstretched arm. As the sun moved farther across the heavens, the scene had undergone an impressive transformation. The mountains of the Dead Sea were blotted out. No longer did bastions of crystal and jewelled towers sparkle from afar, but instead slaty shadows mirrored their unutterable melancholy in the waters of divine punishment. All the light was focused over a bleak, fissured, conical peak that rose to the north-west of the oasis of Jericho. The sun stood right above its summit and transmuted the substance of the rock into a supernatural intangible fabric veiled in soft grey with purple folds. It was as if some mysterious ether, similar to *akâsha*, had permeated the stone and dematerialized it.

"Look at Mount Quarantana," said Burton slowly, "the mount of temptation where, after Christ had fasted for forty days, Satan tempted Him."

They all looked and were silent. Perhaps they were afraid that one of them might say something discordant. But the stillness was broken by a harsh voice that could hardly master its brusque impatience.

"I think we had better be going, Dorothy, if we are to get back to Jerusalem in time!"

Clayton Reeves had spoken at last. All at once the others too were in a hurry to go. Major Shepston called the waiter and then they walked across the salt-strewn shore of the Dead Sea to the waiting car. Dorothy Cowell and Clayton Reeves kept a couple of paces behind.

"What on earth is the matter with you today?" she demanded.

"Nothing," he replied.

"Did you find our conversation so disturbing?"

"Yes," he said.

She looked at him intently.

"You are a very difficult person. . . ."

2

A Journey to Jerusalem

MAJOR SHEPSTON owned a fairly roomy car, but, as his right arm had never wholly recovered from a wound received in the War, he could not drive himself. Before starting out that morning Clayton Reeves had expressed a wish to sit in front next to the driver, and on the return journey he again took the same seat without asking. Dorothy Cowell, Cartwright, Burton, and the major were therefore able to talk about him, as he sat separated from them by a pane of glass, without fearing that they might be overheard. It is doubtful, however, whether Reeves would have heard them even if he had been sitting in their midst. His tortured soul was lost in a confused soliloquy. The three other men knew virtually nothing about him. They had been introduced to him only a few days previously by Dorothy Cowell, who seemed to take a maternal interest in the writer. She had let fall a remark the day before to the effect that she saw in him not only a highly gifted writer but one of genuine creative genius, though her judgment could be based on only a very limited output. Professor Cartwright and Major Shepston had immediately confessed, as if in self-defence, that they knew very little about belles-lettres. It is true that Burton liked reading poetry but, æsthete as he was and immersed in the study of antiquity, he contented himself with verse from Pindar to Swinburne and would have thought it an insult if anybody had imputed to him a familiarity with modern, to say nothing of contemporary, literature. However, it was not Clayton Reeves's literary talent that aroused their interest. It was the brooding shadows on his face, his impossible silence that day, the absorbed way he sat there, holding sharply aloof without being hostile, in short, the disturbing effect of his personality as a whole, that forced them out of their conventional reserve and incited them, quite against their ordinary custom, to interrogate Dorothy Cowell about the stranger. The role of inquisitor was of course taken over from the two older men by Burton. The person of Reeves thus became the theme of an odd quintet, in which he himself developed the leading part, though only in the form of a silent monologue. The engine of the car, which had to surmount steep gradients, whined a melancholy *canto fermo*, while the tragic waste of the Judean wilderness through which they were passing, with its varied shades of red and brown ridged stone, its scarred rocks and jagged ravines, provided a significant background as an outward picture of his inward dissonance.

It is impossible to reproduce a monologue without including in it a certain element of untruth. A man does not talk to himself in terms of "I" or "you." The inward life is expressed neither by thoughts nor by words, though they both have their share in it. Long before the soul has transformed its stresses into speech, it becomes the subject of an infinite sequence of pictures, and even these pictures do not by any means represent the ultimate stratum of the thinking soul. One might indeed believe in the existence of a mental substance, such as Cartwright's *akâsha*, a subtle basic tissue on which the pictures and conceptions of the soul-life are developed. Cartwright, however, and the others who were sitting in the back of the car were no longer thinking either of *akâsha* or of the conversation into which they had been drawn at the sight of a landscape that seemed to lie on the boundary between this world and the Beyond. With the intellectual adaptability of men of the world they had shaken off metaphysics and were now sitting there with sober minds. Reeves alone was unable to free himself from the after-effects of the conversation by the Dead Sea, in which he had refused to participate. Motionless in his seat beside the driver, he stared out into the land and wilderness of Judea.

"I am ill"—with this admission he began his process of introspection—"I have always been ill, ever since my childhood, but it was only yesterday that I became aware of the nature of my malady, when I went to consult the nerve specialist in Jerusalem. Now, if I were a hypochondriac, or even an ordinary invalid, I should not have been confessing my condition to a physician for the first time yesterday, at the age of thirty-three. . . . I never talked about it to my mother . . . and I only hinted at it to Leonora a little while before she died. . . . It is odd that, though I called her by the name of Leonora when we became engaged, now that she is dead she seems to be shrinking away from me back into her old name of Mildred. She was the only one who could have helped me to carry the burden, though she did not take my cautious hints very seriously at the time. . . . Consumption would be worse to bear, it is true. Yet every day I feel that I am burning up more and more hopelessly, that I am growing more and more alien both to myself and to everybody else. I shall never be able to write another line, for the consciousness of my malady robs me of my interest in life. Everything that excites the interest of my contemporaries strikes me as only ridiculous. The books in which they search for a solution of their problems bore me; I am as far from them as the stars. I wonder if this is already a sign of intellectual decay? . . . How disgustingly I behaved today at the Dead Sea! These people could not possibly have any idea that their confounded mention of *déjà vu* touched me on the raw. They could not know that such discussions fill me with fear and embitterment. . . . I suppose I ought to have told the physician that the hours of depression by which I am tortured prior to an attack are connected each time with the feeling, 'I have experienced this before,' and with the ghastly and futile effort to understand what it really is that I have experienced before. . . . It's Thursday again today. It has happened every Thursday for the past four weeks, and each time towards evening. I want to stop it from happening again today, and that is why I arranged with Dorothy to show her the site of the Temple, for I have never had an attack when I was with other people. . . . But take care now! . . . Is there any reason why I should be so sure? . . . I'm not sure at all! Since Leonora died it has got worse from week to week, it gets worse the farther she recedes into the past. During the three years we lived together I was practically free from it; if I had not hinted at it that day, she would not have known anything about it. Leonora was my salvation, and one is not ashamed to make an admission to anybody who is one's salvation. . . . The fact that I am ashamed is very bad. Have I sufficient intellectual vanity to console myself with the thought that it is, at any rate, a noble malady? In antiquity they even used to call it the 'sacred malady.' Great men have suffered from it—prophets, the Apostle Paul, Dostoievsky. . . . They even drew their greatest strength from their abnormality. It brings me only exhaustion and the crippling of my faculties. But perhaps that too is connected with this present age and its flight from the intellect; this age that fixes its teeth like a rabid bulldog into what it calls reality, and needs very different kinds of health and sickness from mine. . . . By the way, the physician did not employ the term 'epilepsy'; he only made me feel it. So he too was ashamed of the word. . . . It is true, I have never lost consciousness and collapsed in the street, or foamed at the mouth, or cramped my thumbs convulsively. The doctor said that it was not so much a real swoon as a deep 'absence' produced in the brain by a lack of blood. . . . An attractive word, 'absence.' . . . Perhaps a commonplace swoon would be more tolerable than this absence, this incomprehensible vacuum, this complete deprivation of one's ego, which is more terrible than annihilation. . . . No, no, what a dreadful thought, God help me, not *that*! I must not swoon, I must not collapse this evening in front of Dorothy. . . . The very fear of it brings it nearer, yet I can't keep my thoughts off it. . . . What happened that day, so long ago, when I had my first attack at the age of six? . . . Mother had taken me with her to a little seaside resort, and the sight of the ocean brought it on, that vast rampart of God towering up to the skies. I was unconscious for a long time. 'A very nervous child,' said the landlady at the pension where my despairing mother had put me to bed. But I remember quite definitely that it was not only the sight of the ocean which had overwhelmed me, but also a question: Why does this monster, this tremendous God, stay within His bounds, why does He stop in front of a ridiculous strip of sand, why does He not break out and seize my mother and me? . . . My little mind had caught a glimpse of God through the gloomy rampart of the northern ocean and had swooned away. That was how my malady started. . . . And now, after an eternity, the terrible emotion inspired in me as a child by the ocean has come back to me through the Bible, through the Book of Jeremiah. What power and beauty there are in the words! . . . I will repeat them to myself softly, perhaps they will help. . . .

" 'Will ye not tremble at my presence, which have placed the sand for the bound of the sea by a perpetual decree, that it cannot pass it: and though the waves thereof toss themselves, yet can they not prevail; though they roar, yet can they not pass over it?' "

He cleared his throat as the chauffeur blinked across at him for the second time. Then he turned his head aside, to hide the fact that his eyes were wet. The car panted its way convulsively up a particularly steep stretch of road.

"What's that you say? His name isn't Reeves?" demanded Major Shepston, who had not quite grasped what Dorothy was saying. She had been making her revelation in a very subdued voice, as if the man in front might overhear her in spite of the sound-proof glass.

"No," she answered. "That is not what I said. Of course his name is Reeves. He was adopted by a Mr. Reeves, his mother's second husband, when he was three years old. He has never had any other name, but his father's name was Paderborner. . . ."

"I thought he wasn't altogether English, in spite of his name," declared Shepston, and he leaned back as if he had satisfactorily solved a problem that had been worrying him. Dorothy Cowell, however, felt compelled to enter a mild protest.

"I am not telling you this for the sake of mere gossip. He talks openly about it himself."

"Such things do happen," suggested Burton good-naturedly.

"Do you think he looks oriental?" Dorothy inquired, to which the men replied in chorus: "Not exactly oriental . . . but foreign. . . ."

Dorothy acknowledged, with slight emphasis: "I think that he looks like a figure from the New Testament; like one of the disciples in the background of an Italian painting. Of course, he would have to grow a little beard. . . ."

"And you, Miss Cowell," declared Professor Cartwright, who was sitting next to Dorothy; his lips did not move and he seemed to be making an objective assertion, "you have naturally been acquainted with Mr. Reeves for some time."

"Longer than I shall admit to him. When we were both children I often saw him in the street, for our families lived not far from each other. I did not really get to know him, however, till much later, in Paris, just before he married. We have related professions, though this he vigorously denies."

The car stopped with a jerk. Like the bluish-black knife of a vast guillotine the sky cut down at the horizon into the wilderness of hills that rose around them. Voices penetrated from near by, a throaty pilgrims' chorus. It was an untidy procession of Arabs journeying on a pilgrimage to Mount Nebi Musa, there to do reverence at the legendary tomb of Moses. From the crown of the road a sidepath led up to the sacred height, and the company of pilgrims was now pouring along it. Their chant was not like that of a pious choir, but resembled rather a wild and mutinous expostulation. From an undulating sea of white, yellow, and brown burnouses, an excited eddy of fezes and coloured turban scarfs, there towered a fat white horse with a gold-embroidered saddle-cloth and bearing the unwieldy, swaying figure of an ulema in a dark-green silken cloak. To the right and left of the colossal horseman were dervishes carrying banners of light green. Major Shepston, who was familiar with the customs of the country, explained with a laugh that the Moslems were well aware that Moses had not been laid in an earthly tomb. Allah, however, had taken thought for "the convenience of the faithful" and had transferred the mortal remains of his first prophet to Nebi Musa, that they might there be revered every year at the time of the Bairam by the true believers. . . .

The wild, spectral confusion of noise and colour was soon swallowed up by the greyness of the thirsty Judean waste. In every sense this region had a wasted look, wasted by some inconceivable spirit. With an easier hum the car glided down a dip in the road as if it were on runners. On both sides jagged boulders shot up like ruined towers from the general accumulation of debris in this valley of despair.

Professor Cartwright announced calmly:

"Only here, and in no other place in the world, could the idea of sin have been conceived."

Reeves still sat as immobile as he had been since the beginning of the drive. He looked neither to the right nor to the left, took in nothing and seemed to see nothing, like a native who expects nothing of a surprising nature to meet his eyes. That which was taking place inside him, and which is crudely termed "talking to oneself," had not suffered interruption even by the Arab pilgrimage, the stopping of the car, or the voices of its occupants which then became audible.

"Here I am in this country, though I never had any idea of coming here. The craziness of fate! . . . No, it isn't fate that is crazy, it is only we who are crazy and stupid and blind.

. . . I might try to deceive myself a hundred times, but I *do* believe firmly in sense and logic. Perhaps it is because I believe in them that I am unable to work any more. That is what makes me different from other people. Everything that is being written today is based on the contrary belief, on the conviction that there is no meaning or coherence anywhere, and therefore nothing is related to anything else. The others are free to think that way, but I am not. Deep down in me there still lives the old causal God, the God of logic. This is His home. . . . Who knows, perhaps it is He who lured me here? . . . Why did Leonora suddenly have that morbid desire to travel? She who usually had to be begged before she would accept the smallest gift, why did she have just this one consuming desire to go to Egypt? She said that if she could not go she would get ill. That is what she said literally. . . . I who am usually so fond of travel, why did I at the time have such an evil foreboding that kept on warning me? Why did I fight down the warnings instead of resisting her desire? And when Leonora took a capricious fancy to live in that Arab house by the water, why did I not simply say no? We could have afforded better quarters, and all our acquaintances warned us of the epidemic which is never quite dormant there. Why did I not persuade Leonora to accept that invitation for a trip up the Nile? I knew perfectly well that it was an offer that would save us from some deadly horror. . . . Why, why, why? . . . All these questionings form a complete chain of causes which contain within themselves intention and guidance. . . . Did it lie within the intention of this guidance that I, Clayton Reeves, the insignificant Reeves, who am not even Reeves, that I should be brought to Jerusalem by way of marriage and death? For it was certainly not by mere chance that Dorothy Cowell roused me from my lethargy three weeks after Leonora died and insisted on my coming to the Holy Land. . . . And why did Providence call me to the Holy Land? Because I belong here by descent? . . . Am I not just as much a Christian and an Englishman and a citizen of the world? More so, in fact? . . . Of course I am! My father was a Jew named Paderborner. I do not remember him at all. He went very quietly out of the world, as if he wanted to wipe out his tracks to my advantage. Nevertheless, he must have been a man of tradition, for I was submitted to the rite of circumcision, which is the token of the covenant of the Lord. I am therefore one of the people of the covenant, and although I did not know my father, yet he is in me, and his fathers and their fathers are in me too, back to the first and last father. . . . And it is this first and last father, the God of my fathers, who sets me in opposition to all the others and has allotted me a fate for which there is no solution. In order to bind myself to Him I have been immersed for weeks and weeks in the study of the Bible—I, whose education has been so very different. . . . At least, that is how I explain it to myself. It is incredible how swiftly the Holy Scriptures pour into me, as though they were wooing me just as I am wooing them. It is no longer a matter of mere reading; it is a repetition, a memory, for without the slightest effort or intention I am able to remember hundreds of verses. So from day to day I understand more deeply many things that the members of my race, who are again taking possession of this land with such ardour and determination, are probably not permitted to understand at all. I do understand it because of the partition or dualism within me, which makes me clairvoyant. . . . There can be no cure for us, no earthly peace or order, so long as it is His wish that in relation to every human community we should be the eternally different. A divine precision has eliminated every way of escape even for me. Perhaps this lack of a way out has something to do with my malady, which began when I, an innocent child, caught a glimpse of God behind His veil of invisibility. . . . But of what use to me is this knowledge of mine? Today is Thursday; in three hours it will be evening and my time will have come. . . . Nothing can save me; I shall fall to the ground, this time perhaps foaming at the mouth, in front of the unsuspecting Dorothy. . . . I feel I could die already with shame and loathing. . . . Shall I make some excuse and find a pretext to go home? . . . This shame is awful, but being alone is no less terrible. . . . It will come, inevitably, I can feel it. . . . The physician called the premonition an 'aura.' I have been living in this aura for hours, and it is growing stronger and stronger. . . . How red the desert has suddenly become! . . . Have I already experienced this before? I must concentrate on thoughts that are stronger than the aura, on memories that cause my own ego to disappear, on the most cruel memory of all . . . how she lay there and was still breathing. . . ."

After passing a precipitous ravine, to the eastern side of which clung the inaccessible stone cages of a Greek penal monastery, the car had climbed to the top of a new and extremely steep incline. Now it was dropping down into a completely different world. The ridges and spines of limestone rocks, the greyness of marl, the peaks and jagged crests of the wilderness through which they had just driven and which seemed to be possessed by the tragedy of despair, had given place to a landscape that was completely characterless and decayed. A vast plain covered with clods and fragments of earth and with weather-worn remnants of rock opened up before them, and everything was of the same unvarying colour, the colour of dried blood. The tragic despair of the Judean wilderness and the dignity that is inherent even in sin had changed to the ultimate catastrophe, to the insipid hell of souls that have lost faith in themselves. At sight of these reddish-brown fragments which covered the earth roundabout, one might have thought of Golgotha, strewn with skulls and bones, on the Day of Judgment. A little way off the road, hidden amidst rusty hollows and mouldering rocks, squatted a family of poor wandering bedouins. Four black and motionless human blobs, two large and two small ones, a low tent and an ass that seemed to have turned to stone, stood out against the dried-blood colour of the undulating ground as though they were the last residuum of life, the bitter lees of mankind before its end. Major Shepston gave the place its name:

"Adumim, the Pass of Blood! The red only comes from iron oxide, but that too is an ingredient of blood."

Burton, who had not been listening to this information, turned to Miss Cowell.

"Why does he wear a mourning band?"

"Haven't I told you about it?" asked Dorothy in surprise. "It was very tragic. His wife died in Cairo last Christmas—of polyneuritis, I think. She was only twenty-three. She was ill for just ten days and completely paralyzed."

The men were silent as a token of sympathy, though they did not show any further interest, but this did not restrain Dorothy from continuing.

"He looked after her as a man rarely looks after a woman, which was a miracle, considering his egocentric nature. When a woman falls ill, her husband generally regards it as an affront to his own sense of importance. Mildred was by no means above the average, though she was charming and had a sense of humour of her own. A solemn husband and a wife with a sense of humour—that's quite a good combination, don't you think? It was almost the only happy marriage I have ever come across. Perhaps that was why poor Mildred had to die, for it seems that such things must not be."

"The men who love most passionately are the ones who are soonest consoled," proclaimed Major Shepston, who was a wiry old bachelor and had gathered only insignificant and cheap experiences in this direction. His dictum appeared seriously to annoy Dorothy, and she retorted:

"So far as Reeves is concerned, you are making a devil of a mistake. I would not wish on any woman the fate of being his second wife. The man possesses a tremendous capacity for mourning."

She was silent and kept her eyes fixed on the writer's back, which expressed so much suffering that it served to confirm her words. His head was bent forward, his narrow shoulders drooped. In his apprehension of an imminent attack he had summoned up the unhealed memories that were stronger than everything, stronger even than his malady, than those most painful moments of his life which were always ready to break forth from behind a transparent veil. His inward monologue was no longer determined by scraps of words and thoughts, but solely by the clear-cut vision of these memories. He saw the little white room in the hospital of the Sisters of Mercy, which resembled a cheap lodging rather than a modern sick-room. For some incomprehensible reason the single window was draped with grey curtains, and about these curtains buzzed swarms of repulsive blue-bottles.

He had constantly to drive them away from Leonora's pillow with a white horsehair switch. She was unable to move a limb, but with angelic kindness she made the most childlike jokes about everything so long as she retained her voice and consciousness. She joked about the doctors, the nurses, the furniture, the wallpaper, and the curtains, but mostly about her own helplessness. Apart from the hours when she moaned out her soul in agonizing pain, she had revealed herself to Clayton only twice. On the first night when she fell ill, she had implored him with a harassed look in her eyes: "Don't let me die." And on the day of her death, after she had received a blood transfusion, she breathed: "Let me die." This was the last short coherent sentence that she spoke. Later the window of the dreadful room stood open. From now on Clayton would always see it open. The bright, deep-blue day of the spring-like Egyptian winter would eternally fill this window with the pictures of its palm trees, rhododendrons, and azaleas, with boats sailing along the Nile in the distance, and with the thousand sparrow-hawks of Ptah hovering with outstretched wings between heaven and earth. Oh, why did this day, which was fixed in his mind for ever, have to be so beautiful! Why was it not clouded, distorted, extinguished by rain or sandstorm! He turned his eyes from the window to Leonora's bed. She would lie eternally in a death agony that could not pass. It was *akâsha*, the mysterious substance that pervades us and allows nothing to perish. How long and difficult a thing is dying! Leonora's lips are still as red as flowers, moist and parted like those of a little girl. But the doctor has put wet compresses of cottonwool upon her eyes, that they may not dry up, then he goes, and Clayton is left alone with Death, longing with a cruel sincerity for its last decision. Death takes its time, however, voluptuously enjoying its victim's youth. One breath and another, rattling in the depths of the throat, then a swift sequence of easy breathing as if things had suddenly taken a turn for the better. The secret that one human being scarcely ever imparts to another, the heavy beating of the heart, becomes perceptible at this moment. The more infrequently it is heard, the louder it sounds, like the hesitating tick of a clock or the chiming of a bell in the misty distance. Then the moment approaches of instantaneous transition, which is more real than all the other moments of time. The experienced hand of an invisible giant passes swiftly over the still-living face of Leonora and robs it of its colour. . . .

"Jerusalem!" cried Burton in a voice so loud and high-pitched that even Reeves heard it. The road turned into the Vale of Jehoshaphat and ran high above the ravine in which the brook of Kidron cuts between the Holy City and the Mount of Olives. Down in the valley extended luxuriant vegetable beds in manifold shades of green, for the town was built on the heights and it was the middle of spring. Dense clumps of willows overarched the water channels, so that nothing of the brook was to be seen; only the white cubes of the houses in the village of Siloah seemed to greet them fleetingly. The road, however, left all this cheerful scene lying to one side, and wound its way up higher to the more austere region of cypresses and twisted olive trees that give the hill its name. They passed by the Hebrew cemetery with its myriads of gravestones crowded together, a slate-quarry of abounding faith. Clinging to the side of Jehoshaphat, the valley of the last trump, the pious dead of centuries and tens of centuries were gathered together. Coming from all the countries of the world, they had crossed the seas in order that they might deliberately choose their place of rest within sight of Jerusalem. Of all the earth's dead, it is they who will have the shortest way to go to their resurrection, only as many paces as will take them down into the valley. Then there loomed up the strange monument to Absalom, an overturned goblet from which the ground had been cut away. When Jesus looked down at this monument, it was in no less crumbled a state than it is today. And He had undoubtedly looked down from the summit, from the cypress grove of Gethsemane, the place of His agony.

The most irresistible power of attraction, however, came from the other side, where from the opposite rock the Jerusalem of earth and the Jerusalem of heaven seemed at this hour to be fused into one. Clouds had risen from the hills and stretched in prophetically radiant bars over the western part of the city. The sun, which was still far from its setting, had absorbed all the gold from the sky and heaped it over the site of the Temple. The towers, cupolas, and minarets all around had become effaced and were fused in a general glitter. Only the spacious central region seemed to be real, the sacred zone that stood out as if it were a separable city distinct from the rest. The Mosque of Omar, overarching with its polygon the sacrificial rock of Moriah, flamed as though it were on fire. The Dome of the Chain at the southern end of the site lay beneath an avalanche of purple shadows. The clear air acted as a magnifying lens, allowing every detail to be clearly distinguished. The slender columns and pointed arches in front of the great mosque extended upwards in a miracle of plastic art. From the grey and brown of the rock sprang the vividness of the city wall, which formed a frame for a picture steeped in gold.

Major Shepston knocked on the window and ordered the chauffeur to stop the car. In silence they all gazed at the

Eternal City in its glory. Jebus, Hierusalem, Jerushalayim, Zion—by whatever name it might be known, it was the city without beginning and without end, older than the oldest memories, of the past, the present, and the future, like the God who had gathered it round the rock of Moriah where Abraham had prepared to make his great sacrifice for his faith. Its earliest king whose name has been handed down to us was called Melchizedek, "the just king," and his memory is preserved in the Liturgy to the present day as a prelude to the coming of the Messiah. The temples of Thebes and Karnak were mighty reconstructions of ruined buildings. But only that which is dead can be reconstructed. Rome and Athens were modern cities with museum-like areas of ruins in their midst. Jerusalem, built upon its rock and flaming there in the sun, possessed no ruins. It had not sloughed off its ages and cast them aside like skins of stone. The daughter of Zion stood in the light again and again, and again and again she lay in the dust. The fires of Nebuchadnezzar, the destructive tools of Titus, the ploughs of Hadrian had scarred her body, but her real existence did not depend on her material existence. Whoever counted her hours was counting the hours of God, which are timeless. Her antiquity was of the present and her present aspect was part of antiquity in the triumphant fusion of the flaming vision that filled the souls of the watching Englishmen, in spite of their self-control, with a breath of magic and with the deepest emotion.

When the car was moving again, Reeves knew that nothing and nobody could preserve him from the attack that was imminent. With the same utter certainty he knew that it would be more grave than any attack with which he had yet been threatened. Perhaps he would never awaken from his unconscious state. Let it be so! Yet in spite of all his shame and apprehension, he had the strange feeling that there was a question in his mind of which he did not know the nature any more than he knew the answer for which he longed. And this convulsive craving for an explanation to which he could not give a name inspired him with the courage to meet the danger that he was about to face.

3

At the Site of the Temple

"I'M LEAVING here next week, Clayton. I am being sent to Central Europe on an important assignment. You will then be all on your own and there will be nobody to worry about you. Now, don't imagine that I think you are going to miss me. You do make it hard for one. Here I am, bringing you into contact with really unusual people, who treat you with extraordinary friendliness, and you sit there, deaf and dumb, haughtily aloof, displaying your pale, proud face at the martyr's stake, a monument of impatience and bad upbringing. I understand your state of mind, Clayton—do believe that—but this kind of thing can't continue any longer. It's quite crazy. Good Heavens, if one only knew what *really* is the matter with you!"

"There is nothing at all the matter with me," said Reeves with a smile of obstinate amiability, and he lengthened his stride.

They had passed the Citadel of Zion and had entered the Bazaar in the old town which, roofed over with gloomy masonry and mouldering beams, leads by way of innumerable uneven steps in a south-easterly direction towards the foundation walls of the Temple site. A twin stream of pedestrians, one flowing up the street and the other flowing down, forced its way with remarkable flexibility through the narrow channel. Although, as in all the bazaars of the Orient, merchants were offering their wares for sale at the dark and cavernous entrances to their shops, hoarse cooks were offering their steaming frying-pans to the passers-by, street pedlars were thrusting their way forward with a vehement impatience as they balanced their baskets on poles, and donkeys, goats, and sheep were being driven through the crowd, yet in Jerusalem's Bazaar Street there prevailed, in spite of all, a deliberate gravity and a solemn sense of tranquillity. The people looked straight ahead with an exalted air of indifference, and the rhythm of their balanced stride could not be disturbed by any passing temptation. Dorothy and her escort were pressed close together in the throng.

"It is not particularly friendly of you to withhold your confidence from me so completely," said Dorothy.

"You have been so frightfully good to me," he replied in a strained tone, "and I don't know how to thank you enough."

The gratitude behind these conventional words, which left an unpleasant aftertaste, was genuine. It was the gratitude for kindly help felt by a man who was seriously ill. Dorothy took off her hat, and it seemed to Reeves that he was seeing her for the first time. He was touched by the grey streak in her ebony hair. Here was a woman who was making her way through life with no help at all, full of vitality, clever, courageous, and no less lonely than he was. This was a vigorous, breathing individual walking along beside him. Through her thin foulard dress he could feel the friendliness of her body every time he touched her. The thought flashed through his mind: "Might not this be my salvation? To tear myself away by making a fresh start! To take refuge with a woman!" But before he could reject the idea with all the fervour of his being, Dorothy seemed to have sensed it. She detached herself from him as though to protect herself.

"I should like to point out, Clayton, that I haven't the slightest intention of intervening in your life. If I find you lacking in sincerity, that is only because I . . . because I have some regard for you as an artist."

They were held up at this moment by a knot of people who were moving towards them. In the centre of the group walked the first of three figures that left a deep impression on the mind of Reeves as he proceeded to the site of the Temple. A distinguished-looking man, in a light-blue burnous that fell in magnificent folds, was followed and surrounded by a host of beggars and street urchins. He was probably an effendi, one of the great landowners of the country. With his right hand he pressed a silk umbrella to his breast, while in his left he tossed and chinked a number of coins. From time to time he threw one or more piastres to the ragged mob, who immediately began to scramble for them, but he did not deign to honour the rabble with a single look as he continued on his way with long and careful strides. At the same time his handsome, masterful face, in its frame of beard, shone with the light of an indomitable cheerfulness. Dorothy turned round to admire him.

"A king out of an old legend! . . . Solomon or Harun al Rashid! Doesn't he strike you like that?"

Reeves, too, gazed for a long time after the royal figure in its light-blue robe, as if he wanted to stamp the splendid form in his memory. Dorothy's voice was infused with a new warmth.

"I know what is wrong with you, Reeves. It is time you started to get down to work again, that's all. After all that has happened, you are going to do something big."

"Yes, I shall soon be compelled to work, Dorothy. That is to say, I shall write some articles which, with your kind help, I may perhaps be able to place."

"Why the self-irony? You know quite well what I mean."

"What you mean is all over. Leonora took it with her. And she left something behind in me which makes further words superfluous."

"Do you mind if I am a little indiscreet, Clayton? . . . When I was in your room I saw heaps of Bibles, biblical commentaries, and theological works. One does not borrow and read books of that kind for pleasure. I hope you have found a theme that will be congenial to you, for you are not one of those writers who study everyday life with a microscope, and you have never been a pioneer in the boring labyrinth of human psychology."

"You are on the wrong track!" Reeves protested sharply. "I am not looking for a theme. I know more or less what I used to be worth, and I am rather proud of the fact that I never wrote a line without . . . without . . . it's a loathsome expression . . . without inspiration."

Dorothy appeared to take offence at the word. "My *métier* is to report what I see and hear. I haven't, therefore, any very clear idea of what you mean by 'inspiration.' "

" 'Absence' with *akâsha*," he said with gritted teeth.

They were standing before a low, dark room, open to the street, that seemed to have been carved out of the front of a dilapidated house. The near-sighted Reeves could not at first distinguish anything in the gloom. In the background glimmered a half-extinguished coal fire, and gradually he saw that there was a kind of revolving mill, with a shaft attached to it, in the centre of the cavernous opening. A giant with the top half of his body bare was working the mill, that is to say, he was walking round continuously in a circle, keeping to a certain rhythm, with his arms pressed against the shaft. It was not possible to see what was being ground in the mill; it was evident only that the giant had to walk round in his circle a thousand times a day like a beast of burden. If this sight itself was horrible enough, the horror was increased when the giant suddenly raised his great head from its bowed and ox-like position and it could be seen that he was blind. His scarred eye-sockets stared out of a face that dripped with sweat. A number of the passers-by seemed to know him and called out to him in Arabic something that sounded like pitiless mockery. The blind slave took no notice of anything, however, as he applied himself to his drudgery, but continued to press against the shaft and to circle unceasingly round the mill. Only once did he bare his teeth in the direction of the street, without taking his attention for a single moment from his work.

Long after this dismal scene had been left behind, Dorothy and Clayton were unable to cast it from their minds. First a legendary king, then a legendary slave. Seeing the blind worker had made Dorothy low-spirited. She looked at Reeves almost humbly.

"Listen, Clayton! I had no intention of saying anything disrespectful about your inspiration. . . ."

"When you have once experienced it," he said with unaccustomed frankness, "nothing seems more worth while living for than such a moment. What is work? A blind man continually turning his shaft round the same central point, without hope. . . . A moment of inspiration, however, or whatever name one gives it, contains everything at the same time, even though the figures, incidents, and ideas throng to one's mind by the hundred. They emerge in a single flash.

No power of imagination, no summoning up of all one's faculties, no insight, no industry, no work can achieve the same end. That is why, since I shall never experience such a moment again, I shall write no more."

"The moment will return," said Dorothy with great firmness, as if she had had a sudden flash of intuition.

They had reached the Wall of Wailing, that sanctuary of enormous blocks of hewn stone which is all that is left to the people of Israel of their former Temple. Since it was a weekday and not the Sabbath, only a few of the pious were standing in front of the great wall, which forms the foundation of the Temple area. They were pressing their faces passionately against the stone as though they wanted to wash it with their tears. At the same time the power of prayer twitched and shook the pitiful figures in their long caftans. Again and again Clayton Reeves's eyes were drawn towards a rather deformed old woman who had been tottering about for some minutes with the aid of a stick as if she were intoxicated. This was the third of those meetings which impressed him with the feeling that they had some disturbing connexion with his condition. She looked like a fortune-telling gipsy and, though she was dressed in European clothes, her garments appeared outlandish. On her short greasy black hair she wore a cap of imitation leopard-skin with a feather sticking out of it. Green glass earrings as large as hazel nuts swayed at every reeling step she took. She also wore round her neck a whole collection of coloured glass beads which jingled audibly. She muttered constantly to herself, and now and then she gave vent to a louder cry. Reeves found himself inexorably compelled to bring this muttering and these cries into relation to himself, as though the old woman were making certain words known to him and communicating with him by signs which she did not wish his companion to see. At the foot of the great staircase that leads up to the Temple area she turned round, and Reeves caught a look of secret understanding which pierced him through and through. Her face was not really so very old. It seemed to him to be that of a woman who was scarcely fifty and yet might be a thousand years old. From her worn visage stared round, disquieted eyes whose sad mockery and sly restlessness appeared to know everything about him. Yes, this old wandering daughter of Israel did know everything about him. She knew that the "aura" was condensing round him more and more inescapably, and that in a few minutes he would be seized by the horror and would fall to the ground, without hope of deliverance. . . .

In great bounds he ran up the high steps; when he reached the top he was out of breath and his heart beat furiously. Dorothy could not think of any reason for this sudden flight, but when they had passed the Mohammedan guard, who collected their entrance tickets, and before they entered the sacred area, Reeves touched her on the arm.

"I have a confession to make, Dorothy. I should like to ask you to do something for me. . . ."

His words sounded so breathless and convulsive that she stared at him in alarm.

"Do not be angry with me, Dorothy . . . but it would perhaps be better . . . it would be better for your sake . . . if we did not . . . if you were to leave me now."

"What do you mean, for Heaven's sake? We specially arranged to come here, did we not, because you were anxious to act as my guide?"

"I do not wish to expose you to unpleasantness . . . to

put you in an embarrassing situation. If anything were to happen . . ."

"An embarrassing situation? . . . What do you mean—if anything were to happen?"

"If anything were to happen to *me* . . . I mean, if I were to be taken ill . . . you must promise me, Dorothy, that in that case you will go away immediately and not bother about me. It is nothing serious, but please, Dorothy, do me this favour and promise. . . ."

She studied his face carefully. How was it possible that she had not long since noticed the disquieting change that had taken place in him? His deathly pale features were growing more strained every second, he was breathing with difficulty, and his forehead was bedewed with perspiration.

"We are going home at once!" she said resolutely. But Reeves burst out in a cry of unconcealed excitement:

"No, Dorothy. I am going to stay!"

"Perhaps there is a café near by. You must have something to drink."

"The body is only of secondary importance, Dorothy. This is nothing physical."

She thought she understood. The death of Leonora had again overwhelmed him. She took his icy hand.

"Nothing is going to happen, Clayton. I am with you and I shall see that everything is all right. Now let us go. I don't generally possess such a thirst for knowledge, but today I want to explore this place in detail. . . ."

Reeves had grown calmer, and he pulled himself together with a jerk.

"All right, let us go. But remember what I asked you."

They emerged from the pillared halls, which still surround

the sacred area as they did in the time of Herod. Reeves kept a full pace behind Dorothy, as if he hoped thereby to preserve a sufficient interval to allow him to disappear from her sight at the last moment. The gigantic proportions of the Temple area extended in front of them, seeming to exceed in size all other sites that enclose famous sanctuaries elsewhere. Jerusalem, like Atlas, bore its burden on its shoulders.

The sun was low in the heavens, but the deeper it sank, the more purple and old gold did it have at its disposal to pour in waves of flame over the cupolas, the arcades, the columns, the steps, and the turrets. Dorothy and Reeves were the only foreigners there. On the following evening began the Mohammedan celebration of Bairam, when the *Haram esh Sherif* would be closed to all unbelievers. So this was the only chance Dorothy would have before her departure of visiting the most important relic of antiquity in Jerusalem, and it was one of the reasons why she had made the appointment with Reeves. There was great commotion everywhere. From every quarter the faithful had poured in for the festival, since the Haram esh Sherif with its mosques was regarded as the most sacred spot in Islam after Mecca. Many pious Moslems had settled down in groups on the great white flagstones with which the ground was paved, and it looked as if they might kindle their fires after sunset and cook their food, eat it, and lie down to sleep as they did in the desert. Perhaps it was part of an old tradition to spend the evening and the day of preparation before the Bairam festival in the Temple area. Other groups were standing about, engaged in animated conversation or ascending the broad steps that led to the Mosque of Omar.

Dorothy felt a sense of unease, for Reeves was not looking

any better. He appeared to have grown even a shade or two more sallow, and she could see from the convulsive prominence of his cheekbones that he was suffering from a tremendous strain. Whatever he might be going through, it was necessary for her to be extremely tactful. It was odd that she, Dorothy Cowell, the independent globe-trotter, who was prouder of her independence than of anything else, should now suddenly find herself in the precarious position of a solicitous woman acting as a kind of nurse to a crazy man. The various changes of scene that day and the discussions in which she had taken part had wearied even her, indefatigable as she was. She would have liked nothing better than to be drinking a cup of hot tea in the lounge of the King David Hotel. But she was well aware that it would not do to make another suggestion about going home. She found herself realizing with astonishment that this madman was exercising a powerful spell over her. His mysterious suffering kept her at his side, and she therefore sought craftily to find a light topic of conversation which might help to avoid the danger that seemed to be threatening.

"I am not very keen on mosques, Clayton. They seem to me to be the profanest buildings in the world. And it's getting late, so a quick look round will be enough. We're not concerned with Mohammed, anyway, but I should like to hear something about the old Temple in which Christ preached when He was twelve years old. . . . These stones are very fatiguing . . . and it is all so vast. Please summon up all your lore. Your attentive pupil is listening."

Reeves nodded, without looking at her. With his body tense and erect he strode straight ahead, so that Dorothy could follow him only with an effort. They reached the steps supporting the spacious platform on which rose the octagon of the Mosque of Omar. The ruins of ornamental and pillared arcades projected into the purple sky. Reeves climbed the steps lightly and swiftly, and when he reached the top he stood still for a moment, looked around, then walked up to one of the columns and leaned against it. He thought that he had found a good support for the approaching moment which he knew to be inevitable. It was possible from here to look over the whole area, and even a part of the Mount of Olives was visible. Dorothy came close to him. Her face, too, was tense and drawn. Stiffly throwing out his right arm, which hung from his shoulder as if it did not belong to his body, he said in a voice that rang out harsh and imperious like that of an angry teacher:

"The axis lies from north to south." The syllables were staccato and breathless. "Up here, from west to east, stretched the Temple of Solomon and also the Temple of Herod, in which Christ preached. . . ."

"You are a more severe guide than Burton," said Dorothy with an unsuccessful attempt to laugh. But he did not appear to have heard her.

"Where we are now standing was once the boundary between the outer court of the people and the inner court of the priests which contained the sacrificial altar. This was where the pillars of the gallery . . ."

He broke off in the middle of the sentence with a groaning sound, as though he had used up all his breath. From the pillar against which he was leaning he stared down at the steps where large numbers of white-clad Moslems had gathered and were preparing to walk with quiet dignity to the house of prayer. His ear just caught an apprehensive inquiry from Dorothy. The red glow of the sinking sun grew more vivid. He knew that it was approaching inexorably. *What* was approaching? Was this the feeling of dizziness already, the fear that he was about to lose his ego? That rushing sound, like steam escaping under pressure, was it inside him? It was approaching together with the white priestly figures that were slowly ascending towards him. And now it had arrived. He tore the spectacles from his eyes, for there was still room in his mind for the thought that he might smash them as he fell. But what was this? He was not losing consciousness. He was not sinking to the ground in a state of "absence." He was standing firmly on his feet. His heart was still beating calmly. But before his eyes everything was growing misty and changing. With a supreme need for assurance and certainty he moved his wrist, on which he wore his watch, closer to his weak-sighted eyes. Before time fell away, it stamped itself on his mind. He saw that it was twenty-three minutes to six.

4

In the Temple

(Incipit vita Hieremiæ prophetæ)

THE man who was holding his hand before his eyes, in order to shield them from the dazzling evening sun, saw with surprise that there was a broad leather band round his wrist. A capsule had been sewn into it, and the capsule contained a strip of parchment with writing on it. It was an amulet, a divine blessing. The man had been deeply absorbed in contemplation of the crown of the Temple which projected above the pillars of the dividing gallery where he was waiting. For a short time he had been lost in thought, and now he had to come back to earth. As he gazed at the leather band containing the blessing he remembered that his mother, the wife of Hilkiah, had attached it to his wrist that morning before he rode out from Anathoth to enter the true and only Temple of the Lord. It was an heirloom, having descended in his mother's family for generations.

This day was a day of honour, a day when the Lord rejoiced in His ancient Temple. How excited his mother had been! She had herself come to awaken him. And her pride was well founded. Of all the families of the priesthood which dwelt in the country roundabout but did not serve in the Temple he, Jeremiah, was the only youngest son who had been chosen for special distinction. His father's family, however, was one of the oldest in Judah and Benjamin, reaching back to the holy epoch as far as Abiathar, the exile, as far as Eli, the Priest of Shiloh, as far as Moses and Aaron themselves. Jeremiah had today been selected to fill a post of honour at the evening Passover sacrifice or perhaps to serve at the King's table. The young man's heart beat loudly, for it was filled with a great joy of anticipation. With his whole soul he loved the sacred festivals and ceremonial, when the fires glowed, the lamps shone, the harps, trumpets, and drums exulted, and the people came together with rejoicing as they united in the Covenant of the Lord.

Jeremiah turned his gaze towards the south. The palaces of the royal quarter, which served both as official buildings and as dwelling places and were separated from the sanctuary of the Lord only by a thick wall, flamed up in a last blood-red reflection. How strong must the soul of the King be to bear the close and constant proximity of God! On the battlements of the wall he could see the sentries of the royal bodyguard pacing slowly to and fro with their long lances. Between the wall and the place where he was standing thronged the vast crowd that had gathered for the feast. What a great concourse of people was contained in this fusion of Jerusalem and the country of the Lord! Neither in Asshur, nor in Babylon, nor in Egypt could more people take part in the feasts of the gold and silver nonentities that they called their gods! These were the thoughts of Jeremiah of Anathoth in his youthful pride, though it is true that he had had no personal experience of the great world and its chief cities. It was, however, well known from olden time that the Baalim of these capital cities possessed the power to whip the blood of mortal men into a fury of intoxication, while the joy of the spirit, free from wine and lust, was solely the gift of the God of Jacob, who bore many names but whose name was never spoken. At the feet of the young scion of a priestly house, below the encircling steps, the invited guests of the Lord pushed and squeezed. They filled the spacious outer court which surrounded the great raised platform of the actual sanctuary. The light of torches gleamed intermittently through the early dusk. Many had given way to the exuberance of their hearts and had kindled torches and coloured lamps, which they now swung in time to the intermingling choirs, even before the first star in the heavens flashed out its sign for the feast to begin. In the intervals when the singing broke off, a muffled diversity of sounds, which seemed to rise from the depths of the earth, became audible amid the general hum and murmur. This was the agglomerate bleating of sheep and baaing of lambs which were being received by the ten thousand in the subterranean halls and stables of the Temple hill by the priests who were appointed for this office. The offerings of the various families in town and country had to be counted, recorded, and provided with distinguishing marks, in order that the precepts of cleanliness might be observed, that no giver of an offering should be overlooked, and that the sacrifice itself should arrive at the altar without blemish. Even the masses of the poor and the destitute had brought their gifts to the Temple on this day. They were permitted to offer fowls instead of the customary yearlings. Those who could not afford even fowls found favour in the eyes of the Lord with a bundle of grain.

Jeremiah continued for a while to gaze in a reverie at the activity below. Then he turned his head and looked round as if something were troubling him. He had not come to the Temple unaccompanied. Baruch, son of Neriah, a sixteen-year-old boy from his district, had passed this day of waiting with him as he passed every other day. In Anathoth they called Baruch "Jeremiah's shadow." Had his shadow again left his side to become absorbed in one of the rolls of parchment that he borrowed from his older friend? Suddenly he heard the panting voice of the lad behind him. Baruch was so agitated from running that his headcloth had worked loose and was fluttering against the back of his neck. His voice broke as he called out:

"Let my master make ready! They are coming to call his name."

Baruch had not recovered his breath before three outstanding figures had mounted one of the pulpits that rose above the steps near where Jeremiah was standing. One of them was dressed, as an official of the royal household, in the sky-blue colour worn at the court of the sons of David. The other two were a priestly herald and a priestly trumpeter. The latter blew a blast without ceremony on his long instrument, which was cast from a mixture of gold and silver, and the herald then called out a number of names in a clear, sonorous voice, making a long pause after each. The last name was:

"Jirmejahu of Anathoth, son of Hilkiah of the line of Abiathar, the High Priest, of the line of Eli, the Priest of Shiloh. . . ."

Jeremiah, whose line was thus traced back to the mists of antiquity, listened to the summons, then crossed his arms over his breast and walked with a tranquil step to the pulpit. There he remained standing with bowed head. As was fitting when in the company of men of advanced years and exalted position, he did not raise his head even when the royal official and the two priests took him between them and escorted him through the dividing corridor into the inner courtyard of the Temple. During the brief journey he received the solemn instructions of the official: "Thus does one address the majesty of the King: 'I have been held worthy to look upon the countenance of the King.' "

The vast inner courtyard presented itself to the eyes of Jeremiah in a flickering reddish glow. The last residuum of daylight was mingled with the shimmering of lamps and tapers on the tables that were laid for the feast and with the distant gleam from the sacrificial altar. Though it was not the first time that he had seen the inner court, he was again startled at its hugeness. How insignificant the white-clad priests appeared beside the altar of burnt offerings, as they constantly encircled it in a double and triple chain. By skilful workmanship it had been fused into a unity with the sacred rock that sprang from the limestone depths of Moriah and formed its foundation. It was approached not by steps, but by a broad ramp leading up to the top. There was a good reason for this. If there had been steps, it would have been possible to see the bare feet and legs of the priests, and the Lord wished that the bodies of His priests should be wholly covered. From time to time a group would detach itself from the circling rows of men and ascend the ramp to the altar in long strides. Most of the groups consisted of a white-bearded sacrificial priest of high degree supported by two assistants, who helped him to carry the oblation, which was of no little weight, on a great golden dish. The sacrifice itself had to be executed with the utmost accuracy and speed, for at the top of the ramp the ministering priest had to bend over a redly glowing sea of fire that was many square ells in extent and covered only with a stone grid, so that it threatened to consume him together with the object intended for sacrifice. He had only a moment in which to lay the offering in its place with one of the gold shovels that lay near at hand and to utter the appropriate blessing. So great was the heat that the four brass horns at each corner of the altar were melted into shapeless lumps after the great festivals and had to be renewed. After each sacrifice—they followed one another without intermission—the group of three priests would proceed to the Molten Sea, there to revive and refresh themselves. The Molten Sea, to the west of the altar, almost equalled it in breadth and height. It was a gigantic basin of chased work, a hand's breadth thick, and the rim was delicately wrought like the rim of a cup, with decorations of lilies, while it rested on the backs of twelve oxen, each more than life-size, which raised their melancholy muzzles, three looking towards the north, three towards the west, three towards the south, and three towards the east. It was the work of Hiram, the famous artist, and Jeremiah was as proud of it as every youth was who enjoyed sufficient acquaintance with antiquity. But it was not the work of an artist, it was the work of the Lord Himself, that a spring of water welled up from the dry rock of the sacred mount directly beneath the Molten Sea, into the basin of which it was led by a clever mechanism. Thus, in accordance with divine precept, a "fountain of living waters" was at hand; not the lifeless water of cisterns from which tadpoles and leeches had first to be removed, but wondrous ice-cold water, the pulsing blood of the earth, with which the exhausted souls of the priests could be continually refreshed.

Opposite the altar, but at a fitting distance, the royal tables had been set up. There was one long one for the princes and the members of the court, and a smaller one, raised somewhat higher, at which the King and Queen would take their seats. All the tables were covered with sky-blue linen and bore basins, plates, goblets, ewers, and candlesticks which without exception were of solid gold. These precious utensils were borrowed for the royal tables from the treasures of the Temple, and were used only for the Passover Feast. God was the Master of the House and the Host at the Feast. He, who loathed all that was unclean with an inconceivable loathing, would not tolerate in His House a vessel from the houses of men. The Temple had therefore to provide eating and drinking utensils for the other guests of the Lord also, but their numbers on this occasion did not exceed a thousand. It was not as it had been years ago, when King Josiah held his first joyous Banquet of the Lord. Then he had gathered round him at least three times ten thousand guests from all the families in the land. If today the inner courtyard of the priests was filled with tables and benches crowded round the dais of the King, at that first celebration it had been the whole nation that sat and sang and ate and drank to the honour of the Lord, both in the inner and the outer courtyards. The King had even had to lend one of the courts of his palace to accommodate the hosts of celebrants. The occasion of that great feast had been more than worthy of it, for the Lord had allowed Himself to be discovered without too diligent a search. In the vestibule of the sanctuary, where Jeremiah pictured to himself the two mysterious brass pillars Boaz and Jachin with their pomegranate capitals in the light of fitful flames, the Lord had revealed Himself to this race anew. It had happened in the following way. Since the priestly mind did not easily decide to undertake the renovations which were necessary in the Temple, Josiah himself had issued an order that the cumulative dilapidations which the sacred buildings had undergone during the course of the centuries must be repaired without delay. To the will and wild tempestuousness of the King it was not possible for those who clung to tradition to oppose any argumentative "if" or "but." With the same wild tempestuousness, believing with a profound faith in the spirit of the Lord, he had once purged the land of the pillars of Ashtaroth, the Queen of Heaven, swept from the heights the sacrifices to Baal, eradicated from the valleys the abominable fires of Tophet, and had shattered everywhere even the secondary altars of the Lord. The Eternal One, whom the Heaven of Heavens could not hold, could not live in an earthly house. When He did descend, however, for a fleeting sojourn, there was only one house that could offer Him shelter, since He Himself was unique. That house shone forth on Mount Moriah. The Eternal One did not fail to show His gratitude. During the repairs to the Temple there was uncovered behind the mouldering cedar panelling of the porch a secret niche in which, amid much decaying debris, was found a well-hidden and well-preserved scroll. This scroll contained the new revelation, or rather the old revelation, for there was written on it nothing less than God's own Word to Moses. It was the long lost Book of the Law, the great collection of precepts which had been handed down only in a falsified and defective version. The High Priest Hilkiah, of the line of Zadok, who was still fulfilling that office as a man of greatly advanced years, had the good fortune to make the discovery. Shaphan, the scribe of Judah, was immediately sent for, and when he arrived the parchment trembled in the old man's nerveless hands. Within three days the learned Shaphan, son of Azaliah, had deciphered and revealed the truth. God had restored the lost Law to Israel.

It was well known that when the scroll was first read out in the palace the passionate Josiah threw himself to the ground and rent his garments, so bitterly was he overcome by his realization of the sins, omissions, and infringements of which he, his fathers, and his forefathers, together with the whole nation, had been guilty. But when his remorse had grown less vehement the King exulted and danced about the room —for the emotions of the sons of David were volatile—since a new Covenant would now be necessary and it was he who had been chosen to make this new Covenant before the Lord at the pillar of the oath in the Temple. Josiah's first decree had concerned the holding of the Passover, the mutual and holy banquet with the Lord that was being celebrated today for the tenth time. Jeremiah thoroughly approved of the ceremony, which caused his heart to leap high. Had God ever performed a greater deed than the liberation of Israel from Egypt, the land of bondage? And was there anywhere a more splendid evening feast than that of the fourteenth day of the spring month Nisan, when the first crops matured and a mild sky embraced the earth with tender solicitude? Jeremiah was well aware that there were many doubting spirits in the world, who winked and blinked when people talked of the rediscovered Book of the Law. Had not Shaphan the scribe taken refuge behind Moses, in order to substitute for the indulgent way of living of the present age one that was more harsh and severe? Nothing angered the man from Anathoth more than such insolent conceit. In long nights of study he had impressed the Book upon his memory from one of the copies that passed from hand to hand. Not that he longed for a life of austerity and self-denial—it was his way to avoid these whenever he could—but he knew that the Word of God was the Word of God and that no man could succeed in imitating it. Only too well had he learned that the Lord possessed a voice, a real voice, a resounding voice, which He employed for the utterance of His Word whenever He so desired. There were even a hundred possible ways of hiding from this voice, of letting it pass unheeded, of drowning it with other sounds, and Jeremiah was well acquainted with them all.

He stared past the sacrificial altar into the weakly illumined porch of the Temple as he pondered on these perilous notions. But his meditations were interrupted and he had to take his place in front of the royal dais together with the other youths who had been summoned to assume the various posts of honour. He found himself standing beside a richly dressed young man who was probably a few years older than himself and was certainly a head taller. It was a handsome head with carefully curled hair and beard, and Jeremiah found himself immediately attracted by his neighbour. The young man, noticing that he was being observed, turned towards Jeremiah with a look in his half-closed eyes that betrayed an unquenchable self-satisfaction.

"Is it Jeremiah beside whom I am standing, the son of Hilkiah of Anathoth? So I have been given to understand."

Jeremiah, who in spite of his office of honour (which was a distinction intended for his family rather than for him personally) regarded himself as a youth of no importance among other unimportant youths, smiled in embarrassment when he heard his name mentioned by the stranger.

"That is my name," he said.

"And I am Hananiah, son of Azur, of the town of Gibeon. I observe that this name means nothing to you. It is true, my father is not a priest and the names of our ancestors are not read out. But from the earliest times my native town of Gibeon has sent forth prophets. That levels things out.

I hope we shall be friends." Hananiah accompanied this jesting introduction with a complacent laugh which Jeremiah could not help finding attractive.

Something appeared to be provoking the man from Gibeon into displaying an uninvited candour towards his neighbour. He confessed even that his father, who was the richest man in the town, had not spared himself in his efforts to ensure that his son should be thus chosen for honour on that evening. By this admission Hananiah disparaged himself, though he appeared to be doing so without intention. He proceeded to explain with a certain vanity, but obscurely, that his own preference was neither for the priesthood nor for the royal service. It lay, he said, in a quite different direction; but he must not talk about it. On the other hand, Hananiah had informed himself very fully about the duties of their present office. It appeared that both he and Jeremiah were to act as cupbearers and that each of them was to hand the King half a goblet of wine whenever he should ask for it.

"You see those two earthenware pitchers? You are in charge of one, and I of the other. Which of us shall pour out the dark wine and which the light?"

There seemed to be a pause in the constant succession of sacrifices. The rows of priests had drawn back from the altar, but only to make way for the procession of the High Priest, which was moving towards the centre of the court from the east. Hilkiah, who bore the same name as Jeremiah's father, was extremely frail, and in the heavy vestments of his exalted office he could move only at a slow and tottering pace. The shield with the twelve gems of the tribes of Israel rattled on his sunken breast and the tall mitre, which bore the four letters of God's name, had slipped down over his narrow and ancient forehead. Only once a year was the famous Hilkiah, who by the favour of the Lord had rediscovered the Book of the Law, brought from his house as from a tomb in order that he might, by virtue of his office as High Priest, offer up with his own hands the King's Passover sacrifice. The sacrifice was carried before him in a great golden cauldron, and he himself swung a richly ornamented censer in his trembling hand, which was supported by other priests.

Jeremiah screwed up his near-sighted eyes as he watched the solemn procession of the venerable old man. Though his neighbour Hananiah nudged him several times in his excitement, he did not notice it. The thousands of spectators had suddenly turned their attention to the royal dais. The flourish of brazen trumpets came nearer and nearer, until it sounded like the cracking of a whip. The first star shone out clearly from a firmament still lurid with the light of the setting sun. Josiah, son of Amon, had reached the steps of the dais and had mounted them unnoticed. Though he had been ruling for many years he still walked with a tempestuous pace, and his courtiers, some of whom were very old men, had long since given up trying to follow closely at his heels. He bounded up to his seat like a lion. A sky-blue cloak enveloped his tall figure, and upon his head he wore a small coronet, since it would have been a culpable violation of the humility which beseems mankind if he had worn the crown of David in the House of the Lord. His fresh-coloured face, framed in a short beard, shone even more than the coronet. It shone with vitality, with physical satisfaction, with the consciousness of power and the assurance that he had deserved and won the approval of the Almighty. The youths who had been summoned to their office of honour, the court officials, the ministering priests, and all the others who had duties to perform threw themselves to the ground. The customary formula filled the air with a confused murmur: "I have been held worthy to look upon the countenance of the King." Jeremiah alone had forgotten what to say when the royal hurricane burst into sight, and he continued to stand and stare until Hananiah of Gibeon tugged at the hem of his garment.

The spacious courtyard was encompassed by a deep silence. The guests of the Lord at the encircling tables—each one a member of one of the most distinguished families of the land—had risen to their feet, waiting for a word from the King. Josiah spoke, and his voice rang out over the courtyard as he cried the watchword:

"Rejoice with the Lord!"

It pierced the stillness like an imperious military command, calling upon the celebrants to summon up all the joy and cheerfulness of heart which they had succeeded in preserving amid the afflictions of life, and to offer it as the sacrifice of sacrifices on this evening. For in the beginning the Lord created heaven and earth out of joy. His spirit, which moved over the waters; the light, to which He said: "Let there be light," and there was light—these were the created tokens of God's joy. The King's shining countenance seemed to say: "Joy is the strength of God. He gives it to us in order that we may return it to Him on the Passover of our liberation and redemption from servitude." The eyes of Jeremiah filled with tears. Across the courtyard, however, there thundered in a thousand voices the cry: "Rejoice with the Lord!"

In the meantime the porch of the sanctuary, between the pillars Boaz and Jachin, was filling with the sons of Asaph. These were the singers and minstrels, two hundred and eighty-eight in number, as laid down for all time according to the commandment of King David and his chief musicians Asaph, Heman, and Jeduthun. They took their places in three choirs divided into twenty-four sections. The lowest choir on the steps of the porch comprised deep, rugged voices such as were suitable for war songs and wild pæans in praise of God. The middle choir consisted of minstrels with richly carved harps, psalteries, and gittith lutes, with flutes, shawms, trumpets, and long-tubed trombones, not to forget the mighty drums which thundered out the beat as the song of praise rose to its intoxicating crescendo. The flower of the voices was contained, however, in the "higher choir," for which the singers were specially selected in early childhood and subjected to the strictest training and most meticulous examination. Even then they were admitted only in rare cases. This choir consisted solely of musical and choral experts, who were intimately familiar with all the hundreds of modes, measures, tunes, intervals, tempi, flourishes, introductions, and cadences of their art, as they had been worked out by Asaph. They sang in accordance with the ancient tradition and—when inspiration from the Lord and the verdict of the judges rendered it possible—they even added to the time-honoured stock of songs which they already possessed. The song that now rose in controlled volumes of sound above the uncontrolled hubbub of the guests was an ancient psalm, a sacred psalm, one that had been composed by David.

Already during the first verses of the song of greeting the courtiers had gathered round the King and seated themselves at the tables. The well-informed Hananiah knew all their names and told them to his more ignorant companion. That very old man sitting between the two princes was Shaphan himself, the great scribe and teacher. He was treated with the utmost reverence, and though he held neither a priestly nor a royal office he took precedence over the Chancellor and the Commander of the Bodyguard; while even the first "Keeper of the Door," who was responsible for maintaining order in the Temple, had to be content with a less exalted seat. Shaphan, however, appeared to take no pleasure in the distinction that had come to him through his long and celebrated life. His little shrunken face, with its red, lashless eyes, was filled with a dull brooding as though he were heaping himself with secret reproaches for having introduced a dubious future by his recognition and deciphering of the newly discovered Book of the Law. For it was worse to forsake a precept that was known than to infringe it through ignorance. The scribe's son Ahikam, who was private secretary to the King, had not taken a place at the table. The eyes of this tall, rather stiff and formal man roved attentively from the one powerful influence in his life to the other, from his great father to his great King. It was obvious that he was prepared to sacrifice his own interests in order to bring these two dominating influences into harmony.

Josiah took no notice of his retinue. He had drawn Hamutal to his side, the wife whom he had made Queen. She was not the mother of his eldest son Eliakim, who sat mockingly in the seat allotted to him and was doing his best to impress his unambiguous disapproval on all those who were present, including his father. He had his own reasons for this attitude, and Hananiah knew what they were. The rank of queen belonged to the mother of the eldest son, and she was the only woman who should have had access to the inner courtyard. But Josiah had disregarded this tradition. He loved Hamutal, and for many years he had shared his couch with her alone. What other woman had the right to be Queen? Hamutal had borne her husband two sons, though Jehoahaz, who was now seventeen years old, seemed unfortunately only slowly to be coming to manhood and understanding. Shaphan, who supervised the princes' education, was in the habit of complaining bitterly that the good, bright soul of Jehoahaz was united to a clouded mind, while the bright understanding of Eliakim was combined with a clouded soul. The characters of the two youths were revealed in their behaviour. Neither spoke a word. Jehoahaz sat bent over the table with a dreamy, childish smile, his fingers playing restlessly with some invisible object which he appeared to be trying to model. Eliakim sat in evident boredom, and now and then he would break a flower from the wreath which he wore according to a foreign custom on his brow, pluck it to pieces, rub the petals between his hands, and then breathe in the fragrance with closed eyelids.

Josiah and Hamutal had eyes only for their youngest child, little Mattaniah, whom they would not allow to be separated from them for even an hour. The five-year-old child was therefore enjoying the banquet instead of his baby sleep. It was clear that he was enjoying it from the exultation in his voice, whose penetrating shrieks were not kept in check by either royal or parental reproof. He was playing and romping about in the free space below the dais with a companion of his own age, by name Ebed-melech, a black boy from Ethiopia who had somehow got cast up in Jerusalem and was a strangely graceful dancer. Every step of the little Cushite was like a step in a dance, and whenever the wild little prince did not happen to be urging him to join in a game, Ebed-melech was turning and turning in the courtyard of the Lord, absorbed in the dance ritual with which he expressed his adoration of some black and heathen divinity.

Though Jehoahaz was already seventeen years old, his mother Hamutal was still a handsome woman of youthful appearance and serene grace. Her large placid eyes radiated a reflective spirit of harmony and peace. One could see that she was aware of the beauty of her body and expended time and discernment on its preservation. Her hair was worn in the decorative style of Egyptian women, with the brow left completely clear. Her nether garment was white and the upper one wine-red, not sky-blue as the court convention required. In honour of the Lord she was wearing all her jewels, a marvellous array of earrings, rows of necklaces, bracelets, circlets, rings, with golden serpents round her ankles and golden varnish on her toe and finger nails. Josiah loved to see Hamutal decked in her rich gems. His reddish hand rested on her indolent white one, and she nodded smilingly at the low words that he whispered to her, but her eyes kept seeking the romping Mattaniah and spurring on the two attendant slaves so that they should not flag in their solicitude for the child.

The feast had long since begun. Rows of serving Levites and priests of the lowest order were hurrying along the tables with dishes and pitchers. With the most minute attention to detail and observance of the laws the banquet had been prepared by the priests who, pursuing their various duties, had slaughtered the animals, let the blood drain out, cut them up, and divided the food intended for the guests from the portion of the Lord and the quota allowed to His servants. Yet this had not been enough, for in the comprehensive ordering of those things which linked the crown of heaven with the centre of the earth there must be nothing overlooked or forgotten. Even the first-fruits of the field, the vegetables, fruits, spices, and savoury ingredients of the meal had to be inspected and examined before they could be accepted. The whole of creation was based on the distinction between what was good and what was evil, what was clean and what was unclean, what was permitted and what was forbidden. By means of this distinction man in his uncertainty acquired direction and a sense of proportion. Several Temple offices had been instituted solely for the purpose of watching with holy scrupulousness over this separation, which concerned everything in the universe both great and small. In the favoured month of Nisan growth was more than luxuriant, but not every plant, not every fruit was equal before the Lord, as by an incomprehensible predestination not all men were equal in His sight. Fennel, rue, and coriander, field mustard and whatever else grew freely and could be eaten by man, were different, in their relation to God, from the cultivated vegetables. No early cucumber, no pumpkin resembled another in its sacrificial value, and every single olive, tiny as it might be, had first to be tested to see that it was worthy. For Adonai Elohim was the exclusive Lord of all that lived, the God of all youth and vitality in the universe. The least defect, the slightest sign of decay, the taint of a worm in the flesh of a fruit, was regarded by Him as a messenger of Death. And although He Himself had set Death as the supreme power over the world, yet He designated that which it had touched as unclean, defiling, and unacceptable.

As the priests hastened from guest to guest, it could be seen that they were not unaffected by the agitation of the occasion and the strain of the preparations in which they had been engaged. If they had been less numerous, or their organization less exact, many of the younger and less skilful ones would have lost their heads.

Jeremiah stood next to Hananiah behind the King's chair. He was able to let his weak eyes roam over the hazy scene of the great feast, for his services had not yet been needed. He and his neighbour were each holding a goblet of gold in the left hand and an unsealed earthenware pitcher in the right. The wine had been specially pressed for the King. That in Hananiah's pitcher was light golden in colour, and that in Jeremiah's was blood-red.

In front of the King lay a pile of flat unleavened barley cakes. He took the uppermost cake and broke it in four pieces. The first he handed to Hamutal, the second to Shaphan, the third to the commander of his bodyguard, whose name was Maaseiah. The last piece of the cake he sent over to the child Mattaniah, who at once pushed it between the teeth of his brown playmate, the dancing Ebed-melech. Josiah's own way of eating was very hasty. Perhaps he knew of the ancient tradition which recommended that food on this evening should be eaten quickly. For the children of Israel had devoured their food hurriedly before they set out under the miraculous guidance of the Lord to cross the Red Sea. The King's hastiness, however, was not due to this old tradition. He was all impatience—perhaps because of a consuming urge to activity, perhaps because of a secret uneasiness. The emotions of the sons of David were volatile. Josiah's rejoicing with God had turned to a sudden restlessness. For some time he had been drumming on the table with his knuckles. Then he called down to Shaphan:

"Has everything been done which is ordained by the Law? Let nothing come between the Lord and me! What are we waiting for? Let the reading begin!"

Ahikam, the King's private secretary, seemed to have been waiting for this command, for he handed the scroll at once to his father. Shaphan unrolled it carefully without paying any heed to the impatience of the King, and began in a low and droning voice:

> "Observe the month of Abib, and keep the Passover unto the Lord thy God: for in the month of Abib the Lord thy God brought thee forth out of Egypt by night."

"No, not that!" the King interrupted Shaphan brusquely. "That is not what I want. I want to know whether everything is being done and observed in the city in accordance with the commandment of the Lord. Are the people eating bitter herbs? Have the doorposts and the lintels been sprinkled with twigs of hyssop?"

Without waiting for an answer Josiah suddenly turned round and, though several goblets were already standing in front of him, he pointed at the one in the hand of Jeremiah. The latter half filled it, as he had been instructed, with the dark-red wine and handed it to the King. Josiah gazed into the face of the youth from Anathoth with a far-away look in his eyes. Then he drank the wine. Immediately afterwards he again grew impatient.

"What is the matter? Why has the reading ceased? No, not Shaphan! Shaphan's voice is weary. Let someone else read! I want to hear the precepts about the waging of war. This youth here, let him read! Who is he?"

The Master of Ceremonies announced Jeremiah's name and descent. The youth, thus singled out from all the crowd, suddenly found himself standing beside the aged scribe and holding the two handles of the staves on which the Book of the Law was rolled. If he had been told the day before that he would be asked to raise his voice in the presence of the King, he would probably not have accepted the post of honour which had been offered to him. He was shy and held aloof from men. He did not like to stand out before his fellows and let his voice be heard. But now that he had so unexpectedly been the recipient of the King's command, he did not feel the slightest timidity. He felt that it had been ordained and that there was a profound significance in it. Shaphan's withered forefinger pointed out the passage which Jeremiah was to read, and he raised the scroll close to his face. In astonishment he heard his own voice declaiming to the King the measured rhythm of the Word of God. As he listened with bowed head to this voice of his, he noticed that there was a strange quality in it, a new tone.

"When thou goest out to battle against thine enemies, and seest horses, and chariots, and a people more than thou, be not afraid of them. . . ."

" 'Be not afraid of them,' " repeated the King approvingly, as though he rejoiced that the Word of God was so near to his own heart. Jeremiah continued to read calmly, and with every line it seemed to him that the strange quality was growing stronger.

"What man is there that hath built a new house, and hath not dedicated it? Let him go and return to his house, lest he die in the battle, and another man dedicate it.

"And what man is he that hath planted a vineyard, and hath not yet eaten of it? Let him also go and return unto his house, lest he die in the battle, and another man eat of it.

"And what man is there that hath betrothed a wife, and hath not taken her? Let him go and return unto his house, lest he die in battle, and another man take her.

"And the officers shall speak further unto the people; and they shall say, What man is there that is fearful and fainthearted? Let him go and return unto his house, lest his brethren's heart faint as well as his heart.

"And it shall be, when the officers have made an end of speaking unto the people, that they shall make captains of the armies to lead the people."

The King had leaned far forward and was gazing intently at Jeremiah as he repeated with him precepts of the Law which must have involved an almost intolerable burden for a king and general. What had caused his handsome countenance to change? It shone no longer, but was as if clouded over by the most secret thoughts. Why had he demanded the reading of this particular portion? He seemed to want to hear still more of the precepts, which sounded mild for the people but severe for the ruler.

"Read on, you from Anathoth. What is your name? . . . I want to hear that passage about the beleaguered city. Let nothing come between the Lord and me!"

Jeremiah lowered his eyes again to the scroll. There was a deep silence. Many wondered at the urgent note of power that the young man's voice had so swiftly acquired.

"When thou comest nigh unto a city to fight against it, then proclaim peace unto it. . . ."

" 'When thou shalt besiege a city a long time,' " the King cried aloud and full of joy at his good memory, " 'in making war against it to take it, thou shalt not destroy the trees thereof, by forcing an axe against them'! That is how it runs!"

Josiah made a quick sign that the reading was over, then he turned to Jeremiah with a thoughtful look.

"You have read well, you from Anathoth. Your voice will become strong and beautiful when it speaks the Word of God. I wish to hear it again one day."

As was customary, this great praise from the King was followed by the acclamation of the princes and courtiers. Even Shaphan nodded his satisfaction and Ahikam, his grave son, smiled with relief as if a difficult situation had been happily averted. Only one grew yellow with rage and was unable to contain himself—Eliakim. The King's eldest son hurled away with a gesture of disgust the rosebud which he was about to pull to pieces, and his lean face, with its puffy lips conspicuous through the sprouting beard, became contorted. Before the King had given the sign for the conversation to become general, Eliakim jumped up and cried:

"May the King's majesty forgive his servant these words. I find the voice of the man from Anathoth far from beautiful. Never again do I wish to hear it, never!"

The whole company sat petrified at the insolence of the eldest prince, who had dared to oppose his immature judgment to the praise of the King. To the ears of Shaphan and Ahikam it was clear that behind the audacious outburst there lay something more than simple contradiction. Could one admit to one's mind the thought that, by blaming the reader, the future king intended to attack that which had been read, namely the Law of God? Nobody stirred. Even the children noticed that an extremely perilous incident had occurred. Mattaniah desisted from his game; Ebed-melech interrupted his dance. Veiled glances timidly sought the countenance of Josiah, which had clouded. They saw that the King's hand was gripping his goblet with a more and more convulsive clasp. In another moment he would have hurled it at his son, despite the desecration of the feast. But a white, plump hand, the hand of Hamutal, was laid on Josiah's tanned fist, which slowly grew less tense and loosened its hold. For the sake of the pure joy of the Passover, the renewal of which was his work, the King struggled with himself till he was able to utter the hoarse words:

"My eldest son is free to say what he thinks. . . ."

Luckily the sons of Asaph just then broke into a new song, which was accompanied by the ample thunder of drums. All the guests joined in, and it was not possible for anyone to hear his own voice. Jeremiah, who had suddenly become the mediator of the divine Law and the subject of a royal quarrel, stood silent, absorbed and unheeding. The King beckoned to him, and at that moment he caught a strangely penetrating look from Hananiah which he did not forget. Josiah took a gold clasp from his arm and handed it to the youth.

"Take this . . . you from Anathoth!" he said brusquely, and that was all he said to him.

His office of honour at the royal table was not Jeremiah's last duty on that evening. The praise from the King and Eliakim's outburst of hatred had endowed the young man with a certain importance in the eyes of the great officers. Thus it came about that, probably at Shaphan's personal suggestion, a further honour fell to his lot, that of "bearing witness." As this had to be performed by two men from the country outside Jerusalem, the choice of the second witness fell upon Hananiah, the rich man's son, who participated in the distinction because he happened to be standing next to Jeremiah.

The following were the circumstances of the ceremony of bearing witness. After the great feasts, especially after the long-drawn-out Passover banquet, the gates of the Temple could not be closed until very late, generally just before the second night-watch, when the starry host had already crossed the zenith of the heavens. Before the Temple was wrapped in quiet and the silent priests had mounted guard, every trace of the sacrificial repast had to be removed. No sign of secular activity, not the slightest disorder, not the faintest stain, must be allowed to disturb the readiness of the Temple to receive the Lord. For now the most dangerous hours of the day were approaching, the hours when men were defenceless, the period of sleep, when the sacrificial office and prayers were interrupted and the hands of the people were no longer raised in entreaty to their Father and Creator, reminding Him of His obligations to His children. Only single individuals were praying in their chambers, men who were unhappy and bowed down with affliction, and these fervent prayers were but despairing will-o'-the-wisps which, even though they called upon the True Name, might just as well have been calling upon Marduk or Ptah or Tammuz or Chemosh or Milcom or Ashtaroth. There was little that could be averted by such individual prayers in times of personal emergency. Even though the compassion of Adonai was a thousand times greater than His anger, yet He was an incalculable God. His creation, organized and maintained in innumerable degrees, from the sun and the stars, from Hermon's snowy crest down to each blade of grass on the plain, was not a permanent legacy to man on which he could presume; it was only a temporary loan, a mortgage that could be called in at any moment. As a worthy father of a family always held himself ready to be surprised by death, and consequently always kept his house in order, so mankind and the whole of creation had always to be in readiness for the Day of Judgment, which might come at any moment. And what moment could have been more favourable for the sudden and final announcement than when the world was hushed in sleep, when the sacrifices had ceased and men's arms were no longer outstretched in entreaty to restrain the arm of God? During these hours of the night one's house had to be properly ordered. The intent of the Eternal One was fulfilled by an ordered existence and it was only by our ordered existence that man could be worthy of Him in whose image he was made.

It was for the purpose of ensuring this order that the custom of bearing witness had been officially instituted. Jeremiah and Hananiah, as the representatives of the people living outside the city, joined the authoritative body, consisting altogether of twelve men, which had gathered in the now empty courtyard before the altar of burnt offerings. There were the Sagan (who was the senior in rank among the assistants of the High Priest), with five fellow officers, the first Keeper of the Door, three representatives of the King, and the two witnesses. It was the duty of these twelve men to make a tour of inspection through the most important rooms of the sanctuary and ascertain whether the divine order had anywhere been infringed and whether any heretic or blasphemer had dared to smuggle any picture, statue, or secret token of a heathen deity—either in human or animal form; either as sun-wheel, crescent of the moon, or star-cake—into the House of the One True God and to set it up sacrilegiously in some concealed place. In attestation of the immaculate cleanliness which they had found, the twelve men had to scratch their names on a wax tablet. The tour extended only to the main buildings of the actual sanctuary, for if the twelve had paced through every part of the whole Temple, however cursorily, it would have required not one hour of the night, but the whole night. The sacred edifice consisted of three sections: the central, nuclear structure, which was itself in three sections, and the two side wings, which rose to a height of three stories. Each of these stories contained thirty-three chambers, cube-shaped rooms whose doors, skilfully carved in oleaster wood, lay exactly along the central axis, so that a spacious suite met one's eyes. This was where the tour of inspection began. Swiftly, with the Sagan at their head, the twelve men walked through chamber after chamber, in each of which a Levite stood on duty to submit a complete inventory of the utensils belonging to the Temple treasure that were in his charge. The walls were several ells thick, so that it had been easy to build into them cupboard-like closets in which the golden splendour stood piled up. Here was an incalculable accumulation of shovels, tongs, pokers, salvers, dishes, cauldrons, sprinklers, lavers, and censers, all of solid gold; while the objects intended for secular use, such as cans, pitchers, goblets, plates, and cutlery, consisted in part of silver. Brass, which was not a precious metal, to say nothing of fired clay or stoneware, was never used in the Temple.

In dreamy silence Jeremiah, walking beside his staring fellow-witness from Gibeon, brought up the rear of the procession through the gold-laden rooms. The immense heap of treasure, which represented only the small part that was in immediate use, excited in his heart neither pride nor admiration. With a thrill of veneration his mind was fixed to the exclusion of everything else on the approaching moment when he would stand before the last and innermost chamber, divided from the rest, where the Lord, whose home was not in this world, had His only earthly dwelling place. No man of the people, not even the King, had access to this most mysterious of all earthly chambers. Even Hilkiah, the High Priest, summoning all his courage, might tremblingly cross the threshold only once a year to enter the place which was filled with the darkness that was before the first day of creation. In the midst of this darkness stood the Ark of the Covenant with the two cherubim kneeling on it, whose gigantic pinions touched the walls on either side. In the Ark were the two rough, jagged tablets of stone that Moses had broken from the Rock of Sinai. Whoever came too near them would be struck dead by their power, for they were the only contact with the world of Him who eternally transcends the world, the unique incorporation of the incorporeal in the great communion between man and God which is the Word.

Jeremiah had no eyes for the treasures in the countless rooms of the two side wings. He paid no heed to the priestly garments that hung in long rows, neither the coats of double byssus tissue that were made in one piece without seam nor the beautiful stoles, thin as a serpent's skin and embroidered with purple and hyacinthine flowers; neither the mitres, the coifs, nor the fillets, gold embroidered and richly decorated. He paid no heed to the magnificent girdles, the hems and borders with their golden bells and silver pomegranates whose purpose was to announce to the people the approach of the High Priest. He passed indifferently by the multicoloured shoulder cloaks of fine weave that were called ephods, and the solemnity of the many ages which they had outlasted meant nothing to him. As in the confusion of a dream he was dimly conscious of the hundredfold shapes of lamps and candelabra, of the artistically shaped censers large and small, the spice boxes and pots of ointment, the beaked receptacles for the sacrificial oil, the crystal phials with anointing oil, the finger bowls and basins chased with fruits and flowers, the jewelled gifts of foreign kings and princes, of every size and for every purpose—all the things that flamed in splendour by the light of the torches and vanished again into the spectral gloom.

Jeremiah seemed to awaken from his apathetic reverie only when the twelve men had again gathered on the steps of the porch. They all drew a deep breath to summon up strength to enter the sanctuary. The Sagan now walked in their midst and called upon them to undertake a minute examination of their consciences, in order that the divine dwelling place might not be marred by the faintest hidden stain. In a subdued voice he enumerated the various conditions that rendered a man unclean in the eyes of the Lord and made it undesirable that he should approach the eternal purity of the sanctuary. In accordance with the precepts he spoke in low, swift tones, for much that he had to mention in the enumeration of impurities had to be said in frank words which would pain the sensitive chastity of worthy men; the possible sources of impurity embraced everything imaginable, from the uncleanliness incurred through the sight of a corpse to secret onanism. When he had finished, the senior priest paused, that each of them might have sufficient time to enter into judgment with himself. None asked to be excluded, so he gave the sign to proceed. Slowly they ascended the ten steps that led to the porch.

The torches were extinguished, for strange fire might not be carried into the innermost sanctuary. The two sons of Aaron had once been overtaken by doom because they had offered strange fire before the Lord. For a while there was deep darkness in the courtyard, against which the moon and a patch of seeping starlight only gradually became visible. The two pillars Boaz and Jachin cast long, deep shadows. The secret of their significance had been lost through the ages, but some wise ancients thought that Boaz absorbed and preserved the power of the sun, Jachin that of the moon. The fruit and lily work of their capitals shimmered faintly, but from within the sanctuary there poured a light so diffused, so rare, so full of meaning, that Jeremiah's heart began to beat uncontrollably. It beat even faster after a few steps had brought them to the chamber which contained the Holy of Holies. Here was the source of the light that caused Jeremiah such deep agitation. On a little altar lay a heap of glowing coals which emitted a reddish light and a steady spiral of smoke. Near by stood a seven-branched candelabrum the height of a man, but only three tiny oil lamps were burning in it with a soft and tranquil radiance that merged into the gloom half-way towards the ceiling. Jeremiah could hardly distinguish the shimmering of the sheets of gold with which the walls were panelled, and still less was he able to perceive the cedarwood carving that reached up into the darkness with all its infinite variations of design—flower-buds, rue, grapes, lilies, and colocynths. The atmosphere of the chamber entered not only into his heart but even into his limbs. He walked on cool, smooth boards of cedar which felt pleasant to the soles of his feet. Nowhere was there any sign of lifeless stone. No nails or rivets had been used in the walls or beams, the ceiling or the doors; nothing had been hammered together, neither had axe or chisel or any other tool of iron been employed. The entire chamber, dovetailed together in a wondrous fashion, resembled the garment of the High Priest, which was without seam. Jeremiah's eyes, however, were fixed on the curtain that filled the doorway of the ultimate mystery, the four-coloured tissue of which could be only faintly discerned.

The six priests had grouped themselves for a short prayer. Then their leader gathered all the men round him and inquired in a whisper:

"Who is the youngest here?"

The youngest was Jeremiah. The Sagan took him by the hand and drew him a few paces into the background. Then he lifted the centre lamp from the seven-branched candelabrum and held it before the youth's face, which he looked at long and searchingly.

"Jirmejahu ben Hilkiah of Anathoth," he whispered in an almost inaudible tone, "you have been chosen as a witness from the people outside Jerusalem to let your eyes rest on the Holy of Holies. Veil your head! You may raise the veil only as far as the lower eyelid and even then for only as long as you can keep your eyes open without letting the lids fall. This glance must suffice for you to see what you have to see."

Jeremiah suddenly grew as calm again as he had been when reading the Book of the Law. Unsuspectingly he had left his native town that morning to proceed to the Temple in order that there might be fulfilled in him a triple destiny. He had proclaimed the Word of God in the presence of the King. For this he had reaped both praise and blame. And finally, the greatest favour of all, he had been permitted to raise his eyes to the only place where the Lord Adonai dwelt on earth. An overwhelming silence ensued. The twelve men seemed to have ceased to breathe. Only Hananiah, who was not favoured in the same way as his fellow-witness, coughed once. Obediently Jeremiah veiled his head as the priest again took him by the hand and led him forward. His fingers touched a doorpost whose age-old cedarwood was still as freshly fragrant as if it had been felled but a few hours before. He knew that all the others had likewise veiled their heads. He turned and gripped the heavy curtain with both hands, then parted it until there was a narrow gap. Obediently Jeremiah uncovered his face as far as the lower eyelid. For one hesitant moment his heart was compressed within him. Then he took a tense decision. He opened his eyes and the Holy of Holies was before him. But all they saw was a thick darkness, a darkness that was not like that of earthly night, the darkness that existed before creation, before light was. Only towards the end of the allotted time, when his eyelids were about to fall, did anything seem to be taking shape out of this darkness. Was it the giant wings of the golden-throned cherubim? A surge of power beyond human conception streamed towards Jeremiah, and the breath of it was still upon him long after the curtain had again been closed.

5

The Voice Without and Within

THE boy Baruch was waiting with Jeremiah's she-ass and his own animal at the Gate of Benjamin. The abundance of the festal evening had yielded to a night that was vibrant with emptiness and silence. A single torch of pitch, already flickering out, hung in its ring on the wall. The priestly sentry sat sleepily at the entrance to the gate, waiting to be relieved. When Jeremiah stepped out into the open and the bolt was shot to behind him, no word of complaint came from the lips of the sixteen-year-old Baruch though he had spent a day of considerable privation as he waited for the comrade whom he venerated. Jeremiah noticed at once that the boy was trembling with cold, and he hung his own cloak round his shoulders. Although he often accepted the boy's strange attachment only with reluctance, he always felt a shy solicitude for him, as he did now. They mounted their animals without a word and rode down into the Valley of Kidron. The great moon and the star of Ashtaroth, Queen of Heaven, still illumined the sky. In their wan light the gnarled sycamores and terebinths were sharply outlined by the wayside. The olive groves clung to the side of the hill like a thin cloud of smoke from a burnt offering blowing gently towards the east. In the villages the dark cubes of houses stood up stubbornly as though angry at some possible disturbance of the nocturnal silence. The wild dogs which roamed the countryside during the day had crept back to their lairs. The two riders heard nothing except an occasional wail, the sharp yelp of a jackal, or the brief note of a dreaming bird, rising on the air and swiftly dying away again, from amid the trembling branches.

As was prescribed by custom, the younger boy did not address the older one until the latter had given him the sign to talk. This was not until they had reached the crest of the hill, where the road turned mournfully away from Jerusalem, set upon its height, to lead down over the boundary between Judah and Benjamin towards the town of Anathoth. Jeremiah told his disciple of the happenings that evening in the Temple, and he tried to make his narration as dry and brief as possible without laying any emphasis on the undoubted significance of what had occurred. He was, however, hardly successful in his attempt to minimize the significance of the three great incidents in which he had played a leading part: the reading of the rediscovered Law for which he, the youngest there, had been selected by the whim of King Josiah; the praise and blame of which he had been the recipient; and finally the distinction of bearing witness before the Holy of Holies. The intelligent Baruch had his own particular views about the future of Jeremiah, and it was this intuition or premonition that kept him close to the heels of the young solitary of Anathoth and filled him every day anew with a thrill of pleasure at the thought that he was an adherent of one who was to be a great figure. Jeremiah's report of what had happened while he was serving in the Temple and at the table of the King dispersed at once the boy's shivering fatigue. He raised himself up in the saddle.

"Now my teacher has received his proof!"

"Why do you call me 'teacher'? Do I not ask you every day

not to address me by a name to which I have no right?"

"What is my master if he is not my teacher?"

"It is a name to which I have no right. Call me your elder brother, or your countryman, or, if it pleases you and it must be so, call me your master. I myself am not even a pupil, so who could learn anything from me?"

There began a discussion which, had it been overheard, would have seemed like a playing with words by two irresponsible persons. Baruch, the son of Neriah, cried aloud into the deserted and echoing night:

"While I was waiting I read something in the ancient writings which I did not learn from my master, but which applies to him!"

Jeremiah almost gave a start and demanded with displeasure:

"Is this again a passage from Holy Writ?"

Joyfully came the response:

"It is again a passage from Holy Writ!"

Jeremiah dug his heels into the withers of his ass and belaboured her fiercely with his stick, so that she changed her amble for the quickest trot of which she was capable. Baruch's smaller and weaker animal could hardly keep up with her; nevertheless the lad began with the panting breathlessness brought on by trotting without stirrups to unburden himself of his newly acquired lore:

> "And the child Samuel ministered unto the Lord before Eli. And the word of the Lord was precious in those days; there was no open vision. . . ."

Without slowing down or turning round, Jeremiah called over his shoulder:

"My countryman Baruch is in error. That passage does not apply to me. My father's house is not descended from Samuel the Prophet. Our ancestor was Eli the Priest, Eli the little old man, whose fame is but slight . . . Eli with his worthless sons."

Baruch panted along on his poor little donkey without letting himself be intimidated, and he continued his chant though he hardly had sufficient breath left in his body:

> "And it came to pass at that time, when Eli was laid down in his place, and his eyes began to wax dim, that he could not see. . . ."

The near-sighted Jeremiah, trotting equably along, replied: "The eyes of Eli, my ancestor, began to wax dim in old age. Mine are already dim and weak in my youth. What do you expect of me?"

The boy expected so much of him that the words of the old chronicle tripped one another up before they passed his tongue.

> "And ere the lamp of God went out in the Temple of the Lord, where the Ark of God was, and Samuel was laid down to sleep; that the Lord called Samuel: and he answered, Here am I. And he ran unto Eli, and said, Here am I, for thou calledst me. And he said, I called not; lie down again. And he went and lay down. . . ."

Jeremiah began to spur his ass and to urge her to an even faster pace. From the words of the boy he heard his mysterious pursuer still calling to him. For years he had refrained from answering the constant summons: "Jirmejahu!" with the words: "Here am I!" His pursuer acquired new power and strengthened the short legs of Baruch's ass so that they rode almost saddle to saddle. And Jeremiah had to hear how the Lord had called the young Samuel for the second time. Perhaps Samuel had been no older than he was himself when the low voice, not yet in its full power, began to seek him out, to weave before his eyes those fleeting phantom visions which inspired in him such longing apprehension and apprehensive longing, and from which he fled with such pitiful cunning. The voice of Baruch pierced through Jeremiah now with every staccato, breathless syllable.

"And the Lord called Samuel again the third time. And he arose and went to Eli, and said, Here am I; for thou didst call me. . . ."

Obedient Samuel! Three times you rose calmly, three times you stepped to the couch of the old man and answered loyally: "Here am I!"

They were riding past the outline of a peasant's low-built house. As they approached, a number of shadows flitted across the roof, fearfully carrying with them as they disappeared a tripod whose scanty flames the riders had seen from afar. Some peasant women had probably been sacrificing to Ashtaroth, offering her incense and consecrated star-cakes. The abomination, the great apostasy, still glowed beneath the ashes in spite of King Josiah, and was ready to flame up at every gust of wind. And the Word of the Lord was precious in those days, for there was little prophesying. Jeremiah allowed his ass to resume its amble, and the boy's voice, husky but no longer breathless, concluded its repetition of the story which had been written in the records and handed down:

"And Eli perceived that the Lord had called the child. Therefore Eli said unto Samuel, Go, lie down: and it shall be, if He call thee, that thou shalt say, Speak, Lord; for Thy servant heareth. . . ."

At the very moment when these words were uttered: "Speak, Lord, for Thy servant heareth," Jeremiah's ass gave such a violent leap to the side that her rider swayed in the saddle. Yet no nocturnal animal had flitted by, neither did a snake, a root, or a shadow lie across the path. The matted flanks of the ass shivered and she spread her forelegs far apart as she emitted with distended nostrils a veritably human and protesting wail. For a long time they could do nothing that would induce her to continue on her way. The two youths had to alight in order to pacify the animal with soothing and persuasive words. Baruch blinked in his excitement, but wisely refrained from any reference to the fact that a new and incontrovertible token had been vouchsafed to them. A light or two at the bottom of the valley showed that they were no longer far from Anathoth.

The estate of Hilkiah lay before the gates of the fortified town of Anathoth on the summit of a pleasant and fertile hill. It was a fine large property and included many acres of arable land. It was to this place that King Solomon, twelve generations before, had exiled Abiathar the High Priest, Hilkiah's ancestor, who had escaped death at the hands of the executioner only by the fact that he had been one of the bearers of the Ark of the Lord on the day when David danced before it. These were old stories from the dim times of legend, but the rambling mansion was still the same as it had been in Abiathar's day, the same protecting wall with the same gates still surrounded the estate of Jeremiah's father. And even the defective places in this ancient rampart had been there as far back as memory reached in the family of Hilkiah.

Not until Jeremiah had unsaddled his ass, rubbed her down, watered her, and given her fodder did he creep across the yard through the little gateway into his father's house. He was afraid that his mother might have remained awake and be waiting for him, as she often did when he was pursued by the mysterious voice at night and left the house in order that in the company of trees, hills, and stars he might not be so wholly alone with Adonai as he was in his chamber. He had never spoken to Abi, his mother, about these visitations, though they had often driven him out of his mind, so that more than once he came to himself in an open field like a man stricken by the hand of God who had been roaming outside his body. But while his mother was unaware of this, her eyes looked as if she guessed a great deal. She was afraid and grieved for Jeremiah's soul and would wait up for him when he left the house suddenly after the evening meal amid the mockery and displeasure of the other members of the family. It was now late, however, and dawn could not be far away, since he had been riding for more than an hour after leaving the capital. His mother had gone to bed, but she had thoughtfully left the back door unbolted and had even set a burning oil lamp upon the threshold.

Shielding the light of the lamp with his hand, Jeremiah tiptoed past the honoured room where his parents slept. The inner part of the house was divided into two by a long passage, at the end of which lay his own bedroom. With a sigh he entered the little, low chamber whose ceiling beams he could touch without difficulty. The large square, unglazed window space faced towards the north, and at this mild season of the year the wooden shutters had been removed from their hinges, so that the exhilarating night air of the month of Nisan, fragrant with honey, streamed in freely. Jeremiah placed the lamp on the parapet of the window as if to give a secret sign to Heaven that he had returned home. At once there began a dance of night moths round the only flame at which they could worship so late. He leaned out into the night. Not far away in the darkness he saw a heap of hewn stones from some structure that had been torn asunder. When he was a child the house altar had stood there, for in those days his father and the whole family had still made their daily offerings to Zebaoth, as had been customary until the decree was issued which forbade the offering up of sacrifices elsewhere than in the one and only House of the Lord. The boy Jeremiah had himself zealously helped to demolish the venerable altar with bare hands, without the employment of any tool. A little to the west of this pile of stones rose a dilapidated square building the sight of which had inspired the children of Hilkiah with a thrill of pious apprehension so long as they were small. For in the time of their forefathers, long, long before the days of King Josiah, this house had sheltered the Lord Himself. It had been the family sanctuary, the estate chapel. Now it was opened and used only on special occasions, when Hilkiah or his eldest son, Obadiah, who was engaged in the management of the estate, entered into a solemn business contract with a neighbour, a tenant farmer, or a cattle dealer and swore the customary formal oath.

Jeremiah's eyes gazed beyond the dilapidated sanctuary and sought the familiar scene of undulating hills and mountain chains that were lost in the moonlight towards the north. He had always loved the view from this window, from the day when the name of the Lord had first awakened in him until this night when he had fulfilled an office of honour in the Temple. It was from this countryside, from the north, that had come all the scenes and incidents which had impressed themselves on his heart. As a boy of seven he had stood at this window when the northern sky had suddenly been darkened by a fierce cloud of dust in the wake of a horde of foreign horsemen. A tribe of Scythians had invaded the country of the Lord. They were pig-tailed men, with wide mouths and slit eyes in merciless, wolf-like faces, a tribe that did not possess even heathen deities. Could they be the instruments of the Day of Judgment which had been prophesied, and which hung now as always like a menacing cloud over Judah? No one knew. With eyes dilated with terror his mother had snatched him away from the window, and Hilkiah's whole household had fled down into the fortified city for protection. But the hesitant Zebaoth had only been warning them, showing them threatening scenes of what the end might be. The galloping hosts had stormed towards the south in the way they had come. Murder and rapine lay behind them. This time the Lord had spared the house of His servant.

Jeremiah's weak eyes were burning with fatigue. He had risen before dawn to make his pilgrimage to the Temple and only a few hours were left before the beginning of a new day. Yet he could not turn away from the view with which he had been familiar all his life. In the waning moonlight, which made the landscape seem more concentrated, he could feel the presence of the highroad in the distance which led across the ridge. A thin whitish mist, a strange cloud of dust that had been whirled up neither by the hoofs of a horse nor by any vehicle, hovered above it. It was as if the whole sequence of scenes and incidents were being drawn together within this gradually accumulating moondust, in order to take leave of Hilkiah's youngest son, who had stood motionless at his window year after year overlooking the world. He had seen the frequent troops of pilgrims from Manasseh and Ephraim, the tribes of the north, whom the judgment of the Lord had condemned to live as shadows. They were proceeding up to the Temple in order to offer the first crop from their exhausted fields. He had seen caravans in endless procession carrying various kinds of commodities, for which no name had yet been invented, from Tyre and Sidon and even farther, from Asshur and Babylon, even from farthest India, travelling by way of Jerusalem down to the House of Bondage by the Nile where the people immortalized their dead. Hundreds of nodding camels, laden with bales, had passed by with their air of aristocratic melancholy, walking one behind the other at a steady pace. Jeremiah had seen the magnificent coaches of foreign princes, preceded by hosts of runners, heralds, and motley fairy-tale figures, and the proud embassies of Asshur with their swiftly trotting escorts clad in armour and wearing peaked or conical helmets. Purple saddle-cloths on gold-bridled horses, a flashing giant at their head . . .

And now the time had come. From sheer weariness Jeremiah had lost all sense of feeling in his limbs. He extinguished the shrivelled wick between thumb and forefinger, and so quickly did exhaustion overtake him that he fell upon his couch without picking up the garment that he had cast upon the floor. His mind was emptied. There was no room for even a fleeting memory of the scenes and happenings of the day. It was a sleep without transition, deep and sudden.

This sleep can scarcely have lasted for the tenth part of an hour before it vanished as swiftly as it had come, leaving him wide awake. The inexpressible mystery of what now took place consisted indeed in the fact that he was less dreamy than ever, that his mind was clear, fresh, and alert as if he had rested for several hours and was completely master of the reality and truth within him and without. He sat up and gazed into the obscurity of the room. Something was happening. The window space had darkened and something was entering from outside, extending in every direction until it filled the whole room. It was not like a misty cloud, but appeared clear in every detail to the last petal. A bough thick with blossom was burgeoning luxuriantly and twining along the walls like a net as it kept putting forth new branches. It was as if a tree had suddenly taken root in front of the window and its boughs were forcing their way into the room. They were the branches of an almond tree, the tree which awakens to life earlier in the year than any other, as soon as winter is ended and before any other bud has begun to unfold. As it was now Passover, the almond had finished flowering some weeks before, yet the branches of this early-blossoming tree of youth and life continued to push their way unceasingly through the window. Countless white and pink buds sprang up, unfolded, drooped, and were replaced by others. Jeremiah could have seized the heart-stirring blossoms with his hands, branch by branch, bud by bud, but he sat motionless on his couch. He knew that this was a vision! It was even not altogether unfamiliar to him, this vision of flowering branches, though it had never appeared to him with a hundredth part of the clarity and maturity in which he now saw it. He held his breath, and strained his hearing to the utmost. The voice must now come, the voice that he knew, though only as a brief and vague whisper or as a hollow, distant call which seemed to be rolling down from a mountainside, an illusory echo, or a prickling exhortation within his own head. Whenever the vision or the voice had come to him he had fled, hiding himself with a wild beating of the heart. Like a child, a youth not yet grown to manhood, he had been terrified of reaching man's estate. Now, however—and this he knew—flight could no longer help him. For God's purpose he was already a man.

The voice came at the very moment when he expected it. It was a clear and gentle masculine voice, filling the room with its dark mellowness. Every chink in the wall, every fissure in the wood, was filled with it equally and simultaneously. Yet in some miraculous way there was no source from which the voice sent out its vibrations. It arose and was diffused everywhere at the same time. It issued from the whole chamber. It was as if it had always been there, submerged by the general noise of the busy world. Now this general noise seemed to be in abeyance, so that the voice could rise to the surface. But Jeremiah, too, was such a chamber. He, too, was filled with the general noise of every day, which was now retreating to make way for the voice. Consequently it filled not only the outer room around him, but also the inner room which was himself. The voice spoke both within and without at the same time, a dual yet a single sound.

The clear and gentle voice called:

"Jirmejahu!"

In a little while, his breath coming with difficulty, he answered:

"Here am I!"

In this answer lay the last residue of cowardly cunning, for the words, "Here am I," did not suffice. The formula of response to the voice of God was different. Eli the Priest had confided the formula to Samuel, the boy prophet, and it had been repeated that evening through the mouth of Baruch, who must have been endowed with the right to do so. Jeremiah was well aware of what he had to say, but he thought that the vision might pass this time too. It did not pass. The room, of which he was a part, was again filled equally and simultaneously with the mellow voice that called:

"Jirmejahu!"

Jeremiah was vanquished and his fear dwindled. He

opened his hands as though in hesitant prayer and replied with the words:

"Speak, Lord, for Thy servant heareth."

The words of the voice now enveloped the couch almost physically and gathered at its head; for the low murmur no longer came simultaneously and equally from everywhere in the room, but seemed to be increasingly concentrated round Jeremiah himself:

"Before I formed thee in the belly I knew thee; and before thou camest forth out of the womb I sanctified thee, and I ordained thee a prophet unto the nations."

Within and without in perfect unison, he heard the irrevocable pronouncement: "I knew thee . . . I sanctified thee . . . I ordained thee." Strange and inconceivable was the message of the voice. Never had Jeremiah in his most secret heart surmised that he could be chosen as the instrument of divine purpose, that he, the son of Hilkiah and Abi, no different from other men, had been predestined to such a future while still within the womb. It had indeed been no secret either to him or to the intuitive Baruch that there must be some meaning and intention in those immature visions and voices that had pursued him since his thirteenth year, but what could be the significance of the words, "a prophet unto the nations"? Which nations? The great nations? Asshur, Babylon, Egypt? And he? What was he? A timid youth who shunned the society of men, who always longed for solitude, who followed no profession, who avoided any conflict. Though Jeremiah sat there in that great hour with no power of movement in his limbs, scarcely breathing and his heart almost stopped, transported from the world by what was happening, yet his mind had lost nothing of its tense alertness and caution. He still sought pretexts for delay and respite. Fully conscious of the inadequacy of his excuse, he stammered with the plaintive pleading of a child:

"Ah, Lord God, behold, I cannot speak, for I am a child."

He felt how weak this pretext was for one who had been called by the Lord and who had passed his twentieth year. The voice, which replied in unmoved tones, hardly seemed any longer to be in the outer room, but to have withdrawn completely into Jeremiah himself.

"Say not, I am a child: for thou shalt gird up thy loins, and arise, and speak unto them all that I command thee."

In the short space of time between his first response and this pronouncement, Jeremiah's courage had grown with an inexplicable rapidity. A great assurance came over him as though he was already old in experience of communion with the voice. He slipped from the couch and sat on its edge. The branches of the almond tree receded a little as if to tease him and now completely veiled the window opening. But the voice did not recede. It still filled the whole of the room like water in a vessel.

"What seest thou?"

"I see a rod of an almond tree."

"Thou hast well seen: for I will hasten my word to perform it."

Jeremiah sprang up. To the courage in his soul was added a sobbing, ecstatic desire to hold Adonai firmly, to belong to Him for ever. With a gratitude that filled his heart to bursting he perceived that this was no illusion, no dream, no enchantment, but as intimate and true and real as he himself was. He opened his arms wide. Suddenly the branches with the flowering buds withered and began to burn. But framed within the window, or rather outside in the now moonless night, a great pot hung between earth and sky on invisible chains, though the flames that licked at it from below were clearly to be seen. This pot, too, possessed a solid reality. The fire reddened the seething steam that hissed from it. It swayed a little on its invisible supports, so that its edge inclined towards Jeremiah from the north and, spilling over, spurted dense, glowing streams of lava, boiling pitch, or melted iron roundabout. For the first time the voice now came from one definite place, close to Jeremiah's ear.

"What seest thou?"

"I see a seething pot; and the face thereof is toward the north."

"Out of the north an evil shall break forth upon all the inhabitants of the land."

These prophecies were far beyond Jeremiah's powers of understanding. He still did not possess the gift of interpreting them. The Lord was free and independent of the mind which He had sanctified that it might serve Him. Jeremiah's strength was beginning to fail. His knees were growing weak and were giving way beneath him. The pot continued to send forth clouds of steam and to strew about the sky the first red gleams of dawn. Once more the voice of the Lord issued forth, and for the first time Jeremiah noticed that the clear and mellow tone was not like that of ordinary men, but like the cool and chanting cadence of the priests.

"I have this day set thee over the nations and over the kingdoms, to root out, and to pull down, and to destroy, and to throw down, to build, and to plant."

The last words, "to build, and to plant," hovered exultingly in the air like a song of the sons of Asaph. Jeremiah wanted to call out that he accepted the injunction and would obey. But he could not speak. His voice died away in his throat and his response was choked by the perception of his tremendous destiny. Then the Lord touched him.

"The Lord put forth His hand, and touched my mouth. And the Lord said unto me, Behold, I have put my words in thy mouth." This was the simple, awkward way in which from now on Jeremiah would describe the indescribable when curious questioners asked what had happened to him. And each time these words tortured his soul as though they were presumption and vain deceit. The Lord God Zebaoth had no hand which He could stretch out from the place where He was. He had a voice, and this voice was His "ruach," His breath, with which He filled Jeremiah and the room about him as though they were a trumpet. It was the breath of Zebaoth that gave rise to the sound, but the brass of the trumpet had helped to bring it forth. Without this instrument His breath would have had no resonance. The voice of the Lord needed the soul of man for a sounding-board. Breath was spirit. A hand was not spirit. Yet, though Adonai possessed no hand, it was His hand that touched Jeremiah; He touched him with a real touch. And this touch was a swift tap on the mouth. He flamed through this man with the agony of agonies, with the joy of joys. If there were a fire that could burn to ashes a being of flesh and blood in the thousandth part of a second, the agony would be like the agony of this touch. On the created earth there were many metaphors for pain. For the joy of that touch there was no metaphor. And in that tap on the mouth was a third component quality: the ice-clear awareness that now and for all time he was different, reborn and regenerated by a process of dying and resurrection.

Jeremiah fell to the ground with a loud cry.

6

The Prophet in the House of His Father

NOBODY in the house had heard the cry in the early morning except Jeremiah's mother, who cast a horrified look at Hilkiah in the bed beside her. The old man, who was mostly in a discontented frame of mind, was asleep. As was his usual habit, he had awakened her twice in the course of the night to have her hear the querulous complaints about his three sons to which he liked to give vent. The intermittent sleep of age, with its frequent interruptions, afforded him numerous opportunities to brood over the unworthy behaviour of Obadiah and Joel and the stubborn reserve of Jeremiah. Towards morning, however, his uneasy sleep grew more profound, and Abi could venture to rise from his side and creep into the chamber of her youngest son. She found him lying in a cramped position on the floor, with his face pressed against the hardened clay of which it was composed. Dropping to her knees beside him, she anxiously felt his ice-cold hands and feet and then put her hand to his rapidly beating heart. At last she succeeded in raising him by the shoulders and pillowing his head on her lap. He was shaken by a convulsive sobbing of which he himself appeared to be unaware, and his whole body was damp with a cold sweat. His mother dried his brow and neck; while she did so she rocked to and fro as women do when they are soothing a baby. Without knowing whether he was unconscious or could hear what she said, she whispered:

"What ails my child? What is the matter with my youngest son? Is he ill, may the Lord protect him!"

At the sound of her voice Jeremiah opened his eyes. The look in them showed that he had understood the question and wished to reassure her. His mother ceased her rocking.

"Has something evil befallen my youngest son? Did something occur to mortify him . . . yesterday?"

The long-lashed eyes of her son rested on her with a faraway look in them and he did not reply. She continued with her questioning:

"Were you not received with honour? Were you passed over? And yet you went forth so proudly to the Temple as the pride of your father's heart. . . . Oh, would that you had never gone!"

Jeremiah, who was once more in full command of his senses, interrupted her softly:

"No, Mother, it is not that!"

"What is it then, my son? Am I to beg of you?"

Her son turned his head away silently. Abi appeared to grow angry.

"I find you lying on the cold floor and weeping for no apparent cause! Like someone who is mourning, like an orphan who has lost father and mother, brothers and sisters, and to whom nothing is left except to cut his cheek with a knife. But, God be praised, we are all alive. Do not by false grief tempt genuine misfortune to come upon you, for one helps to engender that which one imitates. Do you not know that the messenger of death stands in every corner? If you lie here any longer, you will become really ill. Get up, my son!"

Jeremiah obeyed the zealous exhortation, rose from the floor, and stretched out his hand to his mother to help her up. When she began her questioning again, he interrupted her gravely:

"I wish to sleep, Mother."

Without more ado Jeremiah cast himself upon his low couch and did not stir. He had fallen into an immediate and profound sleep, and this frightened his mother more than anything else. She thought that a dangerous fever, some deep-seated malady, must undoubtedly have taken possession of her son. She reproached herself for not having sat up to await his return, when she could have prepared for him a fortifying and purging sleeping-draught which would at once have subdued the evil influences that lay in wait everywhere for those who were loved by the Lord. Yet as she hastened to the fireplace and to the larder in order to brew a belated medicinal drink, she realized with a sudden flash of intuition that it was not a fever, not a malady, not a nightmare by which Jeremiah had been attacked, but something far more powerful than any of these fatal influences. She still did not dare to imagine to herself what this power might be, but Jeremiah's nightly roaming, which had always filled her with such apprehension, must undoubtedly be connected with it in some terrifying way. She had to stop in the middle of her task, for her limbs began to tremble. Her mind could not yet grasp it, but there was something in her blood, with its mystic participation in the life of her son, that warned her what the power was.

When the drink was ready and she had brought it to Jeremiah's bedside, he was asleep and breathing tranquilly. Abi sat down at the foot of the bed with the tray upon her knee, anxious not to awaken the exhausted boy. As she sat quietly and contemplated his face, it seemed as though he were also contemplating her through his thin eyelids and as though he knew what she knew. It was as though *he* were hiding behind his sleep and *she* were hiding behind the rigid watch that she was keeping over his sleep. Now and then she felt the cup containing the hot drink. It became warm, then tepid, then cool, and finally cold. She did not know how long it was before Jeremiah's voice broke upon the stillness:

"Since I may not conceal it from the world, how can I conceal it from you, my mother?"

Her thoughts came back to earth, but she pretended to suspect nothing.

"Conceal what? Of what are you speaking, my son?"

Soberly and briefly the words came from his lips:

"The Lord has been with me."

She stared at him with large, vacant eyes. Then he told her everything.

"He was with me here in this room . . . with His voice, in all His power. . . . And His voice spoke to me . . . and His voice is sending me away from here. . . ."

"Is sending you away from here . . ." she repeated. The words came with difficulty from her tongue, but he made a slight movement with his hand which eliminated her last doubt.

"Yes, Mother, that is what happened and is to be."

Abi's eyes filled with tears. She was not weeping because the Lord was sending her beloved child away. She had never hoped to be able to keep him at her side. Neither was she weeping because the Lord had come to him. Must she not be proud among the mothers of Jacob? The Eternal One, the Terrible One to whom she prayed morning and evening, was kind, and yet her heart was breaking with great sorrow because of the sanctification of her son. Jeremiah, however, kept his eyes closed, as if he wished to hide himself again. Since he had been touched by the Lord it hurt so much to keep them open and look at things. Everything was transformed, revealing other and perilous interpretations—the room he had known since childhood, the window, the very daylight. And even the being most near to him, his mother, had receded further away from him. He found her loving care almost disturbing. It concerned only the welfare and the happy future of a little Jeremiah who no longer existed. The new Jeremiah was an austere and inexorable son, who knew that he must free himself from every tie and learn to hurt both himself and her.

The most important meal of the day was taken, in accordance with age-long custom, by the whole family in the room to which a venerable tradition had given the name of "the Hall of Abiathar." But though it was called after the famous sage and High Priest of the days of David, it scarcely deserved its sonorous appellation. It was nothing but a very large, bare rustic room, whose low ceiling rested on a number of simple stone pillars. Since the Hall of Abiathar lay in the centre of the house, it was never penetrated by the light of day, so that it was always cool and dark, an inestimable advantage for the greater part of the year. It was because of the permanent gloom in this common living-room that there always burned upon the dining-table a lamp known not only to the family but also to all their relations and even to strangers as "the Lamp of the House of Hilkiah," and it was a light that was both useful and pregnant with meaning. When a family had died out people said: "The Lamp of the House has become extinguished." The lamp on Hilkiah's table was, as it were, an ever-burning light whose oil was not allowed to run out, as a token that, by the grace of God, the family had existed for so many generations. The table itself, round which the family had gathered since time immemorial, was spacious, if rather low, and it was of a hard wood that was now worm-eaten. It was essential that there should be plenty of space round it, for, though the number of Hilkiah's sons was but modest, the family table must never be too small for the generations to come. On this particular day, the first day after the eve of Passover, there were only thirteen chairs, which were really short-legged stools covered with skins.

The whole inner circle of the family had assembled for the festive repast; that is to say, the parents, the married sons with their wives and older children, and Jeremiah. There were also two individuals who were the recipients of Hilkiah's hospitality. Obadiah, the eldest son and the future head of the house, liked to talk in loud and throaty tones like a peasant, whereby he gave the world to understand that the whole burden of managing the estate and ensuring its future prosperity rested upon his shoulders. How should the draught-ox and beast of burden of the family find time to polish his manners or to shine in intellectual conversation? How unjust his mother was towards him, honest boor as he was, in bestowing all her love on Jeremiah! And his venerable father as well, who had never had any active understanding of the requirements of life! Obadiah was not the only one to have his views about this supercilious lack of appreciation for solid worth. His wife Mocheleth also had ideas on the subject. Her husband worked for everybody, but received neither reward nor thanks! Mocheleth was very plain, and like many plain people she was inclined to cherish hatred.

The fact that Obadiah had long since ceased to share her couch and consoled himself instead with every young serving-maid or comely slave from the fields was something that she had not only to accept, but even to approve. All the more fiercely was she consumed by the thought of the ingratitude and presumption with which her Obadiah, the benefactor and supporter of the family, was treated in certain quarters. She had never had any doubt from the beginning that the cause of this undesirable situation lay in the favouritism shown by Abi to her youngest son.

A very different type from the heavy-handed Obadiah, with his prosperous belly and throaty voice, was Hilkiah's second son, whose name was Joel. Joel appeared at the table only from time to time, generally on the eve of the Sabbath, at the new moon, and the high festivals, for his business took him travelling. It was his duty to sell the surplus goods produced on Hilkiah's estate, and he journeyed with them in the country roundabout and in foreign lands. With his beasts of burden and wagons laden with barley flour, oil and wine, the skins of lambs and goats, spices and aromatics, flax, yarn, and linen, he traversed the well-kept highroads of the world up as far as Damascus, down as far as Noph in the Land of Bondage, and westwards to the busy ports of Tyre and Sidon. Was it not the duty of such an inveterate merchant to be an observer of human nature and a man of the world? It was easy to see that Joel took an extraordinary delight in his own supple eloquence. There were a hundred languages and dialects between the Nile and the Euphrates, and it was said that Joel was familiar with them all. With amazing skill and in most attractive fashion he mingled foreign words and outlandish idioms in his speech. As though from a spice box he would strew these ingredients of his cosmopolitanism in his native town. Could one blame him if, in the intoxication of his varied travels, he looked down upon his modest place of origin with an amiable pity and a kindly indulgence? With his rapturous predilection for things foreign, this son of an ancient priestly house seemed to be quite unaware of the fact that in the expert weighing of the different racial deities and their forms of worship he sometimes overstepped the limits of what was permitted. That was what Joel was like. And Shua, his wife, was as unlike her sister-in-law Mocheleth as Joel was unlike his brother. In the first place she was still young and of good figure, in spite of her children, of whom the two eldest sat at the table. And though she too lived in a state of almost continual separation from her itinerant husband, this did not diminish her cheerfulness in the slightest degree.

Apart from the parents, the sons, the daughters-in-law, and the grandchildren, there were two strangers who had been invited to the meal—two old men who were looked upon and honoured as God's personal guests, the poor and needy who must not be absent from any well-ordered family table in Judah and Israel. One of them was well known to the household. His name was Shamariah, and down below in the fortified town of Anathoth he occupied the dignified position of chief beggar. Every feature of his arrogant old face, his condescending voice, his well-tended raggedness—all these showed that he was fully conscious of the supreme necessity for his office. Was it not his duty to see to it that the rich man's burden of sin was lightened by the little benefactions of which he was the recipient? What did he receive, anyway, at the tables of the good families? A dish of sour milk, a bowl of lentils, on festive occasions a lamb chop or a wing of chicken—from what was left over after every one else had been served! And how did he return this insignificant hospitality? With the blessings of God, which he showered on his niggardly hosts in extravagant abundance! Every crumb that he consumed, every little bone from which he had ever gnawed the meat, was meticulously put down to his hosts' credit in God's accounts. Thus Shamariah ate and drank, day in, day out, not in order to stay his hunger but in order to promote the credit of his patrons with the Lord. He often betrayed by sighs that it was not really a joyful task to eat his way from house to house as he accomplished his beneficent work. And it was not only to the rich that Shamariah dispensed his charity, for he did not hesitate to allow his fellow-beggars to share in his distribution of blessings. Today, for example, he had brought a second guest to Hilkiah's table, a blind old man whom he had presumably commanded to be dumb as well.

The meal passed in deep silence. Hilkiah, as head of the family, did not please to open the conversation, not even bestowing upon his grandchildren the good-humoured scolding or jesting correction which it was fitting that he should impart to the young people on this festive occasion. The children of Obadiah and Joel felt the depression that was weighing upon their elders, and they sat there with an intimidated air while they furtively kicked each other under the table. Grandfather was worried. "To be worried" was a term applied in Hilkiah's family to any form of gloom that appeared upon his countenance. Even though any tangible cause for anxiety was lacking, the old man did not fail to grow more irritable with the years because of the fate which he imagined to be in store for his house. Was he to be gathered to his fathers as the last of the race of Eli who had preserved the dignity of his descent? Were these sons of his at all conscious of the sanctity invested in a priestly family? There sat Obadiah, his eldest son. An excellent farmer and manager—nobody could deny that! He would crumble a handful of earth searchingly between his fingers, he planted his feet firmly on the ground as he strode across the fields, he filled the barns. But were these suitable activities for a priest's son? Could not a bailiff or a farmer hired for the purpose do the work just as well, and in any case with less talk about it? When Hilkiah himself was in the prime of life were the barns less full than they were today, even though the estate was managed by a bailiff and he himself had not restricted his princely leisure and priestly meditation by contact with material things and thought of profit? Why had Obadiah, who showed himself to be so capable in an essential occupation, not striven to obtain a royal office in order that he might restore the reputation of his house? Though Hilkiah himself had never made any effort in this direction (for which, to be sure, he could adduce the most creditable reasons), he was bitterly aggrieved at Obadiah's lack of higher ambition. And what about Joel, his second son? This travelling about on business, even though it brought a golden harvest, exacted no respect whatever from the old father. Travelling about was a life for vagabonds, for mountebanks and jugglers and pedlars, for drunkards and tramps whose home was not an honourable house in the land of the Lord but the nearest caravanserai. Israel had wandered enough and experienced enough before it won its sacred territory in bloody battle. Yet the disreputable elements in Israel were still wandering and could not even now find rest. All the more was it necessary for a noble child of Jacob, a son of Hilkiah, to stay at home. The present generation had lost all delicacy of feeling and sense of refinement. They thought they could distinguish by instinct between what was allowed and what was forbidden, without having to study the Law and read the ancient writings. That was why they needed so many books and clamorous prophets. To make things worse, he regarded Joel as a braggart who put on airs at home with his traveller's tales and fairy-stories. Even if Joel and Obadiah had been very different from what they were, however, it was still unlikely that Hilkiah would have seen eye to eye with them. This old man of a different generation longed bitterly for that which did not exist, while that which did exist with all its possibilities caused him only displeasure.

So far as Jeremiah, his third son, was concerned, that story which his wife had carefully confided to him was beyond all comprehension. It was the chief reason for his worry today, since he had believed that he possessed in his youngest son a guarantee that the Hilkiah character, the traditional and tranquil priestly disposition, would not completely disappear from the world. As a matter of fact, there was plenty he could find fault with in Jeremiah too. All his reading and studying, his continual practice in writing and his brooding mind—these did not bear witness to a solid temperament rooted ineradicably in his family and in the Lord. Hilkiah himself had not done much reading, writing, or brooding. Nevertheless, he could not deny that there was a certain higher dignity in such activities. The assertion, however, which Jeremiah had boldly dared to make that morning to his mother—an assertion which sent a thrill of horror through one—really ought to be discussed seriously by the members of the family. The meal was over. Hilkiah dismissed not only the children, but also—and this betrayed the delicate nature of the subject to be considered—the daughters-in-law. Only the mother remained behind among the men. The old man lifted the lamp to inspect those present before he opened the council.

"Jirmejahu, my youngest son, your mother has reported to me what you have told her today. And I in turn have spoken of it to your brothers. Let my youngest son now confess, as I hope he will, that he was not yet fully awake when he spoke to his mother this morning, and that he himself now realizes he was visited by a vivid dream."

"It was no dream by which I was visited."

"Even dreams should not be taken lightly, but weighed with understanding."

"I was awake, as I am now awake. Let my father believe me!"

"Do you mean, my son, that it was as real as we who are sitting round this table?"

"It was as real as we who are sitting round this table!"

The short interrogation was followed by an impressive silence. Jeremiah was aware of a new and unfathomable embitterment, even an alien hatred, directed towards him. There had never been friendship between him and his elder brothers, but neither had there ever been dissension. Now, however, Obadiah was glaring at him as if he were a murderer. Was this look already the consequence of his having been touched by the Lord? For the sake of dignity his father controlled his anger and spoke in a low tone.

"Even today there are those to whom the Lord comes with His voice and seeks them out—that is something which we cannot deny. We meet so many who assert this of themselves, but who is able to probe sufficiently into the matter to distinguish deception from reality? The days of antiquity are over, and in this pert generation there will arise no Moses, no Samuel, no Elijah. Why should His voice come to people like us, Jirmejahu, why should it come just to you?"

"Why just to him?" burst out Obadiah. "I will tell you frankly, my father and my mother. Because our mother has pampered him, because our father was no longer in his most vigorous years and did not let him feel the discipline which I enjoyed in abundance and to my great improvement. Nobody said to the youngest son: 'Why are you wasting time?' No! Oh, no! The most expensive scribes had to be brought in to teach him! The most costly scrolls were provided for him! Nothing was good enough or valuable enough for Jeremiah! But nobody ever taught him the only real work, work with one's hands. That has to be performed by someone else, someone of coarser grain, who receives neither help nor thanks. What does it lead to when a man can't hold a spade, but knows instead how to twist and turn what other people have written? It leads to idle fancies, to foolishness and craziness, such as we are now witnessing!"

Such an outburst of dammed-up annoyance and open hostility had never before broken through the discipline of Hilkiah's table. In the presence of their parents the sons took pains to preserve an equable tone and skilfully concealed the bitter feelings which are present in every family circle. Abi raised her hands in horror at the wounding words. Hilkiah kept his eyes fixed wrathfully on the lamp. Shamariah, the chief beggar, nodded approvingly, as he had good reasons for doing, since Obadiah was the future head of the house for whom he had to preserve the credit that would accrue from entertaining him. The blind old man, who did not seem to understand what it was all about, smiled mournfully into space. Jeremiah himself was thinking how audaciously Obadiah lied when he boasted of the work of his hands. For it was not Obadiah who dug the spade into the earth and drove the plough through the furrow. This was done by the serfs and bondsmen on the estate, who in return for their work were swindled every seventh year out of the freedom and just wages which were stipulated for them by the Law of God. The thought of this lay heavily upon Jeremiah, as though it were his own grave omission. Meanwhile Joel, the supple-minded merchant and man of the world, tried to alleviate the effect of Obadiah's words.

"Our eldest brother has uttered forceful words concerning the value of work. One who has travelled far and wide must agree with him that it keeps a man healthy, while immersion in books may only too easily lead to sickness. Books transport him who has no vocation for learning into the underworld, say the sages of Tahpanhes. Many a man makes his head dizzy and loses it in the end, which may God keep from happening to our youngest brother. Perhaps my brother Obadiah will bear with me if I contradict him. There are other kinds of work than with plough and harrow and in the ox-stall. Man should be nourished by the earth, not the earth by man, says a Babylonian proverb. Not everyone is born to be a ploughman or a shepherd. To explore the world with all its nations and countries, to answer them in every language, and with eloquent speech to hold one's own against the foreigner—this, too, is hard and useful work. He who frequently changes his dwelling place and sets sail in his bark is not tormented by the gods, so runs a song which the boatmen sing in Sidon. Let our youngest brother come with me on my next journey and he will see so much at which to marvel that he will no longer be tormented at night by visitations and heavy dreams. I invite him to be my assistant."

The eloquence of Joel, interspersed as it was with so many

foreign references, invariably filled his father with impatience. A scornful gesture signified to the second son that his suggestion was worthless. With persuasive kindness the old man turned to Jeremiah.

"Look, my son. I know so many who assert of themselves what you have asserted to your mother. They are mostly men with disordered hair and tangled beards, over which no comb or razor has passed. They garb themselves in rough cloaks that they may be conspicuous and people may talk about them. With railing voice they interfere in the affairs of the King and his princes, and they incite the people with their prophecies. Of what use are all their prophecies? Before they are fulfilled they bring no betterment, and if they are fulfilled they are of no use to anyone. Do you wish to be like these men?"

"No, I do not wish to be like these men," whispered Jeremiah in torment, and he bowed his head. It had not occurred to him before that he too might become like one of those repulsive figures who wandered about the country, gathered the people about them, and belaboured them with foaming harangues. He shuddered at the picture that his mind conjured up. The white cloth had slipped back from Hilkiah's head so that his pale forehead and narrow skull were uncovered. Never had his discontented father appeared to the son so venerable as now. Never had he so whole-heartedly concurred with anything that his father had said.

"Hear me, Jirmejahu," began Hilkiah. "It is no little thing to belong to a family that reaches back to antiquity. In that chest yonder lie the tablets on which are inscribed the names of the fathers of this house, father upon father right back to Aaron, and all of them priests. Priests preserve the order of the Lord, and do not deviate from it. When your ancestor Abiathar was exiled hither and laid the foundations of this house, for what reason had he incurred the wrath of his king? He had defended that which was lawful against that which was unlawful. From that time until my time we have been settled on this land and we have not moved, nor have we thrust ourselves forward. Of your brothers I do not speak, for their thoughts are not my thoughts. But I, I myself, your father, do you think that I could not have come forward out of obscurity when I was younger? I did not do so, and the Lord well knows why I did not. And now do you come, my son, with visions and voices and divine words? The Lord can step beyond His own order with visions and voices, if it pleases Him. But not you! You may not act like the raving zealots, for you are a priest. Is this not truth, my son?"

"It is truth, my father," said Jeremiah, but he did not raise his head.

Hilkiah was exhausted, and he lifted to his lips the great silver goblet which stood before him, that he might refresh his dry throat. Then he took a deep breath.

"It is good that you believe my words. May we never have to speak of this again!"

Jeremiah looked intently at his father.

"Even though I believe your words, yet it does not depend on me."

"What does not depend on him? And on whom does it depend?"

This question had come from Obadiah in an impatient snarl, but the youngest son did not turn his eyes away from his father.

"It is not I who decide . . . but He who sends me forth."

"Listen to him! Now you have it!" shouted Obadiah, beside himself, and he banged his fist on the table. "That is the speech of those insolent madmen with whom we are all familiar. Do we not give him everything he can desire? Do we not look after him though he himself does not stir a finger? Verily, his portion does not lie fallow."

The mother motioned desperately to her eldest son, pointing to Hilkiah.

"Your father has not yet said all he has to say. He has thought out an excellent plan."

Hilkiah cleared his throat noisily. He was a tired man and no longer equal to lengthy speeches.

"My son, I am about to do for you what I have not done for my other sons, though it is true that their minds are unfitted for it. I, who am very old and ill, will torment my body, and I will set it upon a she-ass and ride up to Jerusalem. I who can no longer endure discomfort and a strange sleeping-place, I will take lodging in the city. I who have never asked a favour of those in authority, I will bow down and plead for you. You have fulfilled an office of honour in the Temple and have read from the Book of the Law in the presence of the King, but in the Temple rule the sons of Zadok, who was the bitter foe of Abiathar. In you I will offer reconciliation between Abiathar and Zadok after many generations and will ask that my youngest son may be received into the highest priestly order."

Anyone who knew Hilkiah—his morose pride of family, his contempt for the present, his crabbed selfishness, his keen aversion to any kind of hardship, even from going a few steps outside the house—would have had cause to be not a little astounded at this truly paternal generosity and self-sacrifice. The older brothers sat rigid and pale with jealousy. They exerted themselves restlessly to promote the greatness and welfare of the house and yet their father humiliated them with every word he spoke. On the other hand, he exalted the idler and good-for-nothing of the family above his own egotistic self. Their mother made imploring gestures to Jeremiah that he should seize the favourable moment and not spoil everything. It had always been her secret wish that her favourite child should be a priest, not only by family but also by office. In the light that came into his mother's eyes Jeremiah could read his own future, rising from rank to rank until he became the High Priest and a new Abiathar. Was there a more noble profession than publicly to serve the Lord in the host of His tried servants? This alone was fitting for a priest's son, as his father had truly said. To venture into the unknown, to transgress the appointed order, to differentiate himself from the rest of mankind—this was contrary to his nature. In the thoughts that thronged into his mind there was a great longing to accept his father's offer and fulfil his mother's wish. But the words that he spoke were not the expression of these thoughts.

"Let my father stay peacefully at home, for I may not serve in the Temple as a priest."

They all started up from their seats. Obadiah burst into a peal of mocking laughter, in which he was joined by the chief of the beggars. Even to the mediating mind of Joel, who disliked conflict and disturbance, this rejection of unprecedented paternal solicitude was too much. He seized Jeremiah by both arms and gave him a shake.

"You raving madman! Tell us what you really want!"

Jeremiah freed himself from Joel's grasp and stood as though enveloped in a dream, his eyes closed as if he were listening to some inner prompting. His lips twitched without saying anything. At last the words wrenched themselves from his constricted throat.

"What I want . . . is that you should no longer have me in your thoughts."

Jeremiah had fixed his secret departure from his father's house for the first night after the week of Passover. It had been a bitter period of festival. His father had addressed no further word to him, while his brothers treated him with open scorn. Even his brothers' children ran away from him with odious tittering as from one who bore a stigma. To his family he did bear a stigma. Because of the visitation of the Lord! It was true that he could not fathom what it was with which they reproached him. Arrogance, aloofness, foolishness? But it was no use wondering. That was their attitude, even though the real reason remained unsaid.

At last the night came for his secret departure. Everything was prepared. Baruch was waiting with the asses at the broken part of the wall. But Jeremiah still hesitated. His heart was not made for battle and conflict. That was why he had resolved to leave the house at dead of night. Not even for the sake of the Lord would he take upon himself the guilt of treating his father with harsh disobedience. Why had the Lord's choice fallen upon him, who suffered so easily and possessed so little strength either to cause or endure pain? Could He not have found harder, colder, tougher souls among this people to carry out His intention? How could Jeremiah, who was not hard enough openly to renounce the community of his father's house, be hard enough to renounce the community of the world if the Eternal One should demand this of him?

He was still standing in the chamber of his boyhood, his eyes turning as always to the north, which was veiled in starless gloom. Not even the outline of the ruined sanctuary could be described. Out there between heaven and earth had hung, seven nights ago, the mysterious pot on invisible chains, its red and seething flood spilling over and spurting the fire of the day of judgment as the Lord Himself had said. But what was the meaning of the words, "the day of judgment"? Hosts of men clad in armour, hordes of horsemen with burning torches who came to devastate the land? Or the last end of all things? How poor and ignorant he felt! He could report only what he had seen and heard, but he could not interpret the riddle or draw deductions. There was no breath of prophecy in him. Dumbly and with hollow eyes the sinister north stared down at him. With a sigh he tore himself away from the familiar view. Then he crept silently along the night-enshrouded passage of the house, as he had so often done. This time, however, he was not coming home but going away, to renounce for ever the ties that bound him to his father's house. Before his parents' chamber he stopped and listened. He had not betrayed his resolve even to his mother, but now he felt suddenly that she, from whom he had never concealed anything, was aware also of his secret departure. Hardly had this thought come into his mind when slender arms were thrown around his neck. Emerging from the darkness, Abi's slight figure stood in front of him. He could not see her; he could only feel that she was there.

"Mother," he whispered, "I always knew that you are aware of everything."

As she was afraid of waking Hilkiah, she breathed her words almost inaudibly.

"I knew that my youngest son was going away without taking farewell of me."

"Did you hear me moving along the passage, Mother?"

"I did not hear you, but I knew that you were there. And I came out in order that Jeremiah might not go without saying farewell."

"What would have been the use of further talk? It has to be, Mother."

"I know that it has to be. For it is He who is sending you away."

He drew her to him.

"I am not disloyal, Mother."

Abi said nothing, and he could not tell whether she was silent in order to hide her tears. He raised his voice slightly.

"Tell my father that I am not disloyal. It is hard for a man to go forth without his father's blessing."

Inside the room the bed creaked. Abi pressed Jeremiah's hands. Her whisper had a passionate note.

"You have taken farewell, my son; now go! It is the Lord who takes you from me. I let you go."

Hilkiah's stern voice cut through the darkness:

"Where are you? With whom are you talking?"

Jeremiah heard his mother's voice. She was already within the room.

"I am here. With whom should I be talking? You have been dreaming."

7

Huldah the Seeress

ACCOMPANIED by the boy Baruch, Jeremiah had betaken himself to a secluded place in the wilderness of Judea in order to cleanse and sanctify himself for the Lord by fasting, vigils, and prayer. Following the example of Moses himself, who had spent forty days and nights apart on Mount Horeb, this was customary for those who were men of God or had reason to consider themselves so. It was only by the exertion of all his strength that Jeremiah had been able to prevent himself from giving up at the very beginning. Words like "sanctification," "cleansing," and "mortification of the flesh" sounded very well when one read them in the Writings as one sat upon a soft couch. The spoilt son of a prosperous house had never learned the meaning of deprivation. He was unfamiliar with hunger, thirst, and fear; he had never slept alone in the open or been exposed to the constant temptation to put a speedy end to a condition that was not founded on any outward necessity. In the first spell of discomfort that he had ever experienced in his life, the result of his own choice, he came out victorious by only a bare margin.

Yet not for a single moment during these days did he feel the satisfaction of having overcome the demons of covetousness and fear. He was in any case not concerned to triumph over his own weakness. Sanctification and cleansing were for him not ends in themselves, but directed towards one definite goal. And this goal he had not reached. Never had the Lord been further from him than at this time, when he suffered hunger, thirst, heat, frost, and fear as he kept his vigils and prayed with inward conflict that He might approach and incline towards him. The All-Merciful One seemed to delight in mocking and tormenting Jeremiah as He withdrew into His most stubborn seclusion. In the same incalculable, even capricious, mood in which He had chosen the youth from Anathoth among tens of thousands and let him hear His voice, He had now withdrawn again and could not be persuaded by any exercise of self-denial on Jeremiah's part to change His mind.

During these days when he was beseeching God most ardently, Jeremiah for the first time in his waking existence experienced the complete absence of God. It was as if in the brief hour between the night of Passover and the coming of dawn too much had been expended both by Him who gave and by him who received. Jeremiah had retained nothing but the memory of two vivid visions and some obscure sayings which were of no assistance on the path that had been pointed out to him and for which he had girded up his loins. The only thing that stood out in clear and real outline was the breach with his father and the departure from the house of his father without taking farewell of him. Could his act of obedience have been in vain, and had the words of his brothers proved true, that he was arrogant and crazed? If the voice of the Lord did not come to him again, what was he to do? Should he roam about the land for a time and then return home to be laughed at and have the finger of scorn pointed at him? Jeremiah shuddered at the odious thought that kept recurring to his mind. If the patriarch Abraham, the exemplar of faith and trusting confidence, had even for an instant been able to conceive the thought that the voice which commanded him to sacrifice the beloved son of his old age might not be serious, might be fickle and false or even a complete illusion, he would in that same instant have fallen dead from horror at the power of doubt. Jeremiah, however, was no mighty man of antiquity. He was the child of a new and faint-hearted, a distrustful generation. He doubted. He doubted even as he prayed and struggled with temptation. Yet the clear and gentle voice of Adonai had revealed mysteries to him that could not have sprung from his own mind: "Before I formed thee in the belly I knew thee; and before thou camest forth out of the womb I sanctified thee." Never had even a breath of such audacity crossed his heart, which was timid and had little confidence in itself. "I ordained thee a prophet unto the nations." Could this have come from within him? Where, in what abyss of his mind, could such a strange and obsessing dream have been concealed so long? Did not these sayings clearly prove that his mission was genuine? Yet Jeremiah doubted and doubted. Supposing that all the visions and voices that had oppressed him since his thirteenth year had been illusions, finally concentrating into one last great illusion before leaving him for ever? The more ardently Jeremiah struggled with such questionings in the days of his cleansing and sanctification, all the more urgently did they emerge from the depths of his own soul.

The Lord seemed to be withdrawing more coldly from hour to hour. Broken in spirit, the doubter opened his heart to Baruch, his disciple. He had to attain certainty about himself. But was there such certainty in the world? And who could give it to him? The discerning boy Baruch had a helpful idea.

In Jerusalem there lived a man named Shallum, son of Tikvath, who was held in great respect. He held office in the royal household as keeper of the wardrobe, but at the same time he possessed a tailoring business which was the largest workshop of its kind. His house lay to the southwest of the Temple mount in the street that was called Millo and formed a bridge between the palace quarter of the ruling kings and the ancient and massive citadel of David. It was one of the stateliest houses in the whole of Jerusalem, two stories high not including the great chamber on the roof. The workshop was on the ground floor and there Shallum, a nimble, skinny little man, was accustomed to stand as he examined the linen, the textiles of flax, yarn, and wool, the single and double tissues of finest purple thread, all the bleached and dyed stuffs that the merchants and market sellers offered him for sale. There also, flitting to and fro like a lizard, he received his customers. He had even been entrusted with making vestments for the Temple, which involved the minute observance of countless regulations and precepts. It was not a matter of indifference how wide the hem had to be in this or that garment, how the cut of the robes for the higher orders was distinguished from that of the lower, whether the sash of a senior priest had to be embroidered with twelve lilies or with twelve pomegranates. Shallum was no less familiar with the intricacies of secular garb. He was the sole arbiter of how the folds of the *simlah*, the cloak, were to fall and how the *ketonet passim*, the sleeved dress of the women, was to adapt itself to the figure and graceful walk of its wearer.

The rooms of the upper story, silent and empty, were dedicated to the royal service. It is true that the court office of a keeper of the wardrobe was titular rather than actual, but it carried certain obligations, for the day might come when it would be necessary to fulfil the duties implied in the title. Therefore a part of the house always stood empty in order to receive the King's clothes if occasion demanded. Shallum was, moreover, an unequalled connoisseur of the costume and ceremonies of all foreign countries, so he was always called into consultation by the court when a foreign prince happened to be sojourning within the walls of the city and the King wished to do him honour by donning the garb of the prince's native land.

Shallum's title, wealth, and knowledge would alone have sufficed to justify the reputation of another man, but in the case of the keeper of the royal wardrobe they were of only minor importance. The real reason for his prominence lay neither in his office nor in his person, for he owed it to another and far more celebrated individual, namely, his wife. This famous woman was none other than Huldah the seeress, whom King Josiah had himself recommended Shaphan the scribe to record for perpetual memory in the Book of Chronicles of the Kings of Judah. Her name was familiar to every child in Jerusalem. If, however, she was called a prophetess, as frequently happened, she was the first to protest against such a crude confusion of terms. Huldah was not one of those persons who were generally called "prophets of God" and who had been so unfavourably commented upon in the house of Hilkiah the priest. The prophets of God, wherever and whenever they appeared, were above all men of God, men whose minds were fixed solely on the will of the Lord in order to make it effective on earth. There had been one single exception in past ages: Deborah the judge, a mother in Israel, who chanted the battle song of the Lord. Huldah was not like Deborah. She was not a prophetess but a seeress.

The Lord had not made her ear to hear His commands, but had opened her eyes to look into the depths. Before her mysterious second sight the hidden lot of men and things was clearly visible, not only so far as the present was concerned but also the distant past and the near future. For thirty years, since her youth, the wife of the keeper of the royal wardrobe had foretold the future, and the cases in which her prognostications had not been fulfilled could be counted on one's fingers. A look into a person's face was sufficient to tell Huldah what was the disease that would bring him to the grave before a year had gone by. By laying her hand beneath the breast of a young woman she could tell the number and sex of the children with which she would be blessed in the course of her life. Yet this gift of foretelling the future, unfailing as it was in its results, could never have brought Huldah the distinction that had made her the most celebrated woman in Jerusalem and caused her name to shine in the Book of the Kings of Judah.

Though her gift had also been efficacious in the case of many sufferers and people who were dispirited, her real fame was based on a number of State oracles of which she had been the medium. The most important of these oracles was in connexion with the rediscovered Book of the Law. After King Josiah had learned the context of this Book through the first reading of Shaphan and had conceived the resolve to institute his great reform, he wished beforehand for confirmation of his assurance that the scroll really came from the hand of God. It was known that, while Huldah could not read, yet she could interpret from writing many things that were hidden in the text. Though she was illiterate, she could by virtue of her second sight see pictures pregnant with fate in the written characters, as though they were constellations in the sky. Josiah sent to Huldah a deputation consisting of the High Priest, Shaphan, the latter's son Ahikam, and two high officers of the court, requesting her to examine the ancient writing from the point of view of its divine authenticity and to pronounce an oracle. The seeress fulfilled the task laid upon her by the State in the most impressive fashion. As soon as she looked at the writing she confirmed its age and divine source. To the astonishment of the envoys she repeated a number of important passages in spite of her inability to read them. Finally she pronounced the oracle, to the effect that the Lord would fulfil all His threats against the land and the people, but not in that generation or in the days of Josiah. Huldah became more than a seeress. She was transformed into a prophetess, since she concluded her foretelling of the future with the following promise of the Lord:

"Behold, I will gather thee unto thy fathers, and thou shalt be gathered into thy grave in peace; and thine eyes shall not see all the evil which I will bring upon this place."

Josiah, who had anticipated immediate vengeance and punishment for the abundance of his omissions, exulted at Huldah's prophecy, which, so far at least as he himself was concerned, had turned out to be unexpectedly favourable. The existence of the kingdom appeared to him to be assured for the duration of his reign. The latter part of the oracle had assuaged the profound uneasiness by which he was so frequently assailed with regard to his own end. He was filled with a splendid certainty that was not far from sinful arrogance. Whenever the burden of kingship threatened to overwhelm this violent man, he would secretly comfort his soul with the thought, "What can happen to me? I shall go in peace."

It may well be imagined that from that day the King's favour shone abundantly on Huldah. The conspicuous reverence with which he treated her confirmed the pronouncement to which she had given utterance, and the King's example was followed by the people. Whenever she appeared, crowds of people gathered to stare at her in fascination. She, however, remained unmoved by her fame, and it never occurred to her to subordinate her eccentric ways to the reputation that she enjoyed. Huldah was a shrivelled little woman. When she walked through the street she swayed as if she were drunk, and she was in the habit of muttering and wrangling to herself. Her attire was as unusual as she was. She did not wear a cloth on her head in the manner of other women, but a broad fur cap, and at all hours of the day she jingled with worthless jewellery. She invariably carried a tall shepherd's crook that was taller than herself. If she had not been the great Huldah, the street urchins and ragamuffins of Jerusalem would have pursued her with grimaces and derisive songs. As it was, however, she was greeted with shy respect as she went on her way swaying and muttering. Shallum, the keeper of the royal wardrobe, paid homage to his exalted wife daily and hourly upon his knees. When she appeared in the streets, the squares, or the outer court of the Temple, he would flit along before her at a rapid pace to clear the way, push back the gapers, and protect her from any form of annoyance. The old demand of the sages, "Let a man precede his wife!" was turned by him into its opposite by the very fact that he did so. At the same time he called out incessantly, in order that the ignorant might be instructed: "Huldah is coming! Make way for the great seeress!"

Shallum also took heed that his divinely inspired wife should not mingle with the unsanctified herd of whom his workshop was always full. She never appeared on the ground floor. Her domain was the large room on the roof through whose four open windows a strong draught was always blowing. It was here that she had received the envoys of the King, and here also she admitted the seekers after truth to whose petitions she gave ear. After sunset a number of men gathered round her regularly to discuss in subdued voices the mysteries of Adonai and His intervention in the affairs of the world, and this they did in a more free and hazardous manner than was possible in the corridors and classrooms of the Temple. In earlier ages there had existed whole communities of revivalists and divinely inspired people who had journeyed through the land with singing and ecstatic dancing, and who were called "schools of prophets." The evening circle that assembled round Huldah bore very little resemblance to those God-intoxicated gatherings. Here conversation was carried on in whispers; no loud tone ever penetrated into the city through Huldah's windows. Such calm was more suitable to the sober atmosphere of those days than raving fanaticism. Sometimes an older man of God would put in an appearance. He was not one of the ordinary preachers of the Temple but had the reputation of being a true and sanctified prophet. His name was Urijah, son of Shemaiah.

Baruch had suggested to his master that he should seek enlightenment and aid from Huldah the seeress and the wise men who gathered round her. Jeremiah, who had become more and more immersed in doubt, did not hesitate for an instant to snatch at this prospect of help. They struck their tent in the wilderness of Judea and proceeded to Jerusalem.

Shallum wanted at first to forbid them entrance. The day's work was over, it was time for the evening prayer, and the house had to be closed. Jeremiah and Baruch waited modestly in a corner. When the last customer had gone and the workshop was empty, the keeper of the royal wardrobe addressed the two young men in a hectoring tone:

"And you . . . what are you waiting for?"

Jeremiah quietly preferred his request that Shallum would grant them the favour of being permitted to look upon the countenance of the seeress. Thereupon the exalted woman's little husband screeched at them angrily:

"There they wait, there they come, young and old, out of the city, out of the towns, every hour of the day! . . . When is the baby going to cut its tooth? . . . What's going to be the result of the dispute among the heirs? . . . All their wretched little worries they would like to heap upon her delicate shoulders! . . . But the seeress of the Lord isn't here to prescribe remedies for everybody and to foretell their uninteresting futures for a shekel. . . . Why don't they go to the witches and necromancers? Why do they come to Huldah, the unique Huldah, to whom the King's majesty sends his royal envoys? . . . He never undertakes anything without consulting her, for she examined the Law of God and found it genuine. . . . She doesn't have anything to do with interpreting the future. . . ."

Jeremiah waited patiently for Shallum's temper to work itself out before he explained that he had not come to have his fortune told, but needed advice in a matter that related to the Lord. And he mentioned the priestly name of his family.

The disfavour and suspicion of the keeper of the royal wardrobe immediately vanished. After a searching look into Jeremiah's pale, absorbed face he suddenly grew quiet and raised no further objection, but motioned to the belated visitors to follow him.

The roof chamber was spacious and almost unfurnished. In the centre stood a low, wide divan, covered with skins, on which the wrinkled Huldah sat with her fur cap on her small head, her coloured glass beads round her neck and her tall crook at her side. A number of men were sitting round her, though some distance away, in a silent circle. The faint light of a single lamp shone dimly, concealing rather than revealing their faces. Through the four open window spaces, which all faced in different directions, could be seen a palely clouded twilit sky. Shallum had brought with him an earthenware bowl of thick cream which he now held tenderly before Huldah's eyes. His awe of his wife was so great that he never addressed her directly, but always spoke of her in a flattering tone as though he were referring to a third person.

"The seeress wears out her poor heart and the strength of her sick body more than other people, who are of coarser clay, but she never thinks of eating and sleeping. She is now going to be sensible and eat this tiny little dish of sweet cream that I have prepared for her because I know the aversion of her palate and am very anxious about her."

He spoke with a lisping voice as one speaks enticingly to a child that has to be persuaded to eat. His old hands, which were still holding out the bowl to Huldah, trembled more and more. With a sigh she accepted the food and began to eat a spoonful or two dreamily, but so that everybody could see she was struggling with herself and eating it only because of her tormenting attendant spirit. The latter watched the wooden spoon anxiously as it was dipped more and more slowly and unwillingly into the thick cream. But he was implacable. Only when the food had been half consumed to the accompaniment of distinct signs of distress on the part of Huldah did he point to the newcomer and announce his name.

"It is no mere desire to know the future that has brought this priest's son of Anathoth to consult the seeress."

Since Huldah could not be persuaded to take another spoonful, Shallum left the room timidly on tiptoe as if it were a sanctuary. Jeremiah looked round with his weak-sighted eyes, but in the faint twilight the men's faces appeared only as vague blurs. One thing was clear, however, even in this obscurity. The attitude of the men, who were sitting in silence and as though turning away from one another, suggested a sadness that weighed oppressively on the room. What could be the meaning of it? The God who demanded from men a festive joy at their sacrificial rites, and who required eternal rejoicing from His angels, was it possible that this same God filled those whom He had "touched with His hand" with the spirit of sadness? Was it their own lot at which they suffered, or was it the inevitable future that they were able to foresee? Huldah alone appeared to be unaffected by the general melancholy. She gazed intently at Jeremiah from the surrounding gloom and a semblance of a smile, as if in recognition of a fellow-conspirator, passed across her wrinkled face. She did not continue the conversation that had been interrupted by the arrival of the newcomers, any more than the men did, and the burdensome silence might never have been broken if Baruch had not been bold enough to offend the proprieties on Jeremiah's behalf. His rough boyish voice stammered agitatedly:

"This man here . . . Jeremiah, the son of Hilkiah . . . to him has the Lord come . . . with word and vision. . . . 'Gird up thy loins and go,' said the Lord. . . . But since then the Lord has not come to him again, and he does not know whether it is true and what he should do. . . ."

After this stuttering description of his master's state of doubt, the courageous Baruch suddenly broke off, and his forehead was damp with sweat. Huldah had listened with her fur-capped head inclined to one side, as though she were hard of hearing, but she did not betray by a single sign that she understood. It seemed as if the oppressive silence was to be resumed. Then a tall, emaciated man rose from his seat in a dark corner, stepped close up to Jeremiah, and gazed at him from between half-closed eyelids. The face of this man, whose age it was impossible to guess, was only slightly less pale than the white head cloth in which it was framed. From his forehead, down past his left eye to the cheekbone, there ran a broad scar, irregular and jagged as if it came not from a slash with a sword but from a blow with the scourge that was called a "scorpion." This scar spoke of other sufferings than the spiritual ones that were torturing Jeremiah. With a thrill of horror he asked himself whether he could ever summon up the strength to endure the humiliation of such chastisement. The man opened his mouth to speak, and Jeremiah saw that his enemies had knocked out his front teeth. But these mutilations were offset by a tender smile and a clear, gentle voice which reminded Jeremiah distantly of the voice that had called him and had since abandoned him.

"Be not afraid to open your heart," he said, "and see that you forget nothing. For he who speaks with you is Urijah."

Jeremiah began hesitatingly, but the sympathetic look of the prophet encouraged him in such strange fashion that his tongue was quickly loosened and he withheld no detail of what had happened between the eve of Passover and the following dawn. Urijah interrupted him now and then and asked him to repeat the description of a vision or the actual words that the voice had spoken. Each of these questions revealed to Jeremiah that his interrogator possessed an unexpected familiarity and abundance of experience in communion with Adonai. His heart grew lighter, for he saw that he was not alone in the world. There lived brotherly men who had shared his experience. A feeling of security came over him. But then his eyes again fell upon the corpse-like pallor of Urijah's face, the flaming scar, the toothless mouth.

When Urijah had come to the end of his questioning, he sighed deeply and said:

"The Lord has been with you, Jirmejahu. Doubt no longer. It was not an illusion that you saw and heard. It was authentic. But this is only the beginning. There are so many who hear and see, but whether they prophesy the truth or prophesy that which is false does not depend on them. When it pleases Him to do so, He falsifies the words of those who are filled with truth, as He fulfils the words of those who are false. Do you understand, Jirmejahu?"

How could the young man understand this cruel paradox which it had taken the experienced communer with God a long lifetime to learn? Jeremiah, however, burned to know the answer to but one question: "Have I been called and at the same time rejected? Have I been sent forth to roam about without purpose?" And he demanded anxiously:

"Is it possible that I shall never hear Him again? . . . That He will never return to me? . . . That He will not keep faith?"

Urijah gave a short laugh that was not without a mocking bitterness.

"Keep faith or not keep faith . . . these are *your* words. You can keep faith or not keep faith, but not He. For in what way is He in your debt? Do not ask, my son, but wait. Wait with great patience. Even if you have to wait until the hour of your death, I say unto you: Wait!"

"And if I should wait in vain?"

"Then it is His decision that you should wait in vain, and perhaps it is best for you. But it is no longer possible for you to turn back."

From the divan came the deep voice of Huldah, which held a note of rebuke:

"Cruel are they who hear only with ears!"

She had seized her crook and was pointing with it more or less in the direction where Jeremiah stood. The latter stepped forward and bowed low. He was about to speak, but she dissuaded him with a violent gesture. Her face seemed to shrink and grow more wrinkled under the inner strain that had suddenly taken possession of her, while the fur cap on her head appeared to become larger. Her mouth began to move with a noiseless babbling. Gradually there became audible snatches of words which followed in rapid succession as if the seeress had not sufficient time to describe everything that was rushing past her mind's eye before it had vanished from sight.

"This man is standing in a house. . . . He is speaking with a woman in the darkness. . . . The woman is weeping. . . . He does well to leave his father's house at night. . . . I see a desolate place. . . . Two people are sitting there, he and the boy. . . . The boy stays at his side. . . . They are sitting before a fire and fear the beasts of the night. . . ."

She paused. The tone of her voice changed to one of displeasure.

"It is not right, what you have done. . . . That is why the Lord is concealing Himself. . . ."

Jeremiah had only with difficulty been able to follow the indistinct phrases as they came bubbling forth. At her last words he gave a great start. In what way had he done wrong? He raised his voice to ask a question, but she motioned him angrily to be quiet. Then she beckoned him to come nearer and laid her small, bony hands on his hips. She commanded:

"Put your hands on my shoulders. Touch my feet with your feet."

Jeremiah did as Huldah had told him, not without having to overcome a peculiar feeling of awe. In sixfold contact with the old woman, his first sensation was of being pervaded by the icy coldness that issued from her limbs. Her head swayed to and fro as she murmured:

"Of one body, as the child with its mother . . ."

Jeremiah's awe deepened, his awe of this new mother, of this artificial unity which enabled her to penetrate to the secret places of his heart. He wanted to tear himself away. The full moon shone brightly through the western window and carved Huldah's cowering figure out of the darkness. The look in her eyes had sunk inwards. She was gazing at him without seeing him. Then her face grew more and more distorted. Her mouth opened and shut. Her breath came in a more and more stifled whistle. All her muscles twitched with swift convulsions. Her vacant eyes filled with the terror of the things she saw within. Her breast heaved with horror at the scenes she was witnessing. Her heavy breathing changed to a loud moaning. Her moans became a wild sobbing that shook her spare figure violently. Jeremiah knew that in her trance she was seeing him, his life, his future, his destiny. He was unable to control himself any longer and he implored her:

"What do you see? I beg you to tell me! I want to know everything!"

She had not heard him. Her breath formed fragments of words as she wept.

"Not in solitude . . . go to the people! . . among the nations . . . to the Kings . . . the sons of David . . ."

Jeremiah's hands gripped her shoulders convulsively, but she was pulled erect by her vision so that he staggered back. And from the frail woman there broke a loud wailing that rose in a piercing crescendo.

The men sprang up to support her as she came out of her trance, or she would have fallen to the ground. Shallum had already come rushing through the door, panting with rage.

"What are you doing?" he scolded. "You will be the death of her one day! Have I not forbidden you to do this and made a covenant with you? Never again shall a stranger be allowed to enter her presence!"

Old Shallum knelt before Huldah and began to rub her forehead with a strong balsam, growling all the while over his shoulder:

"What are you waiting for? It is time for you to go. The seeress must sleep. Huldah must sleep a long sleep. I wish people would learn to have a little more consideration for her. . . ."

In the moonlight the men descended to the street by the staircase that led down from the roof chamber along the outside wall. In spite of his strong emotion Jeremiah suddenly caught sight of a young man whom he knew. It was

Hananiah of Gibeon, who had shared with him his office at the King's table. What was Hananiah doing among the men of God? Could the voice of Adonai have come to him also? Overwrought as he was, Jeremiah wondered.

8

Wandering and Early Vexation

JEREMIAH'S eyes had been opened by the advice of Urijah and the words of Huldah. His suffering was not due to an illusion or to the Lord's not having kept faith with him. The aloofness of God was due to his own disobedience, which itself was due to a misunderstanding. "Gird up thy loins and go!" He had interpreted this command too superficially. It did not mean that he should cast off the burden which was implicit in every form of community, including that of his father's house, in order to be alone with himself in the desert. It signified the contrary: "Take new burdens upon thyself! Do that which hitherto has been least congenial to thee, that which is hardest for thee, that which torments thee most and inspires thee with fear." But what was it that had hitherto been least congenial to him, had been hardest for him, had tormented him most and inspired him with fear? The community of men, the coarse, turbid world that had forsaken God and consisted of his brothers and people like them! The short word "go" suddenly swarmed with new meanings. "Go to the people and speak unto them all that I command thee. Go among them and be not afraid, but trust in me, then wilt thou have no need to fear me!" This was what seemed to have been implied in the words with which the voice had called to him.

So Jeremiah set out in order that he might obey the Lord.

In the sleepless night before he started, however, his mind grew remarkably clear. Adonai had not communicated with him by word or sound, yet he was endowed with an exalted knowledge that grew continuously and undoubtedly sprang from the help which the Lord had granted him in the house of Huldah. He understood in a flash the association between certain things that had hitherto seemed unrelated, and this was something which nobody had taught him.

It was true that the priests, the teachers, and the scribes of Israel had an indistinct realization of the fact that the impulse to create the universe had come from "God's joy," an exuberant urge to love, an intoxication of giving, such as was unknown to human senses. King Josiah had proclaimed these words as the watchword and battle cry of the Passover. And every festival that was dedicated to the Lord was to be an echo of the first primal joy in love, was to remind Him of the time before Time was, when He still grazed "like a young steer" in the uncreated universe. For Jeremiah, however, God's joy was no longer a tenet of the teachers and priests, a cold and dry idea which contained nothing conceivable, but a great rapture such as hitherto he had not known.

When during his wanderings he saw a house in the early dawn, the sun emerging above the rim of a hill, and the dull foliage of an old oak bursting into green fire—that was God's joy. When towards evening the flocks of lambs were being driven across the anemone-strewn mountain pastures into the lowlands like black and white billows, when the warning shadows were lengthening and the thirsty cattle surged round the watering-places—that was God's joy, and he did not know why. It came to him at the sight of children playing or women walking along with full pitchers carefully balanced on their heads. It could overwhelm him suddenly in a scene, a look, or a word. God's joy, the source of the world's creation, the well of adoration and of songs of praise, the union of the engenderer with the engendered, of the father with his children, the satisfaction of mortal impatience. The Lord caused an infinitely faint reflection of His joy to shine in the ecstasy of Jeremiah, that he might understand. And at such moments he understood that the first and primal intention of God was to make His joy an inalterable and uninterrupted condition of creation, an eternal song in praise of mutual and perfect love.

What had happened to make the world so wantonly different? Man had not been content with an ecstatic state of joy which had made him the equal of the heavenly hosts, and perhaps set him even above them. A weak element in his nature had left him accessible to dark whisperings, and to these he had succumbed. He was not satisfied to remain what he was—the created. Arrogantly he wanted to be what he was not—the creator. Through this arrogance he encroached upon and destroyed the order of the Lord and his own life, which henceforth lost its dominion over the earth and became a prey to death. Was it not understandable that Zebaoth should seethe with wrath when His sanctified creature abused his freedom and destroyed the order and plan of the universe? Man on his earth receded from God. And God in His heaven receded from man likewise. Thus began the course of the world. It was like a process of freezing, of hopeless petrifaction. Yet however hardened men's hearts became, in the grimmest waste of the universal frost their memory of the first joy was never wholly extinguished. They kindled fires on their altars and set burnt offerings upon them. And to whom did they sacrifice? To the Baalim on the heights, to

Marduk and Nergal, to Ashtaroth and Hathor, to Amon and Ptah, to Dagon and Milcom and ten thousand others. But these deities among the nations, these filthy abominations, were nothing else than men's clouded memory of the One God; for where a false deity and his heathen cult prevailed, there was no other power than the obdurate weariness of man's mind which was too weak to find its way to the Lord. Time and again had Zebaoth's infinite pity conquered His infinite anger. He saw that men were too weak to find their way to Him, and He therefore graciously stooped to the generations and appeared before them as a pleader that He might conclude a covenant of obedience with them. But generation after generation forsook Him, and after patient waiting He resolved to destroy His godless creatures who rejected the gift of salvation, since they were a futile race and would not allow Him to exert His compassionate will. When He sent the waters over the earth, for forty days and forty nights, and caused the Flood to gather, He took pity on that which He had created and saved one man and his family from destruction in order that He might make with him the first covenant. Yet it was not long before Noah's sons broke the covenant to which they had been witnesses and scorned Him. The world pursued its course, and very soon the generations that came after the Flood resembled in every way those that had existed before the Flood.

And the Lord realized that it was not sufficient to choose one family out of the multitude of families because in one father there was still a trace of supreme memory and he therefore lived a more pious life than all the others. The Eternal One conceived a better plan to prevent the world from coming to a sudden end. From the hundreds and hundreds of nations that peopled the earth He selected a childless old man, to whom He gave a son in his old age that the strength of his attachment to God might be tested. Abraham did not refuse to sacrifice his beloved son and did not fail in his tremendous trial. So great was the merit of this sacrifice that the Lord thought it sufficient to found thereon a whole nation and to sanctify it among all the other nations. From Abraham's seed sprang Israel, the people who extricated the world from confusion and became the people of the joy of God. Henceforth they were burdened with pride and sorrow such as no human race had yet borne. Amidst mighty and menacing nations their only treasure was Abraham's merit, together with the interest that accrued therefrom, and an ear attuned to the voice of Adonai. But the nations hated Israel with a bitter hatred.

In the new understanding of his heart Jeremiah realized that beyond all worldly causes this hatred possessed a deeper root, and that the nations could not even be blamed for their hate. Why had the Lord not knocked at the splendid gates of Egypt, Asshur, and Babylon in order that He might be heard and acknowledged? Though the great world harassed itself with its idols of gold and silver, stone and wood, yet in its inmost heart there still survived a vestige of the memory of the truth that had once been revealed. It was like a sensitive scar that twitched with pain when it was touched by the recognition of this truth. One who was never mentioned by name had created heaven and earth, day and night, sea and land, man and beast. He had always been and always would be. This simple truth lived in the mouth of Israel and not in the wiser or more learned mouths of Egypt or Babylon. Ought not the golden land of Egypt and the lofty city of Babylon to bow their heads in shame that they had not been chosen? Instead of this they proclaimed the simple truth through a multiplicity of false gods. In their most secret hearts they were ashamed. And because they were ashamed they envied the insignificant tribe of Jacob its proclamation of the truth. And because they were envious, they were arrogant in their lies. And because they were arrogant they humbled Israel.

Egypt humbled the House of Abraham for hundreds of years and forced it to slavery. But it was never humiliation and oppression that jeopardized the plan of the Lord and the people of His plan, for it was out of these that He forged His most victorious weapons. When the time was ripe He raised up for the House of Jacob a prophet such as had never been known before and would never be known again. Moses was the leader who preceded Israel, the longing Bride, in the march through the desert on the way to meet the Bridegroom for the consummation of the marriage on Sinai. When the Lord realized that hardening and freezing of the heart were ills which man could not overcome without help, He prepared for the people, as an eternal support, a more splendid bridal gift than had ever before been given to any one. In clear words that could be understood by men He revealed to Moses His Law and His Order so that there might henceforth be no stumbling or going astray. If this order was observed and fulfilled; if it was comprehended with more and more discernment, more and more fully practised; if finally through its innate simplicity and universality it became the order of the world, then perhaps it would be given to Israel to restore that which had been destroyed and to establish the kingdom of God.

But it was not given to Israel to do this. God's plan came to grief through mankind as mankind came to grief through God's plan. The generations did not become purer from age to age, but more and more impure, more and more muddied. Israel's sanctified march through history threatened to disappear like a sluggish brook in the general march of the nations. A landless people had received from the Lord the land of its fathers in order that it might begin to extricate the world from its confusion. But, behold, it was not the people who dominated the land, but the land which dominated the people with all its little gods of the heights, the hills, and the green trees, with the teraphim of its cities and its houses and the horrible tophetim of its valleys. Also from without, from the nations that lived round about, Israel was continually inundated by waves of temptation, seducing it to forsake the Lord and become assimilated. The majority of the tribes abandoned their hallowed focus and gathered in the north. Only the lesser and weaker portion, Judah and Benjamin, congregated round the frozen lightning of the Ark in the sanctuary of the Temple. The tribes that had cut themselves off kept their faces averted and nourished themselves with insubstantial weeds. Thus the inevitable happened. What does the mason do when his chisel breaks against the hardness of the stone? He casts it aside. Why should a people be sanctified over all other nations when it is possessed only by the longing for assimilation? The ten tribes of the northern kingdom, which had taken up their dwelling round Samaria, had become superfluous; they had no further part in God's plan. Woe to him who believed that the Lord loved one nation more than another and held His hand over Jacob for Jacob's sake! It was for the sake of the world that He held His hand over the residue of Jacob. But for how much longer? He had already sent His day of judgment to overwhelm Samaria and the northern tribes; and this had happened not in remote times, but had been horrifyingly recent, for less than three generations had passed since the King of Asshur had marched against Samaria to destroy it, had massacred its people, and led them into exile.

Was this not a warning, a terrible indication which should make one tremble in one's innermost heart? Was it sufficient to trust with thoughtless indifference to the Temple, the Ark, and the sacrifices, as if the Lord were a human father, miserly and mean, who would rescue His treasure from the conflagration whatever might befall? No, the dowry of Israel was not His only treasure. He had no need of the Temple, the sacrifices, the Ark, and the Law. If the chisel Judah should break against the stone, the Lord would cast it aside. "I am that I am!" He was not dependent on the seed of Abraham; He could make new plans and employ other tools. If He should weary of this vagabond creation, He could crush it between two fingers like the flame of a lamp.

Since his visit to Huldah the seeress, all these mysteries had been unveiled in the mind of Jeremiah with the help of the Lord. The seething pot of the north and the threatened judgment grew ever more clear in meaning. He felt with all his being that the world was growing old, that perhaps only one moment was left in which to avert the destroying power of the Lord. A single ray of hope lightened his fear. The Lord had afforded the present generation an opportunity to find itself again in the Law which it had lost. It was, without doubt, a last attempt to rouse the people. The present generation held life and death within its hands, and the life of Judah hung by a hair.

Jeremiah had spent his youth in solitude and meditation. As a child he had held back timidly from the company of men, even from that of his father's house and his own family.

On his roamings through the countryside he had often longed for love and understanding, but when he was again sitting at Hilkiah's table and listening to his father's grumbling, the bitterness of Obadiah, and the bragging of Joel, he could hardly choke down the odious torment that filled him. The others called him a dreamer and chaser of shadows, while they themselves claimed to be attached to what was real, solid, and pious in its actuality. But by the time he had reached his thirteenth year (when the first gentle whisperings had begun to oppress him), he surmised that what men called "reality" was only the name for what was base, renegade, and turned away from God. Now, however, he had been commanded to slough off the arrogance which had come to him through this understanding and to make himself familiar with this very "reality." The divine patience was threatening to run out swiftly. It was therefore necessary that he should go among men and absorb to the full the apostasy which they termed "pious actuality"; that he should begin a great wandering from town to town, from village to village, from house to house, since that was the way in which Huldah had interpreted the Lord's will concerning Jeremiah. He resolved on this journey with Baruch to describe a great circle until Adonai himself should judge that it was sufficient.

After the two young men had celebrated the feast of the New Year in Jerusalem, they set out in the autumn and proceeded towards the south. By way of Bethlehem and Tekoah they came to Hebron, which was the junction of the caravan routes from Egypt. From Hebron they pushed forward as far as the southern border, as far as the Valley of Salt, along which they journeyed until they reached the city of Beersheba. Here Jeremiah turned away from the route he had planned, for he was filled with a great longing to see the ocean for the first time. Therefore they crossed the frontier of Judah and ventured into the land of the Philistines, as far as the populous capital and port of Gaza. There, on the sandy shore, new light came to Jeremiah concerning the Creator and His creatures. Was not this surging and all-pervading expanse of water also a creation of Adonai and, besides, one that possessed infinitely more power than man himself to transgress the limits that had been set to it? But, behold, the monster stayed within its bounds even during the most violent storm. It was hemmed in by a ribbon of sand, and however much its waves might heave and rage they did not pass beyond it, though it would have been child's play for it to have swallowed up the whole country. The more different a creature was from man, even though it were the monstrous sea, the more obediently did it fit into the divine order. During the days that they tarried at Gaza, Jeremiah spent most of his time on the shore. When the wind whistled and the long breakers rolled in, Baruch noticed how his master, who was usually so reserved, would be overcome by the storm within his own soul and would throw himself on the sand, to spring up again with his arms upraised and dance towards the sea as he babbled intoxicated words. At that time the disciple began to pay heed to the ecstatic words of Jeremiah and to note them in his memory.

The Lord had provided in the young Baruch a firm support for His sanctified prophet. It was only through His help that a boy could grow up with no desires or wishes for himself in his soul, but with only a tempestuous craving to follow Jeremiah and smooth his path by serving him. During the months of their wandering (and this too was perhaps part of the Lord's plan) the frail youth had developed into a sturdy man, whose downy beard had begun to grow almost overnight. He might have been taken for the same age as Jeremiah, and he had matured much more quickly so far as knowledge of the world was concerned. His cleverness and adaptability to the ways of life helped them over many a period of hunger and distress, and provided Jeremiah with continual opportunities of becoming familiar with the realities of the world. At home he had uttered the terrible words: "What I want is that you should no longer have me in your thoughts." He had girded up his loins and left his father's house without demanding the slightest portion of that which was due to him, either from the wealth of the fields and stables or from the weighing out of coined silver and gold. Baruch came from a family that had few possessions. They had taken nothing with them but their asses and a tiny store of money which had been reduced to a few shekels by the time they left Jerusalem. Without Baruch it would have been difficult for Jeremiah to make his way across the ways and bypaths of the land. Like all men who had enjoyed a sheltered childhood, he was very proud and preferred to suffer any deprivation rather than open his mouth to ask a favour. Baruch, on the other hand, who had not been spoilt by a wealthy home, did not so easily fall a prey to discomfort. He was not only clever and inventive, but above all he had an impetuous will and knew how to combat hunger, thirst, and lack of shelter by boldness or cunning. While Jeremiah would stand blushingly aside, Baruch would besiege if need be the most miserly doors. He provided food and drink at least once a day and found lodging on rainy nights. If he could not manage otherwise, he hired himself out to a farmer for a spell of casual labour. If Jeremiah wanted to join in the work, however, Baruch would protest. He regarded it as

Jeremiah's duty to gather strength on their journey for the great decision, and not to waste it. It is true that later, when their difficulties increased, he had to withdraw his objection.

Through his good management Baruch had succeeded even in feeding and keeping their animals until they reached Gaza. In the city of the Philistines, however, Jeremiah had to part from the donkey to which he was so tenderly attached. Baruch, who had been in charge of the material arrangements since they first set out, had made up his mind to sell the animals together with their saddles, in order that they might have at least a few shekels at their disposal. They now had their shekels, but they had no asses to help them along the dusty, stony cart-tracks which lay pitilessly before their stumbling feet.

When Jeremiah was at last able to turn away from the astounding phenomenon of the ocean, they set their course eastward again and came to the fortified city of Libnah, which was within the borders of Judah. In Libnah things went well for them. A man had been put in command of the mighty fortress who bore the same name as the youth from Anathoth. Jeremiah of Libnah was, in addition, the father of Queen Hamutal. In accordance with the royal decree concerning all fortified towns, the two strangers were immediately taken before this prince of Libnah for interrogation. Jeremiah of Anathoth returned only brief answers, but Baruch was moved by his fear to act against the will of his master and revealed everything, even the fact that Jeremiah had been sent forth by the Lord and hoped to be rendered fitting to do His will by a long journey of contemplation and study of men. Now it happened that old Jeremiah of Libnah had heard from his daughter at the royal court in Jerusalem about the things that had taken place when the King held the Passover in the Temple. He had remembered about the youth who had been both praised and blamed for his reading, because he bore the same name as himself. The prince of Libnah, a brave warrior in Judah, was known far and wide as a pious man who not only kept the commandments and offered up a daily sacrifice in the Temple, but also liked to indulge in meditation upon the wondrous nature of God. He regarded the necessity of living far from the sanctuary of Adonai as an exile, and this exile inflamed his unbridled ardour. At the western gate of Libnah, where the road descended towards the plain of the Philistines, he had set up a stone monument. On this towering obelisk were inscribed the exalted qualities of the God of Jacob as compared with the brutishness and impotence of Dagon, the supreme god of the Philistines. The latter, who had been reduced by the inexorable course of history since the days of David to a peaceful little mercantile nation, were daily offended by the arrogance of this monument which proclaimed so challengingly the insignificance of their deity. Jeremiah and Baruch were also violently repelled by the bragging inscription.

The King's father-in-law invited them into his house, entertained them hospitably, and passed evening after evening in eager discussion with Jeremiah about the nature of God. The young man soon realized that the prince of Libnah, in spite of his piety and ardour, cherished such stupid ideas about the Lord that they might equally well have applied to Dagon. He could not grasp the fact that the God of Israel was not the God exclusively of Israel, but the God of the whole world through Israel. In the eyes of the old warrior, Zebaoth was a lord of battle breathing vengeance on His enemies (and all the other nations were His enemies); He lay in ambush for them and fell upon them in the flank, in order that His own people might triumph. The young Jeremiah ventured to raise objections, which caused the old Jeremiah to grow heated and argue dogmatically, until the younger man saw that only those minds can be convinced of the truth which are themselves capable of sharing in its lofty quality. To his horror he learned through this encounter what the great and just men of Judah were like. And Jeremiah of Libnah was famous as one of the greatest and most just.

In spite of their arguments the prince let them go after the second sabbath with paternal friendliness and numerous little gifts. As he took farewell of them he even invited them to seek his protection if they should be in distress or suffer persecution. "For few of the princes of Judah," he concluded, "know the Lord, your God, as I do."

Jeremiah and Baruch journeyed for a day towards the east and this brought them to the central part of the land of Judah, where they tarried for a time in the important town of Lachish. There they had a good opportunity to be eyewitnesses of the great apostasy which they had hitherto met only in less blatant form. The commandments of the old and the rediscovered Law seemed to have knocked in vain at the gates of Lachish.

In contrast to Jerusalem the abomination was practised here openly and unashamedly. The men did not keep the Sabbath. Was it possible, were there such brutish souls in Judah, that they did not comprehend the benefit of the day of rest, the solemn mystery of the peace of creation, the hallowing of the pause, which triumphed over toil and the actualities of life so that those who had turned away from God might for a few hours turn back to Him again? Yes, there were such brutish souls and even more brutish ones! The wealthy inhabitants of Lachish lent upon usury to their brothers. The sick and hungry died miserably in the ditches by the roadside, without a helping hand being stretched out to them. Those who behaved worst were the women. They ignored the Lord completely and paid homage exclusively to Ashtaroth, the Queen of Heaven and of the stars. Their bold apostasy went so far that, despite the King's strict command to worship only the One God, they celebrated the great festival of Ashtaroth, "mistress of the blue sky and the green crops," not in whispering secrecy but in colourful processions and with exulting sacrificial dances. During days of preparation they baked star-shaped fruit-cakes and brewed a subtle and intoxicating liquor in deep-bellied pitchers. This drink heated the senses of both men and women. Cakes and drink, consecrated images and flowers were offered to the guests of the goddess in liberal quantities. To make things worse, it was a Sabbath day when Jeremiah came upon the celebrants, who had gathered upon an open height for their burning of incense, their joyous feast, and still more joyous ecstasy. The full moon, which befriended and favoured women, had benevolently expanded almost to the size of the sun. Here Jeremiah for the first time approached people with an exhortation, very hesitantly, very timidly (for they were women), and with conspicuous lack of success. When a girl smilingly handed him a star-cake and a little consecrated image, he hid his hands in horror behind his back.

"What are you doing?" he stammered. "Why are you committing this abomination? . . . And today, which is a hallowed day . . . You are calling down evil upon your heads. . . ."

The girl gazed into Jeremiah's face with such boldness that he lowered his eyes. After this searching look she cried out:

"Oh, you with the long lashes! Are you one of the spies and bigots? Are the Temple priests again going to be let loose on Lachish? Sisters, come hither!"

In a second Jeremiah was surrounded by a crowd of perfumed women; he felt their breath and heard their angry laughter, and he was carried forward as though by a wave until he stood at last before an elevated seat under the leafy roof of a sycamore, where the wife of the prince of Lachish, the arch-priestess of the local Ashtaroth, sat enthroned. This woman, who was still young in spite of her high rank, was called Frustra. She wore an almost transparent robe embroidered with silver stars and golden ears of corn. Jeremiah noticed that a narrow grey streak shimmered in her black hair, which was combed high and decked with jewels. She raised a long-fingered hand, the golden bracelets on her wrist jingled.

"So you are a man of Adonai Elohim?"

There was a pause before Jeremiah answered:

"I hope to become a man of the Lord."

"Then let this young man of Adonai Elohim listen to me," began Frustra in a tone of mocking weariness. "I do not believe that you will have anything new to announce to me. We all know only too well what is in the minds of you and your like. Our thoughts, on the other hand, are unknown to you. For all the zealots only rant about their own imaginings, but they have no contact with the most sacred Being. It is well for us that we cling to Ashtaroth! Has she not been adored by our mothers, our grandmothers, and our ancestresses to their great advantage? So long as we celebrate the

Queen of Heaven, peace and friendliness reign in our midst and not the obscene fury which the slanderers attribute to us. For the Queen of Heaven is herself peace and friendliness and maternal love. Why should we turn away from her maternal love? We take nothing from Adonai, the God of our fathers, when we look up to adore Ashtaroth. Her power rises visibly above us, so bright, so gentle. He does not rise visibly above us. We only hear His voice upbraiding us through the toothless mouths of angry and tyrannous old men. . . . Were you about to interrupt me, young man of God?"

Jeremiah had only given vent to a stifled sound.

"It is good," resumed Frustra, nodding contentedly, "for there is nothing useful that you could say. Therefore learn from us! Does any seed continue to live through itself alone? No, it dies away if it does not find an egg in which to enter. Is it not the night which first turns the day into day? Is it not the darkness which first turns the light into light? How could Adonai, the divine male, rule if his complement did not exist —Ashtaroth, the divine female? She fulfils the most secret prayers of women. She forms the milk in the breast, in order that the sucklings of both man and beast may not perish. And she forms an even sweeter milk in our frequently sad hearts, which we call 'the consolation of the Star Queen.' Now I will hear you, young man of God, should you have anything new to announce to me."

Had the time come when the Lord would loosen his heavy tongue? Jeremiah listened with raised head and wrinkled brow. He heard nothing. The time had not yet come. Jeremiah's word was not yet the word of God. The words that came from him, and were his alone, had little eloquence and did not carry far. Jeremiah suffered greatly from the impotence of his own words, though he had not yet learned the world-wide difference between "speaking" and "prophesying." He said:

"That which you are doing and that which you clothe in such beautiful phrases is abomination. Whether it is hideous abomination or attractive abomination, it is all the same, since it puts that which has been created in the place of the Creator. Cease from this and abandon your feast, for it was on account of no worse abomination that the people of Israel were destroyed from Ephraim to Dan."

These were the words of Jeremiah and not the words of God. They were not the words of a prophet. The women standing roundabout in a circle, who understood little of what was being said, did not even murmur. The princess had been tranquilly gazing at her pointed knees, which could be seen through her transparent robe. She shook her head in disappointment.

"What you say is nothing new, young man of Adonai, nothing new at all, but very old and very trite. We are accustomed to more eloquent reproaches. Your idle talk will not disturb the feast of Ashtaroth, but will only serve to advance it. If you take my advice, you will choose a companion from among our young women so that she may initiate you into the joyful nature of the Queen of Heaven."

Frustra gave a sign to continue the interrupted dance. Confused singing began round Jeremiah, but even if he had been willing to follow Frustra's advice he would not have been able to find the companion she recommended. It was not the girls who were angry at the intervention of the stranger so much as the youths of Lachish who had been invited to the feast, and who grinned significantly as they showed the intruder their unsheathed knives. Baruch considered it advisable to leave the town with Jeremiah that same night.

They turned northwards, leaving Jerusalem and the highlands, which were some way off, to one side. Before them were the cities and regions of Socoh, Jarmuth, Timnah, Beth-Shemesh and Zorah, with their strong citadels, their cube-shaped houses, their farms, markets, streets of shops, mills, forges, potteries, weaving-rooms, bakeries, and slaughter-houses, with their places of assembly, their houses of learning, with all the hundred public and private resorts where men try to evade the Lord even when they imagine that they are seeking Him. Since they had spent their last shekel soon after leaving Lachish, and had already consumed the gifts of the prince of Libnah, Baruch had to seek work of some kind, and he could no longer prevent his master from sharing in it. Jeremiah was now able to estimate both with body and with soul how splendid was the offer that the Lord of heaven and earth had made to His people, and how base the people had been to scorn and reject it. Israel would have had nothing to do but follow the fundamental commandments of the divine Law, and its kingdom would have been firmly established for all time. In the Law it was written: "Thou shalt not oppress an hired servant. . . . At his day thou shalt give him his hire, neither shall the sun go down upon it; for he is poor, and setteth his heart upon it." Jeremiah himself now experienced frequently that his employer did not pay him his hire before the going down of the sun, and that after the rising of the sun he even made some deduction from that which was due to him. It was written in God's commandment to Israel: "If thy brother, an Hebrew man, or an Hebrew woman, be sold unto thee, and serve thee six years; then in the seventh year thou shalt let him go free from thee. And when thou sendest him out free from thee, thou shalt not let him go away empty. Thou shalt furnish him liberally out of thy flock, and out of thy floor, and out of thy winepress: of that wherewith the Lord thy God hath blessed thee thou shalt give unto him. And thou shalt remember that thou wast a bondman in the land of Egypt, and the Lord thy God redeemed thee." This was written in the rediscovered Book of the Law, but Jeremiah saw with his own eyes that nowhere in the land was there an owner who let his bondmen go free after six years unless they were old, frail, and sick. Then he allowed them to starve and die under the open sky of their freedom, since they had not received the share due to them from the flock, the threshing-floor, and the winepress. Everywhere in the ploughed fields, in the stables, and in the workshops worn-out Hebrew men and women were toiling for more than three or four times the stipulated seven years, and these permanently enslaved workers received from their masters neither a lamb from their flocks, nor a bundle of barley from their threshing-floors, nor a single grape from their winepresses. With a burning sense of shame Jeremiah remembered that his own venerable father, a priest of God, acted not a jot better than all the other owners in the land. Every seven years came a year of jubilee, the Sabbath of the week of years, but on the hills of Anathoth no bondman was given his freedom; none of those who were dismissed after years of labour received his portion. He himself had once asked as a boy why of all the commandments just this one was never observed. His father had not replied to the question. Obadiah had evaded it by saying peevishly that when times were hard everybody should be glad to have bread and a roof. Joel, however, trying to find a more subtle reason, had pointed to the possible effect on foreign countries: "What would the great men of Egypt, Asshur, and Babylon say if little Judah made the slaves of neighbouring lands covetous by the conferment of such benefits?" Even as a boy Jeremiah had not been convinced by these answers, and to-day, when he learned what was happening by personal experience, they made him bitter. His heart was filled with unrest, and he felt that he was involved in the commission of a great sin.

Nor was this all by any means. It was likewise written in the Law: "If there be among you a poor man of one of thy brethren within any of thy gates in thy land which the Lord thy God giveth thee, thou shalt not harden thy heart, nor shut thine hand from thy poor brother." But on his wanderings from city to city Jeremiah saw that this commandment of love, just because it was not very difficult to fulfil, was most wantonly neglected. Once more God's offer was transformed into its opposite by the abominable cunning of mankind, for poverty had become a trade and well-doing a subject for boasting. Insolent arch-beggars, like Shamariah of Anathoth, had acquired a monopoly of all the gifts and alms that were distributed. They went from house to house with noisy remonstrations and took their places arrogantly at the family tables, while those who were in genuine need had to starve. Their rags were a lie, but it seemed that this very fact suited the rich men; for the more a man possessed, the more insidiously did he try to pervert the meaning of the Law by the way in which he fulfilled it.

No different from the treatment accorded to the genuinely poor was that which was meted out to the foreigners, the widows, and the orphans; in short, to all those over whom the Law held its protecting hand. When the fields were reaped, no part of the harvest was left lying as a sacred levy for those who were too modest to beg and in their poverty and loneliness resembled Ruth, the noble gleaner. If any "pious" man *had* obeyed the Law, there lay upon the boundary stone an armful of plucked grain which was not good enough for the cattle. And this was worse than nothing, for again the purity of the Law had been sullied.

Slowly journeying from place to place, Jeremiah and Baruch had become abundantly familiar through a hundred meetings and conversations in farms and in houses, in work and in leisure, with the reality by which men were dominated, that is to say, with that which was base and turned away from God. It had been a hard time of training, and full of deprivation. When they came to the city of Ajalon, where the territories of Benjamin and Ephraim met, even the unwearying Baruch looked pale and exhausted, but Jeremiah decided not to return to Jerusalem yet; he wished instead to push forward to the old northern kingdom of the ten tribes of Israel that had been carried into captivity. A longing curiosity, mingled with apprehension, made him want to see the result of Zebaoth's curse and vengeance in the place where it had occurred. Jeremiah had always felt a childlike compassion for the tribes of Ephraim and Manasseh, for they sprang from the brother of Benjamin and it was in the land of Benjamin that he had himself been born. For the first time he was able to realize how ruthlessly Zebaoth had carried out His judgment on Ephraim and Manasseh. In spite of the death and the carrying into exile of thousands of families, the people of Israel had not disappeared from these lands; they had even increased in numbers during the last two generations. Ephraim and Manasseh were still in existence, but it was an existence of the underworld, of Sheol, an uncanny state of decay. The peasants still harvested their barley, the vine-dressers still cut their grapes, the olive-gatherers still pressed their olives into great tubs, the shepherds still drove their flocks to the pasture as if nothing had happened. Even the larger cities were still standing, such as Timnath, Pirathon and Shechem, where the people went to market to buy and sell under the eyes of the tax-collectors of Asshur. But the whole atmosphere was so extraordinarily listless, so stifled, so full of a ghostly mournfulness! It seemed to lack the light of day. It was a world that God had cast away. Nowhere had Jeremiah seen so many people who looked like shadows, such numbers of blind men, cripples, lepers, and raving madmen. Ephraim still kept its face turned away from the Temple, and not even yet had it any thought of turning back. It made no attempt to raise itself up with the help of the Lord, but stretched out its limbs and lived resignedly under the curse. Israel's features could still be distinguished in their countenances, but these features were decadent, marred and effaced through continual intermarriage. The lost tribes were there and yet they were not there. Jeremiah had an oppressive foreboding: "When the divine patience has run out and the time has come, this will be the future of Judah too, and perhaps even more abominable, even more mournful, even more like Sheol."

He and Baruch journeyed swiftly on until at last they stood before the mighty ruins of Samaria, where the feeling of oppression overwhelmed Jeremiah completely. So this was the capital of the Kingdom of Israel, which had wished to vie in magnificence with Babylon, Noph, and Nineveh! The royal palace of Jeroboam and many other proud buildings were still partly intact. But the more undamaged a building was, the greater was the horror of desolation that emanated from it. Samaria was abandoned, not only by men but by God. The successors of Adonai were jackals, wild dogs, snakes, and scorpions, which menaced every step they took. Jeremiah sat upon a block of stone and had ceased to see the ruins of Samaria. He saw Jerusalem in flames and gazed upon the ruins of the Temple. His heart sank within him. How long, O Lord, how long? He thought of the words of Urijah: "Wait . . . even if you have to wait until the hour of your death." He was prepared to wait, but his soul groaned unto the Lord: "For what art *Thou* waiting?"

Adonai was silent. Jeremiah was seized by a wild desire to escape, to leave the place that God had cast aside and reach Jerusalem as quickly as possible. They set out at once. But in Kirjath-Jearim, not far from the gates of the capital, Jeremiah was witness to a scene of apostasy far worse than any he had hitherto encountered on his journeying.

At the entrance to this city rose a stately house in the doorway of which stood a no less stately man who, with his hand shading his eyes, was gazing out into the street and appeared to be awaiting the arrival of belated travellers. The sight of the two weary young men apparently filled him with joy, although, or perhaps because, their shoes and attire showed signs of the long journey they had made. The keen eyes of the majestic old man, who continually stroked his well-tended, wavy beard, recognized immediately that these were not ordinary tramps or vagabonds, but educated youths who were perhaps gathering experience in the Lord or had undertaken a hazardous journey in fulfilment of a vow. It was an excellent opportunity to acquire merit by entertaining such men! He refused to let them continue on their way, although Jerusalem was not more than an hour's journey away. With paternal kindness he invited them into his house, where they were allotted a well-furnished chamber with soft couches and escorted to a magnificent bathroom fragrant with warm, scented water and choice essences. Servants hovered round them as they bathed. Their bodies were washed, rubbed with rough towels, anointed with salve, and massaged. Their hair and beards were trimmed, and the wounds that had been inflicted on their feet and legs by constant walking were carefully tended with various balsams. Finally they were presented with new coats and sandals. As they sat down to the evening meal at the table of their wealthy host, they felt boyishly refreshed and as though reborn. Jeremiah praised in his heart the kindness of the old man, though he was rendered slightly uneasy by the gesture with which he tenderly fingered his wavy beard. Seldom had he known a farmer or owner without priestly rank who was so deeply versed in the Law, who could argue with such surprising skill in matters pertaining to the divine order, and who offered up such a variety of prayers until long after midnight with seemly expression and suitable remorse. The name of this majestic flatterer of God was Meshullam, son of Malluch. Since the seventy Sabbaths of their wandering, Jeremiah and Baruch had never slept so well as they did that night on the luxurious divans of Meshullam.

In the early morning they were awakened by the most mournful of choruses, which seemed to be lamenting the imminent downfall of Israel. The two sleepers sprang up and left the house to seek the source of this heart-constricting chant. Behind the house of Meshullam there stretched a spacious paddock, the grass of which had been burnt and on which twelve mills had been erected such as had been used in Judah since time immemorial. The nether millstone was fixed and immovable, but the upper millstone, which was no less massive, worked on a hub and was set in motion by a long shaft. These mill shafts usually had oxen harnessed to them, which trotted round in a circle throughout the day. The twelve shafts that Jeremiah and Baruch now saw were worked not by oxen, but by men—naked, sweating giants, twelve statues of Samson. As they approached closer they saw that these giants were, in a true sense, like Samson, for all the twelve slaves who were raising their melancholy wailing to the morning sky were blind.

Shaken to his very depths, Baruch shudderingly called out to them:

"Who are you and to whom do you belong?"

The twelve Samsons all stopped in their work at the same time and ceased their chant. With ox-like slowness twelve heads turned in the direction of the questioning voice. They were the heads of aged bondmen. Twenty-four eye-sockets, scarred and fly-tormented, stared empty. Their voices came in chorus:

"We belong to Meshullam the miller. We are his property."

Baruch almost screamed his next question, as though these empty eye-sockets had to be addressed with more than ordinary distinctness:

"Were you all born blind?"

The twelve giants began to move spasmodically, as if they were about to dance. They rocked and swayed to and fro before they wailed in answer:

"We were not blind when we were born. When we were young we were blinded by Meshullam the miller, blinded with fire and iron, with iron and fire."

"They speak the truth. . . ."

It was the dignified voice of Meshullam which had uttered these words. Their solicitous host, whose venerable beard had not suffered the least disorder overnight, had come to seek his guests. With his small white hand he pointed gently to the blind men.

"When slaves have been blinded and can no longer see, their hard work comes more easily to them and they are able to do more. When men who can see keep walking in a circle, they are often struck by the Lord with madness. This I have learned from the nations, in the cities of Babylon and Egypt."

Meshullam had spoken this last sentence with a melodious complacency, as though he expected praise from his young guests for so excellently following the wise example of great and civilized peoples. He gazed at Jeremiah with an amiable air of superiority and seemed to have no suspicion that by this deed alone he had broken the law of God and was helping to bring about the end. Jeremiah said nothing, but merely took off the coat and shoes which he had received as a present in the house of Meshullam and laid them at the feet of his astounded host. Baruch did the same. After this final experience during their wanderings they entered the city of Jerusalem through the Gate of Ephraim barefoot, covering their nakedness only with their cloaks.

On Jeremiah's first day in Jerusalem that happened which had not happened throughout his long wandering. Adonai appeared now to be satisfied with His sanctified prophet's journey in search of reality, but the sign for which Jeremiah was waiting came to him in an unexpected way. It was in the nature of Adonai never to repeat Himself.

In the lower town with its numerous steps, where the craftsmen's quarter was situated, Jeremiah had taken up his lodging over a potter's shop. Since the shaping of the clay needed no hammering and caused no noise, but was a silent craft, he hoped to enjoy undisturbed peace, yet already on the first day he could not endure the solitude and felt an urge to go down into the potter's workshop. It was a strange sight, of which he had hitherto had no conception, that kept him rooted to the spot and compelled him to take a deep interest in the work of the master potter. With an almost physical delight he saw how the formless lumps of clay were first transformed into balls on the swift-moving wheels of the craftsman and his assistants, how they then changed to ovals, how the slender neck of the growing vessel began to extend, how the shape became beautifully convex and the rim arched outwards in the form of a calyx. Finally the master took a graving tool and drew wreaths of flowers and other ornamental lines on the surface of his finished work. The pitchers, bowls, and other vessels were then placed over a fire to be hardened.

Jeremiah noticed that one of the potter's vessels was marred under his hand. The lump of clay seemed obstinately to be resisting the movement of the wheel that was fashioning it. It would not form itself into a proper ball; the convexity was twisted to one side in an ugly way, and the rim was irregular. The whole pitcher seemed to be contorting its mouth rebelliously. The potter grew angry, stopped the wheel, and kneaded the failure into what it had been before —a shapeless lump of clay.

It was at this moment that the Lord spoke to Jeremiah for the first time since the night of Passover. He did not speak in the same resonant, dual voice, clear and mellow, for His sanctified prophet had advanced far enough to hear Him even without that sonorous whisper. Nor did Jeremiah see any particular vision. Everything that Jeremiah saw with a profound insight could be interpreted as though it were a vision. Indeed, it was a vision. Only his eyes and his ears had to be opened by the Lord. The word of which Jeremiah now became the receptacle ran thus:

"O House of Israel, cannot I do with you as this potter? Behold, as the clay is in the potter's hand, so are ye in mine hand. . . ."

Jeremiah perceived that with this parable the Lord was only indicating the final goal of His plan of vengeance. Perhaps His hand was already kneading the clay to shape it anew, but He had not yet announced that His patience was at an end. At the same time as this light broke in upon him, he was beset by an insistent and compelling urge, a restlessness which he could not still and which grew stronger every moment. It was a commandment of the Lord, the first since he had been ordered to gird up his loins and go forth. Tormented though he was by apprehension and the instinct to resist, there could be no question of objection or postponement in the face of the increasing emphasis of this command. The more violently Jeremiah resisted, the more impatiently was the inner whispering repeated, so that it almost filled the room outside him again:

"Go and cry in the ears of Jerusalem, saying, Thus saith the Lord."

It was the first Sabbath after the High Festivals. The popular prophets and promisers of salvation had shone on these great occasions, but on this unimportant day they had stayed away from the Temple. After the early morning sacrifice the inner courtyard was as usual cleared of worshippers by the Temple guard and its gates barred. The idlers of the city were gathered during the hours before noon in the outer courtyard, which stretched between the massive walls of the royal palace and the elevated corridor, or gallery, that surrounded the priests' court and the sanctuary. The great outer courtyard provided a more animated scene on weekdays than on the Sabbath, for the rest day of the Lord required that all the booths which were permitted by the Temple authorities to sell consecrated objects and wares suitable for sacrifice, such as fruit, incense, and doves, or luxuries and refreshments, should be taken down immediately before the appearance of the first star in the sky.

As they promenaded up and down in their best clothes, the people had nothing else to gape at except each other, unless the King, the princes, or a foreign personage happened to be walking to the Temple with a pompous retinue, or some man of God was directing general attention to himself by his rough and rapt voice. If nothing like that was happening and there was no kind of pageantry, commotion, or battle of words, the inquisitive people of the capital had to return home disappointed and with their hankerings unsatisfied.

There was no express prohibition to prevent the populace from entering the great galleries; nevertheless, this part of the Temple, which was built on pillars and reached by a number of steps, was reserved for the sole use of dignitaries of high rank. Unless he was of some importance nobody ventured into this circular structure, which contained numerous Temple offices, rooms for assembly, consultation, and study, and secluded cells. Until after nightfall there was a busy coming and going. Though the Sabbath was a day of quiet, it was no less a day of discussion. With solemn steps, and taking care that they should not exceed the number of paces that a man was permitted to walk on the Sabbath day, the important personages of the Temple and the royal court called upon each other. Guarded views were exchanged concerning the Lord's plan for the universe, and opinions were expressed about home affairs and what was going on among the great nations abroad. Above all, however, over and over again the ticklish question of the relation between the claims of God and the power of the King was circumspectly weighed. As befitted the day when God rested from His work of creation, these momentous discussions were carried on in low, almost inaudible tones that admitted of no display of agitation. In the days of Josiah there was, indeed, no cause for agitation. With the exception of the invasion of the Scythian horsemen there had been profound peace for many years, and only a few people remembered the shedding of blood in battle. The kings of Egypt, Asshur, and Babylon showed themselves favourably disposed towards their little neighbour, and only those who were suffering from delusions failed to realize that a friendly age had dawned, the age of the rediscovered Law and of harmonious relations between Adonai and Judah.

Not everywhere, however, did there prevail the same subdued stillness as among these dignitaries. One of the chief traditional liberties of the Temple was freedom of speech, though it involved no slight risks for the orator. A number of pulpits had been erected on the steps round the gallery, which every adult and trustworthy visitor to the Temple had the right to mount for the purpose of addressing the people. His freedom did not, to be sure, extend further than the pulpit, since he was responsible for the unobjectionable nature and admissibility of every word he spoke and liable to punishment for any deviation from the Law which he allowed himself, as well as for any vexation that he might cause within the sacred precincts. The pulpits of the outer courtyard were thus regarded as snares for inexperienced prophets. This part of the Temple activities was in charge of a very high authority, which possessed its own tribunal and came immediately after the Sagan in rank. This authority was called "the Office of the Keeper of the Door." There was not merely one Keeper of the Door; there were three, in descending order of rank. A few months previously the office of First Keeper of the Door had been assumed by a new man, Pashur son of Immer, but luckily for Jeremiah he was absent from the Temple that day, and his two colleagues closed a friendly eye when the speaker was a youthful enthusiast.

The pulpit on which Jeremiah stood was towards the south, facing the royal palace. He did not know how he had got there, but once he had fought down his overwhelming timidity so that he might obey the Lord, he suddenly grew as calm again as when he had been commanded to read from the Book of the Law in the presence of the King. His heart beat strongly, but unhurriedly, and this was because he was wonderfully sure of Adonai in that hour. He had only to close his eyes in order to be more aware of the Lord than he had ever been. But one thing was essential: he must not desperately seek for words or struggle to express his own thoughts. His task was to entrust himself to the Lord as he did when he slept, to eliminate his own mind and individuality, and to empty his senses of himself almost to the verge of dissolution. The usually hesitant speaker was flooded with the knowledge that up here he would not be forsaken. He looked down from his height upon the close-pressed Sabbath throng, and behind his back he heard the dragging steps of high officials who completely ignored his presence. He took a deep breath and emptied his mind. To his own surprise he suddenly heard issuing from his lips the usual cry with which prophets were accustomed to attract the attention of the people:

"Hear ye the word of the Lord!"

Something in him shrank at the sound of this thundering and compelling voice, which was unfamiliar to him and seemed to have no connexion with himself as he was and had always been.

"Hear ye the word of the Lord! For thus saith the Lord unto you . . ."

The voice had its effect. All noise of movement ceased. Even the steps behind his back were no longer to be heard. This lasted but a moment, however, for the bustle of the crowd was resumed immediately and only a little knot of curious onlookers remained standing below the pulpit to listen to an unknown speaker. Connoisseurs of oratory looked up at him with eyes that were ready to mock, and he heard some disparaging remarks. One or two of them were indignant that he had appeared in ordinary Sabbath costume and not, as beseemed a rough preacher, in a shaggy garment; that is to say, a hairy cloak of untanned skins. Jeremiah's eyes and ears distinguished with great clearness everything that was said and done in front of him, but nothing was able to disturb or confuse him, for in his mind the words of the Lord were beginning to collect like drops of water in a porous rock. His body felt light and exalted, and for the first time in his life he experienced how the voice that dwelt within him detached itself and dominated his hearers.

"Thus saith the Lord; I remembered thee, the kindness of thy youth, the love of thine espousals, when thou wentest after me in the wilderness, in a land that was not sown. Israel was holiness unto the Lord, and the first-fruits of his increase: all that devour him shall offend; evil shall come upon them. . . ."

The knot of listeners had grown to more than a hundred. This was a new voice! It was long since they had heard its like. It did not try to woo their ears with passionate words, but filled them with a mellow and tranquil cadence. The caressing gentleness of the poetic picture was alluring. Of course, the parable of the charming young thing who followed her vigorous bridegroom into the wilderness was not new. The more mature connoisseurs were well aware that Adonai had used the same parable in the mouth of many an old prophet, yet they liked to hear it again and were fond of thinking that they themselves had once been in the heart of the Lord like that maiden in bridal array. They shouted their approval, but Jeremiah had closed his eyes. It was not the thoughts of his own soul, but the whispering within him that came from his lips.

"Thus saith the Lord, What iniquity have your fathers found in me, that they are gone far from me, and have walked after vanity, and are become vain? Neither said they, Where is the Lord that brought us up out of the land of Egypt, that led us through the wilderness, through a land of deserts and of pits, through a land of drought, and of the shadow of death, through a land that no man passed through, and where no man dwelt? And I brought you into a plentiful country, to eat the fruit thereof and the goodness thereof; but when ye entered, ye defiled my land, and made mine heritage an abomination. . . ."

Jeremiah broke off. The vehemence of the last words had taken his breath away. Often as he had been seized with holy wrath at the perversions of the Law which he had encountered during his wandering, his blame had been outspoken but never unbridled. Had he not been taught by his father that a man of culture must under all circumstances avoid calling things bluntly by their name and must always choose palliating forms of expression? And now his lips had been forced to utter the bluntest reproaches, in the place, moreover, which was associated ever since he could remember with his childhood veneration and loving awe. A deathly hush had come over the crowd. Though Jeremiah kept his eyes closed, he knew that the crowd was growing denser.

"Hear ye, hear ye the word of the Lord! . . ." Once more he uttered the cry, as if he wanted to hide himself faint-heartedly behind the actual speaker and impute all the blame to Him.

"My people have changed their glory for that which doth not profit. Be astonished, O ye heavens, at this, and be horribly afraid, be ye very desolate, saith the Lord. For my people have committed two evils; they have forsaken me, the fountain of living waters, and hewed them out cisterns, broken cisterns, that can hold no water. . . . For of old time I have broken thy yoke, and burst thy bands; and thou saidst, I will not transgress; when upon every high hill, and under every green tree thou wanderest, playing the harlot. Yet I had planted thee a noble vine, wholly a right seed: how then art thou turned into the degenerate plant of a strange vine unto me? For though thou wash thee with nitre, and take thee much soap, yet thine iniquity is marked before me, saith the Lord God. . . ."

The hush had changed to a surging murmur. Who was this downy-bearded boy who was thundering out a veritable divine denunciation such as had scarcely been heard since anyone could remember? Was one really to assume that the

Lord could not find a man of more mature years for such a prophecy? The presumption of youth these days was incredible! If one thought of the greybeards who were always summoning to penitence, like the scarred Urijah, for example, it had to be admitted that the latter maintained a praiseworthy discretion in choosing his words since his unfortunate experiences—not at all like this audacious newcomer! And what about the great figures of olden time? Isaiah walked for three years naked through the streets of Jerusalem to punish himself for the bitter words that Adonai had put into his mouth. And this same Isaiah always used to implore after one of his stern speeches: "Comfort ye, comfort ye my people. . . ." What was the meaning, anyway, of the iniquity that could not be washed away with nitre and soap? Had not the present generation rediscovered the Law? Had not Josiah made a covenant before the Lord at the pillar of the oath, and fulfilled this covenant by purging the whole land of idolatrous worship? Had the commandments of the Law not been made the fundamental law of the kingdom? What more could be expected? The demands of the Lord had been satisfied in every detail, and the prosperity of the country was a proof of this. The words of this man were not the words of the Lord, but the culpable insolence of an immature youth who wanted to attract to himself the attention of the venerable dignitaries of the Temple and the honest men of Jerusalem. Scoffing cries and threats began to be heard above the general ill-humour. But Jeremiah did not hear them. His senses had melted away in the furnace of the Word with which he had become one.

"Run ye to and fro through the streets of Jerusalem, and see now, and know, and seek in the broad places thereof, if ye can find a man, if there be any that executeth judgment, that seeketh the truth; and I will pardon it. . . . How shall I pardon thee for this? . . . For among my people are found wicked men: they lay wait, as he that setteth snares; they set a trap, they catch men. As a cage is full of birds, so are their houses full of deceit: therefore they are become great, and waxen rich. They are waxen fat, they shine: yea, they overpass the deeds of the wicked: they judge not the cause, the cause of the fatherless, yet they prosper; and the right of the needy do they not judge. . . ."

From all sides came a yell of rage:

"Where is the Keeper of the Door? . . . Fetch the Keeper of the Door!"

But now Jeremiah was no longer merely the mouth of Zebaoth. His own soul had been carried away in wild indignation by the cadence of the words that came from his lips. He saw the small white hand of Meshullam the miller pointing to the twelve blind Samsons. Below him the people continued to rage:

"Make an end! . . . Stop him from saying any more. . . . Take him to the Keeper of the Door! . . ."

But Jeremiah beat his breast with both fists.

"Shall I not take vengeance on this people? saith the Lord. . . ."

From behind Jeremiah came warning whispers. Someone had mounted the pulpit beside him, had seized his arm, and was trying to drag him away behind the pillars of the gallery. It must have been Baruch. The word of the Lord had not yet wholly left him, but it was less a question that came from Zebaoth than Jeremiah's own cry of apprehension which finally burst from his lips:

"What will ye do, when the end shall come?"

Only then did he open his eyes. The crowd had swelled

to enormous proportions and was quarrelling among itself. For the newcomers had not understood what the speech had been about, while those who were more charitably disposed were rebuking the hotheads. Baruch implored Jeremiah to step down from the pulpit and leave the Temple as soon as possible. But Jeremiah, now that his eyes were open, was staring beyond the quarrelling crowd and the forest of gesticulating fists. Something incomprehensible was happening. The tall figure of an old man was pushing its way implacably through the throng and coming towards Jeremiah with its arm raised threateningly. Jeremiah was paralysed with fright. He saw his father approaching, he also a Keeper of the Door. The proud and weary Hilkiah had set out from Anathoth to bring his son to account for the great vexation, the disgrace which he had inflicted on his family in the Temple this Sabbath day. Jeremiah stepped to the edge of the pulpit that he might go humbly to meet his father, but Baruch threw both arms round him and pulled him back. When they were a little distance away, they began to run like conscience-stricken boys.

9

The Summons of the King

AT THE hour when Hilkiah, of the family of Abiathar and Eli, appeared to his prophesying son in the Temple, he had in reality suddenly died at home on his estate, at the door of his house. He had just been delivering a long harangue of lament and rebuke on the subject of the youngest and most ungrateful of his sons, completely ignoring the mild protests of his wife, when at the words, "but he was always in my heart," he sank to the ground without warning and, with a final rattle of fatherly dissatisfaction, gave up the ghost.

Meanwhile Baruch had succeeded in bringing his master away from the Temple without being pursued. When they were sitting in their little room above the potter's shop, the first words that Jeremiah uttered were a request to Baruch to obtain for him a donkey as soon as possible. He had to set out for Anathoth as soon as the Sabbath was at an end, for he had received an infallible sign that his father was urgently calling him. He foreboded more than he revealed to his disciple. His father's words rang constantly in his ears: "Priests preserve the order of the Lord, and do not deviate from it. . . . And now do you come, my son, with visions and voices and divine words? The Lord can step beyond His own order . . . if it pleases Him. But not you! . . ." Jeremiah had forgotten nothing of what his father had said to him.

He did not reach his father's house on the hill of Anathoth until late at night. The women who acted as professional mourners had gathered round the ruined sanctuary before his chamber window and were rending the stillness of the night, as was their duty, with their outbursts of grief. The more distinguished the deceased, the more clamorous the lament. Jeremiah's foreboding had already been confirmed by their heart-piercing shrieks and gurgling trills when he was yet some distance away.

In accordance with hallowed custom, Hilkiah had been clad in a shroud and laid upon the floor of the Hall of Abiathar. The ever-burning lamp of the house stood beside his covered head and served now as the lamp of the dead. Round his body had been ranged various objects that he had been fond of during his life: several finely wrought boxes of nard and scent-jars of gold which he had always carried about with him, staving off by the thought-deadening enjoyment of the pungent fragrance his discontent with his family and with existence in general. When Jeremiah entered the Hall of Abiathar, his nostrils were assailed by the disturbing odour of cinnamon and other spices. He remained standing at some distance from the extended, white-clad shape, which no longer had anything human about it. How perceptibly the Lord turned away from those who were dead! Jeremiah had loved and venerated his father, in spite of his querulous nature, but now he looked down at the corpse with an aloof and remote gaze, though he knew that Hilkiah's death was associated in some mysterious way with his prophesying in the Temple.

His near-sighted eyes suddenly noticed a crumpled figure crouching on the floor in a corner of the room, which was also completely enshrouded and was scarcely discernible in the scanty light of the lamp. Jeremiah went gently to his mother and raised her from the ground. She seemed to have shrivelled, and lay almost weightlessly on his breast. Though she had lost in Hilkiah the companion and lord of her whole life, she did not shriek and lament as other widows did who had been abruptly bereaved. She appeared only to have withered up. Mother and son remained clasped in a long embrace, but their numbness did not yield and their hearts did not melt.

"My son," she murmured, and in the familiar words there lay a fear and foreboding for which Jeremiah could not divine the reason. Then she turned her head away silently from her son to her dead husband, as if she must not lose a second of the time during which the companion of her life still tarried above the earth. Jeremiah, too, gazed down again at the long rigid form that had been Hilkiah, and he thought of the tall apparition that had pushed its way towards him through the Sabbath crowd with threateningly upraised arm.

"He departed in great anger. . . ." he said. His mother, without looking at him, replied:

"He was angry with his youngest son day and night. . . . And yet, only his youngest son was always in his heart . . . until the moment of his death. . . ."

Jeremiah took a pace back from his mother, as if his proximity might harm her. In his voice was a note of fear.

"Ask of the Lord, Mother. . . . Shall I bring death to all who have me in their hearts?"

That was all that mother and son said to each other in this hour. They sat silently side by side on the ground and kept watch over their dead. A long time they remained undisturbed, for the elder sons of Hilkiah were occupied with preparations for the funeral and their wives did not come near. Only much later, when the footsteps of Obadiah and Joel were heard in the passage, did Abi passionately clasp the hand of Jeremiah and whisper tonelessly, with the foreknowledge that tormented her:

"Be on your guard, my son. . . ."

Custom demanded that the family should mourn for seven days and seven nights after the funeral. The men had torn their garments in certain places and inflicted slight cuts on their cheeks with a knife. The women, completely enveloped in coarse linen, dipped their hands from time to time in a tripod full of ashes which they pensively strewed over their shoulders. Thus they sat for a full week on the floor of the Hall of Abiathar, refraining from looking into one another's eyes, and either maintained complete silence or whispered in the lowest of tones, for loud talking or the mention of any important or controversial matter was strictly forbidden during the days of mourning. Now and then the children of the brothers were allowed into the room to sit in silence at the side of their parents as a sign of mourning for their departed grandfather, and the hypocritically solemn faces of the little ones would twitch with a suppressed desire to laugh or chatter. Those who were already almost grown-up would let their eyes roam about with an exuberant vivacity and pleasure at the thought of the changes that were about to take place. The death of their grandfather was a rare occasion for them, a kind of festival, and it awakened in their hearts a burning expectation and the desire for upsetting things. But the women too, the gross Mocheleth and even the pleasant, good-natured Shua, found it difficult to conceal the joyful feeling of anticipation with which they had been inspired by the death of the old head of the family (involving as it did their own elevation) as they heaved the necessary sighs, let fall the required floods of tears, and invoked the name of God with suitable frequency. For the plain Mocheleth, especially, the great hour of recompense had come, since the power appertaining to the mistress of the house had fallen legally into her lap as the wife of the eldest son and new head of the family.

Throughout the day a succession of visitors came to call upon the mourners in the Hall of Abiathar. From early morning till evening the table was laden with food and drink in abundance, as was fitting in a hospitable and prosperous house. At first the guests would refuse to accept the good things, as the rules of politeness demanded, but then they would willingly allow themselves to be pressed by the persuasive sisters-in-law to partake of refreshment. As they ate, they praised the dead man in edifying phrases and encouraged the mourners to fresh tears.

It was obvious to Jeremiah that the eyes of the visitors kept turning towards him with an odious curiosity. There was no doubt that the rumour of the trouble he had caused in the Temple had spread to Anathoth and was conferring upon him an embarrassing notoriety. Moreover, a conspicuous figure had been making itself at home in the house since the first day of mourning, whose particular interest seemed to be the spreading abroad of Jeremiah's bad reputation. This was Shamariah, the chief beggar of Anathoth, who felt that he had come into his kingdom now that Hilkiah was dead. He stood in the doorway of the hall and invited the guests with a melancholy greeting and well-chosen words to cross the threshold:

"You are entering the house of a priest. The house of a priest is a house of the Lord. A house of the Lord is the house of the poor. Therefore the poorest of the poor, Shamariah, invites you to enter this his house."

The poorest of the poor seemed to have good grounds for feeling so very much at home. Obadiah, the new head of the family, treated him with benevolent condescension, called him frequently to his side, and conversed with him in whispers while he gazed furtively at the younger of his brothers. Both Obadiah and Joel, however, avoided speaking to Jeremiah during the days of mourning. It was only when the end of the week had come that the two elder brothers began to exchange certain remarks and hints.

"Our father's life might have been spared for many years to come," sighed the supple-minded Joel, "for his time was not yet due. But, alas, it was not given him to enjoy his allotted span and sit before his house full of years! A hundred years and more were his merit but he lived for only seventy, no age for a just man."

Whereupon Obadiah, the blunt successor, rejoined ponderously:

"Had not affliction come upon him, I should not yet be drinking from the goblet of the father of the house."

Shamariah nodded as he voiced his approval from the doorway:

"Stately, active, and of rosy complexion was Hilkiah before his heart was broken."

"And what a disgrace for a father and the whole family!" cried Obadiah in sudden wrath, raising his guttural voice more than was becoming. "To stand up in the holy Temple, publicly and on the Sabbath, a son of Hilkiah! . . . To call out: 'Hear ye, hear ye the word of the Lord!' . . . That *he* should do this! . . . Why *he?* . . . Arrogant impudence, to try to supplant in the eyes of men the peaceful, industrious workers. . . ."

Joel at once covered up this unseemly wrath with a seemly melancholy:

"That which my brother mentions was, the Lord be praised for it, spared our father. The news was no longer able to reach his ears. He who dies a day earlier suffers ten afflictions less, as they say on the Euphrates."

On the first day of the new week it became clear that the two brothers intended to render Jeremiah tractable for their purpose by these reproachful references. The house was now empty of guests come to pay their condolences, and only Shamariah had refused to let himself be dismissed. But three kinsmen appeared on the scene, having been summoned by Obadiah as witnesses to his project. The youngest of these was Hanameel, a quiet and thoughtful man, who had been Jeremiah's only playmate as a child. As boys together they had roamed the hills of Anathoth, when Jeremiah's impetuous ideas and passionate schemes had always inspired the slower Hanameel to submission and admiring imitation. Even now his eyes rested on the cause of the vexation with their old loyalty, while the other two kinsmen carefully avoided looking at him. After the meal Obadiah dismissed the women and children with a gracious gesture that he had learned from his father, and he did not invite even his mother to stay behind, though she had hitherto always shared in the council of the men. However, as Mocheleth, the new mistress of the house, also left the table, Obadiah achieved his purpose without detracting from the veneration he owed his mother. Jeremiah realized from this slight indication how times had changed for the former mistress.

Obadiah went straight to the point with an affront which he himself regarded as a pleasant jest and accompanied with a gurgling laugh:

"It is not good to share one's house with a prophet. . . ."

Joel, however, at once interposed soothingly:

"My brother errs. It is very good and advantageous to share one's house with a prophet. Cherish the serpent in your entrance-hall and set the exile in the seat of honour, as the sons of Aram teach in the city of Damascus. But what are we to do if the prophet does not desire to share the house with us of coarser clay? His mind is cruelly intent on leaving us, as the fatal grief of our father has already proved. His mother has been no more successful in keeping him on our estate. How could we succeed, therefore, we who are only his brothers and engaged in earthly activities, not brooders on the nature of God? To us he pays no heed. Yet be his thoughts what they may, it is the duty of his elder and more experienced brothers to provide for the callow youth. And this duty we shall not neglect, either now or later. That is why we are gathered here. Would that our youngest brother might listen to us and consider carefully."

And Joel proceeded to outline in an eloquent speech Jeremiah's situation in life. As third son he was entitled to inherit a considerable share of the fields, pastures, flocks, and farmyards on his father's estate. Since, however, he would not occupy himself with his landed possessions either as a farmer or as a merchant, the right and proper thing would be that he should make a final settlement with his brothers in the form of a covenant. In his immeasurable love for his youngest son, and in spite of all the vexation he had received from him, their father had during the last days of his life laid down in his will that Jeremiah's portion should be worked and administered by the elder brothers, who were enjoined to provide honourably and abundantly for the maintenance of the drone out of the proceeds. The final dispensation of one who had been gathered to his fathers should not and must not be changed by one iota. On the other hand, it would be a praiseworthy act in memory of their father if they made a mutual and just covenant which offered the youngest son great advantages and freed him, moreover, from ties that would only be a burden to him.

Having stated these arguments, Joel offered Jeremiah in the name of both Obadiah and himself to purchase his inheritance from him, since he was childless and independent while they had been blessed by the Lord with full quivers. The covenant could be concluded without delay, for the witnesses were present and the necessary gold and silver that would make the youngest brother a carefree man lay ready to be weighed out.

Jeremiah had listened in tense silence. Though he knew that his brothers hated him because of his sanctification and had thought of this covenant as a means of ridding themselves of him, yet the offer seemed well worth considering, since, as Joel had so cleverly suggested, it would bring him freedom not only from need but also from burdensome ties. One thing alone oppressed his heart. Henceforth he would be a stranger, a guest without rights, in his father's house when he returned home to look upon the face of his mother. He kept his eyes fixed on the ever-burning family lamp which was again gleaming on the table.

"My brothers," he said, "will let me have a little time. . . ."

Obadiah, whom Jeremiah always managed to work up into a temper, burst out:

"This offer is just and proper! Or does our youngest brother perhaps think that we wish to cheat him?"

Jeremiah gazed at the angry man with a sad but steadfast look.

"I do not think that, Brother. But it is not my wish or my advantage that decides."

Derisive coughing broke out round the table, accompanied by much clearing of the throat. Only Hanameel, his boyhood friend, kept his eyes fixed encouragingly on Jeremiah, as though he wished to give him strength to resist any temptation and to do that which he judged to be right.

Jeremiah lowered his long lashes. The swift thought came to him that he would be released by the covenant from the guilt in which his inheritance was involved. Had the Lord not commanded him to gird up his loins and go forth? But the Lord did not speak unambiguously and He was incalculable. Contrary to his expectations, the power of the Lord that was in Jeremiah did not say: "Yes," but: "No." He was not to resign his right to the inheritance of his fathers. Suddenly he put the question:

"When the seventh year comes again, the year of emancipation, will my brothers act on their estate in accordance with the Law: cancel all loans and let their bondmen and bondwomen go with their portion?"

Before Obadiah had grasped the implications of this question, Joel interposed sharply:

"In the year of emancipation your brothers will act as the whole of Judah and Benjamin acts, from the King in his palace down to the smallest farmer. They will do no more and no less."

Jeremiah rose from his seat as a sign that he regarded the discussion as being at an end.

"Then let the will of our father remain in force, and there shall be no covenant made between us."

The brothers had no time to give expression to their feelings, for just then there was a quite unexpected and brilliant interruption. The clatter of horses' hoofs was heard outside, an infallible sign that something important was about to happen. In the land of Judah, saddle-horses were reserved for the sole use of the King, the princes of the blood, the high dignitaries of the court and the army. The clatter that penetrated to the Hall of Abiathar caused such excitement that everybody sprang up from the table with eyes open wide in surprise. Shamariah's beaming face appeared in the door. He beat the air with his hands in agitation and called out something quite unintelligible to Obadiah. Then four armed men walked in, all wearing the sky-blue cloak of the warriors of David and the round golden shields of the royal bodyguard. They, however, kept in the background, for they were merely the escort of a tall, white-clad figure who now appeared in the doorway and surveyed the men assembled round the table with the tranquil gaze of one in high authority. It was only after a lengthy inspection that he opened his mouth, the delicate upper lip of which was clean-shaven.

"I am Ahikam, son of Shaphan."

This name, with its high prestige, came like a thunderbolt to the assembled men. Joel reddened, for in the presence of might and rank the experienced traveller was conscious of his inferiority. The King's private secretary took a pace forward and inclined his head.

"Am I standing in the house of Hilkiah, of the family of Abiathar and Eli, the Priest of Shiloh?"

The faces of Obadiah and Joel shone with a flattered delight, and they beamed like rising suns when Ahikam raised his voice and announced:

"A message from Josiah, son of Amon, King of Judah. . . ."

The elder brothers had no doubt that the long-awaited honour had at last been conferred on Hilkiah's house. Ahikam had brought them preferment from the King, a sign of his gracious favour, or at least a message of condolence on the death of their father. While Obadiah stood with his arms hanging awkwardly and not knowing what to say, Joel pointed to him affectedly and said:

"This is Obadiah, who has become the head of the family, upon Hilkiah's death."

But, alas, Ahikam, the private secretary of the King, appeared to have brought neither preferment, nor a sign of the King's favour, nor a royal message of condolence. Slowly he walked up to Jeremiah, who was standing motionless in his place. The two elder brothers looked at each other sharply. Was there to be a dishonourable arrest at the order of the King instead of the honour they had expected? Was Jeremiah now to expiate his insolent speech in the Temple? Ahikam recognized him whom he had been sent to fetch and touched with a kindly hand the golden clasp on Jeremiah's arm, the gift of the King which had always roused the gall of the two brothers whenever they looked at it.

"Jirmejahu! The King desires to have word with you," announced the secretary. "Prepare to accompany me, for you have been considered worthy to look upon the face of the King."

Jeremiah was startled and turned towards his brothers. They kept their heads lowered as if they had received a blow in the face, but the son of Shaphan put his arm round the shoulder of Jeremiah and escorted him out as a man escorts a younger friend. In the courtyard outside Jeremiah had scarcely time to take leave of his mother.

"This is the work of the Lord," she whispered in his ear. "Therefore be not afraid, my son, and have no thought for me, for my thoughts will be constantly of you."

Her eyes sparkled with hope and faith as Jeremiah swung himself lightly onto one of the royal horses as though he had been used to it from childhood.

"Lamps!" demanded a voice in the completely darkened chamber. With a magic swiftness, as if brought by silent shadows, two candelabra appeared with faintly glimmering lights which gradually expanded and revealed the contents of the room. Jeremiah saw that he was alone with the King. Ahikam had left him when they reached the second court of the guard, which lay between the administrative palaces and the "House of Solomon." The unwieldy eunuch who then became his guide had suddenly disappeared from his side after a strange and labyrinthine walk through gloomy corridors and halls, during which he had held him by the hand. Jeremiah bent to touch with his forehead the sandalwood inlaid floor which had the fragrance of incense, and he murmured the conventional salutation of a subject in the presence of his King. Josiah walked round him as he knelt with bowed head, and repeated his name softly to himself:

"Jeremiah, son of Hilkiah of Anathoth . . ."

It was only after a space of time which seemed unending to Jeremiah as the King continued to circle round him that Josiah cried in a loud voice:

"Up, Jeremiah, up! Why do you remain on your knees?"

He took up one of the lamps and held it close to Jeremiah's

face, as if he wanted to impress it on his mind like a passage from Holy Writ that he wished to learn by heart. In the centre of the chamber was a wide divan covered with a magnificent rug of purple, gold-embroidered byssus. The cushions were disordered, and the King had probably been resting there and dreaming before the entry of his visitor. In the turmoil of his senses, Jeremiah seemed to be aware of a swarm of royal dreams and plans like birds of prey hovering in the lofty obscurity of the room. Josiah had again seated himself upon the couch, and the seven-branched candelabrum at his side threw his face into sharp relief. Now it was Jeremiah's turn to study the face of the greatest king since the days of David and Solomon. But he came to a stop at the eyes, whose vital radiance outdazzled any searching gaze. Here there was only a yes or a no; any other decision was impossible. This man had to be either loved or hated, and for Jeremiah it could be only love, a love intensified by the sorrowful recognition that Josiah's radiance was already menaced by faint early signs of decline and of a burning up within him. Shadows lay beneath the youthful eyes, and the short beard, which gleamed with unguents, was already streaked with white. But his frame, of medium size, sturdy, and deep-chested, showed not the slightest trace of fat or looseness. The play of corded muscles and sinews was visible in his throat and bare arms. If steel could have been flesh, this was flesh of steel.

"I have not forgotten you, Jirmejahu of Anathoth," began the King of Judah. "Since that Passover eve your voice has not left my ear."

Contrary to his usual manner, Josiah spoke the next words slowly and thoughtfully:

"As you read, your voice caused me to pay particular attention, and it revealed to me what it did not reveal to the others, that the Lord is seeking communion with you. And since then you have prophesied in the Temple on the Sabbath . . . wrathful and bitter words of the Lord. They were reported to the King. . . . The people were indignant, and have asked that it should not be allowed to happen again."

At these words Josiah paused and there was a brooding silence. Jeremiah's heart was oppressed with a terrible sense of disappointment. He thought that the King had called him into his presence only to rebuke him. But Josiah suddenly sprang up from the divan. His figure became erect and taut like that of a boxer:

"But it is the King's desire," he cried, "that it *shall* happen again! It is his desire that the Lord's most barbed and bitter words shall be repeated to him and that nothing shall remain concealed! Let no prophet fear my wrath. Fear not, Jirmejahu, for the King puts great trust in your voice. The King cherishes pregnant schemes. . . . He wishes to be the nitre and the cleansing soap that shall wash the iniquity away from Israel!"

After these words, which poured out of him in intense excitement, the King paced swiftly to and fro and appeared to have forgotten the presence of Jeremiah, who put his hand to his breast to control his pounding heart. The King had used words that had come from his, Jeremiah's, lips.

Josiah, however, seemed to have grown suddenly tired, and he threw himself upon the couch as he closed his eyes and murmured:

"Jeremiah will remain in the King's house . . . that is my will. . . . Let him be like a staff, like a rope leading from the Lord to the King. Many a staff has already broken, many a rope has torn. . . . I need the help of those who are able to hear the pure Word."

In the twinkling of an eye Jeremiah's life had been completely changed, and he could not yet grasp it. He stared at the King, who seemed to be sleeping. Josiah's face was pale and stony. Time passed with dragging steps. What burden was it that weighed down this radiant man on the couch? At last Josiah commanded, with his eyes still closed:

"Seat yourself at my feet!" Jeremiah obeyed hesitantly. The King searched his face from between half-closed eyelids.

"What visions did you see? . . . What voices did you hear? . . . Conceal nothing, nothing, that the King too may see and hear and his arm be strengthened."

Jeremiah pulled himself together. He must not allow this great hour of his life to pass without using it for the purpose of his mission. The Lord Himself had brought him into the presence of the King in order that the last respite before His patience was exhausted should not go by unprofitably. He was sitting at the feet of the highest power in the land, a power which was full of a tempestuous readiness to serve the cause of disentangling the world from its confusion and leading the nation back to the Eternal One. To him, perhaps, it had been granted to rouse the strength of the King's arm and to save Jerusalem. Carefully weighing every word, intent only on the accuracy of his report and the truth of his expression, the man from Anathoth began to describe his experiences with Adonai. He told his story backwards, repeating first of all his prophecy in the Temple and depicting to the King with meticulous exactness how the Lord's words had formed themselves in his mind after an endless period of deprivation and without any effort on his part, coming in oozing drops and then flowing strongly like water collecting in a porous rock. The King listened with attentive, almost greedy eyes. Jeremiah continued with his vision in the potter's workshop, which had been both more and less than a vision, which had been an illumination. He dwelt at length on his wanderings, which had been devoted to the study of "reality," as people called their turning away from the Lord. He did not forget the ruins of Samaria, the proscribed shadow-world of Ephraim and Manasseh, the twelve blind giants of Meshullam the miller, or the feast of the Queen of Heaven in Lachish. With the help of the Lord his words grew more glowing and incisive as he thought of the great evasion of the commandments of love throughout the land. As Jeremiah spoke, the King's countenance was gloomy and tense. Only as Jeremiah began to speak of the Passover eve when he had been sanctified by the Lord, did the King's features lose their rigidity. He raised himself up on one arm and inclined his ear to the narrator, who had now reached the vision of the almond tree and the seething pot.

In the middle of his words Josiah interrupted him abruptly:

"Tell me once more, Jirmejahu . . . where did the pot hang? To which side was it inclined?"

"It hung between heaven and earth . . . it inclined from the north towards the south and spurted a boiling flood. . . . And the Lord said: Out of the north an evil shall break forth upon all the inhabitants of the land. . . ."

The King seized Jeremiah by the shoulders and stood erect.

"The boiling flood spurted from the north," he cried, "and not from the south! . . . Praised be the Lord our God . . . The evil will come from the north and not from the south, not from the House of Bondage on the Nile. . . . Nothing has come between Him and me. . . . It is not for me that

He has announced His day of judgment . . . Josiah will go in peace in accordance with the prophecy of Huldah the seeress, upon which I am building. . . . Nothing can befall the King and his plans!"

He tore aside a curtain and thrust open a door which led into another chamber.

"Has Hamutal, my Queen, heard the good news?"

The King stayed his step and remained standing in the doorway. The other chamber was far more brightly illuminated than his own. Jeremiah had risen and he now looked through the door. It seemed to him that it had opened on a blossoming garden. The gardener of the royal park, which lay above the junction of the valleys of Kidron and Ben-Hinnom at the southern end of the city, had heaped up before the Queen an overflowing mass of cut flowers in woven baskets. Fed by an abundant spring which was led through a skilful mechanism, foreign and native plants bloomed with the splendour of spring in the royal gardens at all seasons of the year. Hamutal had evidently been engaged in arranging the day's supply of blossoms, separating those which were to be used by the women whose task it was to bind wreaths from those which were to be distributed about the palace. This was a duty that she had reserved for herself, and she was still holding in her arms a great bunch of burning yellow lilies that fused into a flame with the scarlet of her gown. At her side stood the little prince Mattaniah, who had grown considerably since Jeremiah had last seen him, and not far away was Mattaniah's inseparable companion from Ethiopia, Ebed-melech, who was controlling his limbs with an effort. The two boys were staring with frightened curiosity at a dark apparition that had cast itself at the Queen's feet. Hamutal, who was prevented by this from approaching to meet the King, smiled at him hesitantly.

"Let my lord not be startled! . . . A calamity has befallen the city."

The cowering figure at her feet now raised its head, and Jeremiah recognized Shallum, keeper of the royal wardrobe and husband of Huldah the seeress. The nimble little man was broken, his aged head with its dishevelled grey beard was livid as it swayed lifelessly on his shoulders. Streams of tears poured incessantly from his swollen eyes, and with loud moans he repeated the words of the Queen:

"A calamity has befallen the city and the country. . . . A calamity has befallen the King and his house. . . . A calamity has befallen me, humble as I am. . . . The seeress, the glorious Huldah . . ."

"Is she dead?" asked Josiah curtly.

"More cruelly than with death has the Lord stricken her," wailed Shallum. "In the night she was stricken blind and dumb. Now she lies upon her couch in the roof chamber of my house and cannot see and cannot prophesy that which she saw. But her countenance smiles with great compassion upon Shallum. Woe, woe, what am I without the strength of Huldah! Why did the Lord touch His delicate vessel with too strong a touch?"

Josiah pondered deeply as he weighed the significance of what had happened. Was it really a calamity, as everyone believed? And how did it concern him and his schemes? The Lord had sealed the lips that had foretold his own good fortune, as one seals a vessel that contains the most precious balsam. This was a good omen. The King could doubt no longer. His next words were like a release from his employ of the seeress for whom he no longer had any use:

"She has done great service for the King," he said. "She

gave him strength to swear the new Covenant. She gave him the tranquillity which comes from the expectation of a happy death, for he will die in peace when his work is done. The Lord has willed that her lips should no longer be able to withdraw this promise. May her sufferings be short!"

His final words were the cool dismissal of a whole epoch. Then he turned away and sought the eyes of Jeremiah.

"Huldah has ceased to speak, but on the same day a new voice has been raised up for me. She foresaw my peaceful death in a vision, but you saw the vision of the seething pot which inclines from the north towards the south and spurted the boiling flood of a day of judgment which will not touch me. Whatever I may plan and do, must I not be sure of the Lord?"

Jeremiah's heart was constricted by a sudden fear. He still could not understand the King and the meaning that lay behind his words. But one thing he did understand: that his vision on the night of Passover was no longer a secret between him and God but had begun to influence the course of the world. Responsibility had begun to weigh upon his shoulders like a mountain. And he understood one thing more. This exalted man, Josiah, intoxicated with divine favour, was interpreting the words of Adonai according to his own desire and need. Jeremiah drew a deep breath, and for the first time in his life he stammered the warning which he was so often to repeat:

"It is not good to be sure of the Lord."

10

The Cup of Fury

JEREMIAH had been living for some time in the entourage of the King without having seen him again face to face since their conversation. He and Baruch had been allotted two rooms in the Palace and they were fed from the King's table. Neither did Hamutal forget Jeremiah, and from time to time she would send him a gift. Yet in spite of this pampered existence Jeremiah was very uneasy while he was living in the Palace. The reason was that the King, having brought him to his side, had left him alone again as Adonai had done, not even initiating him into the secret of how he had unriddled for himself the vision of the seething pot. Nor did Ahikam appear to know anything of the great scheme that the King was turning over in his mind. At least, he remained obstinately silent, though he was well disposed towards Jeremiah, when the latter referred to the strangely restive activity which Josiah had been displaying for some time. If the great ones were silent, however, the less important people about the court and in the city could not be kept from whispering. It was not possible to conceal either the warlike preparations and exercises in the gloomy old Citadel of David or the restless journeys of the King which kept him away from the capital for weeks at a time and took him to every part of the land, even up as far as Hermon in the territory of the tribe of Dan, the most northerly region of the kingdom of Israel that the Lord had cast aside. Had Jeremiah's forceful narration induced the King to march through the country in order to wring from the people obedience to the Law with ruthless severity and compel them to turn back to the Lord before His patience was exhausted? Jeremiah did not deceive himself. This unsparing journeying had another cause, which pointed to a perilous undertaking.

Even at his father's table at home the conversation had often turned on the strange happenings that were convulsing the empire of Asshur in the Land of Rivers to the east. The far-travelled and omniscient Joel had talked about the battles in which the new Babylon, under a fresh dynasty, was freeing itself from the suzerainty of Nineveh. And more than that! From the steppes and snowy mountains of the wildest and most remote regions of the world strange tribes, whose very names were unknown, had set out to harass the lords of the earth. Nobody understood the language of these peoples, not even the linguist Joel. Their quiver was as an open sepulchre, and they were all mighty men. Joel's suspicious father had always said that one could not distinguish truth from exaggeration in Joel's stories. But a certain amount appeared to be authentic, for only recently envoys of Asshur had appeared in all the surrounding kingdoms, and in Jerusalem too, and had promised with mild words and fraternal gestures to remit the ancient obligation to pay tribute on condition that none of these kingdoms should send auxiliaries against Asshur in case of war among the great nations. Since the making of this covenant, which was equivalent to complete emancipation, the King of Judah paid minor tribute only to Pharaoh. Could Josiah be thinking of altering a happy situation which everyone was prepared to accept?

What was happening in the world was obscure. But the

relations between Adonai and Jeremiah had also become obscure again. Jeremiah now understood that the Lord could not be faithless, yet it was difficult for one who had experienced the sudden lightning of illumination to endure the long periods of twilight when he was "out of touch." Jeremiah had no illusions on the matter. It was not God who was out of touch, but man. Jeremiah himself had not a quick ear, his eyes were weak, his body was not receptive. The Lord and he were not on the same plane. Each stood alone as though on two remote peaks, calling to each other and making mutual signs which the man was mostly incapable of understanding. Between them lay an unbridgeable distance, a wild underbrush consisting of the whole world of beings. Between them lay the language of mankind, uniting and separating them at the same time, a swaying bridge without railings and whose planks were split in the middle. Who could venture far on such a bridge? Jeremiah, who longed for nothing more ardently than clarity, received obscure words and signs. He received them unexpectedly, when he did not ask. And if he asked, as he did now, Adonai still remained obscure.

He generally passed the morning and the early part of the day with the young prince Mattaniah and the Ethiopian boy Ebed-melech. The King had given orders that Jeremiah was to introduce his youngest son to the elements of the Law. The two older sons had long since passed the age of instruction. Eliakim lived in a state of opposition to his father which could be glossed over only with difficulty. He occupied a magnificent palace outside Jerusalem that he had built for himself and his wife Nehushta. Everything that Eliakim did—and especially his extravagance—aroused Josiah's wrath. The most luxurious caravans from every country thronged to the palace daily. It seemed as if the world could not offer him enough in the way of balsams, spices, unguents, perfumes, and costly incense, which his household consumed in incalculable quantities. What angered the King most, however, was the mastaba, the mighty Egyptian tomb which this young man had had erected for the future reception of his corpse, and to make matters worse, he had shamelessly set it a long way off from the Garden of Uzziah where the sons of David had their simple graves. Eliakim's tomb was painted inside with splendid but blasphemous pictures, and it was to be expected that the future King of Judah, contrary to God's will, would immortalize his lean body with the aid of the natron and wrappings of Egypt.

In truth the Lord had not blessed His servant Josiah in his elder sons. Jehoahaz, the first-born of Hamutal, was a gentle, detached youth, who looked at the world out of vacant eyes and found the things of earth and heaven equally hard to understand. If the people of Jerusalem called their King the swiftest man in the land, they ought to have called Jehoahaz the slowest. Nevertheless, the swift Josiah carried the slow Jehoahaz with him on his tempestuous rides through the various regions, compelling him to sit in the saddle from morning till night and endure every kind of hardship. Perhaps he hoped by this discipline to kindle the faint flame of his son's vitality. The poor youth patiently bore all the discomforts to which he was subjected, his response to them being little other than that of a bale of goods strapped to a horse's back. The only vitality he possessed seemed to be in his fingers, which were always restlessly kneading or moulding some invisible object.

Little Mattaniah's temperament bore more resemblance to that of his father, especially as far as the strange volatility, the ebb and flow of his emotions was concerned. The boy could be tender and sensitive, but at one moment he would fondle his mother's flowers and in the next stamp them into the ground with unreasoning fury. Sometimes he would learn in a flash, as if he possessed the mind of a prodigy. Jeremiah had to repeat a passage to him only once and he would know it by heart. At other times he would stare in front of him in a dull and obstinate manner, and there was nothing that could alter his stubborn temper. Then he almost resembled the dance-obsessed Ebed-melech, who could never manage to concentrate his thoughts on one subject, however hard an effort he made. His thin legs were always twitching and his thick red lips were always babbling questions that were as incoherent as they were inquisitive, until Jeremiah was driven to despair and was compelled more than once to groan: "Enough of your questions, you tormenting little demon!" Ebed-melech would then blink in fright, for by his hundred questions and answers he wanted merely to compensate for the gulf between him and Mattaniah.

The children, however, were deeply attached to their teacher. Particularly when they had finished their writing exercises and Jeremiah began to draw a picture of the world of God and man, they would move closer to him and put their hands on his knees. They preferred to hear him talk about the world of man and the world of nature rather than about the world of God, but one could not love the one without the other. Their teacher sought first of all to implant in Mattaniah's heart a love for the natural world. He sketched, for example, a picture of the wilderness with its melancholy and its dangers. A she-camel had lost her caravan and wandered about in fear, a creature that had become separated from its kind and was a prey to the most terrible loneliness. A wild ass was dying of thirst and panting for air with glassy eyes, until the cry of its mate showed it the way to a waterhole—a case of rescue through loyalty. Jeremiah had witnessed all these scenes himself, and therefore there was nothing didactic about them but only a living power that made the boys open their eyes wide. He described how the huntsmen tied a barn-owl to a pole so that it might lure other birds; he told them about the mutual teasings of maids and youths at harvest time and the dance on the threshing-floor that lasted throughout the night; he imitated the rattling of the water-mills which broke the stillness of the starlit countryside and the urgent note of the horns with which the watchmen on the towers had sounded the alarm when the Scythians came thundering along on their lean horses, ten thousand armed as one man, their voices roaring like the sea behind those who were fleeing from them. He described the vintage and the harvest festival and everything that he had himself seen since his childhood as a country boy, including the days of drought when the people thronged the gates of the city and the grave servants of wealthy families returned home with empty pitchers. He did not forget the nights when the grape-pickers had finished their work and the empty vineyards lay waiting for the moon. Then the Virgin of Zion would take her tambourine and dance over the sleeping hills. These pictures sprang to life on the lips of their teacher and the boys held their breath as they listened to the crowded story.

One day the seven-year-old Mattaniah threw himself on Jeremiah's breast and hid his face. "You know everything," he stammered. "Can you tell me whether Mattaniah will one day be King?"

Jeremiah was startled at these wild words from the mouth

of a child. What was going on in the mind of the prince? Soothingly he laid his hand on the boy's head.

"Your elder brothers must come first," he said briefly.

The boy looked at him with the beautiful eyes he had inherited from his mother, and which were swimming in tears.

"If Mattaniah were King, you would have to stay with him all the time!"

Shortly after the young prince's outburst of tender emotion, Josiah returned suddenly from his journeyings. He immediately called Jeremiah into his presence.

"Has word come from the Lord? . . . Have you dreamed dreams?"

Jeremiah bitterly shook his head. But that same night he dreamed a dream.

At the entrance to the porch of the sanctuary, between the two pillars Boaz and Jachin, a table had been set up and covered with a white cloth. This was a disturbing circumstance which infringed the order of the Temple. The inner courtyard, onto which Jeremiah was looking down, was empty and forsaken. Even the priestly guards who should have been there at that time seemed to have disappeared or faithlessly to have abandoned the sanctuary. Yet in spite of this air of desertion, and the fact that the fire had gone out on the altar of burnt offerings, it was not yet night. It was dusk or rather a steely blue, frosty twilight which preceded no morrow and had been preceded by no day. It was the twilight between two ages of the universe. The Lord had not yet quite cast aside the one world nor quite planned the next.

Jeremiah was standing exactly at the centre of the long table with his face turned towards the spacious porch. His heart was flooded with comfort and peace as it had not been for a long time. He had obeyed his father; he had not rejected Hilkiah's generous offer to petition for his acceptance into the priesthood of the Temple. Now the reward for his obedience had come to him in generous measure, for he gradually realized that the will of the Lord had not only made him a simple priest but had elevated him to the highest rank of all. He could feel the almost unearthly purity of his body and soul, as was required of the High Priest, who, on entering and leaving the sanctuary before and after every sacrifice or act of penitence, had to wash in the bath and be rubbed down by the attendant Levites with fragrant salts and sand-soap. As in the heart of the real High Priest, so in his own was every thought bridled, every picture controlled, that his mind might not be debased by any of the calculating or fleshly ideas that roamed unchastely through the minds of men. Round the first perfect-pure envelope, his body, clung as a second perfect-pure envelope the snow-white seamless coat of cool byssus. Jeremiah turned his eyes from the steely blue dusk of the empty courtyard and lowered them to the table, above which he towered, for the power of his office had also caused his figure to expand to the requisite majestic height of the first servant of God. Beneath his eyes he saw a mighty golden cup standing in the centre of the table. The shape of this cup reminded him a little of the family goblet of the house of Hilkiah, but it was much larger, finely wrought in gold, and strangely ornamented. Intuitively Jeremiah was aware that it was the cup of Joseph which came from Egypt and possessed a special power of compelling truth in intoxication. According to a legend that was well known to the scribes, Joseph's cup had been inherited secretly from generation to generation until, on the day when Israel and the whole of creation should be renewed, it would pass into the hand of him who was responsible for the conversion. Jeremiah saw that the golden cup was filled to the brim with dark wine. As he bent deeper over the goblet, he was surprised to see that the liquid did not resemble the native wine which was pressed upon the vine-hills of Ephraim and Sharon, the heights of Carmel, and the foothills of Hermon. It lacked the blue tinge of the familiar black grape. It was a rust-red liquid, opaque and without the fragrance of berries. And Jeremiah realized that this must be a wine of blood, pressed from a mysterious grape that the sun of Zebaoth had filled with the blood of sacrifice. His eyes were still staring into the cup and his thoughts were still intent upon the wondrous liquid when suddenly, close to his ear, he heard the clear and gentle voice.

"Jirmejahu, prepare yourself! Your guests are coming. Do not forget that you have invited the nations of the world to the banquet."

It was only now that Jeremiah heard a hollow rustling in the twilit air that had been coming nearer for a considerable time and from all sides. He raised his head, and below the stony clouds of the interregnum which had congealed above the Temple he saw a swarm of gigantic, birdlike shapes that were all simultaneously descending in hovering flight upon the porch and landing in a circle round the extinguished altar of burnt offerings. They were all men, but winged giants of the primeval age. What most astounded the priestly host, however, was the hybrid nature of these mighty men with wings. For apart from the pinions of eagle, vulture, and hawk which had borne them to the Temple, each of these human faces and bodies contained within itself a clearly formed heraldic animal: a bull, a lion, a jackal, a leopard, a serpent, or a dolphin. Their dual character resulted in a continual fluctuation between the nature of men and the nature of animals, but mostly their human nature formed a complete outer mask through which the animal nature was visible like the flame in the windows of a burning house.

The clear and gentle voice had assumed the office of master of the ceremonies and was announcing the names of the guests. It began with Egypt. At Jeremiah's right hand a majestic figure, which resembled a colossus hewn from a rock on the shores of the Nile, sank silently into a seat. He sat there motionless, while in his face and body the form of the Apis bull emerged and faded every time he breathed. Then followed Babylon, a long-muzzled lion-man, who took the seat on Jeremiah's left. Next to him sat the man of Asshur, through whose shape the winged bull fleetingly took outline.

And so it continued. The announcement of the name was followed by the appearance of the creature. The animal appertaining to the city of Tyre, which was built into the sea, was a dolphin that twitched within the human body it filled and stared dully out of fishy eyes. Chazor, the nation of Syria, concealed a jackal, Moab a leopard, Edom a wolf, Aram a stag, and Ashkelon a sea-serpent. The heraldic animals of Ammon and distant Elam could not be clearly distinguished. Eleven guests had already taken their seats at the table between the pillars Boaz and Jachin when the voice announced the last of the guests, who appeared to have been delayed:

"The unknown nation!"

At the same time an eagle-man glided down and took the empty seat opposite Jeremiah and the golden cup. And the voice exhorted:

"Why are you waiting? Your guests are thirsty. Give them to drink. Let the banquet begin!"

Jeremiah, the High Priest of Israel, raised the cup and offered it to Egypt, the overseer of slaves, the oldest enemy of his people. Egypt drank and offered the cup to Asshur. Asshur drank and offered the cup to Tyre. Tyre drank and offered the cup to Edom. Edom drank and offered the cup to Moab. From Moab the cup passed to the eagle-man of the unknown nation. From him it passed to Ammon, to Aram, to Elam, and to Ashkelon. Then it came to Chazor, the great nomad tribe that pitched its tents even as far as the mountains of Taurus. The last to drink was the lion of Babylon, who set down the golden goblet on the table before Jeremiah with a heavy thud. The High Priest in his white seamless garment, the thirteenth man at this banquet of the nations, raised the cup again and held it close to his eyes. And, behold, not a drop of the blood-red wine of sacrifice was left that he might drink it and take part in the banquet. But the guests of the High Priest of Israel had become drunk through drinking from the cup of fury. They rose from their seats on the threshold of the sanctuary, swayed down the ten steps to the courtyard, grasped each other's hands (which were also talons, paws, and claws), and began a silent, solemn dance. As time went on the power of the wine of fury which the Lord had trodden out for them increased. The dancing chain broke. Each one seemed to be seized with an immeasurable agony, fell to the ground, and writhed in fiery torment. But the most terrifying thing was that the twelve envoys of the nations had no power of speech and were able to fill the emptiness of the interregnum dusk only with hollow barking, howling, croaking, or grating cries of pain. Had the wine of Zebaoth burned up their bowels? Then Jeremiah recognized the cause of their unutterable agony. The fury was effecting a convulsive transformation in the shapes of his guests. The heraldic animal in each of them, the primal and characteristic nature which was expressed in the clearly differentiated animal forms, was growing more faint through the power of the divine wine. It appeared to be shrinking, to become blurred, to fade, while the human quality emerged to the accompaniment of unspeakable pangs. The lion's maw and the bull's horn grew more and more dim and infrequent. Their hands grew less and less like talons. The one who suffered most excruciatingly under the transformation was the eagle-man of the unknown nation. With piercing shrieks he would rise a little way into the air, and again and again he would fall back to the earth, scattering the brown plumes of his pinions in every direction. Then all the guests lifted their arms and stretched them out towards Jeremiah. Were they about to fall on him and destroy him in revenge for the wine of blood that he had offered them and which was eating away their most inward and vital natures? Were they seeking his help or were they cursing him with the yelling, barking, roaring, and hissing of their voices?

When he awoke he did not know whether the banquet signified blessing or damnation, whether the Lord had offered the nations through Israel the cup of wrath or the cup of salvation. Adonai had again spoken darkly.

The King interpreted Jeremiah's dream of the cup of fury with shining eyes, but by the manner of his interpretation he revealed to the dreamer for the first time the tremendous scheme upon which his mind was bent. The cup that had been offered to the nations was the Lord's cup of wrath and its intoxicating wine of blood was not the sacrificial blood of Israel itself, as the all too scrupulously brooding Jeremiah might perhaps think. The awe-inspiring dance and the convulsive transformation of the nations that had been invited to the banquet signified the final defeat of their beast-shaped deities and their own wicked, covetous natures. That was clear. Verily, the Lord Zebaoth might well veil Himself in obscurity when He revealed Himself to the youthful mind of His prophet; the mind of the King, to whom He did not reveal Himself, was able to pierce through to His intention. The time had come—at these words the King lowered his resonant voice to a whisper—and on him, Josiah, had been laid the great task of founding "the Kingdom of the new David" from which the truth should go forth. Yes, he was the new David, whose coming had been announced by the prophets since olden time. Of that he did not cherish in his heart the slightest doubt. Had he not received abundant proofs of favour? The supreme proof was that the Lord had chosen no other epoch and no other kingdom than Josiah's in which to allow Himself to be rediscovered in the last Law and to offer a new covenant. When Josiah thought of his ancestor David he felt himself to be fully worthy of such a distinction, for his life was not burdened with any great sin as that of David had been. And had he not from the first hour of the new covenant exerted himself for the fulfilment of the Law with the lightning of his sword and his judgment? Had he ever allowed himself, for more years than he could count, to pause in the battle for a single moment? Had he not forsaken his hearth in the service of the Lord and become a dweller in tents, unable to find rest in one place? Did he not ride like a man possessed throughout the land, and not only through his own inheritance of Judah and Benjamin but through all the cast-off tribes of Israel even as far as Dan, in order that he might bring back those who were indifferent and faint-hearted? Truly it was not enough to desecrate the altars of abomination, to hew down the green trees of the whoring gods, and to smoke out the holes and corners in which Ashtaroth was still worshipped. That alone was not sufficient to break the great stubbornness of the people and to extirpate the apostasy which lay everywhere in wait. Nor was it enough to summon the men of the different towns in order to read to them from the Book of the Law, adjuring them to stay their wickedness and obey the commandments which were there for all to see and hear. Man was so slow, so slothful! But Zebaoth and Josiah were not content with smoking out and adjurations. They needed a victory. Until then, let the Lord only have patience with these fools and animals in human shape! Let Him only acknowledge what His servant Josiah intended to do for Him! When Josiah had increased and magnified his own power, when he was no longer a petty king but a great one, then the whole earth would ring with the commandments and fame of Adonai. Then would Israel and Judah, the mourning brothers, be reunited from Hermon down to the Stream of Egypt. Then they would form the gleaming crown of the Kingdom of God. And the centre jewel of this crown would be the Temple of the Lord in Jerusalem.

How Jeremiah's vision had strengthened and confirmed the plans of the King! When, if not now, would the hour come to circulate the cup of fury and wrath? The nations were already writhing in a state of convulsive transition, and it was already the twilight preceding the dawn of a new age. Asshur, the winged bull, was defending itself with its last strength against the lion of Babylon. Both were crippled, and Egypt was lying in wait, cowering for the spring which should tear the prey from the lion. The great nations were draining one another of their life power. Both they and the little nations, all of them age-old enemies of Israel, would drink of the cup, grow drunken, and be won over to the Lord in the end.

The King drew the dreamer to his breast and embraced him, for he himself was drunk with the infinite prospect opened up to him by the dream. Human understanding was by itself adequate, without prophets or prophesying, to measure the uniquely propitious nature of the hour. The lion and the winged bull were engaged in a death-struggle! The world was without a master! Even more, however, was the King intoxicated by the divine assurances which he cherished with a fond complacency in his heart. There was the oracle of Huldah which he repeated again and again to himself: "Behold, I will gather thee unto thy fathers, and thou shalt be gathered into thy grave in peace; and thine eyes shall not see all the evil which I will bring upon this place." It was a precious pledge, doubly precious since the Lord had himself sealed the lips which had announced this glorious truth, as a sign that no word of it would be retracted. What strength did Josiah draw from the conviction that he was invulnerable, that by the express promise of Adonai he could not be overtaken by misfortune in war, that he would go leaving his kingdom in peace! Moreover, the seething pot of the day of judgment had inclined from the north towards the south. The King had no intention of warring against the powers of the north and the north-east. He would craftily put the eventual victor in the Land of Rivers under an obligation to himself, and would establish under his eyes the Kingdom of the Lord. The action that was to emancipate and glorify him was directed against the ancient hereditary enemy of God, against the hated south, against the House of Bondage on the Nile. Here too the Lord had prepared everything favourably, in order that Josiah might be His holy instrument. For many months Necho, son of Psammetichus, the new Pharaoh and kindly god, as he was called, had been preparing a fleet of four hundred triremes which were to land in the bay by Mount Carmel. The army that was hidden in the belly of the ships was to be led by Necho against Asshur through the territory of Israel so that he, the incarnate sun-god, and not the star-kings of Babylon, might gather into his own hands the mastery of the world. Pharaoh had already sent a message to the King of Judah, and Josiah had hitherto veiled his answers, with the help of Ahikam, in prudently ambiguous obscurity. For the King of Judah intended not only to bar Necho's way at the narrow pass of Megiddo, but to hurl the kindly god into the sea together with the mercenaries he had recruited. It was for this purpose that he had during months of breathless and sleepless toil, and with the utmost secrecy, summoned the young men from the melancholy market-towns and hamlets of the northern country that they might be armed and drilled. Captains and other officers of various degrees had been appointed, the day and places of mobilization had been fixed, the hosts had been divided up, and the whole campaign worked out to the minutest detail. In spite of all this open activity he had succeeded in keeping the purpose and ultimate goal of his scheme so secret that the young prophet stood before him in pale confusion at his revelations. Josiah was dizzy with a warlike joy, for his plan had been perfected and he himself was ready to move at any moment. The advantage of his defensive positions against a landing force, even if it should be ten times as great as his own, seemed infinite not only to him but to all his experienced generals. Yet it was not the thought of this dazzling advantage that moved him now, but the new omen which the Lord had sent to him through this man's dream. He stroked Jeremiah's cheek with fatherly affection.

"Jeremiah has again helped the King to see the truth. Who was the first to whom your hand offered the cup of fury? It was Egypt, it was Pharaoh! Do you grasp the significance of the omen? It is I who will offer the wine of blood to Egypt. May my sons one day offer it to Babylon to drink!"

The King had betrayed his intentions point by point, and Jeremiah was excited and dumbfounded at the same time. His soul still glowed with enough fire to be carried away by the schemes of this heroic spirit; none the less he realized with an insight which nothing could deceive that Josiah was irresponsibly interpreting the Lord's will in his own favour. Yet his realization was useless, since he himself had no enlightenment to offer the King, and any objections he might put forward would only be stifled through their obscurity. He tried desperately to think of the right answer, but the Lord was not with him. Josiah had already left the room with his usual tempestuousness; from the courtyard below the window came the commanding tones of his voice and the clatter of horses' hoofs on the stone paving.

At the fourth new moon after this the King summoned his great assembly, that he might speak to Jerusalem and Judah from the throne of Solomon.

The throne-room and the hall of judgment, which together formed one building, constituted the central part of the royal quarter, dividing the first court of the guard from the second and the residential palaces from the administrative ones. They were, so to speak, the sanctuary and the Holy of Holies of the kingdom. In the Holy of Holies, that is to say, the cedar-panelled throne-room, was gathered everybody of high authority in the land: princes and governors, priests and prophets. In the sanctuary next to it, that is to say, the spacious hall of judgment, were crowded in their hundreds the lesser authorities among the people—the city fathers of Jerusalem, the mayors of towns and villages, the holders of various offices, and the heads of influential families in Judah and Benjamin—that they too might hear the words of the King. The hall was filled with an excited clamour. Gradually the King's plans had trickled through to the people and the warlike preparations had been revealed. For several Sabbaths a new watchword had been heard in the streets of Jerusalem and the courtyard of the Temple, and it was growing louder—"The Kingdom of David!" From time to time the gathering in the hall of judgment broke out into this cry with an urgent enthusiasm.

In the throne-room, on the other hand, the entrances to which were strictly watched by a double guard, there prevailed a deep and pregnant silence. The King was seated on the gold and ivory throne of Solomon, which stood on a high dais almost half the height of the room. His hands lay with a royal immobility (which, however, he found hard to maintain) on the widely curved arms of the throne. He looked like a blue flame in a great golden lamp, a controlled flame which obviously would prefer to break loose and burn without restraint rather than shine with a steady light. On the lower steps of sandalwood at his feet sat his sons Eliakim and Jehoahaz between the two golden heraldic lions of Judah. Eliakim, as usual, had excited his father's wrath by wearing a robe of vivid yellow instead of the sky-blue colour of David and by holding in his hands a fan of peacock feathers and a crook, two well-known symbols of Egypt which, on this day and in this place, bore witness to an incomprehensible mentality that could not be indulgently described as "foppishness" or "aping of foreign customs." The tension in the throne-room, however, was so great that neither the King nor anyone else paid heed to Eliakim, who in spite of the assembly had lying on his lap a whole array of little boxes, jars, and phials, the fragrant contents of which he kept testing with the grave air of a dealer in balsams. Now and then he would raise his thin face with its prematurely sunken cheeks, and his puffy lips would twist into a disdainful smile, as if everything that happened under his father's rule, however important it might be, merely bored him. Perhaps one or other of the high dignitaries was beset by anxiety when he looked at the two sons of the King, Eliakim in his glaring yellow robe and the poor Jehoahaz, but this momentary gloom was quickly dispersed, since the blue flame on the throne was the focus of all attention. Below the two princes the whole house of David had taken their seats, and they had been joined by a man who, though he was not a prince of the blood, had been granted the distinction by virtue of his relationship to his royal son-in-law. Jeremiah recognized his old host and namesake, the prince of Libnah, who was so proud of the violent attributes which he conceived to be a part of God's nature.

To the right and left of the elevated throne of Solomon stood the chief dignitaries of the State. Those who filled high military positions presented an incomparably more brilliant appearance than those who were in charge of civil offices.

In spite of the brooding heat of a summer's day they had put on full armour: Maaseiah, commander-in-chief of the whole army, and Assasiah, commander of all the bodyguards. Leaning upon their ornamental golden shields, they gazed upon the assembly with a tranquil absorption, like men whose hour has at last come. Into the space before the dais had been pushed a portable chair in which the wisest and most learned man in Jerusalem had been carried to the chamber. Shaphan, the scribe and revealer of the Law, was now so frail that he could no longer use his legs, and he sat there bent almost double. He could still, however, use his head, shrunken and wasted as it was, and his withered hands. On his lap lay a long open scroll, and his worn fingers crept along the lines and down the columns like spiders of God spinning and weaving invisible threads. His tiny, red-eyed face was so lost in the web of the Law that he did not seem to realize where he was and would suddenly give a little cough of joy when he had hunted down his prey, that is to say, discovered the correct interpretation that he was looking for, or he would scold under his breath when the meaning of a passage could not be unravelled quickly enough. At this decisive hour in the history of the world he presented an exalted picture of absorption in the Lord to the complete exclusion of everything else.

When Jeremiah looked up to the elevated throne, the tense and flushed face of the King appeared far away and blurred. Hilkiah's son was sitting on "the bench of the prophets," of whom a certain number had been summoned to the assembly, along the narrow side of the room farthest from the throne. Despite Josiah's ardent faith in the divine words which were uttered through the instruments of the Lord, the unimportant position assigned to them showed that the great world had no better opinion of the prophets than Jeremiah's father had had. The two longer sides, on the other hand, were occupied by the benches of those who were really powerful, "the bench of the princes" and "the bench of the priests," and these stretched towards the throne. The chief priests of the highest orders had appeared with the Sagan and the Keepers of the Door at their head; opposite them sat all the great and petty princes of the cities, rough peasant kings who were as expert at driving the plough as they were at wielding the sword. Whenever an assembly was about to be held, it was the dreaded duty of the officers in charge of the ceremonies to assign the seats of the city princes in correct order of precedence. Since jealousy was rife among them, a change in the order of precedence had frequently in the past led to quarrels and bloodshed. Jeremiah was relieved, but also oppressed, at finding himself ignored among these great ones of the nation. The vexation which he had excited in the Temple by obediently repeating the words of the Lord seemed after this lapse of time, and in view of the great events that were imminent, to have been entirely forgotten. Also, the King had held his hand over him. Perhaps only his neighbours on the bench of the prophets remembered that outrageous maiden speech of his, for he could feel upon him their probing eyes full of curiosity and suspicion. It may, however, have been that their suspicion sprang from the fact that he disdained, as he had always done, to advertise his mission by his garb. He did not wear like the others a repellent square of shaggy material which was rough to the skin and rubbed the bare places on their arms, legs, and neck. He sat there in his taciturn way and kept his eyes fixed straight ahead, looking neither to the right nor to the left. But he saw a waxen head inclined towards him, greeting him with a melancholy benevolence. It was Urijah, who occupied the place of honour on the bench of the prophets; Urijah, who had interrogated him in Huldah's roof chamber and freed him from his doubts. His heart was again stirred at sight of this man who had had such great experience of communion with God, and he again saw with indignation, shame, and loathing the jagged scar that cut the man's face in two.

Everybody was turning towards the throne, for Ahikam, son of Shaphan, had just introduced the ambassador of Pharaoh into the presence of the King. The Egyptian was a very tall, thin man with a high head-dress, the ribbons of which hung down low on either side. His cape gleamed in seven colours, and the back of his transparent upper garment displayed a yellow, winged sun on a delicate blue background. In his right hand he held a fan of peacock feathers, in his left a golden staff. In a toneless chant he began to recite the introductory formula of his speech, which was translated immediately by an interpreter.

"The King of the Upper and the Nether Lands, the Son of the Gods, who loves his Fathers, the Father of the Gods, who loves his Sons, the Chosen of Ptah, to whom Rā has given strength and Amon his living image, the Son of Rā and of Osiris-Psammetichus, who comes forth in his kindness, the greatest in power who has ever appeared on the throne and raised up the countries, the Lord of the Diadem of the Serpent and Vulture, the Possessor of the golden Horus necklace, which endows men with life and happiness . . ." Here the Egyptian stopped to take breath, and then concluded: ". . . speaks thus unto thee, O King of Judah."

The very sober communication of Pharaoh to King Josiah which followed was veiled in the pleasantly courteous but tortuous splendour of the Egyptian language, as if the exquisite and ambiguous hieroglyphics of Egypt were themselves sounding on the lips of the ambassador. How simple and unhewn, by contrast, did the language of the Lord appear when this speech was translated. Only He could hide His meaning behind such massive blocks of words, not man. The assembly had some difficulty in understanding the true contents of the speech from the interpreter's translation. Again and again occurred phrases like "the Bearer of Beauty," "the Dweller in the Chamber of Light," "He Who Tarries in the Ship That Never Decays," "His Magnificence Who Smilingly Receives the Homage of the Gods," and "His Serenity before Whom the Hearts of Men Grovel." And it was very disturbing that this inexhaustible wealth of pictorial titles was employed solely for the glorification of the ambassador's master, Pharaoh, while the King of Judah, to whom he was addressing himself, and the God of Judah were not even recognized as independent personalities. It was obvious, however, that this was not done to disparage or mortify but only in the smiling and assured consciousness of the all-embracing and universal greatness, wisdom, and beauty of Egypt, beyond whose borders nothing but a melancholy world of shades could exist. Contact with Egypt, the very fact of being addressed by Pharaoh, brought to other countries a redemptive power that put life into the poor spectres who inhabited them. On this point the words and bearing of the ambassador left no doubt in the minds of his hearers. The message itself spoke of the uncountable ships of a mighty fleet which struck terror even into the divine rulers of the sea. This fleet lay ready to sail in one of the channels of the Father of All Rivers, which was swollen every year with the tears of joy shed by the nine supreme divinities, a miracle that gave it the power of bringing life to that which was dead. Manned by invincible warriors, the fleet would set out under the exalted guidance of the divine flagship on the next new moon but one. Innumerable war chariots would accompany the fleet as it sailed along close to the flat shores of the Philistines, until it landed finally in the great bay which lay to the north of Mount Carmel. From there His Magnificence, to whom the gods smilingly paid homage, would illumine the Plain of Israel as he marched through. This was the message of Pharaoh to the King of Judah. It was followed by the request that he should furnish ample provisions for the army in the cities and villages of the aforesaid plain, vouch for the complete peacefulness of the native population towards the warriors who would be billeted on them, and assure Pharaoh of his own dutiful obedience. All this was not put forward as a special demand, but merely as an empty formula which communicated to the King, as a matter of courtesy, something that was regarded as a matter of course. The ambassador's speech was followed by a long and wrathful silence. Josiah, sitting motionless on his elevated throne, let the silence continue until it reached the limit of what was endurable, so that even the stiff Egyptian began to grow uneasy. Only then did he raise his hand slightly to summon his private secretary.

The words which the King now spoke, half to Ahikam and half to the ambassador, were not the words of an angry man, but were uttered softly and with perfect equanimity.

"Tell him that when he has offered up in the name of Pharaoh the seven morning sacrifices which he has hitherto omitted, then I will bring my answer personally not to him but to Pharaoh."

The colourful Egyptian did not fully understand. He was taken aback and looked round uncertainly, but Josiah took no further notice of him. He was dismissed. The ambassador, who had not expected his message to be countered by such royal indifference, touched the ground with his fingertips in homage—an act which he had not considered consonant with Egypt's dignity when he first entered. Some of those present declared later that in his confusion he had sought the eyes of Eliakim.

When Pharaoh's embarrassed ambassador had left the hall a wild and unprecedented roar of approval surged round the throne, but the blue flame in its golden lamp shot erect and the clamour was hushed.

The King spoke to Jerusalem and Judah the words which Jeremiah had already heard. He spoke of the kingdom of the God of Jacob, of the kingdom of the new David, of the kingdom of the triumphant Law, whose hour had come, now or never. Judah was strengthened, Israel was being reborn and prepared to return home to the Lord. Pharaoh's army, cut off from its base and from reinforcements, would not be able to withstand the avenging lightning of Zebaoth. The Lord had ordained a situation which was favourable to a degree that was almost inconceivable. Josiah's voice itself was like the thunder of Zebaoth, and it kindled the inflammable assembly to a frenzy as if the King had offered the cup of fury to his own people and they had been the first to drink of it. The council broke up and thronged round the throne. The most frantic of all was Jeremiah of Libnah, the King's father-in-law. His eyes were bloodshot as if he were in the midst of battle, and he kept thrusting out his arms in rhythmic accompaniment to ear-rending shouts of "The Kingdom of David!"

Only a few were able to preserve their contemplative calm, and among these were Eliakim and Jeremiah. It was not without a feeling of horror that Jeremiah regarded the raving of the prince of Libnah. A terrible question began to harass his mind. Was the King's conception of God essentially different from that of his father-in-law? They both exulted in a warlike Zebaoth who drove His enemies before Him. Jeremiah covered his face with his hands to collect his thoughts. Perhaps the Lord would be favourable and break His silence amidst this clamour, commanding him to warn the King and thus avert disaster. But no divine word came to subdue the clamour of the human storm, which even increased in vehemence when it was communicated to those in the neighbouring hall of judgment. Men embraced each other, uncontrollable tears were shed, cruel oaths were taken, covenants were made, blood-brotherhood was sworn. And again and again there rose through the confused uproar the great watchword: "The Kingdom of David!" In the throne-room, however, the tumult suddenly died away. Cry after cry for silence rang out. It had at last been noticed that old Shaphan had been struggling for some time to get a hearing. The members of the assembly moved back to their seats in order to listen to the words of the wisest sage in Judah, but Shaphan impatiently pushed his scroll backwards and forwards while he was speaking, as if he could not wait for the moment when he would be able to abandon again the fleeting activities of the world and return to the intellectual exercise of interpreting the Word of the Lord, to whom he was anxious to devote every minute that might still remain to him.

"I, too," he began, breathing with difficulty, "agree with this clamorous people in their praise of the King. . . . There has never been a better one in Israel and Judah, nor will there ever be. . . . There are few who remember the far-off days of his fathers, Amon and Manasseh, when the abomination was allowed to prevail unavenged and the flames of Tophet were kindled in the valley of the son of Hinnom that their firstborn might pass through the fire. . . . At that time you were but a child, O great King, no older than your youngest son Mattaniah, and Shaphan sat with you as your teacher. . . . And Shaphan did not leave your side when the horrid murder of Amon by night raised you suddenly to the throne of Solomon. . . . My heart cleaved unto you, Josiah, my pupil, my royal boy. . . . It could not forsake you. . . . How greatly have you rewarded my poor teaching! . . . For the deeds of my King will not be forgotten after thirty generations, nor after three hundred. . . ."

The old man's head sank upon his breast. Many of those present thought that he had either fallen asleep, or lost the thread of his discourse, or come to the end of what he wanted to say. But he was only pursuing his melancholy thoughts, and now he gave them contemplative utterance before the great assembly as though he were alone with the King:

"Shaphan has never heard with his own ears the whisperings of the Lord. . . . He is no sanctified prophet, but only a man who has always toiled industriously. . . . He reads and thinks, draws his conclusions, compares and combines, accepts or rejects. . . . He can announce only what he has learned through the exercise of his own mind, and not: 'Thus saith the Lord . . .' What the Law teaches, that he too can teach . . . but how should an old man who knows little of your activities be able to advise you, saying: 'This is good; do you this!' or: 'This is not good; refrain ye from doing this!' . . . And even if I were nevertheless to utter such words, the people would respectfully incline their ears towards me, but they would not obey. . . . O great King, incline your ear towards me, you whom I still see as a boy with his cheeks flushed from play. . . . O great King, hear me! You have peace before you and many years! Why do you wish to break the peace which is yours, when there is no necessity, and to shorten those years? . . ."

In his agitation of mind Shaphan had muttered the last words so indistinctly that only a very few of those nearest to him could understand them. Like many very old men he was easily moved to tears, and a tear fell just then on the open scroll that he held upon his knees, smudging the ink of one of the letters. In his horror the great scribe forgot everything else and tried tenderly to minimize the damage with the tip of his finger nail.

Owing to its inaudibility his speech lost its effect. Only the King appeared to have been impressed to some extent, for he sat in a reverie with his brow furrowed in deep lines that no scribe could have deciphered. Cries broke out again among the assembly, who were waiting to hear a final word from Josiah, but he made a swift gesture of dissent and pointed with outstretched arm to the bench of the prophets. "Has word come from the Lord? . . . A dream or a vision?"

The soul of Jeremiah was struggling in tempestuous prayer with Adonai. "Speak to me more clearly or enable *me* to speak more clearly," it groaned within him. "Is the kingdom of the new David in truth to be set up by this king? Or is his scheme but a snare, an abyss into which we all are to sink? I have journeyed throughout the land and have learned to know it. Thy commandment lies upon its surface like the languishing green upon the face of a wilderness, but underneath is death. Fearful words didst Thou give me to speak in the Temple. Is all now to be forgotten? Has the Lord changed His mind? And why? Has the Lord suddenly become ready to crown with victory this generation of hoodwinkers and eager stallions?" It was always possible that the Lord might decide suddenly to turn His chariot in a different direction. Jeremiah was well aware of that. He knew also that the thoughts he was thinking and the conclusions he was drawing were delusions and fallacies in the eyes of the Lord. But what was he to do? The King was waiting for a word from his lips and it was in his power to help or to hinder. And he prayed: "Aid me, aid me, for Thou didst know me before I came forth from the womb! Aid me, that I may aid the King and this people! Within me all is confused—yes and no, this and that, fear and certainty. Form within my brain a 'yes' or a 'no' like water, that I may pour it forth as I did that day in the Temple when there was not yet any visible reason to do so!"

"No word has come from the Lord! . . . No dream and no vision!"

These melancholy words had been spoken by Urijah, the oldest of the prophets present. He had taken three steps towards the King and now stood with his thin form bent and his scarred head inclined wearily upon his left shoulder. In this guilty attitude he seemed to be begging the King for forgiveness, not only because the Lord had been silent but also because His prophets had been deaf and unable on this great occasion to report the hearing of a single whisper. But as Urijah stood there so unhappily, a fresh and vigorous voice rang out suddenly:

"Word has come! . . . And a vision!"

Jeremiah turned swiftly. A man detached himself from

those who were standing crowded against the wall and walked with dignified demeanour down the long hall towards the throne. He had doffed his irksome prophet's cloak and carried it over his arm, disclosing the delicate and costly fabric of the garments he had been wearing underneath. His hair and beard had been carefully oiled and curled, and Jeremiah saw with surprise that the years since the Passover eve they had spent together had endowed Hananiah with a convincing and stately manner. There was something in his gait and bearing that inspired trust and confidence. The Lord no doubt paid due heed to the dissimilarity of those to whom He revealed Himself, and He did not seem to insist that all His prophets should be of the same type. Hananiah bowed low before the King and prophesied in a clear voice:

"In a vision of the Lord I saw the Nile rolling through the desert and its waters were making for themselves a new channel. But the Lord opened my eyes and said: 'Behold the waves of the Nile!' And I looked upon the waves. They were warriors with shield and battle-axe, and their horses were prancing in the flood. Then the Lord opened my eyes again and said: 'Behold the waves of the Nile!' And I saw mud and corruption and wreckage. The Father of Rivers had dried up in the desert and the waves that had been warriors were vanished."

A roar of applause followed Hananiah's prophecy, which found a joyful echo in the hearts of the men and confirmed their confident expectation of victory. Josiah himself, strange to say, heard it without emotion. But a weight fell from Jeremiah's breast. The Lord had spoken, even though he had not been the instrument. As the assembly dispersed he stood with bowed head and pondered on Hananiah's vision. Was this the true way in which the Lord revealed His intention?

It was, and yet it was not. How could he decide, since he had experienced only the one way, the way in which Adonai communed with *him.* Perhaps the Lord disclosed His purpose to Hananiah with more friendliness, less obscurely. Yet Jeremiah again felt his heart burdened with a heavy weight. All at once he saw the King standing in front of him. And Josiah said with a smile:

"Whoever else may prophesy, you alone are the rope between Him and me. . . ."

11

Megiddo

JEREMIAH was not allowed to stir from the King's side, for Josiah needed those whose ears were open to the voice of Heaven and in the truth of whose words he could believe implicitly. The man from Anathoth obeyed the King's command and awaited that which was to come, though the silent Adonai had still not revealed to him its meaning and its issue in spite of all his prayers.

After the most sacred fast day of the year, which was kept with the most fervent contrition since men could remember, the King's call went forth to all the tribes and cities. From every direction armed men poured in from the plains to the prearranged centres of mobilization, where they were inspected and allotted to the various detachments of the fighting force.

The distribution and assignment of the people among the variously armed units were not carried out in accordance with a purely secular form of selection, but were based on the mysterious blessing which the dying Jacob gave to his sons. Precedence in war belonged to Judah, for of him the patriarch had prophesied: "Judah is a lion's whelp: from the prey, my son, thou art gone up: he stooped down, he couched as a lion, and as an old lion: who shall rouse him up? The sceptre shall not depart from Judah nor a lawgiver from between his feet, until Shiloh come: and unto him shall the gathering of the people be." The warriors of Judah, whose "eyes shall be red with wine and their teeth white with milk," were therefore assured of their place in the first rank and a commanding position over all their brethren. They rode upon horses and were allowed to use any type of weapon. The most illustrious and royal of all means of battle—the war chariot—was reserved exclusively for them.

The squadron of chariots constituted the central core of the army, and in its midst stood the King himself on his armoured *merkabah*, the earthly equivalent of the chariot in which Zebaoth flashed across the heavens. Jacob had not allotted heroic duties to all his sons equally. Of Ephraim and Manasseh the blessing had said merely that their bow would not break and their arm would remain supple. The cities of these regions therefore sent only archers and men armed with slings. The district of northern Dan, the sight of whose impoverished settlements Josiah had never forgotten, furnished but a few hundred robbers and footpads who were skilled in preparing artful ambushes and harassing the flanks and rearguard of the enemy. Even this dubious heroism had been ordained by Jacob in his blessing: "Dan shall be a serpent by the way, an adder in the path, that biteth the horse heels, so that his rider shall fall backward." And before the hosts moved forward into the field from the centres where they had gathered, Josiah ordered that the commandment of the Lord should be carried out. To every man who had built a new house, planted a new vineyard, taken a young wife, or was faint of heart went forth the summons: "Let him go and return unto his house!" But there was hardly any man who availed himself of this privilege for selfish advantage.

While the fleet of Pharaoh Necho was raising anchor in the delta of the Nile on an almost windless night, and ship after ship was passing in endless sequence through the channel into the open sea, the armies of Josiah were streaming from the north and south towards the green plain which stretched from Carmel to the Valley of Jordan past the hills of Gilboa. The King had divided his force into three parts and had set them three different goals. The western army was under the command of Maaseiah, the oldest and most experienced general in Judah. It was his task to meet the Egyptians with his archers and sling-bearers from the crest of Mount Carmel and to prevent by every means in his power any attempt of Pharaoh to reach the plain. The central army was led by the King himself, who had the assistance of Assasiah, the commander of his bodyguard. His hosts were encamped in an extended line along the main road which cut through the Valley of Jezreel. A number of fortified cities, such as Megiddo, Kadesh, and Taanach, served as supports. The royal headquarters were situated in the citadel of Megiddo. The third and eastern army had been entrusted to Eliakim, in spite of vigorous opposition from the King. Josiah had stood out against the appointment for a long while, but he had finally given in to his advisers, who thought that such a mortal insult to Eliakim (who possessed a reputation for courage without ever having given any evidence of it) might endanger the future. And apart from his various demonstrations of ill-behaviour, self-will, and foppishness the prince had not been guilty of anything that would have justified the King in refusing to entrust his eldest son with the command of one of his armies. Was the King of Judah to proclaim publicly before all the world that he had no confidence in his eldest son? Josiah consoled himself in the usual way with the hope that the terrible earnestness of war, the desire for fame, and the beckoning wreath of victory would subdue, or perhaps even cure, Eliakim's refractory will. In any case the eastern army, which was encamped among the hills of Gilboa, had been assigned the lightest task. In case of emergency it was to provide reinforcements, and if things should turn out well it was to intercept the fleeing hosts of Egypt and lay them low. To this army were also attached a section of the cavalry and the footpads of Dan. As a precaution, the King had deputed as his eldest son's chief of staff a fierce and dreaded warrior named Elnathan, son of Achbor. The fact that Elnathan was related by marriage to Eliakim through the latter's wife Nehushta did not seem to give Josiah any cause for suspicion.

Everything had been wisely thought out and anticipated, even to allowing for chance emergencies, to an extent that had had no comparison in any war of Israel since the days of Joshua and David. There was only One whose plans could not be thought out and anticipated, and it was in order to bind this Inconceivable and Unforeseeable One in some way or other and to draw Him into his scheme that the King took Jeremiah about with him, for he had an unshakable belief in the prophet's unique sanctification by the Lord and miraculous power of assistance. He was convinced that Adonai passed in and out of Jeremiah's soul, and in the simple piety of his mind he imagined that he could fetter the Lord to his side in the person of Jeremiah. During those sad oppressive days the man of Anathoth was not allowed to leave Josiah's presence for a single hour. Even his bed was set up in the King's chamber. The town and citadel of Megiddo were the property of the House of David, and the citadel itself was one of the strongest and most magnificent constructions in the country. It had been known to Abraham when he came from Ur to enter the Promised Land, and Solomon, the indefatigable builder, had nine generations previously given it its towering proportions with its numerous keeps, ramparts, balconies, courts, and dwellings. For many days Jeremiah lived there with the most intimate retinue of the King, who hoped to receive his help by means of the words and visions that the Lord might send him. The prophet himself, however, was fortified by the presence of Baruch.

The worst heat of summer was already over when one morning swift couriers brought news from Carmel that the Egyptian fleet had landed under cover of night, and with astounding rapidity, on the wide sandy shores of Hepha. Deep-bellied monsters, three decks high and each one a citadel in itself, had grounded on the beach almost silently, and showing no lights, in a line many leagues in extent. Their camp, which had shot up overnight as though by supernatural means, resembled a large city whose temples and palaces were represented by the mighty ships. In view of this, Maaseiah, the general in command of the western army, advised that there should be no rash action. It would be best to lie cunningly concealed and invisible until Pharaoh should break camp. King Josiah immediately started off, accompanied only by two members of his bodyguard, for the army on Carmel, where he was able to overlook Necho's camp from the highest observation post. It was not until midday that he returned at a steady trot with hanging reins, and Jeremiah saw that he was very pale and thoughtful. On the same day occurred two events of the greatest significance. The first was a storm such as had not been experienced since the Flood. At midday an indecisive and hesitant thunder began to rumble with stifled resentment from the arch of heaven, and this continued until two hours before sunset, when the great storm broke. The King, trembling with expectation of some important revelation, took Jeremiah with him up to the platform of the highest watch-tower. There they stood and held fast to the battlements, heedless of the unchained torrents that almost washed the clothes from their bodies. Was not a storm the only visible shape in which the Invisible One was wont to appear? Some generations previously the prophet Elijah had declared that a strong wind only preceded the presence of the Lord, who eventually revealed Himself in a still small voice; none the less, who could deny that thunder and lightning were the vestments in which the Lord clad Himself as High Priest, the gold and silver pomegranates on the borders causing the flashes and the peals?

The King and Jeremiah pressed close together so as not to be blown down. The fabric of the heavenly garment strained noisily at every seam. It tore and burst in a hundred places, and through the rents could be seen the higher heavens, the fiery heavens, the firmament of the songs of praise which it is granted to mortal eyes to glimpse for only the space of a lightning flash. As the whole sky was in flames and the storm leapt from one quarter to another, it was not possible to tell from which direction the revelation of the divine will would come. Suddenly, however, a deluge of hail drummed down upon the earth as though Zebaoth were stoning this poor portion of the world. The two men on the crest of the tower had to sit down and press their backs against the battlements, protecting their heads with both hands from the gigantic hailstones. But this hail decided for Josiah the direction of the divine will. In very oblique, dense lines it was driving towards the west, straight towards the encampment of Necho. At the same time a flash of lightning, which seemed by supernatural intention to diverge from the spot where the

King and the prophet were standing, blazed past the high watch-tower and struck a sycamore on the other side of the road in front of the city ramparts. The shattered tree began to flare and smoke in spite of the rain. The lightning had not struck the camp of Judah.

The King exulted aloud, for a new omen had been vouchsafed to him. When he reached his own chamber he tore the wet clothes from his body, and tears ran down his cheeks. He raised his hands and moved in the first steps of a solemn dance.

"Oh, Jirmejahu," he sobbed, "would that I could dance and sing like my father David! . . ."

Hardly had Josiah grown tranquil again when the second and less significant event happened. A messenger from Pharaoh knocked at the western gate of Megiddo and handed to the King a letter from the incarnate Sun God of Noph, whose name was Necho and who added to his signature the circle with a point in the centre which was the symbol of his divinity. The letter was not written in the shortened popular script of Egypt, but had been composed with all the pictorial detail of the sacred characters, whereby it was intended to rank as an imperishable document. It contained very few words. Ahikam read them slowly and with emphasis, and his hairless, delicately curved lip grew damp with suppressed excitement. These were the words of Necho:

"What have I to do with thee, thou king of Judah? Forbear thee from meddling!"

This sounded very domineering and impatient. The Apis bull was switching his tail to scare away the troublesome gadfly of Israel. But the son of Shaphan had inherited his father's capacity for penetrating below the surface of words. The brusque message of Pharaoh concealed behind its majestic taciturnity a silent invitation and offer to the King of Judah which, coming from a ruler of such cosmic arrogance, might almost be regarded as an honour. A war council was hastily summoned and Ahikam submitted to it his interpretation of the letter. The very fact that such a message had been sent showed that Pharaoh had been profoundly taken aback by the impressive and warlike army of Judah. Even though the arrogance of Egypt might have no doubt of victory, yet it could not be a matter of indifference to Necho that he should find himself involved in a bloody war immediately after his force had landed, practically before he had taken his first step, with a consequent weakening of his army and postponement of his purpose. His purpose was none other than the subjection of stricken Asshur, from which he intended to tear all the countries paying tribute between the Land of Rivers and Lebanon. He had thought out a bold campaign which almost surpassed human understanding, a campaign which was not based on his own country and therefore hovered in constant danger from lack of reinforcements and replacements and the possibility that the road back might be blocked. In front of him lay a vast tract of territory, mostly steppe and wilderness. Would the hostile deities of wilderness and steppe not exact the sacrifice of at least half his force, quite apart from his losses in battle? Pharaoh and his councillors must certainly have envisaged such losses from the beginning with deep apprehension. All the more vexatious must appear a bloody encounter with a well-armed opponent on territory where the latter's God held sway. These convincing deductions were drawn by Ahikam from Pharaoh's letter, whose meaning he interpreted as a disguised invitation to enter into negotiations with him. "What have I to do with thee, thou king of Judah?" What this really meant was: "What price dost thou demand, thou king of Judah?" Ahikam believed that the King of Judah would be able to demand a price that he could scarcely hope to wrest from Pharaoh through a bloody war.

Ahikam forgot that he was not speaking to priests and scribes, but to a council of impetuous generals who could hardly wait for the day of honour and fame in battle after such a long and relaxing period of peace. They shouted him down. Pharaoh's message was a confession of fear and weakness; therefore there could be only one suitable answer—none. The King had promised to take his answer personally to Pharaoh. Now the time had come. Josiah, for his part, had his private reasons for being annoyed with Ahikam. The subtly reasoning secretary, who was with him day and night, had still failed to grasp the holy nature of his scheme. The kingdom of God, the kingdom of the new David, the permeation of the world with truth and the Law—these could not be achieved by royal chaffering, but only by royal victory.

When the sun had set on a storm-torn sky, whose aftergleam displayed the four colours of the curtain of the Ark, the King once more ascended with Jeremiah and Baruch to the watch-tower of the citadel. The wind had died down, and it was cool and peaceful. A confused murmur came up to them from the camp, where the long lines of evening fires were burning. Josiah had done all that was commanded in the way of offering up prayers to the Lord and carrying out the necessary rites. He had done even more and had once again ordered the words of the Law to be cried out publicly: "Whoever is faint-hearted, let him go and return unto his house!" Now he was staring silently at the starry host of night wheeling across the heavens. Suddenly, as though struck by lightning, Jeremiah fell at the King's feet and implored him:

"O magnificent King! Consider once more, weigh again, before you march forth. . . ."

Josiah bent a very grave face over the prostrate Jeremiah. "Has word come from Him?"

"No! That is why I am terrified! No single word has come concerning the action of my King. . . ."

"Are there forebodings in your heart which come from the Lord?"

"Neither are there forebodings. . . . Nothing, nothing. . . . From my own soul I cry aloud to the King. . . . Consider once more, weigh again. . . ."

A smile of relief passed across Josiah's features.

"From your own soul? . . . That is the hesitancy, Jeremiah, which besets even the toughened and experienced man on the day before the battle. Be not ashamed of it. Or do you perhaps doubt? Behold, the King is confident! I have kept the covenant. Will He break it, when I am serving not my glory but His?"

The King abruptly turned his head away from Jeremiah and gazed into the darkness. But the latter pressed his face against the cold stone, begging the Lord, like an irresponsible boy, for that which was most forbidden of all forbidden things: the revelation of the future. Night fell and enveloped them completely. After a long while the King again raised his voice and called upon Jeremiah and Baruch to act as witnesses:

"Hearken with your ears, ye witnesses, to the royal oath that I swear to Zebaoth. If Zebaoth will grant me victory tomorrow over the House of Bondage, I will fulfil the Law to the last detail. I shall shun no difficulty. In the seventh year I shall force all the houses in the land to emancipate their bondmen . . . for we ourselves were bondmen in Egypt. . . . Has Zebaoth heard my vow? . . . Do you hear it, ye witnesses?"

The witnesses had heard, but the heart of Jeremiah did not grow lighter.

The western horizon began to take on a purple tinge, so that the shadow of distant Carmel grew distinct. With wide-open eyes they gazed at the expanding glow. Baruch, who had hitherto kept at a respectful distance from the King and the prophet, said:

"Pharaoh has ceased to wait for the answer of the King. The Egyptians are burning their ships behind them."

The clever Baruch had divined correctly.

The battle began an hour before dawn with an attack by Cush and Put, Pharaoh's Ethiopian and Nubian auxiliaries, in the sinister light of the burning ships. They stormed the heights occupied by Maaseiah, but were hurled back time and again by the archers and sling-bearers of Ephraim and Manasseh, who held all the important slopes and passes. When the sun rose, dozens of Negro corpses were already lying amidst the wild underbrush, and the guttural war-cries of the attackers were mingled with the piercing screams and moans of the wounded. But the defenders, too, appeared to be slowly getting into difficulties, for at an early hour Maaseiah sent messengers to the King requesting reinforcements.

Josiah had spent the whole night on the watch-tower. Jeremiah and Baruch had also remained upon the windswept platform, and now they were standing together observing the

King and his generals who were speaking in half-whispers and making motions across the western sky with outstretched hands. Josiah had dispatched his second son at midnight with an important message. The slow-witted Jehoahaz had been ordered to take the swiftest horses and reach Jerusalem as soon as possible, where he was to command the High Priest in the name of the King to ordain forthwith a great day of prayer and fasting in order that Zebaoth, the God of battles, should not remain unsolicited in the hour of conflict. A capable rider would have been sufficient for the transmission of this request, but the dignitaries understood what was in the mind of the King, who wished to withdraw one of his sons from the field and ensure that a descendant of David should hold himself ready in the capital for any emergency that might arise.

When the first reports came in from Carmel, Josiah fell into a spell of deep thought. He walked with swift steps round the battlements and gazed at Jeremiah with vacant eyes as if he did not know who he was. The nocturnal attack by the Ethiopian and Nubian auxiliaries had grievously interfered with his plan of battle. Even if the fight now raging along one part of the line should take a favourable turn for Judah, yet the army of Maaseiah, which had been driven back from the road, would still be held. With his flank secured from attack by this manœuvre, Pharaoh could lead the main body of his troops without hindrance through the narrow pass that led into the plain. Assasiah proposed that the whole bodyguard should be moved forward to do battle with Necho in the narrow pass between the foothills. The King rejected this plan. He wanted to meet and defeat the enemy on the broad plain, not in the pass. The order of battle was concentrated round the citadel of Megiddo, and Eliakim was sent orders to make his way slowly from the east and be prepared to throw in his forces if help should be required.

Among the old women of Israel there was a firm belief in the magic powers of Egypt, and it really seemed as if the incarnate Sun God had employed the arts of magic in leading his hosts through the pass. In the cold light of morning the plain flashed as far as the northern steeps. Everywhere banners had been unfurled and the battle-array of Pharaoh was drawn up in deep formation, wave behind wave. The front line nearest the road was occupied by the far-famed Lubim, sons of the Libyan coasts and deserts, who served Pharaoh as mercenaries. They stood in dense squares and held their lances in readiness. On their flanks were concentrated squadrons of cavalry, with considerable intervals between them, who sat their horses like men of stone. Any child would have known from their voluminous burnouses that these must be the dreaded Anu and Satiu, the mounted auxiliaries of Sinai, who fought with whirling javelins and couched lances. Behind these came the line of battle of the actual Egyptians, who were arranged according to the forty-two regions of "the Two Lands." The generals of Israel recognized them by the mighty images of their deities which towered into the air on the left wing of each regional detachment. There was the oppressive might of "the region of the white walls," Anub Heth, whose capital was the celebrated Noph or Memphis. The wooden image of Ptah rose to the skies as its standard, and it could be seen even from a distance that the hands of the god grasped the sceptre with the sparrow-hawk. On the flank of the detachment from Anub Heth extended the troops of Sepy, at whose head crouched, to the horror of Judah, an alabaster jackal-headed statue of Anubis. Each region with its god, each god with its region.

This was repeated forty-two times and each god bore the shape of a different animal. What made the sight of the Egyptian army even more terrible in the eyes of Jeremiah than the figures of the ram-headed Khnum, the hawk-headed Harakhte, the cow-headed Hathor, the ibis-headed Thoth, or the crocodile-headed Sobek was the magnificent, hardly human rigidity of the armoured ranks and detachments that covered the plain in a silence like that of death.

The disciplined silence of Egypt was so impressive that it stifled every sound even among the ardent hosts of Judah. Apart from the neighing of horses, the scraping of hoofs, the grinding of wheels, and the morning song of the wind, there was not a sound to be heard. Egypt was waiting. Not a lance was raised for the charge. The deep silence and rigid waiting brought a sudden flash of realization to Jeremiah. Pharaoh was displaying before the eyes of Josiah the preponderance of power that lay at his command, and of which he had gathered only a small fraction around him. This was Pharaoh's last warning to the King of Judah that he still had a short respite in which to give up his mad project. Josiah, too, was looking down in silence upon the hosts of Egypt. Assasiah and the other generals having long since returned to their posts, Josiah was again upon the platform with Jeremiah and Baruch. The only other person there was the watchman, who held his curved trumpet in his hand and waited for word from the King.

"Egypt is waiting"—the words came from Jeremiah with difficulty. "Let the King go down . . . and speak with Pharaoh. . . ."

His words did not seem to have reached the ear of Josiah, for almost as he said them the King made a sign to the watchman, who set his trumpet to his lips and blew a long-drawn, wailing note. The horns and bugles of Judah joined in angrily, imitating the roar of the lion's whelp.

After this outburst there was again a short and deathly silence, until Egypt replied with tenfold fury, and the first shower of arrows from the Libyan archers sang past the tower.

The sun had passed its meridian and the attacking waves of Judah had already surged back three times behind the walls of Megiddo. Josiah had suffered heavy losses in men, horses, and chariots, and the field was strewn with dead who lay everywhere in convulsed and distorted attitudes. For the first time Jeremiah smelt the dreadful, sweetish odour of human blood, which was trying to rise from the gigantic sacrificial altar of the Plain of Jezreel but remained hovering in the air without being received favourably by the Lord. For the first time he heard the whimpering of mortally wounded men, which resembled the hundredfold whining of invisible animals and was mingled with the shrieks of dying horses.

The ranks of Egypt also had been thinned, and they had begun to give way under the last fierce onslaught. Judah had driven a wedge through the battle-array of the Libyans, past Anu and Satiu, and deep into the detachments of the forty-two regions, before the superior weight of Pharaoh's hosts again squeezed them out of the wound they had inflicted. Both sides were so exhausted that the two armies had released their grip on each other and seemed tacitly to have agreed to a temporary truce.

Josiah stood in the great courtyard of the citadel surrounded by his generals and a throng of messengers. Where was Eliakim? Several couriers had already been sent galloping towards the east to hasten his steps. Josiah had cast off his tunic and stood with his legs astride and only a short white garment round his loins. His flesh of steel glowed. Servants were pouring cold water over his head and shoulders from pitchers, and the unwieldy eunuch, his chief chamberlain, breathed heavily as he rubbed him down with rough towels. All the while Josiah continued to issue orders without interruption. He himself intended to lead the fourth and decisive attack. All the chariots, together with all the cavalry and infantry who were still alive, were to be concentrated for the onslaught.

The King's chariots were paraded before him in order that he might choose the most suitable one. He decided upon a high-built, two-wheeled car armed with a huge brazen bow, whose protective shield, however, did not reach higher than the hips. The bowstring, woven out of gut, was tautened by means of a lever that the archer worked with his foot, and the golden quiver contained very long arrows whose tips were quite as large as lance-heads. The capering chargers harnessed to this war chariot wore sky-blue ostrich feathers on their heads and gold-embroidered trappings in the same royal colour.

Assasiah tried vigorously to dissuade the King from using this chariot. He said that such a car with its gold and silver mountings was good for ceremonial processions but was no good for battle. Josiah gritted his teeth and averted his face in displeasure from the warning general, for it was just that which he most ardently longed to do: to go out and meet the matchless arrogance of Pharaoh in all the magnificence of his own royal pride, riding in a war chariot with golden spokes and two silver-harnessed foaming horses in front of him with sky-blue plumes that nodded and tossed. How could any man understand him who was not himself a king! He swung himself up into the chariot and tested the resonant bowstring. The driver seized the reins. Suddenly the King turned and shouted for Jeremiah. A new order was issued. One of the great four-wheeled carts had to follow Josiah's squadron. It was to contain no warriors, but a priest of high rank together with the King's two companions, Ahikam and Jeremiah. Israel did not carry statues of gods into battle, but none the less Josiah wanted to bear the Lord with him into the fray in order to arouse His just and warlike wrath. The prayers of the priest would draw Him down, and even more than these prayers was the presence of the man from Anathoth. The King held firmly to this belief. If he knew that Jeremiah was at his back, he knew also that the Lord could not be far away.

Josiah's generals had likewise mounted their chariots. Assasiah, as Commander of the Bodyguard, kept to the left close behind the King, and to the right was the father of Hamutal, old Jeremiah of Libnah, whose coppery countenance already bore a rapt expression in anticipation of the delights of battle. A crack of the whip from the King's charioteer gave the signal to move off. The rattle of the chariots and the clatter of hoofs sounded like a hailstorm, and across the courtyard rang out the war-cry: "The Kingdom of David!" In the creaking cart which dashed breathlessly in the wake of the royal chariot Ahikam, Jeremiah, and the priest were mercilessly thrown about until they were almost bereft of their senses. There was a halt at the north gate of Megiddo, where trumpeters on all sides blew the call to fall in, and other squadrons joined in, taking the King's chariot into their midst. On either side of the King rode the horsemen of the bodyguard, and swift-footed infantry carrying lances followed the whirlwind.

The battle of arrows, spears, and slings had already been resumed and the air was filled with a venomous hissing and whirring. The advance guards of Judah flung themselves against the Libyan ranks and swords and lances were brought into play in a hundred places. Jeremiah's mind was empty and hollow. The surging torrent of carnage filled his ears like dark water in the ears of a drowning man. How could he draw down Adonai from the spheres in which He dwelt! Even if the Lord were not so remote from this battle as He was in reality, Jeremiah would not have had the strength even to direct his thoughts towards Him. From his own state of mind he realized with an icy dread how completely the King would have to rely upon his own resources, without the help of the Lord. The shadows of the horses and their riders were growing longer. Why was the eastern army so long delayed?

A cry of frenzy washed againt the walls of the city so that they seemed to shake. Judah was winning. The far-flung line of Libyans had broken in four places. Disordered knots of Egyptian auxiliaries were throwing away their weapons, surrendering, or fleeing towards the north. Caught up in the wild flight, Anu and Satiu were turning their horses. With a triumphant roar the archers of Ephraim and Manasseh leapt forward and overwhelmed the fleeing men with showers of arrows. The foremost terrain was free, and even the main army of the forty-two regions was reeling under the thrust of a retreat that had to force a way through its ranks. The voice of Josiah cut through the thousandfold cry of victory. The kingdom of God on earth was near and the new David had not been mistaken in his confidence. The royal squadron—chariots, horsemen, and foot soldiers—concentrated into a dense mass. The whole of the mounted bodyguard galloped ahead, thundering into the swept field. A mighty cloud of dust arose in which the new David was enveloped like the Lord in His raging storm. That was all that Jeremiah saw. He had to cling to the edge of the cart to prevent himself from being thrown out. Arrows, stones, and spears hissed and whistled round his head, and in the cloud of dust riders were crashing from horses that continued to tear along as if they themselves were independent fighters. The dead, to whom none paid heed, were left far behind. Suddenly the cloud divided into numerous smaller clouds. A new roar of victory went up. Anub Heth, the region of the white walls, had been thrown down. The statue of Ptah had fallen into the hands of Zebaoth. Jeremiah saw how the mighty wooden figure was lifted up by many men to the King. With almost superhuman strength the new David seized the image of the god who swayed the world and shattered it in the dust. After further surging combats the same fate was meted out to Anubis, the yelping god of the alabaster city, and the cow-headed Hathor of the region of Wath, which carried the orb of the world between its horns. The battle-line of the regions was broken, and again the clouds coalesced into one and thundered across the swept field.

Then the rush of victory came to a sudden halt. A deep ditch, filled with water, cut through the terrain. The chariot horses reared up on their hind legs and shied at the obstacle. Behind the ditch rose the gentle slope of a hill, and on the slope there presented itself to the eyes of the exhausted attackers a sight that froze them in their tracks and struck them dumb. Three lines of bronze giants, one above the other, occupied the height. In close array they stood out sharply against the evening sky, warriors who had not yet hurled a spear or received a wound. Rested, fresh, and calm, with the sun at their backs, they awaited the frenzied, blood-bespattered hosts of Josiah. Their breastplates, greaves, and arm-sheaths sparkled on their slim bodies. Red horsetails and plumes waved upon their helmets, and these were the only moving things that could be seen in the whole line of battle. Through the squadron of Judah there passed from mouth to mouth a word that was filled with dread: "Javan!" These were the Ionians, Pharaoh's auxiliaries from the northern islands and mainlands, from whom he recruited his invincible bodyguard. A harsh word of command echoed from across the ditch. The triple phalanx lowered its long lances. It was as if three gigantic scythes, welded together, lay with their threatening blades turned towards the army of Judah. This, however, was only the setting for a brilliant picture.

On the summit of the low hill, one of the eastern spurs of the Carmel range, a circle of resplendent personages was gathered round a remarkable structure. Jeremiah screwed up his eyes to see more clearly. Then he recognized that this structure, which shone so dazzlingly in the golden rays of the setting sun, was the lofty chariot throne of Pharaoh from which he watched his battles. It seemed to be an ingenious and immobile symbol rather than a real chariot, for no horses were to be seen. In an affected attitude, like a god, a solitary little man stood upon the chariot throne unmoved by all that was happening around him. The double diadem of Egypt with the uræus-serpent jutting out in front crowned the fragile elegance of his form. The colourful councillors of Pharaoh's court who surrounded the chariot seemed to be constantly summoned before their silent ruler, for again and again one of them would advance affectedly towards him, kiss the throne as he writhed in bliss, and trip back to his place again. Behind the symbolic chariot stood another row of officials holding a canopy in readiness, and to the right and left of Necho Jeremiah caught sight of two tall cages. In one of them some motionless object appeared to be squatting, but in the other something was leaping about nimbly. Everybody knew that the earthly Sun God of Noph always carried about with him a golden sparrow-hawk of Ptah and a sacred baboon of the realm of the dead.

Jeremiah's eyes had turned from the picture of Pharaoh, radiant in the sun, to the unkempt picture of his own King. Even now, in this awful silence, no whisper had come from the Lord. Only Jeremiah's own soul shrieked within him, his own poor intelligence. Was not Ahikam at his side thinking the same thing? The Ionian phalanges still stood rigid and motionless. A strong detachment of cavalry appeared on the side of the hill and immediately turned to stone. Flashing chains of war chariots took up positions behind them. Despite the terrible carnage that had taken place, not a single Egyptian weapon was raised in attack. Was this not the work of God? In spite of the blood that had been shed, in spite of the shattered images of his gods, the Autocrat of the Nile still wished to grant the King of Judah a respite in which to reconsider his decision. Jeremiah convulsively seized Ahikam's hand. They saw into each other's minds and leapt from the cart. They began to run, and as they ran they shouted. But more than a hundred paces lay between them and the war chariot of the King.

Josiah, the victor over the Libyans, the Anu and Satiu, and the regions of Egypt, the shatterer of Pharaoh's gods, was not likely to heed their words. During the furious onward drive his helmet had fallen off and strands of his long hair hung plastered with sweat over his face, which was completely disfigured with dust, dirt, and splashes of blood. The frenzy of battle and the intoxication of killing had rendered his features unrecognizable. But his hands were calm. Deliberately he laid one of the long, far-carrying arrows on the bow, which he drew as taut as it would go by means of the foot lever. The sinew hummed like the string of a psaltery. The arrow rose visibly in the air, whistled over the heads of the Ionians in a high arch, and seemed to vanish longingly into the sun, the divine symbol of Egypt. But on the crest of the hill, where Pharaoh's chariot throne was shining, loud groans could be heard. Had Pharaoh been struck? No! Pharaoh's councillors had gathered round one of the cages. Josiah's arrow must have killed or wounded the sacred baboon that was dedicated to the realm of the dead.

All this happened in a moment. That which followed was no longer measured in Jeremiah's heart according to divisions of time. He saw the King whirl a spear over his head and give the sign to attack: "Across the ditch!" He and Ahikam had to dash back or they would have been trampled down by the squadron; they had not yet reached their cart before the crashing onrush began. The ditch was steep and fairly wide. Some of the horses fell, while others were able to struggle laboriously up the hill on the other side. The four-wheeled cart with Jeremiah, Ahikam, and the priest was unable to get across, for the horses refused to move, no matter how savagely they were lashed. And they were not alone. Hundreds of stragglers, fallen horsemen, wounded men, and others who had been robbed of their courage by the sight of Pharaoh and his Ionians—all these stayed on the near side of the ditch. Many abandoned the King in his hardest fight. On the other side of the water a new cloud had arisen, and it enveloped everything as it grew darker and darker with its admixture of dust, earth, blood, frenzy, and shrieks of agony. For it had now mingled with a second cloud that was stirred up by the marching feet of the advancing Ionians and the hoofs of their accompanying cavalry. Now and then it was pierced by the lightning flashes of lances and swords. Fresh fighting had broken out in front of Megiddo as well, where the Libyans had rallied. The sun was already over Carmel, where Maaseiah was still being pressed hard by the Ethiopians and Nubians. Where was Eliakim? For hours the heart of every warrior in Judah had been asking itself the dreadful question. Suddenly the old priest, from whom too much had been expected, burst into loud sobs. He covered his head, beat his breast with both fists, and made childish offers to the aloof and icy Zebaoth.

The great black cloud of dust, blood, and clamour danced and circled round its own axis like a whirlwind. It moved backwards and forwards, opened out and concentrated again. In place of the fighting Ionians, the hill was now occupied by a new phalanx of fresh and gleaming soldiers. When anyone raised his eyes to look at Pharaoh, he saw that the latter had not changed his affected and god-like attitude. He was still unmoved by what was happening, but his chariot throne was closely surrounded by courtiers and guards who protected him with their bodies and shields. All at once the dancing black cloud seemed to stand still. A hurrying group of men tore itself away and ran towards the ditch. They were bent low and seemed to be in dire straits. They were carrying someone. The old prince of Libnah staggered in front of them, made distracted signs, crashed to the ground, and did not rise again. All this seemed to happen remotely, as if in a dream. Even the roar of battle was suddenly hushed. The unconscious King was borne to the four-wheeled cart, where hundreds of hollow-eyed men thronged round, in despair at this final calamity. The cloud was moving sluggishly. Assasiah would fight until the last man had fallen, but little time remained in which to bring the King to safety. Ahikam himself seized the reins, and escorted by only a few horsemen the cart dashed back towards Megiddo by such side-tracks as were available. Jeremiah held the wounded King's head in his lap and gazed down with unspeakable sorrow at the blood-bespattered, sweaty, dirt-encrusted face. At the end of the flight his own coat was soaked through and through with the King's blood. Two Ionian lances had pierced Josiah's breast and left groin. In the citadel, which they reached through the western gate after evading the enemy, there was time only for the physicians and the eunuch to bind his wounds hurriedly. Josiah groaned without regaining consciousness, and only once did he call out: "To Jerusalem!" Ahikam did not cease to urge the necessity for haste. The battle was lost, the future dark. The will of the mortally wounded King must be obeyed without delay. To Jerusalem! That very night and at wild speed. The best of the travelling chariots was heaped with cushions and rugs that the King might lie softly. His head again rested in Jeremiah's lap. Ahikam held his feet.

12

The Great Pleading

"RIGHTEOUS art thou, O Lord, when I plead with thee: yet let me talk with thee of thy judgments: Wherefore doth the way of the wicked prosper? wherefore are all they happy that deal very treacherously? Thou hast planted them, yea, they have taken root: they grow, yea, they bring forth fruit, thou art near in their mouth, and far from their reins."

These were words that Jeremiah often cried out in his affliction. Baruch wrote them secretly on a scroll in which he recorded certain sayings of his master. Before this, however, Jeremiah had listened to the great pleading of a mighty teacher—of Josiah, King of Judah, as he lay wounded unto death. Josiah's great pleading in the days and nights of his dying was concerned less with the fortune of the godless than with the misfortune of the godly.

They had had to change horses several times in the reinforcement camps before they eventually reached the Gate of Ephraim on the second noon, but the King's vitality survived the terrible journey as though by a miracle. Couriers had hurried ahead of the chariot to bring to Temple and Palace the news of Josiah's grave hurt, his approaching return to Jerusalem, and the disastrous issue of the battle of Megiddo. Although the priests and dignitaries of the court, who heard the news with blanched faces, did not open their lips to make it public, yet as always happened in such cases, rumour had found its way to the people through the pores and crevices of silence. In less than an hour after the first horseman had galloped through the Gate of Ephraim, Jerusalem knew everything and more than everything. After such a long period of peace, the nation was like a child that did not realize the full extent of its danger but gave itself up to dull forebodings not unmingled with an ecstatic anticipation of calamity. Every idler in Jerusalem gathered that morning in the outer courtyard of the Temple with a pale curiosity and apprehension. The crowd moved almost mutely from one northern gateway to another. Whenever a priest of one of the higher orders or an official of the court appeared, he was at once surrounded and plied with questions. He would generally murmur something vaguely soothing and force his way with a gentle impatience through the throng. As the day lengthened, so did the weight of unanswered questions increase. Was the King dead? Had he been captured? Was he wounded? Had the army of Prince Eliakim fallen into the hands of Pharaoh? Had Eliakim, the notorious enemy of his father, turned traitor? Was Pharaoh already at the hills of Ephraim, marching towards Jerusalem? Should they flee before the advancing Egyptians, or was further resistance possible among the impassable defiles? All these uncertain rumours had abruptly died away by the time the sun had passed its zenith. Queen Hamutal, heavily veiled and accompanied by a number of her women, had hastened to the smaller northern Gate of Benjamin. The crowd moved after her. The gate, however, was held by a strong detachment of the bodyguard, which turned with lowered lances towards the surging throng and cleared an open space.

The King was swiftly lifted out of the chariot and laid in a deep litter that was like a coffin. Thus he remained hidden from the eyes of the people, and even Hamutal had hardly been able to catch a glimpse of his face. The procession moved at a rapid pace through the suddenly transformed crowd, which broke out into stifled cries of lamentation as if it only now grasped the crushing significance of what had happened and the greatness of the dying King.

Josiah was placed on the divan in his bedchamber. He declined the refreshing drink which Hamutal put to his lips with a hand that was no longer white and fleshy. Neither did he permit his physician to renew the blood-soaked bandages and treat the wounds with the famous healing balm of Gilead. His eyes sought Jeremiah, and there was a command in them: "You stay!" He had still not uttered a word, when he fell into a deep sleep of exhaustion that resembled the endless swoon which had preceded it. In addition to Hamutal, only Jeremiah and Ahikam remained at the King's bedside. Ahikam immediately fell asleep from over-exertion as he sat, but Jeremiah's exhaustion had made him doubly wakeful, like a fire that shoots up into a flame just before it dies out. After a brief sleep, which was almost like a coma, the King woke. He appeared to be somewhat better. The deathly pallor had left his cheeks and had been replaced by deep-red patches. His vitality seemed to be kindled by something that was more than physical, by a fever of the mind. Hamutal, who had up to this moment kept herself under rigid control, now broke down at her husband's bedside; her body was shaken by sobs as she pressed her face to his brown hand. He tried to make the gesture of a fleeting caress, and repeated it impatiently. He wanted to speak with Jeremiah. His voice was low but resonant, as if his lungs had not been torn by an Ionian lance. Now was not the time to take farewell of his beloved wife, to give way to the unutterable grief of a manly heart; it was not the time to think of all that was so intimate and familiar, letting his soul dissolve once more in its harmonious sweetness. A grave hour had come, the ice-cold hour when justice must be demanded. The hand of the messenger of death was already outstretched, and Josiah's moments were numbered. When the King was alone with Jeremiah he breathed carefully, each time as deeply as he could and as well as he could, that he might gather strength for the effort of his great pleading.

"I have kept the covenant. . . . He has broken the covenant." The wounded man spoke with difficulty, like a drunken man, and he no longer called Jeremiah by his name but addressed him as "Anathoth," the name of his native town. Perhaps he had forgotten Jeremiah's name, perhaps the name of one man did not suffice as witness to his pleading.

"He has broken the covenant. . . . Speak, Anathoth, in His name . . . for He comes to thee with His voice and in visions. . . . What hast Thou to say, O Lord? . . ."

Jeremiah avoided answering.

"The King should not talk now . . . the King should sleep, that he may recover. . . ."

Josiah tried angrily to raise himself up.

"There is no time for foolish words, Adonai. . . . Answer me, Anathoth. . . . 'Thou shalt be gathered unto thy grave in peace'—that is what Thou didst say to me through the mouth of the seeress . . . 'Thou shalt go in peace and thine eyes shall not see evil.' . . . When I know what my sin has been . . . when I know my guilt . . . yes, then I will go in peace. . . . But when I do *not* know what my sin has been, when I do *not* know my guilt, how can I . . . ?"

Josiah paused for breath, shaken by a fit of shallow coughing. Jeremiah pressed his hand, and after a time the King regained his strength.

"I speak to thee, Anathoth . . . I speak to Thee, Adonai. . . . Why didst Thou give me Thy Law when it was Thy intention to cast me aside? . . . I did not reject Thy Law . . . I swore to keep it at the pillar of the Covenant. . . . I kept the great Passover with thirty thousand bulls and lambs and wethers and oxen and yearlings for a burnt offering. . . . I have fulfilled Thy Law. . . . Everywhere throughout the land . . . I swept away the high places and hewed down the green trees. . . . By day and by night . . . I did Thy work. . . . I strewed the altars of Baal with ashes and dead bones. . . . And Thou . . . and Thou . . . what hast Thou done for me? . . . Speak, Adonai . . . through the mouth of Anathoth!"

How had the mouthpiece of the Lord been reduced to silence by this pleading! It cut into his soul as with a sharp blade, and he too pleaded and complained. Why had the lightning of the Lord struck this King, who more than any of the sons of David was the epitome of good faith? Josiah fell, but Meshullam the miller stood and stroked his venerable beard with murderous fingers. Jeremiah was dragged from his unanswerable questioning by a hoarse outcry from the King:

"Adonai! . . . I have loved Thee!"

The witness to the great pleading sobbed aloud, but the King in his fever looked at him with a cold gaze. In these tears lay only the common and fleeting compassion of a tender-hearted youth for misfortune. Anathoth was weeping foolish tears of the heart. The Lord did not weep tears of eternity for His servant. He concealed Himself behind His hundred heavens of ice and remained dumb. The soul of Josiah was not crying out for redemption. It was crying out for an explanation of his guilt. It only wanted to know the reason why, after a life spent in the service of Adonai, this same Adonai should cast it aside when He blessed the most wanton transgressors and blasphemers and granted victory to Egypt, His hereditary enemy. Josiah wished to know only what the sin had been that had caused his affliction. This alone would be enough for his questioning soul, that it might go in peace. But not even this final consolation, the least that could be asked, was afforded to his questioning soul. Jeremiah could not help, for he himself was frozen by the immeasurable aloofness of God.

The King's pleading lasted three days and three nights. Jeremiah had to stay at his bedside, and for only an hour at a time, when the wounded man was overcome by fever and pain, was he himself able to fall into an unrefreshing and disturbed sleep. These days and nights forged the prophet's heart on their anvil. His childlike devotion to Adonai yielded to a new resistance and a lurking stubbornness. From hour to hour his intention grew to forsake the Lord and renounce his sanctification. For this, too, was only a covenant, which could be broken as Adonai had broken the covenant with Josiah. The voice without and within had deluded and persuaded him, and he had allowed himself to be persuaded. What had been the consequence of the Lord's knowing him and sanctifying him even before he was born? His youth had been destroyed, his life burnt out! He had fled from his father's house, afflicted his mother with sorrow, brought his father to an angry death, filled his brothers with hatred. He had wandered through the land, trembling in every limb with apprehension lest the patience of the Lord might become exhausted. He had prophesied in the Temple and caused vexation. What was the purpose of all this? How did it help the world that the Lord had revealed to him the danger in which it stood? How had it helped the King that he had kept him, Jeremiah, at his side? He had brought misfortune to everybody with whom he came in contact. His mission was completely useless and worse than useless; it was harmful and embittering. Had not the King in the days when he was preparing his plan continually asked: "Has word come from the Lord?" When He should have spoken for the sake of Israel, the Lord had remained silent and cruelly obscure. Why should the insignificant Jeremiah of Anathoth, who had been called again and again only to be abandoned, assume responsibility for the whole world? To lie in wait again and again in expectation of a sign, this was more terrible than death. Would it not be better for him to live somewhere in the world as a part of the world, regardless of God's cares, and to share with all other men a doom that would be no more and no less tolerable than theirs?

These were the thoughts of Jeremiah when he heard the King in his delirium crying out day and night to the Lord for an explanation. The third night was the worst. The artery in Josiah's neck throbbed visibly. His flesh of steel had wasted like wax in the furnace of his fever and his great pleading. A yellow skeleton lay stretched out upon the bed. His voice had become a hoarse whistle.

"Speak, Anathoth. . . . Speak, Adonai. . . . On the great fast day, the Day of Atonement, I secretly drank a cup of wine. . . . Was that my sin?"

Jeremiah wearily shook his head.

"How could such a slight thing be the cause, my King?"

"Speak, Anathoth. . . . Speak, Adonai. . . . I have often coveted the wives of my neighbours . . . and I have often lewdly followed my desires, a hundred times. . . . Was that my sin?"

"How could it be that, my King? . . . Your father David sinned more grievously with women and he was punished in his child . . . but he was gathered to the grave in peace."

"Speak, Anathoth. . . . Speak, Adonai. . . . I have been full of uncleanness . . . by day and by night . . . in deed and in thought. . . . Was this my sin?"

"How could it be that, my King? . . . Your father Solomon has said, and the Lord knows: 'All flesh is sin.' "

In endless questionings all the grounds were exhausted that might have justified punishment by God. Then the King clenched his weak fists against Jeremiah.

"Curses upon thee, Anathoth, if thou dost not give me answer!"

Jeremiah threw himself down before the couch.

"I will make answer to the King, that his soul may find peace. . . . It is not the King who has sinned . . . but it is the fathers of the King who have sinned, it is they who bear the guilt. . . . They desecrated that which was holy and defiled that which was clean. . . . They did not remember the covenant . . . the King had to purge the land after them. . . . But God says that He will visit the sins of the fathers unto the fourth generation."

This was a clear answer, though it did not come from Jeremiah's heart. The face of the King seemed to grow less tense and his eyes sank into their shadowed sockets. For a while he lay motionless and rigid, then something strange happened. Lifting his wasted legs from the couch, Josiah rose and pushing Jeremiah from him, tottered stiffly to the window of the room which looked out on to the second court of the guard. He pressed his trembling fists against the ledge and his whistling voice rang out shrilly with all the strength he had left:

"By command of the King . . . burn the Temple! . . . Set fire to the Holy of Holies! . . . Destroy the Book of the Law! . . . By command of the King . . . Adonai is the enemy of Israel . . . He has only brought evil upon Judah. . . . He sanctified it only to be the plaything of His hatred. . . . Away with Adonai! . . . Open the gates wide for Rā and Ptah and Baal and Marduk and Tammuz and Ashtaroth . . . for they are great and kind. . . . By command of the King . . ."

The force of this blasphemy caused Josiah to whirl round. He twisted like a dancer and with hissing breath fell backwards to the ground. Blood gushed from his mouth and dyed the sandalwood floor. Hamutal had rushed in when she heard his blasphemous cry, and she saw her beloved husband lying rigid on the floor with half-closed eyes. He had ceased to breathe. She tore open her garment, bared her breasts, and cast her warm body upon the bloodstained form of her husband to snatch him back from death. And her will prevailed. After a period of agonized waiting the shadow of a smile passed across Josiah's features and two long sighs struggled from his torn breast.

On the next morning the King appeared completely transformed. His great pleading was at an end. His wasted face had become thoughtful and shone with a deep peace. Important messages had arrived which caused the measure of misfortune to appear in a milder light than could have been hoped. The generals reported that they had succeeded in saving the remnants of the army from destruction and concentrating them in the hills of Ephraim in order to bar Pharaoh's path. The Father and Son of the Gods, however, did not seem to be considering the idea of a punitive expedition against Jerusalem. He himself had severe losses to recover from, and the goal of his bold march lay not towards the south but towards the north. After a truce of two days and two nights, during which he rested the main body of his troops and his auxiliaries in the Plain of Jezreel, the signal was given to strike camp and the victor marched northwards into the land of Hamath.

In all these messages the unsolved riddle was Eliakim, the successor to the throne, whose delay had partly been the cause of the disaster at Megiddo. It was reported to the King that Eliakim's army had not been engaged in even the slightest skirmish with the Egyptians, but had passively awaited its fate. Pharaoh had then surrounded the army of the prince between the mountains of Gilboa and the Valley of Jordan, and was able to disarm it without meeting with any resistance. The Egyptians were now moving by forced marches in the direction of Riblah, the fortified city to the north of Lebanon, and they were carrying Josiah's eldest son with them, though it was not known whether as an ally or in honourable captivity.

The dying Josiah summoned his ebbing strength and, ignoring the entreaties of Hamutal, Ahikam, Jeremiah, his physicians, and his attendants, he ordered that he should be dressed in his royal robes and carried to the throne-room of Solomon, where the council of dignitaries was in permanent session. The sky-blue cloak of David enfolded all too voluminously the wasted form of the King, whose arms and legs appeared pitiably thin and sallow. His hair and beard had turned very grey, and the crown sank deeply over his waxen and shrunken brow. He had to be tied to the gold and ivory throne with straps, otherwise he would have toppled forward and fallen down the steps. The great assembly presented a very different appearance from that of the day before the war against Egypt, when Josiah's sun had shone down upon a full and brilliant array of princes and priests. Now the harvest of Judah had been mown down and plucked out, leaving a field of stubble on which only a few stalks still swayed in the wind. Many of the princes had met their death in the battle, others were languishing in Necho's chains, others lay with the shattered hosts of Judah in the crevasses of Carmel. On the benches reserved for the city princes sat a few rough elders as deputies, who stared in front of them with frightened eyes and hesitantly gave voice to their views with an awkward embarrassment. It was easy to see that they were trying cautiously to discover what turn events were going to take, so that they might be sure of putting themselves on the right side, that is to say, the side most favourable for themselves. One thing was clear: this King who had to be strapped to his throne could no longer be saved by any healing balm, or even by a miracle. With the diabolical disloyalty of the human heart, which will forget a hundred victories because of a single defeat and a thousand deeds of fame because of a single failure, all these men were turning away gradually and with increasing coldness from the ruler whom yesterday they had acclaimed. The dying man on the throne of Solomon, like a stricken charger that still wore its magnificent trappings, was already finished so far as they were concerned.

The benches of the priests also showed gaps, treacherous gaps. The war against Pharaoh had not been a war of the

Temple, a holy war, a thunderbolt hurled into the world from the Holy of Holies by the frozen lightning of the Ark. It was the undertaking of one individual man—this was now the verdict of the highest priestly orders. With good intentions, but with wanton thoughtlessness, this individual had cut himself adrift from the will of God and must now pay the penalty of his courage. The war had its origin in the mind of the man Josiah, so guilt and penance lay solely upon his shoulders. All those who had a few days before greeted the "Kingdom of the new David" with bloodshot eyes and hoarse excitement now wanted to have no more to do with it and pretended that from the beginning they had prophesied its inevitable failure. In a dread solitude, abandoned on all sides, the King sat upon the throne of Solomon, still burning as a blue flame, but a flame without sustenance, in a golden lamp. With the exception of the steadfast Urijah, the prophets of the Lord had crept away; their bench was empty. The day of Megiddo had been their day of deepest humiliation. Of what power could they still boast, what prophecies would still be believed, when they had not been able to exact a single indication from the Lord on the eve of such a tremendous event? One of them had even foretold a victory, though it was true he was a novice, Hananiah of Gibeon. His prophecy had been unmasked as falsehood and deceit by the bitter outcome. Hananiah, however, did not appear to admit his defeat. On the way to the throne-room he had approached Jeremiah and whispered in his ear that his prophecy concerning Egypt could not be disproved until Pharaoh's campaign against the nations of the Land of Rivers should have been brought to a victorious conclusion. Though Jeremiah was horrified at these arrogant words, yet it seemed to him not incredible that Hananiah too might have been a genuine victim of Adonai's ambiguity. More significant than the absence of all the princes, priests, and prophets from the council of the dying King was that of one single man, the aged Shaphan. He had no further intention of leaving his house because of what was happening in the world. The last days remaining to him were to be devoted to the exercise of his scholarly mind and the interpretation of the Law. He regarded with equanimity the fate of the next few generations if he could only penetrate to the heart of the Law and establish its ultimate meaning. And with the selfishness of age he averted his face from the heart-rending sight of him in whom he still loved the royal boy and pupil.

After his hæmorrhage the King had almost completely lost his voice and could make himself understood only by means of a hoarse whisper. For this reason Ahikam and Jeremiah stood with bowed heads to the right and left of him on the highest step before the throne, to repeat to the assembly every word that he whispered. At the feet of their father sat Jehoahaz and the boy Mattaniah, but no other son of David was present, none of the royal uncles and cousins, not even the few who tarried in Jerusalem at this fateful hour. They too intended to wait cautiously, that they might see in which direction the destinies of the monarchy were going to develop. These princes knew that the future of the monarchy depended on the decision of Egypt, and Egypt had not yet spoken. Josiah, the godly ruler of a day that had run its course, was for them already a corpse, unclean and accursed.

Jeremiah felt that nothing escaped the eye of the King, neither the coldness which was with difficulty masked by an appearance of solemn sympathy nor the awkward embarrassment which garbed itself in a hypocritical humility. The disloyalty of these men was wafted up like a stifling miasma to him who was having to fight for every breath. The two sons held their father's wasted legs, which shivered with a feverish ague. The clear, vacant eyes of Jehoahaz stared with utter lack of comprehension at the assembly. Mattaniah gazed round the hall with the beautiful and placid eyes that he had inherited from his mother, for his time was still far off. The King's whispering voice struggled for words which Ahikam appeared not to have fully understood, but he beckoned to the members of the council to range themselves closer to the throne. Concealing their curiosity as well as they could, they thronged forward from all sides with dignified steps, and a pyramid of closely crowded figures had soon gathered upon and below the steps of the throne. The wretched summit of this pyramid, however, sank more and more towards the left side out of sheer weakness. The voiceless whisper grew more and more sharp and desperate. At last the two listeners realized what he was trying to say and Ahikam was able to announce to the assembly the will of the King. Josiah pronounced his own demise. In accordance with ancient usage a successor had to be elected without delay. Eliakim was a prisoner and had forfeited his rights, but the throne of David must not remain vacant for even an hour. The men of Judah were accordingly called upon to acknowledge the second son as the lawful heir and to elect him King. This was the demand that Josiah had put forward in his hoarse whisper. The men of Judah looked at one another. The expression of anxiety and swift thought on their faces revealed that their minds were all in agreement: it was advisable to fulfil the will of a dying man, and the Eternal One could then turn this will towards His own purposes. Slowly, one after the other, they raised their hands to signify their assent to the election of Jehoahaz as Josiah had desired. It was a reluctant choice, and the murmur of homage which followed was even more reluctant. But since Josiah had prevailed in his purpose, he did not concern himself with what they thought. With an almost superhuman effort he was struggling to raise his stiffened hands to his brow in order to take off the crown of David and set it upon the head of the new King. As he painfully lifted it, the crown of the kings of Judah slipped from his nerveless fingers and tumbled with a malicious agility right through the midst of the men in front of the throne until it reached the farther end of the hall. Somebody sprang after the profaned diadem, but it slid away from his fingers even as he grasped it. Pale with embarrassment and distress, the Sagan, who had been hurriedly sent for, placed the crown of David on the hastily anointed head of the dull Jehoahaz, who still could not altogether comprehend what part he was playing. The oppressive omen of this bungled coronation seemed to have made no impression on the soul of Josiah. He was wholly taken up with a new effort which was beyond his strength. With racked face and gritted teeth he was trying to force himself up from the throne of Solomon to make way for the new King. Ahikam and Jeremiah put their hands under his arms and lifted him up. The maddening pain gave him back his voice. Twice he uttered a piercing cry that shook the hall. Then he hung as if lifeless on the hands that were supporting him as they dragged him down the steps of the throne. The fright in the eyes of Jehoahaz became almost a frenzied terror when he found himself on the elevated throne, alone and exposed to the eyes of the assembly below. He twisted in torment to every side, until at last, the most unroyal cry escaped from his lips:

"Father, come back! . . . I don't want this . . . I don't like it. . . ."

And with the sobbing whine of a child he covered his eyes with both hands. But Josiah did not hear the childish weeping with which the unhappy Jehoahaz, to the abhorrence of the men present, entered upon his kingdom. The litter with the dying man had been hurriedly carried from the hall where stood the throne that he had gambled away.

Josiah's wife and two sons, together with Ahikam, Jeremiah, and a few of those who had remained most faithful to him, were gathered round the couch where he was still breathing. He had not been disrobed and he lay motionless on his deathbed in the blue cloak of his former kingship. With dry eyes, and almost as motionless as he, Hamutal crouched at his feet. Only now did she give him up for lost. Yesterday she had still been making herself beautiful for him, striving with bitter agony of mind to appear as lovely as ever in his eyes. Today she had ceased to dress her hair in the Egyptian style. Her soft body was clad in a drab gown hanging in loose folds to which she had given no thought. No flower from the royal gardens was at her breast. She wore on her wrists none of the jingling bracelets that he had loved. No golden varnish shone on the nails of her fingers and toes, the golden varnish of which he had been so fond. Beauty had been ungraciously dismissed from her service, since it could not accompany him whither he was going. The exquisite Hamutal of yesterday now crouched at the foot of her husband's bed with all her colour and beauty gone.

The silent group in the great chamber no longer expected that the man who was becoming for ever silent would speak again. Yet Josiah spoke, and his voice was full and resonant as in the days of his prime. His eyes opened and were filled with hidden things that he alone could see. Three times he said the same words, and each time with a different intonation. The words were: "The fathers . . ." The first time it sounded like a frightened understanding. The second time it was like an uncertain question. But the third time he sang it with a comprehending smile, as though it were a phrase from one of the melodies of the sons of Asaph. The silent group crowded more closely round the couch, as if they might thereby share in the vision of the holy gathering of fathers which the soul of Josiah seemed to be witnessing with his last gleam of earthly consciousness before he himself was gathered to the realm where sleep is a heightened wakefulness. Had he first of all seen the most recent of his fathers, Amon and Manasseh, the sight of whom had filled him with terror, and was he now seeing Abraham, Isaac, and Jacob, and did he see Moses and David and himself amongst them? Where was this gathering of the fathers? Far from the Lord in the gloomy twilight of Sheol, or near to the Lord and immersed in the presence which He had at last unveiled?

After a further silence that was seemingly endless the King turned his head a little to the side, so that his eyes rested upon the boy Mattaniah. But he did not seem to be conscious that his youngest son was there. Once more his eyes were filled with incomprehensible pictures, and his voice trembled at what he saw. Again he uttered two words, and again he repeated them three times. This time the words were: "The children . . ." And again he spoke each time with a different intonation. The first time it was full of a sighing compassion, the second time like an uncertain question, the third time with a singing intonation of blissful amazement. Even more mysterious than the vision of the gathering of the fathers was the vision of the procession of the children until the end of time. It was only their fusion that constituted Israel, its truth and its sanctification. The king who, according to Shaphan's immortal chronicle, had not his like in Judah and Israel, had perhaps in the hour of his death embraced both beginning and end in one single commanding glance. And with this vision his eyes at last grew dim. Ahikam was already making a sign to the new King to close his father's eyelids, when Josiah gave a deep sigh and called once more: "Anathoth!" Jeremiah cast himself to the ground as one who had been summoned by the King and put his face close to that of the dying man, who spoke the following words slowly and with great clearness:

"To go in peace . . . it was no falsehood, after all. . . . Anathoth, speak to Him. . . . I love Him . . . again . . . still . . ."

Then King Josiah, the son of Amon, turned his face to the wall and died.

Since the days of the great pleading and the King's dying, Jeremiah had ceased to love the Lord, but was angry with Him and bitter, and imagined that he hated Him. He resolved to renounce his mission as a prophet without delay and to take leave for ever. Yet renunciation was not enough. In his own country he would always succumb again to the Lord's persuasion. He must therefore go to another land, where the voice of Adonai would be fainter among alien men and tongues and would leave him in peace. In the night that followed the death of Josiah he appeared in his father's house at Anathoth and spoke in great agitation to his mother of the flight which he had planned. He told her that he was going away for ever, but in spite of this talk her eyes remained dry and she looked at him steadily.

"My son, I shall not worry, for I shall see you again. He has greater power over you than you have yourself."

The Unfathomable One did not make any effort to restrain Jeremiah. He appeared to accept his renunciation, to grant him leave, and even to have planned and ordained the events that occurred soon after this in order to smooth the way for the flight of His sanctified prophet.

13

Among the Flowering Columns of Noph

IN JEREMIAH'S native land this pleasant town was known as Noph. On the shores of the Nile, where its temples, palaces, pyramids, and tombs stretched in an endless line, it was called Men-Nofr, but these syllables were often changed on the unaccustomed lips of foreigners to Membe or Memphi. The priests, however, called it solemnly and accurately "Ha-Ka-Ptah," which signified nothing other than "dwelling place of the spirit of Ptah." This was the most correct of all the names, for Noph was in truth the magnificent "Nu-Ptah," the city of the creative Ptah; and the dwelling place of his spirit, which was itself a city, rose from its busy centre. In contrast to the Temple in Jerusalem, which contained no images, the temple at Noph possessed an incorporation of Ptah in stone which was accessible on certain festivals and could then be seen at least by those of his worshippers who were of high rank. Except on such sacred occasions the Ruler of All Life withdrew to the innermost chamber of his gigantic dwelling, but he allowed free scope to the secondary divinities with whom he formed a trinity and shared his temple. The numerous chapels of Sekhet and Imhotep were filled at every hour of the day with the colourful activity of those who were offering up sacrifices and burning incense. For a stranger, however—even if he were an austere man of God such as Jeremiah—the most fascinating sight in this tremendous structure was the springtime of walls and columns. It was a springtime which lasted a thousand years and was then followed by summer drought and autumn, as could be seen in the decay of so many temples in the forty-two regions. Often, though, the first spring was followed by a second, which was equally intended to last a thousand years. This second springtime had recently awakened in the flowering columns of the temple of Nu-Ptah. It had been awakened by Pharaoh Psammetichus, the father of Necho, the Father and Son of the Gods, who had come down to earth in order to establish anew the eternal throne of Egypt. His radiance caused the grey, withered, and leafless columns of Noph to blossom afresh. The faded colours of their shafts were renewed with fresh purple and scarlet and hyacinth and emerald and gold in both delicate and vivid shades. The vigour of the rising sap showed most clearly when it reached the towering capitals of these columns, which burst into a thousand lotus flowers or clusters of buds of the papyrus bush.

Each of these columns of spring was a world in itself, adorned from root to calyx with sacred hieroglyphics. On their soaring stems of stone had been engraved and painted endless chronicles of the gods and pæans of praise. The eye which was unable to read the writing was none the less held by the illimitable sequence of pictures that had been joyously woven into this imperishable tapestry: the deeds and sufferings of the gods, sacrificial feasts and the sailing of sacred barks, battles on land, sieges, processions of captives, triumphal votive offerings, Pharaoh's hippopotamus hunts; in short, the multifarious and blessed activities of kings and gods. A thousand and more of the flowering columns stood in the temple of Nu-Ptah, diffusing gladness and making young the hearts of those who looked upon them when the eye of Horus shone above and the thousand sparrow-hawks of Ptah hovered over the temple with outstretched wings.

It seemed to Jeremiah that there was probably only one house in Noph that had no part in this gladness. It was the house in which he himself had found refuge and where he lived in company with the exiled Jehoahaz, Hamutal, and the boy Mattaniah, whose education he continued to conduct in obedience to the order of the dying King. When he stepped out of the large and handsome house which Pharaoh had assigned for the use of the banished son of David and stood in the sunny and clamorous street, he was immediately embraced by the serenity of Egypt. The soul would have had to be very bruised that could turn away from this embrace. Where else could such great gladness prevail if not here, where they had succeeded in turning death into the essence of life and rendering earthly comfort imperishable, as was evidenced by the "western city" with its thousand palatial tombs which exceeded in beauty and convenience the homes of the living? The rooms and chambers in which every wealthy mortal was immortalized in identification with the redeemed Redeemer Osiris overflowed with coloured images of that which he had found sweet and desirable on earth. No one had to abandon the things he was fond of. He only moved a little farther towards the west with his beloved chattels, and there he could enjoy in peace his eternally secure retirement and divine privileges. Thus the inversion of values was wisely realized and the enduring dreariness of death transformed into the zest of life. An inexhaustible pæan of praise in honour of everything transitory had the effect of rendering it intransitory, and the land which thought of nothing but death annihilated it by the very thought.

Jeremiah shivered in the embrace of the great gladness of

Noph. Yet every day, an hour before sunset, he was drawn to the great open space in front of the temple of Ptah. He did not venture inside, in order not to defile himself. He let himself be carried along by the stream of people in the outer hall of columns, for at that hour the whole city, young and old, gathered there for an evening stroll. From the numerous inner courts of the temple came the reflection of coloured fireworks and burning incense and the tranquil chanting of endless litanies. Jeremiah turned his eyes and ears away with repugnance, and he felt the truth of the traditional saying that Israel had an aversion for the peoples of other lands. At the same time he recognized that this saying was two-edged. For among the peoples of other lands there was also an aversion for Israel. He saw it in the swift encounter with a pair of eyes or in the aloof hostility of a face that had divined his origin. But he knew also that the cause of this mutual aversion was the Eternal God, who had chosen for Himself a weak people from among the nations of a world which was lapped in a confused dream, and had burdened it with the task of remaining awake and disentangling the confusion.

Moved by his feeling of strangeness, Jeremiah descended the steps of the hall of columns and entered the spacious, handsomely paved square. The stupefying fragrance of flowers was wafted towards him from a whole city of flower stalls, for it was befitting that all the forms and incorporations in which the celestially joyful deities appeared should be approached with flowers in one's hands according to the nature of the god and the season of the year. When Jeremiah had turned his back on the narrow streets that contained the stalls of the sellers of flowers, consecrated articles, and incense, he found himself facing the crowded markets where secular trades were carried on. Each of them seemed to him to be larger than the whole lower town of Jerusalem. He strolled past the long fish stalls, which were strewn with silver scales and splashed with cold, reddish-blue blood. Choppers were driven into the bulging bodies of pike from the Nile and other great fishes. The pieces were thrown on the scales, a man croaked out the weight and price in a hoarse voice, and the goods were nimbly packed in vine or fig leaves. Porters were waiting with poles over their shoulders to deliver the orders at the homes of the wealthy. Similar scenes were to be witnessed in the poultry market. Agile Negro slaves squatted in long rows as with inimitable swiftness, swaying their bodies as they sang, they plucked the feathers from plump geese, ducks, fowls, pigeons, snipe, and moorhens, which were then strung up in long lines. Next to the poultry market were open cook-houses, eating-places, and beer-shops. The sharp tang of roasting meat was mingled with the odour of fermented barley. Jeremiah held his breath. It had been instilled in him that he must guard his soul against defilement, even if only in the form of a thought, a stimulus, or a smell. He swiftly left the street of feasters and topers, and came to the avenue of the barbers, hairdressers, and wigmakers. With the sublime patience of men who had conquered the terrors of death and whom either a luxurious or a modest dwelling, but at any rate a comfortable one, awaited in the tomb, the silent customers sat before the booths and waited until it should be their turn to have their hair cut or their beards trimmed. The barbers and their assistants were stripped to the waist as they worked. Swift razors skimmed over the bowed heads of priests and shaved them smooth as mirrors.

Jeremiah's way led him next past the market of the joiners,

cabinet-makers, and carriage builders. As in a dream his eyes ranged over wardrobes both large and small and of a hundred different shapes, finely carved tables of various sizes, chests and presses of southern woods, gaming-boards inlaid with green and azure stones. In Noph the world of the gods and the world of the dead was ever-present, therefore the world of the living chose to be all the more elegant. These seats and footstools, these armchairs with lion claws, these fragile litters seemed to have been carved for exquisite ladies. At the sight of such charming lumber one could be led to doubt whether this city had furnished warriors for Pharaoh's army since everything seemed to be made only for the limbs of slim dancing-girls.

The noise of hammering, planing, and sawing in the street of the joiners was replaced by a delicate tapping and filing. Jeremiah had entered the street of the goldsmiths and jewellers, and for the first time since uncounted months he heard once more the whispering of the Lord. Whispering? That was saying almost too much. It was a very quiet exhortation in the form of a parable, as if the Lord wanted to show Jeremiah only that distance and an alien country did not set limits to His power and that His eye rested unceasingly on His sanctified prophet in spite of his renunciation and the flight which He Himself had favoured. The parable that came to Jeremiah from Adonai in Noph was rather similar to that which had come to him in the potter's workshop in Jerusalem.

He had become immersed in the work of the goldsmiths, but he was fascinated less by the tapping and beating of the gold than by the stone furnace in which a glowing white mass hissed menacingly and was continually replenished by a stoker. From this dome-shaped furnace, which was of medium size, there issued such an intense heat that the naked bodies of the gold refiners standing near it were scorched and dripped with sweat. Each of the gold refiners held in his hand a long-stemmed crucible, in which lay a small lump of impure gold ore mixed with dross. The stoker would pull open the door of the furnace with a rake, and then the gold refiners approached with distorted faces and pushed their crucibles into the white-hot glow. The furnace spewed sparks and incandescent flakes. The glaring, inflamed eyes of the men betrayed the pain they had to endure, for the gold took time to melt. Their arms were covered with blisters and burns, yet their hands must not shake or falter, but hold the precious crucible firmly until the melting process was completed and the gold was refined from the dross. Jeremiah himself stepped quite close to the open furnace, and simultaneously the parable was in his soul. It was not voiced but appeared as a complete question:

"Did I not make thee a gold refiner among my people, that thou shouldst recognize and test their worth? . . ."

Jeremiah was startled. Had word now come from the Lord when there was no necessity for it, an exhortation that was of profit to nobody? When Josiah had held his assembly, and both before and during the battle, when there was great need of word from the Lord so that he might snatch the King back and save him, he had not heard the voice in spite of all his entreaties. A bitter answer rose to his lips:

"The furnace has been charred in the fire. . . . The suffering refiner exerts himself in vain. . . . The dross cannot be separated. . . . Worthless ore remains in the crucible. . . . It goes well with me where I am. . . ."

Jeremiah intended to be as good as his word. It was not in his mind to plead, as he had done before, that the Lord should possess him. With all his strength he tried to press the whispering of the Lord out of his mind as one presses a thorn out of one's finger. But the more he strained his will, the more forcefully were his thoughts carried far away from the clamorous market of Nu-Ptah, from his own idleness and state of melancholy peace. His thoughts were with the people of whom the Lord had spoken, with Jerusalem, with the way in which everything had seemed to fit into a plan, and with all that had happened.

What had happened was this.

Josiah, the unhappy King of Judah, had been gathered to his fathers in the Garden of Uzziah. There had been no ostentatious display of wailing and lamentation such as the hero deserved, but an embarrassed and strangely hurried funeral. Ignominy has always been the younger sister of misfortune. A dark shadow lay over Josiah's name, and instead of innumerable threnodies by the highest order of the sons of Asaph, a few of them had sung a single song of lament, the words of which had been composed by Jeremiah in praise of his beloved King. The embarrassed funeral had been followed by a no less embarrassed and oppressive interregnum which everyone in Jerusalem and throughout the country felt might come to an end at any moment. During this uneasy interval the ruler was Jehoahaz. The princes and priests still had before their eyes the terrible council when the dying King, strapped to his throne, had exacted the election of his second son and the new King had whiningly protested. Yet when he donned the sky-blue cloak of David even Jehoahaz was invested with a pale dignity, with which he filled the emptiness of his reign. He did nothing evil, he did nothing good, and therefore the nothing which he did was displeasing in the eyes of the Lord.

Jeremiah prepared for his flight, though he did not yet know in which direction he would turn. On the first new moon after the days of mourning he approached the new King and Hamutal and asked them to give him leave to go, since he who had summoned him to his service had been gathered to his fathers. But Jehoahaz and Hamutal grew pale because the man of the Lord wanted to depart, the man to whom the dead King had clung with such passionate faith that his last words had been addressed to him. They stroked and pressed Jeremiah's hands, shed tears, and displayed for him an affection of which he had had no inkling. Yet it was not so much the attachment of Hamutal and Jehoahaz that moved him as the weeping and pleading of Mattaniah, for his heart was devoted to his pupil. He therefore postponed his departure until the hour when things should be more settled, and he continued to live with Baruch in the palace.

The hour of settlement approached and the web of circumstance was so conveniently spun that Jeremiah did not have to abandon his resolve. The rumours that were casting their net over Jerusalem grew more and more disturbing, and it was not long before they were followed by confirmation in the shape of troops of Egyptian horsemen who were roaming through the country. The inevitable happened one morning, very early, when it was still dark. Before the tower-guarded Gate of Ephraim appeared a considerable force of Egyptian cavalry who demanded admittance. One of Pharaoh's generals was at their head and he was accompanied by a brilliant group of high Egyptian dignitaries. Their spokesman called up to the watchmen on the towers that a sacred ambassador of the kindly god had arrived before the walls of Jerusalem with peaceful intentions in order to announce to the King of Judah the implacable divine will. The captains of the guard were suspicious, since the military display seemed too large for a peaceful envoy. They at once ordered the gates to be barricaded, the battlements occupied, and the catapults made ready on the bulwarks.

The sleeping King was awakened and a council hastily summoned. It now fell to the lot of Jehoahaz to do that which in his faint-heartedness he found most difficult, namely, to come to a decision. To decline to give audience to an ambassador of Pharaoh was quite out of the question. Each of the councillors, however, was bound to recognize that the considerable military force which lent emphasis to the ambassador's mission represented an incalculable danger for Jerusalem. It was true that Pharaoh's army was tied down. But could they, after what had happened at Megiddo, afford to fan Egypt's thirst for vengeance by refusing to obey? In this difficult situation Ahikam hit upon the only practicable way out. He suggested that the King should enter into negotiation with Pharaoh's embassy and allow it to enter through the Gate of Ephraim, but only under the condition that the ambassador and his staff should alone pass through with a small escort while the larger force awaited their return outside the gate. In order to guarantee the ambassador's safety they would send Necho's general a number of hostages. After these words of advice Ahikam looked at Jeremiah as if he were expecting him also to express his opinion, but Jeremiah said nothing. It was not his office to speak in the council of the dignitaries. He was not one of them, and it was his duty solely and exclusively to communicate the word of Adonai when it should have framed itself within his mind. This office he had now renounced. Should he then be arrogant and enter into competition with those who were wiser in the ways of the world than he, setting in the place of the Lord's obscurity his own pitiful advice which could only be the result of hasty calculation? Jeremiah kept silent as a modest servant of the King who was not one of his councillors. There was, however, another man in the council who rose up to oppose the advice of Ahikam. This was Pashur, son of Immer, the First Keeper of the Door, a haughty man who wore an ebon-black pointed beard such as was customary in Egypt. His soul seemed to be seething with wrath and his little button eyes flashed. He discharged this wrath first of all against the unhappy and credulous Josiah and the latter's advisers, upon whom he called down all the curses of the Law. He declared that these raving madmen bore the chief blame because the God-intoxicated King had lent them his ear. The Lord be praised, he grated, that the Keeper of the Door still had the right of supervision over the prophets, who deserved to be put in the stocks, and that he could still summon them before his tribunal. As he spoke he fixed his button eyes on Jeremiah with a piercing look, but the young man gently stood his ground. Pashur demanded that the gates should obediently be opened without delay and without proviso. As the Keeper of the Door was the last to speak, his words influenced Jehoahaz, who twisted to and fro in desperation and stammered incoherently. One or two of the dignitaries took this stammering to be an expression of agreement and beckoned to the waiting couriers, who immediately rushed from the council chamber and the palace. The King continued to brood for a while, mistrustfully trying to decipher the faces in front of him, but he suddenly realized what was happening and leapt from his seat, shouting that he had not yet made up his mind and the couriers must be fetched back.

It was too late. The squadrons of Egyptian horsemen were

already rattling through the streets. They occupied the Citadel of David, Millo, and the courts of the guard in the royal palace. Then Pharaoh's ambassador curtly requested the presence of the King of Judah in his own throne-room. All this took place with confusing rapidity. When Jehoahaz, instead of quickly summoning his bodyguard and defending himself against the invaders, hesitantly entered the hall with his heart sinking, he found that another was already seated on the golden throne of Solomon which he himself had mounted only with weeping and trembling. The man who was now seated on high was not by any means weeping or trembling. He was stretching his scrawny figure and laughing. Eliakim was King.

Pharaoh had made him change his name and he now had to call himself Jehoiakim, so that he might have nothing which he had received from his father but only that which he had received from the earthly Sun God, even his name. But what did that matter? It was insignificant compared with the graciousness that had allowed Josiah's outrageous conduct to be forgotten and had restored the lawful succession to the throne of David. Judah was saved. The whole of Jerusalem shared this view. The people thronged through the unguarded gates of the palace to welcome Jehoiakim with their shouts, as if he had not been a traitor, or at least played a dubious part, but had saved the land by virtue of his infallible far-sightedness. If a single defeat outweighed a hundred victories, and a single failure a hundred deeds of fame, yet one successful *coup* balanced a thousand misdeeds. In the fawning soul of the mob everything is justified by the victorious employment of force. It transfigures treachery, desertion, murder, lying, and any kind of rascality, turning them into wholesome necessities which the servile people accept and swiftly forget as a child does a bitter medicine. Jehoiakim was a man of violence and a violent King. This became evident now that the hand of his father, which had weighed heavily on him, was removed. Though he had never before spoken to the people, he delivered to the citizens of Jerusalem a powerful and passionate speech that put all the blame on the previous reign and filled great and small with the diabolical satisfaction of knowing that they had no part in it, that all was now paid for, and that a new life could begin. The princes and dignitaries paid homage to Jehoiakim, the priests blessed him, and the Sagan hastened up breathlessly with the oil of anointing in order to crown him King.

With a sickly smile Jehoahaz stood in the midst of the surging tumult. Jeremiah had to support him, for he looked as if he were going to swoon. The Egyptian general read the message of Pharaoh, in which it was declared that Jehoahaz had forfeited the throne and was condemned to be a State prisoner of Egypt for life. His hands were bound with a long golden chain which did not deprive him of freedom of movement, and then his half-brother pronounced from the throne of Solomon a sentence of perpetual banishment against him, Hamutal, and Mattaniah. On the same day the beloved wife of Josiah had to leave the city, together with her two sons, as a prisoner of Pharaoh. Jeremiah remained faithful to them, and they were accompanied only by the eunuch and the Ethiopian boy Ebed-melech, in addition to a few servants and maids. Since the Egyptian embassy was in a hurry, it had brought with it the necessary horses and swift camels. Only a quarter of the usual time required by caravan was taken for the journey to Riblah, where Pharaoh had set up his headquarters. Neither Jehoahaz nor his mother was introduced into the presence of

Necho, but the dethroned king was relieved of his golden chain as a sign that he was in honourable captivity. A few days later came the order to take the prisoners to the port of Tyre, where an Egyptian ship was waiting for them. Although Jeremiah had not received permission from Pharaoh to accompany the exiles, the captain of the ship did not turn him back but let him go on board. Thus Adonai Himself released him and let him go.

With the whispered exhortation as he stood in front of the furnace in the goldsmith's shop, his native land again forced itself upon his mind together with all the sufferings that he had seen with his own eyes and experienced with his own soul.

Jeremiah was still standing in the same place, absorbed in an imaginary conversation with Baruch. . . . "May my friend Baruch forgive me," he mused, "for having deserted him, too, like a disloyal comrade before my journey was finished. . . . You shared my burden with me, Baruch, when I was still a boy, but I have sinned against you like a potter who has not completed his vessel, like an unworthy father and brother." Now that he felt what was almost a longing for the faithful Baruch, it seemed to him as if his disciple were laughing, as he often did when he wanted to disparage his own service or avoid Jeremiah's expression of gratitude. "Let my master not be anxious," he seemed to say, "but live his life in Noph."

Jeremiah looked up with a start. In his absorption he had not noticed that the craftsmen were everywhere taking down their booths and clearing away their utensils. The spacious square of Nu-Ptah was completely transformed. The people were moving off in the direction of the temple. Jeremiah, too, went back the way he had come and pushed his way among the thousands of people who were now occupying the steps of the hall of columns. He remembered that he had been told about a great festival that was to be celebrated on that day in and around the temple of Nu-Ptah from sunset until midnight. It was the twenty-fourth day of the month of Khoiak, the day of the winter solstice, the day of the redemption of Egypt's dead. They spoke of the "little sun" on that holy evening when Ptah, who had created himself out of nothing, assumed the suffering shape of Osiris. Why was the disk of the sun so small in the heavens? Because the realm of the dead had acquired power over the realm of the living and was drawing the star down with strong chains. That was why Ptah so graciously assumed the shape of Osiris, the murdered and resurrected god who descended into the realm of the dead every year to proclaim redemption and eternal life. By his descent he counteracted the power of the shadow over the living form, freed light from the danger of eternal setting, assured an even balance between the two worlds by restoring equilibrium to the oscillating scales. The hour when the redeemed god prepared to enter Amenti, the western realm of the dead, was celebrated by the priests and inhabitants of Nu-Ptah with the splendid procession that was now approaching before the eyes of the foreigner from Anathoth.

The "little sun" was just touching the summit of the step-pyramid which towered above the "western city" at the edge of the desert. The sunset was dull and misty, without gold or purple, appropriate to the misery of creation at a moment when the scales were tipping in favour of death. Men therefore had to help the deity who had furnished them with artificial light in the form of fire, and in the early dusk lights sprang up everywhere: torches, candles, lamps, chips of resinous wood, and wax tapers which were offered for sale by the thousand at every street corner. On the roofs of the houses and in the windows appeared smoky tripods, glowing charcoal braziers, and little flames without number, which with their dull red glow timorously accompanied the descent of the shivering sun to Amenti. Jeremiah soon distinguished the sound of approaching music. It affected him very differently from the psalms sung by the choirs in the Temple of the Lord. This music in Noph was a pleasant fluting, twittering, and tinkling, which flattered the ear and sweetly lulled the soul. The songs of the sons of Asaph rose to heaven like the arms of giants outstretched in supplication and challenge. The band of musicians who were approaching in rhythmic step was comprised of men and women blowing flutes and pipes, playing on hand harps and lutes, and beating little drums. They were all blind and had to be guided along their path by gentle tappings with a stick, as if they were sheep. In this land where everything consisted of images and idols, where the eye revelled in scenes which intoxicated it, how could the inner ear find the peace in which to listen to the worlds beyond visibility, even if they were only worlds of sound? Therefore the eyes of nearly all minstrels in Noph were closed for ever.

The dancing musicians were followed by the individual corporations of priests according to their rank and the secret significances of the procession. They were distinguished less by their garb than by the way in which their hair was dressed and their headgear. Some wore woven wigs embroidered with pearls; others wore towering head-dresses that reached down to their eyes. Those who belonged to the highest orders, and had therefore been initiated into secret lore, had had their skulls shaved and either went bareheaded or wore veils. All the priests without exception had on the stiff, short kilt, with a lion's tail depending from it, which was the festal garb of the gods themselves, who were imitated by their servants on earth during processions and important ceremonial sacrifices. More and more groups of baldheaded men approached in the flickering light. They walked with very short steps and kept their feet very close together. In the distance, where the red glow of light was most vivid, the sacred object which was the focus of the whole procession was swaying along. Jeremiah was struck by a sudden fear. He would have pushed his way through the crowd and run from the place if he had not been afraid that the worshippers of Ptah would strike him down. In a few moments they would all be bowing down before the deified nonentity that was the false creation of their own minds. And what was he to do? He realized in a flash the endless solicitude of the Lord, who took into account the frailty and wretchedness of His creatures. The commandment on Sinai concerning false gods was of a dual nature: "Thou shalt not bow down to their gods nor serve them!" If one bowed down, it did not mean that one also worshipped; and since one had not worshipped, neither had one broken the commandment. The bending of the back was but an empty gesture which the Lord overlooked when necessary. Now all the others were bowing down to the ground, and Jeremiah too lowered his head. None the less he could see the sacred bark *Hennu* being borne along on two long golden poles by nineteen priests, with the cabin-shrine rising from its midst with the glorious incorporation of Ptah. The keel of the boat ended in a gazelle's head and the bow in a large golden *ankh*, the sign of life. The figure of Ptah was enveloped in mummy wrappings, since he was offering himself up as Osiris and descending into the realm of the dead in order to redeem light. At his feet lay a scourge and a crook, the symbols of sovereignty of the god of the dead.

The sacred bark had swept past and a pious murmur began to rise from the crowd, filling the whole square of Nu-Ptah like a rising storm. Even the man from Judah felt, though he did not know why, a tightening of the heart. The backs of the people were bent lower and lower. Many fell upon their knees and pressed their faces to the ground. The word "Hapi," with its long *ā*-sound expressive of awe, shuddered through the crowd, and then the Apis came trotting along after an interval in the procession, led on a golden halter by venerable priestly attendants. It was not every generation that saw the rebirth of the Apis, which was the purest and most perfect incarnation of Osiris the Redeemer. Whole ages had gone by without witnessing the grace of this incarnation in living flesh. There were twenty-nine essential signs by which the initiated order of priests had to establish the authenticity of the incarnation beyond any possibility of doubt, before they could announce with profound emotion to the world and the age: "We have found an Apis." The most important of these essential signs were as follows: it must be a black bull of more than mighty size; it must have a white triangular patch on its forehead and a larger white patch on its back in the clearly discernible form of a hovering sparrow-hawk; the hairs of its tail must be of two colours, and under its tongue it must have a peculiar growth whose divine characteristics could be identified only by the hand of an initiated priest. Even if all the twenty-nine outward and inward signs were present without exception, there was still a spiritual and general quality that must be apparent before an ordinary bull could be transformed into "the pleasing image of the divine soul." It was the unique and matchless gentleness of the powerful god by which the true Apis was identified. It was the gracious characteristic of divine suffering, of the suffering of Osiris, which he bore in his meek bovine eye and which so profoundly stirred the emotions of Egypt.

In spite of his bowed head Jeremiah could see that the Apis of this age was a bull of enormous proportions. As if it were pervaded by the consciousness of its own divinity, the monstrous beast trippingly set one foot before the other. The pendulous dewlap hanging from its breast shook and swayed at every step. Yet in spite of its gigantic strength the bull was veiled in a cloud of holy gentleness and unearthly benevolence which so affected the inhabitants of Noph that many women burst into tears. Exactly opposite the spot where Jeremiah stood wedged in the crowd, the procession turned towards the north in order to reach the principal gate of the temple. Tripping along slowly, and cautiously treading the ground as if it were pushing the flickering air along in front of it, the Apis approached the place where Jeremiah was standing. With a majestic weariness it swished its tail across its flanks as if to ward off invisible blue-bottles, the troublesome visitants from the underworld. With solicitous attentiveness the two venerable priests who were holding the halter ropes on either side listened to hear the will of the divine bull. They did not lead it as a drover would do, but it appeared to be leading them, for they humbly followed it and kept the halter ropes slack. Just as they were about to turn northward they suddenly stopped, and with them the whole procession. The Apis had been pleased to halt. The enormous bull shook its black, broad-horned head several times, turned round suspiciously, sniffed the air mournfully with raised nostrils, snorted warningly, and finally sent a short accusing roar up to the evening sky. The Apis had called. The Apis had spoken. Nothing like that had happened during the procession of the little sun as far back as mankind could remember. Could the Apis have discovered a foe, an unbeliever, among the crowd, for even a god languished if he was denied? Had he sensed the presence of Adonai Elohim, the Eternal One who did not incorporate Himself in earthly forms, the Creator of heaven and earth who in Himself cancelled out all the forty-two trinities of Egypt and revealed their falseness? Was He whom Jeremiah had renounced still with him?

A tall figure tranquilly approached the Apis from behind. It was a priest with a yellowed, closely shaven skull, and the scourge and crook in his hand told the pious crowd that he belonged to one of the initiated orders and stood high in the service of Osiris. Jeremiah too recognized this authoritative personage, whose real name nobody knew, for in Nu-Ptah he was called only "the Kher-heb," which signified "the Master of Ceremonies of Death." The Kher-heb was the governor of the western city, the highest official and administrator of the realm of the dead. At the same time the government of Pharaoh had put him in charge of everything which bordered on the land of shadows, as for example, the care of State prisoners, the blind and the sick, and the widows and orphans of aristocratic families. He also exercised supervision over the exiled King of Judah, in whose house he appeared from time to time to pay a formal visit.

The Kher-heb stepped close up to the Apis. He laid his left hand, which carried the scourge, lightly on the bull's neck and stroked it almost imperceptibly. Then he inclined his shaven skull towards the gigantic head of the Apis as if he were ready in all humility to hear what it was that had frightened and disturbed the pleasing image of the soul of Osiris. This silent communion lasted only a moment. A dissolving feeling of pleasure, a trembling sense of relief, the joy of being understood, seemed to stream through the divine bull from its horns to its hoofs. It lowered its head with a tender caution, rubbed it twice with a noble gentleness against the shoulder of its understanding confidant, and thrust its brownish tongue between its lips to caress the Kher-heb's sallow cheeks. Then the Apis shook itself once more and resumed the sacred procession with tripping hoofs and rhythmically swishing tail.

The deep anxiety of the crowd was released in a rushing sigh. At the moment when Osiris was about to enter the realm of the dead, the Apis had emitted a sorrowful bellow, a sign that the god was exposed to grave dangers at the gates of the underworld. But when Osiris had overcome the dangers, a shudder of relief went through his pleasing image and he gratefully caressed his faithful guardian with his great tongue. It was a glorious omen! The little sun had conquered its weakness. A new epoch of prosperity was about to begin, a good year with ample inundations, excellent harvests, and busy markets. Subdued applause mingled with reverence showed the people's gratitude to the Kher-heb, the great personal physician of the god, the Pharaoh-like ruler of the other world, who was now again walking gravely and unmoved, with short steps and his feet very close together, after the Apis.

There was a subtle significance in the fact that the supreme controller of the realm of the dead was followed by a procession of gladness. Osiris had burst open the gates of Amenti. Now the beauty of all creation could pour after the resurrected sun. About a hundred of the most beautiful maidens of Noph symbolized this beauty of a world that the god had redeemed by his descent among the shades. The virgins were clad in transparent, gauze-like pleated dresses, adorned with many-hued capes, and wore wreaths of flowers. Each of them represented some branch of earthly activity and carried its symbol in front of her—ears of corn, a dish of fruits or vegetables, the pen, inkpot, and scroll of a scribe, a tiny loom, a dainty spindle, the bow and quiver of a huntsman, and everything else imaginable. The girls also carried hundreds of little papyrus boats, copies of the sacred bark, each with a little light in it, so that they had the effect of transparent lanterns. After the procession the blithe company of maidens would hasten to the shore of the Nile and send their shining boats sailing down the river.

Though this retinue of life and beauty was in charge of a master of ceremonies, yet there was no question of any real discipline. The young creatures seemed to be aware that their part in the procession was to depict not the rigid solemnity of the god, but the surging impulse and charming disorder of the whole breathing world. The delightful nature of the spectacle was, indeed, due to the fact that they depicted nothing at all, unlike the trained dancers who intentionally fitted themselves into a living picture. There was a confusion of laughing and babbling, a turning round and towards one another, a greeting and beckoning, a continual falling out of the ranks and never keeping in step, so that the master of ceremonies and his assistants had their work cut out to keep the procession moving at all. In the long almond-eyes of these young Egyptian women was an embarrassed shyness at thus showing themselves in public and at the same time a high-spirited desire to please and to attract attention. As the wreathed dance passed before Jeremiah's eyes, the hundredfold symbols of the busy world and all the shining papyrus boats of the sun that had set, each of the dancing-girls of Nu-Ptah seemed to look at him questioningly, at him alone. The man of Anathoth felt a painful unease. Was it exhorting him to pursue the consequences of having renounced his mission, to forget his origin and lose himself more and more among the beautiful images of life? Was it exhorting him to return home to the cruel and unfathomable battle for the Lord from whose militant service he had deserted? When the blithe company of maidens had passed, the crowd joined onto the procession with swinging torches. The flood of light stormed up the steps and the flowering columns of Noph blossomed in vivid beauty.

14

Zenua

On the day after the feast of the "little sun" the porter in the house of the exiles announced the visit of the Kher-heb. The day after the solstice and the three other days after the great yearly festivals of the sun were the times prescribed for the Chief Master of Ceremonies of Death in Noph to appear at the house of the unhappy Jehoahaz in his capacity as guardian of State prisoners. The house was in no way different from the colourful and airy mansions of the wealthy Egyptians, who lived outside the busy market quarter in suburbs that were well laid out with gardens. In addition to a considerable number of living-rooms and domestic offices, it possessed a pretty garden and a separate wing for the women. The exiles, however, who appeared to have forgotten the majestic proportions of their palace in Jerusalem, generally gathered in one room. For like all who suffer and mourn, they sought each other's company. It was a spacious and cheerful hall, decorated in a design of red and green, with a painted ceiling supported by three pairs of slender lotus columns of precious wood. Here Jeremiah was giving instruction to the growing Mattaniah and Ebed-melech at the moment when the Kher-heb's visit was announced. Hamutal was sitting by them, as she always did, and listening. Her beautiful large eyes no longer possessed the deep tranquillity with which she had so often soothed Josiah, and she had put off her flaming garments and jingling jewels for ever. None the less the beauty which she had sacrificed to her dead husband still illumined the grey of her widowhood. The one who seemed to bear his misfortune most lightly was Jehoahaz. Since living in Noph he had succumbed to a passionate activity which dissolved all his dull brooding in a zeal that gave him no time for thought. He was carving and carpentering all day long at little wooden figures of dolls, little chests and boxes, and all kinds of other objects whose form it was difficult to identify. His fingers had always been restlessly moulding some invisible material, and now the elegant art of Egypt had awakened his ability to use them in a branch of craftsmanship. A workshop had been set up for him in a corner of the lotus hall from which he hardly ever moved.

When the eunuch who had come with them from Jerusalem introduced the exalted visitor into their presence, Jehoahaz was squatting in his corner with his numerous carving tools, planes, and pots of glue, and he was making the chips fly. The Kher-heb had not appeared alone, but was accompanied by two other priests, elderly men like himself. What was surprising, however, was that the supreme controller of the realm of the dead was leading by the hand a young Egyptian girl, who kept her large eyes fixed with grave attention on Hamutal. Three lion-footed armchairs were placed together at a seemly distance for the Queen Mother, the King, and the Kher-heb, and they seated themselves while the others remained standing, Jeremiah and the boys behind the chair of Hamutal, the group of Egyptians behind that of the Kher-heb. Jeremiah, who had been about to withdraw with his pupils, was restrained by a gesture from the master of ceremonies. He could now examine the bald skull of the priest, his sallow face with its little sunken eyes, which were overhung by thick pads of flesh on which two thinly painted lines took the place of eyebrows. The Kher-heb spoke very slowly and distinctly, as if the correct and apt choice of each word was a matter of conscience. His manner of speaking was also scrupulously exact. The supple dialect of Nu-Ptah, which was perfectly suited to diplomatic conversations, possessed an inexhaustible fund of expressions for the finest shades of distinction and the niceties of privilege. It even furnished an adequate title for a deposed king like Jehoahaz, a prisoner without hope—a title which was neither too important nor too insignificant, so that it should not hurt the sensitive feelings of one who had fallen from his high estate. This title, so far as it could be translated, ran as follows: "His Royal Magnificence in Temporary Retirement." Such was the solemn manner of address with which the Kher-heb honoured Jehoahaz, while he addressed the Queen Mother, since she had not lost her rank, simply as "Your Grace." The guardian of the State prisoners took from his companions a roll of papyrus, which he put to his lips in sign of adoration but did not unfold. Then he announced to His Royal Magnificence in Temporary Retirement that he was to be favoured with the receipt of instructions from the exalted chancellery of the Father and Son of the Gods. Before he revealed the contents, he praised the supreme deities—including, as a matter of courtesy, the deity of the House of David at the end—that now, after sad complications, the land of Judah was entering upon a happier epoch through the favour of the kindly god. He recommended the royal exiles, in view of the gracious preservation of the kingdom and royal house of Jerusalem, no longer to regard their own fate with aversion. Only then did he unfold the roll of papyrus with his long, pointed fingers, cast a fleeting glance at the writing, and report in the following terms:

With the immeasurable kindness that was one of the qualities of light, Pharaoh had decided not to annul the existence of Judah, since he was content with the loyalty of the present King, to whom the overflowing graciousness of his solar nature had granted everything, even the new name which he bore. Jehoiakim had furnished the proofs of his attachment to the full extent that had been required of him, particularly by the punctual payment of the war indemnity which had been calculated in such just and lenient fashion by the exalted councillors of the Sun God on earth.

The Kher-heb mentioned a figure that struck even the dull intelligence of Jehoahaz like a blow with a club—a hundred talents of silver and one talent of gold. This was more than a hundred hundredweight of silver and gold, the transport of which would require several wagons. How must Jehoiakim have despoiled the land, both in the marble palaces of the rich and the clay huts of the peasants, in order to collect this enormous weight of precious metal with which he had purchased the favour of Pharaoh! Jeremiah, however, realized that Necho probably had other reasons for sparing the defeated country than the payment of the indemnity. Could the Lord really have spoken to Hananiah and not to him? Had the handsome prophet of Gibeon, who wore his hairy cloak like a disguise, predicted the truth about Egypt? Had the Nile, streaming northwards with its hosts of armed men, really dried up in the Land of Rivers?

Jeremiah's thoughts were interrupted by the voice of the Kher-heb. It was a strangely faded voice, as faded as the colour of his bare and venerable skull. It was obvious to Jeremiah that what it was saying held no interest for the priest, and that for all his careful choice of words the affairs to which the Kher-heb was referring were matters of complete indifference to him. He was performing a minor duty of his office which left him quite cold.

"The kindly god," he said, "wishes to improve the situation of His Royal Magnificence in Temporary Retirement. He extends the favour, which by his nature as a ray of light he cannot limit, to the whole of the royal house at present sheltering in Noph and grants it freedom to move about at will within the region, under the sole condition that a change of residence shall always be reported to the chancellery of the Kher-heb."

This was an empty formality! What could Jehoahaz and Hamutal do with their circumscribed freedom? It meant nothing at all. More agreeable, on the other hand, was the gift of a carriage and horses, which were to be handed over to them that same day. And yet another privilege, the greatest of all, was to be accorded to Hamutal.

"Your Grace once confessed to me," continued the Kher-heb, weighing each word as he turned to the Queen Mother, "that she greatly felt the lack of the company of a sympathetic and understanding heart. I have therefore chosen for her the sympathetic and understanding heart of a young companion. . . ."

With these words the Kher-heb rose, took the Egyptian maiden by the hand, and led her to Hamutal's chair:

"This is Ha-rekhni. She is a member of the ancient and venerable family of May-Ptah and was orphaned at an early age. Her father, now immortalized in identification with Osiris, was a privy councillor and controller of the staple markets of the kindly god in a northern country beyond the frontiers. Her childhood was passed on the borders of Your

Grace's country and her ear rejoices to hear Your Grace's language."

The rejoicing to which the Kher-heb referred was certainly not evident in the expression on Ha-rekhni's face, which was unusually attentive and thoughtful. She was tall and slim, and her eyes had nothing in common with the inviting almond-eyes of the young Egyptian maidens who had symbolized the beauty of life in the sacred procession of the "little sun" on the previous day. The orphan's eyes were filled with a contemplative peace, and with something else which it was not easy to name. Hamutal, however, was overjoyed, for she really had longed for the sympathetic and understanding companionship of a member of her own sex. She rose quickly from her chair, drew Ha-rekhni towards the light, searched her face with an excited smile, and pressed the alien girl to her heart in a sudden excess of feeling.

The Kher-heb had shown particular perception in choosing Ha-rekhni from among all the orphans entrusted to his care. It was not only in the subtle idiom of a cultured language that a sympathetic and understanding heart had come to join the exiles in their house at Noph. It soon became evident that Ha-rekhni's grave thoughtfulness and contemplative calm did not spring from any hidden melancholy of her nature, but on the contrary from a measured serenity which was very agreeable to a family living in a foreign land. The presence of this alien girl in the lotus hall brought not only to Hamutal, but to all of them, a comfort and relief which prevented the mutual exasperation to which people living too closely together might so easily have been exposed.

Jeremiah usually imparted instruction to the boys during the two hours before noon. As had been the case at home in Jerusalem, the part which the boys liked best was that which consisted of the stories and discussions in which their teacher, following up the passages he had read, touched upon all kinds of matters concerning heaven and earth. As a continual stream of fresh and interesting stories and experience poured from the lips of Jeremiah, the shining eyes of the moody Mattaniah never left his face, and even Ebed-melech's limbs ceased to twitch. The Ethiopian boy had now reached his eleventh year, and was beginning to have an inkling of the honour which had been accorded him by the privilege of participating in religious instruction to which he was not entitled either by descent or by rank. One could see in his eyes the desperate efforts he made to concentrate his thoughts and fight down the demon in his soul which kept on asking meaningless questions. Jeremiah's lessons were listened to not only by the Queen Mother but also by the servants of the household, whenever they happened to be free. They would hang on his lips and repeat to themselves in a murmur the words which conjured up their homeland and moreover refreshed their hearts with the deeds and sayings of the True God who like them was a stranger in the land. Only Jehoahaz did not allow Jeremiah's eloquence to disturb him in his carving and planing, the indefatigable activity of his fingers which provided him with compensation for the bitter stagnation of his mind. Now and then he would hammer away mercilessly in his corner while Jeremiah was speaking, as if he wanted to pierce with angry nails the Law of the Lord who had meted out such grievous injustice to his father and himself.

Jeremiah's most loyal listener, however, was Ha-rekhni. While Hamutal sat on one of the lion-footed armchairs, the girl would squat close beside her on the ground; or rather, she knelt in the charming way that was customary among young Egyptian ladies. The light burden of her body rested upon the heel of her right foot, whose narrow sole was visible, while the left knee, thrust forward at a right angle, was on a level with her breast. She could stay in this position for two hours without growing tired or impatient. Her wide-opened eyes gazed thoughtfully in front of her as she pondered with slightly wrinkled brow on the words which came to her ears, for she was not content merely to listen. The Kher-heb had not exaggerated. Ha-rekhni really did understand the language of the Lord, though not perfectly and not always in the pure dialect of Judah. The longer she lived in the house, the more rarely did she have to ask for the meaning of a word. Even less familiar terms seemed gradually to be recalled to her memory from a fund that she had once gathered, and whenever she discovered such a term in her own mind and gave hesitant utterance to it she would laugh shyly and blush.

The daughter of "the privy councillor and controller of the staple markets of the Kindly God in a northern country beyond the frontiers now immortalized in identification with Osiris" had spent her childhood in Gaza, the capital and port of the Philistines, not far from the borders of Judah. The deceased official had held the office of governor of the port, and this showed that Pharaoh respected the name of the ancient family of May-Ptah, but at the same time desired to keep its bearer at a distance from his court. The reason for this gracious disfavour was apparently unknown to Ha-rekhni. The language of the Philistines had to a slight extent approximated to the language of the Lord in the course of generations, but it was by no means sufficiently similar to explain Ha-rekhni's knowledge. Perhaps she had been brought up by nurses and governesses from the land of Adonai Elohim, whose songs and proverbs she was now recalling to memory. She did not speak about it to anyone, and Hamutal refrained from questioning her.

Jeremiah, who felt his powers of eloquence increasing from day to day, let his glance fall on the Egyptian maiden now and then while he was giving his lesson. In spite of her seriousness and self-control she could not conceal on her still childlike features the look that would come into them when he said something that she recognized. They would be lit up by sudden comprehension or darkened by pondering over something which puzzled her, and they were always filled with a whole-hearted absorption in the words to which she was listening.

One day she went up to Jeremiah after the midday repast as he was walking in the garden, and asked:

"By what name may your servant address you?"

These were the first words that she had ever addressed to him directly. Jeremiah cast down his eyes. The close proximity of a young woman filled him with a torturing shyness. She, however, was not shy at all, but answered the question herself without waiting for his reply:

"I shall call you what Mattaniah calls you: 'My teacher!' . . . That is, if you do not mind and will allow Ha-rekhni to do so."

He looked up, smiled, and nodded. She did not return his smile, but her face showed the serious resolution which often caused her brow to wrinkle.

"I should like to serve your God," she said briefly.

To his own astonishment he felt embarrassed at these words.

"He is not *my* God," he replied, "any more than He

is not *your* God. He is both your God and mine."

She thought over this answer keenly for a while. Then she looked at him with one of her long searching glances. "That which you have said, my teacher, is perhaps very true in so far as it concerns me . . . but I wish that He who is my God should *really* become my God."

She raised her slender hand as if to make a vow, but Jeremiah remained aloof and gave her no further help, though he would have liked to do so. She left him swiftly with bowed head. The first conversation between Jeremiah and Ha-rekhni had been austere and awkward.

Her longing for Jeremiah's God was no light-hearted dream on the part of the Egyptian orphan, but a consuming fire. The first conversation was followed by others, which soon became a matter of daily custom for the sake of which Jeremiah gave up his daily walk to the great square of Nu-Ptah.

In the centre of the garden was a pleasantly walled pool where decorative fishes flitted to and fro in flashes of red and silver light, and whose surface was covered with water lilies which at sunset closed their petals like delicate hands. Ha-rekhni and Jeremiah would sit side by side on the edge of the pool under a sky that was filled with the hovering and swooping sparrow-hawks of Ptah. She sat with knees drawn up and elbows pressed close to her sides, while her long-fingered hands rested with well-bred immobility in her lap; her eyes refrained from meeting his, and she gazed with wrinkled brow at her slender feet, which were always bare except when she left the house.

"I wish that my teacher would reveal to me," she insisted obstinately, "how I am to begin to serve the Lord."

Jeremiah's heart had already been moved by the girl's unceasing attempts to approach the Eternal One. He had never meant to lead any individual soul among the nations towards the Lord. The relations of the God of Abraham, Isaac, and Jacob to His people and to the other nations were too complicated to render desirable a light-hearted and unregulated admixture of faiths. It was not individual souls, but the nations as such, who would one day advance to the pure acknowledgment and service of the Lord, gathering round the sacred focus of the Temple as united peoples. None the less, Jeremiah was pervaded by a pleasurable warmth as he sat at the side of this maiden who was so filled with longing for the Lord, and he said with a smile:

"Ha-rekhni serves Our Lord by loving Him."

This evasive answer dissatisfied her.

"A love which remains within the heart is nothing at all. How could Ha-rekhni love without sacrifice? Let my teacher tell me how I am to sacrifice to the Lord."

"There is only one place in the whole world," Jeremiah replied, "where one can sacrifice to Him."

She tossed her head angrily.

"Jeremiah is very crafty. But Ha-rekhni is not quite so simple as he appears to think. The power of a god lies in the sacrifices of men. His heart is strengthened by offerings, consecrations, and incense. And He finds his greatest comfort in the gifts which we find it difficult to make. When I was a little girl I gave my little singing bird, which I greatly loved, to the cow-headed Hathor; and Isis, who is the wisest of all the supreme gods of Egypt, has received from me more than one golden trinket, though I am poor. Tell me what I am to sacrifice to the Lord, who has created all the worlds and all the gods who are less than Himself."

Jeremiah had to keep his voice lowered in order to remain calm.

"Did not Ha-rekhni hear me repeat the words in my lesson yesterday which the Lord spoke through the mouth of Samuel the prophet? To obey is better than sacrifice! The greatest gift that we can offer Him is to accept His gift, the commandments."

Ha-rekhni's answer was coloured by a slight touch of annoyance.

"My teacher often asks Mattaniah about the commandments and receives only stammering answers. Why does he not sometimes ask Ha-rekhni, who is sitting at his side, in order that he may search her understanding?"

She was silent for a while. Then her voice grew shy and anxious, as if she had made up her mind to ask something which was very foolish and at the same time forbidden.

"Is the Lord really quite invisible?"

"There is no eye of created man which can see Him."

"Yes, but . . . Let not Jeremiah turn away his ear even if I should say something very sinful. . . . The Sun God appears in the sun, as all the world, both wise and simple, is aware. He is visible and at the same time invisible. The god passes across the heavens in his bark, but the eye of created man cannot bear to look upon him."

"The sun is not the Lord, but a creation of the Lord."

"And the lightning?"

"The lightning is not the Lord; the Lord is the power that sends the lightning forth."

"And the storm?"

"The storm is not the Lord; the Lord is the will that unchains the storm."

Jeremiah felt a peculiar joy in the girl's stubbornness. He

took her hand, which was very cool, and in her eyes he could see that her mind was still working. Suddenly he felt a faint pressure from her cool fingers.

"And yet, my teacher, I could wish that the Invisible One would make Himself just a little more visible. . . ."

She lifted her eyes to the deep-blue afternoon sky, under which the proud sparrow-hawks were hovering and wheeling. Her next words sounded slow and weary, as if the agitation within her and her striving to understand the unincorporated God had exhausted her strength.

"Let Jeremiah look at the sparrow-hawks up there, whose dwelling place nobody knows. . . . They are the winged images of Ptah. . . . And the adored Apis, which its attendants serve upon their knees, is the pleasing image of the soul of Osiris. . . . And Osiris, the hero and redeemer who descends into the realm of the dead, has a faithful help in the barking Anubis, with its jackal's head. . . . The priest recognizes in the eyes of many a dog the true image of the soul of Anubis, who runs before the hero in the underworld. . . . Thus every deity has its visible and living image, so that it may be among us . . . and we make images of all these images, not only the great ones in the temples, but also the little ones in our houses. . . . For the hour comes when one is alone and afraid, and one must kindle a light before the deities, consecrate a bunch of flowers, and burn incense, that the anxious heart may be calmed. . . . Now Ha-rekhni is told that this is all very wicked, very sinful. . . . Yet let my teacher at last instruct me which, among all the images in the world, is the image of the Invisible One. . . ."

Under the warm touch of Jeremiah's hand, the hand of Ha-rekhni, too, had grown warm, but he did not loosen his clasp.

"Has my pupil," he asked, "not already received her answer? Is it not said of Him that He created man in His own image?"

For the first time since they had been speaking she turned her eyes full upon him.

"So men are the images of the Invisible One just as the sparrow-hawks up there are the images of Ptah?"

"It is as Ha-rekhni says. . . . But do not speak of the sparrow-hawks, and do not compare the real with the unreal."

Her eyes darkened with her effort to understand.

"All men? Are the sick, the crippled, the possessed, the fools, and the blasphemers also images of the Lord?"

Jeremiah thought that he had never argued with a more difficult questioner and reasoner.

"Let Ha-rekhni understand," he said, "that much corruption has come over the image and many a vessel been marred and cast aside like clay in the potter's hands."

At these words the girl was seized with a strange indignation. She tore her hand away violently and the blood rushed to her cheeks.

"I do not believe and will not believe that all men are the image of the Lord . . . for I firmly believe and insist on believing that only one man is the image of the Lord . . . Jeremiah!"

They both sprang up in sudden fright. She turned her head away in confusion and stammered:

"Let Jeremiah take me to the Temple, that I may offer a sacrifice to the Lord of whom he is the image."

"Ha-rekhni!" he implored her.

With her face still turned away she whispered:

"Ha-rekhni, the daughter of Osiris May-Ptah, is called

Ha-rekhni. . . . Yet once my mother called me by another name . . . by a secret name in the language of the Lord."

"And do you still remember what it was?" asked Jeremiah, who was overcome with excitement.

Ha-rekhni looked at him thoughtfully and shook her head.

"How should I remember the name when I cannot remember my mother, neither her voice nor her face? . . ."

Her confession brought to his lips something that had often occupied his reveries but which he had never consciously admitted to himself. With a tender solemnity he made the gesture of laying his hands on her head, but without touching it.

"I take from you the name of Ha-rekhni and, like your mother, I give you a name in the language of the Lord. Henceforth you shall be called Zenua!"

The Egyptian girl stood motionless for a while with her eyes half closed. Then she moved away from Jeremiah towards the pool and looked at her shadowy reflection in the darkening waters between the closed lilies and the lotus blossoms. She bowed low in farewell and cried out: "Ha-rekhni has gone!" Then she turned her face, which had grown very pale, towards Jeremiah and, without moving from where she stood, announced: "Zenua comes!"

Thereupon she raised her cupped hands to the sky with a joyful laugh in which there was a tremble of ecstasy.

"God of Jeremiah! Receive Zenua!"

15

Zenua Is Received

Jeremiah had long ago heard the voice warning him not to take a wife unto himself, and it had been followed by two further strange admonitions which commanded him never to enter a house of feasting or a house of mourning. They had long since slipped from his memory, perhaps because he had never had any intention of taking a wife. It may often have seemed to him, as to every healthy man in Judah and Israel, wrong and contrary to the will of the Lord that a branch on the tree of Jacob should wither and die without bearing fruit, and his mother had for years implored him not to call down the wrath of God by evading a solemn duty. He had already passed the age considered suitable for marriage and his manhood was approaching its zenith. His mother was not accustomed to using empty words, and she pointed to more than one maiden of their acquaintance who in her opinion would make a suitable and worthy wife for her youngest son. Jeremiah would object and ask: "Why does my mother want to make one of these pleasing creatures unhappy with a man who carries the heavy burden of the Lord and may not speak of it?" "I shall find a wife who will lighten the burden of the Lord for my son." "Every burden is doubled when one takes a wife, Mother!" "What does my son know about women? Your father had much bitterness in his heart, and every night he would wake me twice or three times because he had to speak to someone about this bitterness he bore in his heart. I would awaken and listen and join in his laments and scoldings, even though he included me in his accusations. Who will awaken at the side of my youngest son to listen to him when the time comes that he cannot sleep, as was the case with his father?"

Jeremiah generally broke off these conversations with his mother by pointing out that he could not plan his life without definite sanction from the Lord. The warning that had come to him so long ago had escaped from his mind, yet he was still aware of it in his soul as a vague constraint when the subject of marriage arose.

Now it seemed as if this vague constraint had disappeared for ever and extinguished his scruples, but it merely seemed so, for it was only by a great effort that he had been able to overcome it and banish it from his soul. He convinced himself that the Lord, whom he had renounced, had changed His mind after long hesitation and brought the young Egyptian woman to him in order that he might take her to wife. By this gracious act the Lord had finally granted His sanctified prophet permission to leave His service and share the unburdened fate of mankind somewhere in the world. Were there not signs in plenty that admitted such an interpretation of the Lord's will? Zenua was not wholly a stranger. Though she did not remember her mother, yet there was considerable evidence that the wife of the immortalized governor of the port of Gaza may have been a daughter of Israel. In no other way could it be explained why the orphan of Nu-Ptah had been able to master the language of the Lord with such ease and fluency, recalling forgotten words to memory. Even more significant than this participation in the House of Jacob was the fact that Zenua had always sought the Lord in her heart, offering Him indeed a greater love than He received from His own people. Was it not a wondrously clear proof that this Egyptian maiden, not yet eighteen years old and the heathen ward of the Kher-heb, who controlled the realm of the dead in the name of Osiris, should have seen the light of the Lord with so little aid from any human being despite the fact that her soul was deeply imbued with the gods of the forty-two regions? Was not the hand of the Lord obvious in this miracle? And was not this hand brushing away with unusual perceptibility the familiar reasons which rendered it inadvisable "to love strange women," who smuggled their heathen deities into the House of Jacob through the back door, as had been true with King Solomon? Zenua resembled only one strange woman, Ruth the Moabitess, who had been chosen to be the ancestress of David.

Her ardent love of God went so far that she appeared to love Jeremiah not for his own sake, but for the sake of the Lord who had sanctified him. Hamutal soon realized, to her great joy, that Jeremiah and Zenua loved each other. Yet they never spoke of their love, since their conversation was devoted exclusively to God. Only now and then, for a fleeting moment or two, was there an ecstatic mingling of the two objects of their love. Then their hands would meet in a soft caress, or rather in a rapturous desire to caress, for Zenua would immediately draw back. Thus began a singular betrothal such as had never been seen before, a betrothal in which all the outpourings of the heart were devoted to the things of heaven more than to those of earth. Jeremiah felt a new freedom. While he spoke with Zenua of the Lord he was in reality able to move further and further away from Him. It was only now that he was able completely to escape from the task that had been laid upon his shoulders. Yet there was a paradox in this form of escape, since he imagined that he was again coming closer to Him who had charged him with the task. He had come to Egypt in order to hide from God in the land of the three hundred and seventy-eight gods, but even Egypt had not been able to conceal him entirely from the eyes of his Pursuer. Only his love for a woman had furnished him with an impenetrable hiding-place. Since, however, this love was rapturously directly towards the Lord, Jeremiah had no inkling of his own self-deception. He was guarding himself against the disfavour of the Lord as he had always warned others to do. But frequently, in the darkness of the night, he was assailed by fears for Zenua. He could not help thinking of King Josiah. Did he not bring misfortune upon everybody to whom he became attached?

The betrothal brought radiant happiness to a third person, to Hamutal. Her large eyes recovered their old lustre, and her figure, in spite of the drab mourning garments, almost regained its former comeliness. She loved Jeremiah as the last consoler of the fallen hero and the only friend who had voluntarily maintained his loyalty and not abandoned her in her exile. In Zenua, however, she saw a symbol of love itself, which filled her with a maternal or sisterly satisfaction. Without the Queen, the power that drew Jeremiah and Zenua together would not so readily have become apparent, for they were both shy and elusive. With all the zeal of a woman who had suddenly been given a new interest in life through solicitude and sympathy for others, Hamutal took the girl aside and encouraged her to puzzle out for herself what it was that filled her with an embarrassed and burning rapture. The long, whispered conversations between the two women were also a glorious outpouring of the heart, though in this case it had little to do with the things of heaven. They wove their exciting plans without consulting Jeremiah at all, and Hamutal arranged matters so wisely as far as he was concerned that everything happened opportunely without first having to be discussed in detail. Through her mediation there was no need for words and they became betrothed almost imperceptibly. Hamutal carried her cheerful solicitude even further, so that the essential preliminaries to their marriage passed for the lovers as if in a dream.

Since the earliest time there had lived in Noph a small congregation of Israel which had maintained the purity of its religion. It possessed a house of assembly and teaching as well as its own burial ground, and every year the pious men made a pilgrimage to Jerusalem at Passover in order to sacrifice in the Temple. At the head of this congregation was an old priest who acted as judge in the settlement of disputes, circumcised the newly born boys, received the thirteen-year-old youths into the community of the pious, celebrated marriages, and performed the last rites for the dead. This venerable man was invited by Hamutal to come and see her. He listened to what she had to say and, after some consideration, declared his readiness to introduce the Egyptian orphan into the House of Jacob and to marry her to the priest's son from Anathoth, since she loved the Lord as ardently as Ruth had done.

Hamutal also did what was necessary on the other side, which seemed likely to be more difficult. The month of Nisan had come, the feast of Passover had gone by, and the State visit of the Kher-heb had again become due on the day when Osiris emerged at the other end of Amenti after his journey through the world of the dead. He appeared punctually together with his two subordinate priests. The lion-footed armchairs were again placed in position and the dethroned young King had reluctantly to leave the corner where he was working and exchange courteous conversation with the Master of Ceremonies of Death. His eyes roamed desperately round the lotus hall while his empty hands fidgeted impatiently. The Kher-heb inquired in delicate and tactful phraseology after the welfare of the State prisoners and asked if they had any wishes that he might lay at the feet of the Father and Son of the Gods. He was eager to know whether they were adequately supplied with comforts and whether His Royal Magnificence in Temporary Retirement had discovered any defects in the coach and horses that had been put at his disposal from the divine stables. Hamutal, quite contrary to her usual custom, was enthusiastic and eloquent on the subject of Pharaoh's gracious gifts and the proofs of his superhuman kindness and favour, so that the bald, sallow pate of the Kher-heb turned towards her with grave attention. She declared that, apart from the mournful events which had banished them to Nu-Ptah, the King of Judah and his mother were well content and had no further favour to ask, since through the kind offices of the Kher-heb the sympathetic and understanding heart had become their most intimate companion. Would that their charming friend could be with them for all time! . . . After this significant sigh Hamutal rose and requested the Kher-heb to accompany her to another room, whither Jeremiah and Zenua were soon summoned to join them.

The tall lean figure of the Kher-heb stood in front of the couple, as he regarded the man and the girl with stony eyes whose gaze was turned inwards. There was a long and oppressive interval before he opened his mouth to speak.

It was, he said, a serious matter to change one's gods. Not

serious for the gods, who were immutable, but for the mortals who dared to make the change. Such a venture might only too easily cause the human soul to be transported to the world between, over which neither the old gods nor the new had any power. Then the soul would be menaced by the most horrible of all perils, the danger of "falling out of the world." A soul which had fallen out of the world in this way was "rejected" in an awe-inspiring sense of the word; it was at home in no created place and was excluded from every community, even that of the dead, for the mercies which sprang from the sacrifice of Osiris were available only to those who had been immortalized with holy natron and lasting wrappings and who had never ceased to adore him. Therefore, any soul which intended to change its gods should first envisage with wisdom and forethought the terrible peril to which it was exposed.

Zenua had been gazing fixedly in front of her with wrinkled brow, as she always did when she was thinking intently. Suddenly she tossed back her head so violently that her hair became loosened and fell over her coloured cape like that of a dancer.

"My soul loves Adonai, the God of this man, the Invisible, Unique, and Eternal One, and my soul puts its trust in Him. He does not allow a soul to fall out of the world, and He will not reject me."

Hamutal, who was standing to one side, blanched at the girl's bold words, which regarded a warning of the supreme initiated priest of Nu-Ptah as if it were nothing. The Kherheb, however, did not seem at all put out, but even permitted the shadow of a faint smile to flit across his pale lips.

"I knew that Ha-rekhni of the ancient and noble family of May-Ptah would not speak otherwise. I honour the resolution of her sympathetic heart. But to a guardian falls the duty of instructing his wards concerning the dangers they may encounter. Let Ha-rekhni not put her trust in that which she inherits from her mother. One's gods are determined not by that which comes from the mother, but by that which comes from the father. Nor let Ha-rekhni put her trust in the compassion of the gods. Let her note that it is permissible to implore the compassion of a god, but not to put one's trust in it. Whether the gods will be merciful or wrathful, favourable or unfavourable, is hidden from mortal eyes."

At these words the Kher-heb looked from Zenua to Jeremiah. The latter shivered inwardly at the forbidden and dreadful thought that this man of Osiris, whose mouth was full of the names of vain deities, might also in some mysterious way be in communion with Adonai, the God of the universe. The Kher-heb's eyes, however, moved from Jeremiah as if he found nothing worth fathoming in the face of this alien bridegroom. He addressed no word to him, but raised his right hand, which held the elegant scourge of Osiris, and pointed silently to Zenua's left wrist. Like all Egyptians, both men and women, she wore close-fitting bands of coloured stuff on each wrist. On the inner side of these bands were sewn narrow strips of papyrus covered with delicate writing. That which the inhabitants of Noph wore on the right hand represented in hieroglyphs the spine of Osiris. This amulet was called "Ded" and signified the restoration and resurrection of the dismembered god from the separate vertebræ, and therewith the hope of resurrection for the wearer of the symbol. It was not removed from a corpse, so that it might accompany the mummy until the day of decision.

The strip of papyrus on the left band was called "the secret memorandum of life," in short, "Anekh." The head of the strip was adorned with the *ankh* as the sign of life. Then came most important data for the destiny of the wearer: the horoscopes of himself and his parents, the name of the Apis which had been reborn in his generation, and some highly secret characters which could be understood only by those who had passed successfully through all the schools of initiation. It was this secret memorandum of life that the Kher-heb demanded from Zenua, and she slipped it reluctantly from her left wrist. The Kher-heb became absorbed in his study of the writing of destiny, and it was a long time before he again lifted his head. He raised slightly the bare, fleshy pads of his painted brows, but it was not possible to gather from his pale, immeasurably tranquil eyes anything of the human fate which he appeared irrevocably to have calculated. Jeremiah's throat was constricted by a sudden fear at this cool reserve. The Kher-heb turned slowly towards Hamutal, who was awaiting his words with eager excitement.

"The marriage covenant between Ha-rekhni, the orphaned daughter of the house of May-Ptah, and this man from a foreign country is not opposed by her guardian. . . ."

Jeremiah and Zenua were silent, but Hamutal began to thank him volubly. She had not expected that things would take such an easy turn. The Kher-heb, however, interrupted her.

"I would recommend Your Grace not to fix the marriage ceremony before the little sun of Osiris has completed its transformation to the great eye of Horus, at the beginning of the summer, after my next visit."

The guardian of the State prisoners turned to go. As he took leave he passed his sallow, priestly hand lightly over Zenua's head. It was a gesture that might have had two or even three interpretations. Did it signify felicitation and friendly consent? Was it a kindly surrender of Zenua to her bridegroom? Or was it a caress of pity for what was to come?

On the evening of that day Jeremiah asked Zenua to remove from her wrists the two bands with Ded and Anekh. (They were standing, as they often did, at the pool in the garden, where, thanks to Hamutal's care, there was a profusion of flowers. The sparrow-hawks of Ptah were wheeling and swooping under a sky in which the sun had not yet set.) Jeremiah had never given the girl such pleasure as he did by this request. A little cry of satisfaction escaped her lips. Swiftly stripping off the bands as if they were poisonous, she cast them into the green depths of the water. Her words were a sigh of relief:

"How long Zenua has waited for this command! It is the first sacrifice that she has been allowed to offer to the Lord in Jeremiah and to Jeremiah in the Lord. . . ."

She hesitated, and then added in tortured accents:

"Alas, it is no sacrifice at all! I am only freeing myself. . . ."

Jeremiah did not altogether understand what she meant by "freeing" herself. But she drew him down beside her on the edge of the pool, and he noticed that she was struggling with something which it cost her a terrible effort to speak about.

"My bridegroom should know," she began laboriously, "that something very mysterious, something very terrifying happened to his bride when the Kher-heb read the signs of her destiny. Will my bridegroom be angry?"

"How could the bridegroom be angry with the bride who has made the sacrifice for which he asked?"

"It concerns Osiris. . . . It concerns the teaching in which Ha-rekhni was brought up."

"Then it concerns that which Zenua has cast from her. . . ."

She laughed tremulously, like a child in the dark trying to instil courage into itself.

"Nevertheless, with the bridegroom's permission the bride will regard it as a good and favourable omen."

He put his arm round Zenua's shoulders to help her. With strained eyes she looked down at the ground. Suddenly she pushed three stones together with the tip of her foot and whispered:

"This is Jeremiah. . . . This is the Kher-heb. . . . This is Zenua. . . . The guardian stood between the bride and bridegroom and separated them. . . . Then it happened that . . ."

She ceased to speak. Jeremiah pressed her to him.

"Let Zenua have no fear. Jeremiah is protecting her, and she is protected by the Lord to whom she is going."

"It was my leave-taking from the gods of Nu-Ptah," she whispered shudderingly. "Perhaps Zenua had already fallen out of the world and been excluded from every community after my guardian spoke. . . . For who has ever experienced it and been able to say what he felt? . . . At first I was unable to see Jeremiah, for whom I was longing. . . . He was hidden by the Kher-heb . . . but I could not move either. . . ."

Jeremiah felt that her whole body was trembling and that her limbs had grown cold. Hesitantly, in short sentences, she described her sensation of being far away from this world with her senses fully awake:

"Zenua had become Osiris, the god whose body grows

rigid and for whom Isis and Nephthys mourn. And she grew very tall and was much taller than the Kher-heb and Jeremiah, whom she was again able to see. . . . Let my bridegroom hear me! His bride had become a rigid pillar and could not move. . . ."

She looked at him with a pleading smile.

"It brings good luck to see such things in a vision, doesn't it? Tell me that it brings good luck. . . . For that was not all . . . Zenua was holding Khaïb, the cooling fan, in her stony hand, the fan which is made out of all the shadows one casts. . . . But as she was a nerveless pillar she had to let the fan fall . . . and two great birds flew out of her heart. . . . It hurt so, it hurt. . . ."

She broke off and closed her eyes. There were tears on her lashes.

"Does my bridegroom know what birds they were that flew with such cruel pain from the heart of his bride? . . . Oh, he does not know them. . . . Bā, my spirit, rose up at once to join the other sparrow-hawks of the sun . . . but Kā, the soul of my soul, the love of my love, the swallow, wanted to escape and alight on Jeremiah's shoulder, to stay there peacefully and be quite still and happy. . . . But the swallow was not allowed to do this, however much it twittered . . . the pillar would not let it go. . . . It had to fly round the stiff pillar, round and round, all the time . . . the pillar that was myself. . . ."

Zenua's head had sunk lower and lower over her lap, and she was now shaken by the convulsive fit of weeping that she had been suppressing for so long. Jeremiah spoke to her gently:

"Zenua was taking leave of the twilit house. That is what it was. . . . And the confusion came over her for the last time in the form of a frightening vision. . . . But now she is stepping out of the darkness and coming to the Lord . . . and He is strong as a citadel, and will protect and defend her. . . ."

"Yes, my bridegroom," she cried, though her sobs still came intermittently, "I know that He is strong, stronger than all the others. . . . He must protect me, that I may not fall into the world between! . . ."

Jeremiah felt a rush of apprehension and doubt. How could he, who had renounced his task, assure Zenua of the strength and comfort of the Lord as if he knew His secret intentions? Yet there was no return for him, so he suppressed the painful feelings by which he was assailed and told Zenua of the decision which he came to on the spur of the moment:

"We will take no heed of the Kher-heb's advice. We will not wait until the summer solstice. . . . I do not like Ab, the hot summer month. . . . We shall conquer the world between if we marry after the new moon. . . . Will you marry me then, my bride?"

Her trust in his words and belief that he would save her shone through the traces of her tears.

"I will, my bridegroom!"

They both went to find Hamutal and inform her of their decision. The Queen hesitated as she thought of the Kher-heb's warning, but now it was Zenua who laughingly dispersed her scruples, which belonged to the world of confusion that she believed she had abandoned for ever, having sacrificed it, after a last relapse, to the strong heart of Jeremiah.

Nevertheless, the ceremony of marriage had suddenly to be

postponed, for on the day before the new moon something happened which filled the hearts of the exiles with dread. The sun had not yet risen and the last night watch was still on duty in the waning darkness, when the porter roused the whole household with the agitated announcement that a man had come from Jerusalem who desired to speak with the King and his mother without delay. The secret messenger (for it could be no one else) insisted on his demand in spite of the early hour and the fact that the King was fast asleep. In expectation of important news they all assembled with pale faces in the lotus hall, including Mattaniah, Jeremiah, and Zenua. In the foreboding twilight of early morning and the dying gleam of a coal fire, Jeremiah perceived the presumed messenger, a tall, lank man, casting himself on the ground at the feet of Jehoahaz and Hamutal. He presented a terrible figure, with his cloak and coat hanging from his body in rags as he cowered on the ground. His feet were bleeding and his legs were caked with dried mud to the knee, as if he had been wading through the marshes of the Nile delta. In a voice for which he seemed hardly to have sufficient breath he groaned thickly:

"I have been held worthy to look upon the face of the true King . . . that he may help me . . . against my persecutors. . . ."

With these words the stranger uncovered his mutilated face. From a matted tangle of grey beard emerged a great jagged scar which ran from one fevered, sunken eye to a toothless mouth that was gasping for breath. This old scar was crossed by fresh slashes that were still bleeding or had hardly dried.

"Urijah, son of Shemaiah!" The piercing cry came from Jeremiah, who had recognized the prophet. Urijah looked up at him with a stricken expression in his haunted eyes, and his lacerated tongue formed almost incoherent syllables:

"Jirmejahu, son of Hilkiah . . . help me! . . . Help me! . . ."

Hamutal hastened away and with her own hands brought food and broth, kneeling beside the man of God and helping him to eat. But the food and drink, of which he could take little, seemed to give him no strength. He stretched himself out on the floor and fell into a heavy stupor. Hamutal had a divan brought in upon which the prophet was lifted, but a whole hour went by before he had sufficiently recovered to reveal in broken sentences the agony of his journey.

Urijah had been on the way for more than thirty days since the night of his escape from the prisons of Jehoiakim. He had made his way past the barriers, search parties, and guards of the King until he reached Beersheba. Then came the endless road through the desert, which the old man had to traverse alone, without water and provided only with a handful of dates, avoiding the busy caravan tracks and any lights or camp fires which betrayed the presence of men. The Lord, however, had been with His prophet and helped him to reach the frontier north of the Red Sea near Tahpanhes. But he found that the borderland was barred by strong detachments of Pharaoh's bodyguards. All caravans from Judah, Moab, Edom, Aram, and the Land of Rivers were being compelled to turn back. The catapults of the frontier fortresses were aimed at them menacingly. The reason for this severe measure lay in the imminent return of the incarnate Sun God and his scattered hosts. Pharaoh Necho, the Father and Son of the Gods, had been defeated by a young warrior whose name was gaining more and more repute throughout the world. This warrior was called Nebuchadnezzar, son of

Nabopolassar, who had raised himself to the throne of Babylon and set his heel on Asshur's neck. The most difficult days for Urijah, the aged man of God, were, however, to come only after he had succeeded with great danger to his life in slipping past the frontier guards and reaching the swampy region of Set, the demon slayer of the god Osiris. Leaving the roads and villages to one side he came to the deadly marshlands of the Nile channels, where he would have met a hopeless end from weakness and insanity, amidst the cries of storks, ibises, flamingos, and pelicans, and hunted by croaking animals of the swamps and spectres of the night, if the Lord had not again taken mercy on him and shown him the way to Noph.

At every word that Urijah forced out with his wheezing breath he looked round timidly, blinked his eyes, and tried to raise himself up. He knew who his pursuers were. They were led by Elnathan, son of Achbor, the brother-in-law of Jehoiakim and the fiercest warrior in Judah, whose heart knew no pity. Elnathan and his myrmidons had received full powers from Pharaoh himself to seize Urijah wherever he might be found in Egypt. Alas, he had discovered this too late! His whispers were hardly audible and his teeth chattered, but then he wrung his hands again and implored Jehoahaz to keep him concealed and not to surrender him to certain death.

It was a considerable time before Urijah was in a fit condition to speak coherently of the events which had brought him to the prisons of Jehoiakim and forced him to flee the country. It had been less a matter of individual occurrences than the policy of the new regime as a whole, together with the bold opposition that he had maintained. At first Jehoiakim had been satisfied with slandering his father and his father's reign. The people of Jerusalem, content to have survived the catastrophe with such mild consequences, which they thought they owed to the new King, had received him with acclamation. Moreover, Jehoiakim fanned his spurious fame by an army of agents, gossips, demagogues, and other hirelings who everywhere in the city and the Temple spat their accusing venom against Josiah's reign and the survivors who still remained faithful to his memory. The pestilential odour of these well-calculated lies spread irresistibly, priests and princes succumbing to it and hardly anyone noticing that the air he breathed was corrupt. Jehoiakim managed without difficulty to attribute solely to his father the blame for the crushing levy of a hundred talents of silver and a talent of gold which had been paid to Pharaoh. The wound had not yet scarred over before Jehoiakim grew bolder and decreed a further levy for his own needs, since he had a mania for glorifying himself by means of palaces and magnificent buildings. This second levy was followed by blow after blow. In order to maintain his control over an exploited people it was necessary to drive out the just men and put the most wanton of the exploiters in their places. This was done shamelessly. The last loyal servants of Josiah were expelled from the Temple, the Palace, and the Army; but for the decoys and snarers of men, the rutting stallions, the falsifiers and twisters of the Law, the flatterers, bribers, and sneaking thieves their great day had dawned. The rich men in the land, and particularly their sons, were again able freely to give themselves airs; the proud, the covetous, the wrathful, and the bullies strutted and swaggered without hindrance. Among the priests, positions of authority were given to those who regarded only the sacrificial ceremonies as important but hated God's justice. In this connexion

Jeremiah learned that his venerable old host Meshullam, the miller of Kirjath-Jearim, had been appointed by Jehoiakim to be the royal treasurer. When distributing the rewards and punishments of the new reign, the King found that there was only one family against which he was powerless to act—the house of Shaphan, though the old scribe himself had died on the very day when Eliakim took possession of the throne by his insolent and dastardly *coup.* His most blasphemous blow, however, had been dealt at Passover, when he stood leaning against the pillar of the oath and announced to the people in the Temple that henceforth obedience to the Law and its commandments was dependent on the sanction or veto of the King. The Lord had not sent down fire from heaven even when Jehoiakim, as a threat to Adonai in case He might cherish vengeful plans, set up a golden sun-wheel opposite the Temple. This was indeed sinning with open visor. Nobody could deny the King's tremendous courage and arrogance, and there were even many who saw in Jehoiakim the coming of the new David.

"And all the men of the Lord?" asked Jeremiah with blanched lips. The fugitive, animated by his own narration, burst into a hollow laugh.

"All the men of the Lord? . . . Behold, the Lord is good to them and visits them with friendly words, so that their mouths overflow not with warnings but with promise of salvation and with God's praise for the King. . . . The men of the Lord! . . . The one was far away in Noph . . . and now the other is also far away in Noph. . . . He spoke against the King . . . so he was seized, whipped, and put in the stocks. . . . Though he trembled with fear, he rose and continued to prophesy the words of the Lord. . . . They beat him again and yet again. . . ."

With stiff fingers Urijah bared his shoulders. The weals left by the "scorpions" ran across the old man's back in blood-red lines. He could no longer hold back his tears.

"I lay in dungeons and vaults for month after month. . . . The King pronounced my death-sentence . . . but I was too weak, too cowardly to die for the Lord. . . . Ahikam helped me . . . and I fled, I fled. . . ."

At that moment the porter entered the lotus hall to make some domestic announcement to the Queen. With a stifled cry Urijah started up from his couch and clung tenaciously to Jeremiah.

"They have come," he moaned, "Elnathan and the others. . . . They have found me out and have come to seize me. . . . Let me go . . . I bring danger to you. . . . It is not possible for you to hide me. . . ."

Hamutal put her hand on the old man's shoulder.

"Quiet, O man of God. . . . You are among friends. . . . We shall not let you go. . . . We shall share your danger, for you were honoured by Josiah, the true King. . . . Your chamber is prepared . . . I shall take you to it, that you may enjoy a sound sleep and your soul be at peace, as though Josiah, the true King, were in this house."

Hamutal's soft, rounded hand, which had so often soothed the swift-tempered hero, now soothed this unhappy old man who had at last been broken by tribulation and hardship. As carefully as a mother she supported the tall bent figure in its tattered beggar's robe and led him from the lotus hall to one of the inner rooms. The others stared after them.

Mattaniah, who had shot up from his chair, seemed suddenly to have ceased to be a boy. The blood ebbed and flowed in his cheeks. Had the story told by the persecuted old man filled the soul of the young prince with hatred or with envy of his half-brother's power and brilliance, the royal power of which he had dreamt and from which he was excluded for ever? Mattaniah's large eyes timidly sought those of his teacher, as if he felt himself assailed by a mad longing for something forbidden. Jeremiah's mind was itself in a turmoil, and he did not respond to the appeal in Mattaniah's eyes. At home in Jerusalem a force had arisen which openly opposed the incomprehensible and unfathomable God of Israel. This was no lukewarm apostasy, no equivocal sinning, but resolute disavowal. And its intention was to eradicate by force that which Josiah had done for the Lord. The prophets and proclaimers of the truth were whipped and put to death, and the Lord, who had not tolerated the work of Josiah the just King, appeared to tolerate, and even to favour, the work of the blasphemers. Jeremiah felt glad that he had withdrawn from the general downfall, that he had renounced his task and concealed himself from the Lord in Egypt, whither Urijah, humiliated and broken, had now also fled. No sacrifice was too great to further the work of the Lord. But why sacrifice for nothing, merely that the blasphemers might triumph and bask in the Lord's favour? Despite these thoughts, however, Jeremiah could not quite silence the lurking voice within himself that whispered: "Such thoughts are sinful!"

He turned round and his eye fell on Zenua, who was observing him earnestly. He felt all at once overwhelmed by the greatest gift that God can grant to a human being—another human being. The world might rush to the abyss and nothing stay its course, but for him and his bride there was room enough on the edge of the precipice to build a house and live in it in peace. He could not prevent the downfall of Israel without being shattered himself, as Urijah had been, but he and Zenua could turn two hearts towards the Lord in their own house. Amidst the general collapse they could continue to serve the Lord and listen with ears that would grow ever more attuned. Was this not enough for one of God's dreamers who had not been equipped with the toughness necessary for a fighter?

He spoke to Zenua:

"Evil things have happened . . . but they do not concern us. . . . When one Sabbath more has passed, my bride, then will come our time of rejoicing."

That morning Zenua seemed to blossom as she had never done before. Since she had cast away Ded and Anekh she appeared to have grown more animated, and her spirits improved. She was often to be heard singing in her chamber. Yet now she looked at Jeremiah with veiled eyes as if she were in possession of some knowledge that was hidden from him, and she replied thoughtfully:

"Yes, my bridegroom, it is time that our hour of rejoicing should come."

Before the following Sabbath was at an end the decision of Adonai concerning His future intention was made clear. On the morning of that day all the members of the household had assembled in the lotus hall to hear the reading of the Law. Urijah was there too, for during the past few days he had slowly recovered, under the care and attention of Hamutal, from the terrors and privations of his flight. He still looked mortally ill, but the expression of misery and humiliation in his eyes had changed to the look of noble weariness which had so deeply moved Jeremiah when he first saw his mutilated countenance in the house of Huldah the seeress. As a sign of esteem, the younger man had on this

Sabbath surrendered the office of reader to the older prophet, and Urijah sat in the midst of the group as he read in an exhausted and monotonous voice and interpreted what he had read passage by passage. Yet for some reason, either because he did not speak so clearly and distinctly as Jeremiah or because the little congregation was beset by unusual restlessness, the venerable old man was unable to chain their attention. Zenua in particular increased the general unease and distraction by her attitude. She got up three or four times and walked about the hall, then she went out and returned again immediately as if she had been called by mocking echoes. She had been wont to sit for hours at a time in the charming position customary in Egypt, resting lightly on her right heel, but today she could not stay still for a minute. Though she kept her eyes fixed in front of her, it was no longer with the earnestness of a mind fixed on the Lord. Her brow was wrinkled in its usual childlike way, yet not with the effort to follow the exposition of the Law. Hamutal looked at her searchingly from time to time. She was the only one among those present who felt a vague anxiety at Zenua's lack of repose. Jeremiah, on the other hand, was unable to suppress a slight irritation at the absent-minded, disturbing behaviour of his betrothed. He was aware that Zenua shared the invincible love of beauty of the aristocratic Egyptian women, who lost their composure at the sight of any form of ugliness or distortion, and he therefore suspected that despite her fervent attachment to the truth of the Lord she was unable to endure the scarred face of Urijah, His prophet. He thought that she was filled with disgust at the toothless mouth, the long scar, the fresh weals, and the extreme frailty of the afflicted man. He suffered because Zenua did not seem to realize that Urijah's disfigurement was a more honourable token of battle than all the slashes and scars which the heroes of the nations' wars were accustomed to parade before their admiring womenfolk.

Jeremiah could scarcely await the conclusion of the lesson. His ill-humour increased and he craved for the moment when he would be able to enlighten his betrothed as speedily as possible concerning the vain error of her heart. When they were in the garden again, his suspicion and annoyance vanished, and he could not find words to say. In the space of two hours Zenua had completely changed. She looked fragile and her face seemed transparent, while her brow had lost its little pucker and was quite smooth and white.

"What ails my betrothed?" he stammered.

She looked at him for a long time with a strange expression of mocking love, for she was hiding something of which he had no knowledge.

"It is the joy I feel," she said, "that the Sabbath is coming to an end. . . . And then . . . it is the great rejoicing. . . ."

"This rejoicing of the bride frightens the bridegroom."

She put her right hand over his eyes.

"Let the bridegroom not look upon the bride . . . for the god is struggling with her and is trying to possess her. . . . Perhaps it is the Lord . . . but perhaps it is Osiris."

He tenderly took her hand from his eyes and pressed it to his cheek.

"What are these foolish dreams of which Zenua speaks?"

She seemed too weak to smile, but the right corner of her full lips turned slightly upward.

"Do not say that they are foolish dreams. . . . Rather urge your Lord to win me from him . . . for I have cast away Ded and thereby summoned Osiris. . . ."

"Must I not be angry when my bride speaks so meaninglessly?"

"Do not be angry, my bridegroom . . . for your bride is full of joy . . . full of a great joy. . . ."

Zenua gently released her hand and took a step or two backwards. As if speaking to herself she said:

"When the god comes . . . I must dance . . . I must dance towards the god. . . ."

She crossed her arms over her breast and with a heartbreaking coquettishness tried to pirouette in the first steps of a dance. Before Jeremiah could spring to her side she had sunk to the ground.

Zenua was carried to her room, and after lengthy application of restoratives, such as vinegar, medicinal drops, and pungent odours, she was brought back to consciousness. But she seemed to have lost the power of speech. Her slender body was shaken by cruel convulsions while her eyes, distended with terror, clung to Jeremiah, wandered imploringly to Hamutal, and returned to Jeremiah again. Hamutal understood the look and the entreaty which it communicated. Zenua did not want Jeremiah to see her in the disfigurement caused by her dread disease. Her lips worked incessantly but they brought forth no words. Hamutal gently pushed Jeremiah from the room, and outside the door he collapsed and remained crouching in a stupefied immobility. His numbed mind was unable to pull itself together sufficiently to utter a prayer or a vow. The same thought kept circling with a dull monotony through his empty brain: "Why do the innocent have to endure such suffering; why do they have no respite from this great suffering?"

It was only towards evening that Hamutal called him back

into the room. Zenua could now speak again, though it cost her a great effort before she could frame the words. Her dumbness had given place to a paralysis that held her body in its grip, like an invisible beast of hell firmly clutching every limb. The change in her appearance, which but yesterday had been like that of a tenderly blossoming flower, was unbelievable. In a few hours her body had wasted lamentably. Her paralysed arms and legs had shrunken, while her long-fingered hands and slender feet had swollen out of all proportion. The disease had obliterated the pleasant rounding of her cheeks, as if they had been clay in the potter's hand, and engraved the deep bluish hollows of death under her burning eyes. She spoke with heavy tongue:

"Behold, my bridegroom . . . your bride has after all become the pillar of Osiris. . . ."

Jeremiah behaved as everybody does at the sick-bed of the one he loves. He instilled into his voice a tone of confidence and said, not without a certain austerity:

"The Lord will change the pillar back into Zenua this very night. . . . And tomorrow, on the day of rejoicing, she will awaken lithe and well."

He spoke the words without believing them himself. They were the fruit of his own despair, but they seemed to do her good. With fluttering breath she whispered:

"Yes, let my bridegroom speak of the Lord, only of the Lord. . . . He is the Supreme Being and surely will not let the other god take possession of me. . . . I am lying torn in the world between. . . . Before the day of my rejoicing comes, my ear desires only to hear of Jeremiah's God . . . whom I love so greatly. . . ."

But Jeremiah was unable to do what she asked and speak of Adonai. In no hour of his life would it have been more impossible to do so than it was now. His soul was lying in wait for the monstrous deed of the Lord like an archer lurking in ambush with drawn bow. The arrow lay ready to be aimed at God upon the stretched sinew of his soul. Yet to meet Zenua's wish he did what pious men do at the bedside of the sick and the dying: he sang in a low voice a psalm that David himself had once composed. He was hardly aware of the words or the melody, and the song that was familiar to him from his childhood came to his lips almost involuntarily:

"Bless the Lord, O my soul:
And all that is within me, bless his holy name.
Bless the Lord, O my soul,
And forget not all his benefits:
Who forgiveth all thine iniquities;
Who healeth all thy diseases;
Who redeemeth thy life from destruction. . . ."

When he reached this line his low singing was interrupted by Zenua, who had been listening with half-closed eyes.

"My bridegroom . . . behold, Kā, the swallow, is still within my heart. . . . It does not move . . . I can feel it . . . but Bā, the sparrow-hawk, is fluttering about inside my head and beating against the wall and trying to fly out. . . . It is he who is causing me this great pain . . . but we must protect the swallow. . . ."

Jeremiah lightly touched her swollen hand, that lay lifelessly upon the coverlet. She screamed with pain and he withdrew his hand in fright. But Zenua begged:

"Let your hand rest upon my hand, my bridegroom. . . . It hurts . . . and that does me good. . . ."

Jeremiah sang the remaining verses of the psalm, then sang others, for in this way he hoped to lull Zenua to sleep. Her eyes had closed and her shallow breathing grew more regular. Had the Lord at last extended His mercy to them?

Had He taken pity on the bride who for love of Him had renounced the vain gods? Was this the sleep that would restore Zenua to health? How ready he was to believe that signs were propitious and again to see in the Lord the willing consummator of his own hopes! A prayer of thanksgiving had begun to form within his heart, when suddenly the face of Zenua became distorted and she groaned aloud:

"Why do you let me wander through the land of Set? . . . He is the great slayer in the swamps. . . ."

Her gods were tormenting her and he could bring her no relief, since the Lord was looking down coldly upon her agony. After a few stifled attempts to breathe, words broke from her that were imbued with a deep loathing:

"Black ducks . . . Ha-rekhni did not know that the images of the soul of Set are black ducks. . . . They waddle and splash as they hurry through the swampy pool. . . . Broad red beaks . . . Oh! They gobble and babble and clack hatred. . . . I cannot go any farther . . . they are tweaking me . . . they have caught me . . ."

"Sleep! . . . You must sleep. . . . Then they will go away. . . . Sleep, my bride. . . . Sleep, Zenua! . . ."

Jeremiah repeated: "Sleep, Zenua!" incessantly, as if the empty and monotonous formula might bring slumber to the sick girl like a lullaby. But Zenua opened her eyes and watched his impotent effort with a despairing smile, which concealed in its veiled depths the painful knowledge of a woman, the scoffing of a girl, and the secret mockery of a lover.

"My bridegroom," she asked, "why is the Lord so weak in you today?"

Jeremiah lowered his head and clenched his fist to beat his breast in rage. But his fingers loosened again and the hand which he had raised to dispute with the Lord fell nervelessly to his side. Even now Zenua was as stubborn as ever and would not yield.

"My bridegroom, do not deceive your bride. . . . The Lord, who can do everything, is turning away His eyes. . . . Whatever you may do and however you may pray and implore, it will not help Zenua. . . . Summon all your strength and compel your Lord to drive the sparrow-hawk back into my heart. . . . The swallow and the sparrow-hawk must dwell together if Zenua is to live. . . ."

After the exhausting effort of this speech her lips lost their colour and became bluish, the final dread came into her eyes; she could not catch her breath and panted:

"Do not let me die! . . ."

Hamutal and the maids hurried to the bedside, raised her up, and struck her lightly on the back to prevent her from suffocating. Her head fell back limply, but with all the strength of which she was capable she cried out:

"Jeremiah! . . . Go!"

She did not want him to see his bride in the ugly convulsions of death. Her fear of this was even greater than her fear of dying, and it gave her an heroic courage.

Jeremiah crouched the whole night outside Zenua's room. His soul was numb and he could not think. Maids came and went with candles, pitchers of hot water, cloths soaked in vinegar, and bowls of fragrant incense. They wept and whispered together or murmured prayers. All this reached Jeremiah's senses as if through a thick veil. At last a wondrous spring morning rode over Noph. The waxing sun, joyously preparing to become the great eye of Horus, penetrated every corner of the house and made the red and green paintings on the walls and pillars gleam vividly. Was this not the morning they had chosen for their great rejoicing, and which the Lord was now investing with such a bitter splendour? The weary Hamutal came out of the sick chamber and told Jeremiah with a soothing smile that things were going better.

When he was allowed in to see Zenua he again found her completely changed. Her lips were red and parted like those of a child, while a slight tinge of colour lay upon her cheeks. Only her eyes had sunk more deeply and their whites were like iridescent mother-of-pearl. Again his despairing hope invested him too readily with a fraction of courage. He touched her hand, and this time she did not cry out. He felt the lifelessness and lack of sensibility in her swollen fingers. Nothing could hurt them any more and nothing could give them relief. There was a secret meaning in the look she gave him. With difficulty she whispered, so that no one else should hear:

"It has been decided . . . Zenua does not belong to the Lord of life, but to Osiris. . . ."

The few syllables had exhausted her, and she was silent. A dull compulsion drew Jeremiah's eyes away from Zenua to the window, a compulsion which was already the disloyalty that withdraws the eyes of the living from the face of those for whom there is no hope. The bright deep-blue day of their great rejoicing filled the window with the pictures of its palm trees and rhododendrons, its acacias and azaleas. Boats sailed along the Nile in the distance; the clamorous voices of boatmen, carters, and workers who were beginning their daily toil mingled with the twittering of busy singing birds. The sparrow-hawks of Ptah, the spirits of men which had risen to the sun, were more numerous than ever as they hovered with proudly outstretched wings between heaven and earth. Why was this slowly unfolding day of their great rejoicing so beautiful; why was it not clouded, distorted, extinguished by a sandstorm from the desert! A low whispering recalled Jeremiah to himself.

"The swallows are already fluttering . . . on the edge of my heart . . . as if on a branch. . . ."

He held a horsehair switch in his hand to drive the buzzing flies away from Zenua's pillow. As he bent over her, an almost imperceptible whisper came to him:

"When Kā leaves by the western gate . . . when the swallow settles on your shoulder . . . will you let it rest there?"

She did not speak again for some hours and seemed to be sleeping peacefully. When the sun had passed its zenith he heard her voice once more.

"The land of my mother . . . the land of your Lord . . . why did you not take me there . . . when the hour had come for our rejoicing? . . . We would have built a house . . . you and I. . . ."

Hardly had she managed to utter these broken sentences when she was again seized by a fit of choking, which was worse than all those that had gone before. Neither shaking nor patting on the back brought her any relief. "Let me die!" she gasped, with starting eyes. She no longer thought of keeping the loss of her beauty from the eyes of her betrothed and urging him to leave the room. At the last moment, however, when she seemed on the point of suffocating, the Kher-heb entered. It was significant that he carried in his hand not the symbol of Osiris, as he usually did, but the symbol of the living Ptah, the tall bamboo staff upon which was perched a carved sparrow-hawk. At his entry Zenua immediately recovered her breath, but the Kher-heb addressed himself to Hamutal with stern though carefully weighed words:

"Your Grace has ignored my advice and has acted too soon. Your Grace has sent for help too late. The fluttering Kā of the sympathetic and understanding heart has already summoned her guardian."

Silently, without waiting for an answer or paying heed to anyone, he seated himself at the foot of the couch. The great physician and initiate used neither his skill in healing nor his knowledge of secret arts. Only his bald, shining head seemed to turn to ice, while the lustreless, stony eyes under their heavy ridges were fixed with a weary tranquillity on his ward. Zenua grew calmer. She took short, quick breaths, and seemed to smile as if favourable spirits were fluttering about her. Her eyelids fell and she slept.

After about an hour the Kher-heb rose from his seat and with a brief farewell gravely left the room, carrying his staff in front of him. As he was about to enter his litter at the gate he was touched lightly on the arm by Jeremiah, who had followed him. The Master of Ceremonies of Death stood erect and gazed at the man of God with inscrutable eyes in which there was neither friendliness nor hostility, but only the impenetrability that came from long training in the art of concealing the emotions. He had been chosen by his gods not to be their prophet but to keep their intentions locked in his heart, and his speech was characterized by the carefully thought-out choice between that which was worth saying and that which ought to be left unsaid. The few words he addressed to Jeremiah were unerringly selected to hide at the same time as they revealed.

"The man from a foreign land may set his mind at rest. Ha-rekhni has overcome her foe."

He paused awhile as if he were weighing in his mind whether the delicate consideration which the choice of words demanded might allow him a greater clarity of expression. But instead of speaking he merely stretched out his staff and pointed with the sparrow-hawk at its tip towards the west, where at the edge of the desert the "City of Eternity" rose with its crowded pyramids and temples and the gigantic "Palace of the Divine Workshop." Jeremiah's eyes remained fixed on the western city, which was gilded by the setting sun. When he turned again the elegant and ornamental litter of the Kher-heb was already swaying on its way. Four ugly creatures, however, had just arrived at the entrance to the house. They were redheaded, misshapen dwarfs, small as gnomes, and had brought with them an oblong box that rested on sledge runners. They stood round it grinning impudently. Every child in Nu-Ptah was familiar with the sight of these little men and knew to what mighty god they were dedicated from their youth. They were in the service of Set, the basest and most dreadful form in which death appeared. Though they were despised, what did it matter? There was no palace to which, at some time or other, they were not admitted.

Jeremiah rushed back to the house. Hamutal was waiting for him in the entrance hall and pressed his head to her motherly breast.

16

The Journey through Amenti

JEREMIAH had shot from his soul the arrow he had aimed at the Lord.

He lay stretched out on a hard bench in a chamber of the western city, in the realm of the dead over which the sway of the Kher-heb was more absolute than that of Pharaoh. In the strong light of the torches on the walls he could see colourful pictures which depicted in broad strips the journey of the sun-bark through "the Land of Gathering Glooms." He still could not understand everything that the idolatrous chimeras were supposed to represent, but his heart raged with grief and anger. By everything that he was now thinking, doing, and planning he was laying a curse upon himself, and all in order to punish the Lord who brought death to everyone he loved, and exposed him and brought him to destruction as if He were his worst enemy. His bride had had to die only for his sake, slain on the day they had chosen for their rejoicing—Zenua, who had striven towards the Lord more fervently than any devoted child of Jacob.

Now Jeremiah lay on his hard couch in the western city of uncleanliness and magic. Gauzy bands of mummy wrappings had been wound lightly round his body as a symbol of what he was seeking and the journey he wished to make. He, the pure guardian of the pure Word, lay here in deeper misery than Israel and Judah. He was planning something more iniquitous even than the setting up of a sun-wheel.

Deliberately he was seeking uncleanliness, apostasy, and delusion. His soul cried aloud for vengeance. Yet his soul cried also for his innocent, slain bride. Did the Lord really believe that he would calmly acquiesce? He too was a rebel. He too did not shrink from any means to his end. Least of all did he shrink from the journey which led to Zenua. He was struggling to cross the inexorable frontier. That which Zenua had endured he too wanted to endure. He must see and touch her in her new world; even if he himself should be brought to destruction thereby and extirpated. Ptah, Imhotep, Sekhet, Thoth, Anubis, and Set—these names no longer brought the blood to his cheeks with shame and horror. He was prepared to enter into league with crocodile-jawed, ibis-beaked, hippopotamus-headed spectres, only in order to be nearer to the shadow, the reflection, even a delusive phantom of his dead bride. Seven times already he had omitted the morning and evening prayer and neglected the daily hallowings. For the dead do not pray, and it was they whom he was trying to join. Thus his thirst for vengeance against the Lord and his longing for the lost Zenua were fused into a chaotic, destructive passion which was not further from death than it was from madness.

Jeremiah had set out for the western city and had called upon the Kher-heb in the Palace of the Divine Workshop. The latter showed neither surprise at seeing him nor displeasure at his rash request. He received it with such tranquillity that Jeremiah was afraid he understood it merely as a symbol. The man from Anathoth, however, was in very truth hurling himself against the gates of Amenti. Only later did he discover that he was not the only one to present such a demand. In "the last caravanserai," which bordered on "Ro-stau," the Temple of the Gates, there were many cells like the one in which he was now lying, inhabited by mourners who refused to be separated from their beloved dead. Men were living there while they prepared for initiation and trained themselves for the exploration of the world of death. It appeared that only a few chambers were vacant. The Kher-heb had listened to Jeremiah with an inscrutable expression and, when he replied, he did not deal with the request that was made to him. He did not say that it was possible or impossible, that it was permitted or forbidden. Nor did the fact that he was an alien of a different faith prove to be a bar. Amenti had a tangible existence, and as Pharaoh's deputy the Kher-heb administered it in the same way as the governor of any other region in the kingdom. It was open to all the souls of Egypt, both native and foreign. So the Kher-heb did not discuss the possibility of complying with Jeremiah's request; he returned an indefinite answer by enumerating the various conditions to which Jeremiah would have to submit. He would not be able to return to Nu-Ptah, but would have to remain in the western city and occupy a cell in the last caravanserai as did the other neophytes. Further, he would have to subject himself unresistingly to all the prescribed exercises, readings, and mortifications. He would not, however, be required to deny his own God or violate his conscience by any word or deed. "For the exalted gods of Egypt," concluded the Kher-heb, "are magnanimous."

This proved to be the truth, for nothing was demanded of Jeremiah that might have infringed the commandments. He did not have to bow before any image, call upon any false name, or sully his soul and body with anything unclean, though he was dwelling in the midst of uncleanliness. Thus, in spite of his thirst for revenge and his longing, in a mysterious way his sinning remained incomplete.

The prescribed mortification consisted of almost uninterrupted fasting. During the night Jeremiah was given a hot draught of wine mixed with plant juices, which had the effect of lulling all his physical instincts and senses so that the bounds of reality were effaced. He did not feel that he was fasting, nor did he realize that he did not sleep. Whether he was standing up or lying down, at every hour of the night a herald of the underworld sun-journey appeared in his cell to announce the mystery of that particular hour in elaborate song. The day was no longer altogether day for Jeremiah; the night was no longer altogether night. He saw the light as through dark glass, and the darkness as if by the aid of faint lamps shining from his own eyes.

The exercises required of him consisted of his participation in lengthy periods of study, when priestly initiates chanted with matchless monotony long passages from various writings. One of these important works was called the *Book of Gates;* another was entitled *Am-Duat* or *Concerning That Which Is in the Depths.* The regular and insistent intoning weakened the power of reasoning, relaxed the mind until it drowsed away into a comfortable numbness. Humming swarms of meaninglessly meaningful words brushed past the ear yet penetrated into consciousness, not like the glorious lightning of divine revelation and human intuition, but as a kind of verbal incense which evoked cloudy sequences of dreams and images. The words themselves, and not what they expressed, were like a floating life-stuff which condensed round the heads of those who listened. Enwrapped in these clouds Jeremiah was hardly aware how low he had allowed himself to sink. Yet neither fasting nor lack of sleep, drugging draughts nor monotonous chanting, could stifle within him the angry flame of vengeance and longing.

Even more essential, however, for the purpose of what had not been granted to him and not refused, seemed to be the visits of the Kher-heb, which were paid him by that exalted personage every day before sunset (at the twelfth hour) in his cell. The controller of the world of the dead at Nu-Ptah practised with the man from Judah what was known as "the great exercise of silence." This silence, in which they both shared, was regarded not as an ordinary silence but as an anticipation, while still alive, of the silence of death. Its exercise was for the purpose of rendering Jeremiah's Kā, the soul of his soul, more supple, mobile, lax, and adaptable. For only the Kā, the most inward image, which raised its arms yearningly to heaven, could pass through the gates, provided of course that it could leave the body while the heart was still beating. It was further necessary, according to the science of Nu-Ptah, that the Kā of him who sought to make the journey should be attached to an experienced guide, lest it perish on coming into contact with the realities of the underworld. The exercise itself consisted in Jeremiah's and the Kher-heb's sitting rigidly opposite each other with their bodies completely closed; that is to say, with the inner surfaces of the hands and the feet touching and the chin sunk upon the breast.

One day, when Jeremiah had ceased to reckon the length of his sojourn in the western city, he was sent for and guided through silent streets to the Palace of the Divine Workshop. This mighty building, set amidst gleaming colonnades, rose from a vast square which perhaps even exceeded in size that of the temple of Nu-Ptah. But here was no cheerful activity, no markets, or festive processions; and instead of the smell of oil, fat, roasting meats, and beer, there was the heavy odour of jasmine and acacia mingled with the vapours of bitumen and tar and another bitter, indefinable aroma. There were no crowds of buyers and onlookers, but instead there were swarms of busy servants of Set. The redheaded gnomes hurried to and fro with their closed boxes or carried dishes with little white balls of natron, baskets heaped with amber-coloured resin, transparent jars filled with oil of myrrh and various kinds of flower essences, bundles of delicate, specially selected rushes and stalks of the *menes* plant. The misshapen dwarfs were hastening to store the hundred chambers of ceremonial unguents with the necessary supplies.

Jeremiah was received in a very dark room by a subordinate of the Kher-heb, who unrolled a scroll and proceeded to read the following information with business-like speed: The dismembered and resurrected Osiris was the head of the unit which was formed by the community of the dead. In Osiris alone lay the hope of mortals that they might survive the end of their lives in this world and preserve their most inward personality in all the fourteen sections of decay. Therefore, through the beneficent influence of balsam, oil, natron, resin, and wrappings every man who died was received with his thus immortalized body into the body of the god, into the community of Osiris. Thenceforth he could bear the existence and name of Osiris in addition to his own name and existence. The dead woman Ha-rekhni, of the noble house of May-Ptah, was accordingly now and for all eternity to be known as the venerated Osiris Ha-rekhni. The venerated Osiris Ha-rekhni was about to proceed from the Divine Workshop to the region of the last caravanserai, where his eyes and mouth would be opened in the Temple of the Gates.

After this document had been read out to him a brownish,

opaque mourning veil was thrown over Jeremiah's head and the same silent men who had brought him guided him back. When the veil was removed he again found himself in a dark, bare room where a number of guests who were unknown to him had already assembled to witness the ceremony. There was a long and painful interval before the broad double doors were opened and Jeremiah could see into a brightly lit cell whose walls were covered with strange paintings. In the background, leaning against an imitation door drawn on the wall, was a tall mummy in a coloured wooden coffin fitted to its shape. The lid of the coffin had been turned back and the mummy in its hundred ells of sacred wrappings looked like the kernel of a gigantic fruit. A mask of wax or yellowish plaster had been laid over the face. The most dreadful thing about it, however, was the long streaks of soft dark hair which flowed out from behind the mask.

So this was the work of Zebaoth and the Egyptians! They might both be proud at having so cruelly disfigured the lovely Zenua! Jeremiah lowered his eyes to the ground, and without realizing what he was doing he murmured half aloud the old blessing of Israel in memory of departed souls. He did not raise his head again even when the ceremony began—when the mourning women sang their alternating chants, when the priest called Sem sprinkled the mummy with holy water, when the priest of the offerings perfumed the mummy with incense, and when finally the Kher-heb himself removed the golden fillings from the eye-holes and mouth of the mask so that Osiris Ha-rekhni should be able to see, speak, and recite the names of the forty-two judges of the realm of the dead.

Many hours had gone by and Jeremiah was again lying on

his hard couch, rigid with grief. He had patiently, almost without noticing it, allowed two men to bind him to the couch with a thin strip of gauze. This was merely symbolical, for he could have freed himself from his bonds with the slightest movement. But he did not move. He did not move even when the Kher-heb entered and looked at him keenly. Jeremiah watched with indifference when the priest thrust a long staff into a joint of the stone floor and then turned his gaze towards the sequence of pictures that ran along the walls. The staff cast a deep, clearly outlined shadow against one wall, a shadow which moved with visible speed along the picture representing the journey of the divine sun-bark through the upper and the lower worlds. When the shadow was no more than an ell's distance from the place where the bark of the god left the realm of light, the Kher-heb beckoned. Jeremiah rose and followed him.

They had left the last caravanserai and were wandering through the desert. Jeremiah had doubtless expected something different after traversing under the guidance of the Kher-heb the dark and labyrinthine corridors of the Temple of the Gates. When the innermost and lowest door was opened, however, there lay before them nothing but the desert. Jeremiah now found that they were not walking in the ordinary way, but that he was suddenly endowed with the power to hover, his legs only occasionally moving a little as he progressed over the wind-furrowed desert sand. Usually it was an arduous and lengthy process to wade through it; now it seemed to him as if they had covered a longer distance than that from Dan to Beersheba since leaving the Temple. Their goal lay clear in front of them, where the setting sun was about to cut the disk of the earth. The distance could not be reckoned, but they were apparently approaching their goal at a great speed. Jeremiah had the sensation of being only partially present, as if he were a shadow or one of those spectres that the priests declared to be limbs of Osiris. His thirst for vengeance and his longing had fused in the depths of his soul to a dark defiance. His mind was so numbed and their method of progression so easy that he was hardly aware when they reached the point of intersection of the horizon and the mighty stone gate of the First Hour of Night loomed up before them in the mist. It corresponded exactly to the pylon of Ro-stau, the Temple of the Gates, except that it was a hundred times broader and taller. He could still see the faint reflection of the divine throng which gathered every evening at the gate of Amenti when the god exchanged the bark of day for the bark of night, which was immediately surrounded by the smaller boats of the other gods who were assigned to accompany him. The reflection of the sinking sun soon vanished, however, and Jeremiah and his guide were enveloped in a milky twilight. The first thing they saw was a great host of human figures with jackals' heads that radiated a faint reddish glow as they lolled about in the mist. These were the army of the faithful Anubis, who opened the gates for the god, and they soon revealed themselves as a more or less busy band of attendants. Since there was a continual and exceedingly numerous flow of arrivals from Amenti these jackal-headed assistants themselves possessed a crowd of youthful helpers, little dog-headed monkeys who sprang about round their taller masters with an agitated, officious chattering, romped between their legs, or played at trying to catch each other. The Kher-heb clapped his hands and called as one would call to coachmen, litter-bearers, or ferrymen:

"An opener of the gates for the Kher-heb of Nu-Ptah!"

An old jackal-head immediately detached himself from the throng, approached with the dignified bearing of a princely servant, greeted the Kher-heb with sedate obsequiousness as his master, and inspected the stranger attentively with a doubtful expression on his features. The Kher-heb took Jeremiah by the hand, thereby linking him with himself, and there was a sharp rebuke in the tone with which he addressed the jackal-head by his name: "Battering-Ram!" Battering-Ram appeared to be satisfied and rubbed his snout against Jeremiah as a sign that he was anxious to serve him. The crew, however, was not yet complete. The Kher-heb again clapped his hands and called: "Look-Behind!" Another jackal-head, who seemed to be even older than his comrade, hurriedly limped up. He carried a long rowing-pole over his shoulder, and it could be seen by his gait that he did not feel altogether at home on dry land. He was followed by a number of the dog-headed monkeys, who behaved like inquisitive street urchins hoping to earn a copper or two for some casual service or simply by begging. Battering-Ram strode ahead, the reddish glow he emanated showing them the way. Look-Behind, with his hurried limp and surrounded by the jabbering throng of hopping rascals, formed the rear.

Jeremiah felt himself standing on the swaying planks of a bark. They were journeying along the river Ur-Nes, the Nile of the underworld, in the wake of the sun-bark. Look-Behind rowed vigorously with his pole, which he seemed to be pushing not into black water but into unresisting emptiness. It was undoubtedly a special distinction, reserved for the controller of Amenti, to be allowed to journey through the world of the dead along the river of the nocturnal sun. For on both shores, which stretched unendingly through the milky twilight, could be seen a hazy crowd of pedestrians whose number was no less unending. Was Zenua among these most wretched of the wretched, who were moving so slowly in the land of the First Hour of Night? The Kher-heb made a negative sign with his long forefinger—there was no distinguished Kā in the vast crowd, but only the common people; no soul from the reputable and venerable families of the forty-two regions, but only slaves, bondmen, serfs, peasants, craftsmen, and servants, in so far as these were not required to accompany their masters to a better place of sojourn in order to attend to the latter's comfort and customary pleasures.

For the first time Jeremiah took into account a conviction that was growing stronger and stronger within him. He did not believe that he was witnessing only an unusually vivid dream, yet all this was immeasurably removed from a genuine vision. He saw the thronging processions, from which came low moans, on both shores of the Ur-Nes. He saw the dignified jackal-head glowing reddishly in front of him on the bark. When he turned round he saw the other one rowing through the emptiness with persistent zeal. The dog-headed monkeys were amusing themselves by throwing one another overboard and fishing one another out again. Nothing seemed so definite as the cool, dry hand of the Kher-heb, which was lightly clasping his own. All this was there, but it seemed as if it could be revoked by his own deeper conviction. Was Amenti a real place? The Lord had never given any clear indication concerning the destiny and place of sojourn of the dead. However, this was not the time to doubt and search for explanations. He had to find Zenua, even if she were only a shadow, a phantom, less than a dream.

Whenever they approached the gate of a new Hour of

the Night, the Ur-Nes grew narrower and its nothingness foamed silently and invisibly in a steeper fall. The bark shot along swiftly while Look-Behind pushed his pole against the current in a persistent and praiseworthy effort to avoid disaster. Battering-Ram cupped his hands to his jackal's throat and barked the password at the keepers of the gate: "Your name, O Gate, is the weight that turns the scales of justice!" To this password he added a maxim: "What is eternity? The day! What is infinity? The night!" The land of the Second Hour of the Night was not very different from that of the First. Only the moving throng on both shores seemed to have become slightly thinned, as if they had passed through a sieve which had forced some of them to remain behind. The same thing happened at the next two gates. The moving host grew smaller and smaller, more and more sifted, ever "better." What were they hoping for, since everywhere in these regions the same formula prevailed in all its horror: "Death is tedious!" These Kās seemed to be destined to no real suffering and no real peace, but only to a worthless search, an empty restlessness, which tossed them to and fro in a circle. It was not until they reached the land of the Fourth Hour of the Night that they acquired the capacity to express the state of their being, or rather non-being, in strangely humming song. Here too Battering-Ram addressed the gate of the region by its name: "Gate, behind which the hair is plucked out and its smoothness disordered!" This name referred to Isis, the suffering bride, sister, and mother of the god who was journeying through Amenti. In a drawling and obsequious voice, as if he did not understand its meaning, the jackal-head added the maxim which revealed a great secret appertaining to all worldly images: "The kernel is in the fruit and the fruit is in the kernel."

The bark landed at the shore of this Fourth Hour of the Night, and at once Jeremiah and the Kher-heb found themselves surrounded by a dancing whirl of young women. The two jackal-heads tried angrily, but without success, to push their way through. The whirling ranks closed again immediately. Jeremiah searched for Zenua with a beating heart. She was not there. The women seemed to have no faces. One of them squatted down at his feet and chirped a song like a cricket, at the same time going through the motions of accompanying herself on a long-necked lute:

My husband, my lover, rejoice while you live,
Rejoice in the feasting your world has to offer.
Take other women to your couch in the evening,
Satisfy eagerly every desire.
Hunting and drinking and gaming and love,
Love as you want to as long as you live.

We who are here in the realm of the dead,
Sadly we dwell with our bodies of shadow.
We think not of father, of mother, of brother;
The heart with indifference thinks not of its child.
O death of perfection! So name I the sorrow
That springs from a love which can no longer love.

The living can drink from the waters of life,
But I must languish in infinite thirst.
The stream flows so near and I thirst, I thirst;
I know not my name or in what place I am.
My eyes let fall tears for a breath from the river,
Recalling a love that was given and returned.

The women probably recognized in Jeremiah the flesh and blood of life, for they reached up to him like cold flames whose touch he could not feel. The Kher-heb, the firm grip of whose hand was the only definite thing in an indefinite world, drew him along and swiftly they forced their way through the eddying whirl of insubstantial bodies. It needed only a few negligent movements of their legs to bring them to the gate of the Fifth Hour of the Night, preceded by Battering-Ram and followed by Look-Behind. They were now at the actual entrance of "that which is in the depths." This part of the western land bore the name, "Region of All the Imagined and Imaginable Possibilities of Creation." On this occasion it was not Battering-Ram who uttered the password, but the Kher-heb, for in this land the procession of souls, whose ranks had by now been considerably thinned, were encountered for the first time by an almost equally numerous throng of images which had come to terrify and test them. These images were nothing other than incorporations of the inextricable and intangible growth of extravagant chimeras, incoherent visions, combinations and sudden transitions of thought which had roamed through the minds of gods and men since the beginning of time. The unborn abortions of half-sleep and reverie here found their dwelling place in creation, and the Kā on its journey through the underworld could rid itself of these troublesome phantoms only by calling each of them by its correct name. This was the reason why the mummy had had its eyes and mouth opened. In the uttering of the name lay a paralysing power that bound and disarmed every being or image. To name it was to put a spell upon it. The name alone rooted gods and creatures to the spot, conjuring them up and annihilating them at the same time. That was why the dead were provided by their solicitous relatives or friends with the great *Book of the Dead*, which was bound beneath their wrappings and contained the names of all the beings and images that they would meet on their journey, a complete register, as it were, of the official dwellers in Amenti. Nobody, however, was less likely to need the *Book of the Dead* than the Kher-heb, who administered the realm in the name of Pharaoh. As the supreme initiated priest of Nu-Ptah he was cognizant of the names not only of all the imagined, but also of all the imaginable possibilities of creation, including those which were not recorded in any book or handed down by verbal tradition. Yet the Kher-heb disdained to give himself airs. Only the grip of his hand tightened on that of Jeremiah. The first of the terrifying and testing phantoms sprang in front of them in the form of a fiery circle that hopped along on widespread ostrich legs. It resembled in gigantic magnification the whirling wheels of light with a black spot in the centre which form behind the eyelids when one has been looking at the sun. The Kher-heb stood still, let the will-o'-the-wisp bar their way for a time as it hopped about, and then murmured contemptuously: "Tailed Fiery Eye," whereupon it immediately vanished.

All these phantoms were characterized by the fact that their shapes were completely meaningless. It was their nature to be composed only of such remote components as had not the slightest rational or purposeful association with one another. All the components were fused into animal form, for that was the only way in which both the upper and the lower worlds of Egypt could find expression. The animal form, however, was mingled with absurd elements which were often of a most loathsome and obscene nature. A cock, as tall as a man, strutted about and preened its shimmering feathers, but by the glow radiating from the two attendants it could be seen that instead of a head and neck it bore an erect phallus crowned with a red comb. The Kher-heb caused the monster to disappear by addressing it as "Dual Power of Earth," without revealing the secret significance of the name. A certain order or distribution was to be found in the realm of these imagined and imaginable chimeras, since at different times a definite animal form prevailed. On one occasion it was birds—cocks, turkeys, peacocks, ibises, flamingos, cranes, geese, or ducks. On another it was the dung-beetle, which often reached the size of a wether. And all these insane shapes of animals, men, and plants bore significant names, such as "the Western Stinger," "the Fearless One of the Long Strides," or "the Devourer of the Shadows of the Dead." The feathered and hoofed monsters, spectres, and mad abortions were not so terrifying individually, but collectively they diffused an even more profound tedium and disgust, even a suffocating despair, since they brought into existence that which ought never to have existed.

Jeremiah, who had once searched the very depths of his soul to see that it was pure as he stood before the sanctuary of the Lord on the night of Passover, felt that he would die of shame and loathing as he stood in the abyss of Amenti. He began to realize that by his sinful descent he had punished not the Lord but himself. Were the dissoluteness and unchastity of human thought so vast that a whole realm had to be established for them and no length of time suffice to absorb and eradicate them? Were they, moreover, so diabolical that among all the shapes which concealed the unexpressed thoughts of the soul there was not one that was comforting or godlike?

A side glance at the Kher-heb convinced Jeremiah that the latter did not feel at all uneasy in this hell of intermingled forms. On the contrary, he seemed content to be in charge of a hell whose dizzying mysteries presented no problems to his mind. The two jackal-heads, blasé sons of Anubis who felt quite at home, nestled their snouts admiringly against him. The Kher-heb knew a great deal about the real and the unreal, infinitely more than Jeremiah did, but there was one thing that Osiris had not taught him: to distinguish between good and evil, between the clean and the unclean, between modesty and obscenity. He had no inkling of the flashing sword of revulsion, which extends eternally from heaven through earth into the depths, and divides the universe inexorably into two halves.

The farther they penetrated through the molesting crowds of phantoms, the cruder became the fusions of bestial shapes. Those which looked like hippopotami and crocodiles began to predominate more and more, and this showed that they were approaching the centre of Amenti, the deepest part of the abyss, the region of the Sixth and Seventh Hours of the Night, at the boundary of which the hall where the dead were judged rose on the left bank of the Ur-Nes. Jeremiah again felt the planks of a bark swaying beneath his feet. The Nile of night grew narrower; the gloom thickened. Now and then could be glimpsed the flash of golden gateways and the copper network of tall trellises. The barriers in this region were evidently becoming more numerous. It was not the gates and trellises, however, that presented the real dangers lying in wait for the souls. Whereas the region of terrifying phantoms had been animated by an irritating clucking and cackling, here there was only a fathomless silence, broken at intervals by a frenzied scream. This part of Amenti was allotted to the fearful powers that lay in ambush without becoming clearly visible. Instead of the absurd and monstrous fusions which they had just left behind them, they encountered beings of a very different kind who were called "exhorters" and "subduers." Jeremiah was aware of them though they remained beneath the surface of the Ur-Nes in the shape of crocodiles, alligators, sharks, and water-snakes. Their existence below the surface, their abrupt shooting out and vanishing again, showed the nature of the horrible assaults to which the soul was here exposed. The Kher-heb drew himself to his full height, preparatory to annihilating them by the mention of their names. Their names were lengthy, such as "Stinkface, That Urges Me to Drink My Urine and Devour My Excrement"! Woe to the soul that succumbed to such an exhorter! It would spend an eternity sullying itself. Another was called "Amām, Gorger, That Forces Me to Defile the Corpses of My Mother and Sister"! This was the most accursed of all lusts, which condemned to eternal and unnameable self-damnation the soul which did not know the exorcism. However, the true exorcism was known only to the initiate; that is to say, to him who had drawn into the light of his own consciousness the most secret stirrings of his sinful nature. The Kher-heb continued to conjure the monsters in a loud and clear voice: "Ibu-wer, That Forces Me to Sell My Father and My Ancestors to Their Enemy!" This was the way to exorcize the influence of the evil spirit which urged souls born in foreign countries or in bondage to deny their kindly parents, betray their descent, and try convulsively to be other than they were.

They had only a short way to go before they reached the nadir. Jeremiah felt the hand of the Kher-heb grow icy cold. One of the jackal-heads pressed close up and threw his arms round him; the other withdrew his rowing-pole and did the same to the accompaniment of pitiful snortings. They were passing through the dwelling place of Aapep. The Kher-heb drew a deep breath and thundered into the darkness with a voice of which Jeremiah would never have thought his delicate frame capable:

"Aapep, Primal Serpent, That Wishes to Force Me to Dismember My God!"

Any soul that succumbed to this temptation would die the second death, the death in death, which was not a form of extinction but a conscious state of being dead which was imaginable only to the soul that had died for the second time. Even the Kher-heb appeared to be filled with a profound fear. Jeremiah, however, was not afraid, since of all the evil spirits Aapep had least power over him. Egypt was in a different position, for was it not oppressed by the foreboding that it had long been deserving of the dual death? Had it not long since succumbed to Aapep and dismembered God, tearing Him into uncountable fragments? It was because of this crime against the unity of the Eternal One that Egypt had been conquered by Amenti. For the dismemberment of the one Unity and Truth forced men, however despairingly they might seek to intoxicate themselves, to set up the emptiness of death as their king. A thrill of awe shuddered through Jeremiah in this lowest hell of Aapep as he became imbued with the certain knowledge of the sanctification of Israel. Calmly he asked:

"Where shall I see her?"

The Kher-heb pointed forward into the empty distance without replying to his question. Had Zenua hastened on through all the temptations of the spirits of hell to emerge at last from the exit gate of the hall of judgment, where the region of the western land that belonged to the period after midnight began to rise towards the light? It was no longer possible to distinguish between land and water. They were rapidly approaching the place of judgment and roundabout them yawned the nothingness which swallowed up those who had been rejected by the judges. The two jackal-heads had been joined by others of their kind, who now formed a strong bodyguard round Jeremiah and the Kher-heb, and the snorting, barking group obstructed their view into the gloom. Swiftly as an arrow their bark glided along amidst a splashing and snapping and beating of the watery surface, as if they were surrounded by sharks and crocodiles, and a confused hum of human voices came nearer and nearer. In the wake of the nocturnal sun they would presumably have to dart past the hall where the final verdict was delivered and the silent Osiris, sitting with his forty-two beast-headed assessors, admitted or rejected the waiting souls as the great golden scales were weighted more heavily with omissions or commissions of acts of reverence towards the gods. Gradually the hubbub of agitated voices grew less confused and it was possible to distinguish individual words. Jeremiah listened to the shrieking and wailing confession of sins by a vast concourse of souls standing at the bar of judgment. "O Thou of the Long Strides, I have not done the things that the gods abominate!" "O Fire-Embracer, I have not purloined the sacrificial cakes of the gods!" "O Water-Beater, I have not cheated the dead of the garments and wrappings due to them!" "O Wamemti-Serpent. I have never lain with a man!" "O Robber of the Voice from Urit, I have not polluted myself in the holy places of the god of my city!" All these vindications and others of like nature were to be heard amidst the chaos of cries that came from the accused souls. Now and then they would cease, to be followed by the fateful silence in which the unuttered verdict was delivered. Jeremiah was filled with grief for these souls that were disappointed even in death, but the hall of judgment was soon left far behind and the bark of the Kher-heb had passed the tremendous portcullis which barred the way only to the shades who had been condemned.

The river widened and they had reached the land of the Seventh Hour of the Night, which was also the first hour of the reborn day within the womb. The Ur-Nes was illumined by a faint glow which came from the bark of the god with the nocturnal sun, as it glided towards the farther gate of Amenti in the distance. The bark of the Kher-heb and his guest, however, landed at the shore of the Seventh Hour of the Night, whose region was called "Iaru," meaning "the Fields of the Blessed." But what kind of blessedness was that which was not essentially different from the unblessedness of the earlier regions, and was even more shadowy than the regions of temptation and judgment? Had the souls suffered the earthly torture of dying, together with all the wandering, anxiety, and temptation to which they were exposed on their journey through Amenti, merely in order to chew the cud of the life they had finished with, like the continually recurring stale memory of food which had long since been eaten? On the shore of the Ur-Nes Jeremiah saw a fisherman whose greatest pleasure had once been to cast his line and gaze at it thoughtfully. Now his Kā was making the same movement. With a well-aimed swing his line flew through the air, but there was no line on the rod and no rod on the line, nor was there any water with fish to catch. There was nothing but the empty gesture of a deluded shadow deluding itself. The shades in the fields of Iaru had more distinct faces than those of the earlier regions—exactly in proportion to the lessened gloom—but there was no bliss in their features, rather something forced that seemed to be a wan mingling of the content for which they had hoped and the disappointment they were experiencing. No observing eye could have failed to suspect that all these human phantoms were collaborating only out of kindness and weak compliance in a preconcerted game, so as not to spoil an entertainment with which the gods of Egypt were amusing themselves. The blessed shades resembled a badly ruled people who, because they were compelled to choose between a terrible orderliness and an equally terrible chaos, had preferred the state of order. With an ardour that was heartbreaking they simulated a happiness they did not feel. Scribes sat there writing nothing, without a pen, on papyrus which did not exist. Women were watering the plants of a vegetable garden though there was neither water nor garden. Mowers reaped corn which was not there. Hunters aimed at wild game that seemed to dart past within striking distance, but they held neither bow nor arrow and their prey was a delusion. Families sat at meals, with jackal-heads pushing in front of them the dried-up foods that were the sacrifices to the dead. Fathers, mothers, brothers, and sisters did not look at one another as they put empty hands to their mouths and went through the empty motions of eating; and they were evidently as displeased at their lack of appetite as they were at the inadequate food. Yet this was the highest form of bliss, the fulfilment of all prayers that an honourable father offered up to the gods: that he should one day be united with his family and allowed to sit at table with them in the fields of Iaru. His family? None of them took any notice of the others! It was as if they were in a land of fools. The nucleus of the soul, the soul of the soul, persisted in a state of ultimate, unimaginable egotism which forbade it to show any awareness of its neighbour.

This bitterly insipid activity and feasting culminated in "the Land of Absolute Power and Formal Ceremony," which was the noblest of the regions. Kings sat on frail thrones and presided affectedly before a shadowy assembly as they graciously distributed their favours on all sides. Privy councillors of Pharaoh's personal retinue walked about elegantly, bowing and kissing the empty air or murmuring well-turned, ceremonious phrases. The experienced jackal-heads would occasionally grasp a couple of these councillors for their own amusement and push them forward to make their obeisance to one of the enthroned phantoms. But the king did not see his courtiers and the courtiers did not see their king. There was therefore no point in all the entertainments which the inventive children of Anubis arranged for their charges: ceremonious processions before Pharaoh, pilgrimages, now and then even a little battle. The aping by humorous jackal-heads of customs of the upper world—this was all that remained of formal ceremony and all that remained of absolute power, the most evil and fascinating of the instincts and one which was more deep-seated than love itself. Jeremiah watched the shadowy spectacle with disgust. The Kā had survived as a pale reflection of personality, an Amenti of the ego, aware only of itself and clinging with obstinate selfishness to its delusions. And this abominable state of wretchedness, in which a soul was wholly absorbed in itself without ever feeling the consuming urge to soar up to the one Creator of the Universe, was regarded by the Kher-heb and the whole of Egypt as a state of bliss!

Something happened to Jeremiah which he did not himself comprehend. It was not the voice of the Lord that suddenly came to him, but a heightening of consciousness, the joy of God—that wildly darting flame of his life. All at once

Zenua was gone from his mind. He forgot his will to sin, the thirst for vengeance, and the longing that had driven him to make the journey through Amenti, even his sense of disgust. He was aware only of his certitude that there was a higher salvation, a worthier state of bliss, and of an overflowing pity for the souls whom death had rendered so childish that they repeated their absurd lives in the form of even more absurd mimicry. Though he did not hear the voice of the Lord, he suddenly understood that it was not owing to his own sin, but to divine intent, that he had descended to the realm of the dead. For he had been sent to bring truth to the dead and to comfort them with the news that they too were ruled by the Lord of Life, who rejected death and did not forget that which He had created. And Jeremiah, who had been sanctified as the Lord's prophet among the nations, spread his arms wide and announced to the souls of Egypt:

"Hear ye, too, Amenti! The Lord our God, the Lord is One!"

He could not know whether this glowing message of comfort had any effect on the souls of the blessed. He had time only to feel the hand of the Kher-heb slip from his own, for at that moment the spurious and dubious vision of Amenti was effaced by an authentic vision more burning and absolute than any other he had ever experienced. Before him stood a man of might and radiance, and Jeremiah did not have to ask whence he had come. This was one of the men who had visited Abraham, the man with whom Jacob had wrestled, the messenger of the Lord come down from heaven. In his arms he carried a sleeping woman. Zenua! She was no rigid, enwrapped mummy wearing a mask, no insubstantial shade of the underworld, but the Zenua he had known in life, her lips parted like those of a child, a rosy flush on her cheeks, peacefully breathing; Zenua in a state of salvation, her body preserved intact. And the messenger spoke:

"Behold, this is Zenua Nephesh Hagoim, the chaste soul of the nations, who will remain in the place reserved for her until the time shall come. . . ."

What cry of exultation could be loud enough to give thanks for a message that annihilated annihilation? Zenua lived! Zenua, the sweet soul from the land of the heathen, was waiting for Jeremiah, the soul of Israel! She slumbered until the time should come for their marriage! Jeremiah was unable to give utterance to the great cry that burned within him, for he suddenly heard a clear and gentle voice which filled him with its dark mellowness.

"Thou shalt not take thee a wife, neither shalt thou have sons or daughters in this place. For the sons and daughters that are born in this place shall die of grievous deaths."

The forgotten exhortation of his youth! An exhortation that the Lord was repeating to him in this alien underworld! It ignored his renunciation, his flight to Egypt, and his sinful journey through Amenti as if they were naught. Jeremiah wanted to think it over, to try to understand its significance, and he raised himself on his elbow. The loose mummy wrapping fell away and he found that he was lying on his hard couch with the night far advanced. The white hem of the Kher-heb's robe was disappearing through the partly open door of his cell. It seemed to bear witness to its wearer's confusion, as if he had been put to shame.

Jeremiah was invested with new life. Everything that he had experienced in Noph and Amenti was as though melted away, and only the clear, gentle voice was real. He knew that something must have happened which involved an upheaval in his life. The period of leave granted him by the Lord was at an end, and he glowed with a passionate desire to revoke his renunciation and resume his task. Only now, after his journey through Egypt's realm of the dead, was he ripe for the work for which the Lord had summoned him. His limbs ached from the effects of his fasting and the magic draughts that had been administered to him, but he sprang up and rushed from his cell, leaving the last caravanserai by the light of the stars which illumined the sinister mass of the Temple of the Gates. It was a long walk through the empty western city, and dawn had come before he reached the house of the exiles. There was no porter at the gate; all the doors were open. The rooms were unoccupied and bare as if they had been pillaged. At last he found someone in the garden, the unwieldy eunuch, who groaned and perspired as he bent over sacks and bundles which he was tying together. With tears flowing down his cheeks he informed Jeremiah of what had happened. Two evenings ago the house had suddenly been surrounded by Ionian guards. Elnathan, the brother-in-law of Jehoiakim, had forced his way in with a troop of warriors from Judah and they had ransacked the place until at last they found the man they had come for: Urijah the prophet. The old man was at once bound with heavy chains and dragged away. His Royal Magnificence in Temporary Retirement, together with all his household, had been ordered by Pharaoh to set out for the south on the following day, and the faithful eunuch was about to follow them with their chattels.

Jeremiah pondered for some time with wrinkled brow. Then he stamped his foot.

"No!" he cried; then: "Urijah!" Pointing towards the north-east in the direction of Jerusalem, he said: "You will be able to find me when the time comes!"

Without looking round, he hastened from the garden and the house of his betrothal.

17

The Execution at the Gate of Potsherds

WHEN the news spread abroad in Judah that the greybearded prophet Urijah had been seized at Noph by the fierce Elnathan with the sanction of the Egyptian authorities, that he had been carried to Jerusalem and was being held in strict captivity, Baruch knew that his master would not calmly accept such an outrage committed in the house where he had been dwelling but would immediately set out for Jerusalem in order to come to the old man's aid. Jeremiah, for his part, knew that Baruch must be expecting his return and was probably already waiting for him at some convenient place. It was not difficult to guess where this would be, since the great caravan tracks met at Hebron and travellers from Egypt could hardly be missed there. Jeremiah also suspected that Baruch would have hired two asses, as he had done before, so that the journey to Jerusalem could be continued without delay. And he was not disappointed. After their long separation both master and pupil were impatient to meet, and they were both filled with the same anxiety for the fate of Urijah. Baruch sat waiting day and night in front of the inn at the southern gateway of Hebron, forcibly keeping himself awake that he might not fail to see every traveller who arrived. Jeremiah, however, was journeying with a large caravan that encountered bad weather and other disturbances, so that the cautious merchants who were his companions took their time and covered only short stretches each day.

Would they arrive in time? That was the one question with which the minds both of Baruch and Jeremiah were obsessed. The fact that Elnathan and his myrmidons had not slain Urijah on the way was proof that King Jehoiakim did not intend to dispatch his prisoner summarily, but would bring him before a court of justice and allow him the benefit of the Law. He was probably saving him for some special occasion, yet it was also possible that his mind was occupied for the time being by other diversions. His incalculable moods were the only quality Jehoiakim had inherited from his father, and it sometimes happened that a new building project, the necessity of deciding the colours in which the walls of some magnificent chamber were to be painted, or a fresh consignment of balsams, myrrh, and fragrant essences for his private laboratories claimed his attention so exclusively that his hatred slumbered, the continual chafing of his wounded vanity was mitigated, and for days on end his insulters were forgotten. It might equally well happen, however, that an oppressive dream, a slight diminution of self-confidence, or even a shaming thought would suddenly lash his wrath to fever pitch; then, woe to any poor wretches who were in his power!

In spite of his blasphemous decree at the pillar of the oath, Jehoiakim had not dared to abolish the Law of the Lord. In any case, no man had it in his power to abolish and make null that which owed its origin to God. He could, at the most, disregard and thereby break it. All the commandments relating to the holding of courts of justice and to the carrying out of penalties were accordingly still in force in Judah. The Lord in His compassion did not tolerate that a verdict should be pronounced by a single judge, or even by a judge raised above the others. In every city and in every community a court of elders had to be summoned, in order that a wise judgment might be lawfully delivered after the most minute elucidation of the divine Law and of the crime that had been committed. If one single member of the court found that the delinquency of which the prisoner stood accused was not worthy of death, then the punishment of "extermination from the people" could not be carried out. Even if judgment of death was unanimous, the Lord of Life had still provided that the execution of the sentence should not be too easy.

The other kings and nations of the world, all mightier than Israel, employed in their systems of justice authorized exterminators. These were experienced executioners, headsmen, hangmen, and they were frequently given titles which concealed their real calling. They were men of muscle, with swelling arms and great bared chest, who swung the two-handed sword with unerring aim over the head of a condemned sinner or thrust him with practised grip into the fiery furnace. This was not the case in Israel. Among all the nations of the world Israel was the only one that did not employ executioners, since the wise and cunning kindliness of the Law did not prescribe any form of extermination that could be carried out by one man. And that was the deeper significance of the legal procedure known as "stoning." When a man had sinned so gravely that the divine Law could no longer tolerate his existence among the people, and the stain had to be wiped out in order to preserve the purity and holiness of Israel, then it was necessary to shed blood. Blood, however, was sacred; even the blood of a murderer. The commandment, "Thou shalt not kill!" was always and everywhere valid, without the slightest reservation. No single man in Israel was permitted to take the life of another, not even an official specially appointed for the purpose by the State. Only the people as a whole was allowed to protect itself against a criminal by exterminating him, in the same way that it would have to protect itself against an external foe in time of war. Therefore the divine commandments laid down that all the male inhabitants of a town which had judged a man to be deserving of extermination should assemble before the gates, where, individually and collectively, with sharp stones in their hands, they should put the condemned criminal to death. All blood that was shed, of whosoever it might be, cried aloud to Heaven for vengeance. Even the blood of a criminal cried to Heaven for vengeance, not against an individual but against the whole community of Israel, which had to answer for it and purify itself. This was not possible in the case of a sentence of death ordered by a tyrant and executed by a shedder of blood whom he had specially appointed.

Moreover, the men who constituted the court of justice always had before their eyes the cruel duty of stoning which they themselves would have to assist in carrying out, and this helped to subdue their wrath, quite apart from the oppressive responsibility for bloodshed which they would be laying on the whole people.

Thus ran the interpretation of the Law concerning blood-guilt and blood-penance as Jeremiah had often expounded it to his disciple Baruch and his pupil Mattaniah; and he always used it as an apt proof of the holy commandment of the Lord that men should act together in unravelling the confusion of the world. Now both Jeremiah and Baruch, the one on his way from Egypt and the other waiting for him at Hebron, were hoping that the Law would save Urijah from the vengeance of King Jehoiakim.

Baruch waited day after day, and day after day Jeremiah was delayed as he journeyed with the caravan through the desert by the famous route along the coast which was known as "the Road of Gold and Incense." Neither impatience nor despair could help him, for there was no way of reaching Hebron more quickly. The Road of Gold and Incense was blocked by an incessant stream of merchants with their caravans taking advantage of the fact that the Egyptian frontier at Pithom and Tahpanhes had just been opened again. Pharaoh had ordered it to be closed in order that the roads might be kept clear for the ignominious return of his army, which had been scattered at Carchemish in the Land of Rivers. The last straggler from the boldest and most arrogant of all campaigns had now arrived back in Egypt, but Pharaoh had not grown in the slightest degree less boastful. It was beyond all imagined or imaginable possibilities that the incarnate Ptah could be defeated by any earthly power, and everything that happened, favourable or unfavourable, victory or defeat, took place in accordance with the predetermined plan of the kindly god and exactly as he had intended.

Jeremiah sat round the fire every evening with the merchants. Baruch too sat round the fire every evening with the merchants. Both in the desert and in Hebron the very same matters were related, discussed, and weighed. They spoke of the proclamations made by the royal heralds at Noph who announced that the Sun God Necho had been graciously pleased to bring his light-giving campaign to a conclusion. His purpose, which had been to cause the sun to shine amidst the darkness of the nations, had now been fulfilled. The heart of the kindly god was overflowing with such an immeasurable love that he had resolved to exhibit the robe which he had worn on the day of victory at Megiddo in the temple of Nu-Ptah, before dedicating it to the divinities of his bodyguard at Branchidæ. There it would serve to bring advantage and prosperity to the delighted and adoring citizens. This decree of Pharaoh was discussed by the merchants at Hebron and those who were travelling along the Road of Gold and Incense, but their debates and arguments were concerned less with the Sun God and Nu-Ptah than with the most recent phenomenon in the nocturnal sky. Marduk, the Jupiter of the starry heavens, had risen on earth in a new and brilliant incarnation. Nebuchadnezzar-Marduk had ascended the throne of Babylon in the shadow of the sacred Tower of E-temen-anki. This youthful ruler reflected to perfection the qualities and attributes of the deity that he was. It was the nature of the sun to move swiftly and consume with its rays, but it was characteristic of the stars that they shone with a deliberate light in their ordered courses. The merchants were intoxicated with their own wisdom as they nodded their heads with enjoyment. A hero who belonged to the day sky would have kept at the heels of his defeated enemy and destroyed him, subjugating the whole land down to the Stream of Egypt with the pomp of his victorious gods. That, however, was not the way of Nebuchadnezzar-Marduk; or rather, he did it in his own starry way, cautiously and inconspicuously, in spite of his youth. His conical-helmeted horsemen appeared in the countries of the petty kings, but only as armed escorts for men of peace—paunchy dealers, manufacturers, importers, and exporters, who hid their calculating thoughts behind the dignity of their oiled and artfully curled beards. They examined the barley, smacked their lips as they tasted the new wine, dug their hands into the cool flax, felt the linen that was put before them, called upon their gods to witness the losses they would suffer, and finally sealed the purchase with a bond whose intricate clauses concealed snares for the feet of the unwary.

The ruler of these men was Nebuchadnezzar, and therefore it was the unanimous opinion of the merchants as they sat round the camp fires that his epoch promised to be good for trade. Marduk was a pious and mighty hero, a god who rejoiced in the thought of his divinity, but to the astonishment of his court he had chosen as his symbol not a staff, or a scourge, or a sword, but a golden spade. He signified by this that he was setting himself up not as a conqueror, but as a new architect of the world. The watchword that he proclaimed to the nations was "The Peace of Babylon!"

Thousands of spades were already loosening the earth to make new roads and divert the beds of rivers into straight canals. Marduk's cool strength, however, was derived from the holy science of the starry sky, which he shared with the gods and which was considerably more reliable than they were. For the stars, thought the merchants of every country as they discussed the subject, were true soothsayers and there were no false prophets among them. Baruch at Hebron tried to bring the conversation round to the true prophet Urijah, to King Jehoiakim and the powers that were now ruling in Judah, but his compaions refused to be drawn, blinked their eyes anxiously as they looked about them, and quickly changed the subject.

Late one night, when Baruch was sleeping with his head on the saddle at the crossroads, he was awakened by a subdued bustle and the flare of torches. As he opened his eyes he saw men from Cush unloading bales from the backs of kneeling camels, and when he opened them wider he beheld Jeremiah at his side gazing at him in absorption. Baruch took a firm hold of himself. He knew that his master shyly avoided all demonstrations of emotion. His way was to disappear secretly and return without warning, and Baruch acted as if they had been separated for not more than a few days and had met again punctually in accordance with previous arrangement. He stretched his limbs to give an appearance of composure that he did not feel, jumped up, saddled the asses, tightened the girths, and said: "By the time the sun rises we can be in Jerusalem."

Before they mounted, the two men looked at each other searchingly. Jeremiah had left a slim pale-faced youth whose immature beard grew in untidy and straggling tufts. Now he found a sturdy man, even slightly inclined to corpulence, who wore a pointed beard but kept his upper lip shaved as was the custom. Jeremiah, however, had undergone an even more surprising change in Baruch's eyes. Was it possible that the long-lashed youth with the delicate, girlish complexion that reddened or paled so easily could have acquired so many lines and wrinkles during the years he had spent at Noph? And the man to whom his mother still referred as her "youngest child" had already grown a little grey at the temples, while his cheekbones stood out prominently. "After the great pleading and death of the heroic King Josiah," thought Baruch to himself, "into what hells must you have descended, Jeremiah, during your sojourn by the Nile?" But the man to whom this unspoken question might have been addressed kept the secret of his descent to hell locked firmly within his breast. Never would his lips speak of the unclean apparitions of Amenti. Even Baruch, his old disciple, never learned of the jackal-heads, the tempting spirits, the shades of the unhappy blessed, or the vision of Zenua in the arms of the messenger. Jeremiah had turned his eyes away from his friend and was gazing towards the north, where the hilly region of Jerusalem was mistily outlined in the light of the setting moon. The deep furrow between his brows revealed a passionate resolve and a will to fight which were new to Baruch and filled him with amazement. Jeremiah seemed to have carved a new personality out of himself but to be dissatisfied with his own handiwork. They rode as they had been accustomed to do since their youth, Jeremiah keeping in front and Baruch an ass's length behind.

The fortified gate at which the great southern Road of Gold and Incense ended was called "the Gate of the Valley," since it rose high above the Vale of Ben-Hinnom. To their surprise they found it barred when they arrived that morning, and occupied by a double rank of the royal bodyguard. They therefore had to turn off towards the east and ride along the path at the side of the irregular, turreted city wall in order to enter by the next gate. This was "the Gate of Potsherds," which pierced the wall of Jerusalem at its southern end where it formed an acute angle above the royal gardens. This gate was strongly protected by watch-towers and bulwarks, and in front of it stretched a drear, sloping meadow to which it owed its name, for here was the refuse heap where the whole city dumped its broken pots and other rubbish. Five pyramids of potsherds accumulated in this meadow every year, and morning and evening they were haunted by throngs of beggar women digging among the discarded litter in the hope of finding some lost treasure that a wealthy household had inadvertently thrown away. It was not surprising that the place was regarded as one of ill repute, for it was a favourite resort of evil spirits, of tramps who had been refused admission to the city, and of suicides, who found a few gnarled sycamores on which to hang themselves. That the execution of criminals by the lawful process of stoning was also carried out here was only natural. The meadow bore a number of different names, of which the most usual among the people was "Aceldama" or "the Field of Blood." The more cultured citizens, who in accordance with ecclesiastical custom preferred a euphemistic term to the blunt truth, called it simply the "Potter's Field," for among the wretched booths which supplied the needs of the poor there were two potter's stalls whose owners profited by the fact that broken pottery required replacement.

When Jeremiah and Baruch had ridden round the last bastion, they saw to their further astonishment that the Gate of Potsherds was also guarded by armed troops, while the meadow was crowded with people. They tied their mounts to a ring in the wall near where a sentry was standing, but when they asked him the reason for the multitude he gave only the laconic and peevish reply: "They are waiting for the King." With an intuitive anxiety they hastened nearer. The morning sun stood high above the Mount of Olives and playful reflections were chasing one another across the cedars, columns, domes, and fountains of the royal gardens. They forced their way through the excited crowd, but were continually pushed back. Jeremiah heard scoffing murmurs and realized that the people of Jerusalem had profoundly changed since the days of Josiah. Faces like his own, illumined with the spirit of the Lord, aroused unease, mockery, and hatred. Men with mean, coarse features that betrayed their violent and brutal natures had formerly been despised;

now they were unmistakably treated with respect. The feeling that he was an object of hatred inspired Jeremiah with strength. Conscious that he was superior to these people, he thrust their resistance aside, until at last he and Baruch were standing in the front row. A wide space had been cleared and roped off by the royal guards in front of the gate, and in the centre a low platform, with steps leading up to it, had been erected for the King's throne. A number of dignitaries and officials, nearly all of them new men, were already waiting for their master. Jeremiah could recognize only two of them: Elnathan, the fierce, ill-tempered warrior, who wore a purple cloak and plume, and Jerachmeel, a cousin of Jehoiakim who had never neglected while Josiah was alive to show his disrespect for the great King. This prince of David had a projecting chin and thin, tight lips. Both Elnathan and Jerachmeel stood at the side of the throne.

Baruch drew a breath of relief. The preparations did not indicate that a man was about to be put to death by stoning, but it looked as if Jehoiakim was arranging one of his surprises, for he liked to keep the people in suspense. Presumably he was going to show himself on his throne as a judge and orator, since nothing pleased him more in his office as King than the opportunity it afforded him of exercising his voice. Scarcely had Jeremiah and Baruch taken up their positions when a company of the bodyguard marched through the Gate of Potsherds and lined up in a double rank, bristling with weapons, for the King to pass through. He lived in constant fear of assassination and never took a step without being accompanied by armed guards. As soon as he reached the platform he dashed up the steps, as Josiah had been accustomed to do. It was a mere empty copying of the manner of his father, the father whose work he had overthrown but whom he tried to imitate with his own feeble body. Jeremiah understood from Jehoiakim's attempt to create a startling effect that he was disguising his personal defects. In awkward contrast to his vain will to act the part of the new David was the costume he was wearing, for under the sky-blue cloak of Judah's kings he was clad in the short, stiff kilt of the gods of Egypt and the coloured cape. Behind him stood his chamberlains carrying standards and great ostrich fans, as if he were Pharaoh. When he spoke his voice rang out high and piercing over the meadow, filling the people at first with terror but very soon carrying them away with its power. It had a harsh tone and cracked with hatred, but his cunning skill in playing on his hearers' feelings enabled him to control it.

"Mark ye, people of Jerusalem!" he cried. "The King rules and the King guides you. He abolishes that which does you injury and sets up that which will bring you profit. He alters the commandments of the Law for your sake and because your advantage in the world demands it. He takes upon his own head the blood of criminals, for they are all criminals, these instigators and rebels who cause unrest among the people, who in the name of Adonai fan the flames of wrath against His anointed and the house which He built. The King will not let his right hand grow weary until little Judah has become great and free among the nations! . . ."

A roar of exultation burst from the crowd at these words. Jehoiakim had cleverly touched the nerve of ambition, the easiest way to gain the ear of a people. Amenti lay hidden in the breast of everyone, and particularly in the heart of a mob. The dead wanted to hear that they were alive; little men wanted to hear that they were great; and those who had suffered defeat wanted to be told that they were the victors.

The voice of Jehoiakim rose even more shrilly above the approving roar, lashing the people to renewed excitement.

"Who is it that wishes to cast you out from your inheritance, people of Jerusalem? Who is it that wishes to make you serve your enemies in lands that you have never seen? It is not the Lord, who dwells in heaven above and brought you to this land. It is those who continually bear his name upon their lips because they hate you and want to make you less than the dregs among the nations. Look into their minds and you will not find Adonai in them, but only hatred of you and your King. . . ."

The cry of rage which this denunciation drew from the crowd was so overwhelming and so constantly repeated that even the penetrating voice of Jehoiakim was drowned by it. Jeremiah, the blood draining from his face, seized the rope in front of him as if he would tear it to pieces, but Baruch took a firm grip of his hands to restrain him from committing what would have been an act of madness. The next moment they both grew rigid with horror, as something happened which was over so quickly that no human intervention could have prevented it. Two men in loin-cloths hurled a half-naked figure, almost hidden by the ropes with which he was bound, on the floor of the platform in front of Jehoiakim so that the boards creaked. Whether this human bale was alive or dead, conscious or unconscious, it was impossible to tell. Jeremiah strained his eyes to see if he could recognize the prophet Urijah, whom he had comforted with filial reverence only a few months before at Noph. Would that his hand, which brought death to those he loved, had never touched him! He could not recognize the man of Adonai who had once restored him to faith in himself and the truth of his sanctification. He saw only a yellowish, bony body that was pulled to its feet by the two jailers and cast on its knees again before the King. There was a chill silence. The ghastly figure neither whimpered nor lamented. Its head inclined almost sleepily on its left shoulder. Urijah had to die because of the word of the Lord, and nobody could save him. When would the first sharp stone fly through the air to shatter his skull?

No one in the crowd could have anticipated the horror which rendered even more diabolical the murder of a just man. No men chosen by lot from the community formed a circle round the innocent prophet to exterminate him from Israel by stoning. There was only one who raised his hand against him, and that was the King. A broadsword was handed to Jehoiakim.

That which was done by a king was not the casual act of a mortal, induced by hatred, fear, or revenge. The act of a king was significant; it came from above; it was a flash of lightning that lasted for ever, and the scribes sat down to record it at once and for all time in the Book of Chronicles of the Kings of Judah. Jehoiakim was fully aware of the importance of what he was about to do, and he told himself that neither hate nor thirst for vengeance moved his hand. Since there was no executioner to act as his deputy, it devolved upon him to exterminate his arch-enemy who had spoken the word that must remain unuttered in a land where the word of the King held sway. Jehoiakim had thrown off the cloak of David, revealing his puny figure as he stood testing the sharpness of the sword. Neither the Egyptian cape nor the clasps, armlets, and bracelets that he wore could hide the fact that the arms of the King of Judah were thin as spindles. He raised the sword, swung it over his head to show the people his strength, and brought it whizzing down on the figure in front of him. The blow had been falsely aimed and struck the prophet's shoulder, which was dyed red by a fountain of blood. Urijah screamed once. Jehoiakim sprang back, his face distorted with horror and loathing. He reeled as if he were about to swoon, then hurled the sword away and saved himself in time by pressing a jar of smelling-salts to his nostrils. Meanwhile one of the soldiers had picked up the sword and completed the work of extermination with two strokes that split Urijah's skull. The King and his court left the scene of execution more rapidly than they had entered. Sympathetic spectators wrapped the corpse in the burial clothes that had been prepared and carried it to the burial place of the poor at the edge of the Potter's Field. The rope was taken down and the crowd gradually dispersed, most of them following the court with an excited hubbub of voices through the Gate of Potsherds. A few silent or weeping men gathered round the pool of blood in front of the scaffold, but Jeremiah stood motionless and thought and thought. . . .

Suddenly he raised his head, and his eye fell on one of the potter's booths. "An earthen pitcher . . . the largest there is," he said with an effort. Baruch understood at once that the command came not from a heart torn by its own helplessness, but from the will of the Lord. He hastily sprang to the booth and bought the largest pitcher that the potter possessed. It was a very tall, bulky vessel such as the pilgrims of a village would take to the Temple with their communal drink offering. Fired hard as a stone, smooth surfaced, and adorned with black borders and gilded edges, it could hold two measures of wine, and even when empty its weight was so considerable that Baruch carried it only with difficulty. Jeremiah, however, his eyes swimming in tears and his breath coming sobbingly, seized the great jar with both hands and lifted it onto his head as women carried their water pitchers. Baruch was startled at this proof of a hitherto unrevealed physical strength, which could not be the strength of his master alone. He kept close at Jeremiah's heels so as to be ready in case the strength with which he had been suddenly endowed should as suddenly leave him, but Jeremiah bore the vessel, which it was usually the work of several men to carry by the handles, as if it were weightless, and he did not falter. As he walked he turned slowly on his axis like a dancer, or a juggler at a fair, and by this strange action he succeeded in gathering more and more people round him. They began to laugh and scoff, for they thought he must be possessed, an amiable madman with whom they could have their joke. Gibing at a crazy fellow was just the sort of relaxation they required at that moment, and soon he was the object of the banal jests and jeering pinpricks for which a city mob is never at a loss. But they suddenly grew dumb, and there was a perplexed silence when Jeremiah opened his twitching lips and they heard the unfamiliar or forgotten voice that was the voice of the prophet of Anathoth. He seemed to be completely absorbed in the voice with which he spoke. There was no piercing quality, no penetrating harshness in it. It issued deep, full, and mellow, though shaken by repressed sobs, as he invited the people to follow him.

"Ye kings, princes, priests, men, and women of this city, come with me that ye may see the deed and hear the word of the Lord!"

The people were spellbound by something more than mere curiosity at the action of a presumably priestly man who had cast off his dignity and held a great earthenware pitcher poised upon his head like a juggler. It was also something more than the heart-stirring power of an unfamiliar voice. Even those who were passionately loyal to the new King were impressed by the audacity and tremendous courage of the man. Scarcely the fourth part of an hour had passed since the oldest and most celebrated prophet of the age had been slaughtered as though in a shambles, and already another had arisen with foolhardy daring to proclaim the word of the Lord in terms that would certainly contain nothing flattering for the ear of Jehoiakim. It was as if the soul of the slain prophet had immediately changed its body that it might continue indestructibly to prophesy against the King. Such rashness made even the mob of Jerusalem breathless, fond as it was of violence. Even heroic warriors went to battle in armour and carrying shields, and they stood shoulder to shoulder in their hundreds. But where were the shields and armour of these solitary prophets, where were the hundreds of comrades standing with them shoulder to shoulder? Many a dulled and brutish soul began to have an inkling of the only form of courage that is of any value on the broad battlefield of the earth: the courage of the mind. Moreover, the bloody deed of Jehoiakim, the symbolic significance of which had been ruined by his false aim, had done secret harm to the King's prestige.

At first Jeremiah was followed by only a few women and girls. Then these were joined by a few groups of mostly older men who had obviously overcome their fear of listening to forbidden words for which, after years of oppression, their hearts were craving. Among them were starved and miserable creatures who did not possess sufficient rags to cover their nakedness. Finally, such youths as had remained behind on the Field of Blood attached themselves to the throng with curious, suspicious, and even hostile looks. Was this man, this dancing fool, one of those who did not wish that little Judah should become great and powerful among the nations?

Ten steps before the Gate of Potsherds Jeremiah paused, and the people crowded behind him expectantly. He pressed his eyelids together and swayed as if he were about to collapse under the weight of the pitcher.

Suddenly his face darkened with raging anger. Raising the great vessel high above his head with a strength that seemed superhuman, he smashed it to a thousand fragments on the ground in front of the gate.

"Thus saith the Lord of hosts!" The words broke from him in a loud sobbing cry. "Even so will I break this people and this city as one breaketh a potter's vessel that cannot be made whole again. . . ."

18

With His Feet in the Stocks

VERY few people in the crowd followed Jeremiah and Baruch as they continued on their way to the Temple. The symbolic act of shattering the pitcher, together with the terrible prophecy, had intimidated both those who wanted to hear the word of the Lord proclaimed and those who had watched out of mere curiosity; for it was dangerous to be seen in the company of such a man without summoning the authorities to take action against him. The city was full of Jehoiakim's spies, informers, and agents.

No one had ever heard a prophet foretelling such a fate for a city that had existed since prehistoric times and contained in its midst the only dwelling on earth of the eternal creative God. If the Lord surrendered Jerusalem, He would be surrendering Himself, since He was associated with His city eternally through the Temple. If He smashed Jerusalem like a potter's vessel, He would Himself be without shelter and deprived of sacrifice, prayer, even name, as the High Priest would no longer be able to whisper it in the Holy of Holies. The fall of Jerusalem would be sheer suicide on the part of the Lord. The inhabitants of the proud capital were sufficiently acquainted with the doctrine of the indissoluble interdependence of God and Jerusalem, and it had not in vain been proclaimed with such insistence from the pulpits in the courtyard of the Temple. It was fortunate for themselves that not all the men of Adonai were like the pessimistic and bitter Urijah, who had paid so bloodily that day for his prophecies of calamity. Most of them were benevolently inclined towards the priests, and promises of a brighter future flowed like honey from their lips. How was it possible, the people asked themselves, for a man to live, work, and serve God when he was told that he and his would be shattered on the morrow like a potter's vessel? It was therefore better to inform against this smasher of pitchers or else forget him altogether, if one did not want to get into trouble oneself. By the time Jeremiah and Baruch reached the outer courtyard, the crowd had dwindled to a dozen poor and elderly men.

Baruch was anxious as he walked along beside Jeremiah, and he tried passionately to dissuade him from needlessly challenging the authorities. Otherwise he would probably share the fate of Urijah. Of what further use was the old prophet in his bloodstained burial clothes? Even Adonai, for whom he had battled, could do no more with him and turned away with loathing from his unclean corpse. There was no difference, declared Baruch, between a dead king, a dead prophet, and a dead dog.

Everything that Baruch said was undeniable, and even if Jeremiah had been listening to his solicitous advice he would not have been able to refute it. In any case, he was not trying to challenge the authorities or endanger his life. But what was he to do? His mind was overflowing with the voice of the Lord, whose urge in him was so strong that the idea of danger was grasped by his reason but not by his soul.

On the last working day of the week there was little activity in the outer courtyard. The priests had long since concluded the morning prayers and sacrifices; it was nearly noon. Servants were hurrying along with brooms and pails, while

Levites supervised their work so that the white stone flags should gleam without blemish on the Sabbath. Priests and scribes were walking through the galleries with their pupils, and the voices of both teachers and scholars rose and fell as they grew more and more involved in the intricacies of theological disputation. Attendants carried baskets filled with scrolls to the cells where zealous students were following in the footsteps of the great Shaphan. Other learned men were strolling about by themselves, discussing problems in their own minds with an absorbed smile. Nothing seemed to have changed. Nobody who witnessed this sequestered, priestly activity could have cherished a suspicion that Jerusalem was in the grip of the most deliberate apostasy or that the high dignitaries of the Temple and the Law had suffered one of God's sanctified prophets to be murdered without a word of protest. Among these pillars prevailed not the blatant sin of violence but the abstract sin of the mind, which subtly studied the Word without keeping its commandments, and indulged in hair-splitting interpretation of the Law without shouldering its burden.

Jeremiah shook off Baruch's arm as the latter tried to prevent him from rushing into disaster. With one leap he sprang up the steps of the gallery without entering one of the pulpits, and his clear voice rang far out over the courtyard.

"Thus saith the Lord of hosts, the God of Israel; Behold, I will bring evil upon this place, the which whosoever heareth, his ears shall tingle. Because they have forsaken me . . . and have filled this place with the blood of innocents. . . ."

The scholars walking in the galleries and the people in the courtyard stopped and turned in horror towards the resounding voice. Then everybody began to run silently towards

Jeremiah, until the group in front of him had increased to a hundred or more, and they listened dumbfounded to the monstrous words which this man was daring to utter in broad daylight within the precincts of the holy Temple. The audacious orator seemed, moreover, to be in full possession of his senses, unlike the frenzied, gesturing prophets to whom they were accustomed. It was obvious from his manner that he was not raving wildly, but knew exactly what he was saying, even though the words were wrested torturingly from his lips.

"And I will make this city desolate . . . and an hissing . . . Every one that passeth thereby shall be astonished and hiss . . . because of all the plagues thereof. . . ."

Jeremiah got no further. He felt a hand laid upon his shoulder and heard a voice murmuring behind his back:

"Pashur is hard of hearing. Would the prophet of Zebaoth repeat his words?"

Jeremiah turned and found himself face to face with Pashur, the First Keeper of the Door and the highest official of the Temple, who was responsible for keeping order in the sanctuary and was in charge of a special tribunal. Pashur's button eyes regarded Jeremiah with a fierce benevolence and his square beard trembled in an odd way. But Jeremiah did not lower his eyes, which flashed with anger as they recognized the conspirator who had doubtless been in previous possession of information concerning Eliakim's dastardly invasion of Jerusalem. In a loud voice, as if he were really speaking to a deaf man, he repeated word for word the Lord's threat to Jerusalem. The people assembled on the steps stared open-mouthed and wondered how this battle between the powerful Pashur and the defenceless Jeremiah would end. The Keeper of the Door nodded contentedly.

"Now I have heard quite clearly what you are prophesying."

He stepped close up to Jeremiah while the warden of the Temple and his accompanying guards ranged themselves behind him.

"You are aware," said Pashur in a low voice, "that every one who asserts that the words he speaks are those of Adonai must be prepared to take the responsibility for what he says. I therefore ask you not to cause any vexation and not to attempt to defend yourself, since it can profit you nothing. Follow peacefully the men who are standing behind you and create no disturbance, otherwise you will only make things worse for yourself."

After this calm exhortation Pashur turned away without further formality and quietly disappeared down the gallery, while the warden came forward and ordered the guards to take Jeremiah in their midst. These men were Levite jailers who, because they were equipped with leather thongs, were known familiarly as "thong-swingers." The learned spectators, content with the issue of the unequal encounter, resumed their pensive promenade while the common people dispersed timidly, since Jerusalem was ruled by force. There were only a few who followed Jeremiah as he was led away, and finally the only one to remain was Baruch.

In order to reach the Temple Gate of Benjamin, which was situated in the northern wall of the Temple Mount, they had to walk a long way round the whole outer courtyard. In the thick walls were guard-rooms, offices, dungeons, and prison cells, all of which came within the domain of the Keeper of the Door, and here too lived the "thong-swingers" whose duty it was to keep watch over the Temple night and day, provide the external guards, prevent excesses when crowds assembled on festive occasions, seize anyone who violated the rules of the Temple, and arrest troublesome prophets. Everybody whom they apprehended was brought for swift sentence before the Keeper of the Door, who was allowed to impose various penances but could inflict only two serious punishments: whipping and the stocks.

Jeremiah was thrust by his guards into an empty cell where there was nothing but a mat, and on this he silently sat down. As he was worn out by the hardships of his journey and the dreadful events of the day, he fell into a deep sleep which even the noise outside and the laughter of the jailers were unable to disturb. Suddenly he was pulled up roughly from the mat. He had not noticed the entry of Pashur, who stood and observed him with his little glittering eyes while he tried to infuse into his voice a caustic amiability.

"The son of Hilkiah of Anathoth is again in Jerusalem. . . . He had disappeared after having advised his credulous King so mischievously. . . ."

"My royal benefactor appointed me as tutor to his youngest son."

"And now you have left your pupil! . . . Who summoned you to come hither?"

"I have been summoned by the Lord."

"You have been summoned by the Lord? . . ."

The Keeper of the Door paused for a moment with an air of mockery, before he spoke again in an even more benevolent tone:

"You should praise the Lord for having led you into the arms of Pashur, for you have been a sad blackslider. Were I not the father of all crazy prophets, I should feel it my duty to hand you over for judgment to the court of the King. Therefore be content and grateful that the kind-hearted Keeper of the Door has taken you into his charge."

This was at the same time Pashur's sentence on his prisoner. Two of the jailers seized Jeremiah, who lowered his long lashes and grew pale as he murmured with an effort:

"Let Pashur of the priestly house of Immer consider, before he gives his orders, what he is doing to the son of Eli and Abiathar."

"The son of Eli and Abiathar should himself consider what his own conduct has been. Let him rejoice at the punishment which is to be meted out to him, and that he is not being treated in the way he deserves, as Urijah was."

A cry sprang from Jeremiah's tortured heart:

"Do not touch me!"

But it was no use. Hardly had Pashur left the cell when Jeremiah was dragged by the jailers into a near-by dungeon, where filthy hands tore off his clothes and strapped his white body to a long board with ropes that cut into his flesh. He struggled with all his strength, but he had suffered too much to be able to hold out for long. From the surrounding gloom stepped a man who carried not the ordinary leather strap but a tailed scourge. In accordance with an old regulation this flogger was not a pure Levite, for the office had always to be filled by someone who had sprung from the unlawful union of a Levite with a bastard female slave. Though his trade was plied within the precincts of the Temple, it was still regarded as being in the same category as the despised trades of the barbers, bath-attendants, washers, and tanners. His bared breast shone with oil. When the warden of the Temple signalled, the first light stroke lashed down on Jeremiah's back.

Then something occurred which filled the jailers and the flogger with the utmost confusion, since interruption of the punishment was not allowed and no unsuccessful blow could be repeated a second time. Baruch had managed to slip into the dungeon by bribing the sentry at the gate. At first the warden paid no attention to him, as he presumably imagined him to be a witness appointed by Pashur. But when the first blow struck the delicate body of his master, Baruch roared with the voice of a lion:

"You know not what you are doing! You are striking your God in this man!"

With a strength that would not have been suspected from his incipient corpulence he sprang at the throat of the flogger, who dropped his scourge and crashed to the ground. Then ensued a wild struggle which seriously disturbed the dignity proper to the carrying out of a legal sentence. Woe to the captain of the guard if Pashur heard of the incident! Even here, on the margin of the Temple Mount and during the chastisement of a delinquent, the first precept to be obeyed was the preservation of order. Baruch's intervention, however, was decisive for the further course of the proceedings. He shook off the jailers who hurled themselves upon him like a wild boar freeing itself from a pack of hounds, and his voice reverberated terrifyingly through the vaulted chamber: "You are striking Adonai, your God!" Every time the flogger raised his arm to deal a fresh stroke, Baruch hurled himself between Jeremiah and the lash, so that both he and the jailers who were clinging to him received a goodly portion of the blows. His face, already dripping with sweat, was soon covered with red weals, but he did not give up until at last a blow from a cudgel hurled him into a corner. The breathless warden did not know whether the full number of strokes permissible, "forty less one," had been dealt, and in order not to infringe the Law, which had already been violated by what had occurred, he signalled to the agitated flogger that the punishment was at an end.

Jeremiah had swooned, not on account of the physical pain, which he hardly felt, but because of the overwhelming humiliation to which he had been subjected. Nobody had ever before raised a hand to strike him; not even his stern father. The burning lashes on his back had not affected him, but he could not endure the dishonour, the ignominy to which he had been so savagely exposed by order of Pashur. Two strokes with the sword had split the skull of Urijah, and then he knew no more. Jeremiah, on the other hand, was acutely conscious of his galling degradation, and he bit his tongue to prevent himself from crying out, until at last his soul sank into darkness. The jailers quickly brought him to by throwing bucketfuls of cold water over him; he fell into a state of dull apathy. Let Pashur's will prevail. The desecration of his body and the humiliation of his soul could never be forgotten. When the jailers carried him out he felt as if it was someone else they were carrying. Even the burning weals were not part of him, but seemed to be outside him. He looked numbly at the wooden stocks, sheathed with iron, in front of which they set him down. He felt a remote twinge of pain as his feet were twisted outwards and the stocks closed over his ankles. The sun poured down hotly on the white stone flags, but Jeremiah could see only a number of creeping shadows that seemed to be peering in at him—shadows of Amenti. Someone moved stealthily and sat down beside him. The warden had locked up the disciple with his master as a punishment. Jeremiah suddenly sank backwards and his head fell softly on Baruch's lap. Above his head he saw a scarred face, like an unwavering star. Baruch's lips moved, but he could not find the right word to say. Now and then a heavy drop fell on Jeremiah's cheek, compounded of blood, tears, and sweat.

The stocks of the Temple were set up at the Gate of Benjamin and there delinquents were exposed not only to public contempt, but, what was even worse, to the jeers of the populace. Contempt is revocable when men realize that it rests upon a legal error or upon slanderous gossip; the poisonous jeering of a mob cannot be washed away. It is like a scorpion's venom that corrodes for all time. It cannot be erased from the memory and leaves a permanent scar, whether it is nourished by truth or by lies. No time of the day was more favourable for the exposure of a prisoner in the stocks than towards evening, when the outer courtyard of the Temple was filled with idlers and the rumour quickly spread which sent them all hurrying to the Gate of Benjamin that they might lend emphasis to the penalty by their jeers, which they regarded as an elevating duty.

Broken by his degradation, Jeremiah lay apathetically with his head in Baruch's lap and resigned his soul to the punishment which made him "desolate and a hissing," as he himself had prophesied concerning Jerusalem in the name of the Lord. He could now feel in himself what this meant. The hissing and murmuring, the coughing and laughter, the curiosity and even the sympathy of those who crowded round the stocks, seemed to bury him under layer after layer of shame like dust in the desert. He closed his eyes and sank into the hell of his misery, where he could find no comfort—not even in the thought of Zenua, for her time had not yet come. From the ring of onlookers he suddenly heard a toothless voice that he seemed to recognize, and it rose loud above all the other mocking noises. This was what Jeremiah heard:

"Just look! Whom have we here? . . . The youngest son of the priestly house of Hilkiah of Anathoth. All his life he has been an idler and a sluggard, and now he has become a corrupter of men to boot. I, Shamariah, the poorest of the poor of Anathoth, I know his father's house, for it is as good as my own and I sit at table there as the least of God's guests. Praise be to the Lord our God that Hilkiah has not lived to see his youngest son in the stocks! The good-for-nothing broke his heart even without this disgrace. And he is bringing his mother's grey hairs to the grave, for he lets her languish in her anxiety for him. How little he resembles his estimable brothers, who bear the burdens of life and fill the plate of the poor with generous gifts! Shamariah, a poor but godly man, was not good enough for him. He was always a man of ambition. And now, just look at him! A prophet of the Lord! This is where he has got to after pushing himself into the presence of kings and making himself conspicuous—sitting in the stocks, like a drunkard or a thief! A precious honour, a delightful exaltation for a prophet of Adonai and a guest at the table of the King, forsooth! Even the poorest of the poor can envy him. If it were not on the eve of Sabbath, so that a pious man may not undertake a journey, Shamariah would run to Anathoth, in spite of his eighty years, that he might be the first to bring the news of this precious honour for the house of Hilkiah, this delightful exaltation. . . ."

Such was the mocking speech, delivered with obvious enjoyment, of Shamariah, the chief of the beggars, who had come to Jerusalem for the purpose of offering up a burnt sacrifice in the name and at the expense of a number of his benefactors. The eloquence of the filthy old man seemed to fill the onlookers with pleasure. He acted as the leader of the scoffers, and they kept on interrupting him with their laughter and applause. Only once did Jeremiah open his eyes and turn them towards his tormentor. The face of the beggar, with its tousled hair and beard, sweated with self-satisfaction. Since Jeremiah had been touched by the hand of God, men seemed to hate him, yet there was no reason for their hatred.

The trumpets of the priests sounded for the evening sacrifice and the people began to disperse. When the courtyard had emptied, the guards took pity on the prisoner and loosened the stocks a little so that he could move his ankles in the holes. A mat was spread beneath him and Baruch was given a blanket, while both of them were refreshed with food and drink. The night was mild and Jeremiah sank into a semi-stupor which brought him oblivion, but about the time of the change from the first night watch to the second he was awakened by something that made him raise his head. He saw that a man had approached and was bending over him. He did not at once recognize Hananiah in the gloom. During the fateful years that had passed since their last meeting in the days of King Josiah, Hananiah seemed to have prospered in his mission as a prophet. His pleasant face was still full and youthful, while Jeremiah's cheeks had grown hollow and his temples grey. Hananiah's soft little beard glistened with perfumed oil, his coat was of the finest purple tissue, and his rough prophet's cloak was folded over his arm, for he regarded the hairy mantle as a banner rather than a garment. With well-tended, milk-white hands he set a little lamp on the ground. Then he sat down carefully so that the faint light flickered between him and Jeremiah and cast queer shadows.

"Let Jeremiah not suspect my motives," he whispered. "A brother comes to comfort his brother. Base and unjust is the treatment which has been meted out to you."

He untied a little leathern bag from his girdle and took from it a sponge soaked in vinegar, together with a number of phials and jars. The sponge he tore into two pieces, giving one to Jeremiah and the other to Baruch. The jars contained pungent essences, and in the phials were narcotics and a sleeping-draught, of which he made Jeremiah drink a little. After this work of charity he sat silent and declined to listen to words of gratitude.

"My comrade from Anathoth should not thank me. We went forth together into the world. . . ."

He resumed his silence and shifted his position, as if he were prepared to spend the night in company with the prisoner. As he gazed thoughtfully into the smoky flame of the little oil lamp, there was not the slightest trace of malicious pleasure on his features at the wretchedness of his rival, but rather a secret sorrow of which he hoped to free himself by opening his heart to Jeremiah in the hour of the latter's humiliation.

"I know," he began, "that my comrade has no faith in me. . . ." And as if it were necessary to speak more clearly, he added: "He believes that the words which issue from the mouth of Hananiah are lies and deception."

Seeing that Jeremiah was about to reply, Hananiah sadly raised his hand to prevent him, as though any word of protest would hurt him more than an affirmative silence.

"And yet," he continued with a slight emphasis, "Hananiah was the only one to prophesy the truth concerning Pharaoh, when Urijah and Jeremiah did not speak and no one understood my words."

This proud assertion could not be disputed. Hananiah had darkly foretold the downfall of Necho's army. On the day of the great council it was he, and none other, through whose mouth Adonai had delivered His ambiguous oracle. Jeremiah, however, was thinking of what Urijah had once said: "He who prophesies the truth is not necessarily a genuine prophet of the Lord, nor he who prophesies falsely necessarily a deceiver!" Hananiah raised his voice a little, as if he had divined Jeremiah's thoughts:

"Jeremiah is very arrogant, that is what it is. Jeremiah believes that a soul which is not like his own cannot be sanctified. But Jeremiah does not seem to know that Zebaoth looks into many mirrors . . . and that in each mirror He sees Himself differently."

Jeremiah raised himself on his elbow and stared at his midnight visitor. Had this suave man of the world a profounder knowledge of communion with God than he had himself? Was this dreadful thing Hananiah had said true? Were there as many divine truths as there were souls to mirror them? Was the suffocating truth with which he was tormenting his soul not even the sole truth? Had he been flogged and put in the stocks for something which was valid only for his own soul, and not the universal and urgent reality of God's unwavering purpose? Had the Lord selected Jeremiah to prophesy doom while He made other ears happy with the promise of salvation? And was the one as true or false as the other? A stifled sigh escaped from his breast, but Hananiah continued with a kindly smile:

"I came not hither to indulge in vain boasting, but to warn my brother. When you offer up petitions to the Lord, does He fulfil them all? Why, therefore, do *you* fulfil all the words that He speaks unto you? Why do you always go forth and speak in His name when He summons you and says: 'Go forth and speak in My name'? The more you indulge the Lord, the less indulgence will He have so far as you are concerned. Would that you might see the wisdom of my words, for you are helping God to play a game with your own life. And if you lose it, the Lord will care less about you than the King cares about the life of a common soldier slain in battle. That is the nature of kings!"

These well-intentioned and well-directed arguments struck Jeremiah as with a lash. He sank back as though the life had gone out of him and was hardly aware when his comforter picked up the lamp and left him. Less than twice twelve hours had passed since his return to Jerusalem and already the Lord had overwhelmed him with a measure of affliction that would have been sufficient to cast down another for life. Could not his Persecutor grant him respite for even a single day? Words formed in Jeremiah's soul like a chant. They were not the words of Adonai, but an expression of revolt over which Jeremiah's will had no control:

"Thou hast again ensnared my mind . . . and I have again let myself be ensnared. . . . Rejoice, O Lord, for Thou art stronger than I and Thou hast gained the victory. . . . I have become a laughing-stock and all men jeer at me. . . . Once I thought: 'Behold, I will think of Him no more and I will cease to prophesy in His name.' . . . And fled from Thee and hid . . . but Thou wast ever with me . . . in my heart and in my bones, like a burning fire. . . . Thou art still within me, Thou burning fire, but I cannot bear it and I must perish. . . ."

He felt that his endurance was at an end and he could no longer live, but he was not allowed to cast off his burden so lightly. Though he could not bear it, he was not allowed to perish. Between the two rocks, Adonai and the world, he was crushed yet could not die. It was an evil moment for Jeremiah, when he believed that he must escape from the imprisonment of his own soul or sink into madness. He started up, fettered as he was in the stocks, so that his legs almost snapped. There was nobody to help him, as Baruch was sleeping the sleep of the dead, and from his lips burst the bitter curse:

"Cursed be the day wherein I was born! . . . Cursed be the man who brought tidings to my father, saying: A man child is born unto thee, making him very glad. And let that man be as the cities which the Lord overthrew and repented not: and let him hear the cry in the morning, and the shouting at noontide, because he slew me not from the womb; or that my mother might have been my grave. . . . Wherefore came I forth out of the womb to see labour and sorrow, that my days should be consumed with shame?"

Baruch woke from his deep sleep and asked stammeringly if Jeremiah had called him. But Jeremiah only lay down again as well as he could and stared up at the starry sky, where Marduk, Ishtar, Nergal, and Ninurtu, the planets and a thousand constellations, circled tranquilly above the Temple of the Lord. When Ishtar, the morning star, caused all the other stars to pale with its brightness and cast faint shadows, a new warning came to Jeremiah. The bringer of the warning was none other than Ahikam, who had been the private secretary of King Josiah. Against the sons of Shaphan, whose house stood in such high repute because of its purity and divinely inspired intellect, the malice of Jehoiakim had been impotent. The change of regime had left them with nothing but their honorary offices and Shaphan's study in the Temple, but there they were inviolable. Yet even Ahikam would hardly have dared to visit a prisoner, who was being disciplined for rebellious speeches, at any other hour but this, on the threshold between night and dawn. Since the death of

King Josiah he had aged visibly. His beard shimmered white, and the finely curved upper lip, which was now bordered by two deeply etched lines, had lost its fullness. Taking a torch from the hand of the servant who accompanied him, he let it shine on Jeremiah's face. Then he sat down on the ground beside him with a sigh.

"Ahikam," he said softly, "has not forgotten his friend, to whom the true King turned his countenance. . . ."

Jeremiah touched Ahikam's knee, but kept his eyes averted. Ahikam was silent for a time, then he continued:

"I hold my hand over Jeremiah. . . . But you must be reasonable. . . ."

"Is the Lord reasonable?" cried Jeremiah. "Is it not *He* who bids me speak of the evil which is to come?"

"Of what use is it to speak of what is to come? There are no ears to hear, but there are many hands waiting to grip you by the throat."

With the skill in logical argument for which the house of Shaphan was celebrated, Ahikam began to point out to Jeremiah the uselessness of continuing to fight. The tyranny which held sway over Jerusalem, like every tyranny that stood above the law, was uncertain of itself and sensitive to opposition. Jehoiakim had established his rule by betraying his father, invading Jerusalem, and spreading falsehood; therefore he was secretly trembling lest he be unmasked and punished. An empty tyranny, moreover, cared for nothing but itself, wanted to preserve nothing other than itself; therefore it feared only its own defeat and was not concerned about the possible implication of the whole nation in an eventual catastrophe. Nothing was more abhorrent to it than the truth, the spirit of the Lord, which it could not fetter. It could, however, fetter him who spoke the truth, as Jeremiah himself knew from his own experience; and a tyrant could even slay a true prophet with his own hand. The only result was that the spirit and word of the Lord were no longer reverenced by the people, since they had proved so weak and impotent in the fight against tyranny. When a prophet sacrificed his life, he only harmed the prestige of the Lord. Urijah, who died because he could not lie, would not be remembered. The truth must choose more subtle ways, the mind must employ more cunning arts than open attack, by which it only destroyed itself. Jeremiah listened to these arguments, which were convincing and very much to the point, as was everything that clever debaters said. But the Lord did not argue, He did not try to be convincing, and He did not work by logic. Though Urijah might not be remembered by the people, perhaps He would remember him. If the death of the prophet diminished His prestige, perhaps it was by this very death that He would re-establish it. There was nothing that could not be expected from Adonai.

The only reply Jeremiah made to Ahikam was: "When *He* speaks, how can *I* be silent?"

"I will hold my hand over Jeremiah," urged Ahikam, "but let him swear to me in the name of the Lord that he will not prophesy again in these days, neither in the Temple nor in the city."

"How can I swear against the Lord in the name of the Lord?"

Jeremiah sat motionless, and the voice of Ahikam became sharper:

"Is it your will to challenge the King and his princes?"

"My will," said Jeremiah with a faint laugh, "my will is for nothing other than peace. I long for rest. I wish only to know nothing and to dwell in peace. . . ."

Ahikam interrupted him at once:

"Your word is enough . . . I take it as a covenant sworn between us. . . . Wait in peace until your day shall come, as I am doing. . . ."

Jeremiah pressed his fists against his temples in despair, but Ahikam rose and went before any new argument could detract from the promise that he was taking with him. Ishtar, the Queen of Heaven, dissolved in the approaching dawn, and the outlines of the sanctuary loomed greyly as the darkness began to fade. As the sober world emerged once more from the embrace of night Jeremiah vowed to himself that he would heed the injunction of Ahikam, that he would prophesy no more but return to Anathoth as soon as he should be freed. He took this resolve though he knew that his brothers would scoff and he feared their scorn. Then, until the sun rose, his thoughts were of his mother.

After the first trumpets had sounded, Jeremiah was released from the stocks. Pashur was present at the freeing of his prisoner in accordance with custom. When Jeremiah was able to stand on his feet again he reeled, and would have collapsed if Baruch had not supported him. Pashur stepped close up to him and said:

"Are you thankful, son of Hilkiah, for the lenient punishment which has saved you from a worse penalty?"

Jeremiah gazed silently into the little eyes that confronted him. Then the Keeper of the Door dismissed him with the words:

"I hope that you will never show yourself here again."

He turned and walked away, but Jeremiah called to him in a low voice: "Pashur!" The Keeper of the Door could not refrain from turning back. Jeremiah took a step towards him and murmured:

"Pashur, Pashur! In your name was the Passover. It denoted joy and freedom. . . . But now you shall have a new name in which is desolation and captivity in a strange land."

The Keeper of the Door raised his hands as if to parry a blow and grew deathly pale. Against this dark prophecy his scourges and his stocks were powerless. It closed round his throat with the suffocating terror of a prediction that would be fulfilled.

19

Jehoiakim and Coniah

IT WAS some time before Jeremiah was able to use his tortured legs. He had visited the Beth Hamoked, the "house of the burning hearth," which was situated on the eastern side of the Temple Mount. In the centre of this structure was a walled pool containing warmed water for ordinary bathing and baths of purification, and there were also little rooms in which one could rest for a time on a divan. Baruch had meanwhile gone down to the town to look after their animals and find lodging where he too could rest. It was their intention to set out for Anathoth that evening, as soon as the Sabbath was over, by the city Gate of Benjamin which was to the north-east.

The Sabbath day, with its fine weather, had brought a large crowd to the Temple both from Jerusalem itself and from other cities in Judah. It was refreshingly cool, for the sun was hidden by clouds. Only a few of the pilgrims were admitted to the inner court of the priests, in order to take part in the burnt sacrifices; the majority of the people were, as usual, crowded in the outer courtyard and moving in two opposing streams. There was an air of festive cheerfulness owing to the laughter and jests, the psalms and joyful songs of praise which could be heard on all sides. Jerusalem might be weighed down by tyranny and oppression, but nobody seemed to notice it except the few rebels and restless minds against whom they were directed. Whatever may have been the means by which Jehoiakim had come into possession of his throne, the Lord had undoubtedly blessed his reign. During the past five years each harvest had been more abundant than the preceding one. The sun and the rain appeared in their due seasons as if the Lord tolerated no negligence that might harm the prestige of King Jehoiakim. Wheat and fodder, hemp and flax, wine and oil, accumulated and increased in the granaries and storehouses, and no one complained any longer about Jehoiakim's two great levies of gold and silver, which in any case he had laid to the charge of his father. So far as the luxurious palaces were concerned, which the King had built outside the city, these served only to nourish the people's new-found pride. The summer palace in particular, on the airy heights of the Mount of Olives, with its hundred halls and chambers, was regarded as one of the wonders of the world, and the youth of Judah was intoxicated with delight at a brilliance and grandiosity that put the emperors of Babylon and Noph in the shade.

As Jeremiah left the Beth Hamoked and stepped out into the courtyard, he was again oppressed by the vaunting pride of the people, which had been fostered by Jehoiakim. It was at the same hour on the previous day, just before noon, that he had uttered the prophecy which brought him to the stocks. He was immediately carried along by the crowd and had not the strength to resist. He moved forward with the stream and his ear was filled with the insipid worldly cackle of voices that discussed profits and losses, house and farm, parents and children, cattle that had calved or died of sickness. The holy Temple was like a daily market, and hardly one person in a thousand was capable of elevating his mind beyond his everyday needs to meditate on his Creator and the universe that He had made.

Jeremiah's only desire was to escape as quickly as possible. There was no longer any room for him here. Whatever might happen, his lips would henceforth remain sealed, as Ahikam had demanded and he had promised, a promise which he had confirmed by making a solemn vow to himself. But it was not easy for him to escape with his aching limbs. Again and again the Sabbath crowd formed currents and groups that hemmed him in as he slowly moved along. The priests on duty were coming out from the inner court after the last morning sacrifice. The crowd was thickest, however, in front of the pulpits, each of which was occupied that day by a prophet anxious to take advantage of the presence of a multitude of pilgrims such as the Temple did not see every day. Jeremiah, tightly wedged among the throng, was compelled to stand in front of the pulpit where he had first caused vexation to the authorities, and which was now occupied by one of the popular prophets of salvation whose passionate voice rang out over the courtyard. This prophet not only wore the shaggy cloak of his kind, but himself presented a most shaggy and hairy appearance. His face was almost hidden by his beard, his eyes were hollow, his garments were tattered and filthy, and his whole person seemed to reek with his prophetic mission. Compared with him Jeremiah, to say nothing of Hananiah, might have been taken for a well-groomed, pampered courtier. The orator, however, appeared to take an extreme delight in debasing the inward mystery of sanctification by the outward neglect of his body. The most incredible thing about him was that he did not even take the trouble to pretend that he was inspired by the promptings of the Lord, but quite unequivocally prophesied in his own name.

It was the usual ranting of the day—about the greatness of King Jehoiakim and the re-established glory of Israel—the fraudulent demagogy that stops up a nation's eyes and ears, and leads it drunkenly to destruction. Under the eyes of the Keeper of the Door, his wardens and his jailers, within the hearing of the twenty-four orders of priests and all the scribes and scholars of the Temple, the insolence of this speech went unpunished though the orator did not shrink from the most monstrous blasphemy. Jeremiah felt himself suffocating with rage and hatred, for the shaggy blusterer was inventing the order of the world. He spoke as if it were not the Lord who raised up Israel, but Israel who raised up the Lord. Through Judah's greatness, he bellowed as he slavered into his matted beard, Zebaoth would grow among the gods of the nations. Jerusalem must become mightier and more populous than Noph and Babylon. Only then would the Lord become puissant; only then would He be the one supreme God.

A struggle was going on in Jeremiah's heart: "Do not listen! Shut your eyes and ears! Keep silent, keep silent!" He tried convulsively to concentrate his thoughts on the disgrace and humiliation to which he had been subjected. He thought of the warnings of Hananiah and Ahikam and of the promise he had made. If only the Lord would have pity on him and be reasonable and not overwhelm him. When one needed Him, He kept aloof and was inaccessible, but when one did not need Him, He was as near as if He were behind a papyrus screen. If His voice should make itself heard only once within Jeremiah, then Jeremiah was lost and there was no more hope for him than there had been for Urijah.

The shaggy prophet stood on tiptoe to add height to his tattered insignificance, waved his arms wildly within his hairy cloak as if they were a pair of wings, and bellowed:

"The Temple of the Lord! The Temple of the Lord! The Temple of the Lord! When Judah is great and powerful, then it will build a new Temple to the Lord that shall be mightier than all the temples in the world!"

Intoxicated by his own prophecy the man stamped about on the pulpit as if he were indeed filled with the rapture of Adonai, and not with human megalomania. His words tumbled over one another.

"Therefore I cry: 'Hail to the great Temple of the Lord!' Therefore I cry: 'Hail to the King who will magnify Jerusalem! Hail! Hail!' "

The crowd, however, turned with a jerk to stare at Jeremiah, from whose lips the same word suddenly began to issue repeatedly in a voice that drowned every other sound: "Hail! . . . Hail! . . . Hail! . . ."

An empty space was soon cleared round the mighty voice as the people moved back expectantly. Jeremiah had succumbed to the Lord, had forgotten all exhortations, warnings, and promises, together with the vow he had sworn to himself. His resistance was broken. The cry that came from his lips rose more and more mockingly above the heads of the crowd, so that the hairy orator gathered his cloak wrathfully around him and shook his fists at the disturber, who kept calling up to him implacably:

"Hail! . . . Hail! . . . Are these the arts with which you heal the wounds of my people?"

The crowd listened in awkward embarrassment as Jeremiah imitated the passionate croaking of the shaggy prophet:

"The Temple of the Lord! The Temple of the Lord! The Temple of the Lord!"

Then slowly, in tones that were audible even in the court of the guard in the royal palace, he thundered:

"Thus saith the Lord; If ye will not hearken to me to walk in my Law, which I have set before you, then will I make this house like Shiloh, and will make this city a curse to all the nations of the earth!"

Jeremiah's overpowering prophecy was followed by a horrified silence, which was soon broken by a murderous outburst of hatred so violent that it came within a hair's breadth of taking the law out of the hands of the tribunal whose office it was to punish blasphemers. He was struck in the face, hurled to the ground, and kicked. But the Lord seemed to have come to his help in that perilous moment, making his body invulnerable and his soul insensitive. He felt neither the effects of his former ill-treatment nor the wounds which were now being inflicted on him. His mind was calm and he felt only a dreamy curiosity, as if he were a disinterested spectator. He stood outside himself and looked on. The knot of raving men that hemmed him in pressed round him even more closely as they were pushed forward by the great mass of the people who had heard his blasphemous words. Their eyes gleamed with hatred, but it was mingled with pleasure at finding the dull monotony of their Sabbath promenade unexpectedly broken by an incident of such enormity. From the gallery dashed the wardens on duty, followed by jailers who thrust the crowd aside with blows and lashes. Jeremiah was pulled to his feet and dragged towards the southern part of the Temple amid a roar of execration, to which he listened as calmly as if it were only the rumble of a distant storm.

The southern wall of the Temple area and the northern wall of the royal palace were linked together by means of two mighty gateways. The one on the left was reserved for the

King and his family when they walked to the sanctuary. The purpose of the one on the right could be gathered from its name, for it was called "the Gate of the Bodyguard." Between them lay a third structure, extensive and with numerous pillars, which also formed a link between Temple and palace. The double means of access, for the ecclesiastical power on the one hand and the secular power on the other, was symbolic of its use both for the affairs of the Lord and for the affairs of the King; that is to say, matters which pertained equally to both spheres. The building was called "the House of the Joint Tribunal," and every day it was the scene of an assembly composed of Temple priests and royal officers whose duty it was to dispense justice. There were usually twenty-three judges present: eleven ecclesiastical and eleven secular, with a president who was chosen alternately from among the priests and the officials. The court sat on the Sabbath too, since even on the Sabbath there was no rest from sacrilege; it was only in recess on New Year's Day and the Day of Atonement, the "dreadful day" when God Himself sat in judgment. The acts for which men were brought before this tribunal were often grave infringements of the divine commandments, and in such cases the jurisdiction of the Keeper of the Door could not assign adequate punishment.

This was the tribunal before which Jeremiah was brought. The crowd streamed in the wake of the prisoner until the inner hall was packed, and only then did the guard close the gate, since it was not lawful to refuse admittance to the court so long as there was room. Jeremiah was bound by the jailers to a pillar that stood apart from the others and was rubbed smooth. The twenty-three judges, who always had to be assembled in readiness at certain fixed hours, sat in a half-circle as was prescribed, "in order that the one could see the other" and no member should be able to come to an understanding with another member by means of secret signals. The eleven officials who were present on behalf of the King were all prudent old men, and this was to the advantage of the delinquent. There was no Elnathan or Jerachmeel among them, nor any other of those by whom the tyranny of Jehoiakim was upheld. It was, however, not to the advantage of the delinquent that the president on this occasion was one of the secular dignitaries—Meshullam, the miller of Kirjath-Jearim, the master of the twelve blinded Samsons. He had multiplied his fortune so wisely and co-operated so successfully in the collection of the great levy of gold and silver, that the King had appointed him to be his treasurer. Meshullam did not appear to have changed since the day when the guests whom he had received so hospitably laid at his feet the garments which he had provided for them. He was the same handsome, dignified old man they had known, and his gratified fingers still stroked the wavy white beard, which had not grown more sparse. His heavy eyelids seemed to droop with the weight of his dignity, and he returned the greeting of his fellow-judges with a weary, melancholy nod as if to say: "We already know, you and I, the kind of thing we are going to have to deal with."

Among the eleven judges from the Temple sat Pashur, together with the other two Keepers of the Door. For the time being, they kept silent and left the charge to be made by the tattered prophet whom Jeremiah had robbed of the frenzied applause which he had a right to expect. He was still foaming with rage and he reiterated with inexhaustible invention the accusation of blasphemy which he was bringing against Jeremiah, in whom he saw something that he hated with an elemental hatred. The eyes of the prisoner looked round the half-circle of judges for a single face, the face of him who had said: "I will hold my hand over you." But Ahikam had not come, though he was a member of all the tribunals: the tribunal of seventy-one, the tribunal of twenty-three, and the tribunal of three. Perhaps he was unaware of what had happened. Perhaps it was not his turn to serve on the present court. Or perhaps he was angry with the untrustworthy friend who had broken his promise, and refused to have anything more to do with him. Then Jeremiah's eyes lit on two men of his own age who had just joined the half-circle and were taking their places, as the youngest members of the tribunal, to the right and left at either end. He recognized Gedaliah and Micah, the twin sons of Ahikam, who had been serving in other cities in the days of King Josiah and whom he had therefore seldom met. They were very much alike in feature, but Gedaliah was sturdily built and of healthy complexion, while Micah was pale and sickly. Jeremiah was so bitterly disappointed at not seeing Ahikam, that he could find no comfort in the fact that he was represented by his two sons. Neither Gedaliah nor Micah knew much about him, and they would take care not to throw the weight of their great name into the balance for the sake of a blasphemer. He was overcome by a great despair, which sapped his courage, so that he was filled with fear of his fellow-men; this fear grew into a fear of death and his teeth chattered. His hands gripped the pillar to which he was bound and his head swayed on his shoulders. He gave himself up for lost.

The accuser in the hairy cloak ended his wrathful speech with wild gesticulation as he stood in front of the judges:

"And therefore it is lawful that he should be put to death!"

". . . That he should be put to death! . . ." echoed the

chorus of fascinated hearers who had followed him into the court.

The consciousness that he was doomed had penetrated to every fibre of Jeremiah's being, but, strange to say, it was this very consciousness that supported him. He took several deep breaths to overcome the weakness of his spirit. He thought of Urijah, who had died like a lamb led to the slaughter, and he determined that he would not die as Urijah had done. Though his forehead was damp with an icy sweat and his hands still trembled, yet he raised his head and gazed steadily at Meshullam, his judge. And again it was strange that the sight of this just man, who was one of the secret blasphemers of Israel, gave him back his faith. Meshullam, however, caressed his wavy beard with his small white hand and put the first question:

"Is it true, Jirmejahu of Anathoth, that you have committed the crime of blasphemy by prophesying in the Temple: 'The same will be done to this Temple as was done to the old sanctuary at Shiloh and this town will be a heap of ruins and lie desolate'?"

Jeremiah's voice was calm as he assumed responsibility for his words, and his hearers listened to him with profound attention.

"That is not true. I have not committed the crime of blasphemy, since the Lord Himself compelled me to prophesy concerning the Temple and the city as you have heard with your own ears."

Before Meshullam could continue his examination, or one of the other judges interpose a question, Gedaliah rose and said in a loud voice:

"I protest against the accusation, for it does not correspond to this man's offence! A man can blaspheme the Lord only out of his own heart, but not when the words are put into his mouth by the Lord Himself. Can God be guilty of blasphemy? No! The charge contradicts itself and is therefore meaningless. . . ."

Pashur stood up with a tranquil air and smiled courteously, but his little eyes gleamed as he said:

"Behold, Gedaliah, son of Ahikam . . . gladly would the Keeper of the Door learn from your great wisdom. . . . But he has had much experience, for he has been appointed these many years to keep his eye on these prophets and he knows their ways. No prophet is so foolish as to blaspheme from his own heart. When he blasphemes, he always hides behind the Lord."

Gedaliah retorted with a certain sharpness:

"How does Pashur distinguish between truth and blasphemy? There are, no doubt, lying prophets who go about among the people. But how can you fathom whether they are lying? It is not possible to prove that they are deceivers. There are deceivers who are not even aware that they are deceiving, and not even these can be judged guilty of blasphemy. Let Pashur provide me with proof that all the prophets who promise salvation are speaking the truth, while all those who prophesy evil and summon the people to repentance are blasphemers. If he can prove this, then the charge against the prisoner is justified. . . ."

Meshullam interrupted the dispute, which had turned to the advantage of the accused man, by requesting Jeremiah with a graceful and weary gesture of his hand to continue with his defence. The latter did not take his eyes off his judge all the time he was speaking, and this made Meshullam visibly uneasy.

"The Lord did not say through my voice: 'I shall destroy

this Temple!' but He said: '*If* ye will not hearken to me to walk in my Law, *then* will I make this house like Shiloh.' "

Jeremiah had hardly come to an end before Gedaliah began a fresh assault:

"The judges have heard with their own ears. There is no witness to refute what this man has said. It is not God against whom this man has railed, but the people. He railed against us; no, he warned us that the Lord will take vengeance if we do not turn back."

Micah, Gedaliah's twin brother, now raised his hand pensively at the other end of the half-circle, and his low voice supported the defence of the accused:

"I should like to put a question to the court. Is there any law to be found among the writings which forbids a man to rail against his fellow-men? Does this court know of any precedent which forbids the utterance of a warning?"

This query provoked arguments and counter-arguments both among the judges and among the public. The forensic skill and elasticity of mind of the sons of Ahikam had undermined the charge before the judges had time to think. They put their grey heads together and debated hotly the question, so cunningly presented by Micah, whether there was any precedent which would enable them to pronounce the prisoner guilty of blasphemy. The case showed clearly how passionately the people were divided under the cover of fear. Those who were intoxicated with the arrogance of the new reign wanted the condemnation of Jeremiah, whether he was guilty or not. The others, who had been merely overawed or rendered numb by the tyranny, appeared suddenly to awaken from their stupor and acquire new courage. The effect of the grandiloquent boasting to which they had listened for so long was dispersed, and their own sense of weakness made them rally to the side of the accused man. When the shaggy prophet realized that victory was slipping from his grasp, he broke into a fresh torrent of slavering vituperation, and his behaviour was so unrestrained that Meshullam was forced to protect the dignity of the court by ordering him from the hall. This incident strengthened the cause of Jeremiah, who stood erect at the pillar to which he was fettered and tranquilly addressed both the tribunal and the public.

"I am in your hand," he said. "Do with me as seemeth good and meet unto you. But know ye for certain, that if ye put me to death, ye shall surely again bring innocent blood upon yourselves, and upon this city, and upon the inhabitants thereof. . . ."

His speech was simple and dignified, and it was followed by a deep silence. The reference to the slaying of Urijah made many of them feel ashamed. Even the blood of the guilty cried to Heaven and had to be answered for by the whole nation. Pashur, however, in view of his position, could not admit defeat. He tried to put the charge which was brought against Jeremiah in an even more serious light, emphasizing his incurable stubbornness and the fact that he had committed the same offence twice within the space of a few hours. But Gedaliah again intervened:

"Has the Keeper of the Door already caused this man to be punished by his own tribunal?"

"The Keeper of the Door," replied Pashur, "did less than was his duty." The pale Micah immediately retorted in his weary voice, as if it had been prearranged with his brother:

"I wish to put a question to the court. Is there any law to be found in the writings which declares that punishment can be meted out twice for the same offence? Does the court know of any precedent? . . ."

"There is a precedent in the records of this land!"

Everyone pricked up his ears, for the cry had come from among the public, through whose ranks somebody appeared to be pushing his way. A very old man emerged and stood before the judges. He was obviously one of the elders from the country outside Jerusalem, the chief of a village community who had come on a pilgrimage to the Temple in order to offer up a sacrifice on behalf of his congregation. And this sturdy ancient, an untaught peasant whose memory reached far back in history, calmly faced the scholarly priests and dignitaries as he apprised them in a hesitating but clear voice of what had happened when an earlier prophet warned Jerusalem of the coming doom:

"This is the precedent. . . . Micah the Morashite prophesied in the days of Hezekiah, King of Judah, and spake to all the people of Judah, saying: Thus saith the Lord of hosts, Zion shall be ploughed like a field, and Jerusalem shall become a heap of ruins, and the mountain of the Temple shall become the high places of a forest. . . . Did Hezekiah, King of Judah, and all Judah put him at all to death? . . . Did he not fear the Lord, and besought the Lord, and the Lord repented Him of the evil which He had pronounced against them? . . . And ye want to procure great evil against our souls? . . ."

An ignorant man from the plains, an old peasant, had not only apprised the scholars of Jerusalem of a precedent that they should themselves have borne in mind, but he had also rebuked them by his speech. And the worst of it was that the rebuke not only came from the simple mind of the people, but was based on a knowledge of the past which had been able to provide a parallel to the present case in accordance with all the recognized arts of argument. It was not the students and interpreters of the Law who had reminded the court of the prophecies of Micah and cited a legal precedent which could not be overlooked, but an uneducated rustic. The people rejoiced at a victory won by a simple man over the scholars of the Temple, and from all sides rang the cry: "Hear him, for he has told you that which is meet and proper!" The judges were silent and embarrassed. Jeremiah's fate was settled, and in a favourable sense. A final attempt on the part of Pashur to renew the charge was drowned by the cries of contempt and mockery from the crowd, whose attitude had changed completely in the course of a single hour.

Meshullam signalled to the Keeper of the Door to resume his seat and then gave the order for the customary vote to be taken. The voting of the joint tribunal was equally divided, so the decision lay with the president. With a benevolent smile Meshullam cast his vote for acquittal.

"Unbind the prisoner," he ordered.

When the guards untied the rope by which Jeremiah was fettered to the pillar, Meshullam withdrew his hand from his white beard and commanded silence. Then he spoke:

"Jirmejahu of Anathoth! You have been adjudged innocent of blasphemy by this court. But before the eyes of a thousand witnesses you have been guilty of inciting revolt among the people in the Temple on the Sabbath. For this offence the King of Judah demands that you be called to account. You will therefore be carried into the presence of the King, and he will be your judge."

Meshullam looked round benignantly. Both the ecclesiastical and the secular authorities could be grateful to the craftiness of the venerable president of the court for having at the same time preserved the prestige of an incorruptible justice and prevented a dangerous prisoner from slipping out of their hands. There could be no appeal against his decision. Pashur and his friends nodded in approval, but the two sons of Ahikam bent their heads sorrowfully. The spectators were silent, for any sign of protest against reference of the matter to the King as judge might have to be dearly paid for. Meshullam probably expected that Jeremiah's pride would now be broken, and that he would have the gratification of being able to reject a weeping plea for mercy with a compassionate sigh. He was disappointed, for Jeremiah only smiled to himself. His feeling of despair, his faintheartedness, together with his fear of the men around him and his apprehension of death, had vanished completely and yielded to an inexpressible and sublime confidence such as he had never known. Often as he had been bereft, maltreated, and exposed to shame, he knew that the Lord would not abandon him in *this* battle and that he would emerge unharmed. Had not the old peasant come forward on his behalf like an authentic, secret messenger of God? A feeling of irresistible strength streamed through him and he rejoiced inwardly in the certainty that the Lord was by his side, causing his persecutors to stumble and come to grief.

Jeremiah bowed to the twenty-two judges and to Meshullam their president, as he said with a smile:

"I shall enter the presence of the King and speak with him!"

He was surrounded by the guards and led away, but Meshullam did not order him to be fettered.

Early that morning the King had left Jerusalem in his Egyptian chariot, a present from Pharaoh, in order to drive to his summer palace on the Mount of Olives. This was a dual breach of the Sabbath, since it was forbidden both to use a vehicle and to go such a long distance. Jehoiakim, however, did not worry if he broke the Sabbath sevenfold and twelvefold, for he even compelled the free citizens of Judah, his brothers and sisters, to work as bondservants on the holy day and help to build his palaces. The judges of the tribunal, on the other hand, were faced with the painful necessity of making up their minds what they were to do. It was the inviolable right of every accused man to be brought before his judge before sunset. Postponement for even a single night would involve infringement of the Law, and a pious tribunal could not be a party to this. They were therefore forced to search for precedents and precepts which would enable observers of the Sabbath, however strict, to regard the commandment concerning the distance a man was allowed to walk as being temporarily in suspense. There were several such decisions recorded in the writings. The Sabbath could be regarded as being in abeyance on the occasion of war, persecution, or revolt, and it was eventually agreed that the last of these hypotheses would meet the case since it could only refer to the *prevention* of revolt. Jeremiah was to be taken forthwith to the summer palace, and a deputation of seven members of the tribunal was chosen to accompany him and prefer the charge. Gedaliah and Micah were not included, but in spite of his age Meshullam would not allow himself to be deprived of the pleasure of escorting his victim into the presence of the grateful monarch. The day was already far advanced when they reached the summer palace. A number of people had attached themselves to the procession and thronged round the guards who were in charge of the prisoner. Jeremiah felt a light touch on his shoulder; when he turned round he saw that Baruch had discovered his whereabouts and was indicating his readiness to follow him through thick and thin.

The summer palace presented a scene of immense activity. Jehoiakim was not only a great builder, he was an even greater rebuilder. He was never granted the peace that comes from work completed, but a vague dissatisfaction with the finished product always compelled him to pull it down and build it up anew. For example, he had just torn down the Egyptian tomb that he had prepared for himself some years before, in order to erect a new mastaba of truly prodigious proportions in the neighbourhood of the summer palace and with an outlook over the Temple Mount. No king in the world had ever had, or ever would have, such a colourful setting for his immortalization, and Jehoiakim was already examining with an uncanny passion whole bales of byssus tissues for the wrappings of his mummy, together with a hundred kinds of balsam, oil, and perfume for the final rites.

All around was a hammering, sawing, and filing. Now and then could be heard the urging voice of an overseer of slaves. The work went on unceasingly, and Jeremiah looked steadily at the priests who were taking him before his judge. In the face of this immeasurable violation of the Sabbath by the King himself, they were compelled to lower their eyes before the gaze of their prisoner. Some of them probably felt an inclination to let him go, but old Meshullam kept the procession moving so that they might reach the gate as soon as possible. The palace was guarded by more than a hundred soldiers, for Jehoiakim lived in fear of being assassinated as his grandfather Amon had been. With the exception of the bodyguard, the eunuchs, and the servants, there was nobody in the summer palace except the royal family, for Jehoiakim's constant friends and companions, Elnathan and Jerachmeel, had been granted leave that morning. This was a dispensation of the Lord in favour of Jeremiah.

When the seven judges, with Meshullam at their head, presented themselves at the gate, it was opened readily. Escorted by eunuchs they walked through one luxurious chamber after another. No eye in Jerusalem had ever seen such magnificent interiors, compared with which the House of Solomon in Jerusalem and the adjoining House of Pharaoh's Daughter seemed crude. Each room was decorated in a different colour and panelled with a different wood. The builder had not economized on ebony, cedar, sandalwood, acacia, and oleaster. The tints in which the elegant sequences of pictures had been executed were remarkable for their particularly vivid lustre. The brilliance of vermilion contrasted with the dullness of red lead, while four or five different shades of purple astonished the eye. And not only had the colours been chosen to harmonize subtly with the woods, but each room was pervaded by a special fragrance which harmonized with both. The smoke of incense curled up from delicate bowls or drops of perfumed oil fell at intervals from unseen alabaster vessels.

All the sons of Josiah resembled one another, as Jeremiah well knew, in their enslavement to beauty. Poor Jehoahaz sat in his corner all day long carving skilful imitations of the elegant images of Egypt, and even the eyes of young Mattaniah would fill with rapture at sight of a delicately wrought trinket, a flashing gem, or even a heap of coloured glass fragments.

King Jehoiakim must have been extremely surprised at the sudden invasion of his palace on the Sabbath by a deputation from the joint tribunal. He was wearing a loose, thinly woven dressing-gown, such as Pharaoh was accustomed to wear, which fell in soft folds to his ankles, and he let them wait what seemed an endless age before he gave them audience. They had been introduced into a spacious hall known as "the summer hall of judgment," and long before the King appeared, the old judges, even the indefatigable Meshullam, looked yellow as wax with weariness and could hardly stand on their feet. In his inmost heart none of them wanted anything except a seat and a refreshing drink. Jehoiakim obviously had no idea why he had been thus disturbed and what had brought the pious dignitaries to consult him on such a day. He incessantly rubbed his thin hands together, putting them from time to time to his nostrils, and it was not only the courtiers who were able to gather from this gesture that he had been interrupted in the occupation which, next to building and rebuilding, fascinated him most. The dreaded tyrant whose sword of vengeance rested so loosely in its scabbard, the seductive orator who knew so well how to sway the people's feelings, possessed in each of his palaces a private laboratory where he brewed and mixed the queerest things. He compounded draughts out of different wines, juices, and spices; he mingled perfumes made from the oils of pressed flowers and fruit kernels. He mixed colours; he mixed various kinds of incense. He mixed aromatics with a deep-seated craving to produce something new, something unknown, something that would have the magical effect of preserving life. Though this passion had long since become an end in itself, his thoughts circled continually round the possibility of perfecting his future mummy, so that it might far excel the work of Egypt through the refinements he was able to produce in his balsams, myrrh, natron, resins, and newly invented ingredients. The time spent in his wizard's kitchens seemed to be having a deleterious effect on his health. His sunken cheeks showed red spots as if he were feverish, his eyes were veiled like those of a man stupefied with drink, and his puffy lips were parted as if in exhaustion. He mounted the steps to his throne as if he were walking in his sleep, and as he leaned back he made an effort to control his dissipated features and invest his manner with a regal dignity. Meshullam and the others bowed down till their heads almost touched the sandalwood floor, and they all murmured together:

"We have been held worthy to look upon the countenance of the King. . . ."

Jehoiakim appeared to be unaware that he was being addressed. His nostrils still craved the odorous delights that he had been compelled to abandon, and it was some time before he was able to rouse himself from his abstraction. When he saw that he was alone with these annoying men from Jerusalem, he looked round him fearfully. Where were Jerachmeel, Elnathan, and the rest of the princes who endowed him with the courage of his tyranny and released the bonds of his tongue? Meshullam stood in an attitude of flattered humility and pursed his lips as he announced the reason for his presence:

"May the majesty of the King hearken unto me. . . . This man whom we have brought before the countenance of the King, Jeremiah of Anathoth, has been prophesying in the Temple. . . ."

Jehoiakim was growing more and more uneasy and he hardly listened to Meshullam, but fidgeted and twisted in his seat as if he were about to jump up at any moment. Suddenly his face lit up with a smile of relief, as he heard a voice call: "Father!" A pale, delicate child, a boy of some twelve years, came running into the hall, but hesitated when he saw the men standing in front of the throne. It was Jeconiah, the King's son, whom every one affectionately called Coniah, for a more beautiful boy and charming prince had never sprung from the House of David. Though he was very short for his age, Coniah looked like one of the dainty, shining figures in the hosts of Zebaoth. His large eyes, in a white, almost transparent face that seemed hardly to veil his soul, measured the venerable strangers with melancholy and dislike. The King called to him to come nearer, pressed him to his heart, and bade him sit down on the steps between his knees. Coniah was the son he loved, the only one he loved. Meanwhile horrified chamberlains and other officials of the court had hastened into the hall and taken up their positions round the steps of the throne. They had not expected a deputation to be calling at such an hour, or that the King would leave his laboratory.

Meshullam seized the hand of the accused Jeremiah and tried to begin his speech again, but Jeremiah tore himself free and stepped forward to address the King:

"Yes, I prophesied in the words of the Lord concerning the Temple, but now I shall prophesy in the words of the Lord concerning you, O King of Judah, who are sitting upon the throne of David! Hear the word of the Lord, you and your servants and your people and all that enter in by these gates. . . ."

Meshullam and the other prosecutors were thunder-struck. They grew red and pale alternately. The miller at last managed to find his voice and implored: "May the majesty of the King . . ." but Jehoiakim signed to him with an impatient nod of the head to keep silent. He had eyes only for Jeremiah, and it could be seen that he was making a determined effort to shake off the stupor which even yet had not quite left him. He had recognized Jeremiah, the last friend of the father he had betrayed; he remembered the voice that had driven him into a frenzy one distant Passover night, but as his hands felt for Coniah's slender shoulders there was no rage to be seen in his features, only fascination and suspense. While Jeremiah, for his part, was completely filled with the promptings of the Lord, he realized with no possibility of doubt that his life depended on his ability to keep the King fascinated and to cast the same spell over the others too.

"Thus saith the Lord, Execute ye judgment and righteousness, and deliver the spoiled out of the hand of the oppressor: and do no wrong, do no violence to the stranger, the fatherless, nor the widow, neither shed innocent blood in this place. For if ye do this thing indeed, then shall there enter in by the gates of this house kings sitting upon the throne of David, riding in chariots and on horses. . . . Ye, however, do violence and shed blood! Yea, sacred, innocent blood have ye shed with your own hands!"

Jeremiah's voice had not once risen in tones of loud solemnity, as was customary among prophets, yet its very soberness enhanced the penetrating quality of his words and caused the courage with which he hurled the truth in the face of the King to appear ten times more audacious. It was an audacity which deprived his hearers of their power of action, and everyone looked up helplessly at Jehoiakim. An angry command to the bodyguard and Jeremiah's strangled body would be lying on the floor, strangled so that no blood should stain the precious sandalwood. That was not what happened, however. The King did not open his mouth, but remained sitting on his throne without uttering a word. Like every man of violence who hurts others without compunction, he was immeasurably sensitive so far as his own person was concerned and full of self-pity. He was merciless in assailing others, but when he himself was directly assailed he lost his nerve and collapsed, as he did now. The King's paralysis was communicated to all the others, so that Jeremiah dominated "the summer hall of judgment" and could even feel sorry for the innocent boy whose ears he could not spare at this fateful hour. Coniah, however, the prince with the face of an angel, gazed at him with the frozen horror of a gazelle that suddenly finds itself looking into the eyes of a lion. Even now Jeremiah did not raise his voice, rather did he speak still more softly:

"Ye have built your house by unrighteousness and your chambers by wrong. . . . Think ye that ye are like Pharaoh, or the King of Babylon, because ye enclose yourself in cedar? Did not your father eat and drink, and do judgment and justice, and then it was well with him? . . ."

Jeremiah had exploited to the full the advantage which the King's silence afforded him. The mere mention of his father in the presence of Jehoiakim was a bitter accusation that sent a thrill of dread through all those who heard it. The hands of the guards gripped the hilts of their swords, but Jeremiah bent forward to whisper, since what he now had to say was intended only for the ears of the house of David and not for the others.

"Therefore thus saith the Lord concerning Jehoiakim, the son of Josiah, King of Judah, They shall not lament for him, saying, Ah, my brother! or, Ah, sister! they shall not lament for him, saying, Ah, Lord! or, Ah, his glory! . . ." He drew a deep breath and then did for Urijah what had to be done:

". . . He shall be buried with the burial of an ass, drawn and cast forth beyond the gates of Jerusalem. . . ."

Jehoiakim did not start up from his throne, but leaned back shrinkingly as if the terrible fate prophesied for him were about to be fulfilled at once. Was he thinking of the pompous tomb that he had built for the reception of his immortalized body? The men roundabout, who had heard nothing of the whispered prophecy, looked at one another with grey faces. Slowly Jehoiakim's fingers curled convulsively round the arms of his throne. The paralysis that had held him in its grip was gone, and the reddening of his cheeks showed that he had thrown off the stupor. His eyes sought the captain of the guard, but at that moment the Lord intervened to save Jeremiah. Little Coniah, sitting at his father's feet, had heard the inexorable prediction and he suddenly swooned without a sound. His beautiful face was white as death and it seemed as if his heart had ceased to beat.

The King screamed, snatched his beloved son into his arms, and began to call frenziedly for water, physicians, and help. But he was answered only by a wild confusion, for everyone thought that God had punished Jehoiakim by striking down his son, and he stretched out his arms with the boy's body towards the prophet, imploring him hoarsely:

"Ask your Lord to save him! Ask our God to save him!"

Jeremiah tranquilly laid his hand on the waxen forehead of the child. After no more than twelve heart-beats Coniah opened his eyes. At first there was a faint smile in them, but when they recognized their awakener they were again filled with unspeakable horror.

Sadly Jeremiah turned away. Walking slowly past Meshullam and the judges, through the midst of the guards, and from one chamber to another as if he were invisible, he at last stepped out through the gateway into the setting sun, and there was no hand stretched forth to restrain him. He thought it strange that he seemed to be invisible not only to the others, but even to himself.

20

In the Place of Hiding

THE hills of Anathoth lay under a moonless sky. Since the two dreadful days Jeremiah had passed in Jerusalem the air had grown sharper, and a colder wind disturbed the silvery foliage of the olive trees that surrounded the estate of Hilkiah. There was a dark, mysterious rustling everywhere as Jeremiah and Baruch crept silently along the ancient wall that protected the farm as if it were a fortress. For many months they had lain concealed in the neighbourhood of Jerusalem, only Ahikam and his two sons knowing their place of refuge. Now the hue and cry raised by Jehoiakim, with the aid of Elnathan and Jerachmeel, seemed finally to have died down. Parties of men had scoured the country, their search extending to all the adjacent countries and even as far as Noph, but now that winter had set in, the King appeared to realize that he must acknowledge defeat by someone who was stronger than himself. It was rumoured in Judah that Jehoiakim had fallen into a state of gloomy brooding since the day when Jeremiah had flung his great challenge into his face. Could a tyrant still feel that his rule was safe when someone lived within his domain whom his power could not touch and on whom he could not take vengeance? A tyranny was weakened when revenge was not possible.

Jeremiah felt, however, that the hour had come for him

to return home. After so many months the spies of the King would expect him to be anywhere but in his father's house. None the less, it was essential for him to exercise the utmost caution, if only for his mother's sake. This was already the second night that he and Baruch had secretly crept round the wall of the estate. The disciple was pale and downcast, for he had learned down in Anathoth that his own parents had died within a short time of each other while he and his master were in hiding. He had not been able to take farewell of them or attend their burial. The Lord, who inexorably compelled Jeremiah to carry out his mission, cast a shadow also over Baruch, who grew more and more sombre. It was his fate as well to be set apart from his fellow-men and kept aloof from all human activities. Yet it was the very death of his parents, and the fact that he could not mourn for them, which formed a strong reason for his urging Jeremiah to return home, for Abi must have grown very old and on the morrow it might already be too late.

They had reached the broken part of the wall over which Jeremiah had so often climbed when, after his flight from the uncomprehended promptings of the voice, he returned from his nightly wandering and found the gate closed. Again he swung lightly from one projection to another, for, in spite of all he had suffered, his lean body had lost nothing of its agility and youthful vigour. He sat astride on the top and warned Baruch in a subdued voice to keep a strict watch and inform him, by the signal they had arranged, of the approach of danger. They had encountered armed men on the highroad, and it was possible that they might have been recognized.

Leaping down onto the soft grass, Jeremiah lay there for a while with the comforting feeling that it was all a dream, that he was still a boy and Adonai had not yet singled him out for his fateful task. He allowed himself to be lulled by the thought that he was returning home as he had so often done, and had not yet experienced what it meant to be the mouthpiece of the Lord and come into conflict with the world. He felt that he was retracing his steps of yesterday and that the years had passed as if they had never been.

Slowly he rose and crept along the familiar path to his father's house. His old boyish fear came over him that the noise of his return might awaken the sleepers. The cube-shaped buildings loomed out of the darkness, and he paused. There were probably even more sleepers now than there had been then. Mocheleth and Shua, his two sisters-in-law, would have given birth to other children, while their older sons and daughters would have grown up and must now be married. There must be grandchildren of his brothers to sit round the massive table in the Hall of Abiathar.

Jeremiah felt a slight shock of apprehension; not because he was thinking of the enmity borne him by Obadiah and Joel, but because his mind was occupied with the thought of his mother. Perhaps the increase in the family had necessitated a new distribution of the rooms, and she may have been compelled to give up the old bedroom she had shared with Hilkiah. What if he was unable to discover in which chamber she was sleeping? It was not safe for him to enter the house by daylight. His heart grew more and more oppressed with a secret fear of meeting his mother again after the years of separation. She may have become so dreadfully changed by age that he would hardly recognize her. Perhaps he would find her bent to the ground, or blind, or with her mind dulled. The boldest of the Lord's prophets, who had told the King to his face that he would suffer the burial of an ass, was unnerved by terror. It would have needed little to make him turn and creep away again as he had done the night before. Breathing heavily, he stared into the darkness.

He could feel rather than see that the gloom was broken by the faintest of flickering reflections. He obeyed his presentiment, but even before he discovered the source of the almost imperceptible illumination his heart told him what it was. His mother had set her little handlamp on the outer threshold as she had always done, so that her youngest child, amid the persecutions of heaven and earth, might find his way home to her when every other way was barred. Had she been doing this on each of the thousand nights that had passed since he left his father's house? Or was she giving him a sign on this night alone that she was aware of every stirring of his heart even before he had translated it into an act? Jeremiah had seen again and again how the simple, untaught mind of Abi was in secret touch with everything that concerned her youngest son. Not the slightest emotion of sorrow or wrath in Jeremiah's soul was hidden from her, however far away he might be. She was the only being on earth who, in some inexplicable way, shared even in the possession of him by Adonai which caused him so much suffering.

The night must have been far advanced, for as he lifted the little lamp from the threshold he saw that the oil was almost used up and the wick smoking. Slipping through the door, which was slightly ajar, he stood in the long, dark passage where he had spent so many agitated moments as a boy and wondered that he felt so little surprise at being there at all after such a long interval. Moving on tiptoe, he measured the steps that led to the old bedchamber of his parents in the way he had always done when he crept past timidly in the dead of night. Then he stood still, drew a long breath, and raised the lamp higher. The door was open. Was his mother still sleeping there? The wick flared up with one last effort, and as it tore the darkness of the room into tattered shadows Jeremiah saw his mother. She was sittting fully clothed on the edge of her couch.

Slowly she rose and went towards Jeremiah, who did not move. She had not changed. Age had not bent her, and her eyes were clear and tranquil as ever. They embraced gravely and neither of them wept.

"Peace be unto you, Mother!"

"Unto you be peace, my child!"

"I want you to understand, Mother . . ." he began.

She shook her head in protest.

"Why do you talk about it? It is not necessary to say anything."

She took his hand and led him to the couch. He sat down, but she moved hastily about the room, noiselessly locked the door, lit a fresh lamp from the wick of the one that Jeremiah had brought, and placed it on the floor, so that it cast the hollow-cheeked, lined face of her son into sharp relief. The furtive looks with which she studied his changed features grew more and more anxious. As if the ravages inflicted by struggle and hardship must be repaired without delay, she hurried to a cupboard in the wall and fetched strong wine together with fresh fig cakes, urging him to eat and drink. The taste of the newly baked cakes, sweetened with honey, brought back memories of his boyhood and he thought again of the nights when the voice of the Lord, coming as though from afar, had not yet commanded him to fulfil a task which involved the death of those he loved.

He drew his mother down beside him on the couch, but she could not stay still. She kept jumping up to do something else for him. His clothes were not only old and worn, but full of dreadful holes! So she brought him fresh linen and a new coat of the finest weave, spun in the house itself. In spite of his protests he had to change his garments, but before he did so she rubbed his skin with the cool salve that had long been used in the house of Hilkiah for the treatment of infants. She saw with horror the red scars and weals on his back, but she did not ask about them and he was spared the pain of telling her how he had come by them. The odour of the healing salve conjured up all sorts of hidden memories, and it was almost as if his mother in her solicitude was trying to help him to keep silent about all the things he longed to say to her. When she had done everything she could possibly think of and was again sitting at his side trying to keep her hands still, even then she asked no questions, but told him what had been happening during his absence:

"Five times this house was visited by armed men of the King, who had come to seize my youngest son. . . ."

Jeremiah nodded to himself.

"That is why I stayed away from my mother . . . and for that reason I have come stealthily at dead of night. . . ."

Abi raised her voice slightly and declared in a stern tone that brooked no contradiction:

"But now I shall not let you go again!"

He pressed closer to her and whispered almost harshly:

"Where Jeremiah is, there is suffering and death. My mother knows much but she does not know that I have cursed the day on which she bore me. For, behold, I am dumb—yet I must cry aloud. I am timid—yet I must strive against kings and priests. I wish to be alone—yet I must mingle with the people. I beg on my knees for peace—yet I must go forth to war. . . ."

Old and frail as she was, his mother exhibited a strength of will which Jeremiah had never suspected in her while his father was alive. Under the domination of the peevish and arrogant Hilkiah she had seemed to possess no powers of resistance, but now her eyes were flashing with a determination that sprang from the depths of her soul.

"I cannot protect my child from the Lord. . . ."

She said no more, for it was not necessary to assert that she could and would protect him from men.

"Can my mother really protect me from my brothers?" he asked doubtfully.

She was silent, and in her silence he read the truth. After the abundance of vexation they had suffered on his account and the ransacking of the house by the King's men, his brothers' wrath must have become intensified to a white heat. It would have been troublesome enough for an honest, simple family to harbour a prophet among its members, even though he enjoyed fame and esteem throughout the land, but the name of one who had been put in the stocks, a rebel with a price upon his head, involved them all in a disgrace equivalent to the stigma of leprosy. Jeremiah saw this when his mother's face darkened at mention of his brothers. There could be no question of reconciliation, for nothing but his death would relieve the minds of Obadiah and Joel. So long as he was alive they could expect further shame to be brought upon their house, and Jeremiah was convinced that they would surrender him without mercy to the vengeance of the King, unless indeed they decided to rid themselves of him with their own hands. Who would call them to account if they did so? The blood of a rebel might cry out to Heaven even though he were an enemy of his country, but the courts of justice in Judah would not be particularly concerned. Jeremiah smiled almost mockingly at Abi.

"And how does my mother intend to shield me from my brothers?"

She rose without a word and took from the cupboard a great, rusty key. Jeremiah did not at first realize its significance, but she said with a sly pride:

"Your father bequeathed this key not to Obadiah, his eldest son, but to a woman."

Then Jeremiah remembered the dilapidated sanctuary in front of his window, the sacred building in which the Lord had been honoured in ancient times but which was now used only when a covenant had to be sworn with farmers, landowners, and cattle dealers. This happened very seldom when he was a child, and since the death of Hilkiah it had ceased to be used at all. His mother smiled with an air of confidence.

"My son will not sleep in his old room."

Jeremiah found that preparations had long since been made for his comfort and security. Abi had worked with her own hands at night to render the old sanctuary habitable, carrying mats, cushions, even a couch, and all the little things that add to the amenities of life. No one had the slightest suspicion that the bare ruin, formerly dedicated to divine worship, had been turned into a snug hiding-place where a man could live. Even though he would have to remain in concealment by day, Jeremiah would be free to roam at will by night. There could be no inkling in anyone's mind that a living soul had taken shelter in a place which, on account of its former usage, still inspired most of the members of the household with vague fears. Abi had forgotten nothing. She alone possessed the key to this lair, where her intuition told her that Jeremiah would feel himself very near to the Lord.

He thought over all the possibilities of refuge that remained to him. He was unutterably weary of his wanderings and rejoiced in the clever solicitude of his mother. Though in hiding, he would still be near her and would feel every day the comfort of her love. Baruch would, of course, share his shelter with him. Jeremiah and Abi slipped silently from the house, though the rough key grated so noisily in its rusty lock that they were both terrified and held their breath. The sanctuary consisted of one large chamber with a smaller room behind, and it was this smaller room that Abi had fitted up for the fugitives. As he entered, Jeremiah felt at once in his heart the faint vibration and tugging which announced the approach of Adonai. This time, however, the prompting of the Lord was more gentle than usual. This time He demanded not deeds but meditation. "Think, ponder, and search your heart!" the walls seemed to whisper. And amidst the whispering he heard a word that had not come to him before. It was repeated continually and was a command: "Write!"

"Take thee a roll of a book, and write therein all the words that I have spoken unto thee . . . from the days of Josiah, even unto this day."

Jeremiah did not carry out this command quite literally, for his handwriting was hasty and illegible. Baruch, on the contrary, was a master in the art of calligraphy; there was no one in Jerusalem who wrote a more elegant hand. So Jeremiah dictated the words that the Lord had spoken to him and his disciple wrote them down, at first in abbreviated signs and then with loving care and at length in the actual roll. This was the way they passed the time and arranged their work:

At midnight they would stealthily leave their hiding-place, climb over the wall where it was broken, and go for a walk beyond the boundaries of the estate. On the wooded hills of Anathoth they sometimes received messages from their friends in Jerusalem. Ahikam, who held his hand over Jeremiah, or his two sons, Gedaliah and Micah, would send reports or warnings to the fugitive through trustworthy agents, informing him of new decrees or designs of Jehoiakim and exhorting him not to leave his place of concealment. The sons of Shaphan were artfully leading the King on one false trail after another.

After their exercise and refreshing sojourn in the open air they would return an hour before sunrise to their sanctuary, where they slept till the day was well advanced. When the sun was high in the heavens and the members of the household as well as the farm workers were drowsily taking their midday rest, Abi came tripping along cautiously, choosing a devious route and keeping a good look-out on all sides. Arrived at the shelter, she put on the ground outside the door a covered tray she had brought. Immediately the door was opened from within and the tray silently disappeared. It contained the midday meal of Jeremiah and Baruch: wine, cream, milk porridge, a dish of lentils, barley bread, fig cakes, and occasionally a couple of lamb chops.

When they had eaten and drunk to their hearts' content, they set to work promptly, if one could compare with earthly work the tremendous effort it cost them to recall with meticulous exactitude the words with which Jeremiah had been inspired. In this symmetrical division of their days the time passed until Jeremiah had no idea whether months or years had gone by since he had so furtively returned home, for his communion with the Lord obliterated his sense of time, as it had always done. And it was a novel form of communion for him, since it was indirect. He had to search his memory and bring the past back into consciousness. It is true that the danger to which he had always been exposed after receiving a direct command from the Lord was lacking, but on the other hand he found himself involved in fresh mental torment as he laboured unremittingly to record the true text of the divine words, adding nothing and taking nothing away.

The difficulties were almost insurmountable. When the words originally formed themselves in his mind, like water in a porous rock, and when his own power of will and reasoning had been eliminated so that no evil impulse should dim or falsify the divine prompting, then the prophecy was pure and true as long as that condition lasted. But humanly it was almost impossible when delivering a prophetic speech of any length to keep one's own thoughts from finding an echo in what one was saying. The egotistic and importunate stirrings of the heart corrupted the truth and purity of the divine word. It could therefore often happen that a man who began his prophecy as a genuine prophet of Adonai concluded it as a false prophet. And if this danger of falsification threatened the spoken word even when it flowed directly from the Lord, must it not threaten a hundredfold when Jeremiah tried to reproduce it from memory?

The speech that came from a man's lips was liable to alteration and decay like every manifestation of life. Its meaning changed even in the mouth of the speaker. On its way from mouth to mouth a simple statement of fact could be distorted until eventually it was unrecognizable. Yet even the word of Adonai in the mind of a prophet needed the vehicle of human speech if it was to be heard at all. It had to be clothed in the corruptness of that which was more fitted to veil than to reveal the truth. Therefore, even when it was given to man, it was trying all the time to escape from its earthly limitations.

Jeremiah understood how difficult it was to retain the word of God as he struggled despairingly to record it in writing. He did not flag in his efforts to recall the past. He sharpened his memory as though it were a knife with which he was trying to cut into the blackness of time. Again and again he returned to the assault until he could again see clearly every vision and hear every word. Baruch frequently had to revise a part of his record seven or eight times until what he had written was as near to the original as Jeremiah could make it; and the latter would sometimes become so exhausted in the effort to cast light into places that were dark and obscure that he had to cease dictating for a while and lean against the wall in his corner until he recovered.

The record began with the night Jeremiah was first sent forth upon his mission, when he was informed of his sanctification and saw the visions of the almond tree and the seething pot. Then he put down as faithfully as possible all the things that the Lord had caused him to see and hear, distinguishing carefully between the divine essence and the human adjuncts. His usual method was to relate at length everything he could remember, after which Baruch would read what he had written. With this first version Jeremiah was always disgusted. The second version would be somewhat more concise, and after repeated further attempts the text was laconic to the verge of austerity. This was his procedure with most of the visions, whether it was that of the "clay in the potter's hand" or the "cup of fury," the "shattered pitcher" or the "furnace of the gold refiner"; and he scrupulously eliminated everything that might have appertained merely to ordinary dreaming or imagination. When it was a matter of recording the actual words of God, Jeremiah was even more exact. Here there was no elimination to be done, for he was able to differentiate clearly between his own words and those of God, his power of distinction being so keen that there was no danger of mixing the two. At some particularly inspired moments it seemed even as if Adonai had resolved to collaborate in His own way in the work of the prophet, replying to questions and elucidating or supplementing certain passages. When Jeremiah came in his record to the incident of the "great pleading"—"Righteous art thou, O Lord, when I plead with thee: yet let me talk with thee of thy judgments"—he suddenly received the momentous answer:

"If thou hast run with the footmen, and they have wearied thee, then how canst thou contend with horses? And if in the land of peace, wherein thou trustedst, they wearied thee, then how wilt thou do in the swelling of Jordan?"

This rejoinder neither brought him comfort nor implied that the Lord was excusing Himself on account of the delay and vague nature of His justice. On the other hand it was a pregnant warning against self-pity and the belief that his sufferings in the past and the present represented the climax of evil. Jeremiah was to encounter greater peaks of calamity amid the dreary wastes of the future, and he must summon all his strength and passionate resolution if he was to surmount them.

Such hours of condescension on the part of the Lord were balanced, however, by other hours of utter barrenness when his mind was completely empty and he was overwhelmed by despair. It was only when he was making these laborious efforts to write down his experiences that he learned, somewhat belatedly, that the proximity or aloofness of the Lord was closely related to his own spiritual condition. The prophet was not always successful in keeping his own impulses and the divine word apart. The nearer he approached in his recollection to the terrible days of his return to Jerusalem, the more fiercely did wrath, hatred, and the thirst for vengeance take possession of his soul. He grew pale and trembled when he thought of Pashur, of Meshullam, of his shaggy accuser and his judges. He lost control of himself, and his voice became shrill as he broke into curses which his disciple wrote down as faithfully as he did the pure word that came from above:

"But thou, O Lord, knowest me; thou hast seen me, and tried mine heart towards thee: pull them out like sheep for the slaughter, and prepare them for the day of slaughter!"

This outburst was followed by the Lord's withdrawing his collaboration, and Jeremiah's soul grew sterile. Day after day he wore himself out in the vain attempt to record his further experiences. He could not produce a single sentence. His mind was like a stone through which not even the most ordinary memory could percolate. All his communion with God seemed to have been but a torturing delusion, only dross was left. Frequently weeks would go by before the Lord relented, but one day he was vouchsafed a promise:

"If thou return, then will I bring thee again, and thou shalt stand before me: and if thou take forth the precious from the vile, thou shalt be as my mouth."

Then Jeremiah understood. It was forbidden to combine the design of God with the insignificant desires of human frailty. The attempt to join forces with the Lord was wanton arrogance. Jeremiah now realized this clearly, though it did not help him very much. Again and again he relapsed, and again and again the unfathomably sensitive and jealous Lord punished him by holding aloof. Jeremiah had to pay the penalty for even lesser offences. Once, when he had denied in one of his sentences that it was possible for Israel to repent of its iniquity because it could no more transform itself than "the leopard could change his spots," he had to make retribution for his doubt by wasting two full months.

Because of this jealousy of the Lord and Jeremiah's own conscientiousness, the work proceeded very slowly. Outside their place of concealment the seasons alternated, but the fugitives realized the change only by night when they wandered about the hills and slopes in the neighbourhood of Anathoth. In the dark back room of their sanctuary, illuminated solely by a narrow window high up in the wall, the frost of winter and the heat of summer were alike mitigated. It was a veritable miracle that they remained undiscovered for so long by anyone in the house. By day the children and grandchildren of Jeremiah's brothers played about the hiding-place, which fascinated them at the same time as it filled them with uncanny fears. Jeremiah and Baruch listened uneasily to the voices of the boys and girls as they discussed ways and means of finding out what was inside the mysterious structure. Luckily the copper-bound oaken door was firmly locked and bolted, and the window was too high for them to reach. Nevertheless, the two were more than once in great danger of discovery. There was a very adventurous boy who did succeed, thanks to the numerous crevices and projections in the back wall, in climbing as far as the window from time to time and putting his head through the opening. Jeremiah would look up in affright at the sparkling eyes of the lad as he peered curiously in their direction. But whether the occupants of the room were enveloped in the natural gloom, or whether it was the will of the Lord that they should not be seen, the prying eyes could discern nothing. Nor did the daily visits of Abi awaken the suspicions of the other members of the family, ready though they always were to ferret out anything unusual.

When Jeremiah and Baruch had faithfully recorded all the words and visions of Adonai from the days of Josiah to those of Jehoiakim, they could justifiably hope that their task was fulfilled and that they had accomplished it creditably. Yet Jeremiah had scarcely begun to rejoice in the lightness of heart which came from work well done when he was once more disappointed. He again heard the voice within and without, commanding him: "Hearken, and write down these words!" And as he hesitatingly spoke the words for Baruch to write down, his mind grew numb with horror and he trembled in every limb. Despite all the prophecies, exhortations, warnings, threats, and curses which he had uttered hitherto in the name of Adonai, he had himself only half faced the truth, hoping always that the Lord did not wholly mean His menaces seriously and that He would eventually deal kindly with Israel. But the words he was now compelled to dictate froze him to the very marrow. For the first time he understood that it was not possible to cherish any more sanguine hope for the survival of Israel than for the life of a dying man. This was the most fateful part of the new prediction:

"From the thirteenth year of Josiah the son of Amon King of Judah, even unto this day, the word of the Lord hath come unto me, and I have spoken unto you, rising early and speaking; but ye have not hearkened. And the Lord hath sent unto you all his servants the prophets, rising early and sending them; but ye have not hearkened, nor inclined your ear to hear. They said, Turn ye again now every one from his evil way, and from the evil of your doings, and dwell in the land that the Lord hath given unto you, and to your fathers for ever and ever. And go not after other gods to serve them, and to worship them, and provoke me not to anger with the works of your hands; and I will do you no hurt. Yet ye have not hearkened unto me, saith the Lord; that ye might provoke me to anger with the works of your hands to your own hurt.

"Therefore thus saith the Lord of hosts; Because ye have not heard my words, behold, I will send and take all the families of the north, saith the Lord, and Nebuchadnezzar the King of Babylon, my servant, and will bring them against this land, and against the inhabitants thereof, and against all these nations round about, and will utterly destroy them, and make them an astonishment, and an hissing, and perpetual desolations. Moreover, I will take from them the voice of mirth, and the voice of gladness, the voice of the bridegroom, and the voice of the bride, the sound of the millstones, and the light of the candle. And this whole land shall be a desolation, and an astonishment; and these nations shall serve the King of Babylon seventy years."

Jeremiah paused and covered his eyes with hands that were cold as ice. It was unthinkable that he could have uttered with his own lips the words: "I will send Nebuchadnezzar, *my servant*." How could one who did not know the Lord be His servant? How could He be served by one who mocked Him amidst the hundred starry gods of his own creation? Was not the most wanton blasphemer and corrupter in Judah a holier servant of the Lord than Nebuchadnezzar, whose heathen soul sought the truth not in the pure Word but in the stars, the passing of the clouds, the flight of birds, and the livers of animals sacrificed upon the altars of his deities? Even Jehoiakim's sinning was only an error and a swerving away from God. Where there was error, there also was always at least a shadow of the truth. In Marduk-Nebuchadnezzar, however, there was not even error; there was only a void, shallowly joyous and with no hope of salvation. Yet the Lord called this thing of naught His servant, a name of honour which He had conferred only on Abraham, Isaac, Jacob, and Moses—not even on David!

Jeremiah groaned, sank to the ground, beat the floor with clenched fists, and wept like a boy who had been unjustly chastised by his father.

One mild winter's night Gedaliah, son of Ahikam, appeared among the hills of Anathoth at the prearranged meeting place in order to speak with Jeremiah. The twin brother of Micah was known as "the Senior," a name which he owed not only to the fact that he really was the firstborn but also to his more spacious nature and power of inspiring confidence, which invested with a genial humanity the usually austere intellect and logic of the sons of Shaphan. His influence in council was due both to his skill in rational and incontrovertible argument, which he shared with Micah, and to a benignly buoyant spirit whose vitality and reliability had a soothing effect. Jeremiah, too, felt his own burden alleviated when Gedaliah was with him.

Ahikam and his sons were worried because mysterious things were happening at Jerusalem which they, who lived in honourable exile from the royal court, were unable to fathom. It was whispered that a secret embassy from Pharaoh had been received in the winter palace to the west of the city. Elnathan, on the other hand, was alleged to have gone to Noph with a deputation from Jehoiakim. These were only rumours and no authentic confirmation had reached the Temple from the royal circle. It was not merely a rumour, however, that preparations were being made throughout the land which recalled the days when Josiah had conceived his unhappy plan of attacking the hosts of Pharaoh. As on that occasion, though under some harmless pretext, the princes of the cities and the various regions were being ordered quietly to recruit young men and drill them in the use of arms. Suspicious-looking caravans were arriving from Egypt with great bales which were unloaded in the gloomy old Citadel of David. Nobody could say for sure that they contained consignments of weapons, for this state of oppressive uncertainty and irresponsible secrecy was an integral part of any tyrannous regime. None the less, Ahikam and his sons were convinced that all these signs pointed to the fact that there was some evil project on hand in alliance with the House of Bondage, Israel's arch-enemy. Jehoiakim owed his throne to Pharaoh, and perhaps he was now being compelled to pay his debt by entering into a perilous pact that would serve the schemes of Egypt.

What frightened Gedaliah most was Jehoiakim's sudden change of heart, which he had paraded with disturbing and deliberate emphasis. The sun-wheel on the Mount of Olives had been taken down overnight and the construction of the royal tomb discontinued, while it had again been decreed that the Sabbath was to be observed as a day of rest—a decree to which the King himself, to everybody's astonishment, was strictly conforming. As Gedaliah said, however, a hypocritical change of heart was even more abominable than naked apostasy. Jehoiakim's ostentatious observance of the Law indicated merely a fraudulent attempt to secure God as an ally in a scheme that was contrary to the divine commandments. He was acting like a horse-coper who groomed and smartened up a broken-winded jade in order to outwit a prospective buyer. The Lord was to be outwitted in order that He might help to further the King's sinister plans. And at this perfidy the prophets were beside themselves with delight, while the high orders of priests ecstatically sang the praises of Jehoiakim and his court on account of their new-found piety. In honour of his conversion, and as a general penance for the nation, Jehoiakim had ordained a day of fasting for the whole people. Strange to say, this coincided with the arrival in Jerusalem of an embassy from Babylon to receive, as the heir of Asshur, the yearly tribute: a merely nominal sum that was not a real tribute but only an acknowledgment of the fact that Marduk-Nebuchadnezzar was the new architect and supreme master of the world.

Jeremiah and Baruch sat for the greater part of the night under a tree and anxiously discussed the news brought by Gedaliah, who requested the prophet to inquire the will of God in order that he might have a divine basis for the deductions he drew concerning the situation. Gedaliah believed that even the obscurest prophecy contained the grace of providence, the sacred sequence of cause and effect, which could be correctly puzzled out only by the impartial and intellectual process of logical deduction. Jeremiah gazed contemplatively in front of him. Without mentioning the work they had been doing in their place of hiding, he promised Gedaliah that he would communicate with him immediately word came from the Lord.

When Jeremiah and Baruch had returned to their room

just before dawn and were lying on their couch preparing to fall asleep, the disciple asked a question which led to a long discussion between them.

"Is there not," he inquired as he lay in the darkness, "sufficient prophesying for Gedaliah's purpose in the roll of the book?"

Jeremiah allowed some time to pass before he answered, so that Baruch imagined his master must be asleep. Then he said in a low voice:

"Tell me, what is likely to happen if I speak all these words in the ears of the King?"

Baruch started up in affright.

"Does Jeremiah intend to seek a useless death that will not even help the Lord and His people?"

"The words concerning Nebuchadnezzar, whom He called His servant, must be spoken," replied Jeremiah.

It was now Baruch's turn to think a long time before he asked another question, like a pupil inquiring of his teacher:

"Will my master tell me why the Lord created the rolls which are called books?"

"The purpose of books is to enable men to realize the error of their ways, to change their hearts, both now and in the future. Books are an exhortation for everyone."

"Am I right," the intelligent Baruch asked modestly, "in thinking that books are intended to be read by those who are able to read and to be listened to by those who are unable to read?"

When Jeremiah did not answer, he continued:

"Does one need a strong voice in order to read to others? Is it not sufficient if one reads with a weak voice?"

Jeremiah understood his disciple's meaning, but declined firmly to accept his offer.

"Since when does a warrior send his younger brother into the bloody fray in order that his own life may be spared?"

"Your younger brother will not be entering a bloody fray. Who is there that knows him? The Lord, moreover, did not command us to write this book in order that it should remain unread."

Baruch unfolded to Jeremiah the plan he had in mind. He would appear in the Temple with the roll they had written in their place of hiding and read it first of all to a gathering of chosen men in the chamber of the sons of Shaphan. This could not involve him in any serious danger. If necessary, he would pretend to be simple-minded. Nor would anyone discover in what way the book had fallen into his hands. In any case, Jehoiakim's hypocritical change of heart required him to take less tyrannical measures against his enemies.

Baruch's arguments could not be controverted and his plan was a good plan. Yet Jeremiah hesitated for three days and three nights before he would allow his disciple to expose himself to risk. At last, on the fourth night, he gave him permission to go. For the first time since the beginning of their companionship he laid his two hands on Baruch's head and spoke the blessing which, as the son of a priestly house, he had the right to give:

"The Lord bless you, and keep you, and make His countenance shine upon you!"

21

Glowing Coals and Poisoned Wine

One day, when the lonely Jeremiah was sitting in his room thinking anxiously of Baruch and his daring undertaking, the door abruptly opened and Obadiah, his elder brother, stood before him. The shock was so sudden that he could scarcely realize the full extent of his peril. Slowly he rose from where he was sitting. On returning home the previous night he had forgotten to fasten the inner bolt. He stared in horror at Obadiah, the ill-tempered peasant who had become an old man in the course of the years. His beard was now long and grey and he seemed to have learned self-control, for the eyes with which he looked at his brother were neither angry nor hostile. Silently they took each other's measure, and during the brief respite Jeremiah feverishly considered all the ways of escape that might be open to him. Obadiah, however, who appeared to have divined his thoughts, was the first to speak:

"Why does my younger brother hide himself from his kin? It is true that he has brought sorrow and little honour to his house by his activities, but surely he does not think that sedate fathers of families will help to augment the dishonour?"

In spite of the rebuke, Obadiah's words were spoken in a friendly tone. Moreover, his question held an implied assurance of protection. Yet it was just this friendliness, and even the implied assurance, that filled Jeremiah with anxiety. He would have been less disturbed by the open malice to which he was accustomed. He knew that the Lord had withdrawn from him the blessing of concealment and was commanding him to devote his puny strength to a struggle, old and yet new, he had thought was long since ended. Obadiah sighed as if his prediction had been fulfilled; belatedly, it was true, but yet fulfilled.

"The world is one thing . . . and a family is another. . . ."

Obadiah spoke not as an elder brother, but as if he were Hilkiah himself, a father responsible to the Lord for the continuance and unity of an ancient family of Israel. With a certain astonishment Jeremiah realized that a considerable part of his father's spirit had entered into the firstborn son, mitigating his clumsy manner and investing him with the tranquil dignity appropriate to the head of a priestly house. It was not only his elder brother who stood before him, but the man who had inherited his father's office, and Jeremiah was ready to humble his soul before him and offer him the veneration which was his due. He bent his head before his fatherly brother and kept it lowered in the manner of one who is full of remorse. This humility was very pleasing to Obadiah and he nodded magnanimously.

"The waves have cast my younger brother forth. Let him return home to the Hall of Abiathar, where a place will be assigned to him at the table of my house. Let him acknowledge the error and arrogance of his ways and return to his family, where he will find a safe refuge at Obadiah's table. Verily, I will strangle you with my own hands rather than give you up to your persecutors!"

Obadiah had not only acquired a new dignity; his rough vocabulary had also become more polished, as was evident from this well-turned speech, at the conclusion of which he lightly touched Jeremiah on the shoulder before adding:

"It is well! Let those things be forgotten which can be forgotten!"

Their horrified mother suddenly appeared behind Jeremiah. She motioned imploringly to her youngest son, who smiled with an effort, raised his arms, let them fall again, raised them once more, and finally drew his brother into a fleeting embrace as a sign that there was now peace between them.

At the evening meal the prophet who had been appointed by the Lord to speak unto kings and nations sat in depressed silence at the ancient table in the Hall of Abiathar, occupying the place which had been allotted to him as a boy. He again felt the burden of the mysterious law of sanctification, which alienated him from his home and made strangers of his nearest kin. During the period of his wanderings the house had filled with new faces, and even those he had known were changed. He hardly recognized those who had been children. Mocheleth, who was now the mistress of the household, was as grey-haired as her husband. But whereas Obadiah, in the full consciousness of his position as the head of a great family, was careful to maintain his courteous and sedate attitude, she was apparently even more spiteful and bitter than before. Her eyes glittered with malice and she was unable to control her voice even in the presence of the men, but upbraided the children and on one occasion vented her anger against her venerable mother-in-law, who received the outburst calmly and made no reply. Mocheleth seemed to be beside herself with disappointment at Jeremiah's return, and he could feel the burning hatred that was consuming her. She did not make the slightest attempt to conceal her embitterment. Though Jeremiah had always been aware that she could not endure him, he was deeply perplexed at her present manifestation of a hatred for which he could think of no grounds. Shua, on the other hand, the wife of Joel, who had grown fat and lethargic, kept her eyes fixed on him with her old, dull look of curiosity and seemed still to be making an effort not to laugh. Even the numerous children whom he had never seen before cast furtive looks at the notorious uncle whose name had become an abomination in the house of Hilkiah, while the older ones inspected him arrogantly as if he were a wild animal in a cage whose appearance did not come up to their expectations. The little boys and girls pushed past him in shy haste as though he were something forbidden and unclean.

Obadiah and Joel, however, enjoyed an evening of glorious self-satisfaction. They were now receiving their reward for that humiliating and unforgotten moment when a king had sent his messenger to summon a stubborn idler instead of honouring honest, hard-working men. To this day the wound to their vanity had not healed. Joel, man of the world as he was, was not ashamed to overwhelm the defenceless prophet in front of the women and children with a flood of insipid advice, precepts, and maxims in various tongues. His restless life of travel had dealt more kindly with him than a stay-at-home life on the farm had dealt with his brother. He had remained young and agile and had lost nothing of his skill in well-informed repartee. But that evening, drunk with their triumph at the ruin of Jeremiah's fortunes, they both succumbed to the temptation of flaunting their victory before his eyes, an exercise in which one tried to outdo the other. With great complacency they praised their own works and deeds as the only earthly activities that were pleasing in the eyes of the Lord. Obadiah began by referring to his invention of salted cattle-fodder, which had done more for the nation and the country than all the wordy speeches of the prophets, since it had doubled the size of the herds and even trebled the weight of fat. What would all the scholars who wasted their time in the Temple and elsewhere do if Obadiah's unwearying toil on the hills of Anathoth did not supply them with sweet milk and fine wool? Joel nodded graciously in confirmation of this truth, extending its scope with the assertion that the sweetest milk would become sour, the finest wool would deteriorate, all the produce of the earth would decay, if his linguistic and persuasive powers did not succeed in disposing of the excess products to hesitating customers as he travelled so courageously about the countries of the world. This was the only real and true cycle of earthly blessings, as the priests sang in the temple of E-sagila. Moreover, all the Lord demanded was a solid, not too feverish piety; that is to say, the regular offering up of seasonable prayers and sacrifices together with the customary observance of the most important commandments and festivals. Everything that exceeded these clearly defined limits was merely an unnecessary evil, especially the uncalled-for listening to secret voices whose authenticity could not be proved. This sprang from a vaulting ambition and could lead only to the abyss, as was clearly to be seen in the melancholy return home of the failure and fugitive now seeking refuge with compassionate brothers to whom he had imagined himself immeasurably superior both in mind and in destiny. Joel and Obadiah exhorted their sons and daughters again and again to learn a pious lesson for their future lives from this miserable example.

Jeremiah, now mature in experience, had to listen in silence to the unfriendly boastings and disparaging remarks of his brothers. They no longer sent the blood rushing to his head as they had done in earlier years. He listened in complete humility and said nothing, thereby giving the women and children a lesson in the patient endurance of injustice. But they did not understand and only despised him for a silence which they regarded as an acknowledgment of his guilt.

The one who was most irritated by his tranquil reticence was Joel, who would have been glad to have his eloquence kindled by contradiction. Jeremiah remained mute until the self-satisfied bragging of the two men died down for lack of fuel, then he raised his eyes and said:

"I honour the work which is done by my elder brothers. Perhaps in their kindness they will instruct me how to follow in their footsteps, that I may learn from their knowledge that which I have neglected."

This modest request surprised the two brothers and took the wind out of their sails. They exchanged glances with each other and their wives, as do merchants who suspected that a particularly favourable offer conceals a cunning snare.

During the following days Obadiah and Joel, together with their eldest sons, accompanied Jeremiah on a tour of the fields, so that he might see with his own eyes the blessings of their work. It was the first time since his boyhood that he had visited the ploughed acres and pastures, the vineyards and olive plantations, the dairies, mills, and sheep-folds that comprised the great estate and a third of which was his own inheritance. He had to acknowledge that his brothers, by their industry, had increased its prosperity and incidentally made him too a rich man, though the night he entered his mother's chamber he had been clad in a tattered mantle and coat. After the death of Hilkiah he had hardly once asked for anything from his share of the estate, since, while living at the court of King Josiah and as the tutor of Mattaniah, he had been provided for as a member of the royal household. He had no desire to be counted among the prosperous people of this world, who were all without compassion and did not live in the spirit of the Lord, as was shown by the example of Obadiah and Joel. On the other hand he had no desire to surrender the inheritance which was due to him, for he regarded it as a sacred inheritance in the land of the Lord. Every clod of earth in Judah was connected with the far-reaching plan of God, and nobody ought voluntarily to resign his share in that plan. Yet the Lord had specially exempted him, Jeremiah, from the duty of settling on his portion of his father's estate, since He had forbidden him to take a wife and have children. A man's inheritance was meaningless when he had no son to whom he could bequeath it.

Jeremiah's mind was in a turmoil. He was only too well aware that the disturbing friendliness of Obadiah and Joel was founded on the hope that their earlier attempt to purchase his inheritance from him might now be brought to a successful conclusion. As their younger brother had returned home a fugitive with a price on his head, he was completely at their mercy. His life was not safe for a moment, and his presence menaced the whole house of Hilkiah. Joel made a point of referring to this fact at every possible opportunity; the dignified Obadiah would add, not without a certain unction, that none of them had the slightest thought of surrendering one of their own kin to the minions of the King, especially as he was so full of remorse for his erring ways. It was clear to Jeremiah that all these speeches, with their emphasis on his helplessness, were intended to render him tractable and ready to accede to any suggestion that his brothers might make.

Mocheleth, however, appeared to find the charitable attitude of her husband and brother-in-law not to her liking. She could not bring herself even to return Jeremiah's greeting when he appeared at table, but would turn her head away abruptly. Presumably it had been her hope that he had disappeared for good, having met his death somewhere. She had three sons of her own and had long ago divided Jeremiah's inheritance among them in her thoughts. It had been a shock to her when the object of her hatred turned up again and brought to naught her dreams, which she had regarded as certainties. Those two clumsy men, the simple-minded Obadiah and the loquacious Joel, did not realize that any covenant they might make with their brother would be revoked if his divine Master should be pleased to command it. Mocheleth was fully aware of that possibility, and she also believed that in spite of all her prayers and sacrifices Jeremiah's Master cherished only malevolent inventions towards her and her family, while He would never withdraw His favour from Abi's youngest son. The two men, with their obtuse, earthly minds, had no idea of all this, but Mocheleth was ardently convinced that Jeremiah's death was the only thing that could free them from the ill-will of his heavenly partner and assure her sons of the inheritance she coveted. When one shattered the vessel of the Godhead—so argued this erring daughter of Israel—one destroyed its shelter and annulled its harmful power. Mocheleth was thus the only person in the house, apart from Abi, who was deeply convinced that Jeremiah was a true prophet. At meal times he seemed always to be watching her, until she reddened to the roots of the grey hair which straggled from under her head cloth. His understanding gaze confused her and intensified her hatred to a feverish mania. Jeremiah's eyes followed her everywhere, until she sometimes felt like screaming without any apparent reason.

When Jeremiah saw that the hearts of his brothers grew more covetous of his inheritance from day to day, his hesitancy began to disappear as his mind inclined towards a definite decision. He thought seriously of acceding to their avaricious desire and thereby purchasing peace for himself in at least *one* sphere of his life. Though he felt repelled by the insatiable greed of the wealthy, this did not make him love poverty and misery the more. He knew only too well that physical deprivation tended to prevent rather than to promote the concentration of one's thoughts on God. Only voluntary fasting could sometimes help to illumine the obscurity of Zebaoth, never involuntary hunger. It was his intention, therefore, to demand from his brothers a just and proper price.

For the time being he concealed his decision from his mother, for she would never have agreed to the surrender of his inheritance. Things came to a head one Sabbath when they had concluded their meal. Obadiah and Joel began to clear their throats with a certain embarrassment and to speak of that which lay nearest to their hearts. They pointed out how tactfully they had acted since Jeremiah's return by refraining from inviting any friends, or even a guest of God, to their table in order not to imperil his safety. Jeremiah listened attentively and did not interrupt them, until his constraining gaze brought them rather more quickly than they had intended to the object of their desires. Joel declared magnanimously that their younger brother would not lose contact with his family by selling his inheritance, but would as a matter of fact be taken more closely to its bosom—especially if he avoided any further foolish activity in the future. To their great surprise Jeremiah nodded as a sign that he did not reject their offer. The dignified Obadiah could hardly disguise his delight as he suggested that witnesses should be invited to assemble on the following day, in order to establish the just price of Jeremiah's portion. Jeremiah, however, damped his brother's enthusiasm by saying that a message was already on the way which would decide his future. He had to await its arrival before the decision he had come to could be put into valid form. One always had the same trouble with this fellow, thought the brothers; as soon as one imagined that he was pinned down, he slipped away again. Obadiah's face showed his disappointment, and he seemed about to lose the control that he had so lately won. Joel soothed him with a meaning glance.

"A slow fire hardens the pitcher," he said in the guttural language of Aram.

On the following day Jeremiah went for a walk by himself across the fields. An agony of restlessness drove him to inspect once more the inheritance that had hitherto meant so little to him. He was finding it difficult to take leave of possessions which he had never really owned. In a strange, melancholy mood he strolled along the paths and the margins which ran between his fields. He guided his steps deliberately over the soft earth as if he wanted to enter into loving contact with it, and the earth seemed to respond gladly to the touch of his foot. A fresh breeze was wafted across the stubble, filling the air with fragrance. It was the time of the new sowing and everywhere the crude wooden ploughs were driving their furrows through the soil. Teams of oxen plodded along and the ploughmen drove their ploughshares into the earth, intent on cutting their furrows as straight as man could make them. Behind the ploughmen walked the sowers casting seeds. These again were followed by women and children who bent down and heaped the soil over the precious grains with their hands. The spacious fields of Hilkiah were full of busy peasants, but peasants who were not free men and women with the same rights as their brothers and sisters in Judah. They were serfs and bondmen, to be bought and sold. They belonged body and soul to the owners of the land, that is to say, to Obadiah, Joel, and Jeremiah. They were offered for sale in special markets and their emaciated bodies bore the brands or other signs of slavery. The Lord had delivered the Israelites out of Egypt, the House of Bondage, only for these children of Jacob to be cast into bondage in their own land. It was true that the Law made special provision for such afflicted people and that the Lord spoke again and again in their favour, but none of the commandments was more openly flouted by the rich men of Judah than this one. At the sight of these slaves in fields which were partly his own, Jeremiah felt a stab of fear and shame. He, who in the presence of kings had boldly demanded the fulfilment of the Law, had been faint-hearted enough to stand by with closed eyes when it was ignored on his own estate. When the day of reckoning came, his hands would not be cleaner than those of his brothers and he would have to condemn himself as their accomplice. From every direction the mournful songs of the serfs were borne on the wind and filled the ears of Jeremiah, whose steps grew more and more weary and hesitant. In front of him there loomed one of the miserable huts that the peasants built out of baked clay and straw, near which a group of women was tending an old man who had been overtaken by weakness or some sudden malady. One of the women was trying to pour a few drops of milk between his lips. Jeremiah approached, sat down on the ground, took the sick man's head upon his lap, and laid his hand upon the cold, damp brow. The stricken serf quickly came to, and his wrinkled, weather-beaten face stared up at Jeremiah with vacant eyes. Then a faint gleam of recognition flickered across his grey features. Perhaps the old man had watched the dreamy boy in bygone days as he strode with an abstract air across his father's fields. His hands sought to caress the son of Hilkiah as his dying voice came rattling from his throat:

"Behold, this is our good master. . . . This is our good master who is well inclined towards his servants. . . . Oh, my good master, nine times seven years have I served you and soon there will begin a new period of seven years. . . ."

"A new period of seven years," repeated Jeremiah with pale lips. But the women roundabout only laughed and looked at him with twinkling eyes. "He is always counting," they said. The counting of the years of jubilee, the remembrance of the commandment, all this seemed to them only the foolish hallucination of an old man's mind. They had long since lost any desire to be free. But Jeremiah gave the old bondman the new clothes which he had received from his mother, though he knew that, unless they were stolen by the other serfs, they could serve him only for funeral clothes. He also gave away the golden clasp of Josiah, a sacred memento which he had always worn. To the annoyance and scorn of his family he returned home almost naked, clad only in a loin-cloth.

The two brothers had to restrain their covetousness once again, for Jeremiah disappeared and they did not see him for some time.

One night Baruch had come to his window, and they at once shut themselves up in the old sanctuary. The disciple seemed to have come unharmed through the perils to which he had been exposed, but he did not have the roll with him.

"The King has burned my master's work. . . ." These were the words with which Baruch commenced the report of his adventures. "Your farewell words," he said, "strengthened my timid heart and I did not tremble. . . ." In spite of this assertion Jeremiah realized from Baruch's story what an alarming experience he had gone through.

The sons of Shaphan occupied a large chamber in the Temple, adjoining which were a number of little rooms for the purpose of study. After preliminary arrangement with Baruch they had invited about a hundred pious, God-fearing men, who had ears to hear, to assemble in order that Baruch might read to them from Jeremiah's book, which was not a human document but a continuation of the prophecies vouchsafed to Israel by the Lord since the earliest times. The disciple confessed to his master that his voice had failed him through excitement and that he had read the first few lines as if he were choking. The word of Adonai had been like a burning fire in his throat, and he could only slowly become accustomed to it.

Nevertheless, the effect of the divine prophecies read to them by the disciple was so tremendous that Ahikam and his sons were shaken to their very souls. When Baruch had ceased his audience sat thunder-struck, then cast themselves to the ground as one man and began to beat the floor with their foreheads. In a flash they had all become conscious of the endless sequence of iniquities in which Judah had participated, of the Lord's exhausted patience, and the doom that could no longer be averted. There was a great wailing and gnashing of teeth, followed by tears of despair and heart-breaking entreaties which, Baruch hoped, must surely have penetrated to the Lord. Ahikam and his sons had waited calmly until the agitation died down, and then the clear headed Micah took advantage of the general remorse by proposing that they should not hesitate another moment, but should go down to the administrative quarters in the Palace and acquaint the authorities with what was written in the book. They would declare that in their opinion it was equal in importance to the Book of the Law which had been rediscovered in the reign of Josiah. Everyone had raised his hand in agreement. Fearlessly and without delay the King should be compelled to acknowledge a sincere change of heart. It was not a raving rabble that accompanied Micah and Baruch to the Palace, but a silent band of venerable greybeards each of whom was a man of rank and position in Jerusalem and could not be ignored by the royal officials. In the rooms of the new Chancellor, whose name was Elishama, the deputation was received at once. Micah, who was their spokesman, requested Baruch to wait for the time being in an antechamber, and there he stood with beating heart for what seemed an endless age, until a young man appeared to bring him into the presence of the great dignitaries of the realm. This good-looking young man was Jehudi, of the house of Cushi, the King's chief reader, and his eyes rested amiably on Baruch, inspiring him with courage at one of the most fateful hours of his life.

When he was standing in Elishama's chamber, however, and saw the stony faces of the princes of the court in front of him, his heart again grew weak and despondent. One of them had placed his naked sword before him on the table and sat there with folded arms. It was Elnathan himself, the friend and brother-in-law of Jehoiakim and the cornerstone of his tyranny. In the presence of this immobile fire-eater, Baruch felt a hopeless desire to flee. Yet it was Elnathan who was to provide the great surprise of the day.

With condescending courtesy Elishama bade the disciple sit down and begin his reading of the divine book. Baruch found it even more difficult to start than he had the first time. He felt that he must either stop reading or swoon. Through the veil of his overwhelming agitation he saw the eyes of the great princes fixed on him with grave attention, while those of Elishama seemed to pierce him through. Then Baruch knew that the whole future course of history depended on his voice alone. The thought cleared his head and dispelled his fears. His life was nothing; his spiritual victory over these men was everything. He raised his voice, trying to instil into it the power of mastery with which Jeremiah was able to cast a spell over his opponents in the hour of need. And for the only time in his life of service the Lord enabled him to imitate that which was inimitable. Baruch concluded with the prophecy of the downfall of Jerusalem and its destruction by Nebuchadnezzar. When he came to the appellation "my servant," with the terrible humiliation of Israel which it implied, he hurled the words fearlessly and inexorably in the faces of the princes.

Not a hand moved to draw a weapon and chastise the speaker of such an audacious prophecy. Silently and with lowered heads they sat motionless. Only Elnathan sprang up and flung his sword into a corner. Then he turned away his face that the others might not see the agony which distorted his features. Among all those who listened to words such as man had never heard before, there was none so aghast as he. He pressed his hands to his throbbing temples, and the words that wrenched themselves from his breast were like a deep groan: "We must tell this to the King."

Elishama, however, addressed to Baruch the dangerous question: "Tell us now, how did you write all these words?"

The disciple hesitated a long time before disclosing the name of his master. But now a lie would have seemed too base a thing to utter. He revealed the true origin of the work they had done in their place of hiding:

"Jeremiah pronounced all these words to me with his mouth, and I wrote them with ink in the book."

Elnathan gathered his cloak around him and urged the other princes:

"To the King! Let us go to the King! Is there one of us who will hesitate?"

Jehudi raised his voice and advised against such a sudden incursion into the King's presence. It would be better to wait for a favourable moment when they could have the book read to Jehoiakim, not by a stranger, who would only arouse his anger, but by someone in whom the King had confidence. Jehudi's prudent advice was approved by the majority of those present, and even Elnathan eventually agreed that it was best to walk warily. When the men were dispersing after their fateful meeting, Jehudi took Baruch aside and warned him:

"Go and hide, both you and Jeremiah, and let no man know where ye be!"

Baruch found shelter in the house of Gedaliah, where he was safe, only Jehudi knowing of his presence there. The day seemed endless as he waited, but during the night Jehudi appeared at last to inform him and the sons of Shaphan what had been the fate of Jeremiah's book.

It had not been easy to discover the whereabouts of the

King, since during the past few months he had been in the habit of changing his place of residence several times a day. He did this not only from fear of assassination, but because he was afraid that he might be forced to make decisions. Already he had allowed the embassy from Egypt to depart without fulfilling its mission, while the embassy from Babylon was still waiting for his reply. The ruler whose throne was founded on tyranny, and who knew so well how to carry the people away by his oratory, had been unable, since the day when Jeremiah had foretold his end, to make up his mind about anything whatsoever. For days at a time he would shut himself up in his laboratories or lie tossing on a couch in one of his painted rooms. Elnathan and the princes who accompanied him eventually surprised their King in a dark chamber of the new winter palace, though he had at first refused them admittance. He sat shivering in front of a brazier, staring as if hypnotized into the glowing coals. His spindle legs were closely pressed together and his bony hands now and then moved over the fragrant flames as though in entreaty. Elnathan reported in an agitated voice that a book of divine origin, but written down by Jeremiah of Anathoth, had been brought to the Temple, and he asked that the King might order it to be read to him. At the mention of Jeremiah's name the King gave a start and looked in consternation at Elnathan, who had hitherto been the fiercest of the prophet's persecutors. Then he pretended not to have heard words that were unwelcome to him and endeavoured to open a conversation that had nothing to do with the matter in hand. He was not successful. Elnathan, the general who had from the beginning been Jehoiakim's companion in treachery, violence, and sin, was facing one of the gravest hours of his life. He had rent his robe in twain and cut his scarred cheeks as a token of lamentation and remorse.

Jehoiakim twisted and turned in discomfort. He, who inspired fear in others, must not exhibit signs of fear himself, especially fear of mere words. Elnathan stood implacably in front of him. With a slight gesture that betrayed his annoyance, he gave Jehudi permission to read the roll. The voice of the court reader was resonant and the words of the Lord issued melodiously from his lips, but their fire did not burn him. Jehudi told Baruch later that the King had seemed ashamed of his surrender, for he let his eyes roam from one to the other in simulated abstraction and rose to his feet now and then to speak in loud tones with one or other of his chamberlains. Then he sat down again and was silent, until at last he appeared to be gripped by what was being read. Elnathan, however, who had based his hopes on the emotional nature of the King, was bitterly disappointed. Jehoiakim neither broke down and wept nor tore his garments, and he showed no signs of swooning with remorse. When Jehudi had finished reading one of the closely written columns, the King asked for the roll to be handed to him, cut the column from the rest of the roll with a penknife, and threw it carelessly into the fire, causing a flame to leap up. After this, no scoffer could assert that the King was a coward. As each column was consumed, Elnathan grimly signed to Jehudi to continue. The latter read tranquilly until he came to the end of another column, which then shared the fate of its predecessors. Since Jehudi did not omit a single sentence, it was several hours before the whole book was destroyed, but when the last column flared up, Elnathan took two heavy steps towards the King and kicked the brazier over with his foot. Jehoiakim gave a loud cry as the glowing coals were scattered over the floor, filling the room with smoke before the chamberlains could hurry to remove them. Elnathan fixed his eyes sadly on the monarch, then turned on his heel and left him.

As he listened to Baruch's story, Jeremiah covered his eyes with both hands. His throat was constricted with the pain of unshed tears. The work that had cost him so much effort during untold days and nights was gone, and he was overwhelmed with agony of mind at the thought of the irreparable loss. He hardly listened to Baruch's further report concerning the renewal of Jehoiakim's furious attempts to discover his place of hiding. The craftiest spies had been sent out to seize both him and Baruch, and it was essential for them to seek a new refuge. No sooner did Jeremiah realize this than the thought flashed through his mind: "Do not accept defeat! The Lord does not intend that His word shall be lost. Write it down a second time from beginning to end!" The resolve to do this brought him comfort.

His mother was again able to help him. Near the northern boundary of the estate there was a dilapidated hut in an outlying fallow field that nobody ever went to. It would make a safe shelter, since the serfs who lived roundabout and loved Jeremiah could easily warn him of approaching danger.

This hut became their new place of refuge, and they again set to work laboriously to write down the words of Adonai on a roll of papyrus.

For the second time Jeremiah searched his memory to recall the visions and words with which the Lord had visited him. The Lord favoured his work and prompted him, so that the book was an even more faithful record than before. He also held His hand over the two fugitives, and not even Jeremiah's brothers succeeded in discovering their whereabouts, to say nothing of the pursuers who appeared several times on the hills of Anathoth. After a time Jehoiakim seemed to weary of his vain attempts to capture his enemy. The prophesied doom was coming nearer and demanded daily decisions, which he tried to avoid by locking himself in his laboratories. His regime was built on weak foundations, and after a temporary period of success the first jolt caused it to totter. The King of Babylon, the unsuspecting servant of God, lay with his army at the gates of Damascus in the land of Aram. The neighbouring nations had not understood his watchword, "The Peace of Babylon!" taking it for a confession of impotence. Marduk, who had set himself up as the architect of the world, was therefore forced to prove his mettle first of all as a general. Large troops of cavalry, wearing conical helmets, appeared everywhere before the open towns of Judah and their warning presence put a stop to the warlike preparations in the land. It was rumoured—and the rumour reached even Jeremiah in his concealment—that Marduk, the lord of the starry sky, had commanded Jehoiakim to break off his relations with the sun of Noph and acknowledge the King of Babylon unconditionally as his liege lord. Jehoiakim's reply was not known.

The smoky winds of autumn were again blowing across the fields. The vintage was over and the year was approaching its end. The next year would be the Sabbath of the years, the year of jubilee, when all serfs had to be freed from their bondage and loans of property returned to their original owners. One day Jeremiah unexpectedly appeared in the Hall of Abiathar and announced to his brothers that he was ready to accede to their wishes and resign his inheritance to them. He requested them to summon all the men of their kin before the festival of the New Year, that he might state in the presence of witnesses and arbiters the conditions on which he would be prepared to swear a covenant forthwith. Joel asked suspiciously whether it would not be better to talk the matter over first of all among themselves before calling in their cousins. And he asked, besides, whether Jeremiah would not be afraid to show himself openly to men who were virtually strangers to him. Jeremiah assured him that he was not afraid; that he intended to depart immediately after the covenant had been sworn, and that, so far as he and his personal advantage were concerned, he would submit reverently to the advice of his brothers. The word "reverently" was very comforting to the heart of Obadiah. He magnanimously motioned to Joel not to say anything more and declared his agreement with Jeremiah's proposal. Mocheleth, however, who was just filling the men's wine cups, snarled in her husband's ear:

"This trickster of Adonai will cheat you yet!"

Three days before the New Year all the adult male descendants of Hilkiah assembled in the Hall of Abiathar together with those of their cousins who lived at Anathoth, including Hanameel, Jeremiah's boyhood friend whose little estate bordered on that of the three brothers. There was also a stranger whom nobody had invited—the brazen Shamariah. It was a healthy life and kept a man vigorous, being the chief beggar of one's town. One acted as a kind of counter where earthly good deeds were exchanged for divine rewards; the rich were granted favours strictly in proportion to the charity they dispensed. Eighty or even eighty-five years could not wear down an arrogant arch-beggar whom not even the

King dared to turn from his door. Shamariah limped actively on his bandy legs from house to house, and the road was not yet made that could tire him. In the course of the years he had acquired considerable power in the house of Hilkiah, and he had so cunningly mastered the art of mingling servility and insolence that the slow wits of Obadiah repeatedly succumbed to him. Everybody feared this inevitable Sabbath guest, this unpleasant purveyor of scandalous gossip who insisted on his customary rights and took his place at the table without being invited. Even Obadiah was afraid of him, but since he swallowed even the basest flattery in his thirst for praise, he protected Shamariah against those who disapproved of his presence. Even the favour of the head of the house, however, did not help the chief of the beggars this time, for Jeremiah took the matter into his own hands.

"Are you a member of this family?" he asked sharply, as he seized Shamariah by his stained cloak. "One of our cousins, perhaps? If not, then your place is not in the Hall of Abiathar but outside the door!"

A gentle but relentless pressure helped the old man on his way, so that he did not have time even to begin one of his venomous and eloquent lamentations or entreat the protection of his patron. No one uttered a protest, for most of those present sympathized in their hearts with Jeremiah's resolute action. Obadiah clenched his teeth, but he too remained silent. His younger brother had usurped a right which did not belong to him, but he was justified in expelling a man who had not been invited and had come only to spy on what they were doing. Jeremiah took advantage of the silence to open the proceedings. It was the first time that the prophet who had made Jerusalem ring with his name and cast a spell over kings and priests had raised his voice to address his own kin assembled in his father's house. Curious eyes scanned the black sheep of the family as he spoke.

"Men and cousins of this house," he began, "may you decide wisely concerning the proposal that I am about to lay before you! Do not imagine that we intend to chaffer about boundaries of fields and weights of silver. The youngest brother will be content to accept that which his elder brothers consider just. But there is one thing that must be settled first of all. Hearken unto me when I tell you that the word of the Lord has gone forth concerning this whole land and therefore concerning this house. Little hope remains that Adonai will take pity on this people, for abomination and apostasy are practised not only by rich and poor, but even by priestly houses descended from Eli. We have failed to heed the Sabbath year, the year of emancipation, and have rejected the commandments and the Law. May my entreaty find favour in your ears that you respect the jubilee, set free your bondmen and bondwomen, giving them their just share as your brothers and sisters, and so avert the great wrath of the Lord!"

Jeremiah had spoken with the utmost deliberation and gentleness, not as a prophet demanding a change of heart, but as a modest member of a priestly family imploring those of his own kin to realize the desperate nature of their situation. Yet the effect was as if he had hurled bitter insults in their faces from a pulpit in the Temple. The men sprang from their seats and burst into cries of anger, mingled with jeers and scornful laughter. Obadiah forgot his dignity and raved imprecations at Jeremiah. Joel clapped his hands to his forehead and walked swiftly up and down the room on tiptoe like a dancer, laughing to himself with an excruciating expression on his features: "A poor madman! A dangerous fool since the day he was born!" They had all been touched in a tender spot, their cupidity, hence their wrath and outcries. The only one who did not join in the general gnashing of teeth was Hanameel, who stood to one side absorbed in his own thoughts. Among all his nephews and cousins Jeremiah did not find a single supporter, and his worst antagonists were the young ones, whose rage at their disreputable uncle knew no bounds. Gradually, however, the more moderate among the landowners began to exchange their empty wrath for more solid arguments, with which they replied to the demand of Adonai and Jeremiah. And as usual there were arguments in plenty why the commandments of the Lord should not be obeyed. If the old serfs were emancipated, for example, would it not be necessary to acquire new ones? How would that alter things? Since the beginning of the world there had been bondmen to cultivate the fields of their masters, and whom else had the Lord appointed to do such work? Were they not well treated? Were they deprived of anything they needed? Did they not receive as much bread and clothing as they required? Would a single one of them be so unthinking as to exchange bondage and a full stomach for liberty and starvation? And what would be the result if everyone throughout the land were to keep the year of jubilee, which in any case was not laid down in the original Law but only in the Book that had been rediscovered in the days of King Josiah? Disorder, confusion, and revolt—that was what would happen! The crops would fail and there would be a famine!

Jeremiah sadly faced the storm of anger and argument. It was a long time before the excitement died down and he could announce the decision to which he had come:

"My entreaties have not been received with a favourable ear. . . . My heart is heavy because my brothers refuse to stand on the side of the Lord. . . . I, however, must do so, even if I cause them pain. . . . Let me go in peace, though I fulfil the Lord's commandment on the fields and pastures of my inheritance. . . ."

Obadiah, who had come close to his brother and now stood facing him, was trembling in every limb. He pressed his left hand to his side, for any agitation always affected some internal malady from which he suffered and caused him intense pain. In guttural tones he muttered:

"And yet I spared . . . and protected . . . and tolerated you. . . ."

Suddenly he raised his fist and dealt Jeremiah a violent blow in the face. Jeremiah did not wince, but only put his clenched hands slowly behind his back.

After this odious incident the men quickly dispersed. Obadiah, attacked by agonizing convulsions in his intestines, went to bed cursing but remorseful. In spite of the imminence of the New Year, Joel had ordered his animals to be saddled for a short business journey to Ajalon. Jeremiah remained alone with Hanameel in the Hall of Abiathar.

"I am poor," said his cousin, "and have only one servant and his wife. But I will do with them as the Lord demands."

Before Jeremiah could reply, Hanameel implored him:

"My friend should not stay another hour in this house. Let him come and take shelter for the night with me, where he will be safe. . . ."

Jeremiah unhesitatingly declined the kindly offer, but Hanameel stayed for some time in the hope that he would change his mind. When Jeremiah left the hall, the women and children who had been listening outside drew back from him in horror. Only Mocheleth planted herself in front of him in all her bony length and stared at him murderously, as if it had not been her husband who struck Jeremiah but the other way about.

"You have made your brother ill," she panted, "and he is in great pain because of you! . . ."

She could not say any more, as her hate stuck in her throat. She made an effort to swallow and fell into an uncontrollable fit of coughing that shook her whole body, until at last she dashed sobbing from the presence of the diabolical wizard.

Later on, Jeremiah's mother drew him into her chamber and they entered into one of their taciturn conversations which concealed more than they revealed.

"I am afraid for you, my son," she said gravely and not without a certain sternness. He did not know why the same words came from his own lips:

"And I am afraid for you, Mother."

They sat down side by side on the couch, as they had always done. Abi could not repress a heavy sigh.

"Many men have been here. They have heard and seen, and their hearts are filled with wrath. My son had better seek another place of refuge, where the Lord will keep him safe."

"They are men of our own house, Mother," he said soothingly. "They will not betray Hilkiah's son."

Abi was not so sure that the cousins would be so generous, and she urged him further:

"Open your ear to my entreaty! Hanameel is still waiting. I beg you to go with him."

"Can I admit defeat and seek a place of hiding?" he

asked stubbornly. "No! I must stay and hold my own, fulfilling the commandment of the Lord on the fields which are mine."

At these words, which he uttered with compressed lips, Abi sighed even more deeply than before. Then she went to the cupboard and took out something that was carefully wrapped in a cloth. It was a full weight of solid gold. As she spoke she held it out to her son:

"On the evening before he died your father spoke thus to your mother: 'If one of the children or grandchildren of Hilkiah should suffer dire affliction through the will of Adonai, then give him this. Let him take it and go where he will be safe.' "

Jeremiah took the gold into his hands and murmured dreamily:

"Who knows whether the hour of dire affliction has yet come?"

That evening he appeared at table as if nothing had happened and sat down in his usual place. The others were all dumbfounded, and into the eyes of Mocheleth came a brief glitter which Jeremiah did not fail to notice. She announced sharply that the head of the family would not be present at the meal, since the insolence of a certain wicked creature had cast him upon a bed of sickness. Because of the absence of the two brothers and their eldest sons the table was much emptier than usual; Abi took advantage of the greater space available to move next to Jeremiah, as if she wanted to protect him and at the same time seek his protection for herself. When the meal began it was like a funeral feast. Not a word was spoken. The grown-ups and older children helped themselves to food from the common dish with their flat slabs of bread, chewed it slowly, and kept their eyes fixed in front of them in embarrassment. The stifling feeling of uneasiness was like a thick fog in the room and even the ever-burning lamp on the table flickered as if in torment. Its flame seemed to be blown this way and that under the influence of hostile breaths. No one moved except Mocheleth, who stood up from time to time and went to the door to give orders in a half-whisper to the serving-maids, who looked no less disconcerted than those sitting round the table.

Ever since anyone could remember, it had been the custom in the house of Hilkiah for wine to be brought to the table in silver cups after every meal. The tall, finely wrought goblet that had been in the family since the days of Eli belonged to the head of the house. The others, each differently fashioned, were not reserved for any particular person but might be used by anyone. According to custom the mistress of the house filled the cups as they stood before her from a large earthenware pitcher containing wine pressed on the hills of Anathoth. Then she offered the drink to each of those present with her own hand. Jeremiah noticed that one of the cups stood apart from the others, and that Mocheleth's eyes kept returning to it though it was already full. It must be for him, he thought, who also stood apart; the hatred of Mocheleth must be strangely deep when she would not hand the cup to him herself, but ordered a maid to set it in front of him. He fell into a reverie and was hardly conscious of the fact that his mother had changed her cup for his. When he raised his head, he saw that they were all waiting for the blessing before beginning to drink. As he was the oldest man present, he stood up and said:

"Blessed art thou, O Lord our God, who hast created the fruit of the vine!"

They all set their cups to their lips and drank, each in his own way, some greedily and others with deliberation. Mocheleth drank her wine at one draught as if she were a man. Abi, however, examined the colour and inhaled its fragrance before she smiled tranquilly and took three small sips. Jeremiah was very thirsty, but he paused with the cup still at his lips. He had suddenly realized what his mother had done. A dreadful suspicion seized his mind and he turned towards his mother with frozen eyes. She had just put down her cup and she nodded to him cheerfully. He looked at Mocheleth, who had risen from her seat convulsively and was staring with distended eyes at the cup which he still held in his hand. The others, too, were gazing at her with horror. Her chair fell to the ground behind her as she tore the head cloth from her dishevelled grey hair, that seemed to be standing on end, and she rushed from the Hall of Abiathar with a wailing moan that was scarcely human. Jeremiah and the others sat as if turned to stone. His mind was paralysed. Then Abi sank slowly sideways and fell with her head in his lap. He shook her, but she lay lifeless in his arms. Then he raised her frail body and carried her through the dark passage into the sleeping-chamber of his parents. He could hardly breathe; the few steps seemed endless. As he laid her down on the couch with stiff hands, he seemed to hear her whisper the words: "My son . . . my child . . ." He held the lamp, which she had so often set for him on the threshold of the house, close to his mother's face. The light had already gone from her eyes.

The first thing Jeremiah did was to bolt the door and barricade it with furniture. Then he threw himself at full length on the couch beside his dead mother and knew nothing more. Occasionally words flashed through his mind during the night without his thinking them. For his sake she had made the last sacrifice of all, she had herself experienced the final agony a few hours after she had repeated to him his father's words: "If one of the children . . . of Hilkiah . . . should suffer dire affliction . . ." The Lord had now taken from him his last possession. He who took pity on all servants had slain everyone who was the object of His own servant's love. Jeremiah did not think, did not weep, did not live, he only lay there. As from a great distance he heard voices throughout the night, hollow steps, and a dull, incessant knocking at the door. When the dawn came, the knocking changed to thunder and the door was battered in. Rough hands tore Jeremiah from his parent's couch and he saw armed men standing in the chamber where the sacred body of his dead mother was lying. More odious than the sight of his captors was the spectacle of Shamariah's grimacing features as he urged them on. Jeremiah was bound and made no attempt to resist. Reeling like a drunken man, he followed the soldiers of Jehoiakim.

22

The King of Babylon

THE escort sent to arrest Jeremiah consisted of three lightly armed soldiers of the royal bodyguard under the command of a corporal. By the time they reached the wall that surrounded the estate, they had been joined by Baruch, who kept a few paces behind as if he had no connexion with the prisoner. In their hurry the guards had presumably not received orders to seize the disciple too, for they paid no attention to him as he trotted along behind. Once, when Jeremiah turned round, Baruch raised the book which they had written to replace the burned copy and waved it in the air, as if to console him by this reminder of his sanctification. But Jeremiah seemed to recognize neither the book nor Baruch himself as he staggered along between his captors.

The highroad rose fairly steeply out of the valley towards the mountainous country around Jerusalem; in the fresh morning sunshine and clear autumnal air the ridges stood out sharply against the sky. For a long while it was possible to distinguish every bush and every wild dog that appeared on the horizon, but at such an early hour there were neither men nor horses to be seen. The world seemed as empty as Jeremiah's bowed soul.

Suddenly the leader stood still and snapped out a sharp command. The soldiers seized their prisoner and drew him off the road into a bare field, where they crouched down.

The corporal pointed in alarm to the nearest ridge, where a long file of horsemen was outlined against the light-blue sky as it approached at a steady pace. The peaked helmets of the Chaldeans were unmistakable. It was a portent of what was to come! A reconnaissance party from the main body of the Babylonian army had already reached the vicinity of the capital. Jeremiah's captors discussed the advisability of continuing on their way, or, on the other hand, whether it would not be more prudent to retire behind the walls of Anathoth with their important prisoner. Before they could make up their minds, Baruch came and sat down close to his master and pointed agitatedly to the still distant horsemen, in whose opportune appearance he saw an unexpected chance to escape. Jeremiah, however, did not hear his eager whispers and kept his eyes fixed on the blood-red clods of earth as he murmured to himself:

"The name has been fulfilled which my father and mother gave me before I came forth from out of the womb . . . Jirmejahu . . . God builds, God destroys. . . ."

"What is my master saying?" asked Baruch in surprise. But Jeremiah only gave a start and seemed to realize for the first time who was sitting at his side. Meanwhile the file of horsemen had disappeared behind the ridge and the corporal decided not to go back but cautiously to press on towards Jerusalem. He had received strict orders to bring his prisoner alive into the presence of the King.

Hardly had they reached the top of the hill, keeping to the sidepaths and avoiding the main road, when they suddenly found themselves face to face with a troop of soldiers sitting their horses like a wall in front of them. The Chaldeans seemed uncertain which way to go. One section was looking towards the south-east in the direction of Jerusalem the other towards the north, where in the distance, beyond the Plain of Jezreel, must lie the encampment of the mighty army to whose vanguard and skirmishers they belonged. These horsemen of Babylon were not lightly equipped as they usually were when acting as escort for large trading caravans, but were heavily armed. Their steel helmets flashed in the sun. The soldiers of the baggage-train, who could be recognized by the fact that they were in charge of led horses, wore round leather caps with cheek-pieces instead of helmets, but the sturdy bodies of all the troops without exception were clad in coats of mail and breeches of scale-armour, even their legs being protected by greaves. The two sections belonged to different branches of the army. Those turned towards the north were lancers with long convex shields and gleaming trappings to their horses, while those facing Jerusalem were archers with round shields and mounted on agile little horses whose reins and bridles were of light leather. Somewhat apart from the rest of the troops were three sunburnt men with neatly plaited beards, whose chargers were distinguished from the others by their scarlet saddle-cloths. They were the officers in command; the "senior captain," who was called (as everybody in Judah knew) a "Tartan," appeared to be giving orders for the day to his "Rhabsakim," or "junior captains."

The corporal raised his hand as a signal to his men to take cover, but at that very moment one of the Rhabsakim happened to turn his restless horse and caught sight of the little group with the prisoner in their midst. He at once made a sign to the Tartan and a rough command to halt stopped the men of Judah in their tracks as they were about to disappear. The Babylonian captains rode up to them at a slow trot, their heavily armoured bodies jogging and rattling, for they did not use stirrups and they rose and fell with every movement of their mounts. The Tartan pulled up and made his horse prance in front of Jeremiah.

"What are you doing with this man?"

"This man," stammered the corporal, touching the ground with his hands as a mark of respect, "this man is a corrupter, a criminal. . . ."

"What was his crime?"

"He has prophesied evil concerning the majesty of Jehoiakim, our King. . . . May my lord be pleased to have consideration for us and let us go in peace. . . ."

While the Tartan was making up his mind, Baruch suddenly sprang forward and waved the book up at him.

"May my lord," he almost shrieked, "be pleased to have consideration for the innocence of this guiltless man! . . . He has foretold the downfall of the King of Judah and the victory of the King of Babylon. . . . It is all written in this book, and that is why he is being persecuted. . . . For he has heard the voice of God prophesying the misfortune of Jehoiakim and the fortune of Babylon. . . ."

The hard little eyes of the Tartan wandered away from Baruch and fixed themselves on Jeremiah, who, as if he were walking in his sleep, seemed not yet to grasp what was happening. Then the Babylonian turned to his Rhabsakim and curtly enunciated one of the important military maxims of his country:

"The oracles of the stars and of the prophets must be closely scrutinized and compared with one another!"

With these words he took the roll from Baruch's hand and thrust it into an empty quiver which hung at his saddle. A brief order or two issued from his lips and Jeremiah's fetters were removed. Three archers took aim at the desperate corporal of Judah, who prayed and entreated that he should not be deprived of his prisoner, but an arrow hissed past his ear to show him that the Babylonians were not jesting, and the soldiers of Jehoiakim quickly made off. Jeremiah and Baruch were ordered to mount two of the led horses and the lancers closed round them. The heavy cavalry then rattled away towards the north, while the archers moved off in the opposite direction.

The Babylonian encampment had been pitched in a huge arc round the slopes of Mount Tabor. Among the hundred tapestried tents of the Tartans and the thousands of canvas ones for the common soldiers was a leaky shelter that hardly deserved the name of "tent," and this was allotted to Jeremiah and Baruch. They were given a blanket each, a few barley cakes, and a large earthen pitcher with fresh spring water, but Jeremiah, without waiting either to eat or to drink, fell at once into a deep sleep that lasted for twenty-four hours. It might have lasted for twenty-four days without his being disturbed, since nobody bothered about the newcomers and the camp was not struck.

For many days Jeremiah hardly spoke to his companion, confining his remarks to essentials, and even these he uttered as if lost in the remoteness of a mournful dream. His voice had entirely changed; it was low and hoarse as though his throat was sore. He left the food and water almost untouched; in his sleep at night he sobbed and tossed about as with dreams too cruel to bear. After the death of Josiah and Zenua he had disputed angrily and struggled with God, resigned his mission, and defiantly pursued the path of sin, descending even down to Amenti. After the death of his mother he did not dispute again with the Lord, who had shown Himself to be stronger than His prophet; but neither did he acquiesce and become reconciled. He only lay in a state of dull apathy. Baruch was deeply worried as he bent over him at night while he slept. "He has lost the only soul who loved and cared for him," he thought. It never occurred to the disciple to regard himself as worthy of Jeremiah's love in return for the loving care he bestowed upon his master.

At last the time came when Jeremiah seemed to have resolved to pull himself together, and one bright, moonlit evening they went for a walk along the paths between the tents. Everywhere were crackling camp fires, on which the men were cooking their meal. The long wait in the fertile land of Zebulon had cheered the warriors of Babylon, and to the accompaniment of clashing cymbals and the clapping of hands they sang their lively songs in celebration of the victory of the starry sky over the sun at Carchemish. They glanced curiously at the two men of Judah, but their looks were not hostile. No one tried to bar their path or question them. They were allowed to leave the confines of the encampment without hindrance; it seemed as if orders had been issued that Jeremiah was to be treated with respect.

The prophet and his disciple ascended the treeless slopes of Tabor, and when they were some way up they sat down on a bare projecting ledge where they could not see the smoking fires or hear the drunken clamour of the camp.

"We are not being held as prisoners," suggested Baruch, "so we can go where we wish."

Jeremiah shook his head:

"Where do you wish to go? Which way can Jeremiah turn?"

Baruch realized that Jeremiah would never leave without

the book, which was in the hands of the Babylonians.

The clear disk of an enormous moon rode over the mountain with its innumerable escort of stars, inviting the worshippers of Ashtaroth and the constellations to bow down and adore. In front of them stretched a landscape flecked and shrouded with an unearthly light. One range of hills succeeded another until the last merged into the misty distance. Mount Tabor rose between Issachar and Zebulon, but Jeremiah looked down towards Mannasseh, where the level fields of Megiddo extended from Carmel to the hills of Gilboa. Josiah's name was forgotten, for the Lord had not allowed His prophet to save him. Beyond the bloody plain, where the mountains rose again, lay Ephraim, the Amenti of Israel, a land of shades, with a few ghostly cities and many ruins. In the nebulous light of the horizon Jeremiah thought he could see the quarry of stones that had once been the palaces of Samaria and was now the home of vipers and scorpions. Farther off, beyond the steeps of Ephraim, smiled the broad hills of Benjamin in whose earth his mother was now buried. And beyond the hills of Benjamin was the Daughter of Zion, lost in pleasurable dreams and blind to the coming doom. For how long? The evil from the north was gathered round Mount Tabor, and the pots in which Babylon cooked its food were spilling over on the camp fires. As Baruch cast a sidelong glance at Jeremiah, he saw in his features a sadness that was not only his sorrow for the death of Abi. The disciple was alarmed and said:

"Let Jeremiah inquire of the Lord whether Judah may yet be saved from *this* evil and *this* end!"

But the prophet of doom, who in this hour had lost all hope and saw in his mind the smoke of the burning Temple rising beyond the hundred undulating hills, lifted his arms to the sky as though he were swearing an oath, and in a suffocated voice the cry was wrung from him:

"Thus saith the Lord which giveth the sun for a light by day, and the ordinances of the moon and of the stars for a light by night, which divideth the sea when the waves thereof roar, the Lord of hosts is his name. If those ordinances depart from before me, saith the Lord, then the seed of Israel also shall cease from being a nation before me for ever."

Jeremiah and Baruch had been in the camp for three months, when one morning two Babylonian dignitaries appeared and escorted them to a luxurious tent where henceforth they were to dwell. The dignitaries inquired with a respect that bordered on homage whether the men of Judah, whom they addressed as the "Guests of the Planets," had any further wishes. The incident showed that their fate must have taken some significant turn of which they knew nothing, for such courtesy would not have been offered to ordinary prisoners or unimportant strangers. From that moment Baruch continually urged his master to wait no longer in idleness, but to insist on an audience with the princes of Babylon, even with the King himself, who had recently taken up his quarters in the camp for the purpose of deciding the destiny of the nations of the world.

Jeremiah listened tranquilly to Baruch's entreaties, but it was not his habit to run with wringing of hands to meet the inevitable half-way. He bided his time, and that was what distinguished him from those of little faith and the petty-minded who craftily assumed that it was never too late, since even at the eleventh hour the Lord could be bribed by an importunate attempt at piety. His crushing experiences had taught him that one could not bargain with the will of the Lord, who did not tolerate any intervention on the part of man which was not pure and untainted by selfish aims. Therefore he remained passive and waited, though Baruch and the astute sons of Shaphan, who liked to prepare against eventualities, frequently disapproved of his attitude.

And, indeed, he was summoned into the presence of the King of Babylon without any overtures on his part. On the "Feast of Spring and the Manifestation of Marduk in the East" he was visited by seven star-councillors of Babylon. Their tall figures were radiant in close-fitting robes of dark purple which reached to the ground. Across their left shoulders hung coloured sashes with silver fringes, while their oiled and curled beards were decked with rubies and emeralds of astonishing size. It was not possible to see whether they also wore jewels in their long, wavy hair, for their heads were covered with tall cylindrical hats of some shiny blue material. At their embroidered girdles, where the Tartans wore their short swords, gleamed elegantly wrought spades of gold, Nebuchadnezzar's symbols for the turning up of the soil and the metamorphosis of the world. They bowed their heads before Jeremiah, and the senior among them announced in polished phrases to the soothsayer of Judah and his assistant that they were commanded to appear before the countenance of the Sacred Being who reproduced, ordained, and fulfilled in earthly reflection the destined cycles of the starry sky. Then thin sacks of linen were placed over their heads, in accordance with the custom of the court of Babylon, and they were gently guided out of their tent.

After walking for some distance, which in their blindness seemed long, the same gentle hands indicated that they were to halt and pressed them to their knees. The linen sacks were slowly lifted from their heads and they found themselves in a lofty, spacious pavilion in which little could be discerned at first, since it had no windows. Thin rays of sunshine trickled through a narrow opening and a number of small slits in the material of which the sides were made, but instead of dispersing the gloom they rendered it only more confusing. Gradually Jeremiah was able to make out twelve little altars that were set up against the circular wall of the great tent, with the smoke of incense curling up from them. The symbols above these altars showed that they were dedicated to the signs of the zodiac; for some reason he could not fathom, two of these—the ram and the archer—stood out in a stronger light than the others. In addition to the twelve smaller altars there were seven rather larger ones forming a second circle nearer the centre, from which rose smoky flames of different colours, one for each of the seven planets. The yellow flame was dedicated to the sun, the silver one to the moon, the red one to Nergal (Mars), the blackish one to Ninurtu (Saturn), the blue one to Nabu (Mercury), the green one to Ishtar (Venus), and the tawny or sandalwood-coloured flame to Marduk himself. Jeremiah was most surprised, however, by the incessant twittering, croaking, and cawing that filled the pavilion; when he looked up he saw a flock of birds both large and small flitting about under the lofty roof: ravens, starlings, popinjays, and grosbeaks that had been tamed and trained to talk. The feathered host broke the solemn silence below them with their shrill, human cries and it sounded like a chorus of spirits jeering at the gravity of mortal men.

The councillors of Babylon seemed not to notice the mocking clamour above their heads. If the altars of the zodiac and the planets constituted the outer orbits, they formed the inner one nearest the centre. They stood immobile, with lowered eyes and gently smiling, to symbolize the perfect contentment and equanimity of soul evoked by the presence of the Supreme Being. They kept their hands folded in a horizontal position to represent the fitting together of the two halves of the universe and its blissful union under the newly incarnated Marduk.

Marduk himself, so far as his garments and method of wearing his hair were concerned, was the least striking personage in the royal tent. But the planet of Jupiter, the architect of the world, was likewise inconspicuous in the starry sky. Nebuchadnezzar sat in the exact centre of his tent on a kind of folding chair, his short, sturdy figure clad in a tawny robe and a simple cap upon his head. In front of him were rolls of papyrus and heaps of tablets with writing on them. He would dig among the rolls, pick one out, read a line or two, cast it aside, and then choose another. His restless hands betrayed his impatience with the swift passage of time, which allowed so little to be perfected. "Why do kings, who are born for action," thought Jeremiah, "all have such restless hands?" From time to time Nebuchadnezzar raised his round face with its short beard and listened with an exhilarated expression, which still retained a certain boyishness, to the incessant twittering and croaking of the birds. His nose was rather snub, and as he listened he smiled with an arrogant and at the same time roguish enjoyment, even laughing loudly to himself, which was in strange contrast to the dignity of his jewel-decked councillors.

At Nebuchadnezzar's side stood two magnificent figures. The one on his right was Nergal Nebuzaradan, the chief marshal of Babylon, and he was clad in fiery red like the planet of war which he represented and whose functions he performed on earth. In his radiant handsomeness he looked almost a youth and nobody would have thought that the power of destruction and death appertaining to Nergal rested in his hands, but he seemed to be penetrated with a blissful consciousness of his military might, which had been conferred on him at an early age. No less handsome was the man on Nebuchadnezzar's left, though he could not be compared with Nebuzaradan, since he was no longer young. The age of Samgar Nebo, chief soothsayer of Babylon, had never been discovered. Old greybeards remembered him in their youth, but he still looked like a man of twenty with the eyes of a man of a hundred. His unlined but waxen face under the blue-dyed, curled hair seemed really to have been spun from the rays of the stars which he spent his life in studying. Samgar Nebo was like a tall plant that grew at night or in the shadow, sickly and indestructible. The holy secrets in which he was an adept raised him beyond all other men, beyond youth, age, and death. Not every epoch in Babylon saw the birth of a supreme soothsayer who united in himself both sexes, who was not sexless like a eunuch but man and woman in one. Ishtar and Nabu, Venus and Mercury, whose colours he wore, cancelled each other out in him. Unburdened with sexual instincts and fruitful interdependence as he was, with the two opposites completely harmonized in his own person, Samgar Nebo was free to roam among the forms of knowledge like no other mortal.

Jeremiah had to wait a long time before Nebuchadnezzar deigned to notice him, and even longer before he took the roll that Jeremiah had written from among the others that lay heaped up before him and held it out. When he spoke

—he used the language of Aram with which many people in Judah were familiar—he was curt and impatient, in contrast to the polished and conventional speech of the court. He looked at nobody but adddressed his words to all:

"The oracle of the stars . . . the oracle of this man . . . they agree."

A fleeting movement of his hand sealed the fate of Judah. Jeremiah, who was still on his knees, let his head drop upon his breast. A gesture from Nebuchadnezzar gave him permission to speak, and he too employed the language of Aram:

"May the majesty of the King lend a favourable ear to the words of his servant!" he began tranquilly, without being overwhelmed by the presence of Marduk and stammering, as most people did. "The Lord our God has granted you victory; He has made you His good servant that you may execute His will. Nothing will prevent you, not even the Lord, from destroying Jerusalem and burning the holy Temple. . . ."

The councillors blinked in amazement, though they did not raise their heads and their faces still wore an expression of gentle bliss. They had not expected to hear words like this addressed to Marduk. They had expected not this sad firmness of tone, but servile lamentation and whimpering entreaty. And, strange to say, the confused, mocking clamour of the birds had abruptly ceased as soon as Jeremiah began to speak. The airy spirits seemed to be listening intently to the further course of the conversation below, and there was no doubt that the King himself had been struck by the unusual silence of his birds, who did not as a rule stop chattering even for him. For some reason which he did not himself understand, he found himself referring in his reply to the inevitability of all that happened in the world:

"The actions of the King," he said, "proceed from the law of the stars."

"But the law of the stars proceeds from the actions of the Lord," said Jeremiah slowly, adding in a whisper: "He leaves you scope to do or not to do."

Nebuchadnezzar turned his head slightly towards Samgar Nebo and inquired just as softly, without looking at him:

"What does he mean by 'scope to do or not to do'?"

A shadow of pain flitted across the handsome features of the youth with the aged eyes. It was as if Samgar feared to destroy, by the effort of speaking, the splendid work of art that was represented by his blissful attitude and transfigured smile. With his lips hardly moving, he did not seem to be speaking himself, but to have deputed an indescribably pale voice, like that of a very old woman, to speak for him. To those who listened it sounded less like a direct statement than a monotonous report concerning a statement made by someone else. In general, explained Samgar Nebo, mortals had no scope to do or not to do and thus confuse the patterns of the stars of their own free will. But this freedom was possessed to some extent by the gods, who used it only with the greatest moderation since the visible, manifest part of their being was itself bound up with the stars in their courses. Only a god, therefore, possessed in extraordinary circumstances the power to weave a new causal chain into the illimitable fabric of the universe, thereby creatively influencing its ordered symmetry and ultimate destiny. The god-like nature of the King of Babylon contained a material and mortal admixture in its human elements, it was true, but its actual essence was a manifested form of the divine Being who rose as the royal star in the nocturnal sky. Let Marduk on earth therefore be graciously pleased to know that he alone, in all creation, had the right "to do or not to do" and thus weave a new chain of causes into the fabric of the world. "For," said Samgar Nebo, "one thing follows from another."

With this maxim he concluded his obsequious and informative statement, relapsing immediately into his previous state of smiling rigidity. Jeremiah, however, at whom Nebuchadnezzar was gazing steadily with his sparkling black eyes, took Samgar's last sentence as the text of his reply:

"One thing follows from another. . . . The Lord our God has given you His city and His Temple to plunder. No power can deprive you of the Lord's favour. But what follows from this? . . . The majesty of the King will conquer Judah as it has conquered greater nations, and then will come that which must inevitably follow. . . . Scattered and cast aside will be the house of the King who has been chosen to execute judgment on the holy land of the Lord!"

The air was filled with the menace of death for Jeremiah at that moment. The smiling faces of the councillors darkened, and one or two of them looked round for the guards. It was unprecedented to utter such an oracle in the presence of Marduk, and the fact that it coincided with the oracle of the stars, rendered the utterance ever more audacious. The King's hands had ceased to grope restlessly among the rolls of papyrus and hung loosely at his sides. The eyes in the arrogant, boyish face were fixed intently on Jeremiah as if he were amiably pondering on the most impressive way to put this insolent man of Judah to death. No one knew what would have happened if the fateful silence had not been broken by one of the starlings up above, which screeched out as if in warning:

"Melech Babilu! . . . Melech Babilu! . . . Melech Babilu!"

There was a second's pause, then the other birds joined in with a furious clamour:

"King of Babylon! . . ."

It was a confused warning, wailing, and mocking. Nebuchadnezzar stood up, and said in a voice that was quiet but high-pitched with suppressed resentment:

"He is a traitor—your King! . . . He has not kept faith with me. . . . He does not understand my will. . . . The Peace of Babylon! . . . None of them understands my will. . . ."

Jeremiah threw himself on his face.

"The King of Jerusalem is not Jerusalem!" he urged. "The house of David has other sons. . . ."

Again the birds were silent. Nebuchadnezzar looked down at the prophet and retorted sharply:

"A vicious dog has vicious whelps!"

The sinews in Jeremiah's throat grew taut. He knelt again, and his hands seemed to be clenched round invisible reins as if he were driving a chariot. A wild cry burst from him:

"Remember the king who barred Pharaoh's path for your advantage and fell in battle! . . . Josiah still has a son whom Egypt holds in captivity, his youngest son who should be on the throne of Judah. . . ."

Nebuchadnezzar was taken aback. He sat down and remained lost in thought. The birds under the roof, however, again burst into a bedlam of screeching, mocking cries.

23

The Burial of an Ass and the Keys of Heaven

AFTER journeying for many days Jeremiah and Baruch reached the little town of Michmash in Benjamin, which was at the junction of important crossroads. Though the King of Babylon had not again summoned the prophet to his presence, he had dismissed him graciously with gifts and excellent riding-horses. He had also given orders to return the book that Jeremiah had written. The two men of Judah knew that the army of Babylon would be following them within a few days, for they had everywhere seen the hurried preparations for departure as they left the camp by Mount Tabor. The inhabitants of the cities they passed through on their way were like men who had been awakened from pleasant dreams by the house burning over their heads, and had not yet been able to rub the sleep out of their eyes. The wealthy refused to believe it possible that their prosperity could so soon have turned to ruin without any visible cause, while the common people had grown bold and were assembling in crowds to raise an outcry against those who ruled the land. The object of their curses and wild imprecations was, above all, Jehoiakim. They again remembered the two levies of gold and silver, and the baseness which had degraded free men to serfs working to build palaces for the King. The power of a tyrant was strong when directed against the weak, but when a power arose that was stronger than his, then he collapsed with a squeak like an empty bladder! Jehoiakim had flaunted his strength in the face of Babylon as if he had the whole might of Pharaoh at his back. And where was Pharaoh now? Nothing had been foreseen and no precautions taken. Since for years nobody had dared to speak openly, the rumours became inflated like sails as soon as the winds of death began to blow. It was said that Elnathan, the great general of Judah, had refused to gather an army for his brother-in-law, and that Jehoiakim had sent one embassy after another to Noph to plead with Pharaoh for help, but without success. It was impossible, however, to distinguish truth from rumour amid all the wild reports that were passing from mouth to mouth.

Jeremiah and Baruch sat down in an open field before the gates of Michmash, to which they came when the sun had already passed its zenith. The prophet was meditating with wrinkled brow and Baruch firmly believed that he intended to return to Anathoth for the purpose of calling his brothers to account. The horsemen of Babylon were ranging the countryside and the main army was approaching from the north. Jeremiah's enemies were scattered and powerless. No Jerachmeel, no Pashur, no Meshullam would dare to raise his hand against the prophet whose words were now being so inexorably fulfilled. Jeremiah was safer and in a stronger position than he had ever been. He had only to league himself with his cousin Hanameel and a few men of good-will in Anathoth in order to wreak vengeance on Mocheleth and his brothers, and enforce the observance of the jubilee on the estate of his father.

Jeremiah's thoughts, however, were very different from

those of his disciple. He had no intention of returning to Anathoth under the protection of Babylon and revenging himself on the murderess Mocheleth, who had intended the poisoned wine for him and not for his mother. Neither was he thinking for the moment of the emancipation of the bondmen. Time was pressing; nobody could know who would be a slave and who would be free when the sun rose again. When the whole house was falling in, there was no longer any point in propping up a single wall. To a cautious question from Baruch he replied, with a shake of the head:

"I am not thinking of Anathoth. I am thinking of something much farther away."

"May the Lord assist your thoughts!" said Baruch, and he prepared to leave his master to himself for a time. But Jeremiah bade him stay and drew him closer to his side.

"It is hard for Jeremiah to take leave of Baruch, who knows the Lord and is full of faith."

Scarcely ever had the master opened his heart to his disciple. Baruch lowered his eyes and held his breath, as Jeremiah gravely laid his hand upon his knee and said:

"This is the work that has to be done . . . and it is a great task that is placed upon the shoulders of Baruch. Behold, there where the roads divide is where we shall take leave of one another. And Baruch will go down towards the land of Egypt to do my work. . . ."

The following was the task that Jeremiah set his disciple:

Baruch was to proceed first of all to Anathoth. There and in the neighbouring cities he was to choose a few reliable youths who were on the side of God to accompany him on his journey and give him the help he would need in carrying out his daring venture. The exiled House of David was living in Shefit, the city of crocodiles, and it demanded no little courage on the part of a stranger to penetrate beyond the closely guarded gates. Whatever happened, Baruch must not fail to find Hamutal and speak with her in complete secrecy, for the purpose of the task assigned to him was to effect the escape of Josiah's youngest son, Mattaniah, from the House of Bondage and bring him with all possible speed safely to Jerusalem.

Jeremiah reckoned in his mind how old Mattaniah must now be. His restless pupil had grown to manhood. He was twenty years of age, and Jeremiah did not need to tell Baruch that the last hope of Judah rested on Josiah's youngest son. At the mention of Mattaniah they had both seen how Marduk gave a start, sat down, and remained lost in thought. Though he had not said another word but dismissed the prophet with a slight gesture, perhaps the evil that was to come upon Jerusalem had again been postponed through the intervention of Jeremiah!

When he raised his eyes and looked at his master, the colour had ebbed a little from Baruch's cheeks, but he acquiesced in his difficult task without putting forward any objection to the plan or seeking a pretext to avoid having a share in it. He was oppressed less by fear than by the thought of leaving Jeremiah at a time when, if they separated, it might be for ever. They walked together as far as the crossroads and then mounted their horses. The road to Jerusalem lay straight ahead, while a narrow cart-track at the side led towards Anathoth. Before they parted, Jeremiah said:

"Take from Mattaniah the name of his boyhood and give

him a royal name. Let him henceforth be called Zedekiah, 'God is just,' for he shall sit upon the throne of David and judge the people!"

Jeremiah found himself wedged amidst a crowd of wailing peasants pouring in from the neighbouring countryside when he entered Jerusalem by the Gate of Ephraim. Only three or four of the gates were open, the others having been barricaded to prevent access and their towers and bulwarks occupied by men of the garrison. With pale, anxious faces the guards looked down from the battlements, for no pretence of cheerfulness or vigorous speeches on the part of their officers could hide the fact that the fate of Jerusalem was in the balance. The reconnoitring horsemen of Babylon had concluded their task and nipped in the bud any preparation for resistance in the cities of Judah. The actual vanguard of Marduk's army had reached the heights of Zion that very day and was taking up its positions in a wide semicircle round Jerusalem. The summer palace and the tomb of Jehoiakim, built on treachery, had already fallen into their hands. The magnificent painted rooms, full of the elegancies of Egypt and the aromas of Arabia, had been ransacked within an hour and were now picked clean like the bones of a horse that had fallen in the desert. The "summer hall of judgment" and the house that Jehoiakim had erected for the reception of his immortalized body rang with the stamping hoofs of the horses of the Tartans and Rhabsakim that were tethered to rusty iron rings fixed into the precious cedar panelling. The sandalwood floors were torn up by the grooms to provide an easy kindling for their fires of dried dung. No tears were shed by the inhabitants of Jerusalem for the destruction of Jehoiakim's glory, but their hearts stopped beating every time they thought how the Babylonian noose was tightening round their throats. Already the ox-teams that drew the siege batteries of Nebuchadnezzar were thundering down into the Valley of Kidron. The guards looked down grimly at the scene opposite the Temple, where, to the accompaniment of curses and amid the clang of hammers and axes, row upon row of gigantic catapults, battering-rams, and ladders was being set up. No order had yet come from the King to disturb the Babylonians at their work.

The crowd entering Jerusalem continued to force its way irresistibly up towards the Temple. All the streets and lanes of the upper and the lower city were packed to bursting with whole families of homeless fugitives, who slept with their backs resting against the walls of houses, ate their meals in the open, quarrelled among themselves, and filled the air with a desperate clamour. The population of Jerusalem had trebled in a few days and the elders of the city were tearing their hair and beards, since they had managed to collect no more wheat and cattle than would suffice for a single month. After that they would have to resort to the stores of food that had been accumulated in the fortified granaries of the Citadel of David for use in case of extreme emergency.

The stream of people that pressed through the ranks of the hollow-eyed, shelterless fugitives gave loud expression to their bitter feelings. What had happened to the promises of Jehoiakim, the braggart orator whose words lashed his hearers like a whip? The scraggy buffoon was going to make Judah great and populous among the nations, forsooth! The Lord was striking at him as if he were a gadfly whose buzzing annoyed Him, but if He crushed Jehoiakim He would with the same blow crush the whole nation. It was too late to save the people of the Lord. But the tyrants who ruled the country, the oppressors, the exploiters, and the fowlers had succeeded in saving themselves in time. Meshullam had fled to Noph with his venerable beard and the taxes he had squeezed out of the people, on which he would be able to live for the rest of his life as comfortably as the richest of Pharaoh's councillors. Elnathan had withdrawn into the desert with a handful of brave warriors to wait for a favourable moment, but how was that going to help? The moment had not come, nor was it likely to! And where was the King? Why did he not show himself to his people? Now that the day of reckoning had come, perhaps he was hiding behind his bodyguard in the House of Solomon, which hitherto had not been luxurious enough to satisfy his arrogance!

Again and again the same questions were to be heard as the crowd gave voice to its hatred and resentment, but Jeremiah also saw a number of older men who tore their clothes and wept like children for King Josiah, whom they now called "unique" and "holy." To his astonishment he frequently caught the name of Urijah, as well as his own. Yes, people were saying, Urijah and Jeremiah had prophesied the truth, but the boasting tyrants had prevented the pious and willing inhabitants of Jerusalem from giving ear to those who called them to penitence and foretold the coming doom. Jeremiah's surprise was even greater when he was pushed through one of the gates of the Temple and saw the outer courtyard. Not one of the lying prophets was missing from the pulpits, not even his shaggy denouncer, though at this hour of crisis they were prophesying anything but salvation.

The whole Temple was pitching and tossing like a ship in

a storm. All the twenty-four orders of priests were on board trying to avoid shipwreck. Day and night without cessation the sacrifices smoked upon the altar, while the sons of Asaph did not pause for a single hour as they stood between the two pillars, Boaz and Jachin, and sang psalms of penitence and remorse on behalf of the whole nation. At the approach of the Babylonian army the High Priest had ventured to do what was permissible only on the Day of Atonement: he had entered the Holy of Holies and, in the profound darkness that was before the creation of the world, he had pronounced the name of God.

The guards kept a strict watch over the entrances to the inner court of the priests, allowing no one to enter of whose purity and worthiness there was the slightest doubt. The crowd remained dammed up in the outer courtyard, giving way to pressure now and then and moving as a whole to one side or the other. As they stood wedged together in this perilous way, so that they could hardly breathe, the loud voices of the prophets wailed and screamed over their heads from every pulpit. There was no trace of pity in the exhortations and harsh words of condemnation with which they overwhelmed their hearers. Those who in happier days had flattered the Daughter of Zion and predicted a glorious future could not find words of reproach and castigation bitter enough now that the opposite had happened. The persecutors and haters of Jeremiah went even so far as to steal the sayings of the Lord that had come to him and repeated them almost unwittingly as their own prophecies. Jeremiah, however, knew that these men were worse than cunning deceivers. He knew that they were reeds in the wind. Therefore his heart rejoiced that Hananiah was not among them. From all sides his own denunciations struck his ears:

"Why has the Lord brought all this evil upon us? you ask. . . . Because your fathers have forsaken me, saith the Lord. . . . But you have done worse than your fathers. . . . Because you walked in the pride of your own hearts, you did not hearken . . . I will scatter you among the heathen, whom neither you nor your fathers have known. . . . And you shall serve strange masters, by day and by night, and I shall give you no rest. . . ."

These were the bitter prophecies that the pitiless creatures thundered down upon the wall of helpless people. Jeremiah's soul revolted. It was true that these men did not know what he knew, but what cruelty must dwell within them if they could revel in prophecies of destruction at the very hour when it stood, visible to all, before the gates of Jerusalem and nothing could avert it but the Lord's secret resolve, in which Jeremiah believed with an intuitive faith that he nursed like a tender flame in the wind! He was sorry for the men and women roundabout him, with their faces pale as death, who sighed heavily and now and then broke out into hollow cries of despair. But as the hammering and thundering of the newly converted preachers seemed to be endless, Jeremiah was carried away by wrath and compassion, and he determined to put an end to it. Drawing a deep breath, and clearing a little space round him with his elbows, he infused into his voice all the power of which it was capable. The words, however, that issued from his lips were the words of Isaiah:

"Comfort ye, comfort ye my people! . . ."

The effect of his voice, even though he spoke only a few words, was as profound as it had always been. Hundreds of heads were at once turned towards the man who could speak like that and who had found the only exhortation that befitted the hour. Of these hundreds, at first only six or seven recognized the prophet whose prediction had come true. The cry of "Jeremiah!" which was raised here and there in the crowd gradually grew stronger and stronger and at last developed into a storm. Jeremiah had never imagined that the syllables of his name—"God builds when He destroys"—would ever be wrung from innumerable hearts in a cry of such fervent hope and faith. The man who had been derided, persecuted, and maltreated stood now as a firm pillar to which the people of Jerusalem were clinging. His short hour of love and fame had dawned, but it filled him with anxiety only. Meanwhile the people had lifted him onto their shoulders that he might answer the scolding of the preachers with words of truth. As he swayed over the heads of the thousands assembled in the outer court who were looking up at him expectantly like thirsty children, a change came over him and the Lord breathed into his soul. Jeremiah comforted his people:

"Thus saith the Lord: Again I will build thee, and thou shalt be built, O virgin of Israel, thou shalt again be adorned with thy tabrets, and shalt go forth in the dances of them that make merry. Thou shalt yet plant vines upon the mountains of Samaria, the planters shall plant, and shall eat. . . . Sing with gladness for Jacob, and shout among the chief of the nations: publish ye, praise ye, and say: O Lord, save thy people. . . ."

A surge of joy answered him. His words, spoken slowly and as in a dream, were like a spring of fresh water in the desert. The man who had harshly proclaimed the doom of Judah in the midst of prosperity and good harvests now announced salvation and the eternal establishment of Zion at a time when destruction was waiting at the gates. Was this an unexpected change of heart on the part of Adonai? Since the old prophecy had been fulfilled, might they not hope for the fulfilment of the new one? Jerusalem was still standing and the Temple was not destroyed. The Lord of hosts was hesitating before plunging His holy land into ruin. Perhaps the evil would once more be averted. They must now do precipitately everything that the commandments ordered. As the crowd eddied wildly, thousands of voices called up to Jeremiah in a confused clamour that drowned what they were trying to say. One man, however, at the far end of the court, launched a cry among the people that radiated like a star and finally merged into a general shout: "To the King, to the King!"

The hour of reckoning had come. The King who had betrayed his father and murdered Urijah, who had persecuted Jeremiah and the truth, the tyrannical ruler and introducer of abominations, now had to answer to his people and cast his own life into the scales to save Zion. No longer would his laboratories furnish him with protection against the wrath of Jerusalem. Before Jeremiah could grasp what was in the minds of the shouting throng, the whole mass had begun to move slowly like ice breaking up in a frozen river. He was still being carried on the shoulders of the enthusiasts who had lifted him up, and from this elevation he could see clearly everything that happened.

The mob at once stormed the double walls which separated the Temple from the palace. The gates creaked heavily as the wildest and strongest of the men hurled their weight against them. Up above, on the battlemented pathways that ran along the top of the walls, the sentries and jailers were hastily assembling, but there were only a few of them, since nearly all the armed men had been withdrawn to garrison the city defences. A lively dispute began between the sentries and the crowd at the same time as the blows of axes and clubs thundered against the doors. But the little group of guards made a fatal mistake. Instead of gaining time by negotiation and sending for reinforcements, they lost their heads, allowed themselves to be carried away by fear and rage, and hurled their spears into the crowd, killing a woman and wounding several men. This monstrous act was followed by a piercing yell of rage from thousands of throats. The mob again hurled itself in frenzy against the walls, as if to tear them from their foundations by sheer weight. Suddenly tall ladders that reached up to the battlements appeared on the scene. Men stormed up the rungs, only to be hurled down again, but they were followed by others. A few minutes sufficed to overcome the defenders; then there was a creaking of hinges and planks as the mighty gates were slowly opened from within. The streaming multitude split into three sections as it flooded into the royal palace through the right and left gateways and the hall of the joint tribunal, Jeremiah still swaying above their heads as he was borne along.

The court of the guard which surrounded the living quarters of the royal family was very spacious, yet it could not hold all the people who tried to swarm in. Before the portal of the House of Solomon were a few members of the bodyguard, together with servants and eunuchs of Jehoiakim, and these tried to bar the way. The enraged mob would have given short shrift to these pale, only partly armed men, if Jeremiah had not managed to press forward as far as the entrance. He calmed the people with his words, begging them not to commit fresh violence and suggesting that they should choose twelve worthy and judicious men from among them in order that they might speak to the King in the name of Jerusalem. And they did so. Twelve honest citizens came forward and stepped with awkward dignity to Jeremiah's side. The latter, however, kept looking round restlessly in the hope that one of the sons of Shaphan, whom he had originally come to the Temple to see, might have been attracted to the scene by the uproar. Neither Ahikam nor his twin sons, nor any other member of the gifted family, was anywhere in sight. During the days when the streets were overrun by the common people, every man of culture or rank seemed to have disappeared from Jerusalem.

Jehoiakim's servants breathed again when the crowd drew back a little to make room at the foot of the steps for Jeremiah and the twelve deputies. The chief eunuch and two other chamberlains undertook to lead them into the presence of the King; when they had passed through the portal a deserted and melancholy aspect presented itself to the eyes of Jeremiah, who was walking through the corridors of the ancient palace for the first time since the far-away days of Josiah. In the rooms where Josiah and Hamutal had lived, he thought he could still detect the faint fragrance exhaled for so many years by the Queen's flowers.

They hastened through the whole palace, but found it empty. There was no trace of the King. Had he left the palace? Nobody knew. He had been there only a few hours ago. And the Queen? The chamberlains exchanged furtive glances. The Queen had gone on a journey, but they did not know where. Where was Coniah, the King's son? The gracious Prince Coniah was always at his father's side. Jeremiah did not give up, but continued with his interrogation. Where did the King spend most of his time? The chamberlains refused to say and gave evasive answers. Someone mentioned the King's laboratories. Were there such chambers only in the new palaces, or were there some in this one too? The chief eunuch lowered his eyes and was silent. So there *was* one of these laboratories in the House of Solomon? Where was it situated? The chamberlains turned away. Jeremiah promised that no harm would come to the King if they revealed its whereabouts, that on the contrary it would enable them to protect him. The chief eunuch fixed his eyes on the prophet's frank face, then he sighed and whispered one word: "Below!"

By secret passages they reached the vaults, which were cut out of the rock of Mount Moriah. Here, amid the foundations of the Temple and the palace, they walked a few steps in clammy darkness until they reached a low door that looked like the entrance to a tunnel. The chief chamberlain knocked obsequiously, but there was no answer. He continued to knock with growing agitation. There was still no response. He shook the door and found it closed. Then he called out in a coaxing voice:

"Will not the King deign to listen to me! . . . My dear, dear Master . . ."

As there was still no sound from within, he repeated the words in a tone of increasing despair, until at last he was screaming with fear and horror in a voice that echoed from the vaulted roof. The twelve men whispered briefly together and decided to break in the door. Two of them flung themselves against it with all their strength, while the others pushed with hands and knees. The mouldering wood creaked, but did not yield, and they finally had to use an axe to smash it in.

A couple of torches fixed to the wall illumined the room in front of them with a flickering light. It looked like one of the great tombs in the western city at Noph that had been burst open by robbers. Jeremiah reeled and felt as if he were about to swoon as a sweet and heavy, unspeakably fulsome odour streamed through the doorway and struck him in the face like the blow of a fist. They all had to protect their noses and mouths with their cloaks or they would have been overpowered by the narcotic fumes, which were rising not only from the smoking censers gleaming in the corners but even more from the essences that had been poured on the floor and formed little pools everywhere. Innumerable fragments of broken glass showed that some crazy hand had smashed the jars and phials in which the variously blended perfumes had been contained. Stretched out on the floor amidst this confusion were the bodies of two men: Jehoiakim and Coniah. The body of the father was already rigid; the son was still alive though his heart beat but faintly. Coniah was quickly carried up into the palace and gradually the colour came back into his cheeks, although he did not regain consciousness. The King, however, could not be brought back to life. With the sensuous love of beauty that was characteristic of the sons of David, he had chosen to die in the voluptuous embrace of his myriad perfumes.

The twelve men carried the corpse of Jehoiakim past the sorrow-stricken chamberlains and showed it to the people, who suddenly grew dumb at sight of a judgment so swiftly executed. The King who had delighted in power and pomp was sewn into a sack. While the horses of Babylon were eating out of their mangers in his gaudily painted tomb, he was dragged like a dead ass through the Gate of Potsherds to the parched verge of the Field of Blood in order that the prophecy concerning him should be fulfilled to the letter. With wild gestures the people drew the attention of Marduk's sentries to what they were doing. Perhaps the

King of Babylon would be reconciled by the death of the traitor whom he had set out to punish. Before they left the dead Jehoiakim lying on the ground, someone painted the following strange words on the sack: "This and even more."

The news came only vaguely to the ears of Jeremiah as he sat sunk in thought at the bedside of Coniah and waited for consciousness to return to the youth who had been so near to death. Coniah was now seventeen years old, but his delicate body was like that of a younger boy. The last time Jeremiah had seen him, he had been unconscious as he was now and it had been his hand that brought the child back to life. Coniah's narrow chest rose and fell as he breathed heavily, and his slender limbs, which were not yet fully developed, twitched convulsively. Through the pallor of his face shone the radiance of the heavenly hosts which Jeremiah had observed at their last meeting, and he could not turn his eyes away from such heart-rending beauty.

Meanwhile Ahikam and his two sons, together with a number of dignitaries who had not yet left their posts, appeared at the couch of the heir to the throne. They held council in a low tone and came to an important decision. In the existing circumstances it was impossible for the throne of David to remain unoccupied for even an hour, leaving the country and capital without a lawful king. The heads of the priesthood, together with all the princes and elders who were still in Jerusalem, were therefore summoned to assemble without delay in the throne-room of Solomon.

Jeremiah remained behind with the physicians and attendants at the sick lad's side. He had promised to bring the prince to the anointing ceremony as soon as his strength had returned. The physicians sprinkled Coniah's chest with lye, sprayed his face with pungent essences, and held vinegar to his nostrils, but none of these stimulants seemed of any avail. Time passed and Jeremiah knelt down by the couch, gently calling the unconscious boy by his name:

"Coniah! . . . The Lord and your people are calling you! . . . Coniah! . . ."

At last a reluctant twitching of his features showed that Coniah had heard the implacable voice calling him from a distance. He drew a deep breath, stretched his limbs, and sat up with a sudden jerk. His eyes, which were wide open but still seemed clouded over, sought the owner of the voice that had called him back from the depths of unconsciousness to the unwelcome world of reality. When he saw Jeremiah's face close to his own the recollection of his terrible experience at their last meeting came back to him in full force. There seemed to have been no interval at all since the time when he sat at Jehoiakim's feet and heard the whispered prophecy of his father's end. He did not know from which swoon he had just awakened, whether it was the one into which he had fallen at that moment or whether it was a subsequent one. Covering his eyes with both hands he uttered a strangled cry of fear. In a tone of profound sorrow Jeremiah repeated:

"Coniah! . . . The Lord and your people are calling you! . . . Coniah! . . ."

Coniah murmured with trembling lips:

"Not the Lord and my people . . . it is you who are calling me. . . . You are the messenger of death. . . ."

"It is Jeremiah who is calling you back to life. It was not he who persecuted your father, but your father who persecuted him. . . . Yet I will not leave you, Coniah, until I have brought you to your place. . . ."

The chamberlains hurriedly brought the royal robes, the

snow-white coat of double byssus tissue and the sky-blue cloak in which the sons of David were crowned. The Sagan had already entered the throne-room with holy oil to anoint the head of the new King. Coniah stood up and allowed them to garb his slender body in the exalted garments that were much too wide for him. With an heroic effort he repressed the feverish shiver that shook his frail form and stood stiffly in a haughty attitude that could not hide his feeling of helplessness.

The supplies of food in Jerusalem had come to an end, and Nebuchadnezzar had not yet flung a single stone from one of his gigantic catapults or hurled a single blazing torch into the city. Friend and foe were alike amazed at the strange hesitancy which was in such extreme contradiction to the usually resolute nature of Marduk. They wondered what secret reason he might have for this prolonged postponement of the work of destruction, since nearly three months had passed since the beginning of the passive siege.

Angry mobs, infuriated by hardship and the failure of their tyrannous rulers, were still raging through the streets of Jerusalem. Looting and murder stepped hard upon the heels of hunger like the sower behind the plough. The complete collapse of order was leading to the inevitable end. Then early one morning a frenzied clamour broke out in the great circle of the Chaldean camp and continued without interruption to beat like a hurricane against the walls of the city. The blare of rams' horns, horns of bulls, and brazen trumpets was mingled with the noise of cymbals, kettle-drums, rattles, and chains, and this din was augmented by the thunderous war-cries that went up from tens of thousands of Babylonian throats. Nebuchadnezzar's warriors were shouting the ineffable name of Adonai, threatening the Eternal One with annihilation. So terrible was the effect of this storm of blasphemous voices, that the people of Jerusalem, who were running wildly about the streets, were thrown to the ground. They covered their heads and pressed their burning foreheads against the walls of the houses. The awe-inspiring uproar outside was made even more intolerable by the screaming of thousands of children within the walls, and there was fulfilled in every soul in Jerusalem the prophetic words which Jeremiah had written in his book: "My bowels, my bowels, I am pained at my very heart, my heart maketh a noise in me, I cannot hold my peace, because thou hast heard, O my soul, the sound of the Trumpet, the alarm of war. . . ."

After about an hour the frenzied clamour subsided as suddenly as it had arisen. Before every gate in Jerusalem appeared Marduk's heralds, clad in shimmering silver, who announced that the respite granted to the city would expire at the new moon. In the throne-room of Solomon the council sat night and day with the boy-king Coniah, helplessly discussing the situation. Ahikam, whom sorrow and exhaustion had aged until he looked almost as old and frail as his father had looked, had been arguing for days in the endeavour to persuade the council to accept his advice. It was both senseless and blasphemous, he said, to think for even a moment that the city could be successfully defended. Though the warriors and bulwarks of Jerusalem were strong enough to hold out for an indefinite length of time against the superior forces of the King of Babylon, they would still have to reckon with a populace that was herded together in inadequate quarters and was frantic with disappointment. The people were not capable of enduring even another three weeks of such hardship. Nothing could avert the fall of

Jerusalem; it could be alleviated only if they were prepared to humble themselves completely. There was but one purpose left for which they must strive: by the ruthless sacrifice of their own pride they must save the Temple from destruction and maintain the worship of the Lord. No thought of national disgrace must deter them. The preservation of the Law was everything; the preservation of their pride was nothing.

After long opposition the minds of the majority accepted the wise arguments of Ahikam and his sons. When the decision to surrender the city had already been reached, however, some of the high officials of the former regime, who had hitherto remained in hiding, suddenly appeared before the council. Their spokesman was Pashur, the First Keeper of the Door. He stood in front of the assembly like a gaunt rock, his little eyes gleaming in scorn, and hurled unbridled abuse at Jeremiah and Ahikam. Adonai, he shrieked, would blot Himself out from the minds of men, would annihilate Himself, if He delivered His city up to the pitiless enemy! Only godless heretics, only deceivers and those who had escaped from their judges as did the blasphemer of Anathoth, could suggest that the Lord was capable of such a heinous paradox. The only true injunction of the Lord of hosts was that they should defend the Temple and the city to their last drop of blood. These were the passionate arguments put forward by Pashur, Jerachmeel, and the handful of men who accompanied them. A gleam of relief in the eyes of the young King showed that his heart was with the friends of his father, but in this perilous hour Gedaliah acted with unhesitating resolution. As if he were speaking in the name of the King, he ordered the palace guards to seize the bold intruders and cast them into the dungeons in the house of the Chancellor. Coniah's face became even more transparent than before. His lips trembled, yet he said nothing and permitted the once powerful administrators of Jehoiakim's reign to be arrested, buffeted, and finally dragged away scratched and bruised.

Jeremiah stood silently beside the King, but Coniah refrained from honouring with a single glance the hated prophet who had twice awakened him from a swoon. Though he had received nothing but kindness from Jeremiah, he always felt a sinking of the heart in his presence. Distrustful and abstracted, the beautiful boy-king looked down on the noisy scene as he sat helpless, a victim decked for sacrifice, on the golden throne of his fathers.

A day of bright sunshine, which seemed to be holding its breath as it waited for the final decision, was followed by a night of deep darkness. The thin crescent of the waning moon rose late in the sky. The young King, with Jeremiah at his side and accompanied by a few of his most intimate attendants, had climbed to the roof of the palace. From the Temple were wafted the imploring psalms of the sons of Asaph, and over the inner court hung a pall of redly gleaming smoke which ascended from the continual burnt sacrifices but was prevented by a hostile wind from rising to the Lord.

When the trumpets of the priests, sounding more muffled than usual, announced the beginning of the second night-watch, a sad procession could be seen approaching from the Temple by the fitful light of torches. With the High Priest at their head, an aged man whose frail form was supported by his Sagan, the princes and generals of Judah were coming into the presence of their King. Their heads were all bowed low and enveloped in their cloaks. In their midst walked a tall man carrying a massive bowl that was covered with a white cloth and resembled one of the sacrificial vessels in which the chosen portions of the food offerings were carried to the altar.

Silently the procession mounted to the roof of the palace. Silently the covered bowl of sacrifice was raised up before the face of the King. Silently the High Priest withdrew the cloth. Coniah saw in the reddish light the great keys of the Temple and the city, the humiliating offering that he would have to bring to the King of Babylon on the morrow with his own hands. The flickering light played over the keys with dancing patterns and Coniah closed his eyes tightly as he turned his face away. He had understood the silent request of the High Priest and the princes, and a shudder ran through his slender body. He swayed, but Jeremiah held him firmly. The King's lips moved.

"Was it for this that you awakened me and called me back? . . ."

There was a tense pause that seemed endless, nobody daring to move or breathe aloud. Only the bowl of sacrifice trembled in the hands of its bearer. Coniah wept soundlessly until the misty crescent of the moon had vanished from the sky and the light of the crackling torches began to die away. Suddenly he pulled himself together, took the bowl into his own hands, and set it on the parapet of the roof. Below the place where he stood was a little garden court, over which two sycamores spread their branches. His eyes wandered from the darkness of the garden below to the darkness of the heavens above. Like a dreaming child he took one of the great keys in his fingers and played with it, turning it this way and that with an air of abstraction. Jeremiah saw by the smoky gleam of the almost extinguished torches that there was a pathetic look of cunning in his eyes. Raising his face to the sky, Coniah pleaded with the Lord in a penetrating whisper:

"What guilt hast Thou found in me? . . . Why has the lot fallen on *me?* . . . Why dost *Thou* not do it? . . . Why not *Thou?* . . ."

With parted lips he waited for an answer. Then he swung his right arm and hurled the key with all his strength up into the sky. Silently it disappeared in the darkness, for at that moment a breeze rose and shook the rustling branches of the trees. The men on the roof did not stir, but no sound of metal striking the ground came to their ears. As if hypnotized they kept their eyes fixed on the King, who seemed to be playing a childish game with God and at the same time having mysterious communion with Him. One key after another vanished into the air and each was accompanied by the same plea:

"Why must I do it? . . . Why not Thou? . . . Why not Thou? . . ."

When the last key had been hurled into the heavens, Coniah sank to his knees before the parapet and pressed his cheek to the cold stone. His audacious game with the Lord had sapped all his strength. The keys had been swallowed up noiselessly in the rustling wind. The men looked at each other. Who could tell, perhaps the Lord, whose dwelling place was on high, had received into His hands the keys of His city and sanctuary?

Though there was no solemn ceremony of handing over the keys, the Babylonians found the gates of Jerusalem wide open on the following morning. Shortly after sunrise the first vanguards moved towards the city from three directions amidst the blare of trumpets and the rolling of drums. For the first time since the days of Sennacherib the foot of an enemy trod the holy Citadel of Zion. In two or three places there was a short but bloody encounter, since the soldiers occupying the bulwarks, chiefly members of the royal body-guard, were overwhelmed with rage and grief and refused here and there to lay down their arms. These dying convulsions of the beleaguered city could not affect its fate. Before three hours had passed, the banners of Babylon were flying over all the towers and fortifications of Jerusalem. The victorious army, however, belied the evil reputation which had preceded it. In orderly array the conical-helmeted hosts marched through the streets. A strict order must have been issued that no man was to leave the ranks, and not a single company fell out of the line of march to loot and slay as was the conqueror's right. The incredible happened. No blood was shed and no woman ravished. The people could venture without fear to leave their barred houses.

Marduk-Nebuchadnezzar entered Jerusalem towards noon, his jewelled litter swaying along in the midst of his retinue of conquered kings, royal princes, generals, councillors, and standard-bearers. The procession of the starry sky on earth mirrored accurately the cycles of the stars in the heavens above. They all smiled in blissful harmony and held their hands folded horizontally one upon the other. To right and left of the litter walked Nergal Nebuzaradan, chief marshal of Babylon, in his fiery red robe, and Samgar Nebo, the soothsayer, in deep blue. Nebuchadnezzar himself was not even now in the garb of a warrior, but was again clad in the sandalwood-coloured robe that Jeremiah had already seen, only instead of the leather cap that he had worn in his tent, he now wore a narrow, plain circlet of gold on his head. His slightly wind-tossed hair was far less curled and oiled than the elaborately dressed hair of his courtiers. His round face, with the snub nose so uncharacteristic of his people, showed a lively curiosity as he looked round at the subdued city.

Marduk's way led first to the Temple. In the outer courtyard were assembled the lower orders of priests, more than a thousand men, all clad in white as on the Day of Atonement. When the litter came in sight they cast themselves to the ground in silent entreaty and lay motionless, like freshly fallen snow. The King of Babylon alighted. Perhaps he wished to show by this action that he was prepared to respect the god of a strange race whose prediction had agreed with the oracles of the stars as interpreted by his soothsayers. But he ignored the priests and passed indifferently through the recumbent ranks in his gilded sandals, which were raised at the heels like buskins. Slowly he crossed the gallery with his retinue and approached the inner court, which no worshipper of the stars or other false gods was allowed to enter, under pain of death. The priests of the higher orders, who were ranged round the cold altar of burnt offerings, the Molten Sea, and the twelve portable lavers, and also on the steps of the porch below the pillars Boaz and Jachin, shuddered with awe at this violation of the holy Temple. Many of them covered their eyes with their cloaks so that they should not witness such desecration.

Jeremiah, who was standing between the altar and the porch, did not veil his eyes. He gazed steadily at Marduk and his councillors. The frail High Priest tottered towards the King of Babylon in his hampering robes and raised his hands with the palms turned upwards in pleading, as he moaned some unintelligible words with averted head. It was an ambiguous gesture which might have been taken either for a reluctant blessing or a despairing protest. But Nebuchadnezzar disregarded the whiteheaded old man. His eyes scrutinized the inner court with the keen glance of an experienced architect, and then he slowly walked round the altar of burnt offerings and inspected its impressive proportions with a calculating wrinkle of the brow. Everyone knew that Nebuchadnezzar was not only a mighty builder of cities, but also a connoisseur and collector of ancient works of art. In the temple-city of E-sagila, in Babylon, he had erected a special palace to house his collection of sculptures and writings from Ur, Akkad, and Asshur. With the screwed-up eyes of an expert he examined the Molten Sea and stroked the flanks of the great brazen oxen with the short fingers of his sinewy hands. The old High Priest, breathing with agonizing difficulty, kept close at his heels as if his presence might prevent the most infamous desecration of all. When the thoughtful King turned his calculating glance towards the porch and the two strange pillars with their exuberant ornamentation of pomegranates and lilies, something unexpected happened. The fragile form of the High Priest was suddenly endued with youthful vigour and agility. Leaping swiftly up the ten steps that led to the porch, so that the little silver bells and golden pomegranates on the hem of his robe began to ring, he flung himself across the threshold of the sanctuary to prevent with his own body the entrance of the unclean star-worshipper. Nebuchadnezzar did not allow himself to be disturbed in the slightest by the sight of the venerable old man lying stretched out in his priestly garments, but merely gathered his robe round him and stepped over the High Priest of Israel. A wailing cry rose from all the hundreds of priests as they saw this outrage.

Nebuchadnezzar had motioned to his retinue, even to

Nergal Nebuzaradan and Samgar Nebo, not to follow him. This again could be interpreted as a mark of respect and a concession to the holiness of the place. Very calmly he disappeared into the dusk of Adonai's dwelling place on earth. But he did not remain hidden from their sight for long. When he emerged again, he was smiling thoughtfully. Halfway down the ten steps, which had meanwhile been vacated by the priests, he paused and called out to the patiently waiting Samgar Nebo a single word: "Nothing!" Then he slowly continued on his way towards the altar, this time carefully inspecting the faces of the priests. Suddenly he stood still. With the infallible memory of great rulers he had at once recognized Jeremiah, who was standing apart from the others. He gazed at him for a long while with a distant look in his eyes that had in it something of the remoteness and friendly indifference of the stars. Then he called out to him too, very softly, the word "Nothing!" as if he were slightly amused and tolerantly making fun of the soothsayer of Judah, tacitly inviting him: "Now try to interpret *my* oracle!" Jeremiah understood and interpreted it at once in his own mind. Marduk had found "nothing" in the almost empty sanctuary that could shake his conviction. This "nothing," the agreeable allaying of a secret fear, had put the King of Babylon in such a cheerful and benevolent frame of mind that he would do "nothing" detrimental to the God of this temple who had been presumptuous enough to occupy his thoughts more than was fitting. The disparaging word was, so to speak, a diffident token of his favour, guaranteeing that the Holy of Holies would remain unviolated.

Nebuchadnezzar did not accord the same favour to the Temple treasure stored in the ninety-nine chambers of each of the two wings. The accountants and treasurers of Babylon were immediately summoned, and they set to work to prepare on great piles of writing-tablets an exact inventory of all the valuables: the golden vessels and weights of gold, the jewels and the fine stuffs. For this work they needed more than a whole week. Then there appeared within the precincts of the holy Temple an army of porters, who packed the treasure of centuries in sacks and bales under strict supervision and carried it away. The priests were broken by this blow and crept about like shadows. But the heart of Jeremiah was glad. The judgment of Zebaoth had been infinitely lenient. The Temple was still standing and the worship of the Lord suffered no interruption. What did it matter that the treasure chambers had been plundered? Perhaps this very misfortune was a blessing in disguise!

Jeremiah's relief and gratitude, however, were clouded by far more oppressive measures on the part of Marduk than the ransacking of the Temple. Judah was compelled to pay heavy tribute in men. All the princes, priests, high officials, and citizens who were suspected, justly or unjustly, of having favoured the regime of Jehoiakim were seized and gathered into special camps. Together with the bravest warriors on whom it was possible to lay hands and the most capable craftsmen of Jerusalem, they constituted a considerable host of more than ten thousand. Among these ten thousand—and this was the bitterest drop in Judah's cup of sorrow—were many of the oldest and most venerated families in the land. They were condemned to be expatriated and carried away to Babylon. Kinship with the House of David was of as little avail to Jerachmeel as high priestly rank was to Pashur. Jeremiah's persecutors were all overtaken by the fate they had deserved, but on Ahikam and his sons Nebuchadnezzar conferred many favours and they were frequently admitted into his presence.

The Temple had been plundered, the oldest families borne into captivity, the land impoverished both in men and wealth. Yet was this severe blood-letting not a purge carried out at the command of the Lord by His unwitting "servant"? The nation still lived, though reduced in numbers and humbled. It was not important that the nation should be great and proud, but it *was* important that it should be pure. The Lord had granted it a further respite in which to clear up the confusion. It was like a fresh beginning after a great act of expiation, and these days of misfortune were for Jeremiah the most hopeful ones of his life. Yet his heart bled for one guiltless victim, who had been destined to become the scape-goat in order that Judah might be saved. The boy-king Coniah had to pay the full penalty for his father's reign. He was still in the palace, but was bound with iron chains and nobody was allowed to see him.

Jeremiah occupied the same chamber in the House of Solomon as he had done in the days of King Josiah. He walked restlessly to and fro, his soul longing to speak with Coniah, until at last the evening twilight darkened the window looking onto one of the inner courts and a servant brought a candelabrum, as he always did at that hour, on which three lamps were burning. Jeremiah, absorbed in contemplation of the flickering lights, did not notice that two men had entered behind the servant and remained standing in the shadow. As he pondered on ways and means of alleviating Coniah's lot, he heard his name called by a familiar voice. Starting up in affright, he cried: "Baruch!" and already he had drawn his faithful disciple into his arms, overcome by the thought of all that had happened since their last farewell.

Baruch pointed silently to his companion, who was standing shyly near the door. He was rather tall and wore a dusty travelling-cloak, which could not hide his radiant youth and manly bearing. His face was very handsome, but not with the transparent beauty of Coniah. There was an imperious light in his large, lustrous eyes, which none the less held an irresistible charm. The sight of Jeremiah seemed to fill him with agitation and embarrassment, and in order to master his emotion, which he perhaps regarded as a weakness, he threw his head back and stood erect. The prophet recognized the characteristic gesture of Josiah, and his voice trembled as he murmured:

"Mattaniah, my young pupil. . . ."

The voice of the newcomer was steady.

"No longer Mattaniah, your young pupil, but Zedekiah, to whom you gave the name, 'God is just'! . . . This is the name I shall bear when I sit upon the throne of David and judge my people."

Jeremiah thought of the boy who had once asked him eagerly: "You know everything; can you tell me whether Mattaniah will one day be King?" The intuition of a child, which had at that time seemed so utterly improbable, had now been wondrously fulfilled. And Jeremiah sank to the ground before his pupil to pay him homage.

"You are Zedekiah, the true son of my King. May the Lord be praised in all your deeds!"

Zedekiah raised Jeremiah from the floor. The prophet felt strangely old in the presence of this imperious youth whom he had last seen as a moody boy. They looked at each other with eyes that no longer tried to conceal the tears of deep emotion or the question that was in their minds: whether they could be sure of each other in the future too. Baruch felt awkward at witnessing their touching reunion, so he broke the pregnant silence by beginning his report on the task he had so efficiently carried out. The difficulties, he said, had been much slighter than in his fear he had anticipated. As a matter of fact, there had been no difficulties at all, since the new Sun God at Noph, Pharaoh Hophra, the grandson of Necho, was personally very friendly to Mattaniah-Zedekiah and had agreed unhesitatingly to his ascending the throne. Jeremiah had no need to feel alarmed at this sign of favour on the part of Pharaoh, since it would of course remain a well-guarded secret. The King of Babylon would confirm the anointing of Zedekiah as King of Judah only if he regarded him as one who had been held captive and eaten the bread of affliction in the House of Bondage, but not if he knew that he was a favourite of Pharaoh. Immediately upon arriving in Jerusalem, Baruch had spread a highly coloured story about Zedekiah's flight from Egypt, and on his way to find Jeremiah he had met the sons of Shaphan in the Temple. Gedaliah, who had access to the ear of Nebuchadnezzar as had no one else in Judah, had straightway set forth to speak with the King and inform him that the youngest son of Josiah had taken refuge in the arms of Babylon. There was no doubt that Nebuchadnezzar would raise Zedekiah to the throne of David if he cast himself at his feet and petitioned him to do so. Jeremiah said nothing. Baruch's report had dimmed his joy. Zedekiah, with his keen intuition, realized at once that his teacher's mood had imperceptibly changed to one of sadness, and he also understood the reasons. He looked at him with a smile in his eyes and said:

"I know that it is not Pharaoh and not Nebuchadnezzar,

nor even Ahikam and Gedaliah, by whom I have been raised up, but that it is Jeremiah alone who has raised me up and will set me on my throne."

As Jeremiah still did not speak but only made a deprecatory movement with his hand, Zedekiah lowered his eyes and went on:

"To my father and mother I owe my life . . . but to my teacher I owe everything else."

This was a significant admission, acknowledging an obligation on the part of the future King towards the prophet. Zedekiah reddened, as if he was fully conscious that it would not always be easy to stand by this avowal. There was a pause, during which the two men were engrossed in their own complex thoughts and feelings, until Baruch put an end to it by reporting that Coniah had that morning been taken to the camp in an iron cage and was shortly to be carried away to Babylon. Jeremiah was taken aback at the news, but Zedekiah made a gesture of disdain, mingled with pity, consigning his unhappy predecessor to his fate as if he had no further concern in the matter. Then he gently touched Jeremiah, as though to hold him fast, and said:

"Henceforth I shall not let you go from my side."

"You will let me go from your side," replied Jeremiah, "until I return from Babylon."

"From Babylon?" asked Baruch and Zedekiah together in surprise. In a tortured voice Jeremiah grated:

"Is this man Coniah a despised and broken idol? Is he a vessel wherein there is no pleasure? Wherefore is he cast out, when he might have been the signet upon the right hand of the Lord?"

He stepped to the window and became absorbed in a brooding reverie. His soul was torn with doubt. Could he abandon the pitiful youth on his way to exile? Could he leave the immature Zedekiah during the first days of his reign? It was equally unjust to leave the one or the other. Which of them needed him more? Only Adonai could decide. Baruch and Zedekiah went softly from the room, for they divined that their teacher was about to converse with the Lord.

24

The Journey through the Starry Sky

JEREMIAH grew constantly more distrustful of his own deeply rooted instincts which tempted him to regard things more optimistically than was warranted, and his ear had consequently become keenly attuned to the promptings of the Lord. Other men had visions and other men heard the voice, but it was not alone their sanctification through these divine gifts that could make them genuine prophets. The divine inspiration was not enough if the human instrument was not equal to the unceasing and holy effort of collaboration. In His compassion the Lord condescended to reveal Himself in words audible to human ears, and their supreme purity was therefore exposed to the danger of becoming dulled by admixture. The art of the true prophet consisted in hearing "aright," that is to say, in eliminating from what he had heard all the confusing elements which sprang from the passions, desires, and ambitions of his own nature. Jeremiah had discovered various criteria by which to distinguish the pure word of the Lord from the promptings of his own heart. For example, the more novel and startling the word of God seemed, the less did he suspect it of being mingled with anything of his own.

During these days, when the Lord took pity on His people and once more snatched them back from the abyss, Jeremiah was filled both with gratitude and with apprehension. His great fear sprang from his surmise, nay, certainty, that the Lord had granted another respite only because of his own mediation. Who had led him to Nebuchadnezzar, so that he might avert the destruction of Jerusalem and the Temple by his advice? The King of Babylon had allowed Zedekiah to be anointed with holy oil and crowned with the crown of David. At the same time, however, Coniah, the dethroned boy-king, had been taken to the Babylonian camp in an iron cage.

In whom could Jeremiah put more trust than in the favourite son of Josiah and Hamutal, who had received instruction in the Law from his own mouth? But who needed support more than Coniah, the outcast? The poor captive filled his heart not only with pity but even more with a peculiar sense of guilt. He would none the less have been unable to come to a decision between remaining in Jerusalem and accompanying Coniah to Babylon if he had not heard the voice of the Lord commanding him to do something more strange than had ever been the case before.

"Go and get thee a linen girdle," said the voice, "and put it upon thy loins, and put it not in water."

Hardly had Jeremiah had time to obey this curious order, when he was told how to proceed further:

"Take the girdle that thou hast got, which is upon thy loins, and arise, go to Euphrates, and hide it there in a hole of the rock."

Jeremiah saw in this mysterious command the granting of permission to undertake the journey to Bablyon, so that the boy Coniah should not be alone in his wretchedness.

He went at once to the camp and submitted his petition. The Tartans who were appointed to supervise the expulsion and carrying to Babylon of the ten thousand captives were not a little astonished that one who had been spared such a bitter fate should plead so eagerly to be allowed to accompany them. They had their hands full in any case with the appeals and lamentations, the importunate requests, the secret and open attempts at bribery, with which the expatriated men of Judah and their families tried to induce them to concede forbidden favours. How different this nation was from all the other nations they had subdued during their campaigns! All the other peoples had resigned themselves dully and without protest to the fate of the conquered after they had been abandoned by their gods in battle. Everywhere else the attitude seemed to be: "We should have done to you what you are now doing to us if your gods had not been stronger than ours. For such is the bitter way of the world!" But that was not true with the people of Judah! They did not acknowledge that the way of the world was bitter. They were wholly recalcitrant. They had not the faintest intention of exchanging their One God for other gods. Every son of Israel, or so it seemed at least to the Babylonians, felt himself exalted far above the general fate of mankind. The leniency of Nebuchadnezzar, who had not even ordered the walls of Jerusalem to be razed to the ground, was not sufficient to make them resigned to their defeat. The camp was overrun with screaming women demanding their husbands back; many of the exiles feigned illness or exhibited ancient wounds which made it impossible for them to undergo any exertion, while others tried to purchase their freedom or sent slaves to impersonate them. All the more incomprehensible, therefore, was the request of Jeremiah, a man who had never been a member of Coniah's retinue.

Since the name of the soothsayer was mentioned with respect among the dignitaries of Babylon, his petition was at once brought to the ears of Nebuchadnezzar, who unconditionally acceded to his desire. It appeared even as if the King of Babylon was gratified at the thought of the man of Adonai visiting his capital city, where the shadows cast by the stars of the nocturnal sky converged. As an additional mark of Nebuchadnezzar's high favour, Coniah was released from his iron cage that very day and allotted a comfortable tent in which to live. On the following morning two magnificent camels were grazing in front of Coniah's tent, a present for him and his travelling-companion. This pointed to Nebuchadnezzar's decision to take his prisoner with him to Babylon among his own retinue before the exiles and their escort set out from Jerusalem. So far as the latter were concerned, they were not particularly harshly treated. They were not chained together, but were allowed to use horses, camels, asses, and draught-animals, in so far as they possessed or could procure them. A wave of love and generosity swept over Jerusalem and the rest of the country. In order to help the exiles, the people gave whatever they could and even deprived themselves of necessities, so that many a poor craftsman had received an animal to ride on and all kinds of victuals for the journey by the time the trumpets of Babylon gave the signal for the march to begin.

Nebuchadnezzar and his staff set out a good seven days before the columns of the returning army and the ten thousand banished men of Judah. At a remarkable speed they passed through the valley of the Jordan, and it was not long before they had left the mountains of Lebanon behind them and reached the city of Riblah, which was a junction of roads from all points of the compass. Light and heavy cavalry covered both flanks and also furnished the vanguard and the rearguard, Nebuchadnezzar himself riding most of the time on a long-legged camel whose sprawling stride made it seem to hover in the air as it trotted over the grassy plains. Now and then he exchanged this mount for a dun-coloured horse, and occasionally he used his travelling-chariot for a part of the way, but he always rode in the centre of his escort, whose positions never varied. Nearest to him was the inner ring, consisting of four groups of horsemen representing the planets Nergal, Ninurtu, Nabu, and Ishtar. To his right were the men of Nergal, clad in fiery red, and the men of Ninurtu, clad in black. These were Marduk's generals and chief warriors, under the leadership of Nergal Nebuzaradan, together with his supreme judges, augurs, and priests of the dead. To his left, the side of his heart, rode the men of Ishtar, clad in blue and light green, under the leadership of Samgar Nebo, who combined both forces within himself, the masculine, rational element of Mercury and the feminine, emotional element of Venus. Samgar Nebo did not ride on a saddle, but sat with his legs crossed beneath him in an upholstered basket that was buckled to his camel. On account of his epicene nature it would have been improper and inauspicious to ride astride. Nebuchadnezzar himself sat his mount with a sturdy ease. He knew that his every action, whether of construction or destruction, was an imperishable impress formed by the rays of Marduk in the shifting sands of time. The star-priests attributed a healing power to his nature. In all the cities and villages through which he passed the people of the various nations thronged to him. The very sight of Marduk in his simple, sandalwood-coloured robe and flowing hair "edified" them in some mysterious way, and they came from far and near to be uplifted by the architect of the world, the royal star and star-king.

Only very rarely did Marduk address a word to Nergal or Nabu. He was usually absorbed in his schemes and silent, as befitted the solitary royal planet. Now and then, however, his features would light up as he gazed at the cloud of birds, which obediently flew above their master's head throughout the long journey. In the opinion of many soothsayers these birds were a shrunken residue of the stars of a former creation. With their gift of flight, they were to some extent superior to man himself, and it was not fortuitous that they were the first creatures on earth to have been endowed with the power of song, the divine and original form of human speech. The oracle of the birds had been the first of all oracles, and Marduk's birds were a lively confirmation of this truth. Their confused and mocking cries never ceased, while the boldest of them would perch on his shoulder and impertinently screech their incoherent and unintelligible prophecies in his ear. Nebuchadnezzar never wearied of this amusement, occasionally even bursting into loud laughter at some particularly droll caricature of human words.

The order of march did not consist only of the inner ring of planets in the immediate proximity of Marduk. There was also an outer ring representing the twelve signs of the zodiac, each of which comprised exactly the same number of noble riders as the constellation contained stars. Only the star-councillors of the court of Babylon knew what complicated problems of rank and dignity had to be solved, what disappointments and triumphs were experienced, what intrigues and sycophancy were employed before the constellations were eventually composed. While Marduk and the planets kept to the roads, the groups of the zodiac moved over open ground in a far-flung circle, and thus the eternal cycle of the stars was mirrored day in, day out, in the march of the nocturnal sky across the earth. But beyond the planets and the circle of the zodiac, in the freezing realms of outer space where the innumerable swarm of lesser stars had their being and the order of the universe was less strict, the dethroned King of Judah rode side by side with Jeremiah in the midst of a company of keen-eyed guards armed to the teeth.

Coniah was tied to the hump of his camel by a chain round his waist, so that he could move in the saddle only with difficulty, and to his left foot was attached a long rope which one of the guards held in his hand. Whenever the guard's camel moved too far to the side or happened to jump, the rope tightened round Coniah's foot and would have torn him from the saddle if he had not been chained to the hump; each time both the rope and the chain cut deeply into his flesh. He sat upright and paled, but no sound of anguish escaped his lips. He remained silent, his haughty hostility growing more intense as he almost savagely rejected every attempt on the part of Jeremiah to comfort him. Jeremiah realized that Coniah hated him with an irreconcilable hatred, and he humbled himself to look after the unhappy youth as a servant, taking him his food, waiting on him, and attending to his physical needs. He said no word unless he was spoken to, refrained even from attempting to raise Coniah's spirits by pointing out to him that by his sufferings he was fighting for the continued existence of Jerusalem and the Temple.

One evening, as he was undressing the young King, he saw that Coniah's white undergarment was soaked in blood. The festering wounds caused by the pressure and chafing of the chain round his waist had burst open, and the bleeding could not be stanched. Coniah looked down at his body but said nothing, though his austere and boyish face, more transparently beautiful than ever, was flushed with fever.

Jeremiah, who was allowed to move about freely when they pitched camp, went in spite of the lateness of the hour to the zodiac constellation of the Fishes, which practised the arts of healing and medicine. The Fishes reported to Marduk and at once sent a physician. But Coniah's eyes flashed angrily, he gritted his teeth, and clenched his fists. He would have sprung at the physician's throat if the latter had dared to approach him. He would allow no one to wash and dress his wounds. Coniah did not want to be healed. The agony he was suffering was as a crown, the last reality left to him in a world bereft of all else.

Jeremiah spent the whole night watching beside the fevered boy. He had begged for a small lamp, which he placed on the ground. Every now and then Coniah opened his eyes, and his faithful companion caught a look of such loathing that he was shaken, yet he continued to hold his cool hand on the boy's forehead. That it soothed his pain was shown by the suppressed moans that broke from him when the hand was removed. Towards morning the fever abated and a copious perspiration heralded a change for the better. Coniah lay awake and did not turn his eyes, in which hatred had yielded to an unutterable sorrow, from Jeremiah's face. The latter kept silent, as he had vowed to himself to do, in order not to irritate the patient. Coniah, however, began to speak in a low voice. He pleaded with God, but very differently from the way in which Josiah had pleaded. His grandfather had been lying mortally wounded on his death-bed, but the young Coniah, who was suffering only from the wounds caused by his conqueror's chains, had to anticipate countless days of captivity.

"Is it true," he whispered, "that it is written in the Law: 'Thou shalt love the Lord thy God with all thy heart and with all thy soul'?"

Jeremiah gently stroked Coniah's hair as if to dissuade him from fruitless questioning. But he would not be dissuaded. His lips, which he had been biting in his fever, were like those of a child asking why it had been hurt.

"Why should I love the Lord? . . . Has He done that to me which should make me love Him? . . . Where does He dwell? . . . He is far away. . . . There is nothing between Him and me. . . . You alone are the mediator between Him and me. . . ."

He had spoken the last words very slowly, his eyes resting on Jeremiah with the old look of horror, and Jeremiah felt the awe with which he inspired him. For it was true that he alone stood between the Lord in His infinite aloofness and the soul of this outcast King. Coniah again stared up to the roof of the low tent which was pitched for him every evening.

"Why do you persecute me," he murmured, "you who stand between Him and me? All you have is the Word, just as all that He has is the Word. . . . But I hate the Word, both yours and His . . . for it has plunged my father and me into ruin. . . . Yes, you are the cause of my ruin, even though you are now sorry for me and oppressed by your feeling of guilt. . . . I wish that you would leave me alone in my wretchedness and not disturb me. . . ."

Jeremiah quietly went over to the curtain which hung at the entrance to the tent and lifted it so that the early morning breeze might refresh the sick boy. The paling stars were wheeling towards the edge of the immeasurable plain, a section of which could be glimpsed through the doorway. Coniah raised himself up on his elbow, with a far-away look of despair on his emaciated face.

"How I envy those who worship the stars," he cried, "to whom the stars belong! Their gods rise and set before their eyes. It is not He whom I love! I love the stars! O beautiful morning star, thou who art sinking in the heavens, would that I could bow before thee and worship thee! But even though I would, I may not . . . I may not. . . ."

Coniah was already falling asleep as he murmured the last words, and Jeremiah continued to bend over him long after he had closed his eyes. Just as once he had accompanied Jehoahaz, the simple-minded son of David, into a captivity that was easy to bear, he was now accompanying Coniah, another son of David, into a captivity that was harsh beyond measure. But Coniah was not simple-minded. In him the Lord had broken a hero and plucked the signet from His right hand. Was it weariness, or was it the increasing years, that made Jeremiah less rebellious than when he had fled from Adonai into the western underworld of Egypt? Now, on his way towards the eastern world of the stars, his heart wept silently for Coniah until the sun rose.

That morning Marduk ordered the camp to be struck at a much later hour than usual. He doubtless wished to give his prisoner time to recover and collect new strength. It was by no means his intention to leave the corpse of a dethroned king to be devoured by the beasts of the field and the birds of the air. He regarded the prisoner as not only a valuable hostage taken from an alien and mysterious god, but also as a guarantee of the destiny foretold by the stars. So long as he lived and was held captive in Babylon, the dominion of Nebuchadnezzar's house was assured. So ran the interpretation of the complex orbits of the planets in the zodiac. Marduk sent specially to inquire whether the patient was capable of continuing the journey, but before Jeremiah could reply, Coniah had walked to his camel, pulled it to its knees, and swung himself into the saddle. His beardless cheeks were sallow and sunken, but his face was set in a smile so that no one should see the agony that was his crown and his hope of death. With tremendous self-control he held himself erect and looked neither to the right nor to the left, as if he wished to ride into Babylon like a true king and not like one who had been cast out.

By evening they had reached the Euphrates, on the west bank of which they pitched camp for the night. Coniah at once fell into a deep sleep of exhaustion, and in the last rays of the setting sun Jeremiah stealthily crept away. Vivid white cliffs of chalk rising from the shore of the river had caught his eye. In a short time he came to a massive rock in which steps had been hewn; he knew at once that this was the place which the Lord had indicated to him. He quickly removed his loin-cloth and saw to his wonder that in spite of the arduous journey the fine linen was still as clean and white as if it had never been worn. Climbing up the steps, which cut more and more deeply into the steep hillside, he found that they led to an ancient inscription. The letters were weather-beaten and he was unable to read them, but he decided to use one of the carved runes for the purpose whose meaning was still hidden from him. Folding the loin-cloth and pressing it between two flat stones, he thrust it into the cleft and sealed the opening carefully with fragments of chalk. Neither water nor rain could enter, and no animal or insect, not even an ant or a worm, would be able to penetrate between the stones.

On the following day their march took them upstream

along the bank of the Euphrates. Coniah's courage did not fail and only once did his strength give out, so that he nearly sank from the saddle. Jeremiah urged him to rest a little, but his features became distorted with shame and anger. His only reply was to hit his camel over the muzzle with his stick and make it gallop even faster.

As the sun was again about to set, all the horsemen suddenly halted as though rooted to the spot. A transparent, spectral structure loomed above the horizon in the reddened evening mists of the Euphrates. It rose massively from the vaporous earth in seven steps, each of which was narrower than the one below. The men of Babylon descended from their mounts and cast themselves with a shudder of awe to the ground before E-temen-anki, the tower that had been built up into the sky.

Jeremiah and Coniah had not been able to bid each other farewell. At the hour when Marduk and his accompanying retinue were preparing for their entry into the capital, the two had been abruptly separated and the State prisoner again placed in the iron cage that he might be carried before Marduk on his triumphal march. This was the last time they ever saw each other, and Jeremiah could not banish from his mind the memory of Coniah's last look, a look from which all self-control and effort to appear proud had dropped away, leaving only an utter wretchedness that he no longer attempted to conceal. Now it was not hatred and loathing that Jeremiah saw, but the dumb appeal of a victim who knew that he was being led to the sacrifice; not fear of a swift death at the hands of a slaughterer, but fear of the life of captivity in darkness and solitude which stretched endlessly before him. When Coniah looked for the last time at the man who had taken care of him on his journey, his eyes had revealed the realization that he was cut off now and for ever from everything that made life worth living: from the land of his birth, from the house of his ancestors, and from the waiting bride whose destiny it should have been to become a wife and bear children to her husband so that his memory might not perish from the earth. What were the agony of chains and the tortures of captivity compared with the consciousness of being cast aside in early youth and vigour like an outworn garment, of being a useless torso lying in a corner whose hacked-off limbs continued to move! "Falling out of the world" was the way the Kher-heb had described the danger of exchanging one's gods, but every captive, too, fell out of the world into a barren "world between" that was even more melancholy than Amenti. That was why Coniah, who had so heroically conquered his agony and so haughtily despised Jeremiah, cried out suddenly with eyes opened wide in horror and arms outstretched in pleading as the guards dragged him away.

For months Jeremiah haunted the straight streets of the capital trying to find a way to Coniah, but in vain. The laws of Babylon were inexorable. They were far more rigid than those of Noph. When anybody had once been swallowed up by the black-painted citadel, which was used as a prison for rebels and was under the influence of the star Ninurtu, he could hope for no mitigation of his sentence or lessening of his hardships until the day of his death. Among the hundred prohibitions which hemmed him in, the most important was that which forbade him to see any of his countrymen or relations, or any envoy from the god of his native land. The audacious request that this supreme veto should be set aside for Coniah made Jeremiah an object of suspicion when he presented it to the authorities in Babylon. In any case, things were different for him in the capital from what they had been in the camp. He was no longer treated with respect. Nobody knew him. When he waited for days at a time before the closed doors of the star-councillors, he was eyed askance as a member of a distrusted nation.

Marduk and his councillors were as remote from him as were their corresponding planets in the sky. He did not succeed in getting even as far as the guards at the gates of the great palace, and at last he realized that there was no way of obtaining permission to see Coniah and being able to share his terrible solitude for a single hour. When, after unwearying efforts, the futility of making any further attempt came home to him, he began to think of returning to Jerusalem, for he was assailed by uneasy fears concerning Zedekiah during nights when he could not sleep. There were, however, two obstacles in the way of his return. No further word had yet come from the Lord with regard to the mysterious loin-cloth. And further, when he applied to the competent authority in the new city, which was charged with the supervision of strangers, for permission to return to his native land, this permission had first been granted to him and then suddenly withdrawn. The officials had treated him with an inquisitive curiosity, so perhaps it was Marduk himself who had ordered that he should not to be allowed to leave Babylon. He found these hindrances not altogether a matter for regret, since he still could not reconcile himself to abandoning Coniah.

Day after day he roamed restlessly through the streets of Babylon. One evening he let himself be carried by the crowd along the street which was known as "the Holy Way of Processions and Festivals" and bisected the city in a prolonged straight line from the Gate of Marduk to the temple area of E-sagila. He gazed around. The dual Gate of Marduk, through the tall arch of which he had just walked, shone in the rays of the setting sun. The whole structure, including its towers, battlements, and bays, was faced with deep-blue glazed tiles and shone like a colossal jewel. Right up to the top the blue surfaces were ornamented with coloured bas-reliefs arranged harmoniously in groups of seven. The lion of Babylon, with its slender body, gaping jaws, and raised tail, alternated with Babylon's dragon on the projecting, giraffe-like neck of which was set a triangular serpent head. There were other beautifully modelled animals standing out from the shining blue surface of the tiles, such as the defiant wild bull with lowered horns which was dedicated to the stars that influence the weather.

As he stood in front of these carved and painted fabulous beasts, Jeremiah did not feel the thrill of awe and the longing which had come to him under the flowering columns of Noph. He gazed abstractedly at their splendour and thought of Coniah, who so loved the stars of the pale morning sky.

Nowhere was the burden of the Lord heavier than in an alien country. In the throng of people idly strolling up and down the street, Jeremiah more than once caught a look of malice, and more than once he heard an imprecation or a jeering cry. The hostility towards Israel was perhaps even greater in Babylon than it had been in Noph. Yet the people of Noph were children of Japhet, while those of Babylon and Israel were children of Shem. Their hatred had nothing to do with blood-kinship or the lack of it. It sprang from the will of the Lord, who had founded a nation, sanctified it, and set it against all the other nations of the world. The aversion which high and low, the finest and the coarsest natures, felt for Israel was rooted in religion and hardly rational. The bitterest aspect of it for Jeremiah was that he was in revolt against his own people. He began to meditate on the fate of the ten thousand whom the King of Babylon had settled in two neighbouring districts, in Borsippa and Tel Abib. Only the princes and men of high rank among the exiles had been ordered to live in the capital, so that they might always be under the eyes of the authorities and any attempt at conspiracy ruthlessly crushed. Jeremiah took care not to encounter Pashur and his other persecutors while he was in Babylon, but before he left the Land of Rivers he would perhaps go to Borsippa and Tel Abib, so that he could report to King Zedekiah on his return to Jerusalem concerning the life the exiles were leading. He raised his eyes to the cloudless sky, which was beginning to fill with the gold of sunset. "A weak myriad of Israel," he thought, "among the myriads upon myriads of Marduk! Will they succumb? Will they survive?" He held his breath and pressed his eyelids together in order to listen to the voice within him, but now as always there was no clear answer to his bold questioning.

When he opened his eyes again, the mighty city of Babylon seemed even more illimitable, even more oppressive than before. From the twenty-four main streets, which intersected it in endless straight lines, a hubbub of excited voices rose into the air. On the twenty broad, embanked canals of the Euphrates, which crossed the network of streets, sailed innumerable barks and long native rafts supported by inflated goatskins. Dense crowds were flocking from the country to the gates of the town. Not only E-sagila, the central temple, which was ten times the size of the Temple of the Lord, was festively decked with wreaths and banners, but also all the other fifty-three temples that were contained within the environs of the capital. At every street corner stood beflagged shrines and chapels with incense smoking on their altars. Three hundred of these small sanctuaries were dedicated to the constellations of the zodiac alone, chiefly that of the Ram, which was also called the "Workman" and was the sign of the age. On the following night, at the beginning of the month of Nisan, when Marduk entered the sign of the Ram, the zenith of the age would be reached and a new cosmic spring begin, the spring of Nebuchadnezzar. Therefore the greatest festival was being prepared which that generation had ever been privileged to witness. While tens of thousands were streaming into Babylon from all sides, Nebuchadnezzar had secretly left the city to pass the night of dedication before the great spring festival in a bleak mountain cavern, where he was divested of all his power and forsaken by his retinue as if he were an outcast or dead. When his hour came and the priests had ceased their prolonged lamentations, he would emerge from his obscurity as a mighty god, return to his city, and knock at the Gate of Marduk. There he would be received by all the gods of the starry sky and their priests, who would form a sacred procession round him and lead him to E-sagila, that he might ascend to the "Chamber Where Destiny Is Determined," on the highest level of the tower.

Jeremiah's eyes rested on E-temen-anki, which rose like Mount Hermon high above the royal and divine palaces of E-sagila. Was it really, as they said in Judah, "the Tower of Babel" which arrogant men had tried to build up to heaven? If that were so, then the Lord had at last yielded to human pride, for it undoubtedly looked as if the topmost starry chamber merged into the radiance of the evening sky. Each of the seven stories of this "Foundation Stone of Heaven and Earth" comprised a whole world in itself. The seven worlds above the earth were strictly reproduced in seven worlds below the earth, for that which was above was also below. The vastest of these great stories was the lowest one, which contained a little city within its walls. Each story rose up more slenderly from the one below, differentiated from it in material and colour in accordance with the planet it represented. The lower stories were in dark colours and heavy metals, and the tower gradually grew lighter in tone and less massive towards the top. The story of Ninurtu was built of lead and coloured black, shading into earthy brown at its upper limit. The story of martial Nergal was in dark purple and fiery red, growing lighter as it stretched upwards, and all the metalwork was of iron and steel. The story of the sun, richly ornamented with pure gold, ranged from deep orange to clear saffron. Ishtar, goddess of fertility, displayed the hues of green vegetation and burnished copper. Then came the mercurial blue of Nabu, in whose hall the rare metal quicksilver was preserved in little urns. The story dedicated to the moon shimmered with silver. The seventh belonged to Marduk and was the colour of sandalwood, a pale ashen-grey with yellowish and bluish tints in it. The star-king's metal, tin, was as unpretentious as himself, and his story was overtopped by a small cube-shaped chamber erected on its roof. The colour of this "Chamber Where Destiny Is Determined" was an indefinite milk white that seemed to fade into the heavens.

The stories of the tower of E-temen-anki were linked together by broad outside staircases; Jeremiah knew, though he was unable to see them from where he was standing, that priests were moving to and fro along them in orderly procession as they went to or came from their duties. He stood absorbed in thought as he gazed at the tower which men had built, contrary to the will of the Lord, to reach up to heaven. The sun was setting and the colours were slowly paling in the twilight, the purple and fiery red of Nergal still glowing vividly after the others had lost their brilliance, until it too faded and dissolved into a faint violet hue in which the lofty E-temen-anki was wrapped as in a priestly cloak. The bustle in the streets ceased, and all eyes were turned in rapture towards the storied tower as if they were awaiting a miracle. The miracle happened, as it did every evening, and drew dreamy cries of ecstasy from the spectators. Ishtar, the evening star, had risen in a sky from which the light had not yet gone. It did not remain alone for long. One star after another emerged to keep it company. The pale-violet mist in which E-temen-anki was veiled darkened to a cloud that concealed its contours. Then the starry chamber on its summit began to glow with a light that was not of the earth. The walls and roof were made of some special crystalline vitreous flux produced by the priests, who alone knew the secret and used their own furnaces, from a formula that had been handed down from ancient Ur. This translucent material possessed the quality not only of magnifying the stars so that the soothsayers could interpret their mysteries, but it was also endued with the power of absorbing their rays from the depths of the celestial hemisphere and gathering them in the Chamber of Destiny. It was therefore no light kindled by human hands that shimmered on the top of the tower, but the hidden radiance of the gods descending upon mankind; and the thrill of awe evoked every evening in the citizens of Babylon by this wonder found voice in a hymn which the crowd sang in a low tone.

Jeremiah stood silent and thoughtful amid an alien people. Then as he turned to go, he saw that he was surrounded by four blue-clad figures that had apparently been waiting for him. For a moment he was startled and imagined that he must have violated the laws of Babylon by his petitioning for Coniah. Perhaps Nebuchadnezzar had sent these men to arrest him! His fears were calmed when they bowed deeply before him with folded hands, and his heart leapt with joy. Perhaps the blue-clad priests of the stars had come to take him to the gloomy citadel that he might look upon the face of the unhappy boy-king! They were priests of Nabu, interpreters and soothsayers, and were therefore to a certain extent his brethren, since he himself in his quality as a prophet was called both in Babylon and Jerusalem by the same title, "Nabi." The envoys of Nabu, however, did not lead him in the direction of the citadel. Ranging themselves courteously on either side of Jeremiah, they escorted him through the curious crowd and along the processional way until they reached the strictly guarded temple area of E-sagila, a group of buildings clustered round the tower of E-temen-anki. By the time they crossed its boundary the last rays of the setting sun had disappeared from the sky, and the streets and squares of E-sagila were illumined solely by an occasional ever-burning lamp.

It was too dark for Jeremiah to discern the way they were taking, but their destination appeared to be a building distinguished from the others by the faint shimmer in which it was enveloped. When they reached the gateway he was received by no less a personage than Samgar Nebo, and he was dumbfounded at being greeted with a brotherly kiss by the highest dignitary in the realm, second only to Marduk himself. Jeremiah had no conception of the mysterious part he had been chosen to play even when Samgar Nebo invited him, a member of a conquered and despised race, to share in the feast of the order and brotherhood of Nabu. The meal was as silent as it was frugal. It took place in a blue-painted hall at a table covered with a blue cloth, and the only illumination was provided by the little blue flames that burned in silver censers. While the attendants handed round dates and figs, barley cakes and cakes sweetened with honey, the deep silence of the brotherhood of Nabu seemed to be intensified by the voice of one of their number who sat apart from the table and chanted not hymns or lays, as might have been expected, but figures from the calendar of the cosmic year, with the times of rising and setting of the constellations and the calculated dates of eclipses of the sun. The meal came to an end with the drinking of a sweet wine from little tin cups. Then Samgar Nebo rose, took Jeremiah by the hand, and led him to a comfortable chamber containing a broad couch.

Here the star-councillor explained to the prophet of Adonai that he had been appointed by order of Marduk to fulfil a holy office. On the following night, at the hour of the rejuvenation of the world and the determination of destiny, he was to be the foreign star-witness of Marduk. This was a custom that had been followed since the founding of Babylon, and the choice usually fell upon an allied king, but this time Marduk had been graciously pleased to confer the distinction upon an alien soothsayer who had proved himself to be cognizant of so many truths of the dawning age. As Samgar Nebo went on in his gentle voice, Jeremiah felt a pleasurable weariness drawing him irresistibly to the couch. He tried to smile at the councillor as if to excuse himself for appearing so inattentive, but was asleep before he could do so. Never in his life had he slept so profoundly. When four men clad in blue came later to awaken him, he did not know whether it was morning or evening. His sense of time had become confused while he lay unconscious. It was evening, the greatest evening of the age, for the royal star of Babylon was about to mount to its zenith. A blue veil was thrown over the head of the star-witness before he was conducted from the palace, but it was wide-meshed and did not obscure his view. He found himself standing among the brotherhood of Nabu at the foot of the mighty tower, between the two outside staircases that led right and left towards the dizzy height. The head of Marduk's procession had long since entered E-sagila, and a great host of star-gods of gold, silver, copper, wood, and alabaster, many hundreds of them, could be seen swaying in the air as their bearers carried them towards E-temen-anki. They had awaited Marduk at the gate of pilgrimage as he came, newly resurrected, from his solitary cave, and were now escorting him to the holy temple. When they reached the tower, they all disappeared through the black gates of the story of Ninurtu. Marduk was not riding, or travelling in his chariot, or being carried in his litter, but walking—a short, sturdy figure in an unpretentious robe, his round face looking rather tired and very thoughtful. The empty space around him, like an icy vacuum, denoted his unique importance and the awe-inspiring task of determining the destiny of the world which he was about to undertake. But beyond this space, and seeming to wall it in, rose the chanting of priests and the stirring, cacophonous music of hundreds of drums and other instruments of various kinds. Jeremiah was able to distinguish Nebuchadnezzar's salient features; the broad, implacable mouth and the tilted nose that projected with such an air of defiance from his still boyish face. In his right hand he carried a silver thunderbolt and in his left a gladiator's net. As he approached the staircase of the tower, he suddenly raised his thunderbolt on high. The chanting was hushed; the minstrels ceased their discordant din; the procession of priests came to an abrupt halt. Alone, and at a steady pace, the King of Babylon continued on his way towards the tower of E-temen-anki. At that moment Jeremiah felt the light touch of Samgar Nebo's hand upon his shoulder.

The Chamber Where Destiny Is Determined was far more spacious than it looked from below or from a distance. Jeremiah found himself alone there with Marduk and Samgar Nebo, the blue-clad brotherhood of Nabu having ascended no higher than the story of Nabu and entered the hall of the quicksilver urns. The Chamber of Destiny was almost empty, but in the centre of it stood Marduk's bejewelled chariot. This vehicle, which was let into the floor, was half-chariot and half-boat, and instead of movable wheels it had curiously formed golden runners on which the body of the car rested with an elevated seat behind for the driver. In the rays of the setting sun it flashed with the thousands of gems, arranged in the shapes of the constellations, which encrusted it. The walls and ceiling of vitreous flux were not wholly transparent, but rather translucent, resembling very clear alabaster; and one could not be sure whether the reddish cloudiness in them came from the sky or was inherent in the substance of which they were made. The red tinge deepened until the chamber was flooded with the colour, and now Jeremiah noticed that an animal was harnessed to Marduk's car. This was not a horse, but a little winged, giraffe-necked dragon that hovered in the air and was fashioned out of some rough, brownish material.

Time passed on leaden feet and Jeremiah felt that he could almost hear each slow heart-beat. Years before, when he had stood at the entrance to Amenti, at the rocky gateway of the First Hour of the Night, he had experienced the sensation of being only partly present. Now he was experiencing the same sensation, except that this time the part that was present was his head, which seemed to be attached loosely to his almost numb body. He though of the words that Zenua had uttered as she lay dying: "Kā, the swallow, is still within my heart . . . but Bā, the sparrow-hawk, is fluttering about inside my head. . . ." The man from Judah was so absorbed in his solemn thoughts that he was oblivious of the events of the past twenty-four hours, and even of the fact that he was standing in the Chamber of Destiny at the side of the King of Babylon on whose word the fate of all the nations of the world depended. So deeply occupied was he with himself and his mysterious condition that he hardly noticed Samgar Nebo place a lofty crown upon his master's head and garb him in a jewelled cloak, nor did he catch the half-murmured words they exchanged in the process. When Marduk, now flashing with gems, climbed into the car, Samgar Nebo, who had taken hold of Jeremiah's hand, found it necessary to repeat his whispered command that the latter take his stand on the broad step reserved for the witness. Then the star-councillor swung himself up into the high charioteer's seat to take the reins in the name of Marduk.

As the glow from the windows faded, the dusk grew deeper, and the three men were so silent that they seemed not to breathe. When their faces and hands were no longer visible except as shimmering patches, the four doors of the chamber were flung open with a sudden jerk and four black figures were silhouetted against the twilight of cosmic space. Each of these heralds called out a short formula in an echoing voice: "Ishtar is here!" "Let the journey begin!" "Climb to the zenith of spring!" "Determine the fate of the world!" Hardly had the voices died away and the doors closed again, when Samgar Nebo pulled on the reins. Crackling sparks sprang up and set the dragon alight as it hovered in the air, the brownish substance of which it was made revealing itself as a rare kind of incense. The odour it emitted was of an intoxicating sweetness such as Jeremiah had never breathed either in Jerusalem or in Noph, and clouds of smoke filled the chamber. Strange to say, the darkness did not become more dense; it even lessened gradually as tenuous rays of light penetrated the curling fumes from every side and formed mysterious but meaningful patterns. The car was now in the centre of an arching, hollow sphere of fragrant smoke that grew more and more transparent until it merged with the night sky itself, through which the vehicle began to move.

The first clear sensation of which Jeremiah became conscious was that, though they seemed really to be travelling through the sky, it was an oddly motionless journey. He could not tell, in fact, whether the car was moving through the sky or the sky moving past the car. It was not, he thought to himself, motion away from or towards any particular point, not a rising into the air or flying onwards, but a joyous heightening of consciousness. In a little while he realized that he was seeing in a manner hitherto unknown to him, that scales had fallen from his eyes. The night sky was beginning to bud and bloom like a watered meadow in the month of Nisan.

This transformation took place not so much in the space ahead of the car as in Jeremiah's own sense of space. Everything appeared to him both far and near, above and below at the same time. Such words were deprived of meaning, since that which was infinitely remote was near at hand and vice versa. Whenever, in his boyhood, he had roamed the hills of Anathoth by night and looked up to the stars, a feeling of oppression had come over him which even the presence of the Lord had not helped him to conquer. The mind of man is silenced with confusion at sight of a symmetry that he cannot comprehend, and the blossoming sky was revealing its symmetry to Jeremiah's opened eyes. His senses suddenly acquired the power of interpreting the vision of reality that he saw. In some miraculous way he was able to see with the eyes of Samgar Nebo, the charioteer, who was sitting on the elevated seat behind him. At first he was filled with a rare ecstasy of figures and dimensions as his mind partitioned the starry heavens into interrelated sections.

"Behold the houses, the temples, the gardens of the upper worlds," announced Samgar Nebo in a velvety voice. Jeremiah saw houses, temples, and gardens, but these words described his vision very inadequately. He could not yet give his undivided attention to that which stood still and yet moved, since his eyes were attracted by four moving figures which appeared to be imperceptibly approaching Marduk's car, though they were far apart from each other. As their radiance vibrated through the fumes of incense, they more and more clearly took physical shape. Samgar Nebo continued:

"The messengers are advancing towards the King in order to receive his commands." The words of Samgar helped Jeremiah to discern the true shapes of the four messenger-planets. The swiftly moving figures formed the terminal points of a gigantic cross, in the centre of which was Marduk's car. From the west came Ishtar, from the east Nabu, from the north Ninurtu, from the south Nergal. Evident though it was that they were hastening towards the car, the distance between them did not diminish. None the less they were present simultaneously in the four corners of the sky and in the hollow sphere of incense. The summery Nergal appeared in the shape of an armed man, a Tartan in redly glowing armour. In place of a heart he had a shining, pointed star that waxed and waned. He retained this shape, however, only so long as Jeremiah did not examine him more closely. When he did so, Nergal changed into a seething panorama which seemed to be fashioned out of a fiery fabric. In this panorama Jeremiah saw great armies clashing in battle, mighty ramparts being stormed with the aid of ladders, conquerors hurling blazing torches into the temples of the gods (he wondered whether the Temple of Adonai was among them), bandits pillaging peaceful villages by night and setting fire to the huts, women being dragged from their chambers by the hair and carried away to a shameful fate, executioners hacking off the arms of defeated enemies and thrusting captive princes into boiling oil. Red blood flowed in streams, but also red wine with which the victors made themselves drunk. Their shouting and laughter drowned the wailing of their victims. In the evening, when the fighting was over, they siezed one another by the hand and stamped about in a wild dance. Nergal was dominated by blood and fire, yet there were also impetuosity, spirited pride, and simple manliness.

In Ninurtu, Nergal's wintry counterpart, there was neither blood nor fire, neither turbulence nor youth. At the first glance Ninurtu appeared as a very old man walking on a crutch. The star which took the place of his heart glowed with an icy calm. But he too presented a rich panorama when looked at more closely, a scene that lacked the storminess of Nergal but was filled with an insidious haste. Jeremiah again saw crowds of people and great cities, though the people were not assailed by visible foes and the cities were not on fire. There was an invisible foe stalking about in Ninurtu that was far worse; not the death that came in bloody battle, but the death that grew and did its work from within: sickness, infirmity, plague, and madness. Jeremiah saw streets desolated by pestilence, in which putrescent corpses lay about and were being devoured by jackals, hyenas, and clouds of vultures. At the gates of the cities crouched lepers with their warning rattles, waiting for alms that were thrown to them from a distance. Men possessed by devils and driven from the company of their fellows reeled, dishevelled and naked, screaming through the desert. Crippled beggars, both men and women, loitered in front of palaces of dark stone in which dwelt kings who had been born under the influence of Ninurtu. Ninurtu was crowded with sorrowful faces distorted with suffering. Jeremiah wondered where he had seen such faces before. Then he remembered the countenances of Ephraim and Manasseh, the features of the tribes that had been cast aside, the voices of Sheol, the eyes of Amenti, which he had encountered in the land of Samaria. So it seemed that the tribes of Israel whom the Lord had rejected were assembled again in Ninurtu, and not without reason had Babylon dedicated the Sabbath day to Saturn.

Jeremiah turned with a shudder from Ninurtu to rejoice in the sight of Ishtar. At first glance she appeared to him as a mother suckling a male child at her breast. The panorama which revealed itself to him as he watched was utterly different from those of Nergal and Ninurtu. He saw no forces of battle and destruction. Everything was rural, full of the green crops of spring, full of the friendly shade of trees and ordered activity. Peasants with wide hats worked in the fields, and sheep, heavy with wool, were being driven to their watering-places. Broad-hipped dairymaids sat beside the distended udders of cows, milking them into earthenware pitchers. In the cities was the joyous bustle of marketing. Jeremiah could see through the walls of the houses, where families sat together in harmonious accord at meals and there were no disputes between parents or children. In the bedchambers were husbands and wives lying heart to heart in youthful beauty. Betrothed couples sat silently with clasped hands. Marriages were being celebrated, virgins were dancing round the happy pairs, and wine was being poured out for the guests. If there was suffering in Ishtar, it was only the pangs of motherhood or the tortures of unrequited passion.

Different from the deep and simple joys of Ishtar were the gifts of Nabu, who first revealed himself as an elderly priest with a colossal, clean-shaven skull. Whereas Ishtar wore the largest star of all the planets in place of her heart (it covered the whole of her left breast, which she was giving to the child), Nabu possessed but a tiny, faintly shining star. In contrast to Ishtar the scene he presented was autumnal. Mist and clouds shrouded the countryside, rain swept obliquely across the fields, winds began to blow and whirl the dry leaves in a circling dance. Men wrapped themselves in their cloaks and took refuge in the cities. The world of Nabu was mainly a world of cities and temples, and there were innumerable altars dedicated to innumerable gods, with sacrifices smoking on them that were being offered up by priests of every kind. The real sons of Nabu, however, were not the sacrificing priests. Quiet cells were visible to Jeremiah's penetrating gaze, where solitary blue- or white-clad scholars, versed in secret lore, were holding converse with the forces of creation. Most of them were practising their art by night, with windows opened wide that the powers of the upper and the lower world might enter. A tiny, smoking lamp sufficed to illumine their secret work of study and instruction. (That was why all the sons of Nabu had weak, near-sighted eyes, and why blindness was the infirmity peculiar to the planet.) Everywhere Jeremiah saw tall piles of clay tablets, on which the hermits had inscribed the symbols of the sky. They compared the tablets of antiquity with their own and smiled faintly when they found that the experiences of the ages were in accord. Jeremiah thought that in the faces of Nabu he could recognize not only the countenance of the Kher-heb, but also the waxen, undecaying beauty of Samgar Nebo with its unlined cheeks and aged, reddened eyes. In the faces of all those who were so unwearyingly copying the symbols of the sky, calculating orbits, courses, and cycles, and mapping the holy outlines of the upper world, he saw the same marks of suffering: forswearing of the joys of the flesh, renunciation of love, and conquest of self.

Long before he had seen enough of Nergal, Ninurtu, Ishtar, and Nabu to satisfy his inquiring mind, his contemplation was interrupted by an announcement that Samgar Nebo made to Marduk:

"The messengers are assembled to receive your commands."

These words, together with Marduk's response, must have been a formula prescribed since the earliest times. Marduk said in a concise, rather high-pitched voice:

"I send forth the messengers. Let them hasten to the heavenly Euphrates, that the powers from whom they come may hold themselves in readiness!"

Jeremiah raised his eyes from the moving figures to the starry sky, where the Milky Way formed a clear arch, slightly inclined towards the east, above the Chamber of Destiny and the journey of Marduk. He understood that Babylon possessed a Euphrates of the heavens just as Noph possessed a Nile of the underworld, that this Euphrates was the Milky Way, and that the messengers drew from it the mysterious forces which they brought on this night of destiny to Marduk. It really looked to his eyes like a whitish river, and seemed to consist of countless waves and ripples that formed little playful eddies as it rushed along in an incomprehensible kind of motionless movement. Each single drop in these waves and ripples revealed itself to the penetrating gaze of the star-witness as a brilliant spirit-being, a thousand times more insubstantial and remote from anything earthly than the more solid beings who were the four messengers. Jeremiah felt strangled by a terrible sensation of joy which brought irresistible tears of ecstasy to his eyes. He was himself caught up in the process of supreme transmutation brought about by the stars and, like Marduk-Nebuchadnezzar, he became a "man of the sky." The upper and the lower worlds fused in him to a joyous unity. The Milky Way ran through his own body, from the crown of his head to the soles of his feet. He was pervaded by the eternal cycle of the stars, and there was no ray or ripple which did not also have its source in him. In his rapture it seemed as if his own flesh and blood were made of stars. A vast love-urge took possession of him, a longing to hurl himself out into space and dissolve into the universe. At that moment he forgot Jerusalem and Israel; even the name of the Lord was no more than a remote and hollow warning in the fathomless depths of his soul.

Meanwhile there ensued between Marduk and his charioteer a whispered exchange of question and answer that were evidently as ancient and traditional as the formulas that had preceded them. They concerned the periods of time through which Marduk had passed on his seemingly short journey through the sky.

"You have passed your *Soss*," announced the charioteer, as if he were calling out the first stage of the journey. Jeremiah knew that this was the term used in Babylon for a period of sixty years.

After a while Marduk inquired: "Where am I now?"

"You have passed your *Ner*," was the answer. Six hundred years had gone by.

When Marduk next asked how far they had come, he was told that they had reached his *Sar,* six times six hundred years. After this stage had been passed, Samgar Nebo chanted:

"Enter into possession of your cosmic year!"

A cosmic year was sixty *Sars* and constituted the great epoch through which Marduk was journeying and over which he held sway.

The winged dragon, now no larger than a hawk, emitted another great cloud of incense that enveloped them in its fragrant fumes. Gradually the space around the car grew brighter, until Jeremiah could distinguish the gems on Marduk's starry cloak. It was as if the moon were rising within this space, but on the first night of the month of Nisan the moon did not rise at that hour. The light must be issuing from another source. Samgar Nebo's voice vibrated with suppressed excitement as he announced to his master:

"The messengers are approaching, Marduk. The trinities of powers from whom they come are holding themselves in readiness."

"Whom does Nabu bring?" asked Marduk.

"Those who are under my influence," replied Samgar, deputizing for Nabu; "those who are light and airy. The Water-Bearer—your planning in solitude among the nations. The Twins—your omniscient scepticism, which carries you to your destination through *Soss* and *Ner* and *Sar* and the cosmic year. The Fishes—the deep humility of your supreme arrogance when you enter the lower cavern. Under their sign you rise when you descend."

"Whom does Ishtar bring?"

"Those who are under my influence," replied the charioteer on behalf of Ishtar; "those who thrive and in whom you take pleasure. The Goat—under whose sign you sow the seed. The Bull—under whose sign you tend the hidden crops. The Virgin—under whose sign you gather the harvest. For she gives birth to the son by whom you will be perfected."

"Whom does Ninurtu bring?"

"Those who are under my influence," was the reply; "those who are unconquerable and cause you torment. The Crab—which scatters you and fills you with fear. The Scorpion—which gathers your hatred and sets you like a leech on the artery of the world. The Scales of the Judgment of Death—on them you will lie."

"Whom does Nergal bring, that executes my will?"

"Those who are under my influence: the glowing trinity of fire. The Lion—the heart-bright prodigality of your power. The Archer—the purposeful frugality of your power. The Ram—you yourself under your own sign! Your enterprise, your work, the question to which you supply the answer."

Jeremiah tried with his newly opened eyes to penetrate the inner nature of these beings whose home was in the girdle of the zodiac, but the scenes that were enclosed within them could not be interpreted in an earthly way as could those of the planets. They eluded his scrutiny and all he saw was little groups of stars, embedded in light clouds, whose shapes had no relation to the mysterious names they bore. Did the Water-Bearer really pour broad beams of infinite force from his pitcher? Were the Fishes swimming in the heavenly Euphrates? Did the Archer loose an arrow from his bow? Jeremiah could no longer imagine what he saw or see what he imagined. In a blissful state of infinite peace he floated on the step of Marduk's chariot as a man of the sky, formed of the substance of the stars. And as his eyes had been opened that he might see things previously hidden from him, so his ears were now opened to hear. Again Samgar Nebo began to speak in his velvety voice:

"Now that the four and the twelve are gathered round your godhead, be graciously pleased to sound the keynote!"

Nebuchadnezzar's voice was not beautiful, but high-pitched and of little volume. He seemed to be ashamed of it, for the note he sang was short and discordant. It was answered by a low humming from above, but before Jeremiah could analyse this sound into its individual notes the music of numerous harps and lyres joined in from below. The priests of E-sagila were reproducing with their earthly instruments the music of the temples of the sky, and a faint shadow from this world dimmed the rapture of Jeremiah.

Samgar warned his master:

"Your star, O Marduk, is climbing to its zenith."

Nebuchadnezzar sat erect. Even his imperturbable calm

seemed to be shaken at such a tremendous moment, when the destiny of the world was about to be determined amid the stars of space. His heavy breathing could be heard as he began softly to utter an incantation, but with the last words his voice grew louder and more peremptory until it rolled like thunder.

"Ye four, whose fifth and Lord I am! Sun and moon, who are now in concealment! Ye twelve who are turned towards me! Ye myriads who are turned away from me! And Thou above all, O Ram, servant of my age under whom I shine! Hearken unto me! I who am called on earth Nebuchadnezzar, son of Nabopolassar, in this hour of destiny I bind you to me with all your forces, to me, my sons, and my house, for a *Soss*, for a *Ner*, for a *Sar*, for a cosmic year I bind you! Let me be the sieve through which trickle the destinies that are under your sway, so that through war and peace my work may be perfected!"

Marduk had uttered the incantation which was to introduce the new cosmic spring. His heavy breathing could again be heard in the sudden deathly silence of space. Jeremiah did not at first realize that it was the godless evocation which had startled him out of his ecstasy and pulled him back to earth. His immediate feeling was one of disappointment, which changed to uneasy doubt and finally grew into the definite suspicion that this vision of the stars was not a true vision, any more than his journey through the Egyptian realm of the dead had been a true vision. If the revealing thought had crept into his mind in Amenti that death was tedious, he was now beset by the no less illuminating thought: "The stars are vanity." The star-beings that he had imagined he saw a few minutes before amid the incense fumes of the Chamber of Destiny had disappeared, had again become mere gleaming sparks in the nocturnal sky. Their icy solitude now seemed to him almost blasphemous; the measured harmony of those who were absorbed in and filled only with themselves was infamous. If the stars were heavenly hosts of angels, then they had forgotten their Lord and were singing the praises of their own self-delusion. In their twelve shining palaces of the sky they resembled puffed-up servants adorning not the King, but themselves, with borrowed powers and forces. Just as the Ḳās in Amenti were merely masks to hide a clamorous emptiness, so the stars in Babylon's vision were merely masks emitting false and ineffectual rays. Jeremiah remembered an old saying of which his father had been fond: "Israel has no star of destiny," and for the first time he understood its significance. At that moment he knew that the four and the five and the seven and the twelve that were turned towards Marduk, together with the ten thousand times ten thousand that were turned away from him, were only a world of delusion between the joy of God and the sufferings of Coniah, which were for him the two great realities.

Could you not be silent, man of Judah? Did the restless urge within your heart again spur you on to stir up trouble? The King of Babylon had raised you, the insignificant man of Anathoth, above man's stature, appointing you to be his witness when he determined the destiny of the world amid the stars of space. You should have been proud of such elevation and have held your peace! But how could Jeremiah have held his peace, when a true vision broke through the vision of the stars before his eyes? He saw Coniah, the boy-king, chained to a dank and massive wall with wrists and ankles chafed and bloody. In his misery, where he no longer had to hide his agony from the eyes of a mocking foe,

Coniah whimpered softly like a child and called again and again into the empty air upon the name of Jeremiah. But other faces obtruded themselves in front of Coniah. Was that not Josiah with his twisted lips in the days of his great pleading? Then he thought he could recognize the young Zedekiah, groaning as he pressed his clenched fists against his eyes. The face of Coniah changed continuously into a hundred different faces that Jeremiah knew and yet did not know, but all of them belonged to men who had been defeated and cast aside and were as if living in Ninurtu. Jeremiah heard his name being called incessantly. It had to penetrate many thick walls before it reached his ear, but in the voice of Coniah, which sounded so muffled and yet so clear, there were a thousand other voices, an army of captives, an ocean of torment. He could no longer restrain his heart and dared an unprecedented thing. He spoke to Marduk when the latter had climbed to his zenith and entered into possession of his cosmic year.

"O King," he whispered, "as you bind to yourself at this hour the powers and forces of the stars, remember the man who lies bound within your city, remember the youth Coniah! Be graciously pleased to raise him up out of his affliction and to set him at your table!"

The holy rite was not yet concluded, for a fragment of the incense dragon was still glowing and the royal star had not left its zenith. It was therefore to be assumed that Marduk would ignore for the time being the grave offence of his witness. If that was what Samgar Nebo thought, he must have been surprised to hear Nebuchadnezzar utter the command: "Answer him!"

After a brief pause his voice came from the darkness above Jeremiah's head:

"A cosmic year lasts sixty *Sars.* What is man that Marduk should remember him?"

"The sufferings of an innocent creature," whispered Jeremiah, "last more than a cosmic year."

"Answer him!" ordered Marduk for the second time.

Again there was a short pause before the reply came, this time more emphatically:

"Tell me the history of a crushed worm since the beginning of creation and I will prove to you that your foot did not tread upon an innocent creature."

Jeremiah had to summon all his strength to control his trembling limbs, which no longer partook of the quality of the stars. "Is there then in the law of the stars no room for compassion on a man in fetters?"

Marduk's jewelled cloak jingled. For the third time he commanded: "Answer him!"

The answer came now without hesitation:

"In the law of the stars there is no compassion other than the preordained compassion."

Jeremiah raised his eyes to the faint shimmer of the Milky Way, which still showed above the Chamber of Destiny. Samgar Nebo had spoken the truth. How could the stars above, those that were known and those that were still uncounted, be free to exercise compassion, which was an attribute of the one true God? The multiple deities of the nocturnal sky were but gleaming slaves pretending to be masters in the temple of E-sagila. They may have been assigned the power of controlling the flow and ebb of the tides, health and sickness, birth and death, or Adonai might use them to pour out over the earth the waters of the flood and the fires of heaven. But they were servants of the Lord, not the sources of His power, and all knowledge which took them as its basis was therefore false. They were less free than the son of David in his prison cell, for whose sake Jeremiah uttered the words that he now spoke. Though he knew well what it meant to speak as he did in Marduk's holiest sanctuary, yet he could not help himself. Even before he came forth from the womb he had been sanctified as a prophet among the nations, and he now proclaimed to the star-worshippers of Babylon what he had proclaimed to the inhabitants of the realm of the dead in Egypt:

"Hear ye, Marduk and all the stars, the Lord our God, the Lord is One!"

The voice in which Jeremiah made this tremendous avowal was neither solemn nor loud. He spoke gently, as if abashed at having said what he could not refrain from saying. The stars took heed. Marduk pensively turned his head with its high crown towards him.

Perhaps the prophet's life was saved by the fact that only Marduk and his councillor heard the words that he had uttered in the starry chamber of E-temen-anki. At that moment the last ashes fell from the wire frame of the winged dragon. The four doors were opened and the brotherhood of Nabu could be seen waiting with burning torches to fetch Marduk from the chamber and escort him down to the temple which was called "the Bond of Union of Mankind," where he would spend the remainder of the fateful night keeping watch. At the foot of the staircase Nebuchadnezzar paused and turned to the foreign soothsayer whom he had appointed as witness to the dawn of spring. In the bluish light of the torches of Nabu, his face looked like the phantom spirit of his own planet. His lips moved, but the words did not come.

His curious yet mocking eyes rested on Jeremiah's face, and at last he murmured two words which were a command: "Return home!"

The caravan to which Jeremiah had attached himself encamped on the bank of the Euphrates at the place where the road turned off towards the west. When the merchants had fallen asleep, he climbed in the bright moonlight up the steps which led to the ancient inscription and found the cleft untouched by human hand and sealed as he had left it. It needed an effort to extract the two flat stones which he had inserted, but he found them clean and dry; neither rain nor trickling water had found its way into the crevice, there was no trace of any animal's having been there, and neither ant nor worm had forced its way in between the stones. Yet the firm white linen, which seemed to have been woven to last for an age, had completely decayed in the course of the year during which it had lain in its clean, dry, and protected hiding-place. Jeremiah held the costly fabric in his hands with disgust, as if it were a putrescent body. Frayed, tattered, and yellowed, there was nothing left but a threadbare web that could have been concealed in a clenched fist. There was nothing to show what had marred it. Jeremiah sat down on the bank of the Euphrates and stared at the babbling water, with the faded remnants of the linen lying on his lap and wisps of mist from the river curling round him in the moonlight. The parable of the loin-cloth was revealed to him as the parable of the clay in the potter's hand had once been revealed to him. The snow-white cloth had been wound round his body, encircling his waist, where the nerve-fibres formed a living network. When this contact was lost the linen decayed in some mysterious way. In His parable the

Lord had wrapped Israel round Him as Jeremiah had wrapped the cloth round his loins. When it was near to His heart it remained pure, intact, and white as snow. When banished from the presence of God, within a short space it became defiled and was destroyed.

Jeremiah wondered whether this interpretation applied to the ten thousand exiles in Babylon. It was like a load on his heart that, in his vain attempt to save Coniah, he had avoided the captives lest he incur their displeasure. Restlessly he turned the tattered tissue this way and that. Perhaps the parable had other meanings which he had not been able to fathom! As the wearer of the loin-cloth, had he not been appointed by the Lord to bear Jerusalem's fate upon his shoulders? Through his instrumentality the Lord had once more granted a respite. Yet he had accompanied Coniah to Babylon, divested himself of the loin-cloth, and closed his heart to thoughts of Jerusalem and the Temple. He had put his trust in Zedekiah, the devoted pupil whom he had helped to ascend the throne of David. Now he was holding in his hand a piece of marred linen. What was happening in Jerusalem?

The hours crept by all too slowly for the impatient traveller. The greater the distance he put between himself and Babylon, the deeper grew his anxiety for the exiles. On the back of the camel that had been allotted to him he wrote a rough draft of a message which he copied out that night by the light of the lamp in his tent. It was a fairly long letter addressed "to the elders in captivity."

"Build ye houses," it began, "and dwell in them, and plant gardens, and eat the fruit of them. Take ye wives, and beget sons and daughters, and take wives for your sons, and give your daughters to husbands, that they may bear sons and daughters, that ye may be increased there, and not diminished. And seek the peace of the city, whither the Lord has caused you to be carried away captives, and pray for it: for in the peace thereof shall ye have peace. . . ."

He urged them not to cleave to vain hopes, not to let themselves be deceived by the prophets and diviners in their midst or put their trust in dreams. He warned them that their exile would be of long duration and would not come to an end until the downfall of Babylon.

After Jeremiah had concluded his epistle, he preserved it in a place of safety until they reached Riblah, where he found an opportunity of sending it to Babylon. When it had left his hands, however, he became a prey to sudden fears. He had written in his letter: "Seek the peace of the city, whither the Lord has caused you to be carried away captives, and pray for it"! Pray for your jailers! Seek the peace of your destroyers! Bless the arch-enemy who hates you! Had he really written down these words, which upset the order of the world? He was asking the human heart to belie itself. What nation would not have stoned a man in its burning wrath for such an exhortation? Why had he not written: "Pray day and night to the Lord for the downfall of Babylon and the day when you will return home"?

Jeremiah knew that in asking the exiles to pray for Babylon he had issued a wanton challenge to man's nature, and that retribution for these words would surely be demanded.

25

The Yoke

FOR days Jerusalem had been living in a whirl of festivities. The citizens had made a strenuous effort to erase from their minds the memory of the siege by the army of Babylon, which had been so much less onerous than they had anticipated; if anyone ventured to mention it, he was angrily silenced. Festivities served as an agreeable antidote to bitter memories, and Jerusalem had in these days good grounds for rejoicing. In the first place there was the radiant young King Zedekiah, who far excelled Jehoiakim even as a builder, since his works were intended not for the satisfaction of his own desires but for the welfare of the whole nation. Hardly a year had gone by since their misfortune (of which they preferred not to speak), and already Zedekiah had strengthened the walls of Jerusalem, supplemented them by new rings, and added a number of magnificent towers and bulwarks. A feat without compare, the very sight of which was overwhelming! Anyone who refused to recognize that Zion was now impregnable was looked upon as a traitor.

The completion of the new fortifications was not the most important reason for the joyful celebrations. The King had been responsible for an even greater achievement. By a brilliant stroke of diplomacy the youthful Zedekiah had succeeded in doing something which had not been possible even in more auspicious times. He had invited the kings of the neighbouring countries to visit him at his court in Jerusalem. The unexpected had happened: they had all accepted his invitation. Even mighty rulers like the Phœnician sea-kings of Tyre and Sidon were not too proud to honour the little kingdom so soon after its defeat by Babylon. The kings of Moab, Edom, and Ammon, hostile neighbours who had despised Israel since ancient times, even appeared highly flattered at receiving Zedekiah's hospitable message, and each of them had prepared to set out for Jerusalem with much pomp and ceremony. Success was crowned by the acceptance of Hophra, the kindly god of Noph. It was true that he was not present in his own divine person, but he sent his only brother, who stood very close to the throne, that he might preside as Pharaoh's deputy at the sealing of a new pact of peace between kings and nations. Six kings, whose power extended from the cataracts of the Nile to the isles of the north, from the oases of Arabia to the coast of Libya, were about to recognize the humbled capital of Judah as the focus of world events. If Zedekiah in his wisdom and with the help of Pharaoh should succeed in welding all these kings and peoples into one power and one will, then a new world order would have been created before which even Babylon would have to bend the knee. At the same time, however, Zedekiah had sent an envoy to Marduk with rich gifts and assurances of his most faithful devotion. No prophet could now complain that the House of David was thwarting the holy plans of the Lord. The ways of God were good ways. No one could charge Him with hostility to His people, and He was undoubtedly content with His servant Zedekiah. As the shaggy prophets stood in the pulpits of the outer courtyard there was no thought in their minds of scolding or threats. They had long since forgotten the last days of Jehoiakim, when they had been unable to restrain the bitter accusations and warnings with which their hearts had been full. They were again prophesying nothing but good, and their vigorous voices were mingled with the general exultation.

Banners and flags, palm leaves and olive branches, wreaths and decorations, adorned the gates, towers, battlements, and houses of the city. The six royal guests had been preceded by royal gifts. Herds of oxen and flocks of sheep, each yearling a splendid specimen of the ancient art of breeding, had been furnished as a sacrifice to the Lord, the strange invisible God whom the visitors were preparing to honour in His Temple. The presents sent by the kings to the House of David were on public view—several strings of thoroughbred horses and swift camels, together with rows of war chariots and state coaches, before which admiring crowds were to be seen all day long. Itubaal, the King of Tyre, had brought with him a skilfully wrought model of a seagoing vessel in precious wood, which was set up in the first court of the guard before the amazed and enthusiastic eyes of the people of Jerusalem, but it was only a miniature of the actual gift which was waiting with a full crew in the port of Tyre for the orders of its new owner. During these festive days nobody went to bed. The streets were crowded all day and all night.

The culmination of the celebrations was a banquet—at which the public was allowed to be present as spectators—offered by Zedekiah to his guests on the day before their departure in the palace known as the House of the Forest of Lebanon. He had chosen the spacious pillared hall of this house partly because of its venerable age and great fame, but chiefly because it was open to one side and the people could therefore see what was happening. There were more spectators than the court of the guard could hold, and even beyond the walls of the palace there were people standing with open mouths though they could see nothing at all and could have no idea of what was going on. Among those who had succeeded in gaining admission was Jeremiah, who stood wedged amid the throng and unrecognized. He had returned only a few hours before and had scarcely had time to seek a lodging, which he eventually found in the lower town in the house of a saddler. It had been his intention to go first of all to the Temple, where he had hoped to meet Baruch, but it was useless trying to force his way through the crowd that was going in a different direction, so he gave up the attempt and allowed himself to be swept along to the court of the House of the Forest of Lebanon, where he had now been waiting for what seemed an age in a state of complete exhaustion and with no chance of getting away.

Like all the others, he stared through the double row of guards, carrying their golden shields, who occupied the broad steps of the pillared hall, but the chamber was in darkness and it was not until after sunset that their hours of waiting were rewarded. Gradually the hall was illumined by numerous golden seven-branched candelabra with lamps of different colours, and a reddish-golden light shed its rays over the spectators too. Between the cedar columns they saw a mighty dais upon which the royal table had been set up like an altar. It was covered with light-blue cloths and the plates and goblets were of gold, all from the treasure of the sons of David which had been hidden in the vaults of the palace and thus saved from the looting hands of Babylon. Seven thrones were set at the table, which was in the shape of a semicircle, each some distance apart from its neighbour. Garlands of foliage hung from the ceiling, wreaths had been twined round the pillars, and the floor was strewn with fresh flowers. From these fresh flowers Jeremiah guessed that Hamutal had returned to Jerusalem.

Behind each of the thrones stood the retinue of the king who was to sit on it. The spectators saw the stiff purple robes of the Phœnicians, with their hundreds of embroidered silver dolphins, the seven-coloured capes of the Egyptians, and the flowing burnouses of Ammon and Moab. Tall conical hats contrasted with coloured cylindrical ones, with jewelled caps and two-horned, gleaming helmets. After a long fanfare of trumpets, which was answered from each of the towers, the kings all entered together with swift step from the throne-room of Solomon. Each of them stood in front of his throne clad in the colour of his house, the same royal colour being repeated in the robes of the retinue which stood behind him. Zedekiah, radiant with youth, was in light blue and stood as host in the centre of his guests. On his left was Pharaoh's brother, on his right Itubaal of Tyre. Next to Itubaal were Sidon and Moab, next to Egypt were Ammon and Edom. The servants of David hastened along with covered dishes and pitchers which they handed to the servants of the various kings, for each king was served by his own chamberlains. Simultaneously the High Priest in the Temple was carrying to the altar the portion of the royal banquet reserved as an offering to the Lord.

The kings raised their hands and began the feast with a solemn breaking of bread. The spectacle offered to the eyes of the people was indeed a solemn one, for the guests sat upright and rigid and took only a tiny piece from each dish, putting it slowly to their mouths and eating it as if they were fulfilling a duty towards their subjects but were not enjoying it. After each morsel they washed their fingers wearily in gold finger bowls that were constantly changed. But they partook more freely of the wine of Sharon, which stood before them in gold goblets. The royal table was wrapped in silence, since the words of a king are far-reaching and portentous, for which reason they are best left unsaid. The inquisitive throng of spectators was also silent, because they were straining their ears to catch words which might flash like lightning through the darkness of the world. The kings, however, chewed, drank, and maintained a cautious and stubborn silence. The fact that seven kingdoms had gathered together in the persons of their rulers spoke louder and more clearly than words, and all that could be heard was the soft music of concealed psalteries, flutes, and singers.

After his endless journey and hours of waiting Jeremiah was almost fainting with fatigue. He had caught a fever on the shores of the Euphrates and his veins seemed to be filled with fire. The scene in the brightly lit hall wavered before his eyes as his head began to reel. The anxiety by which he was oppressed had not yet yielded to a clear understanding of his future course of action. What had happened to the clean linen when he removed it from his body? It had become marred and had fallen into decay!

When the last dish had been taken away by the servants, a tall, slender man came to the side of Zedekiah and set before him a great goblet which he filled with spiced red wine. As he raised his head, Jeremiah saw the dark-skinned face of an Ethiopian! Was it possible that this staid chamberlain who moved so sedately could be Ebed-melech, his other pupil, the little dancing Moor with the restless limbs who had asked so many questions?

Zedekiah raised the heavy goblet of the House of David, set it briefly to his lips, and then sent it round the table before the eyes of the people. Jeremiah felt a sudden compression of the heart. Was this the Cup of Fury? Just as it had happened in his dream, the goblet had returned to the centre of the table after each of the kings had drunk from it. But their faces did not become convulsed with agony; rather did they smile contentedly as if they had achieved something of which they could be proud. They rose from their seats and grasped one another by the hand in brotherly fashion, presenting a picture of unity for Jerusalem to witness. The music was hushed and the silence grew more expectant. If it had not been for the fever that raged in Jeremiah's brain, Adonai would at that moment have found it difficult to speak through the mouth of His prophet. It made Jeremiah oblivious of everything and sapped his resistance. His voice pierced the stillness, not in a tone of passionate declamation or entreaty such as had often held his audience rooted to the spot, but in a weary, monotonous chant such as beggars use to excite compassion:

"I have made the earth, the man and the beast that are upon the ground, by my great power and by my outstretched arm, and have given it unto whom it seemed meet unto me. . . ."

The people round Jeremiah, who imagined that this chant was a song of blessing for the King's banquet, pushed back a little in order to give him more room and encouraged him with murmurs to continue. The fevered prophet went on in his singing tone:

"And now have I given all these lands into the hand of Nebuchadnezzar the King of Babylon, my servant, and the beasts of the field have I given him also to serve him. . . ."

The people could not believe their ears and looked at one another in astonishment. Even the kings turned their heads in curiosity. But to the fevered eyes of Jeremiah the semicircle of kings, who were still clasping one another's hands, seemed to be a team of seven yoked oxen walking before the plough with heads lowered and arched chests. In his monotonous tone of lament he continued to chant the words of Adonai:

"And it shall come to pass, that the nation and kingdom which will not serve the same Nebuchadnezzar the King of Babylon, and that will not put their neck under the yoke of the King of Babylon, that nation will I punish with the sword, and with the famine, and with the pestilence, until I have consumed them by his hand."

The festive throng could still hardly believe that they had heard aright. Such a chant on such an evening was so monstrous that none of them would admit to himself that he had understood. Had the kings heard the words? There were signs of restlessness in the banqueting hall, where the guests were whispering with Zedekiah, but from the crowd of spectators came a cry which opportunely broke the painful tension:

"He is possessed! . . . He is a sick man. . . ."

The words brought a feeling of relief to Jeremiah. "Verily," he thought, "I am a sick man!" Then the fever took hold of him again and he would have sunk to the ground if those nearest to him had not caught him in their arms.

Jeremiah did not allow his sickness to master him. On the following morning he rose, poured a bucket of cold water over his shivering body, descended to the workshop of the saddler, and purchased an old, worm-eaten yoke together with a clumsy, heavy cudgel such as was used by drovers. Mocking eyes stared after him as he staggered out of the workshop, supporting himself on his stick and almost collapsing under the weight of the yoke.

Jerusalem was even more animated than it had been on the previous day, for Zedekiah was taking ceremonious farewell of his royal guests. It was a busy day for Zedekiah and his court, and also for the inhabitants of Jerusalem, who did not intend to miss any of the magnificent spectacles provided by the departure of each of the kings. Very few women stayed at home that day to prepare the family meal; though it was contrary to custom, dignity, and good taste for women and maidens to show themselves publicly in the streets, they refused to let pass an opportunity such as that generation would never see again. They walked about in couples or in small groups, dressed in their best, their bracelets jingling, their cheeks rouged, their eyebrows plucked and replaced by a painted line, and their finger nails stained with gold varnish. To increase their seductiveness they wore high heels to their delicate sandals and little silver bells round their ankles. It was not in order to be displeasing in the sight of the Lord that the Daughter of Zion adorned herself with such special care, but in order to be pleasing in the sight of the strangers who had come to Jerusalem in the retinue of their royal masters.

Since the mothers and grown-up sisters were not at home as they usually were, the children who were left without supervision had also gone into the streets and an army of urchins was running about the city looking for mischief. These street urchins were the first to gather with screeches of joy round the bowed figure of Jeremiah as he staggered along under the weight of his yoke, and they followed him like the tail of a comet. They did not know whether he was a clown who was about to show his amusing tricks, a man possessed by evil spirits, or merely a harmless fool, but any of these three possibilities promised to provide an equally welcome entertainment for the exulting children. They were joined by their laughing elders, and soon there was a large crowd following in the train of Jeremiah curious to see where he was making for. A few of the more responsible citizens, recognizing the prophet whose predictions had so recently been fulfilled in the days of affliction that had befallen Jerusalem, shook their heads sadly at the man whom Adonai had sanctified but who had now fallen so low as to expose himself to the laughter and jeers of the populace. It was a repellent spectacle on such a day of triumph. But that was the way of these prophets! They wanted to attract attention and make themselves conspicuous at any price, no matter how low they stooped! The worthy citizens turned away in disgust from the inventive charlatan. Jeremiah forced himself to continue on his way like an apathetic beast being driven to the sacrifice, nor did he stop to consider whether his sacrifice would bear fruit or be futile. His soul was burdened only with the dull conviction that it was necessary and that he must not fail.

When they arrived at the gates of the Temple the scoffing crowd was dispersed by the guards, but it was not until a priest of one of the higher orders had recognized Jeremiah that he was allowed, though with a certain hesitation, to enter the precincts. On account of the attractions elsewhere, the Temple was fairly empty, except for the priests, and only a few small groups of people were waiting to join in communal prayer or in case there should be something to hear from one of the pulpits. Before Jeremiah had reached the gallery, Baruch came running towards him. The news of Jeremiah's return having got about, Baruch had been wandering all round the city trying to discover the whereabouts of his master. An expression of bewilderment came into his eyes as he saw the yoke round Jeremiah's neck, and he scrutinized Jeremiah's features apprehensively. It was a melancholy and uneasy reunion. Not only Jerusalem, but Baruch, too, had changed. The understanding disciple, who had possessed such a keen insight into Jeremiah's heart, appeared now to be at a complete loss; at sight of Baruch's embarrassment Jeremiah realized that the Lord had estranged from him even this last friend.

"The city is in festal array. . . . And Jeremiah . . . what is the burden that Jeremiah is bearing? . . . What has befallen my master? . . ."

"I have seen that which is about to befall Jerusalem," said Jeremiah brusquely, "and I bear the burden that has been laid upon me."

There was note of protest in Baruch's voice as he asked: "Are the things that have been done in Jerusalem not good? Has the King not brought great benefits to the city and the nation? Never again will an enemy dare to disturb the peace of Zion."

"Who knows what the King is bringing to his people?" replied Jeremiah hoarsely. "Good can turn to evil as evil can turn to good."

Baruch was silent, and his master felt that, like all the others, he thought the prophet's mind was distracted and overwrought. Gradually a curious crowd again assembled round him, for the rumour had spread that the eternally refractory prophet was not even now content with the glorious days that Jerusalem was experiencing, but had thought out a particularly startling parable for his homecoming. Among those who disapproved were Ahikam and his two sons, who gazed with pained eyes at their old friend for whom they had fought so courageously in the days of Jehoiakim. They could not imagine what he intended by his eccentric action at a time when the whole of Jerusalem was rejoicing at the successful conclusion of a work that had been blessed by God. They all thought as Baruch did, or rather, Baruch thought as they did. The keen-minded sons of Shaphan were agreed among themselves that Zedekiah's alliance with the six kings would lead to their ultimate salvation, and they had actively assisted both by word and by deed in its preparation. And now this hothead, this man with a caustic tongue who could not tolerate anything that did not spring from his own mind, had returned from Babylon and wanted to disparage their achievement! Jeremiah was more alone than he had ever been, but he was careful not to dispute with them. At last an elderly dignitary joined the throng, who blinked mildly at Jeremiah's yoke and rubbed his hands with a chilly benignity. Zephaniah, the First Keeper of the Door, formed a striking contrast to his predecessor, Pashur. His manner was propitiatory and soothing, though not without a certain artfulness. He did not look directly at Jeremiah, but his words were obviously intended for him. The raving and ecstatic prophets, he declared, whom it was his duty to supervise, would find in him their most solicitous friend so long as they kept their ecstasy within suitable bounds, did not cause offence, and, in short, did not inconvenience him. Any inconvenience due to their vexatious conduct was liable to make him, who was generally of a calm and peaceful temperament, as excited as themselves. Having warned Jeremiah in this oblique fashion, he pointed to the steps of the gallery where one of the prophets to whom he had just referred was preaching to a small audience. The new Keeper of the Door mentioned the name of Hananiah and singled him out for praise as a happy example of good behaviour and moderation.

Leaning heavily on his stick, Jeremiah approached the pulpit of his old companion, who looked vigorous and in the best of health, for he knew how to use his gift wisely without letting himself be swayed too far in one direction. In the days of defeat Hananiah had held aloof and could not be charged with inaccurate predictions. Neither had he grown hollow-eyed in the service of the Lord, but looked more robust than ever. He still carried his shaggy cloak over his arm as a ready concession to his prophetic calling and his voice was no less radiant than his countenance.

"Thus speaketh the Lord of hosts," he cried, "the God of Israel, saying: I have broken the yoke of the King of Babylon. Within two full years will I bring again into this place all the vessels of the Lord's house, that Nebuchadnezzar, King of Babylon, took away from this place, and carried them to Babylon. And I will bring again to this place Jeconiah the son of Jehoiakim, King of Judah, with all the captives of Judah, that went into Babylon, saith the Lord, for I will break the yoke of the King of Babylon . . ."

He broke off in the middle of a sentence as he recognized Jeremiah, and reddened. His lips twitched and the words seemed to stick in his throat with shame and hesitation. The sophisticated Hananiah had suddenly become like a boy caught doing wrong by his master. Jeremiah, however, greeted him respectfully with his hand on his heart.

"Amen," he said in a calm voice. "May the Lord do so, may the Lord perform the words which you have prophesied, Hananiah! May He bring Coniah and all those who were carried away captive back from Babylon to this place."

Hananiah breathed more freely after this sigh that came

from the heart of Jeremiah. At the unexpected sight of the returned prophet, whom he had thought far away, a cold tremor had run through him. He had expected words that would put him to shame, anticipating a bitter reproof from the incorruptible and unyielding man of Anathoth, and Jeremiah's mild language filled him with gratitude. He, too, put his hand upon his heart and bowed.

"Behold, O people of Jerusalem!" he cried in a flattering tone. "Jeremiah has returned home from his journey across the world, Jeremiah in whom dwells the truth of the Lord. . . ."

This announcement was greeted with a murmur of surprise that was occasioned less by the presence of the prophet than by the yoke he was wearing. Jeremiah ignored the flattery.

"Let Hananiah hear the word that I speak in his ears and in the ears of all the people. The prophets that have been before me, and before you of old, prophesied both against many countries and against great kingdoms, of war, and of evil, and of pestilence. But whether a prophet prophesy war or peace, evil or good, not by the prophecy will it be known that the Lord hath truly sent him, but by that which comes to pass, even though it be long after him. It is hard to know if the words of the Lord have been rightly heard. . . . May the truth be with you, Hananiah, and not with me!"

While Jeremiah was thus sadly questioning the whole art of prophecy with the modest caution of an experienced master, Hananiah seemed to be sunk in a reverie. Suddenly, however, his figure, which had become slightly corpulent, jerked itself erect and his features became tense as if the voice of Adonai had just come to him like a lightning flash. He swiftly stepped down from the pulpit and, before Jeremiah could realize what he was about to do, he had taken the yoke off his neck. Then he held it high above his head so that all the people could see it, and his face grew purple with the effort to break it. The veins and sinews stood out on his neck and he looked like a Samson trying to rend the pillars asunder. The worm-eaten yoke creaked, split, and at last broke into two pieces. Hananiah had performed not only a symbolic action, but also a miracle of strength. Panting for breath, he exulted:

"Thus saith the Lord . . . Even so . . . . will I break the yoke . . . of Nebuchadnezzar, King of Babylon . . . from the neck of all nations . . . within the space of two full years."

The people exulted with Hananiah. By his action he had done more than merely predict. He had forestalled the future and, with the help of the Lord, shown it the way. The broken yoke was a significant symbol that could not but affect the destiny of Judah. Even Jeremiah felt a strange sense of relief. His heart had always been inclined towards Hananiah, though he had never been able to put his trust in him. But now he was ready to believe unreservedly in the man whose hand had taken from him his dreadful burden. Body and soul rejoiced in a feeling of freedom. The miracle-worker basked in the praises and blessings that were showered upon him, though his eyes kept wandering anxiously towards Jeremiah. The latter once more said: "Amen!" and, like a brother, put both hands on the shoulders of the prophet with whom he had served at the King's table as a boy. Then he went gladly on his way, though as a prophet he had suffered defeat before his fellow-men. He blessed this defeat. Would that the Lord might approve and that it might be complete and final! Baruch followed him dejectedly, suffering from the incomprehensible behaviour and failure of his master.

They turned towards the southern wall of the outer court, but before they had reached it Jeremiah gave a sudden start, moaned aloud, and began to stagger about. Baruch leapt to his side and held him tight. The eyes into which he looked were wide open and staring with horror, while a hoarse, feverish voice that he did not recognize groaned:

"The yoke of wood is broken . . . but the yoke of iron is already forged. . . . Henceforth I must bear the iron yoke. . . ."

Jeremiah hid his face on Baruch's shoulder. He saw Hananiah dying a horrible death, his body that had been so strong and full of health twisting in fiery agony. Large brown worms were crawling everywhere through his cracked skin and twining out of his seething entrails. Baruch did not know what Jeremiah was seeing in his vision, but only heard him sigh again and again:

"Unhappy Hananiah! . . . Woe to thee, Hananiah! . . . Why hast thou done this thing? . . ."

26

Zedekiah and His House

FROM now on Jeremiah wore an iron-sheathed yoke round his neck when he appeared in the streets or in the Temple, and he felt the weight of it all the more since he had grown very frail after his bout of fever. None the less, he took it off only when he entered the inner court or a dwelling. Like Hananiah he was anticipating the future, and his wearing of the iron yoke was a symbolic act to influence the destiny of Judah, though in a very different sense from Hananiah's breaking of the wooden one. Humbly he accepted the most ominous promptings of the Lord as immutable predictions, and by his own sufferings he forestalled those that were to befall Jerusalem. In this way he was making amends for the guilt of the nation even before the account was presented. Perhaps his sufferings would help to diminish to some small extent the great affliction through which the land would have to pass; perhaps (though to follow up such a thought was in itself a sin) his insignificant but constant agony might even excite the Lord's pity!

Some time had passed since Jeremiah's return, yet from day to day he kept putting off his visit to the King, his former pupil. For this hesitation he found many reasons in his heart. Zedekiah's confession after his return from Egypt still rang in his ears: "To my father and mother I owe my life . . . but to my teacher I owe everything else"; and also:

"Henceforth I shall not let you go from my side." The glowing words spoken by the young man in his hour of good fortune must be felt by him, now that he was on the throne, as a binding and burdensome vow. Jeremiah saw that clearly. Nor was it by chance that Zedekiah, for his part, had not sent for his teacher during all these days. He could not but be aware of the eccentric behaviour of Jeremiah, who not only was alone in holding aloof from the general rejoicing at the King's diplomatic and peaceful triumph, but even publicly rebuked him by voluntarily undergoing the torture involved in wearing a yoke round his neck. Thus both Zedekiah's exuberant expression of gratitude and Jeremiah's repellent burden cast a shadow between them that caused them to look forward uneasily to their next meeting. Not until the prophet received a clear command from the Lord, did he set out with a sigh and knock at the gate of the House of Solomon.

The first to receive him in the palace was the unwieldy eunuch of King Josiah, whose flabby face showed no trace of the passage of time. The old chamberlain had transformed himself into a complete Egyptian, not only so far as his costume and manner were concerned, but even in his speech. In Jeremiah he greeted above all the old companion who had been with him in Egypt during the pleasant and easy days at Noph, which was a veritable Garden of Eden compared with the gloom and seriousness of Jerusalem. From the loquacious chatter of the communicative eunuch Jeremiah learned of many trivial matters and one that was of great importance. His Magnificence in Temporary Retirement, the dethroned Jehoahaz, had died suddenly in the old house at Noph, whither he had been graciously allowed to return by Pharaoh. At mention of the house Jeremiah again saw

Zenua sitting in the lotus hall, resting on her right heel and looking up into his face with her characteristic air of gravity. He passed his hand across his eyes. Jehoahaz had been very young! What had been the cause of his death? The eunuch informed him long-windedly that His Magnificence, as Jeremiah well knew, had been accustomed to pass his time carving the elegant and charming objects of Egypt. At first he had confined himself to little chests and ships and cars and such-like, but as he grew more skilful he had tried his hand at copying living models—a little lion, or bull, or ass—and then, yes, and then he had tried human figures, such as an archer or two, a lancer, a boatman, and so on. The chamberlain paused. The presence of the prophet made the offence of his royal master seem more blasphemous than ever. He continued his story in a melancholy and disapproving whisper. Fate had overtaken His Magnificence while he was in the act of carving a wooden figure of the cow-headed Hathor. It had only been a very tiny image, hardly an ell high and only suitable to be used as a child's toy. Yet a small cut in the hand with his knife and Jehoahaz had died from the festering wound before seven days had passed. Not even the Kher-heb, the governor of the western city, had been able to help his protégé with all his draughts and attempts to exorcize the demon responsible for the abscess.

The old chamberlain bowed his head as if, in spite of his hankering for the old days at Noph, he was prepared to listen piously to the moral that a prophet of the Lord was bound to draw from such a divine punishment. But Jeremiah merely requested curtly to be introduced into the presence of the King. He was informed that this was not possible for the moment, as His Majesty was in council with the princes of his court, but the eunuch declared that he would incur a grave rebuke from Hamutal and her daughter-in-law, the young Queen, if he allowed Jeremiah to leave the palace without their being advised of his visit. The Queen Mother asked after him every day and could not understand why he had not been to see her.

The eunuch took the prophet by the hand and waddled along at his side through the inner court of the palace until they reached the women's quarters, which were in the building known as the House of Pharaoh's Daughter. Here he was asked to wait a little while and his guide disappeared inside. The first evening shadows were touching the white walls. Very soon Hamutal herself appeared on the threshold to press her old friend to her heart. She led him to a chamber that was already wrapped in twilight, and there they sat down side by side on a divan. They could not say much to each other. As so frequently at such a reunion, the measure of that which they had in common was less in comparison than that which tended to estrange them after such a long separation. Hamutal sat with her chin supported in her hand and gazed at her son's teacher. Could this emaciated man, she thought, this man with the deep lines round his mouth, be the same gentle youth to whom Josiah had been so attached that he would not allow him to leave his bedside as he lay dying? It was easier for Jeremiah to recognize his kindly patroness, the queen who had protected the woman he loved and had lost a daughter in Zenua. Hamutal had grown very stout, but despite the changes wrought by the years one still would not call her an old woman. Her faded beauty still faintly illumined her features like the last afterglow of sunset. Jeremiah looked down at her shimmering hands, which were as white and rounded as when he had last seen them. When the two had said the little that could be said without touching what it was not possible to put into words, Hamutal asked with a smile:

"Why does the dear companion of our days at Noph scorn to share our bread now that we have returned to Jerusalem?"

A tense look came into Jeremiah's eyes.

"Is it the will of the King that I should share his bread in this palace?"

Hamutal was startled at this earnest question, and Jeremiah felt that he had invested with a painful significance a friendly remark that was intended only as a sign of affection. She was silent, obviously seeking for words with which to defend her son from the reproach of faithlessness. When she did speak, it was only to depress the prophet even more:

"The King is grateful to his teacher."

Grateful! Jeremiah thought of Zedekiah's words: "But to my teacher I owe everything else!" He deprecated Hamutal's feeble rejoinder with a gesture.

"A boy sitting at his teacher's feet is one thing; a king seated on the throne is another," he said. Hamutal had been thinking only of the instruction he had given to her son, not of Zedekiah's elevation to the throne, which had also been Jeremiah's work.

Their conversation was interrupted by the entrance of serving-women with lamps and flat earthenware bowls containing heavily scented narcissi, which they put on the table. Behind them was a young woman, who started at sight of the stranger and remained standing at the door.

"Maacha!" cried Hamutal. "Let not the Queen be afraid! This is the loyal friend of Josiah and Zedekiah sitting at my side."

Maacha timidly came nearer. Her almost immature figure, her hovering step, her shy reserve of manner—all this gave her the appearance of a young girl, though she had already borne the King two sons and suckled them herself. Jeremiah rose to touch the ground at her feet, but she prevented him by taking his hands and holding them fast. They stood face to face without speaking, looking gravely into each other's eyes like two people who had a presentiment that the future would link their fates together.

Hamutal, however, suddenly became very animated and began to sing her own praises. It had not been easy, she declared, while they were exiled in Noph, to choose from among the princesses of Judah the one who was most suited to be the wife of her son. Yet amid all the misfortune that the Lord had inflicted upon her during her life she had always had a faculty for doing the right thing, and not least in her selection of a daughter-in-law. Maacha seemed to be paying no attention to Hamutal's laudatory remarks. She wrinkled her smooth forehead impatiently, and then suddenly averted her face. Her scrutiny of Jeremiah had apparently allayed some secret fear. When Hamutal continued to praise the virtues of the young Queen in front of Jeremiah, Maacha grew annoyed and rebuked her in a severe tone: "Mother! . . ." But Hamutal had got under way and refused to stop. Had Maacha not borne her husband splendid sons, she asked, and would they not be followed by others, so that the throne of David would be supplied with true kings until the end of time?

"The children!" she cried suddenly. "The children! . . ." And she sprang up as if she had unpardonably forgotten the most important thing. "Shall not our friend see the children of his King?"

She insisted on going herself to bring Zedekiah's sons and introduce them to the prophet. Breathlessly she returned from the inner chambers with a boy holding onto each hand and nurses following behind. The older child, the heir to the throne, who was called Adajah, was four years of age, while the smaller one was not yet three. They both had their father's beautiful large eyes, which he had inherited from Hamutal. When they saw that there was a stranger in the room, the two boys became refractory, tugged at their grandmother's arms, and refused to go any farther. Only by furtively whispered promises could they be persuaded to take another step or two into the room. Jeremiah stooped to regard more closely these youngest descendants of David, whose fate the Lord had not yet revealed to him. Adajah stood his ground and even returned his gaze with the irritation of a proud child that did not like to be inspected by strangers. However, Ichiel, the younger boy, let his mouth droop and burst into a disapproving wail, refusing to be comforted by anything Hamutal said to him. When Jeremiah tried rather clumsily to stroke his hand, his wailing turned to screams of fear that made the walls tremble. At a sign from Maacha the nurses picked up the children and hastily carried them from the scene of the unfortunate introduction. Hamutal had not even had time to ask Adajah the question she had carefully prepared, whether, when he grew older he would not like to have the same teacher as his father. Maacha, who was embarrassed at her child's behaviour, smiled at Jeremiah as if asking his forgiveness, but the latter merely nodded pensively. He seemed to see nothing unusual in the fact that, among all his other afflictions, he had become a bogy of whom children were afraid.

Ebed-melech came to lead Jeremiah into the presence of the King; as the Negro walked ahead, the prophet observed with surprise the sedate step of the former restless dancer who had now become the epitome of dignity and calm. He had grown tall, staid, and composed. It appeared almost as if he had forgotten his teacher who had guided the alien and superstitious child of Cush to the Lord. Jeremiah, however, was mistaken about the changed character of Ebed-melech, for suddenly the latter turned round with eyes that were filled with tears of joy. Snatching Jeremiah's hand, he covered it with kisses, then he continued on his way with the same grave step. He had no command of words with which to express his feelings.

At the door of the King's chamber they encountered the princes who had just left the royal council. They were all new faces with the exception of the old warrior Elnathan, son of Achbor, whom the events of the past year or two had changed profoundly. In place of his fierce and gloomy air there was a look of sadness. Jeremiah looked round in vain for Ahikam and his sons, but they had apparently not been invited to the council. Were they intentionally being kept in ignorance of the matters that were being discussed?

The King came to meet Jeremiah and, with a forced smile, reproached him mildly for having kept away so long. Jeremiah remained completely formal, bowed to the ground, and murmured the usual formula with which the King was greeted by his subjects, but Zedekiah made a gesture of protest. In his eyes Jeremiah could see at once the inward uncertainty that tormented him. They were not alone in the faintly illumined chamber, and Jeremiah recognized in a third person present the new Keeper of the Door, Zephaniah, who hated nothing so much as the vexation caused by turbulent prophets.

"Letters have come from Babylon," said the King casually,

as if he did not attribute much importance to them. He paused for a moment, evidently waiting for Jeremiah to show signs of curiosity, but when the latter did not move, he added:

"Among them is a letter that affects you. . . ."

Jeremiah still appeared to take no interest, but gazed thoughtfully in front of him as if he had long been familiar with the contents of the letter in question. The reply of the captives in Babylon to his warning epistle had been late in coming. His silence increased the King's uneasiness, but then he caught sight of the obsequious Zephaniah and grew angry. In a brusque tone he ordered: "Read!" The Keeper of the Door quickly drew a sealed scroll from his girdle, unrolled it, bowed twice to the impatient King, and read the letter without casting a single glance at Jeremiah:

"A letter from Shemaiah, the Nehelamite, from Babylon to Zephaniah, the Keeper of the Door in the Temple of the Lord . . ."

The receiver of the letter appeared to be filled with pride as he read the ceremonious form of address. He paused and cleared his throat portentously. Jeremiah remained unmoved. He now knew which way the wind was blowing. Shemaiah the Nehelamite was a son-in-law of Pashur. Zephaniah continued:

"The Lord has appointed you to your holy office, to be in charge of the mad prophets in place of your predecessor, that you may put them in the stocks or at least cast them into prison. Why then, Zephaniah, have you not strictly forbidden Jeremiah of Anathoth from continuing to publish his predictions? This man has dared to send his exhortations to us in Babylon, writing thus to the elders: 'Long will be the duration of your captivity. Therefore build ye houses and dwell in them! Plant gardens and eat the fruit of them! Take ye wives in Babylon and beget sons and daughters! And pray unto the Lord for the peace of the city in which ye dwell.'"

Here the King interrupted the reading:

"Are these your words, Jeremiah?"

"They are my words!"

"And what have you to say to the letter of the Nehelamite, whose heart is so filled with wrath?"

There was a far-away look in Jeremiah's deeply sunken eyes, which appeared only as shadows to the King as he listened to the prophet's reply:

"The Nehelamite! And Pashur! And all the others! Their names no longer live, even though their bodies are not yet dead. They will not be remembered!"

Zedekiah sprang from his seat and his handsome face was flushed. This was a matter that concerned his honour as King. He had to prove to the Keeper of the Door that he was strong enough to put his former teacher in his place. Stepping close up to Jeremiah he cried:

"Do you know what you have done in your ruthlessness? You have robbed of hope those who have nothing to live for but their hope. 'Build ye houses!' Where? In the land of the enemy? Who will build a house that can be taken from him on the morrow? 'Plant gardens!' Where? On foreign soil? Who will cultivate fields from which he may be expelled without warning? 'Take ye wives in Babylon!' Why? So that feeble generations may grow up who believe neither in the Lord nor in the stars? 'Pray unto the Lord!' How? Without a temple, without sacrifices, without holy rites? 'Pray for the peace of Babylon your great enemy!' Shall a man pray for the peace of his slayer, who sets the sword to his breast? . . . And now tell me, man of Anathoth, do you realize what you have done in your letter to the captives of Babylon?"

"I realize what I have done," said Jeremiah calmly.

The King struggled for words.

"And you do not shudder with horror at . . . at . . . at the impossible?"

Jeremiah bowed his head, so that his brow gleamed white in the light of the lamp.

"The Lord demanded of them and of us . . ."

With a violent gesture Zedekiah dismissed the Keeper of the Door. When they were alone, he grew quieter. "The positions are reversed," he murmured to himself. "I am speaking like a prophet and Jeremiah like a sinner."

"The Lord," said Jeremiah with a heavy tongue, "declares His will but not His intention."

The King stared at him with his large eyes.

"I have heard of your chant," he murmured, "concerning Nebuchadnezzar . . . and the yoke of the nations. . . . Is this His will?"

"The Lord of hosts has made Nebuchadnezzar His sword-bearer."

"Then He loves those who hate Him and hates those who love Him?"

"Do *you* love your sword-bearer?"

"Verily, Jeremiah, I grow dizzy. . . . How shall I comprehend Him?"

"Do not try to comprehend . . . only listen to His words!"

"Listen to His words? . . . Are you the only prophet in whom is truth? . . . Even if I wish to believe that you are the only one, *may* I believe it? . . . The King hears the voices of many prophets and they foretell many different things. . . . He has to choose not according to his inclination, but according to his judgment, between Hananiah and

Jeremiah. . . . The incomprehensible is not the concern of the King, but only that which can be clearly comprehended. . . . It is his duty to calculate and plan and care for the nation and for Jerusalem."

Zedekiah was again overcome by his excitement and jumped from his chair. He placed both hands on Jeremiah's hips.

"I have formed a league of kings"—he whispered the words, though there was no witness in the room to hear them—"and we have sworn a solemn oath to be *one* body, from the borders of Ethiopia to the isles of the north. . . . Now we are stronger than Babylon. . . . But you revile my work, the only man in Zion to do so. . . ."

"May my King be victorious, may he prove to be right and so be revenged on me," cried Jeremiah in a voice distorted with pain, "and may he never become caught in the toils of this league of blood!"

The King's hands dropped to his side.

"And for whose sake did I do what I have done for this people? Was it not for Him, for the Temple, for the sacrifices and the prayers?"

From Jeremiah's heart was wrung the cry:

"It is not the Temple, not the sacrifices, and not the prayers which are important in the eyes of the Lord!"

The King took a step backwards.

"It is good, my teacher," he said, "that these words have been heard by no one but your pupil, who is willing to forget them."

He allowed a long silence to ensue, that the blasphemous syllables might dissolve in the air. Then he struck a new note, and said in a tone of appeal:

"Let us find a way between you and me, Jeremiah! . . ."

In words that had presumably been carefully rehearsed, the King declared his readiness to follow up the league of kings already in being by entering into another league with the Lord. He would do no less for God than his father had done. He fully realized that in order to have Zebaoth on his side he must make Him feel at home in Zion. Like a wary bargainer the King proposed to the prophet that the Lord should be paid by instalments; namely, a further purge of idols throughout the land, stricter observance of the Sabbath, the decreeing of a new day of fasting and penitence. But to all these offers the uncompromising Jeremiah shook his head. If the King really wished to bind the Lord to his side, then an act was necessary that far transcended the ordinary conduct of nations. Then indeed must the Lord fear that if He destroyed Israel, He would be destroying for ever in the world a supreme law that Israel had fulfilled. This supreme law had nothing to do with the Temple, the sacrifices, the fasts, or the Sabbath; nothing to do with serving the Lord but everything to do with serving the poor and toiling multitudes of Judah. Jeremiah demanded of the young King that he should not wait for the beginning of a new year of jubilee before ordering the godless employers, who had already allowed one period of seven years to pass after another, to emancipate their bondmen and bondwomen and give them their portion. Zedekiah stared at him helplessly.

"You always make things more difficult and ask the impossible," he groaned. "It is *I* for whom you make things more difficult and whom you urge to do the impossible. . . . It is not the poor and toiling multitudes who strengthen the King's right arm but the rich men and the princes."

"Let us find a way between you and me, my King," Jeremiah quoted the King's own words.

"I intend to find this way, however hard you try me, my teacher. Hearken to my words! At the turn of the year I shall proclaim the jubilee and emancipation of the bondmen and bondwomen on the estates of the House of David. Will that suffice?"

"What a single person does, my King, will not suffice. The jubilee and emancipation must be proclaimed throughout the land."

"Do you want my princes to strike me down like a dog!" shrieked Zedekiah, beating his breast with his clenched fist. For a long time he walked to and fro unceasingly and without speaking. His face grew clouded as one thought after another coursed through his mind. There were moments when he seemed about to accede to Jeremiah's demand, tremendous as it was. Suddenly he turned to the prophet with a swift, angry movement.

"Will you take off the yoke?"

"When my King proclaims the jubilee, I shall take off the yoke."

"I have promised nothing!" muttered Zedekiah resentfully, and the audience was at an end. He had not invited Jeremiah to share his house and bread.

27

Caught in the Toils of the League

BEFORE the time had yet come for Jeremiah to take off his yoke, his presentiment that Zedekiah would find himself caught in the toils of the league he had founded was most terribly fulfilled. Itubaal, the King of Tyre, was a vassal of Babylon, but he suddenly announced his refusal to pay further tribute to Marduk. Perhaps the rich and powerful sea-king of Phœnicia hoped that Nebuchadnezzar, in view of the new league between the seven nations, would think twice before sending an army to collect the tribute and thereby disturbing the peace of the world. But Itubaal had made a grievous mistake when he took Marduk to be a vulgar calculator like himself. The King of Babylon certainly made his calculations in this case as in every other, but not with the aid of earthly alliances. He consulted the starry messengers and the twelve mysterious forces of the zodiac, and before three months had passed he sent Nergal Risua with a considerable body of fighting-men to the seacoast to punish the rebellious ruler and destroy his city. Tyre, however, was more favourably situated than most capitals, since it was built on an island off the coast and could be reached only by means of a long bridge.

In former times such an occurrence would not have been of any particular concern to Jerusalem, but in present circumstances the league involved obligations which overshadowed the sky like a coming storm. If the King of Tyre should be attacked, the oath of alliance expressly stipulated that the kings of Sidon and Judah should be the first to hasten to his aid with a military force, just as Itubaal had to fling an army into the field if either of them should require his help. Zedekiah's course of action as laid down in the terms of the alliance was therefore clear, and Itubaal had at once sent an envoy to Jerusalem demanding the immediate fulfilment of the pact. The young King of Judah was now floundering in the net which he himself had prepared amid the rejoicings of his people. It seemed that a more than human power had woven the meshes of this snare, for whichever way he turned he could not find a hole large enough to slip through. If he carried out his duty to his ally and sent an army northwards to Carmel, he would be inviting the fearful vengeance of Nebuchadnezzar, who would not hesitate to invade Judah and besiege Jerusalem for the second time. Even if the other kings kept loyally to their bonds, the whole world would flame up in a senseless war that would, moreover, be fought out on the soil of Israel and Judah. If, on the other hand, Zedekiah declined to carry out his obligation, then as the founder of the league he would have broken his oath and would appear before the eyes of men as a perjurer, disgraced for all time, a coward instead of the royal hero in whom his people had exulted. Jerusalem, which had set itself up as the focus of world events, would be a laughingstock and a thing of scorn among the nations. Yet even if Zedekiah possessed a soul sublime enough to bear the humiliation of the misunderstanding that would inevitably arise, he still would not have been able to save his kingdom. Nebuchadnezzar would hardly hesitate to crush for all eternity the despised originator of the futile league. And that was not all; in any decision he might take, Zedekiah had to think of the possible fate of the ten thousand captives in Babylon, whom Nebuchadnezzar held as hostages and who might be massacred without mercy. This was the hopeless position in which Zedekiah found himself entangled even before the rejoicing at his diplomatic genius had died away.

During the days when Itubaal's envoy was waiting in Jerusalem for the answer that Zedekiah still hesitated to give, Jeremiah returned one evening to his lodging in the house of the saddler. He still wore the iron yoke round his neck and was utterly exhausted, while the fever had not yet left his limbs. Baruch, who had avoided him for some time, was sitting in a distracted state of mind in a corner, and at his master's entrance he threw himself on the ground and clasped Jeremiah's knees with the tears pouring down his face.

"May Jeremiah never let me leave him again!" he moaned. "I thought that my own heart would enable me to recognize the truth and I doubted the voice of the Lord, which never speaks except through your mouth."

Jeremiah wearily released himself from his disciple's embrace.

"It would have been better," he said, "if you had not returned to me and the judgment of your heart had proved truer than my words."

Baruch began at once to busy himself, as he had been accustomed to do in the past, with putting into order Jeremiah's numerous scrolls and the few other chattels that lay about the room. But his eyes suddenly remained fixed in horror on his master's sunken cheeks. Jeremiah had probably eaten nothing for months but a little dry bread. Baruch ran to the nearest cookshop and came back with a hot meal and a jug of wine. The prophet ate with ravenous hunger and refreshed himself with the wine, while his disciple, with a feeling of guilt, informed him of the reasons which had convinced even the sons of Shaphan that the league of kings was a masterpiece of statecraft. Alas for these clever men, the pride of the Temple, who fasted every week and never let a day pass without studying the Law! They were all worshippers of a false god, the god of their own minds! Jeremiah listened with bowed head and said nothing.

None the less, he allowed himself to be persuaded to go that very night to Shaphan's chamber in the Temple, where a number of despairing men, who all shared the same view, had assembled to discuss the menace that was hanging over Jerusalem. Even Ahikam was there, though he suffered from a disease of age which had paralysed his legs and left him unable to drag himself along except with the aid of two sticks. The combined wit of all these scholars had been able to produce nothing other than a letter, composed in tortuous and involved phraseology, which they intended to send to Zedekiah and which put forward the following proposals for his consideration:

If he should refuse to dispatch the aid demanded by Itubaal of Tyre, it would not legally constitute a breach of his oath, since the pact referred to *one* body whose parts were united and inseparable. In a united and inseparable body, however, it was impossible for one of the parts to act according to its own judgment without orders from the whole unit. Yet this was what the King of Tyre had done. The unity of the body of nations had been annulled and therefore, in this particular case, the joint obligation of the individual parts to help one another was also annulled.

The arguments put forward in this letter were neither unplausible nor dishonourable, but it was an ominous sign that a man like Gedaliah should have to give his advice in writing to a young king for whose elevation to the throne he had once interceded so passionately in the camp of Babylon. Ahikam and his sons had long since ceased to be councillors of Zedekiah. The change had come quickly and they had not publicly fallen into disfavour, but their place had been taken by others, less inconvenient to the King, who made up for their lack of intellectual power by an enthusiasm for horse-breeding, gorgeous Egyptian chariots, tournaments, and banquets. Their cheerful companionship and hearty songs were far more to Zedekiah's taste than the eternally anxious and hair-splitting arguments of the scribes.

Zedekiah was as careful to preserve the formalities as he was meticulous in his personal appearance. Could one expect such a king to stain his honour by a breach of faith based on such crafty arguments? The men assembled in Shaphan's room were not very hopeful, and they implored Jeremiah to go as soon as was seemly to the palace and speak with the royal ladies. With all the energy and eloquence of which he was capable, he must exhort Hamutal and Maacha to restrain the King from any military enterprise. There was no one who was likely to influence the mother of Zedekiah more than the prophet who had been her companion in exile.

Jeremiah accepted the mission and appeared at an early hour in the House of Pharaoh's Daughter. Hamutal was unwell and was keeping to her chamber, but he was received by the young Queen. Maacha's eyes rested on Jeremiah with disquiet as she invited him to sit down beside her. Though her face looked so virginal, it was shadowed with a vague sorrow which could not have its cause in any outward experience of her life hitherto.

"The Lord is preparing the end," began Jeremiah, "but He

still holds His hand. Will the Queen not help to lengthen the days of our life? Will the Queen not perform a supreme service for the King?"

Maacha was immediately aware of the reason for his visit. She sat upright and assumed an air of reserve.

"It is not the business of women to perform such a service!"

Jeremiah sought her eyes, which she at first kept lowered but which were finally drawn to his.

"That which serves life is the business of women," he said.

He proceeded to describe to her the most horrible pictures of war that he could draw from the depths of his soul. He did not depict men fighting in battle, which, in spite of the thousands of killings and the bloody clamour, took place amid excitement and frenzy and soon came to an end, but he depicted a war which did not come to an end before it was gorged and could find nothing more to feed on. Decaying corpses lay strewn about the streets—men, women, and children alike. From the furrows of untilled fields the hands of the slain stretched up to the clouded sky but were seen only by the carrion fowl. The horses of the conquerors trampled on the crowds fleeing from their burning houses. In the besieged cities wild dogs, which roamed the streets at night, sought their prey among those who had died of famine and the plagues which followed in its wake. When the last drop of water had gone from the cisterns, men dying of thirst drank their own urine. When the last blade of grass had been plucked from between the stones, mothers devoured their prematurely born children. . . . What king could venture, unless supreme necessity should demand it, to take the first step that must lead inevitably to such horrors! Must he not exert all his powers to avoid rousing the terrors of destruction that lay dormant in the world? If Zedekiah sent armed help to Itubaal, it *would* be the first step, and there was no supreme need to justify it.

Jeremiah's irresistible voice and the scenes it had conjured up had their effect. Maacha had grown very pale, but she still hesitated.

"The King does not speak with women about the cares of his realm."

Jeremiah was not to be denied.

"But the King's wife must speak with the King about the cares of his realm . . . at once . . . before it is too late."

Maacha turned her head away in torment.

"The King is sitting in council with his princes."

"Then let the Queen go in to him. He will listen to her words."

"He does not even listen to the exhortations of his mother. Why then should he listen to Maacha?"

Jeremiah bent his head towards her, and he spoke in a very low voice.

"For whom will you be doing it? You will not be doing it for others, but for yourself . . . for the children of the King are the first to . . ."

Maacha shrieked aloud and put her little hand to his mouth.

"Do not say it," she panted, "for everything you say is fulfilled! . . ."

Quickly, almost running, she left the room.

That evening, just as Jeremiah had retired to rest, there was a knock at his door and a tall man entered with a sedate step. He walked up to Jeremiah's couch and seated himself on the floor. It was Ebed-melech, the Ethiopian chamberlain, who had been sent by the young Queen to inform the prophet that her warning to Zedekiah had come too late. Elnathan had already ridden away to the north with a small army composed of sections of the royal bodyguard. Zedekiah thought that he was thereby formally fulfilling his obligation and preserving his honour, without really intervening in the war and risking the vengeance of Babylon. By taking this decision without summoning the assembly he had acted contrary to the usage of former kings, and the responsibility rested on his shoulders alone. He must realize what the possible consequences would be, for he had at the same time sent recruiting officers throughout the land to summon all the male population to arms, from mere boys to old men. And this burden was being imposed on the people at a time when the harvest was not yet gathered and the olive and the vine had not yet ripened.

Ebed-melech delivered his message with a grave face and in an unemotional tone. It was not for him to criticize his master's decisions. Yet Jeremiah could see that the Ethiopian's heart was consumed with anxiety. When he had finished speaking Ebed-melech did not prepare to depart, but looked round timidly and whispered:

"Pray to Him, my teacher; pray night and day!"

"Of what use are the prayers of one man?"

"Your prayers will be of use, my teacher. . . ." The thick lips of the Ethiopian parted in a smile of childlike pleasure. "I, too, will pray to Him, my teacher," he said. Then he added: "But He will not look at Ebed-melech. Or if He does, it will only be with loathing. For I do not belong to the people of God, whom I wish to serve. . . ."

Jeremiah supported himself on his elbow, and there was a gentle gladness in his voice as he spoke.

"Though your skin is dark, Ebed-melech," he said, "and it cannot be made white, yet you belong to the people of God. Many of those who have their portion in Abraham only by virtue of their blood will be cast aside, but you have been adopted by Him as one of His children because of the piety of your heart."

Hananiah had suddenly been overtaken by a mortal sickness, as Jeremiah had foreseen in his agonizing vision. And Jeremiah went to visit him in his wretchedness as he had once visited Jeremiah when the latter sat wretchedly in the stocks. Hananiah lay stretched on a couch in his princely house, moaning with pain, his robust frame reduced to a shadow in a few days. His body, which was naked and uncovered (since in his agony and fever he could not bear the touch of a blanket), was all spotted with sores and suppurating boils that had a bluish tinge from the poison in his blood. Beside the couch stood earthenware pitchers filled with fresh water, into which his son Irijah, who served as a captain in the royal bodyguard, kept dipping linen cloths to cool the burning ulcers. Silently Jeremiah sat down beside him and helped the son of the dying man in his work of love. It was a long time before Hananiah awoke from his delirious dreams and recognized his visitor, but then with a weak gesture he motioned his son to leave them together. Irijah, however, bestowed on Jeremiah a piercing look of hatred, as though he attributed to him alone the blame for the pitiful end of his brilliant father. When they were alone, Hananiah spoke in a voice that rattled in his throat and was like that of a drunken man.

"You have come. . . . I knew that you would come, my brother . . . as the messenger of death. . . ."

Jeremiah, who in the course of his life had so often stood at a death-bed, laid his hand upon the forehead of the sufferer. Hananiah's expression of pain grew less tense as he felt the soothing touch.

"Now at last I can tell you the truth, my brother," he whispered. "In order to deceive Jeremiah I deceived the Lord . . . for His voice was not within me. . . ."

Jeremiah bent over him and said gently:

"His voice was within you, Hananiah, when you prophesied concerning Egypt!"

A strange smile illumined the features of the dying man.

"Perhaps . . . perhaps not. . . . But I envied you from the depths of my heart . . . from the hour when you were privileged to read the Law in the presence of the King . . . you and not I. . . ."

"Envied me?" asked Jeremiah in a tone of sorrow and incredulity. Hananiah drew a deep breath.

"Yes, envied you . . . for you alone are to be envied, unhappy Jeremiah. . . . I said to you: 'The Lord looks into many mirrors' . . . but do not believe what I said . . . I only wanted to confuse you. . . . It is you alone who hear the truth . . . you alone . . . you alone. . . ."

The rattle in Hananiah's throat became more pronounced and he seemed to have lost consciousness. Jeremiah was about to call the dying man's son when his hand was again held tightly.

"Why you? . . . Why not I? . . . This is the reason. . . . I wanted to bend the Lord to my will and compel Him to speak to me. . . . But then I saw that I did not need Him in order to appear great in the eyes of other men. . . . I could manage without Him . . . things went better without Him. . . ."

Hananiah began to laugh, but his pain increased tenfold with the effort. When Jeremiah tried to calm him, he suddenly raised himself and cried:

"In two ways has He punished me, my brother . . . by your disbelief . . . for you have never believed in me. . . . No, do not pretend that you did. . . . It was only you whom I wanted to win over. . . . And then this . . . these boils and sores . . . I rejoice in them. . . . When you speak to Him, who holds communion with you alone, then tell Him . . . Hananiah rejoices in his affliction. . . . He thanks Him for the punishment He has sent. . . ."

The sick man fell back and said no more. He ceased for a moment to breathe, but once again he recovered and put his hand over his heart, on the only part of his body that had not been attacked by his malady.

"Here, my brother . . ." he muttered thickly, "here . . . there are no sores . . . no poison. . . . Though I shall not be remembered . . . behold the merit of Hananiah, you who have been so hated . . . my heart did not hate you. . . ."

The voices of the shaggy prophets were again thundering down from the pulpits in the courtyard of the Temple. But it was not the words of the Lord to which they were giving voice. Intoxicated with news of victory, every day they reported fresh defeats inflicted by Elnathan and his glorious army on Nergal Risua before Tyre. Jeremiah did not leave his lodgings. If he had appeared in public with his yoke on his shoulders, he would no longer have had to suffer merely the usual jeers but would certainly have been stoned to death. The prophets' clamorous announcing of daily victories did not fill the Daughter of Zion with a humble sense of happiness and gratitude, but degraded her to the condition of an intemperate woman. Whoever tried to advise and warn her was destroyed.

Hanameel, who had come from Anathoth to speak with Jeremiah, took half a day to discover his whereabouts. In order to protect himself against pestering visitors, who regarded him as a kind of master magician and importuned him with their requests, the prophet had given orders that he would see no one, neither man nor woman. But his cousin did not rest until he stood in the narrow room and had put down a sack containing various kinds of nourishing fruits that he had brought with him as a gift. In spite of his kindly solicitude Hanameel looked exceedingly grave and worried. Unbelievable things had happened at home in Anathoth, and he had come on Obadiah's behalf to entreat Jeremiah's help. According to his cousin's report something very serious must have occurred to call down once more the ancient curse on the arrogant children of Eli. The real cause of Abi's death had never been cleared up, but it had not remained unavenged. By slow degrees a deep depression settled on the members of Hilkiah's family. The change began with Mocheleth. At first it was noticeable only in her neglect of her housewifely duties and certain irregularities of behaviour. Then one night she went out and roamed the fields with her hair flowing loose and singing psalms. She returned to the house on the following morning wet through, her clothes in disorder, and unable to speak for hoarseness. The attacks grew more and more frequent and her periods of absence more and more protracted, until eventually she did not return home at all. Before long the crazed woman, as she wandered over the hills of Anathoth on moonlit nights uttering ugly, owl-like screeches, had become an apparition of dread to the superstitious people.

When Joel realized that his sister-in-law was irrevocably possessed by evil spirits, his suspicion changed to certainty. He rent his garments and said to Obadiah before witnesses: "I am weary of this. Let my elder brother weigh out my share of our inheritance in gold!" Obadiah, with his heart still set on his old ambition of becoming the sole owner of the estate, agreed to the transaction and paid over all the ready money he had at his disposal. Joel left the land of Benjamin with his wife, his children, and his grandchildren, and went to live in the heathen city of Ashkelon, which was an important seaport and provided greater opportunities for a merchant than were to be found in inland trade. Besides, his prudent mind told him that the heathen city was more likely to offer a safe refuge than the holy land of the Lord. Obadiah, however, who had put too much trust in his own capacities, experienced bad harvests and lean years. When he parted with the supple-minded Joel, all his good fortune left him. He was forced to seek loans in Jerusalem, and now that advancing years had sapped his strength, his creditors were pressing unmercifully for payment. In addition to all his other troubles, the King's recruiting officers had recently appeared on the estate, conscripted a proportion of his menservants, and carried away all the adult sons and grandsons of the family to serve in the war. Obadiah sat with only a few women and half-grown children at the table in the Hall of Abiathar. At night, as he tossed on his couch unable to sleep and his limbs racked with pain, he thought of the blessings which had been heaped on his parents, while the wind brought to his ears the wild cries of his crazed wife who was roaming about somewhere among the bushes and mingling her wails with those of the nocturnal beasts and birds.

Hanameel concluded his story by telling Jeremiah that his brother asked his forgiveness in the name of the Lord, imploring him to forget the past, return home, and by his wisdom bring new blessings to the decaying house of his father. In return Obadiah promised to fulfil the prophet's old demand and unconditionally to proclaim the emancipation of his bondservants on the whole estate. Like most people, Obadiah was hard in prosperity and weak in adversity. Not so Jeremiah; he was unmoved by Obadiah's entreaties and merely shook his head.

"My elder brother will not see me again while we both live."

"And the emancipation?" urged Hanameel.

The prophet gave him the same answer that he had given to the King:

"What a single person does will not suffice."

"And what will happen to your inheritance?" his cousin pressed him further. "Times are bad and there are few buyers in the land."

Jeremiah started up angrily.

"I shall not sell my portion in the land of the Lord!"

"It will become a wilderness and nothing will grow in your fields but thistles," Hanameel warned him. But Jeremiah seized his hand, looked keenly into his eyes, and said:

"You shall administer my inheritance. Everything that thrives upon it shall be yours. Let there be a covenant sworn between you and me!"

At first his cousin protested against this offer. But he was a man of little wealth, with only a field or two, the produce of which was meagre; with a peasant's covetous desire for land, he soon yielded. Cautiously he began to draft the text of the covenant. He indignantly refused to take over the property without rent, and bound himself to transfer to Jeremiah at regular intervals a portion of the produce or profit. The latter instructed Baruch to see that the covenant was sworn that very day before witnesses according to law and custom. And so it was done. When Hanameel was again alone with Jeremiah and preparing to take his departure, he said with a deep sigh:

"We have sworn a covenant between us, but who knows how long it will endure, both for you and for me? . . ."

Scarcely had Hanameel gone when an order came from the King summoning Jeremiah immediately to his presence. Zedekiah appeared to be overwhelmed with joy, for he ran to meet the prophet as he entered without waiting for the usual greeting.

"Let Jeremiah rejoice!" he cried. "The King is about to accede to his astounding demand. . . . Your pupil is about to show his gratitude and pay his debt to you, my teacher. It is a tremendous thing he is doing for you. Be comforted and cast away your yoke at the gate of Potsherds!"

Jeremiah was alarmed at the King's high spirits. The more exuberant he became, the greater was the anxiety he provoked in the prophet. Zedekiah's voice grew more and more triumphant.

"Have you already divined my will, you seer and soothsayer? The King does not intend to wait for the New Year. He intends here and now to put into effect the most difficult of God's commandments. You do not know the obstacles with which the King has had to contend, my teacher! For days and nights, for nights and days, he has argued with the princes and the landowners of Judah. But you knew nothing of all this, and you condemned your pupil. Listen, then! On the next Sabbath day the emancipation will be proclaimed and carried out. Already the order has been sent to all the elders and governors in every city and village. I am myself making a beginning in my own house. . . . But why are you silent? . . ."

Jeremiah's heart was beating so wildly that he had to press his hand to his breast. The King's voice took on a defiant tone.

"Zedekiah has done what his pious father did not do, what his exalted forefather Hezekiah did not do, what Solomon and David did not do! Verily, it is enough and more than enough! Thousands of bondservants will become free and receive their portion in accordance with the Lord's command. It will change the order of the world! Plead with Him ardently, that He may look with favour upon Zedekiah and the King's great deed rise up before Him in supplication!"

Jeremiah bowed down and kissed the hem of the King's robe. The great battle of his life had been crowned with victory. Yet he could not feel glad. The shrill note in Zedekiah's excited speech made him distrustful. He knew that there were ulterior motives for this fulfilment of the Lord's commandments. Was not any such fulfilment worthless and utterly without merit if it was done not for its own sake but for secret considerations of profit, even if only in the expectation of divine reward? The King seemed to be conscious of Jeremiah's suspicion. He looked at him once, then turned round to Ebed-melech, who was standing stiffly behind him.

"Ebed-melech, my chamberlain! Tomorrow you will be free! You have served me since you were two years old.

Have you reckoned out in gold, day by day, what is justly due to you? Open not your mouth to contradict my words! Do you know the punishment that the Lord has appointed for those who refuse their freedom? 'Then thou shalt take an awl, and thrust it through his ear.' . . . Take good care of your ear, my dark-skinned chamberlain!"

Ebed-melech bowed very gravely.

"May the majesty of my King not be wrathful if I none the less open my mouth to contradict his words! . . . Your chamberlain does not belong to the blood of Jacob, for whose people alone this supreme commandment was intended. Your father purchased me, a lowly child of Cush, in one of the slave-markets of Moab. With the price he paid for me all my rights were extinguished. It is therefore permitted me to continue to serve my King."

"Have you heard," scoffed Zedekiah, "the dismay with which this child of Cush regards the prospect of acquiring his freedom? Tomorrow there will be many children of Jacob who will envy him his black skin, when they receive their freedom at the Lord's command."

Jeremiah listened to Zedekiah's scoffing words in silence. He was well aware that for many bondmen their emancipation would be as terrifying as the open air would be to those who had lain long in dungeons. That, indeed, was why it had been ordained that nobody was to remain in bondage for more than seven years, lest he lose his memory of what freedom was like. The King, however, drew himself up to his full height and continued:

"I have done this against the will of all, even against my own, solely that I might obey His commandment. But now it is enough and more than enough! Let Jeremiah not venture to exhort me to fulfil the commandment concerning war!

He who has taken a young wife or built a new house shall not be allowed to return home before the battle, but the cowards who make faint the hearts of their brothers shall remain and shall die in the forefront of battle!"

By this threat Zedekiah had revealed, without knowing it, the desperate truth of which he was conscious in his own heart. The war would inevitably be carried into Judah. Those who lulled themselves with vain hopes still believed that Nebuchadnezzar would hesitate to set the world on fire, but it was already plain that this was a delusion. The young King was gnawing his underlip as if to keep back dreadful news of which he alone was cognizant. Jeremiah stared at him with eyes full of burning questions, but Zedekiah reddened, turned away, and dismissed him with an impatient gesture.

It happened as Zedekiah had said. Two months before the commencement of the new year the jubilee was proclaimed and carried out after solemn sacrifices and swearing of covenants in the Temple. Even the most foolish among the people of Judah realized that a day of affliction was drawing near which would be more terrible than anything that had gone before. Yet the false prophets continued to announce victories in the little war before Tyre, where, according to their hymns of praise, Elnathan was daily covering himself with fresh glory. They even boasted of the emancipation and of the fulfilment of God's promise that Judah would be raised above the other nations of the world. They acted as if it was their exhortations and prophecies to which the King had at last given ear, and they were able to do so without contradiction, since Jeremiah, though he had taken off his yoke, did not appear in the Temple. It was because of his constant urging that the bondservants had been released, but if one looked more closely it could be seen that their newly won freedom was outweighed by a hundred new abuses and difficulties. Zedekiah had correctly foretold that it would upset the order of things, with all the suffering and confusion that such a disturbance entailed. Many men and women now lacked bread, while fields remain untilled and flocks untended. The young King intervened with a strong hand. Like a true son of Josiah he rode unwearyingly throughout the length and breadth of the land, collecting the emancipated serfs, who at no time and in no nation had ever been considered worthy of bearing arms, into troops and companies and assigning them to the command of various captains. Through his energetic efforts they were eventually organized into a considerable force, comprising many thousands of excellently armed men. Jeremiah now realized the ulterior motive that had inspired the King's decision to proclaim the jubilee. Zedekiah had used the divine commandment for the purpose of reinforcing his army by the recruitment of every man in Judah who was capable of bearing a weapon.

One day the prophets in the Temple announced that Elnathan had won a great victory at Endor. The people stared at one another in alarm. Where was Endor? Was it not a little town on the slopes of Mount Gilboa? A few days later came news of an even greater victory at Taanach. Then the faces of even the most stupid grew pale as chalk. Taanach was the next fortified city to Megiddo, a strong citadel of the Kings of Judah! If an enemy should take possession of this citadel, the road to Ephraim lay open in front of him.

After this the false prophets had no more victories to announce. On the very next day these reeds in the wind were again summoning their hearers to repentance and thundering their denunciations of Judah's offences and backsliding, threatening punishment from Heaven. Judah, they shouted, had but a few thousand trained warriors, while Babylon had hundreds of thousands who had been accustomed to bear arms since their childhood. Gradually there began a fresh influx of fugitives into Jerusalem, melancholy processions of peasants with their wives and children, their cattle and their household goods. The city was again filled with people as it had been only a short while before, and this time the multitude was even greater. The new rings of walls that Zedekiah had erected soon after his accession to the throne proved their value, for it was possible to shelter twice as many people within the fortifications as had found room there during the earlier siege. Josiah's youngest son could not, in any case, be compared with his half-brother Jehoiakim, who had been great only in oratory and intrigue but had lost his head in the hour of danger. Zedekiah did not lose his head. His messengers flew to Noph and Edom, to Moab and Ammon, and he himself seemed to be with his army and in Jerusalem at the same time. Like all handsome, upstanding men he inspired those around him with confidence. Every road was congested with wagons, camels, and asses bringing vast quantities of corn, wine, oil, and other necessities of life to Jerusalem by order of the King.

Later, though at first only in straggling groups, soldiers began to retreat into the city. Then appeared whole companies, more and more of them and at frequent intervals. The shafts of their lances were broken, their swords notched, their bows slack. Their hollow eyes, no less than their tattered, bloodstained cloaks, told of the fierce fighting, in which they had been engaged. As soon as they arrived they were re-armed, re-clothed, and distributed among the forts and bulwarks of Zion, so that the people, seeing the energy and determination with which the defences were being organized, grew calmer. The King's bitter resolution was a steadying influence; moreover, as the prophets never ceased declaiming, Jerusalem did not stand alone. The one essential was to gain time, since the nations with whom Judah was in league were hardly likely to cover themselves with ignominy by breaking the oath that had been taken by their rulers. Pharaoh's name was on everyone's lips, and even those who had never expected anything good to come from the House of Bondage no longer dared to doubt that Hophra's mighty army must already be on the way, together with his auxiliaries from Ethiopia and Nubia, from Libya, Ionia, and Sinai.

One fresh, wintry morning, when the sentries looked out from their watch-towers in the early dawn, they saw that the whole countryside round Jerusalem appeared strangely deserted. It was like the deathly stillness of creation before the Day of Judgment. A few hours later the vanguards of Babylon came into sight on the hills to the north and east. As they rode along in close order, with the Tartans and Rhabsakim at their head, they really did look like the heralds of the last day. Marduk, with his unwearying invention and search for novelty, had introduced into his army iron masks that his soldiers wore like visors. Painted black or red, they sparkled in the sun and gave their wearers the appearance of starry messengers from Nergal or Ninurtu, emissaries of the nocturnal sky, as indeed they were. The hearts of even the bravest of Judah's warriors trembled at sight of these terrifying masks.

28

The Triumph of Zedekiah

THE walls of the Temple lay within and on a higher level than the rings of walls that surrounded the city, and from their towers and battlements the priests could look far out over the countryside to the heights beyond Jerusalem. On one of the towers of the east wall Jeremiah stood with Baruch and Gedaliah watching the Babylonians, who had invaded the land in three columns and had now covered the slopes of the Mount of Olives with their thousands of tents. The encampment curved in a wide arc almost to the hills of Gareb, so that the city was gripped within gigantic pincers. Only the unscalable south wall, which rose from a steep rock and reared itself high above the Vale of Ben-Hinnom, was left free by the besiegers, since it could not be stormed even by the might of Babylon. The names of Marduk's generals had become known. In addition to the youthful Nergal Nebuzaradan, who was chief in command, the siege was being conducted by the two next most important marshals, Nergal Sharezer and Nergal Sarsechim. To ensure success, Marduk had sent even his chief councillor, Samgar Nebo, to bring the plans of Nergal Nebuzaradan into harmony with the predestination of the stars. Hardly had the tents been pitched before they began to build a miniature E-temen-anki, to serve both as a military temple and as an observatory where Samgar could watch the sky and make his calculations.

According to report, the King of Babylon was equipping new armies with the intention of placing himself at their head and enforcing the great decision on the Phœnician coast, in Syria, Israel, Judah, the neighbouring kingdoms, and, if necessary, even in Egypt. Only then would the sacred symbol of the Ram, the golden spade, be able to dominate the world as had been ordained. Marduk, the Lion of the North, had wearied of his indulgence and generosity in merely playing with his prey and allowing the weaker creatures to fool him. It was no longer enough to strike a lazy blow or two with his paw. The hour had come for the world to be refashioned. The unsymmetrical diversity of nations must be abolished and mankind brought into line with the ordered unity of the starry sky, where everything was in harmonious relationship and there was no room for any arbitrary and confusing remnant. Once more blood was about to flow in streams, so that Marduk might bring the earth into unison with the beatific symbols of the heavens. The wisdom of the soothsayers had revealed the symmetry of the stars, their grouping in constellations, and explained their influence on the destiny of men. But the nations of the world lived in disorder and confusion, unconscious of their destiny. The multitude of different races, especially the small ones, was not in accordance with the law of the stars and was therefore an evil that could not be tolerated. What were nations, indeed? They owed their very existence to the stars, yet they insolently held themselves to have been created by their gods and insisted on their independence! The smallest of them, moreover, were superfluous and disturbing notes in the celestial symphony. They must be extirpated as a jarring element in the harmony of the universe, and their gods with them, who were mere clumsy deviations from the eternal truth of which

Babylon was the sole repository. Could there be any different truth from that which presented itself every night to those who gazed up with awe at the starry sky and which was realized every day by those who studied the mathematical mysteries? One of the tribal gods in particular ventured to set himself above this evident and rational truth. He opposed his unity to the multiformity of the gods of Babylon. Through the mouth of his soothsayer he had even dared to call Marduk his servant! Yet nothing pleased Marduk more than an arrogance which surpassed his own. The very fact that such arrogance existed acted as a spur and warmed his heart. He rejoiced at having found an antagonist who was convinced of his own superiority, and his campaign was directed not at the people of Judah, but at their god. He felt no hatred for Zebaoth, only a furtive curiosity which he could not shake off. The servant of the Lord was prepared to challenge Him in His own Temple, and the weight of armed power behind the challenge was manifest on the first day of the siege when Jeremiah and his friends looked down from their tower onto the swarming camp of Babylon.

The Babylonians refrained this time from splitting the air with their wild blare and din, and did not even send their heralds to the gates of the city to demand its surrender. The purpose of this war was not merely to enter and occupy Jerusalem, but to conquer and destroy it. Without wasting time, the generals brought their ordnance into position. There were battering-rams to break down the walls; ladders and tall, slender wooden towers to attack the stone-towers of the defenders; catapults and flame-throwers for use against the inner town. The battle began without delay. The iron tips of the battering-rams crashed against the granite ramparts so that the stone was ground to powder and spurted like water. Great rocks whizzed through the air in a high arch. The ladders and wooden towers, drawn by teams of oxen, swayed towards the battlemented bulwarks, with men in armour standing on their rocking platforms ready to bridge the gap and board the city as if it were a ship. Thousands of archers knelt behind the parapets of hastily prepared breastworks and launched one hurricane of arrows after another at the defending garrison. For a full thirty days, from sunrise to sunset, there was no cessation of the colossal efforts of the Babylonians to take the city by storm. Yet the result was not only the collapse of the attack, but very serious losses to Babylon in men and ordnance, without even a breach having been made in the walls or one of the outer battlements being captured.

The successful defence was the work of Zedekiah, who hastened from one scene of battle to another and foiled every attack by a series of cunning artifices and stratagems. Each time he allowed the enemy to move his wooden towers close to the wall while the defenders retired in simulated flight, then at the last moment men would come running from their places of concealment and pour burning oil over the portable bridges. Only rarely did the towers and the soldiers who manned them escape destruction. And while the King supervised the defence by day, Elnathan harried the enemy by night. All the troops who were not being used to garrison the city had been withdrawn, under the command of Elnathan, to the wilderness of Judea, the pathless mountains of the south, and the Arabah by the Dead Sea. Elnathan had already practised the advantageous method of guerrilla warfare under Jehoiakim, but as he now had a real fighting force at his disposal instead of the scattered bands which were all he possessed before, he was able to threaten the communications of the Babylonian army. He not only overwhelmed reconnoitring parties in Nebuzaradan's rear, and destroyed smaller garrisons and detachments, but frequently ventured under cover of night into the vicinity of Jerusalem and invaded the Babylonian camp. The night was sacred to the Babylonians and Nebuzaradan's warriors disliked fighting in the dark. When the wild battle cry of Zebaoth suddenly rang out in the pitchy blackness before the breastworks of the encampment, they started up from their sleep with terror-stricken faces; in vain did their officers urge them on to face the attackers. More than once Elnathan succeeded in striking down the sentries and advancing some way into the camp, massacring all he met. The damage he inflicted on the Babylonians was considerable, but even more effective was the state of uncertainty which made the besiegers anxious for the safety of their flanks and rear. Nergal Nebuzaradan found himself compelled to weaken his main army and send a large force under Nergal Sarsechim to seek out Elnathan in the Judean wilderness and destroy him. The result was the opposite of what he had intended. In the steep ravines, dry valleys, and wild gorges it was possible for the men of Judah to hold their own without difficulty against ten times their number. Elnathan decoyed the Babylonians into one of the boulder-strewn hollows and annihilated them almost to the last man as they were pitching camp. Henceforth the place was called Adumim, the Pass of Blood. Sarsechim managed to escape with his small bodyguard and made his way back to Nebuzaradan.

With the siege going so favourably for Judah, the inhabitants of Jerusalem lived in a state of almost drunken hope. Jeremiah had been deceived by the voice within him. The Lord was not going to forsake His people and make them an object of contempt among the nations. He would show by the example of Babylon that greatness and strength were in His sight but a breath of wind. The first-fruits of Jerusalem's successful defence were already to be seen. Moab, Edom, and Ammon had all promised to fulfil their obligations under the pact and were preparing armies. The most glorious sign of all was that Pharaoh had sent three of his privy councillors (in spite of the fact that the city was in a state of siege) to discuss the situation with Zedekiah. After the first audience it was said that the King's cheeks had glowed with a wild joy.

Once more the Temple was pitching and tossing like a ship in a storm. The fire on the altar of burnt offerings never went out, and it was impossible to renew the four brass horns at each corner which were melted into shapeless lumps. Since orders had been issued by the High Priest for the more strict observance of divine worship, the priests virtually never slept. Their insistent appeals and prayers rose to Heaven day and night like the undying flames of sacrifice.

Not only was there no famine in the beleaguered city, but there was even a superabundance of provisions. Herds of cattle grazed in the fields between the inner and outer rings of walls; the warehouses were stocked from floor to ceiling; the pools and cisterns were filled to the brim with fresh water from the winter. Rain fell to replenish the springs, brooks, and wells, and there was no more disease than in time of peace. Since the gates to the south were open and in no danger from the enemy, it was possible to replace whatever was consumed. Elnathan's captains not only intercepted supplies intended for the camp of the Babylonians, but were able to convoy along the Road of Gold and Incense every caravan that ventured the journey northwards from the Nile. Under cover of night, hundreds of heavily laden camels were driven into the city. Jerusalem flourished under the sword as it had never done before, so when the name of Zedekiah was mentioned it was always accompanied with blessings.

Jeremiah and Baruch, together with Gedaliah and Micah, met almost daily in the Temple. They too participated untiringly in the sacrifices and communal prayers, the fastings and the vigils. When Jeremiah was alone in his chamber he would try to enter into communion with the Lord, but Zebaoth seemed to have grown weary of Israel and of Jeremiah. If He occasionally condescended to favour the prophet with an obscure utterance, it seemed like an ill-humoured rejection of his supplication.

One Sabbath, when there was a pause in the fighting at the walls, the aged Ahikam had himself carried to his father's room in the Temple. His yellowed skin, the fixed look in his eye, his quick breathing, and the faintness of his voice were signs that his life was drawing towards its close. Motioning to Jeremiah to come nearer, he asked:

"Is there any change in the attitude of the Lord?"

Jeremiah shook his head.

"I knew it," sighed Ahikam with an effort, "and the favourable beginning does not deceive me. What I know comes to me not as it does to Jeremiah, but as the result of my own deductions. For I am not a prophet, but only the poor son of my father, whose powers of logical deduction were more far-reaching than those of any other man. Yet this time my conclusions agree with what Jeremiah has learned from his communion with the Lord."

He beckoned to his servant to place pillows behind his back so that he might assume a more dignified attitude, but his sons hastened to raise his paralysed body, over which he had no control, into a sitting position.

"Is there anybody here," he whispered, "who is not one of us? . . . Baruch, Jeremiah's disciple, may remain and listen and give his opinion. . . . Gather round me and incline your ears, that we may discuss what is to be done when the end has come, which will be when I am no longer here."

The men formed a circle round Ahikam and bent down so that he should not have to strain his voice, also that his words should not penetrate beyond the room and bring danger on their heads.

"When the end has come," the old man began, his breath coming in quick gasps, "and everything is destroyed and burned, the people massacred or carried away into captivity, there will still be a Remnant left in Judah. . . ."

At these words they all bowed their heads in dread. However strong their presentiments of the awful truth may have been, it had the force of a blow when they were thus put into words. Ahikam, however, had little time or strength left.

"The last Remnant of Judah," he repeated, "let us think only of them, let us make plans only for them. . . . They must not remain without shepherds. . . . That is all I have thought of during my sleepless nights . . . who will be the shepherd to gather the Remnant of Judah when the hour has come? . . . Do you hear me, Jeremiah? . . . It must be a man who is loyal to the Lord and does not look to his own profit. . . . It must be a man who enjoys the favour of Babylon, so that he may have its power on his side. . . . It must be a man who is able to leave this city today or tomorrow, that he may prepare the folds in which the last Remnant of the flock is to be gathered. Do you hear me, Jeremiah?"

Jeremiah raised the palms of his hands towards Ahikam.

"I shall not leave this city until its last day has come. Let my benefactor remember that Jeremiah is not a shepherd in whom the flock trusts. Whenever he approached it, he filled it with abhorrence. I am not the man you seek."

Ahikam had expected no other answer. His eyes rested on his twin sons, who were themselves growing grey.

"Then the father," he said, "lays the burden of his cares upon the shoulders of his sons and orders them to carry out his will. . . . Gedaliah and Micah are both loyal to the Lord and do not look to their own profit. . . . Gedaliah is in favour at the court of Babylon . . . I therefore order you, Gedaliah, with my last dying breath: 'Leave this city today or tomorrow and prepare the folds in which the last Remnant of Judah is to be gathered when the hour is come.' "

Gedaliah's face turned to stone.

"Let my father hearken to my words," he stammered. "Whatever may befall, Gedaliah will be regarded as a traitor. . . ."

Ahikam remained unmoved.

"Do not ask what men will say of you before the day has come when you will be able to justify your action . . . and that day will come. . . . What need will you have then to be concerned at what has gone before?"

His strength left him and he sank back in spite of the pillows which supported him. With the last ounce of strength he could summon up before he died, Ahikam had ordered his sons to fulfil his final wish. He was about to be gathered to his fathers, an endless sequence reaching back to the first man and hence to the Creator Himself. His countenance was marked with the sign of death, which was a sign of his return to those from whom he had sprung. Pious sons could not refuse to obey the last request of their dying father, who was at such a moment invested with more than earthly authority. The pale Micah had turned even paler than usual. He crossed his hands over his breast as he addressed his father.

"One sends at first him who is of less account. . . . Of the two of us who were born at the same time, Gedaliah is called the elder brother and he is of greater account. . . . He is not only wise but strong, and the people put their trust in him. Let my father send Micah, who is of less account, to prepare the fold. . . . He will not rouse the hearts of the people to anger by leaving the city. . . . Gedaliah can follow him as the shepherd of the Remnant when the time comes."

Ahikam smiled weakly at the loyal spirit of his son. Micah had divined well and proposed the best course.

Maacha, the young Queen, had begged Jeremiah with tears in her eyes not to leave the King's side during the execution of a perilous enterprise that he and some of the young princes had planned. As he was unable to resist her anxious pleading he had given her his word.

On the evening of the new moon, long before it was dark, Zedekiah's companions assembled near the Gate of Potsherds and the double wall that led to the royal gardens. They were waiting for the King, and with them were a few picked detachments of soldiers under the command of Irijah, Hananiah's son. They were all clad in dark garments to make them as little visible as possible; they had even painted their armour and weapons black. Among the friends of Zedekiah was a man of royal blood, Prince Ishmael, a younger brother of the Jerachmeel who had been one of the bitterest persecutors of Jeremiah and Urijah before he was carried away into captivity in Babylon with the other exiles. It was strange that the Babylonians had allowed one of the brothers to stay in Jerusalem, when there was nothing to choose between them either in rank or in the irreconcilability of their temper. Nor was it less strange to find in the personal retinue of the King a son of Pashur. His name was Malchiah, and he had managed to return home by bribing some high official in Babylon. In addition to Ishmael and Malchiah, two other young princes who enjoyed the close friendship of Zedekiah were waiting for him to join them. These were Shephatiah and Jucal, and by an ill fate they too were the sons of men now in exile who had been among Jeremiah's most inveterate opponents.

These four were known as inseparable companions of the King, so that his closest friends were all enemies of Jeremiah, sons and brothers of those who had held positions of power in Jehoiakim's reign and had inherited a burning hatred of the prophet. It was an incontestable fact that Zedekiah had gathered round him, not men versed in the Law who honoured the true prophets, but men who arrogantly despised the Law and rejected the commandments of God. The four young princes spared no effort to make Jeremiah aware of their hostility and contempt. They ignored his greeting, turned their backs on him when he appeared, and made mocking observations in a loud voice which he could not fail to hear. Their attitude was copied by the soldiers, who added their own jeers and behaved even more coarsely than their superiors. Jeremiah stood alone. He had been forbidden to communicate the plan to Baruch or to take him along, and he began angrily to consider whether he should not renounce his promise to stay by the King and return home. For what purpose and to whose advantage had he agreed to expose himself that night to the sight of bloodshed, which he loathed with all his soul? What was it that had led him since his youth to serve with such utter selflessness these sons of David, who disregarded his words when they were the words of the Lord, cast him aside when things went well, and exploited him in times of misfortune? No, there was no place for him in the palace and he had no concern with the military adventures of the King! Jeremiah had already made up his mind to return to his lodging when Zedekiah appeared, just as the last of the twilight was fading, accompanied by Ebed-melech and followed by his shield and sword-bearers. As if he had divined the prophet's thoughts, the King walked very deliberately past his four friends without responding to their greeting and approached Jeremiah at a quick pace. Embracing him affectionately, he addressed him as his teacher and thanked him for having come to protect his pupil that night with his godly presence. Zedekiah spoke so loudly and demonstrated his favour so clearly that the men roundabout, who had just been openly mocking Jeremiah, were overcome with embarrassment. Even after they had moved off, the King allowed only Jeremiah to stay at his side, while the princes followed a short distance behind.

The heavy gate was silently swung open and the soldiers marched out noiselessly. They at once scattered into small groups and vanished in the darkness. The moonless night was stormy, and this was very favourable to their enterprise. The flood of light that came from the Babylonian encampment rose mistily to the sky, where low clouds were driving towards the east. The route had been arranged beforehand. They had to keep carefully outside the extensive circle of light thrown by the camp fires. The men of Judah flitted swiftly through the gloom like shadows, and Jeremiah had to exert himself in order to keep pace with the young King.

On the way Zedekiah revealed his plan to the prophet in

a whisper. The attack was to be carried out in three waves. The first was under the command of Elnathan, who had collected for the occasion from their various hiding-places all the troops at his disposal and was going to lead them at the appointed hour against the southern breastworks of the encampment, which on that side reached down as far as the Vale of Jehoshaphat and was protected only by weak bulwarks. For this reason it had often been the objective of Elnathan's nightly incursions, though he had never before used more than a small force. The Babylonian generals, in the expectation of further assaults of a like nature, had recently doubled and even tripled the sentries on the south side. To the east and north, where the breastworks ran along the heights and there were no paths by which to reach them, the enemy had little fear that the men of Judah would indulge in similar daring exploits. Zedekiah was reckoning on the sentries on the Mount of Olives having been lulled into a sense of security. He had succeeded in inducing one of the Rhabsakim, a man of Aram, to turn traitor. This man, in charge of the guards on the eastern side of the encampment that night, had promised Zedekiah to leave the breastworks and the gate undefended as soon as the attack to the south should become audible. Nergal Nebuzaradan had issued a special order that in case of a night attack all the sentries and available guards were to rush to the threatened quarter. So while the noise of the fighting was drawing to the south of the camp all the Babylonians on watch, as well as those aroused from sleep, Zedekiah intended to penetrate as far as he could from the unguarded eastern side and start a wild slaughter. When the battle was in full swing in the valley and along the heights, and the camp had been set on fire in different places, this would be the sign for the garrison of

Jerusalem to make a general sortie through the gates of the city.

They crept along silently in the pitchy blackness, invisible even to one another. They carried no shaded lanterns to guide their steps, but every now and then a low, monosyllabic cry was passed along to indicate a change of direction. There was no path for them to follow, yet Jeremiah did not find it difficult to keep up with his companions, in spite of his feverish condition and the undulations of the terrain. He suddenly trembled at the thought that the Lord might be favouring Zedekiah's daring exploit, and a wild hope surged up in his heart that the proclamation of the jubilee, even though it had been clouded by ulterior motives, might once more have excited the Lord's compassion. Supposing they should succeed in weakening Babylon in the eyes of the world and hurling it into confusion! It was a thought that made him almost sink to his knees. The powers of the night were unfavourably disposed towards Babylon. Its gods had withdrawn behind a veil. Neither Marduk nor Nergal could be seen in the sky. The whining west wind at their backs lent wings to the attackers' silent onrush and at the same time drove the clouds towards the north-east, towards the Euphrates, as if it wanted to warn the soothsayers of Babylon of the evil that was about to befall them. Jeremiah began to murmur to himself the psalms he had learned in his childhood. His prayers were as if flung from the catapult of his soul, rising up to heaven to besiege the Lord. If they could only succeed! If the Lord would announce His change of mind this night!

A sudden, brief cry, and the invisibly flitting shadows stopped with a jerk. Noiselessly they all dropped to the ground, Jeremiah being pulled down with a grip of Ebed-melech's hand. The watch-fires of the outposts shone through the undergrowth and the twisted branches of the olive trees, with the breastworks looming up behind. In the topmost chamber of the little tower, which was built of painted wood, gleamed a solitary light where Samgar Nebo was presumably trying to unriddle the clouded sky. The three generals were probably standing restlessly at his side, waiting to hear his interpretation of the menacing positions of the stars and chafing at the enforced restriction of their activities. Jeremiah closed his eyes. In the darkness around him he could hear nothing but the heavy breathing of excited men. Straining to eliminate from his mind everything outside himself, and concentrating wholly on the world within him, he besieged the Lord more and more insistently with his supplications. Thus it was that he hardly noticed when the far-flung watch-fires gradually began to go out one by one, to be replaced by a dull gleam.

All at once the air was split by a distant din and shouting. Jeremiah was borne along by scurrying, panting shadows until, before he was aware of it, he found himself in the Babylonian encampment on the farther side of the breastworks. He heard Zedekiah give whispered orders and saw Ishmael, Malchiah, Shephatiah, Jucal, and Irijah dash down the radiating pathways at the head of whirling groups of black figures. But he planted his feet on the ground and stretched his arms up to heaven, as Moses had done in battle. He stood and did not let his arms sink when the first piercing cries of alarm rang through the camp, when swords began to clash and the first blazing torches to hiss, when a confused turmoil of fighting surged round him and arrows, spears, and stones whizzed through the darkness in aimless flight. He was still completely heedless of what was going on outside himself, and his concentration did not lessen even when triumphant fires sprang from tent to tent and embraced the great camp in one increasing conflagration that was fanned to fury by the exulting storm. Jeremiah did not exult with the wind and the flames, for he had become aware of startling words within him, seemingly contradictory and for that very reason terribly authentic. The soul-shattering words he heard were:

"For though ye had smitten the whole army of the Chaldeans that fight against you, and there remained but wounded men among them, yet should they rise up every man in his tent, and burn this city with fire."

Slowly he let his heavy arms sink to his sides, and was only roused from his reverie by a joyful shout from Zedekiah as the latter darted towards the wooden tower with a burning torch in either hand. Together with his bodyguard he set fire to the temple of the Babylonian gods, which was protected by but a few hastily collected and disorganized troops, yet long before the wreathing flames shot heavenward from the miniature E-temen-anki, the gates of Jerusalem had been flung wide and the beleaguered garrison had poured through the defences of the terror-stricken Babylonians with a roar as of thousands of lions.

When in the early dawn the gates of Zion had again closed behind the last warrior of Judah, they were able to celebrate not only the success of a cunningly planned sortie, but the fighting of a great battle and the winning of a decisive victory. The Babylonian camp had been set alight on two sides and was almost completely burnt out. Nebuzaradan had not merely lost a third of his army; he had no means of providing shelter for the rest. Zedekiah's men had levelled the enemy's breastworks and entrenchments to the ground and, what was the most serious blow for Babylon, captured or destroyed all his ordnance and siege-towers. It would be months before Nebuzaradan was in a position to resume the siege. The Lord who ruled the stars had caused the star of destruction to feel the weight of His hand, and the people of Jerusalem, as unbridled in their pride as they were extravagant in their remorse, danced frenziedly in the streets from sunrise to sunset. Women and children could not be prevented from climbing onto the walls, so that the showers of arrows and spears which greeted the homeless enemy were accompanied by no less violent storms of gibes and hisses. The warriors of Nebuchadnezzar no longer filled the watchers on the walls with awe, in spite of their iron masks of black and red. Even they themselves seemed to feel that their reputation as the unconquerable lords of the earth had been struck a mortal blow, and to have lost their self-confidence now that the stars had permitted a despised and insignificant foe to burn down the divine temple of their army. Not only did they refrain from answering the mocking shouts and ignore the clouds of arrows, but in the course of the day they began to withdraw to some distance from the city and set up an exiguous, inadequate encampment on the heights. When the sun rose for the second time after the great victory, the sentries on the walls of Jerusalem saw that the miracle of miracles had happened. Vanished were the humiliated hosts of Nergal Nebuzaradan; none but the keenest eyes on the topmost towers could still discern the billowing dust that showed where the rearguard of the Babylonian army was riding towards the south. The ignominious retreat must have seemed to them a matter of such urgency that they had executed it, contrary to all custom, during the night.

Jerusalem rang with shouts and cries that never ceased. The people were not merely exulting, they had gone mad, and in their frenzied joy there were few to ask themselves the decisive question why it was that Nebuzaradan had marched off towards the south instead of towards the north. The answer came that evening and it served to make the miracle complete. Zedekiah himself appeared before the people in the Temple; he was quite pale and faint at so much good fortune as he announced in a breathless voice that Pharaoh had resolved to fulfil his obligation under the pact, that he had just crossed the Egyptian frontier near Pithom with his army, and that within a short space he would have reached the boundaries of Judah. The holy alliance of kings had roused itself from its early state of impotence and was approaching from every side to punish the arrogance of Babylon for all time.

This was too much for the people of Jerusalem to bear. Their frenzied cries gave place to a deep silence. Their silence turned to stifled sobs. A whole nation was weeping, weeping at its own obduracy and at the divine compassion that had forgiven them at the eleventh hour. That night not a soul left the Temple. The priestly guards and their assistants were not strong enough to prevent the invasion of the inner court by the crowd, who threw themselves on the ground and kissed the stone flags that were wet with their tears. Their confessions of sin rose unceasingly to Heaven with the smoke from the burnt sacrifices. Without any order from the High Priest, their souls felt a passionate need for national fasting and penitence, and there ensued seven memorable days of contrition when the hearts of the people were so deeply stirred that even Jeremiah was led to believe that the true conversion had come at last. Yet only a few days after this penitential period there occurred something so abominable and monstrous that Jeremiah refused to believe it until public proof left him no alternative. The crime originated not with the King, but with the princes of the court and the great landowners—people, for the most part, who were not very different from Meshullam the miller. It was wrapped in fine words and justified by the pretence of necessity. The jubilee, so these wealthy men declared, had borne evil fruits. Great areas throughout the land that had been spared by the war had fallen into neglect from lack of peasant labour. Even the manufacture of the utensils of peace and of the weapons of war had suffered to a dangerous extent. Without the incessant toil of the bondservants it was impossible to manage when times were hard, and it was to the Lord's own advantage, since His Temple was being defended, that the King should restore the order of their fathers and with it the old and regular system of employment. By the gracious intervention of God the siege had been raised. Thousands of bondmen who had been recruited for service in the army were no longer needed for that purpose and would be eating their bread in idleness, which was detrimental to the welfare of the country. The King was therefore petitioned to decree without delay that every emancipated servant should return to his lawful master, and that if he did not do so voluntarily he would be subjected to severe punishment. The King issued the decree as the princes and landowners demanded. Though he suffered deep pangs of conscience, yet he yielded to Ishmael, Malchiah, Shephatiah, Jucal, and the rest when they assailed him with cogent arguments and declared that the monarchy could thrive only if the common people were kept in the state of thraldom, which was all they were fitted for. Particularly in times of unrest they must not allow the monopoly of power enjoyed by the noble families and wealthy landowners to be weakened by the sullen independence of the lower orders, who were always filled with hatred and malice.

The King's evil counsellors did not realize that they were tendering him this advice not from considerations of advantage to the State, but from their own intuitive hatred of the common people. They were careful to refrain from mentioning the fact that the emancipation was not a demand put forward by the bondmen themselves, but was a divine commandment of love. Time and again they repeated the same argument in different words—that God's place was in the Temple and the King's place was on the throne! A nation surrounded by other nations could not be governed by over-conscientious laws. None of them seemed to be aware of the abominable iniquity, the diabolical treachery, involved in the withdrawal, at a time when fortune favoured them, of the liberty which had been granted in the hour of peril. Or rather, there was one who was aware of it. Zedekiah was fully conscious of the foulness of his sin. While his governors and overseers throughout the land were restoring what was called the order of their fathers, the King did not revoke the emancipation in his own house and on his own estates. Jeremiah, however, was not in the least degree reconciled by this concession. It was now his turn to weep to himself with a helpless indignation that knew no bounds. And when it became known that the re-enslaved bondmen had been forced to return to their masters the portion they had received, Jeremiah was carried away by his wrath and uttered a solemn curse. For the first and only time in his life he repudiated the people for whom he had struggled so passionately and selflessly with the Lord since the night when he first assumed his task. Tossing sleeplessly on his couch, he sobbed into the darkness:

"Thou hast said, O God of Jacob, 'Behold, I will feed them with wormwood, and give them water of gall to drink!' . . . Thou hast said, 'I will scatter them among the heathen, whom neither they nor their fathers have known.' . . . Lord, Lord, I will not hold back your arm."

In the days that followed this act of base treachery to God, the King sent Ebed-melech three times to Jeremiah, summoning him to his presence. Three times the prophet sent the Ethiopian away with the same message:

"Speak to your master in my name: 'What has Jeremiah to do with thee?' "

Then one day he received a visitor whom he had least expected. Maacha, the Queen, whom custom strictly forbade to show herself outside the royal palaces, came at nightfall to his lodging, heavily veiled and accompanied by a single attendant. She advanced towards him in great agitation and seized his hand.

"Why has Jeremiah renounced his loyalty to his master and mine?" she asked, and flushed at her temerity. Jeremiah looked away from her.

"Your master," he said, "who rules over a small portion of the earth, has renounced his loyalty to the Lord who rules the world."

The strange shadows on Maacha's thin, virginal face deepened.

"No one knows better than his wife," she said with an effort, "how faithfully the King serves the Lord. It is easy for a prophet to judge sternly. But the King is chained to the world. He is ensnared in the pride of his generals, the will of his princes, the covetousness of powerful men. What does a solitary prophet of God know of the difficulties the King has in keeping to the narrow path between the jaws of the beasts of prey."

"Let him keep to the narrow path of his own weakness until the end!" replied Jeremiah harshly.

The Queen ignored the discourtesy of his answer. She was prepared to hear even harsher words. Though the whole town was still echoing with joyous shouts Maacha had come to offer the angered prophet a veiled apology for the king who had broken his oath. She seemed to be under the influence of a more or less vague apprehension, a foreboding of what was to follow the present triumph.

"Great things are happening in these days," she urged. "The King desires your counsel, but the only answer you give him is: 'What have I to do with thee?' "

"Of what use is it to him to hear my counsel," Jeremiah protested, "since he acts only according to the counsel of his princes!"

Maacha defiantly withdrew the hand with which she had been holding Jeremiah's as she pleaded with him.

"But it is my will that he should hear your counsel, and not only the counsel of his princes! He shall listen to you this very day!"

Jeremiah turned away his head, for the purity and devout urging of the young Queen sapped his resistance. He reminded her of what had happened long before:

"For words that were not my words I was beaten, put in the stocks, and pursued by those who desired my death, year after year. . . . Shall I again venture my life fruitlessly? And for whom?"

Maacha's childlike mouth quivered.

"Will you be doing it for the King," she asked solemnly,

between Noph and Babylon? Have you seen it in a vision or heard the voice of the Lord?"

Before Jeremiah could reply, the son of Pashur intervened. "Does the King not see how it pleases this man to prophesy misfortune? Do you not see how he rejoices at being able to belittle your mighty victory and call it vain? He cherishes but one hope, your downfall, that his ravings may be fulfilled. It would delight his heart to see you slain and Jerusalem in flames, for he hates you and this people. Can you not perceive this?"

"I perceive nothing," the King murmured, and he looked round in perplexity.

Chamberlains entered with lights, two large candelabra being set on the floor near to Zedekiah's chair and a number of gold candlesticks distributed about the room. In their bright radiance the face of Ishmael seemed to Jeremiah like a seething furnace whose flames could be faintly perceived through strong, dark walls. The prince's hand played with one of the massive candlesticks on the little Egyptian side-table near which he stood, and he thoughtfully extinguished the flame between two fingers as if he did not want his face to be illuminated too clearly from below. His voice sounded hoarse as he turned to Zedekiah.

"The King has subdued the Land of Rivers as no King has done before him. A weak army confronts Pharaoh. Is it likely that he will hesitate to free himself from Babylon for ever?"

"But if what we have been told concerning Noph and Babylon is really true!" said the King uncertainly, with his eyes still fixed on Jeremiah. "They show no sign of preparing for battle. . . . What then?"

Jeremiah laid his hand on his heart and bowed.

"May the King now give me leave to go from his presence!"

"So there is ill news from the Lord?" whispered Zedekiah.

The prophet took three steps back, as if he were about to go without waiting for permission, but the King started up from his seat.

"You are to speak!" he commanded. "I wish to hear the words of the Lord!"

Jeremiah lowered his head and remained obstinately silent. The King was unable to control himself any longer.

"If you do not hate me and this people," he cried, "then speak! How is it with Babylon?"

"Babylon will come again," Jeremiah replied calmly.

There was a burst of scornful laughter from the princes: "Let Babylon come again!"

Jeremiah did not heed their mockery, but gazed steadily at the King.

"You have defeated Babylon in battle. But you cannot conquer him who is the Lord's servant. He will come with new armies to besiege you."

The others bent down to whisper in the King's ear:

"Our King, are you not yet weary of this repeated babbling? Did he not predict the same thing before your victory?"

The King ignored them. His eyes had suddenly lost their lustre.

"These are not the words of Zebaoth," he said in a stifled voice. "I wish to hear the words of Zebaoth."

Jeremiah held back no longer. Advancing until he stood directly in front of the King, he revealed the words which the Lord had spoken to him:

"Ye have not hearkened unto me in proclaiming liberty

every one to his brother, and every man to his neighbour: behold, I proclaim a liberty for you, saith the Lord, to the sword, to the pestilence, and to the famine!"

The princes stared at one another. What could be the meaning of this threat? Zebaoth veiled his intentions in obscure language which the prophets could use as a mask for their own audacity. Only slowly did they grasp the significance of what they had just heard. As a punishment for revoking the emancipation of the bondservants, the Lord had proclaimed that they themselves were free, but it was the freedom of the hunted birds of the air and of the wild beasts. Ishmael was the first to understand, and his face seemed to contract till it was thinner than ever. The sinews of the hand that gripped the gold candlestick grew taut, but he kept his voice under control.

"Does the King, who had the courage to defeat the Babylonian general in his own camp, not possess the courage to deal with this man here? Must the swords of his princes lie idle in their scabbards while the King is insulted?"

Zedekiah, who had flushed scarlet, looked in helpless anger from one to the other.

"These words do not apply to me. I have no concern with them. In my own house I have revoked nothing. In my own house I have kept my oath and not infringed the commandment. But you, my companions"—the accusation burst from him in rage and grief—"you have deceived and outwitted me. You, and you alone, have broken your oath and sinned. It is not to me, but to you, that these words apply. On your souls rests the curse. . . ."

He covered his eyes, and the deep silence that followed his outburst was charged with hostility. Never had the King spoken so harshly to these princes, who were his most intimate friends. They were struck dumb with mortification, but put all the blame for the estrangement that had arisen between them and the King on the hated prophet, who even now dared to raise his voice again and repeat his request: "Does the King give me leave to go?"

"No!" Zedekiah fulminated. "Though you were my teacher, I order you to stay! My commands are for you no less than for everyone else!" Then he added in a calmer tone: "I know that you have not yet told me all. There is still something that you are keeping back!"

"Why do you force me to speak, when you will not listen?" asked Jeremiah sadly.

The King seized upon the implied admission.

"You see! You yourself confess that there is more to tell. How well things went without you! How ill they go when you are here! An hour ago I was rejoicing in my victory. And now? I command you, speak before me and these princes, that your words may penetrate to their stubborn hearts. If the Houses of Bondage should conclude a treaty, if Babylon should come again, if new armies should march against Jerusalem . . . what then?"

Ishmael jerked the candlestick from the table. He wanted to anticipate the prophet that the King might not be rendered faint-hearted, and he hissed:

"If they should come again, if new armies should march against Jerusalem, what then? You will defeat them as you have done before!"

For the first time during the audience Jeremiah turned to face Ishmael, and he gazed mournfully into his eyes as he repeated the words that had come to him while Zedekiah was making his successful attack on the Babylonian camp:

"Though ye had smitten the whole army of the Chaldeans

that fight against you, saith the Lord, and there remained but wounded men among them, yet should they rise up every man in his tent, and burn this city with fire!"

"But you will not rise up again," said Ishmael in a hoarse but tranquil voice. Flinging back his arm, he dashed the heavy gold candlestick right into Jeremiah's face.

The dreadful blow struck the prophet between the eyes and he sank to the floor at the King's feet without uttering a sound. There was no one in the room who would not have sworn that Jeremiah was dead. Even the faint glimmer of consciousness that dwelt in the most inaccessible depths of his numb soul believed that this was so.

29

Between the Walls, in the Dungeons, and in the Court of the Guard

FOR more than three months Jeremiah hovered between life and death. But the sensitive son of Hilkiah and Abi had a hard skull that withstood the force of the massive weapon and saved his life. Slowly the wound healed as the splinters of bone were removed, but the scar that it left on his forehead between the eyes was as deep as the wound itself. Luckily the blow had missed his shapely, aquiline nose, so that his face was not disfigured by such an unsightly and terrible scar as Urijah's had been. His mind took longer to heal than the wound. For some time after the hand of death had been lifted from him, he lay stretched on his couch motionless and dumb. When Baruch, who was tending him, offered him liquid nourishment, he would open his mouth obediently and swallow like a child, his eyes fixed with a far-away look on a corner of the room. From time to time the two Queens, Hamutal and Maacha, came secretly to visit the patient, bringing with them pomegranates, fresh dates, and grapes, and they would sit for a long while at his bedside. But he looked through them as if they were transparent. On one occasion the King himself appeared; it was obvious from his words that he was deeply sorry for what had happened, but Jeremiah did not even flicker an eyelid. They all thought, therefore, that he had lost his sight and hearing, as well as the power of speech, though

whom he had sprung. He smiled gently at his reflection, to the astonishment of the saddler and his assistants, who showed by their meaning looks that they took him to be a harmless simpleton. Jeremiah, however, regarded his changed countenance, his outward rebirth, as a mysterious token of distinction.

It was another month before he regained the full use of his legs, but when he did, he took full advantage of his restored health, for he was possessed by a strange impulse to wander about. As the city was surrounded by the enemy, there was no way in which Jeremiah could get out into the open country; he had to confine his walks to the space within the walls. He roamed in circles, but visited neither the palace nor the Temple, avoiding even the outer courtyard, which seethed from early morning till late at night with the clamorous preaching of the prophets and the hubbub of agitated voices among the bitterly disappointed people. During these days Jeremiah gave those who saw him the impression that he had become demoralized; that the great healing forces of prayer, penitence, and sacrifice no longer meant anything to him. When Baruch frankly questioned him on the subject, his answer was: "Know you not that liberty has been proclaimed for you and for me?"

Every morning at sunrise he left the saddler's house. The narrow streets were still empty and there was little likelihood of his being stared at and annoyed. When he appeared at other times of the day in his weather-worn cloak and leaning on the clumsy, gnarled stick that he had retained after discarding his yoke, foolish mothers would point to the man of God as he tottered on his way absorbed in his thoughts and frighten their little children with the words: "Look, the prophet will take you away!"—as if he were an evil spirit.

He carefully kept out of people's way, until eventually he discovered the most suitable spot for his daily walk. Between the outer and inner rings of fortifications ran a broad belt of grassland in a great right angle, a town within a town. Here grazed the cattle that served to feed the besieged inhabitants, though their number had shrunk to an alarming extent, since the herds could not be replenished. Belated fugitives from the plains, who had not been able to find shelter in Jerusalem, had pitched their tents in the open space, and it was also used as a centre for the sick and wounded, so that the inner city should be free from the danger of epidemics. In addition, the troops and their officers were quartered here while waiting to relieve the garrisons that occupied the walls and bulwarks. When fighting was taking place on the walls, reinforcements of men, weapons, and munitions were made ready so that the supporting companies of soldiers and the necessary war material could be thrown into the fray in good time. As this area was therefore the most important military depot that the defence possessed, access was not granted to everyone; the officers in command at the inner gates were provided with lists containing the names of all those authorized to enter.

Most of the soldiers knew Jeremiah by sight and let him go through with a careless wave of the hand when he appeared every morning at the inner Gate of Benjamin or Ephraim. Though they were not amiably inclined towards any of the prophets, and least of all to the most implacable of them, they did not prevent the former teacher of the King from attaching himself to a company that was going up to relieve another; occasionally they allowed him even to climb up to a sentry-post on the wall or to ascend one of the towers. He would spend hours at a time silently looking out over the countryside where, strange to say, there was little to be seen of the war or of the Babylonians, since Nergal Nebuzaradan had learned his lesson after Zedekiah's successful sortie and had altered his method of siege. His cordon was drawn completely round the city, but in a much wider circle than before, and now, with the serene patience that befitted a man of the stars, he was waiting for the most suitable moment to tighten the noose. The Babylonian encampment no longer stretched along the slopes of the hills, but along the crests. Six separate camps, guarded by strong breastworks, could defy any daring assault on the part of Zedekiah or Elnathan. All the roads were under enemy control, even the Road of Gold and Incense having been blocked after their pact with Pharaoh, so that neither camels nor asses, sheep nor cattle, could enter Jerusalem. The vast no-man's-land between the Babylonian camps and the city rendered impossible any attempt at an effective sally, since it would only be swallowed up in the empty terrain like water in the desert. Yet there was no sign of anxiety in the eyes of Zedekiah's warriors. They did not look beyond the present, and seemed long since to have forgotten that Pharaoh's disloyalty had caused everything to take a turn for the worse again. The heroes of the bodyguard roared their battle songs, in which they boldly, even shamelessly, summoned Zebaoth to keep his promise and, if necessary, to perform a miracle as He had done in the days of Joshua. They went about their duties cheerfully, for up till now it had not been a bad war. Jerusalem had so far proved impregnable, and the infrequent, half-hearted assaults of Babylon seemed to indicate a healthy respect for the warriors of Judah.

Jeremiah kept his eyes fixed in the direction of Anathoth.

He was filled with an unfamiliar nostalgia for his father's house and for the land of Benjamin, where he had spent his childhood. The hills of Anathoth called to him, though he did not know why. In his heart was a vague foreboding. During Jeremiah's illness Hanameel had twice managed to slip into the city to pay the interest due to him, but four months had gone by since his last visit. Jeremiah felt that his father's desolated estate needed him, perhaps for the first time. Belatedly he realized that his heart clung to the house and farm which he had so often forgotten in the course of his life, and he considered how best he could leave Jerusalem in order to go to Anathoth. All the gates were strongly guarded; night and day they were in charge of officers of high rank. None the less, there were numerous deserters. Marduk had issued a special order that deserters were to be received not only considerately, but with open arms, and that each of them was to be promised a share of the estates owned by the King, the princes, and the magnates. By such inducements the Babylonians planned to depopulate Jerusalem with the minimum of bloodshed and, at the same time, to take vengeance on Zedekiah and his advisers.

Jeremiah craved only one thing: to return home to Anathoth for a few days in order that he might visit his father's house, wander through the fields of his inheritance with Hanameel, and lay a consecrated offering on the tomb of his parents. He felt as if his mother were waiting for him at home, and that he must show her his changed countenance so that she might recognize her youngest child in spite of it. He revealed his deep longing to Baruch, but the latter was so startled, and warned him so vehemently against any unconsidered act, that he did not speak of it again.

One autumn night, when there was no moon and he was

again roving restlessly between the walls, he was suddenly stopped by a man who shone a screened lantern in his face. As the man's massive form was wrapped in a voluminous travelling-cloak, it was only when he lifted the lamp to his own features that Jeremiah recognized Gedaliah, the older of Ahikam's twin sons.

"I know a way," whispered Gedaliah, "that is without danger if we hurry. Follow me!"

The prophet did not stir from the spot, and Gedaliah grew more urgent.

"Everything has happened as you predicted and as my father deduced before his death. I have waited and hesitated and could not persuade myself to go, until this hour. Now that all is lost, I am no longer concerned with Jerusalem or the Temple, but only with the Remnant of Jacob. Micah has gone before me to prepare the fold. Now the time has come and he has summoned me to take over the task. He has summoned you too."

Jeremiah slowly shook his head.

"This is your concern and his, not mine."

In truth, it was not his concern to act, like Ahikam and his sons, on the basis of logical thought and argument. He did not need to learn afresh that the sum of all calculation was invariably naught. The fact that Gedaliah and Micah had convinced themselves logically that the end would be evil, and that they expected no change of heart on the part of Judah, filled Jeremiah with a strong antipathy. Men did not change. Their ridiculous self-confidence and assurance were due to their childish overestimation of the empty conjecturing they called reason and foresight. Greatly as he honoured this faithful son of Shaphan as the best man in Judah, there was an unbridgeable and fundamental difference between them. In a hurried whisper Gedaliah informed him that Nebuchadnezzar was expected in the Babylonian camp within a few days and that he was prepared, as Micah had declared in a secret message, to exercise mercy after he had exterminated the House of David. He had promised to spare the people and appoint Gedaliah governor over the Remnant. Until that every day Gedaliah had wrestled with himself before deciding on the step he was about to take. But there was no other way of preserving Judah and rescuing it from the abyss. It was Jeremiah's duty to help in the work of salvation, for he stood high in Nebuchadnezzar's esteem.

Jeremiah realized what a bitter struggle it had been for Gedaliah, in spite of all his clear arguments, to forsake the beleaguered city, and how deeply his heart craved the help and comfort of his friend. Yet he refused to go with him.

"Neither Nebuchadnezzar's desire nor Gedaliah's plan will be fulfilled," he said.

"Do not delay another moment," urged Gedaliah, "but let us go to Marduk, that you too may lay your entreaties at his feet."

"My place is not with Marduk in this hour," said Jeremiah; "but repeat to him the words I am about to say to you."

Anxiously Gedaliah put his face closer to that of Jeremiah, and these were the words he was told to carry to Nebuchadnezzar:

"You will slay a people that is already dead. You will burn a Temple that is already burned. You will grind corn that is already ground."

Swiftly the rumour spread in Jerusalem that Gedaliah,

the honourable and widely respected grandson of Shaphan, had turned traitor and fled under cover of night to the camp of the Babylonians. It was a blow more discouraging than a reverse to their arms would have been. The King, his generals, and his princes were furious and determined that the treachery of desertion to the enemy should be punished without mercy. The sentries and patrols along the walls were doubled during the three night-watches and received strict orders to put to death without hesitation anyone caught trying to escape from the city. The northern sector of the walls was placed in charge of the sternest of the captains of the royal bodyguard, who was none other than Irijah, the son of Hananiah. Irijah took up his quarters in a chamber of the outer Gate of Benjamin, from which a great road led to the northern provinces.

Some days after Gedaliah's flight, Jeremiah appeared as usual in the belt of grassland between the walls and wandered about undecidedly for an hour or so near the Gate of Benjamin. Every now and then he would pause and cast a longing glance through the dark archway, in front of which a redheaded corporal and a few soldiers were sitting idly while the sentries marched up and down with their lances across their shoulders. At last he walked up to the corporal and pointed to the gate.

"Open it for me," he said calmly, as if he were asking nothing out of the ordinary. "I am the man of Anathoth. I wish to return home for a few days to settle my affairs on my estate in Benjamin."

With a swift step he walked past the redheaded corporal and entered the gateway, but the man gripped him firmly by the arm and stared at him with venomous little eyes.

"The man of Anathoth," he nodded, "wishes to return to Anathoth to settle his affairs. . . ."

Ere Jeremiah had time to grasp their intention, he was roughly seized by the soldiers and taken before their captain, who was sitting in his underground chamber in front of a glowing brazier like a patient spider in a web waiting for victims to be brought in by his spies and familiars. Even before they reached the door, Jeremiah's captor called out exultingly:

"We've got him! . . . He walked right into our hands!"

Irijah raised his head, and his finely chiselled face gleamed redly in the light from the glowing coals. For some time he did not speak, but his eyes betrayed the pleasure he felt at the prospect of his long-delayed vengeance. At last he had in his power the man whose name had haunted his father until the day of his death, and who had come to revel with a diabolical joy in the sight of his defeated rival as the latter lay dying in agony. Either Jeremiah was a consummate liar who had by his magic arts prejudiced the Lord against Irijah's father, in which case he deserved to be put to death; or else he truly was a sanctified prophet and Hananiah the charlatan, in which he doubly deserved death in the eyes of Hananiah's son. Irijah gave no indication of what he was thinking, but turned to his prisoner with an air of official calm.

"So you want to go to Anathoth?" he asked thoughtfully, as if this was a request that might well be considered. Hope rose in Jeremiah's heart. "I wish to return home for a few days to set my estate in order."

The captain carefully pushed the glowing coals together in the brazier with a pair of tongs.

"When were you last in Anathoth for the purpose of settling your affairs?" he asked in a tone of unconcern. Jeremiah hesitated. The question was undoubtedly designed as a trap! Yet he had to admit the truth and say that he had not been in Anathoth since the days of Jehoiakim. Irijah smiled gently as he listened to the prophet's answer.

"It is somewhat late in the day to begin taking an interest in your farm, Jeremiah. You appear to have waited patiently for the arrival of Marduk and his generals before making up your mind to return home."

"I know," said Jeremiah, "that the Babylonians will not prevent me from going to visit my estate."

The son of Hananiah smiled with increasing delight.

"I can well believe that you do. And you know much more. It is not for nothing that you have been spying into all the gates and climbing the towers during the past few months. We know quite a lot about you."

In spite of his innocence Jeremiah was so confused by Irijah's smile, the angry looks of the guards, and the circumstantial evidence which seemed to prove his guilt, that he began to stammer incoherent explanations as if he had been caught red-handed. But Irijah only bowed his head before him in mocking respect.

"True prophet of the Lord," he said, "grant a simple warrior, who is unversed in the ways of God, permission to assume your prophetic office and tell *you* the truth for a change. . . ."

With these words he rose from his seat in fury, then shouted:

"You have fallen away to the Babylonians like the others, like Gedaliah! You are a traitor, a spy of Marduk! We have known it for a long time. . . ."

Jeremiah's soul was torn by a wild grief, and he too began to shout:

"It is false! It is false! . . . I fall not away to the Babylonians . . . I yearned for my home in Anathoth. . . ."

His impotent outburst brought forth guffaws of laughter. He continued to shout and protest, but this served only to make his guilt appear more evident. Irijah ordered him to be fettered, and as he did not dare on his own authority to execute summary judgment on such an important prisoner, he set himself at the head of his men and led Jeremiah through the streets of the city and the precincts of the Temple. The guards thoroughly enjoyed their task, and the arrest of the prophet who had so undeviatingly predicted disaster came most opportunely for the inhabitants of Jerusalem. After the joyful mood in which they had celebrated the league of kings, the depression which had ensued on his failure, their renewed joy at the defeat of Babylon, and their further disappointment at the enemy's return, the people were in a state of utter bewilderment and at a loss to know which way to turn. They thirsted for a scapegoat on whom they could discharge their hatred. It was immaterial whom they chose as a victim, but they had to attribute the blame to someone if they were not to stifle in their wrath and despair. For more years than they could remember, Jeremiah had been prophesying the downfall of Jerusalem; now nothing was more natural than that they should regard him as the cause of their misfortune. The people were profoundly distrustful, and they suspected that every prophet put forward his own passionate hopes as the word of God. He who predicted fire must in his own heart be an incendiary. Jeremiah had predicted nothing but fire; it was now clear that he was an incendiary not only in his heart but in his deeds as well. A rumour sprang up that he had visited the camp of Babylon every night. In a few minutes the streets were crowded with people whose hatred in many cases was mingled with a strange feeling of relief that the stern, incorruptible, implacable prophet had been unmasked as a base and treacherous knave. For nothing brought greater comfort to trivial minds than the knowledge that one far superior to themselves had been reduced to the general level or below it. Men and women rushed wildly from their houses, shouting and shaking their fists, and soon stones began to fly through the air. Irijah ordered his guards to place their shields together as a moving wall round the prisoner. When Baruch, undismayed, tried to force his way through the raving crowd, he received a blow in the face from the flat of Irijah's sword that flung him to the ground. The man of Anathoth was friendless and alone.

Irijah, who had judged the situation correctly, led his prisoner not before the King but before the so-called "daily tribunal," which met in the house of Jonathan the scribe. This was a permanent court martial which dealt with traitors, deserters, cowards, profiteers, and hoarders of food. The president of the tribunal on this day was Pashur's son, Malchiah, whose features lit up with pleasure at the sight of his father's enemy in fetters. The representative of the priests was Zephaniah, First Keeper of the Door, who was breathing on his gnarled hands in an effort to warm them, an occupation in which he was completely absorbed. The hearing did not last long. Facts spoke too strongly against Jeremiah. His name had been for months on the daily lists made by the guards of the different gates. There were witnesses who alleged that they had seen him in conversation with

Gedaliah. Even more benevolent judges would have found it difficult to believe that the evidence admitted of some harmless explanation, and since Jeremiah had given himself up for lost, he refused to defend himself or to answer their questions. Things had been very different on the previous occasion when his enemies had dragged him before the tribunal of twenty-three and charged him with blasphemy. This time he was not tossed about between fear of his fellowmen and apprehension of death on the one hand, and anger and the will to fight on the other. He was filled with a deep peace such as he had never felt before; or rather, he was embraced by it. It seemed to stand behind him with outstretched arms like an angel of God, against whom he had only to lean gently for everything around him to recede into the remote distance. Whatever might happen to him, he would not protest. The angel of peace did not desert him even when he was condemned to forty strokes less one and the jailer's scourge lashed down on his naked back. On this occasion there was no Baruch present to intercept any of these blows, and after the flogging he was thrown into the State prison in the cellars of the house.

When Baruch, years afterwards, recorded his master's sufferings in a special book, he referred to it in the words: "Jeremiah was entered into the dungeon, and into the cabins, and remained there many days." These words were a true record, yet they were not wholly true. Jeremiah did remain for many days in his dungeon, but they were days without morning or evening. He spent a single, endless, unbroken night in the bowels of the earth. Compared with his prison, Amenti was a place of delight, for it knew the passing of the hours and a changing scene. In Jeremiah's cell there was neither. It knew no variation and was therefore more oppressive than the realm of the dead. The darkness in which he was confined never grew less black and the hours knew no procession. Unintermittent, too, were the wailing and chattering of teeth of his fellow-prisoners, who were fettered like Jeremiah to the rock with chains and iron balls. In the unending succession of sighs and groans even the strongest spirit could fall a prey to madness. Was the groaning at his side something that he had heard yesterday, or would he not really hear it until tomorrow? Neither bliss nor damnation could be measured by time, and both were more than human nature could bear. But the angel of peace did not forsake him, and in his loving care Jeremiah lived and breathed even in his timeless purgatory. In this endless, fetid night, his senses became even more acute than they had been before. Yet he did not hear the voice of Adonai. Its peculiar attribute was never to speak to him when his whole being was tense and prepared to receive it. On the other hand, his ears were opened in a new and wondrous way. Suddenly he was able to hear, or believed he could hear, what was happening far away. It began with the regular step of marching troops high above his head, ordinarily inaudible to the sharpest ear, as the guards were being relieved. He heard a confused murmur of voices that first approached and then receded. After a time, by dint of much strain, he was able to disentangle the threads of this web of sound and distinguish individual voices. In this way he overheard conversations taking place in the House of Solomon between the King and his princes, and the voices were so clear that Jeremiah did not realize it was his own brain and not the royal palace from which they came.

Zedekiah was speaking in a hesitant and anxious whisper. He reported that the envoys to Pharaoh and the other kings had been unable to achieve their purpose. Babylon's allies had increased tenfold and Pharaoh had no intention of involving Egypt in war with Marduk, while the little kings were glad to keep in the background and avoid bringing themselves to the notice of their powerful neighbour. Zebaoth Himself had gone over to the enemies of Judah. The King raised his voice in anger, accused his princes of giving him advice that had brought only disaster. The princes also raised their voices in angry retort. They seemed to have lost respect for their royal master and called him faint-hearted, declaring that he was an enfeebled lion whose mind was so intent on the future that he could not see the needs of the present and the deeds which beckoned. Jerusalem, they said was impregnable. Two harvests had already been lost, the King rejoined heatedly, the granaries had been stripped to almost the last measure of wheat, the stores of oil and wine had been almost used up. It would be criminal to deceive the people any longer, and to refuse to admit that they were menaced by famine and the plagues which came in its train. It was criminal, cried the princes, to speak of famine and plague when the army still stood unconquered behind its leaders. Only one thing was essential: to lose no time, but to prepare a blow that should be as glorious as the previous one had been. . . .

Here the web of voices grew so dense and confused that Jeremiah could no longer distinguish what was being said. But he heard voices elsewhere: the distant singing of the guards, the watchmen on the towers calling the hour, men talking in their houses in anxious whispers. He heard the weary voices of the sons of Asaph and the sobbing entreaties of the High Priest at the threshold of the Holy of Holies. Then his ear became attuned to sounds of a different kind.

There came to him in the darkness an excited twittering of numerous birds. It was more than an empty twittering. The birds were actually speaking. They screeched, jeered, laughed, chattered, and imitated human voices. Jeremiah realized that he was listening to the clamour in Marduk's tent, where the King of Babylon sat alone with his parliament of birds. He made a supreme effort to distinguish clearly what these shrunken images of the stars were debating with their master, but his inner ear could decipher neither Nebuchadnezzar's questions nor the shrill answers of his mocking companions.

Once, when he was again straining to overhear the inaudible, the endless night of his dungeon was torn by the jagged light of torches. Men entered and freed him from his chains.

He was taken not to Solomon's Palace, but to the House of Pharaoh's Daughter, where the King sat with his family waiting for him. The age spent in his pitch-black cell had so weakened him that he was unable to stand upright when he emerged once more into the light of day and the fresh air. He had almost to be carried by the men escorting him, and when they reached the chamber of the royal ladies he sank into a chair and found it difficult to catch his breath. As he gradually became accustomed to his changed surroundings, the first thing he saw was that Hamutal and Maacha were sitting side by side on a couch, with the two little princes standing next to them. Adajah, the older boy, had grown considerably since Jeremiah had last seen him and he regarded the prophet with a distrustful look in his alert young eyes. A melancholy shadow, as of coming flight and exile, seemed to hover over the small group. Abruptly the King, who was sitting behind Jeremiah, called out to him.

"Thank these women," he said, "not me, that you have been remembered. . . ."

Jeremiah did not turn round; he had not the strength to do so. He waited for the King to come forward a couple of paces and speak to him face to face. But Zedekiah deliberately refrained from moving. He apparently found it easier to converse with his former teacher from behind his back.

"Never would I have thought it possible," he murmured with an exaggerated sigh, "that you could become my enemy."

Not only Jeremiah, but Hamutal and Maacha too, ignored this empty and insincere accusation. Zedekiah's attempt to put him in the wrong, in spite of the unjust way he had been treated, failed of its effect, but Jeremiah's pointed question did not fail to hit the mark.

"What have I offended against you, or against your servants, or against this people, that you have put me in prison?"

Before the King could collect himself sufficiently to answer, Hamutal intervened. The malady from which she suffered was now far advanced and she looked old.

"Our friend," she said in a tone of indignation, "could never have offended! . . ."

"It is for the King to speak, and not his mother," interrupted Zedekiah cuttingly. His discourteous and angry retort indicated the discomfort under which he was labouring. Jeremiah, however, addressed him in the formal phraseology of the court or the Temple, as one spoke not to another human being but to a king on his throne or to the Lord in heaven:

"Hear now, I pray thee, O my Lord the King; let my

supplication, I pray thee, be accepted before thee, that thou cause me not to return to the house of Jonathan the scribe, lest I die there!"

The obsequious formula seemed to please Zedekiah and he came forward from behind Jeremiah's chair. Gazing at him with his large eyes, he said:

"What are you thinking of, Jeremiah? Your offence has been grave. . . ."

"My King knows in his heart that I have been guilty of no offence. . . ."

"Even if your King knew it, yet Ishmael, Malchiah, and the others believe in your guilt, for you have never given proof of your innocence. That is why I am receiving you secretly in the house of the women."

At this point Maacha rose from the couch where she had been sitting. Her face bore traces of the anxiety which consumed her. The strange look of sorrow that shadowed her virginal features had deepened. Touching Zedekiah's hand with the tips of her fingers, she pleaded with him:

"May my King hearken unto me! Let this man of the Lord be held as his own prisoner, and not the prisoner of his princes!"

"My wife speaks wisely," said Zedekiah with a smile. By his gentleness to Maacha he wanted to make up for the brusque way he had spoken to his mother. "Her thoughts are akin to those of the King."

He turned to Jeremiah.

"You once greeted me as the true son of David. Do you remember?"

"I remember."

"Since you remember, I also remember that after my father and mother it is you to whom I owe the deepest debt of gratitude. I have remained loyal to you despite your disloyalty to me, and despite the fact that your behaviour and the favour I show you have estranged my friends from me. You should not and cannot go free! But I have brought you out from the dungeons and you shall be kept in honourable captivity as the prisoner of the King. You shall be lodged in the great court of the guard in my palace, where you may dwell and move about as you will, though you must not go beyond its boundaries. As you served Josiah, my father, so faithfully, I will do even more for you. Let my mother rejoice! It may be that the time will come—though I do not expect it to come—when it will not be easy for you to obtain food and you may go hungry. Because I am still grateful to you, I will arrange beforehand for your needs. Let my mother and Maacha hear my words! Orders will be given to my steward that Jeremiah is to receive daily a piece of bread out of the bakers' street, a portion of meat out of the butchers' street, together with wine, oil, and all necessities from my own table. Though I must keep you as my prisoner, at the same time I receive you as my guest who breaks the King's bread. . . . Now it would befit the King to be silent and leave it to his prisoner to acknowledge the generosity of such gratitude. But I know Jeremiah and realize that even the impossible seems to him modest."

Jeremiah raised both hands in horror.

"The King must not do the impossible for me!"

"For you or for Adonai," the King replied with a deprecating gesture, "it is all the same! In return, however, I demand that you tell me the whole truth, honestly and concealing nothing. Let the truth be favourable, Jeremiah, for I am very downcast. Is there any word from the Lord?"

Jeremiah's eyes rested for a long time on the two women

and the boys, but he said nothing. The King flung himself into a chair and his voice sounded constrained.

"Jeremiah does not wish to speak before the ears of the women, though they are the mother and wife of the King. He does not wish to speak before the ears of the King's sons, though they can as yet comprehend but little. Jeremiah is right. Let my children be spared, before they have reached their thirteenth year, from hearing the bitter words of the Lord!"

At a nod from Zedekiah the two queens left the room with the young princes. Hamutal, whom her malady had made very obese, was able to walk only with difficulty, and Maacha had to support her. The King waited impatiently until they had gone, then he demanded in great agitation:

"Now speak, whether what you have to tell me be good or ill! May it be good! It must be good! Yet my sorrowful spirit has the strength to bear it even if it be ill."

Jeremiah lowered his head, so that the King could not see his emaciated face and his eyes which were still half blinded from the endless night he had spent in the dungeons.

"Look at me, my King," he implored, "and do not compel me to speak!"

"I have shown you immeasurable mercy," said the King with rising wrath, "and what I have done for you has caused me to quarrel with my princes. Yet you are full of malice and refuse to answer me, though I know you are concealing something, whether it be good or ill. Have a care, lest you return once more to the dungeons! I command you to speak!"

Jeremiah shuddered at the threat, and he whispered sadly:

"You will be delivered into the hand of the King of Babylon, both you and your house!"

The King stared at the prophet, but his thoughts were far

away. At last he collected himself with an effort and burst into a convulsive fit of laughter.

"My one consolation is that I know you so well, Jeremiah. You would rather bite your tongue through than speak that which would comfort my spirit, even though each word I uttered was an entreaty that you should comfort me in my sorrow."

"Should I have lied to the King when he demanded that I speak the truth?" asked Jeremiah in astonishment.

The King's twisted smile vanished and a stream of words poured from his lips. "Do lies consist only of that which it is agreeable to hear?" he cried. "Is the truth only that which chokes one? You err grievously, for you are ignorant of the complexity of life! And your grievous error gives me strength to laugh at your words. Perhaps I shall be delivered into the hand of the King of Babylon. But perhaps I shall fall on the battlements, pierced with spears, or on the field like Josiah, my father. Perhaps I shall grow old in peace, and songs of lamentation will be sung at my burial in the Garden of Uzziah. Nothing is yet decided, neither the hour that will come after this, nor tomorrow, nor the day after tomorrow. My teacher, your pupil confutes you with your own teaching! You have always said: 'Adonai is a patient and hesitating God.' Do you tell me that He will not hesitate before He destroys the House of David? You have always said: 'Josiah, your father, died because he was too sure of the Lord.' I, however, am not sure that I shall be favoured by fortune, just as I am not sure that I shall be overwhelmed by misfortune! Are you listening to me, Jeremiah? You have predicted this and that, and what you have predicted has sometimes come to pass. But what prophet does not sometimes see the fulfilment of his predictions? I am certain of nothing, Jeremiah. And this gives me the courage to laugh at you and your words, and to hold to the generous promise I made because of my gratitude."

"It is permitted," said Jeremiah in a low voice, "to be uncertain even of uncertainty."

The great court of the guard, which was also known as "the King's court of the guard," extended from the royal palaces to the northern wall that bordered on the Temple. It was the most spacious of all the courtyards and, together with its various rooms, stables, turrets, and vaults, was used as service quarters and parade ground for the royal bodyguard. A gloomy cell situated in one of the walls was allotted to Jeremiah; there he lived among the soldiers whose generals were his mortal enemies. The men were neither friendly nor hostile, but treated him partly with a condescending respect, partly with good-humoured mockery. Whatever their attitude, they all felt a secret awe of the uncanny stranger. These soldiers performed arduous duties, yet their rations were none of the best. The barley bread they ate was hard, and the flat loaves grew smaller and of poorer quality from week to week. Jeremiah, on the other hand, received a daily supply of excellent food from the King's table, which he gave away to the soldiers with the exception of the small amount he needed for himself. Many of them were grateful and hung round his cell expectantly, but their gratitude did not lead to greater friendliness. Sometimes, when a company of the guards had returned from a period of duty on the bulwarks and the men, wrapped in their filthy cloaks, had thrown themselves down on the ground in front of Jeremiah's open cell to snatch a brief sleep, one or other of them would start up from an uneasy dream and awaken the prophet with a hoarse cry: "Prophet of the Lord, what will become of us?"

Jeremiah would soothe the restless sleeper with obscure and comforting sayings that allowed him to go on hoping but did not pervert the truth. Every day, as he sat with the soldiers for hours at a time during their periods off duty, he was careful to avoid saying anything that might render them faint-hearted. When he first came among them they had talked roughly and boastfully, but as time passed they grew more and more subdued. Nebuchadnezzar had brought a hundred new pieces of ordnance with him from Babylon, together with storming ladders of a novel type that projected above the walls of Jerusalem. A new attack had been in progress for some weeks, with heavy casualties daily. Battering-rams and rocks hurled by catapults thundered incessantly against the walls, but without success. Jeremiah only half listened to what the men were saying, whether they were bragging of their deeds or giving a gloomy account of the fighting. His thoughts returned again and again to Anathoth. He could see the defective place in the wall that surrounded the estate, the threshold of the house where his mother's lamp had so often waited for him, the dark passage that led to his parents' bedchamber, and his own room where the almond tree had spread its branches on the night of his first vision. Never again would he journey to Anathoth!

But Anathoth came to him. And it came, as was to be expected, in the person of Hanameel. The worthy farmer, who usually presented such a neat appearance with his well-trimmed beard and simple but spotless garments, had for some reason become slovenly and ragged. His hair hung over his eyes, his beard was long and tousled. The rents and holes in his dirt-encrusted clothes bore witness to the thorny undergrowth and mud through which he had made his way in the attempt to reach Jerusalem. Though the soldiers crowded round inquisitively, he squatted down on the ground beside Jeremiah, and they both sat silent for a long time, as befitted men whose hearts were full of anxious questions and answers to questions. Jeremiah was the first to speak.

"Hanameel, my cousin and friend, I was thinking of my father's house when you appeared."

"Jeremiah, my cousin and friend," nodded the faithful Hanameel, "I knew well that your thoughts were of your home in Anathoth; there is every reason why they should be. Therefore, amid great peril and discomfort, I have crept into this city for the last time. Behold, I bring you the last instalment of the interest that is due to you. It is but a lean portion. A little sack of lentils, a little sack of dried figs, and a pitcher of last year's wine. More I could not bring."

"Distribute the lentils and the figs and the pitcher of wine among these brave soldiers, my cousin! For there is famine in the city and the men go hungry. Then tell me the reason why my thoughts are of my home in Anathoth, and why you speak of the last instalment of interest."

Hanameel did as Jeremiah bade him and gave the things he had brought to the soldiers. Then he began to tell his ill news, relating one item after another without any change in his calm voice.

"When Obadiah, your elder brother," he began, "was dying with agonizing pains in his bowels, he sent for Hanameel, for he was quite alone. The long war and the wrath of the Lord had scattered all his family. Only the murderous screech-owl still remained, whose voice could be heard at night like a watchman on his tower calling out the passing hours of God's vengeance. In his last hour Obadiah spoke thus to me: 'Joel, the traveller, has been paid his due and has gone. My sons have been torn from me by the war. My daughters and my daughters-in-law have taken their children and have departed. I have been struck down by the Lord because of Jeremiah. Gird up your loins and go hence to speak to my younger brother in my name. Tell him that he, who has no children, is now the father of the family and the master of an empty house.' . . . It is more than two months since we buried your elder brother. I had already girded up my loins to set out and come to you when the great disaster befell Anathoth. The men of Babylon came and burned your house, with the Hall of Abiathar, the chamber of your parents, and many good things that your mother had accumulated. They took everything that was of any value. They drove away the cattle, drank up the wine, devastated the fields, and slew the peasants. My own farm did not escape the same fate. There too they pillaged and burned, as they did throughout the countryside so that there might be no place from which Jerusalem could receive food and supplies. I hid with some of my neighbours in the mountains and was in great fear, before I turned my feet towards you for the last time."

Jeremiah had listened intently without interrupting the tranquil flow of Hanameel's story.

"Verily, now am I the childless father of my family and the master of a house that has been burned down," he said after a long silence. But Hanameel laid his large rough hand upon the prophet's knee and demanded:

"What will be the end? Tell me! For in accordance with your words shall I order the rest of my days."

More and more soldiers had joined the group, until there was a dense ring round the two cousins. Jeremiah kept his eyes closed and, to his misfortune, he forgot that they were not alone. Though he spoke very softly and almost tonelessly, yet his dangerous words were overheard and understood by some of the listeners.

"This city, this people, and this whole land will be delivered into the hand of the King of Babylon."

"You have spoken," nodded Hanameel, as if he had expected to hear nothing less, "and I shall order the rest of my days in accordance with your words. I shall leave this country, as the wise traveller Joel did long ago, and shake off the burden of this people and this God. But to you I return that which is yours, since I can no longer be responsible for it. My own fields and my pastures, moreover, I give to you, though the soil lies fallow and is worthless to you."

At the word "worthless" Jeremiah sprang to his feet .

"May God forbid," he cried in a ringing voice, "that fields and pastures in the land of the Lord should be considered worthless! You should be rebuked for this word, my cousin! Behold, I stand before you as a buyer. There is nothing to prevent you from casting off the burden of this people and this God, that you may go hence while there is yet time. But I will buy your fields at their full value, that I may further increase my great inheritance in this land. You must obey me in this, for according to law the right of redemption is mine alone."

Jeremiah had spoken so loudly that a murmur of surprise broke from the crowd. His eyes warned Hanameel, who was about to protest, to be silent. Gradually the worthy cousin realized that it was not a foolish offer made by a madman, but a symbolic act which the Lord had imposed on His prophet when the word "worthless" was uttered. Jeremiah summoned the soldiers of the royal bodyguard who were standing roundabout to be lawful witnesses of the transaction, and drew from his girdle the gold that had once been given him by his mother, at his father's wish, for his hour of "dire affliction." The paymaster of the bodyguard was called, and he weighed Jeremiah's gold on a balance against shekels and pieces of silver. Baruch, who had succeeded in obtaining permission to visit the prisoner every day, had to sit down forthwith and prepare evidence of the purchase according to law and custom. Hanameel, still unclear about what was happening, was paid the full value of his land, the amount being reckoned according to the price obtaining during the last years of peace. The sum total was seven shekels and ten pieces of silver. Then Jeremiah told his bewildered cousin to cast from his mind his belated intention of leaving the country, advising him to return home, to build himself a modest shelter on his old farm, to wait, and to hope. With tears in his eyes Hanameel promised to obey, and Jeremiah dismissed him with the ringing words:

"Houses and fields and vineyards shall be possessed again in this land!"

Baruch was ordered to place the sealed document, the evidence of purchase, in an earthen vessel and preserve it in a safe place, that it might continue as a token for future generations in the years to come. The men standing roundabout had seen and heard all that was being said and done, but their simple minds were puzzled by the contradiction between Jeremiah's prophecy and his action. Had the prophet not expressly foretold the end? Then why, if he was convinced of the imminent downfall of Judah, had he purchased with his last remaining money a desolate and useless piece of land? It was not only the simple minds of the soldiers that found the contradiction surprising. Jeremiah himself was puzzled at the sudden transaction into which the Lord had prompted him to enter, and which filled him with a dreamy delight as if he surmised a change in the divine plan.

On the following day the King appeared in the court of guard surrounded by his inseparable friends and other princes and generals. Clad in his golden armour and sky-blue cloak he was a vision of splendour. His companions, too, wore magnificent armour with Egyptian battle-helmets, plumed with ostrich feathers, on their heads. The King had ordered a sortie to be made from the Gates of Ephraim and Benjamin in the late afternoon, with the object of destroying the new pieces of ordnance that Nebuchadnezzar had brought from Babylon. The plan had sprung less from calculation of the possibilities of success than from despair, for Zedekiah and his generals had been guided by the two thoughts: "Something must be done!" and: "What have we to lose?" They knew their rashness would cost many lives, perhaps even that of the King, but the proximity of death filled them with a dark ecstasy which made them welcome the thought of bloodshed, however futile. At a command from Malchiah the guards on duty seized Jeremiah, thrust him in front of the royal group, and forced him to his knees.

Zedekiah's nostrils quivered as he stared straight ahead. His restless movements betrayed the impatience and uneasiness he felt. His right hand nervously gripped an ivory sceptre, with which he gave Malchiah a reluctant sign to state the charge against the prophet.

"Do not deny your crime," began the son of Pashur in a bullying tone to Jeremiah, "for there are witnesses in plenty. In front of the King's warriors you spoke the following words: 'This city, this people, and this whole land will be delivered into the hand of the King of Babylon'!"

Jeremiah took time to consider before he answered in a low voice:

"There was one who wished to know how he is to order the rest of his days. . . ."

"Good, then you do not deny it!" Malchiah interrupted quickly. "But that is not all. You have sold your spacious lands in Anathoth to a peasant for seven shekels, to show how worthless the Kingdom of Judah has become. . . ."

"It is a slander!" burst out Jeremiah. "It is a lie, a shameless lie! I have bought land in order to show the value I set upon it. Let Baruch bring the sealed document, the evidence of purchase. . . ."

"True or untrue," intervened Ishmael with cold arrogance, "to whose advantage is this investigation? Are we to waste time talking with this man when there is so little left to us? Has it not at last become clear to the King that this man must die? Without mercy we slay those whose hearts grow faint before the enemy and who seek to take flight. Yet is this man to live, whom you have allowed to dwell among your warriors and have fed from your own table? When the men of war should be roused by fiery speech and encouraged by glowing exhortations, he speaks words that weaken their hands and make the people dejected. Does the King need further proof before delivering him to us? This man loves only Babylon, and hates the land of his fathers with a fearful hatred!"

The King continued to look high over Jeremiah's head. He had given up all hope of saving him. The letter to the elders in captivity, the attempt to desert to the enemy, his words in the presence of the soldiers the day before—each of these offences was deserving of death. He could not even accuse his princes of being unjust. Ishmael had spoken no differently than any prudent general would have done. Yet Zedekiah flushed deeply and rocked to and fro on his toes. At last he cried abruptly, but in a strangely uncertain tone:

"Behold, he is in your hand! Do with him what you will . . ."

He left the sentence unfinished, hesitated a moment, then swallowed his shame and added in a faint voice, disclaiming any responsibility for what they were about to do:

". . . For the King is not he that can do anything against you."

He seemed to tear himself loose from the ground on which he stood and hurried away with fleet steps. Only his shield- and sword-bearers followed him. The princes made no concealment of their delight. Amid bursts of laughter they discussed in detail what exquisite form of death would be most fitting for the most unrelenting of their enemies. The example of the princes was followed by the common soldiers, who immediately turned their hearts against the prophet. Those with whom he had shared his food now took a special pride in excelling their superiors in the coarseness of their words and actions. They struck him, spat in his face, defiled his garments. But Ishmael soon put a stop to this by ordering the condemned man to be bound hand and foot and placed against a wooden gate. Jeremiah allowed them to have their way calmly and without protest. The Lord had compassion on him in this hour, and he knew that he would not die at the hands of the soldiers. Even when they began to hurl lances, arrows, and knives into the wood all round him, he uttered not a single cry of fear. Strangely enough, it was Irijah who unintentionally saved him from death. Throwing up his arm as a signal to his men to cease their torture, he said:

"Hearken unto me, O princes of the King! Shall this man die by the sword or the lance, as some of us are about to die this very day? It would be no disgrace, but an honour he does not merit. Therefore I beseech you, cease to cast your weapons at him! I know of a more fitting death for this abominable carcass, in whose slimy filth he pretends the word of God has taken up its dwelling. Thus saith the Lord of hosts, forsooth! It would appear that the word of the Lord of hosts prefers a sewer to a noble house! Well, since it delights in fetid odours rather than in pleasing perfumes, let us take the word of God to its proper place, where its vessel can languish at leisure without taking bread from the mouths of the starving inhabitants of this city."

The princes applauded Irijah's speech. Perhaps the less hotheaded among them were not sorry that the shed blood of a prophet would not be crying out for vengeance against them before the coming battle. The soldiers dragged Jeremiah to the place referred to by their captain, the so-called "Cistern of the King's Son." This was the ancient name, of unknown origin, for a receptacle which was anything but a cistern to receive and store the pure rains of heaven. It was a large cesspool, situated on a gentle slope near the eastern wall of the city. Twelve feet deep and eight feet square, it acted as a drain for waste water, and all the filth and refuse of the neighbourhood was dumped into it. When Jeremiah was thrown into this pit he came to no harm, for he fell on the soft mire with which the bottom was covered. Above his head he heard the mocking laughter of his persecutors:

"Now let the word of God issue from your lips!"

30

From the Depths and from the Heights

THE dank filth came up to Jeremiah's knees. He stood upright and still. Even when he looked down at his defiled body, the slight movement stirred the loathsome mass so that he thought he would swoon. He was enveloped in darkness and foul odours. Perhaps the putrefying carcasses of animals were lying below the miry surface and adding their corruption to the tainted air. Now and then a rat squelched out from the ordure and shot past him, to disappear into a hole in the earth. The day had not yet gone, but in this pit, this Sheol of pollution, how could he survive the night, how could he continue even to stand upright during the night that was to come? Before long Jeremiah was in the grip of uncontrollable fear and nausea. His mind began to work quickly, searching for the reason why the Lord had allowed him to come to this pass. The Lord would not have submitted him to such a repulsive ordeal if there was no meaning in it. There was nothing that could not be interpreted significantly. Everything that happened had a meaning and itself expressed that meaning, like clay in the potter's hand. Every incident in the history of the world, whether it was the flight of a gnat or a great battle, revealed by the very fact of its occurrence the mystery that was inherent in it. That he, the Lord's sanctified prophet, was standing immersed to the knees in a stinking pit, through no fault of his own—even this expressed something significant or it would not have happened. He found a clue to the explanation of his suffering in the words of Irijah that still rang in his ears. There was no doubt that the Lord had saved him from certain death through the instrumentality of Hananiah's son, but at the same time He had used this man's spiteful mouth to speak of the "word of God," which had entered into an "abominable carcass full of slimy filth." In a sudden flash of understanding Jeremiah realized the aversion with which the Lord must be filled when He sent down His word to be spoken by human lips. The prophet's repellent situation in the cesspool corresponded to the repellent situation in which the divine word found itself when it descended again and again in order to save Israel, but had to languish unheard. The loathing inspired by his noisome surroundings was a faint semblance of the divine loathing evoked by the noisome minds of men, by their backsliding, disloyalty, sin, idol-worship, and other abominations; in fact by everything that diverged from the primal joy of God. Jeremiah's heart was flooded with a warm compassion for the suffering Compassionate One, and he raised his hands to Him fervently from the depths.

During all the hours that he stood in the foul pit he did not grow weary, for he exulted in the tremendous discovery of the significance attaching to his ordeal. He had wished to help his people and had devoted himself to their service. In return he had been humiliated and cast down to a slow death. Yet in the secure knowledge that his suffering for and at the hands of the people of Jacob was only a symbol, he fell into a trance-like state such as he had not hitherto experienced. He was hardly conscious of his defiled body or the nauseating emanations of the pit, and this enabled him to endure the long hours of his confinement. As in a dream he heard the sound of trumpets and the clamour of battle, which began in front of the north gates and died away only when night had fallen and the stars were rising above the Cistern of the King's Son. Suddenly, by the light of the stars, he saw some large object dangling against the wall of the pit on the end of a rope. It was a chair, to the legs of which extensions had been hurriedly nailed. From one of the arms hung a little basket containing food and a sealed wine jar.

Who could have thought of him? Who had dared to save him from death by hunger and thirst? Could it have been Baruch? Could it have been Hamutal or Maacha? But that was impossible! The entrances to the court of the guard had been barred by order of the princes. Neither Baruch nor the queens could yet know of Jeremiah's fate. It must have been some man of mean estate who had taken pity on the prophet without making his identity known to him. Far greater than this kindly deed was the help of a different kind that came to Jeremiah. Just as the angel of peace had embraced him in the endless night of the dungeon, so in this malodorous abyss he was transported to a more and more remote and untrammelled state of being. And as his ears had then been opened to a tangled web of distant noises, so now his mouth was opened to utter bitter-sweet songs of lamentation. Involuntarily words and melody streamed from and enveloped his rapt soul. His voice rose gently from the depths, yet it filled the night with its resonance and floated in the waxing light of the moon through the open windows of the palace, so that all who heard it knew that Jeremiah was suffering in the pit. Maacha, who lay sleepless on her couch, listened in horror to his lamentations and broke into sobs as she distinguished the words:

"I am the man that hath seen affliction by the rod of
His wrath.
He hath led me and brought me into darkness, but
not into light.
Surely against me is He turned, He turneth His
hand against me all the day.
My flesh and my skin hath He made old, He hath
broken my bones.
He hath builded against me, and compassed me
with gall and travail.
He hath set me in dark places, as they that be dead
of old.
He hath hedged me about, that I cannot get out:
He hath made my chain heavy.
Also when I cry and shout, He shutteth out my
prayer.
He hath enclosed my ways with hewn stone: He
hath made my paths crooked.
He was unto me as a bear lying in wait, and as a
lion in secret places.
He hath turned aside my ways, and pulled me in
pieces: He hath made me desolate.
He hath bent His bow, and set me as a mark for the
arrow.
He hath caused the arrows of His quiver to enter
into my reins.
And I said, My strength and my hope is perished
from the Lord:
Remembering mine affliction and my misery, the
wormwood and the gall.
My soul hath them still in remembrance, and is
humbled in me.

This I recall to my mind, therefore have I hope.
It is of the Lord's mercies that we are not consumed,
because His compassions fail not.
They are new every morning: great is Thy faithfulness."

With knees drawn up Jeremiah sat on the chair that had been let down to him by his unknown friend. He had again been attacked by a bout of his old fever, but, when it came so violently as now, he welcomed it, for it took the place of his rapt trance and spun round him in his exhaustion a network of sounds and visions in which the sufferings of his body were resolved. He had no idea how much of the night had gone by. He had not heard the trumpet calls of the priests when they announced the passing of the hours, but the stars were already less numerous in the sky, a sign that it was past midnight. To Jeremiah's senses it seemed as if some transformation had taken place, though at first he could not tell what it was that had changed. Only gradually did it become clear to him that the transformation had something to do with the mephitic odour of the pit, which was slowly dispersing and being supplanted by a fragrance that reminded him of incense and then of liquid myrrh such as queens used to perfume their skin. When this aroma had overcome the last breath of tainted air, Jeremiah happened to look up. In the open top of the pit, above which trembled the pale stars of the spring night, appeared a bird with widespread wings that hovered and wheeled in the air. He wondered what bird of the night might thus be seeking its filthy prey. Yet in spite of the hour it was no bird of the night, but a large swallow that had probably wakened too early and was easily recognizable by its whirring and the lightning swiftness with which it fluttered its wings. Was there any swallow, thought Jeremiah in astonishment, that swooped down at night on rats and toads? Even as the thought passed through his mind, he was already convinced that the swallow was none other than Zenua come to visit him. "When the swallow settles on your shoulder, will you let it rest there?" He remembered her whispered entreaty as she lay dying. The swallow, however, seemed to hesitate a little while longer, folding and unfolding its wings and hovering uncertainly before it darted down and settled on Jeremiah's left shoulder, near his heart, so lightly that he could not feel it at all.

"My bridegroom," said the swallow. It was not a bird-like twittering, but Zenua's own voice, now strangely reduced, subdued, and remote. Cautiously, so that he should not hurt the frail soul-image on his shoulder by any sudden movement or heavy breathing, he whispered:

"Zenua . . . my bride . . . chaste soul of the nations . . ."

"I have come," she said in her small, clear voice, "that you may grant me the favour I have asked of you. . . ."

"My bride," lamented Jeremiah, "this is a sorry bridal-chamber to which you have come to meet your bridegroom."

The delicate, weightless bird on his left shoulder seemed to smile.

"Do we not bear our bridal-chamber within us?"

Suddenly Jeremiah and Zenua were together in a festively decked chamber. He was leaning back in a broad, lion-footed chair, and she knelt at his left side in the manner of noble Egyptian ladies. He felt her breathing, virginal presence beside him, yet he did not see her.

"My bridegroom," she said, "you have not been released from our betrothal. Your bride is waiting in the place decked and reserved for her until the time shall come. . . ."

"Chaste soul from the land of the heathen! How many days and how much sorrow must pass before the time of our union will come?"

The charming mockery that Jeremiah remembered so well was discernible through the gravity of her words:

"My teacher, did you not tell me yourself that the sky is a wanderer like the race of Jacob?"

"When, Zenua, when will it have come to the end of its wandering?"

"When it lets Khaïb, the fan of shadows, fall as I, little Zenua, had to let it fall."

"My bride knows things," praised Jeremiah, "that her bridegroom does not know. Tell me more. . . . When will that be?"

"When light has become so tenuous," said the invisible Zenua, "that bodies cease to cast shadows."

"O chaste soul of the nations, of what use is that?"—the words broke from Jeremiah with a sob. "For my suffering through the sufferings of this people is of the present. . . . Help me, Zenua!"

And Zenua helped her bridegroom. By her aid he himself became a bird, though he did not know of what kind and his body felt no change. Only one thing in him seemed different —his power of vision. His sight was like that of a bird, looking down from above out of round, lidless, sleepless eyes. And out of these round, lidless eyes, as he perched among the birds of Marduk resting with ruffled plumage high up under the roof of a luxurious tent, he looked down at the royal couch supported on the backs of two long-necked, golden dragons. It was night, but Nebuchadnezzar was not asleep. He sat in his sandalwood-coloured robe on the edge of the couch and held council with his birds. The ruffled councillors under the roof seemed displeased with Marduk, for they listened with a keen and censorious air.

"What is the matter with us?" cried the King of Babylon in ill-humoured bewilderment. "For three years we have been beleaguering this wretched city and allowing it to defend itself and remain intact within its walls. Time is passing and three jewels have been sacrificed from my imperial crown. When shall I complete my work and bring the universe and the nations into edifying harmony?"

A croaking and screeching broke loose round Jeremiah. The angry, mocking words that the birds uttered with their human voices came tumbling over each other in clumsy haste, were repeated and distorted, until at last from the incessant clamour of "Melech Babilu, Melech Babilu!" the calmer voice of a grosbeak became audible.

"Why does Marduk always hold back the arm of Nergal?" croaked the grosbeak.

Nebuchadnezzar rebuked him.

"Nergal's work on earth is not my work. Nergal must serve me."

"But you are serving Nergal," croaked the grosbeak, "throughout your age. He does not serve you. Take the golden shovel of the Ram from your girdle and cast it away."

At once the confused screeching of the other birds began again.

"War! . . . War! . . . War!" they clamoured turbulently. "There is no end to war. . . . Cast away the golden shovel. . . . Your time is passing. . . ."

With clenched fist Nebuchadnezzar ordered them to be silent.

"My time is passing," he cried, "and this foul dog of a

traitor, whom I myself placed upon his throne, resists me."

"He resists you," mocked the grosbeak, who was presumably the spokesman for the birds, "he resists Marduk because Marduk is afraid."

"What reason has Marduk to be afraid?" shouted the King of Babylon threateningly.

There was renewed croaking and screeching until the spokesman raised his voice.

"You are afraid of the consequences! You are afraid of the god whom you do not know! The writing in the sky and the writing of the soothsayer are in accord!"

Nebuchadnezzar said nothing, but let the minutes go by, until at last he confessed to his council:

"It is true. The consequences will be grave if I fail to set the world on a new course. My cosmic year will last but a short *Ner.* After seventy years everything will fall in ruins. An unknown god has appointed me his servant."

"Melech Babilu, Melech Babilu! . . ." clamoured the birds in agitation and beating their wings with fright. "Free yourself! . . . Make yourself free! . . ."

"What, then, is your advice?" cried Marduk impatiently. "If I destroy this wretched city and its temple, the sacred dwelling place of its god, I shall be destroying myself after seventy years."

"Don't destroy it! . . . Don't destroy it! . . ." shrieked the birds, beside themselves.

"This is no idle counsel and no magicians' babble. It has been calculated from the stars," muttered Marduk to himself. Then he turned again to his advisers and asked: "But if I do not destroy the dwelling place of this god, what then? I shall have made Marduk's honour a thing of naught among the scoffing nations. I shall inspire traitors with fresh courage. I must destroy this wretched city, if Babylon itself is not to be destroyed. . . ."

"Destroy it! . . . Destroy it! . . ." interrupted the forgetful birds.

As he looked down, Jeremiah saw for the first time that a man was kneeling at the entrance to the tent. By the flickering light of one of the lamps he saw that blood flowed down the man's forehead and that four swords were buried to the hilt in his breast. It was Gedaliah, son of Ahikam. With his last strength he raised his arms imploringly to Nebuchadnezzar, who hardly heeded him, and cried in a voice that rattled in his throat:

"Let the King of Babylon separate the House of God from the House of David!"

With these words Gedaliah sank to the ground. But his bloody death made not the least impression on Marduk. Turning his boyishly defiant face up towards the roof, he spoke, so it seemed, not to the grosbeak or to the birds in general but solely and directly to Jeremiah.

"Let the son of David," he said, "come barefoot in sackcloth and ashes, cast himself down before me and humble himself in every way. Then will I spare the dwelling place of his god, and he and his house may live."

Jeremiah wanted to cry out and ask whether this was Marduk's definite and final decision, but his throat was incapable even of uttering an incoherent, bird-like sound. In the torturing effort to speak, everything became confused, and he found himself sitting with cramped limbs on his chair in the pit.

As Jeremiah awakened, the last words spoken by Marduk in the dream vision sounded in his ears once more, this time in a clear, gentle voice. He looked up. The grey light of early dawn was visible above his head and his body was rigid with cold. Suddenly he shrank into himself as he became aware that someone was calling to him in a more and more urgent whisper from the edge of the pit:

"Jeremiah! . . . My teacher! . . . Jeremiah! . . ."

Jeremiah glimpsed a dark head bending over the pit. It was Ebed-melech the Ethiopian, who hurriedly explained to the prophet what he wanted him to do. Ropes had been made ready, and two strong men were standing by to help him out. Ebed-melech asked Jeremiah to catch a bundle which he was going to throw down to him. The bundle contained old clothes from the storeroom of the palace.

"Put them under your armpits and knees and tie the ropes firmly over them!" he called. At the same time the bundle flew down and the ropes were cautiously lowered. As Jeremiah caught them, he asked Ebed-melech:

"Do you come of your own accord or have you been sent by the King?"

"I come of my own accord. But I have spoken with the King and he knows what I am doing."

So the plan to save him had come not from the guilty heart of Zedekiah, but from the innocent heart of Ebed-melech! The latter had evidently begun his preparations for Jeremiah's rescue as soon as possible, and it was he who had let down the chair at great risk to himself, in order that the prophet should not collapse into the pit. "Oh, Zedekiah," thought Jeremiah, "though you reddened with shame when you uttered the words, 'Do with him what you will!'; though your reasoning mind could find no fault in him, out of cowardice you gave up your prisoner to the hate-intoxicated princes. Then, in spite of your cowardice, you went out to do battle with wild, heroic courage. Shouting your battle-cry you sowed death before the gates with unflinching arm, prepared with a joyous heart to meet death yourself. So bold in battle and so cowardly in mind, who can unriddle the puzzle?"

"Hurry, my teacher, before it grows too light!" whispered the Ethiopian urgently. Jeremiah protected his armpits and the hollows of his knees with the old rags and tied the ropes over them as Ebed-melech had instructed him. As he was pulled up jerkily by the men above, he was roughly jolted against the wall and suffered slight injuries. When he reached the top he remained lying on the ground, stiff, wet through, covered with filth, and incapable of moving. The powerful Ebed-melech picked him up and carried him to the palace in his arms, with his face covered by a cloth as if he were a corpse. The sentries tried to bar the path of the Ethiopian, but he thundered at them in an awe-inspiring voice: "By order of the King!" He carried the prophet to his own chamber, where he undressed him and washed his body with hot water and strong soap. Then he brought bread and wine and prepared a couch, where Jeremiah slept dreamlessly in a state of utter exhaustion for many hours. When he awoke, Ebed-melech bent over him and said agitatedly: "The King awaits you."

Zedekiah was in the building known as the Gate of the Bodyguard, which linked the palace with the Temple but was opened solely on the occasion of ceremonious entries or processions. At other times the gateway was barred and deserted. It possessed a number of small, windowless rooms which allowed hardly any light to enter even by day, and into one of these, a place well designed for a secret meeting, Ebed-melech led the bowed Jeremiah, who leaned heavily on his arm and could walk only slowly. The room in which the

King was waiting was entirely unfurnished. A narrow bench ran along the walls, as in most guardrooms. Zedekiah was sitting not on this bench, but on the stone floor. He was not wearing his golden armour, but was piously enveloped in burial clothes. After the battle he had probably rested only a short time before betaking himself to the Temple in order to pray in the sanctuary beside the High Priest. Jeremiah remained standing at the door, which Ebed-melech closed softly behind him. His eyes took a little while to grow accustomed to the twilight and to recognize the white figure crouching on the ground in its voluminous garments. The King's voice sounded strident and his first words were:

"Perhaps it would have been better for us both if we had met our deaths yesterday, each in his own way, you and I."

This was an unexpected greeting. When Jeremiah did not answer, the King continued in a defiant tone:

"Or perhaps it is better that we did not meet our deaths, you and I. You, Jeremiah, have been saved by my intervention. I have been fighting against the Babylonians and have ravaged them, though this time the hurt was not very great. I shall, however, repeat it day after day until I have sapped the enemy's courage. We still hold firm, though our belts grow looser. Hunger is more endurable than thirst. The springs, the wells, and the pools are full of fresh water. Verily, the King is not discouraged and he knows not what it is to despair. But, Jeremiah, it was you—did you believe that I wish to deny it?—who brought me back from Egypt and set me on the throne. Yes, you wrested me from the House of Bondage, which was, if I remember aright, a pleasant, peaceful, and very comfortable house. Therefore it is only just that you should ward off despair from the pupil whom you wrested from the mild air of Noph. So I ask you, prophet, what I have always asked you, and this time I hope for a favourable answer: Is there any word from the Lord?"

Jeremiah stood, weak and faint, before the king who had humbled himself and sat upon the floor like one who mourned or as one doing penance. Leaden minutes passed before he spoke.

"My King! Many a time have you asked me this question and many a time have I answered, as I answer now: To what purpose, to what end? You will not act according to the word of the Lord whether He speaks or is silent. Twice you have cast me into the jaws of death. The third time they will hold me fast."

There was a note of supplication in Zedekiah's voice:

"Hide nothing from me . . . and have no fear, for I shall protect you."

"The King cannot protect me . . ." And Jeremiah repeated the King's ignominious words: "For the King is not he that can do anything against you."

"Hearken unto me!" cried the King, and he bade the feeble Jeremiah sit down beside him. "It is true I said these words, but do you believe that I can do nothing against these men? They serve me with their blood. They hate you not for your sake but for mine, because they love me and because they delight in war, which you profane. And are not they, who are royal heroes and warriors, justified in their hatred of a man who gave up all hope for their city before the first blow was struck and urged the soldiers to fall away to the enemy? You too, Jeremiah, should try to see with their eyes! But concerning what passes between us in this hour, both you and I must be silent. . . ."

Zedekiah paused as if he suspected eavesdroppers. Then he lowered his voice and continued:

"Be not afraid of my princes! Jucal is dead. Ishmael's left shoulder has been pierced by a Babylonian arrow. But even if this were not so, my resolve would remain firm. I will not put you to death, neither will I give you into the hands of these men that seek your life. Henceforth you shall dwell in my house and be guarded from all your enemies. You shall dwell in the innermost part of my house and not in the court of the guard. And the King swears to you with upraised hand, as the Lord liveth who created this life, thus shall it be done! If a simple vow is not enough, the King is prepared to renew his oath before witnesses in the Temple."

Jeremiah turned two heavy eyes towards him.

"It is not necessary for the King to renew his oath. God, who created this life, has heard him. . . . Yet even without your oath I would have spoken to you, for there is word from the Lord of hosts, and His word is favourable. . . ."

"His word is favourable. . . ." stammered Zedekiah. He grew deathly pale, then flushed a deep red, and his lips twitched. "His word is favourable. . . . Blessed be your coming!"

Jeremiah drew a deep breath.

"My King! It is in your power to save this city, this people, and the whole land. . . ."

"It is in my power to save this city, this people, and the whole land," Zedekiah repeated like a child learning its lesson, yet with a faint foreboding of approaching disappointment.

Jeremiah spoke of the reward before he told the King what was demanded of him.

"If you save the holy land of God, then you will save your own life, yours and that of your house, and you will be remembered in heaven and on earth until the end of time!"

Verily, a great reward! For to be remembered in heaven and on earth was to obliterate the power of death, a sign of the Lord's high and mysterious favour. But what tremendous sacrifice would be exacted for such recompense? The King's voice sounded stifled as he asked:

"Is it a grievous deed that I must do?"

"It is not a deed that you must do; it is a path that you must tread." . . .

"Stop!" whispered the King. "Speak no further, but give me time to think. . . . It is no deed that I must do, it is a path that I must tread! . . . No, no; speak quickly, speak, that I may hear the word of the Lord. . . ."

Jeremiah lowered his eyes to the ground as he told Zedekiah in a low voice of the sacrifice that was demanded of him:

"The King must go out before the gates of the city with upraised hands. His garments must be rent like those of one who mourns, and his hair sprinkled with ashes. The princes who follow after you with upraised hands must be garbed like you. Then you must enter into the presence of the King of Babylon, cast yourself at his feet, and humble yourself in every way. If you do this, your life will be spared and the lives of your sons, and this city together with the holy dwelling place of the Lord will not be burnt with fire."

Zedekiah seemed to shrink into the voluminous burial clothes he wore. He was unable to speak. Only when his silence had reached the limit of what could be borne did he mutter brokenly:

"Now the word has been spoken and the path that lies before me leads to a bottomless pit. . . . But you, Jeremiah, do you see clearly before you that which comes so lightly from your lips?"

"My King, I see it clearly before me."

"You see nothing!" shrieked the King. He was like a man who had been struck a mortal blow. "I alone can see what lies before me. . . . I see myself going out in beggar's rags and with upraised hands from the Gate of Ephraim. . . . But my princes and my generals do not follow me with upraised hands. . . . I am followed only by the jeers and mockery of the warriors I have betrayed. . . . They spit after their pitiable King. . . . Yet I must bear it and enter alone into the presence of the King of Babylon, cast myself down before him, humble myself in every way, and lick the feet of this fool of a star-worshipper like a beaten dog—I, a son of David! . . . All this I can see. . . . Do you see it, too, Jeremiah? . . . Do you see Nebuchadnezzar signing to his executioner to slay the humbled King of Judah as he lies in the dust? . . ."

"Not thus, my King, not thus!" Jeremiah's voice was choked by a stream of hot tears. "You shall live, you and your house."

"Live!" Zedekiah laughed out loud. "Coniah lives, but is he alive? . . . I shall be placed in a cage and put on show. And not only the soldiers in the camp of Babylon will gather round to feast their eyes on me. Gedaliah and Micah, the sons of Shaphan and all the others who have escaped from the city and deserted to the enemy, hundreds and hundreds of them, they will all come to look at me. They will mock at me and defile me . . . for I shall be less than Jehoahaz, less than Coniah. . . . I shall not be a dethroned king living in exile, but a miscreant, a snake crushed in the sand and full of maggots, a crippled jackal, a stench at which men hold their nostrils. . . . I can hear their songs of derision. Do you hear them too, Jeremiah? . . . They are carrying the women away in chains from the House of Pharaoh's Daughter, Hamutal and Maacha and their waiting-women and their handmaidens. . . . I hear a weeping and a chanting:

> The friend who led you to disgrace,
> Now he dare not show his face.
> Curse him for an evil liar,
> For he's left you in the mire. . . .

Do you hear it, prophet?"

"I shall not leave you," said Jeremiah, but the King continued to cry wildly:

"No, you will not leave me, as you refused to leave Coniah! Behold what a joyful companion I shall have in my good fortune! . . . My house too will be spared. . . . That was the promise, was it not? . . . But I see them carrying my sons, Adajah and Ichiel, to their necromancers. And these necromancers will castrate my sons, that the seed of David may be utterly destroyed. Traitors will be set to govern the people, quibbling corrupters but never a king, since a King of Judah once sullied his honour. . . ."

Jeremiah's heart beat so furiously that he had to struggle for breath before he could speak.

"These are reckless words, my King! Verily, the sacrifice demanded of you is the most grievous that any king has ever made. Yet I entreat you, let me show you the things I see with my own eyes! If you do not go out before the gates of the city with upraised arms, how long will it be before a breach is made in the walls? For you are alone, betrayed and lost, as you well know in your heart. You will be dishonoured and put to death, and there will be no recompense, for a conquered king is likewise but a snake crushed in the sand. Three years, three jewels from his crown, has Marduk lost because of you. Perhaps he has destined you for a worse fate than swift death! How do you know they will castrate your sons if you submit to Marduk? You have been promised that their lives would be spared, but this would not be life! If, however, your sons fall into the hand of Babylon as captives, then they will be not castrated, but cruelly slain. As the Lord liveth who created this life, I implore you to consider whether a choice still remains to you. For if you go forth with upraised hands, then the Temple will not be burnt with fire, this city and this people will live. The wounds will heal, the land will prosper once more, and this will be due solely to the holy conduct of the King. What signifies the scoffing of your heroes compared with the praises of a whole age? Saul, they will sing, was the first King, but a shadow lies upon him, for his kingdom was established against the will of the Lord. Zedekiah was the last King, and he is bathed in radiance, for he sacrificed his kingdom and his honour to the Lord."

When he had spoken Jeremiah cast himself on the ground and kissed the King's feet in homage. But Zedekiah withdrew from the prophet's touch.

"You have forgotten one choice that still remains to me," he reminded him hoarsely; "death before the gates, death that comes as a kindly, cheerful brother in the ecstasy of battle. I shall go to meet it and be free, and then I shall know no more."

"Death before the gates is commonplace and vain. Thousands of your captains and common soldiers meet the same end. From the King a greater sacrifice is demanded."

"You demand a sacrifice, Jeremiah, you who have never circumcised your heart? When have you ever sacrificed a fraction of your stubborn will? Would that I had fallen yesterday, before I heard the favourable word from the Lord with which you have rejoiced my ears! Verily, I am but a weak man, and the Lord is a strong God . . . but why should the weaker sacrifice to the strong, and not the stronger to the weak, who has need of Him?"

"Will you not understand, O weakling," breathed Jeremiah, no longer trying to keep back his tears, "that this sacrifice is your only strength?"

Zedekiah drew his burial garments closer round him, as if he wished to avoid contact with the prophet.

"Perhaps," he said, "you know what God is. What a man is, what a king is, that you do not know."

With these words he covered his head. For a long time they sat together on the floor, but they did not speak again.

31

Through the Darkness

THE King kept his oath and did not deliver Jeremiah into the hand of his princes, who were seeking him like bloodhounds and lying in wait in all the places where they thought he might have taken refuge. He remained hidden in the House of Pharaoh's Daughter, which he left only at night to walk in the inner garden court, where there were no sentries. During the day he sat with Hamutal and Maacha in the Queen Mother's chamber. Hamutal was very ill, and neither physician, nor herbalist, nor exorcist was able to help her. Her limbs were swollen with malignant waters and she lay breathing heavily on her couch. She did not complain or stare silently in front of her. There was a staring look in her eyes, it is true, but she talked incessantly and her mouth never ceased moving, as if she were afraid that she might not have time completely to unburden her soul. The words she spoke never referred to the rising flood that was surging more and more tempestuously round the House of David. For her there was neither Babylon nor Marduk, neither hunger nor deprivation, neither fighting on the walls nor a son in danger. In a tranquil voice she spoke of Libnah and the house of her father, the prince of the city. Her mind dwelt on the auspicious years when her husband was King, when he celebrated the Feast of Passover and the renewal of the Covenant with the thirty thousand guests of God in the

Temple, when the lilies and anemones bloomed more beautifully in the gardens and on the hills, and Josiah's watchword—"Rejoice with the Lord!"—rang throughout the land. She spoke also of Noph, of the airy, wooden houses of Egypt with their painted walls, of her little garden with the pool filled with floating lotus blossoms, of Ha-rekhni, who was given the name of Zenua and had died young.

Maacha sat with bowed head and appeared to be listening patiently to the voluble, wandering monologue of the sick woman. Only now and then she moved restlessly as a shadow of despair veiled her eyes for a fleeting second and as swiftly vanished. In truth, she could no longer bear to listen to the babbling voice of the Queen Mother, whose bedside she could not leave. This recalling of the faded past, in which Maacha herself had played no part, made her throat seem dry. Instead of sitting still and hearing old tales retold, she had often felt like bursting into a long hysterical cry of uncontrollable fear. But custom forbade the mistress of a house even to raise her voice in speaking; far less therefore could she dare to scream. Custom further forbade a youthful daughter-in-law, even though she was the wife of the King, to be so lacking in respect for her husband's mother as to interrupt her while she was speaking. Thus Maacha was unable to escape from the web of memories that Hamutal was so busily spinning. Hamutal was living in the past, but the young Queen felt stifled and wanted to hear only of the present and the menacing future, for there was no hope left in her. Now and then Jeremiah caught a look from her roving eyes, in which he could read not only the silent protest at being thus tied to Hamutal's couch, but also hatred of the monotonous voice to which she was compelled to listen. The prophet knew what was in Maacha's mind, and he offered to fulfil an old wish of Hamutal. He had once been Zedekiah's teacher, and now he had sufficient leisure to be the teacher of Zedekiah's sons. During his lessons, which were to be held in the family living-room as at Noph, there would be a pause in the sick woman's flow of talk. And so it happened, to Maacha's great relief and gratitude. When Jeremiah began in the first lesson to speak to the children of the beginning when God created heaven and earth, the young Queen forgot both the present and the future.

Adajah was eight years of age, Ichiel not yet seven. The two last branches on the tree of David had developed very differently from each other. Adajah was his father's son through and through, both in looks and in character. Zedekiah had commanded the royal armourer to make him a little suit of armour and a helmet plumed with ostrich feathers; in this warlike garb the boy strutted about attractively and with full consciousness of his rank. There was something about the boy, half-aloofness and half-condescension, that prevented even his mother and grandmother from rebuking his self-will too severely. He would allow himself to be reproved only in private. If anyone made a request to him in the form of a command, he would turn his back. Small as he was, he insisted on keeping even Jeremiah, his new tutor, at a distance. Let anybody be a sanctified prophet of the Lord if he wanted to; royal blood in one's veins was the highest sanctification of all! Adajah seemed to be conscious of this in every game he played.

The younger boy, on the other hand, took less after his mother than after his grandmother. He had inherited not the austere character of Maacha, but the softer character of Hamutal. For suits of armour or plumed helmets he had little use, and he joined without enthusiasm in his brother's war games. He would best have liked to wear girl's clothes and trinkets. One of his favourite pastimes was to ferret about among the women's baubles, among their jars of myrrh and unguents, their work-boxes and ribbons. The little silver dishes with sweetmeats and comfits, which always stood ready for the ladies of the royal household, were never safe from his fingers. In his perverse love of perfumes and fragrant essences Ichiel had inherited a weakness of the sons of David, one of the vicious qualities of ancient blood. His obsession went so far that Maacha often had to rap him over the knuckles for pouring a phial of liquid myrrh or Arabian perfume over his clothes or even, in a stupor of the senses, setting it to his lips. Yet though he was still babyish and had wheedling ways, his mind was much more alert and responsive than that of his proud and self-centred brother.

Jeremiah's spirits were cheered during the few short hours when he was teaching the two boys, looking into Ichiel's eyes, which were continually wandering away to gaze at a fly on the wall or some other distraction, and trying to keep the child's attention fixed on the stories of the patriarchs. When Ebed-melech heard that the prophet was giving lessons in the House of Pharaoh's Daughter, he slipped out whenever his duties permitted and joined the circle. The tall Ethiopian would then crouch on his heels in a corner and listen intently, with a far-away look in his eyes, to the expounding of the Law. When Jeremiah was carried away by his own words and his voice took on a singing tone, Ebed-melech too began to hum to himself and rock to and fro, while his great jaws moved as though he were chewing the holy nutriment of the commandments. In this way he again listened to the instruction that he had received in his own youth, as if he, an alien child of the south, wished to attach himself with a thread of double strength to the sacred garment of Jacob.

When Jeremiah's work was done, Baruch came every evening to his chamber, and there, in their second place of hiding, the two of them prepared a second book containing all the promptings and visions that had been disclosed to the prophet since the days of Jehoiakim.

The House of Pharaoh's Daughter, with the peaceful life within it, was like a ship sailing placidly on the tides of the siege. Little was to be heard through the windows of the angry clamour of war. Though the bread in the city grew more and more gritty, until one day the supply ceased altogether, there were still stores of the finest white flour, of milk and butter, of oil and wine and honey, in the royal larders. Instead of bread they ate sweet cakes, to the great delight of Ichiel. During this time the King appeared only twice, to spend a fleeting hour with his mother, his wife, and his children, but he seemed each time to be in a happy mood. He boasted and jested, yet the more high spirited he became, the less was Maacha able to keep her fears from showing in her face, though Hamutal was contented and went on with her voluble chatter.

"Did I not always tell you, my daughter, that the King would be victorious? Things will be different from what they were when Josiah, his father, set out from Megiddo with five hundred chariots to attack Pharaoh's army, but in his boldness ventured too far and found himself facing the Ionians. . . ."

Her thoughts were again flowing along the old channel of the past. To her great disappointment, her son did not let her continue with her dreams. He interrupted her, for he could not stay long, and stretched his limbs with exaggerated cheerfulness as he spoke encouragingly to the apprehensive

Maacha and the others. It was as if he knew of something that was concealed from them, and final victory was now only a question of weeks. Yet Jeremiah had learned the truth from Ebed-melech. Through the continual sorties and the fighting in front of the gates, a game of hazard which Zedekiah was playing with a rare audacity, he had not only already lost one half of his brave bodyguard but had given hundreds of malcontents, who were adherents of the sons of Shaphan, an opportunity to desert to the Babylonians. In spite of these experiences he did not change his tactics. He sapped the courage of Babylon and performed wild deeds of bravery that were worthy of being remembered. But they were not remembered, nor did they make the heart of Zion proud. Jeremiah knew why the King was doing this. He was trying, by a laudable death in battle, to avoid the sacrifice that had been demanded of him. For that very reason, however, he seemed to be invulnerable. With a company of storm troops that he had recruited from the most reckless of his warriors, he succeeded on one occasion by means of a lightning coup in breaking through the ranks of the besiegers and fighting his way to where Nergal Sarsechim was standing. He challenged the general to a duel and seriously wounded him, but even this tempestuous sally into the heart of the enemy's army did not bring him the death he coveted. Zedekiah's way of saving Jerusalem was not the way of Zebaoth. None of the thousands of arrows and lances even grazed his flesh; no sword, trident, or net could prevail against his charmed life. After his victory over the Nergal, he was bold enough to challenge Marduk himself to single combat. The answer he received was a final opportunity offered by the Lord to the king who was defending his honour with such supreme temerity in the effort to evade the divine command. With aloof and annihilating dignity Marduk ignored the ridiculous challenge of an inferior. If the King of Judah, he said, would surrender himself and acknowledge the overlordship of the King of Babylon by new moon in the month of Ab, then Jerusalem would be spared the dominion of Ninurtu, the star of destruction. These words fully confirmed what Jeremiah had seen and heard in his dream vision. Once more the prophet cast himself at the King's feet, but Zedekiah put his hand over his mouth and would not let him speak. Everything had been discussed that there was to be discussed; there was nothing more to be said. Again they sat together in silence. Later Zedekiah ordered Ebed-melech to go to the storeroom of the palace and seek out some old and tattered garments such as were worn by the lowest menials. Picking up the least soiled of them with the tips of his fingers, he put it on with an expression of loathing. Then he looked down at himself, turned white with misery, and ripped it from his body. Ebed-melech had to rub his skin with rough towels and anoint it with unguents.

The days passed, but Zedekiah made no further attempt to do what Jeremiah had urged. The month of Tammuz was nearing its end, the scorching month which preserved the name of the mutilated god for whom the heathen women lamented on the heights. It had brought a drought such as the oldest in the land had never experienced. No rain had fallen on the earth for weeks and wild beasts emerged from the wilderness and the mountains, roaming through the fields and venturing into the villages that had not been burnt down. Even the hind on the hills abandoned its newborn young, for all the grass was brown and there was no milk in her teats. The wild asses came out from the thicket snorting and howling like jackals, despair in their bloodshot eyes. Wealthy people sent out their bondservants to dig wells in likely places, but they returned despondent. It would have been easier to find water in the desert. At first the copious spring which filled the channels in the royal gardens ceased to flow. Then within a few days all the other springs and wells in the city ran dry. Everybody rushed to the cisterns and reservoirs, and finally to the two pools of Siloah, that they might fill their pitchers. But the level of the water in the great pools sank from hour to hour, and in a short time that which was left had evaporated. It was true that the drought affected the besiegers as well as the besieged, but it was of no advantage to Jerusalem, since it compelled the Babylonians to use their superior weight of men and material in order to bring about the speedy surrender of the city. Inflamed by the deprivations from which they were suffering, the Babylonians renewed their fierce attack against the walls and bulwarks. The patient lion of Babylon was roused to fury, and he did not cease to fight even when darkness had fallen.

The men of the defending garrison lined the walls. Emaciated, parched, fighting wildly under the burning sun, they did not even perspire. As they stood behind their parapets aiming spears, shooting arrows, or hurling stones, they sucked at thin twigs held between their teeth. The city was filled with the wails of mothers and children who wandered through the narrow streets, peered in at doorways, or burst into the Temple to beg for some of the sacrificial fruits which they imagined were to be found there. But the priests, who were walking about like spectres, had nothing to give them. As time went on these roaming women and children were joined by numerous criminals, who formed bands that went about looting and murdering, for a rumour had spread that some of the well-to-do citizens were concealing hundreds of jars of wine or great pitchers full of other refreshing drinks. Every woman suspected every other woman of possessing stores of preserves and sweet fruits for the use of her own family and refusing to share them with her neighbours. The looting bands shed much blood, but found little to drink. In their train came that which was bound to come, the scourge of all besieged cities: pestilence, the offspring of hunger and thirst.

During the last three days of Tammuz all the gates of the palace had to be barred and guarded by soldiers, for the lives of the King and his family were in danger. On every side could be heard the incessant shouts of the mob demanding water and bread from those within. The King, however, stayed all this time on the bulwarks and did not return home.

In the women's quarters they sat together hour after hour—the two queens, the boys, Jeremiah, Baruch, and Ebed-melech. Hamutal lay as usual on the couch, though now she only dreamed and did not talk. Adajah did not leave the window, but stood there all the time looking out and listening. His younger brother took matters less seriously and his eyes kept wandering round for sweetmeats that were not there. All at once the days seemed to be rushing past and they were already in the month of Ab, with its consuming heat that turned every meadow into a desert, the month that Jeremiah had hated since he was a child without knowing why. With the new moon Zedekiah's last respite had come to an end. His last chance to sacrifice himself for his people was gone. Yet encouraging messages began to arrive in the House of Pharaoh's Daughter, and they were like a breath of fresh air to the little company. The King had succeeded in beating off every attack, and in a sortie by night his storm troops had destroyed a large part of the enemy's ordnance with burning pitch. At the same time Elnathan had managed, by means of a caravan disguised as a consignment of fresh supplies for the Babylonian army, to smuggle large quantities of water, wine, and figs into the city through the subterranean passage of Siloah. Though these treasures sufficed for only a small part of the population and lasted no more than a few hours, yet their value was inestimable, since it was said that ten times the amount would follow before another week had gone by. Even those who had not benefited were fortified by this hope. But the end came suddenly. And it came when it was least expected.

Jeremiah was asleep in his room. Baruch, wrapped in blankets, lay on the floor beside him. During these days, when they had all been enjoying a feeling of relief at the apparent change in the tide of fortune, the prophet and his disciple had been engaged in recalling the words of the Lord so that they might record them in their book. It was not yet midnight when the house suddenly reverberated to hollow cries and the banging of doors. Servants hurried through the corridors with candles in their hands, and Ebed-melech, his teeth gleaming white in the darkness, put his head in at Jeremiah's door.

"They have torn a breach in the walls," he said breathlessly. "Every one to the King! . . ."

Jeremiah and Baruch sprang up and dashed to the living-room, where they found women and girls running about in confusion. They had completely lost their heads and were collecting useless possessions and packing them into travelling-bags. Even the sick Hamutal had risen from her couch and was being dressed with difficulty by her waiting-women. Maacha had her hands full with her two sons. Impatiently she was trying to dissuade Adajah from putting on his suit of armour and plumed helmet, but the stubborn lad refused to yield. Ichiel, in a bad humour at having been awakened at such an unusual hour, pouted and scolded his nurse as she dressed him. Amid all this bustle of women and children the King stood erect and motionless. Only now and then he tapped the floor with his foot as a warning to them to hurry. During the past weeks of the siege he had become almost as thin as a skeleton, and his large eyes glowed twice as brilliantly in his emaciated face. He showed no sign of despair at having been taken by surprise, nor even of disquiet. He wore an air of content as if everything had gone according to a well-thought-out plan, and when he caught sight of Jeremiah he beckoned to him with a smile.

"It is better that we should leave Jerusalem; and you will come with us." This was a command that could not be ignored. "It will be an easy task for the King to augment the hosts of Elnathan and lead them to the city as reinforcements for the garrison. During my absence Ishmael will be in command. Everything was planned and prepared long ago. Horses, asses, and camels are waiting for us in a safe place, and we shall go to meet Elnathan at the Sea of Salt. Away from Jerusalem the King will be more powerful than lying here in a trap, and he rejoices at the prospect of open warfare. Rejoice with me, all of you!"

With these words Zedekiah laughed as though he had not painted the situation more brightly than was warranted and pretended that a dire necessity was a crafty stratagem. He laughed like the incorrigible optimist he was, remaining self-willed to the last and refusing to budge; until eventually, being forced to shift his ground, he asserted that he was moving of his own free will. At that moment, when he had no choice, Zedekiah did not ask his old hesitating question: "Is there any word from the Lord?" and his confident laughter was singularly comforting to all who heard him.

"You may take your disciple with you," he said graciously to Jeremiah.

Within an hour everything was ready for their departure. Zedekiah had arranged that the flight from the city was to take place in two groups. One of these consisted of two princes of the court, a number of bodyguards, a few servants, and the baggage, and it was to attempt to gain the open by way of the royal gardens. The main group, consisting of the King himself with his wife, mother, and the boys, together with Jeremiah, Baruch, Ebed-melech, and two soldiers of the bodyguard, intended to creep through the subterranean passage of Siloah and reach the Vale of Kidron where it joined the Valley of Ben-Hinnom.

This subterranean passage had a curious history. More than a hundred years before, King Hezekiah had built two pools between the Citadel of David and the outer walls to the east in order to store the copious rains of winter. Since there were also wet years when there was more rain than the reservoirs could hold, a conduit had to be provided for the overflow from both pools and particularly for the waters of the brook of Siloah which fed them. A channel was therefore bored through the rock to the south-east of the hill on which Jerusalem stood, and it was called "the subterranean passage of Siloah," a famous piece of engineering of which the citizens were inordinately proud. The implacable Hezekiah did not rest until the work was completed, though all his wise men threw up their hands in horror at such an undertaking. Boring was begun from both sides simultaneously, from the valley and from the city, and the miners hewed their way through the living rock, often losing their direction, until at last they met. But it was years before the two parties heard each other's hollow shouts and knew that they were separated by only a few feet. When the channel was finished and the waters flowed down, there were seven days of feasting and sacrifice, while at the place where the miners had met, Hezekiah had an inscription engraved in the rock as an eternal memorial.

From its entrance to the east of the pools till it emerged in the Vale of Kidron was a distance of twelve hundred ells. In order to deceive the enemy its exit was disguised as an abandoned quarry, of which there were several in the precipitous slopes of the hill, and therefore none of the Babylonian officers had any suspicion of its existence. Since the commencement of the siege, the sluice which allowed the channel to take the overflow from the brook of Siloah had been closed, and as the exit lay below one of the steepest and most inaccessible parts of the fortifications, where no assault was ever attempted, there were very few of the besieging troops to be found on that side. Nergal Nebuzaradan had no reason to take any particular precautions in such a desolate spot, particularly at that stage of the siege when he was gathering all his forces for the storming of the north wall, where the first breach had already been made. Zedekiah was reckoning that this would be the case, and his watchmen on the towers confirmed the fact that only a few scattered outposts were sitting round their camp fires on the farther bank of the brook of Kidron.

The flight of the royal household began with a grave misfortune. Hamutal heroically exerted herself beyond her strength. Almost carried rather than supported by the two soldiers, she kept up with her companions, though she was breathing with greater and greater difficulty. For some unknown reason she had had herself clad in a red mantle such as she had not been accustomed to wear since the death of Josiah. The King had been startled at the vivid colour, but he refrained from saying anything that might hurt his mother's feelings, resolving to throw a black cloak over her shoulders when they reached the open. By the light of a single flickering torch they entered the dried-up channel, and in spite of its comfortable breadth and height they were able to move forward only very slowly in the spectral gloom. The boys, now fully awake and excited at the unexpected adventure, were thoroughly enjoying themselves and shouted at the top of their voices in order to hear the echo that reverberated from the arched roof. Their father had to threaten them with punishment before they could be persuaded to stop. When they had reached about the middle of the winding passage, where Hezekiah's proud inscription was cut in the face of the rock, Hamutal suddenly swayed and sank to the ground.

"Leave me, my children," she murmured. "I shall not find a better place. . . . I am very comfortable here. . . . It is good to rest. . . . You go on and let me stay here. . . ."

Zedekiah bent over his mother with flickering eyes, but Maacha carefully adjusted the red mantle round the sick woman's body and put beneath her head one of the pillows they had brought with them.

"Come, Mother," urged the King, "come! You must try to rise! Never before have you left me, not since I was a child. . . . I will carry you. . . ."

By the unsteady light of the torch they saw Hamutal making an effort to smile and her pale lips forming the words "good" and "go" as she again tried to persuade her son to leave her. Her last wish, that she should not be a hindrance to them, was soon fulfilled. She made a slight movement, as if she was seeking someone upon whom she could rely to stand by the children of David in their need—perhaps she was looking for Jeremiah—then her heart gave up the struggle and ceased to beat. Hamutal, the wife of one king and mother of two others, was dead. She had seen one reign when the Lord looked kindly upon Judah and another when the Lord had cast Judah aside, and death came to her half-way along the subterranean path that led from the direst straits to even deeper misery.

The King was the first to collect himself.

"Good," he said, repeating the last word his mother had uttered. "Yes, what you have done is good, Mother, now as always. It is a good, deep grave that you have found. . . ."

He broke off and tore himself away, pointing onward with a swift gesture as if, for the sake of Jerusalem, even a mother's death must at once be erased from the mind.

Jeremiah, Baruch, and Ebed-melech hastily performed the last rites for Hamutal, covered her body in a blanket, and leaned it against the wall in a deep cleft so that her face was turned towards the sanctuary of the Temple. As they neared the exit, the torch was extinguished and they crept along the last section of the passage in deep darkness, their hearts heavy with grief for the death of Hamutal and their abandonment of her. But soon they could see a glimmering light like a star that gradually grew larger.

Under the mild night sky the Vale of Kidron lay deserted. Perhaps Hamutal in a dying prayer had pleaded for succour for the last sons of David. The fires of the distant outposts gleamed faintly, and there was no patrol to be seen far and wide on the heights beyond. To the north, on the other hand, a battle was raging round the Gate of Ephraim where the wall had been breached, and arcs of flame showed where burning torches were being hurled into the city. Zedekiah paused. Up there in the north Ishmael, whom he had appointed in his place, was fighting to the death. His heart was torn in two directions. Was it right for him to leave Jerusalem without even asking whether there was word from the Lord? Ought he not return and fling himself once more into the battle? Would it not be better for him to be buried beneath the ruins of his city? Was this flight after all only a cowardly pretext, and his hope of open warfare a mere delusion? His mother was already dead, a martyr to his plan. His hesitation, however, was soon overcome, then he turned away and began to run in a southerly direction along the stony bed of the brook of Kidron. The others followed him, Ebed-melech carrying the two princes in his arms. They did not know how long they ran, stooping low to avoid being seen, but they were exhausted and breathless by the time they reached a little gorge, covered with underbrush, where the other group was already waiting for them and the riding- and draught-animals had been hidden. Both the animals and their attendants belonged to one of Elnathan's disguised caravans. A gentle camel, which had been provided for Hamutal, was assigned to Maacha.

This second group had not escaped from the city without loss. One of the servants, who had a very heavy load to carry, had not been able to keep up with the others and he had fallen into the hands of an enemy patrol. Among the treasures which had thus been captured was the golden Cup of David, a loss that could bode no good.

Worse than this was the fact that they had to envisage

the possibility of the man's being tortured into betraying the King's flight and the direction he had taken. There was no time to lose. The riding-animals were quickly distributed, the King and his bodyguard taking the horses while Jeremiah and Baruch rode on asses, as did Ebed-melech, who was ordered to follow as quickly as he could with their possessions. Zedekiah took the older boy with him on the saddle and Maacha insisted on carrying Ichiel, who objected to his uncomfortable seat between the camel's humps and began to whimper. So Ebed-melech took him from his mother and put him on his own mount, while Jeremiah rode alongside and told the child stories until he fell asleep.

The first part of the dangerous journey was over. In the wilderness of Judea, however, to which they soon came, it was possible to go only very slowly, since they had to avoid the road. The horses and asses stumbled along amid the heaps of rubble, the crevices, and the uneven folds in the ground, and the men had to descend from their mounts again and again to examine the animals' fetlocks for injuries. It was not till after midnight that the thin sickle of the new moon gave them a faint light on their way, for which Maacha thanked the Lord in her heart. By this time they had reached Adumim, where the soil was more friable and the horses were able to step out more freely, followed by the sturdy, shuffling asses. Suddenly the King signed to the others to halt, and they all held their breath to listen. From a distance came the sharp clatter of horses' hoofs, which continued to echo for a while and then ceased abruptly. There could be only one explanation. The captured servant must have betrayed their flight under threat of torture, and the enemy was on their heels. There was no possibility that they were being deceived by their own echo in the silence of the night, for their pursuers continued to trot for a time after they themselves had stopped, as if they were waiting patiently to hear in what direction the fugitives were making. Shortly after the arduous journey was resumed, Zedekiah's horse fell and was unable to rise again. The King, unhurt, mounted the horse of one of the soldiers, who had to remain behind in the desert. Though they took a devious route and more than once changed their course, they could not shake their pursuers off their trail. The Babylonians were sure of their prey and kept always the same distance behind the royal party. Zedekiah had no time either to speak a few words of encouragement to his companions or to grant them a short rest, however much his heart tightened every time he looked at his young wife. The sorrow that had shadowed her face in happier days had now sufficient cause, and as she swayed on the tall back of her camel it was apparent to the King that she and Jeremiah were the only ones in that company who cherished not the slightest hope of their reaching safety. Whenever she caught his eyes she gave him a confident smile, but he knew that it was forced, that she was dissembling her fears out of her love for him. Each time it struck him like a blow, so that his heart failed him and he wanted to leap from his horse and creep away to some solitary cavern in the wilderness where he could spend the rest of his life in solitude. Luckily the children were sound asleep, Adajah at his father's breast and Ichiel in the arms of Ebed-melech.

As there was no sign of slackening in the pursuit they extinguished their torches, in spite of the dangerous and precipitous nature of the path they were compelled to take. When the first grey streaks of dawn appeared in the sky, all sound of horses' hoofs behind them had ceased. The King had eluded his pursuers. By morning the main part of the

troop rode with mocking deliberation towards the King of Judah. When Zedekiah tore at the reins to pull his horse round, it was too late.

The sun was darkened by an eclipse. The sun, which had left its chamber like a bridegroom and entered like a hero upon its victorious course, covered its flaming head. Gradually it was hidden by the black shadow until nothing remained but a narrow ring. A moaning wind rose up that was like no other wind on earth, that was only the phantom, the echo, the ghost of a wind. Before it were driven the birds of night, the owls and bats that wondered at the unaccustomed hour of their awakening. Men, animals, plants, everything took on a pallid aspect and the nations of the world trembled in their hearts, for they recognized the existence and power of God in unusual phenomena rather than in familiar miracles of everyday life. The sun began to darken at the third hour after reaching its zenith, and when the black shadow had consumed three-quarters of its disk the clear light of Marduk and his two mightiest messengers, Nergal and Ninurtu, shone forth amid the pale stars. At the same moment Nebuchadnezzar emerged from his house, for the great hour of his career had come, when the nocturnal sky was visibly overcoming the sky of day and he himself, together with the servants who executed his will, could be seen in the firmament coming out from the house of the fiery lion. This hour had been calculated by the astrologers at his birth, when they foretold that kings and nations would be crushed beneath his heel at the darkening of the sun and his dominion over the world be complete. Marduk's great hour could be only the hour of judgment of his *Ner.* Judgment was, indeed, an inadequate term. It presupposed justice, a just weighing of deeds according to laws and precepts to which even a king had to bow. Marduk, however, did not acknowledge the justice which condemned or set free after due consideration of laws and facts. Marduk was not just, but mighty. His justice consisted solely in the preservation of a sacred symmetry, and he regarded this duty as the noble privilege of his power. Whoever pretended that little things were great or great things small; whoever confused figures or distorted values, thereby denying the evident and calculable proof of the eternal symmetry of the universe, was guilty of violating the natural order that had been predetermined by Marduk and must inevitably be hurled into the abyss of nothingness. Zedekiah had pretended that little things, namely, himself and his kingdom, were great; he had confused figures and distorted values, namely, those of Jerusalem and Babylon; he had denied the evident and calculable superiority of Nebuchadnezzar by founding a league of nations to oppose him. The symmetry of the world had been violated. He must therefore be hurled into the abyss of nothingness. It was not as a judge that Marduk came forth from his house when the sun grew dark. A judge's task was to examine the question of the prisoner's guilt, listening to arguments and the evidence of witnesses. Marduk came forth as the absolute power whose task it was to preserve symmetry; it was not even his duty to administer punishment, but only to effect the inevitable consequence that must ensue from Zedekiah's disturbance of the world order.

Those who saw Nebuchadnezzar's face in the hour of the sun's eclipse did not fail to notice its expression of melancholy, a melancholy different from that engendered on the lonely heights of absolute and triumphant power. Marduk, the Lord of the starry messengers and the constellations of the zodiac, Marduk, the King of the stars that were turned towards him and those that were turned away from him, was dependent on the countless stellar forces and orbits of which he was the focus. His actions were guided by those whom he himself controlled. It was not his plan that was now being fulfilled. Jerusalem lay in ruins and its Temple had been burnt to ashes. Marduk was forced to be the instrument of a destiny that did not spring from his own will. He was the servant, and not the master, as was written in the book of the soothsayer of Judah. Now, when he appeared to be the undisputed Lord of the world, he had by some inescapable confusion become the tool of an alien plan. What he had wanted had come to pass, but not in the way he had intended. The only free being in the universe, who determined destiny in the Chamber of Destiny, had in some mysterious manner become, together with all his starry forces, subservient to a strange god. The realization of this put the world out of joint. The darkening of the sun cast shadows that enveloped him too. He was oppressed by the sorrow of a god who is conscious for a moment that he is not a god. And this sorrow could be read in the round, youthful countenance before which heaven and earth trembled.

Marduk was at Riblah, the city where he had set up his headquarters, at the junction of many roads and where many nations met. People from different countries had gathered at Riblah to witness the victory of the nocturnal sky over the sky of day and to enjoy the sight of the punishment that had overtaken the King of an unloved nation. The great square could not hold the throng; it was only with the utmost difficulty that the bodyguards were able to keep a clear space round the pyramid of the star-throne and the scaffold at its base. High above sat Marduk in his jewelled cloak, forming the peak. To his right, and lower down, stood twelve Nergals clad in fiery red. The brilliant figure of Nebuzaradan was not among them, since he was still tarrying in Judah to complete the work of destruction and dissolution. To Marduk's left stood twelve Ninurtus garbed in black, mostly peevish old men who coughed a great deal. Between the red and the black councillors, four steps below the throne and exactly in the centre, Samgar Nebo stood alone, the only one clad in blue. His beardless, unlined face expressed a weary loathing of that which he was about to see. It was not sympathy that caused the youthful-looking councillor with the aged eyes to appear sick at heart, but an unspeakable distress at anything coarse. Nergal could be transformed into Ninurtu, and Ninurtu could even be transformed into Nergal, but between them and the sensitive, blue-clad Nabu there could be nothing in common. If Marduk was the Lord of symmetry, Nabu was the Lord of the beauty and harmony inherent in the precision of mathematical laws. When he was forced to witness anything ugly or gross, his fastidious mind was nauseated. On the steps below Samgar Nebo were crowded the other star-councillors, arrayed in the most varied colours and their hands folded tranquilly one above the other.

The scaffold had been set up before the pyramid like a vast table, as if Marduk intended to offer a banquet to his gods. Great rust-red bloodstains marred the surface, for in the course of a few days more than three hundred of Zedekiah's princes and officers had been executed on this scaffold by the sword. After the final battle they had fallen into the hands of Nebuzaradan and been taken forthwith to Riblah with a strong escort. Among them had been Malchiah, the son of Pashur, and Irijah, the son of Hananiah. The greater part of Jerusalem's dignitaries, particularly those who held priestly office, had been hanged in the Temple without more ado. A small group, under Ishmael's leadership, had bravely cut its way through to Baalis, the King of Ammon. In front of the steps that led up to the scaffold stood Jeremiah. He was at liberty, for Marduk still showered favours on the soothsayer of the alien god, though Jeremiah did not know why. After passionate pleading he had been allowed even to pass some hours of the day and night with Zedekiah and his sons in their prison. In this most bitter hour of all he was not separated from them. Otherwise the sons of David were guarded by an inexorable wall of swords and lances. No one was allowed to approach them, particularly no one from Judah, even if he was an adherent of the sons of Shaphan. Maacha and the faithful Ebed-melech had been forbidden under pain of death to enter the city, and they waited outside the walls, where Jeremiah and Baruch came from time to time to bring them news. Maacha lay on the ground with closed eyes as if she were in a trance. In spite of all his exhortations the Ethiopian had not been able to make her eat or drink for eight days.

Slowly the sun's disk was filled with the shadow that foreboded the eventual end of the world, when it would grow colourless and cold, the chain of causation being exhausted. Marduk and his messengers still shone but faintly. The trembling shimmer of the other stars could hardly be perceived in the hollow pallor of the firmament. On all the towers of Riblah stood the astrologers of Babylon, watching through polished crystal the growing shadow on the sun and the gradual brightening of the royal planet. It was their duty to announce the moment of total eclipse. The blanching hand of death passed over the faces of the assembled people. Only Marduk's tanned, tense face did not lose its living hue. The jewels of his cloak sparkled with a more and more sinister light as the sky darkened, retaining their lustre even in the indescribable twilight when the rams' horns announced from every tower that the time had come. An abysmal silence followed, the last terrifying respite before the approach of doom. In this solemn stillness Zedekiah and his sons were led to the scaffold.

The King of Judah and the two boys were naked for the sacrifice. Even their loin-cloths had been taken from them, and they were exposed in their shame before the eyes of the nations. But in this hour of darkness the Lord had endowed them unstintingly with inward light. Zedekiah was radiant with beauty. The delicate loveliness of the boys wrested a deep sigh of sympathy from the hearts of the watching people. The father's wrists had been chained to the thin arms of his children. Adajah held his head high and kept his grave eyes fixed on Zedekiah, as if he was resolved, come what might, to model his demeanour on that of the father he idolized and to endure his ordeal no less courageously. Ichiel, however, looked round tremulously, with wondering eyes that were on the verge of tears. The older boy was silent. The younger boy whimpered:

"Father . . . what do all these people want? . . . Why are we here? . . . When are we going home? . . ."

Zedekiah soothed the child, and his voice did not tremble.

"Have patience, Ichiel. . . . It will not be long now. . . . We shall soon be home again. . . ."

Ichiel began to wail a little:

"Let us put on our clothes and go to Mother and Grandmother. . . ."

A ripple stirred the ranks that lined the pyramid. Marduk had handed a small clay tablet to the chief Nergal and it was being passed down to the base. At the same moment a procession of shrouded figures in voluminous, fiery-red cloaks mounted the scaffold and formed a circle round the three sons of David. The first of the red-clad figures received Marduk's tablet and read out to Zedekiah and the assembled people the inevitable decree:

"At first you will see and then you will not see, because when you could see you would not!"

Marduk's divine decree was dark, like all divine decrees. Zedekiah's eyes, distended with horror, sought Jeremiah. Now that the end had come, did he regret not having accepted the sacrifice that had been urged upon him? Jeremiah tried to go to him on the scaffold, but four blue-clad brethren of Nabu suddenly came forward and barred his way on every side, so that he was unable to move a step. Again the rams' horns were sounded. The eclipse of the sun was complete. In the square, in the rest of the city, perhaps throughout the inhabited world, began a wild uproar of rattles, drums, triangles, and other percussion instruments in which even the trumpets and chanting of the priests were drowned. It was as if the people were trying by their clamour to stave off the end of the world as well as to smother the screams of the victims. Only now were Zedekiah's children seized by panic. As they pressed their little faces against their father's burning flesh, Samgar Nebo slowly turned his back upon the scaffold and looked wearily into Marduk's eyes. The latter raised his hand almost imperceptibly. Six of the muffled figures in red stepped behind Zedekiah and his sons. Loosening the fetters that bound Adajah and Ichiel to their father they led the screaming boys three paces in front of him, one to the right and one to the left, so that he could see what was being done with them as Marduk had decreed. Zedekiah flung himself forward with such force that he pulled with him to the ground the two giants who were holding him fast. Before he could rise again the men standing behind the boys had thrown off their red cloaks and revealed themselves as black-clad executioners. Their swords flashed swift as lightning and split the heads of the last sons of David. Neither the screams of the boys as they were torn from their father nor the sound of their fall as their spurting blood dyed his naked body was heard in the savage uproar. Once more Zedekiah put forth all his strength and hurled his captors aside, but they flung themselves upon him, forced him to his knees, and bound his arms so that he could not move. With heaving breast he cried in a terrible voice:

"Now I have seen! . . . Why are you waiting? . . . Hurry, that I may no longer see. . . ."

Zedekiah, however, had misunderstood Marduk's decree. With the exception of the two giants who guarded him, the red-clad executioners again formed in procession and left the scaffold. The condemned man gazed after them, his eyes filled with the torture of disappointment and delay. As they disappeared he glimpsed another figure coming towards him from the opposite side of the scaffold, a figure that was not only clad from head to foot in saturnalian black but might have been taken for Ninurtu himself. White-bearded and morose, with the air of a man who had a duty to perform, he limped painfully towards his victim. One of his legs was shorter than the other and in his hands, which he kept concealed behind his crooked back, he carried two thin iron rods that glowed white hot. As Zedekiah turned his face towards him, he thrust the glowing tips abruptly and with an incredibly skilful aim into the lustrous eyes. The blinded King's maddened scream was lost in the increased din that greeted the disappearance of the shadow and the end of the eclipse. Men came and carried away the gory corpses of his two children. Others poured buckets of water over him as he lay where he had fallen. The agony had been more than he could bear and he had lost consciousness.

The four brethren of Nabu stepped back and left the way free for Jeremiah. Dragging himself to the scaffold, he pillowed Zedekiah's head in his lap. Where the King's eyes had been were bloody, charred cavities. With the tears running down his cheeks the prophet spoke to him without knowing what words he was saying:

"My King, my child . . . you will live. . . . And he who lives may know the reward he merits for so great a sacrifice. . . . Your sacrifice has been very great . . . for you have drunk the bitter lees from the cup of all the generations. . . . Now you have swooned with the agony . . . but in a few days it will leave you. . . . And when the time has come, the Lord will not refuse to let you share in the joy He will dispense. . . . Rejoice, Mattaniah, for you will be remembered and your soul will go to join the souls that live. . . ."

Bending low over the unconscious Zedekiah, the prophet sobbed words of comfort that perhaps did not go unheard. When he looked up again, he saw that Nebuchadnezzar was standing before him. The King of Babylon had ascended the scaffold with his councillors of Nergal and Ninurtu; and his eyes, for all their far-away look, rested keenly on Jeremiah as he cooled Zedekiah's wounds with wet cloths. In his high-pitched voice he addressed the prophet of Judah, a mark of honour that provoked the envy of his retinue:

"The prisoner," he said, "will be carried to Babylon tomorrow. No one is to accompany him, neither man nor woman. But you are free to stay or to go. Even, if you wish, to go with him."

After this signal mark of esteem from the Lord of the earth, the Babylonians expected that Jeremiah would cast himself at Marduk's feet and kiss the spot where he stood. But the prophet sat motionless and silent. Something stirred within his crushed soul and gave it strength. He had been appointed as a prophet to speak unto the nations of the world and he was not afraid. He therefore spoke to Marduk, Lord of the nations, in the name of the One God:

"You could have been a foundation-stone and a corner-stone. . . . But now you are only a dead block that lies in the way. . . ."

There were three seconds of dumb horror. The councillors of Marduk paled and seemed to shrink. Their folded hands sank helplessly to their sides. Nebuchadnezzar's lips twitched. Life and death depended on what they would say. Jeremiah's words had pierced to the core of his secret sorrow and revealed the truth. The sword-bearer of God knew that though he had laid Jerusalem in ruins and burned the Temple, yet his work was in vain. The fingers of his right hand played with the little golden shovel at his girdle. At this moment, however, he proved that he was a great man worthy of the height on which he stood, and not a little man striving to appear greater than he was. With no sign of malice or apprehension, of wrath or desire for vengeance, he bore the truth with a tranquil spirit. His twitching lips curved into an inscrutable smile and he turned with a slight inclination of the head to his horrified councillors. The words he spoke were a pledge of life and liberty to the prophet who had outraged the majesty of his omnipotence.

"Let him stay or go whithersoever he will! Let him say and prophesy what he must! For his god is very strong within him!"

That night Jeremiah had a vision in which the Lord appeared to him. For the first time in his life Adonai was not only a voice but something more. He did not see a definite apparition with his eyes. Yet a masculine figure, erect, luminous and almost youthful, was in some inexplicable way within the range of his senses. Even this fails to describe the nature of his dream vision. It was not that Jeremiah perceived a figure in the room, but that he was imbued with a consciousness of its presence. He seemed to be in an open space, a sand-blown caravan route in the desert. Far in the distance, on the edge of the desert, he saw the violet spectral shape of E-temen-anki, towards which he was moving. Every time he halted, exhausted by his lonely journey, and turned round, he saw in the distance, at the opposite edge of the desert, the black columns of the temple Ro-stau in the western city of Noph, which guarded the gates of Amenti. In between stretched a vast waste of ruins and ashes. Suddenly a deep crevasse opened in the road ahead of him. He felt within himself the strength to leap across it but was held back by the consciousness of the luminous figure, which spoke to him in the voice he had so often heard:

"The longing of thy heart draws thee to Babylon. But it is opposed by *my* will. Turn back!"

"Lord," answered Jeremiah, overwhelmed by the genuineness of the vision, "Lord, Thy compassion endureth for ever. Mine endureth for but a short time. Grant thy servant leave to accompany the blinded King to Babylon, for he is alone!"

"Thou shalt not go to Babylon," said the voice, not without impatience, "for I will send thee back to the Remnant."

Dusk had fallen. In the starry chamber of E-temen-anki the gathered radiance of the firmament began to shimmer. The dreamer protested with all his strength:

"Not only the blinded King is being led to Babylon, that like Coniah he may spend the rest of his days in captivity, but all in the land who are young and strong, both men and women. Bowed beneath the yoke, fettered one to the other, they are being driven with sticks and iron goads, ten thousand upon ten thousand. The roads are choked with their misery. But the Remnant, who are they? They are the traitors, the deserters, the timorous, the quibblers, the old people, and the rabble who sow and reap wherever they may be and whatever may befall. They do not need me."

"Do not dispute with me," said the voice, not without impatience, "but obey and turn back!"

At these words the crevasse widened and deepened to an abyss. The luminous figure had receded slightly. Jeremiah decided to argue in more subtle fashion.

"Has Thy servant not always obeyed Thee, Lord?" he asked. The figure appeared to grow thoughtful, and this was in itself a kind of gracious affirmation. More could not have been expected. Jeremiah continued craftily:

"This time the desire of my heart is stronger than my obedience, Lord. It clings to the blinded King; it clings to the prisoners of Zion. Does not Thy promise hold good for them?"

"My promise holds good for them."

"And yet Thou wilt drive me away? Though I have worn myself out in Thy service, wilt Thou after so many weeks of years withhold my reward?"

Behind his back the dreamer was conscious of the desolate

ruins of many cities and villages. In the distance he saw the lighted chamber of E-temen-anki, and in front of him the gaping abyss over which he would have to leap. The voice of the invisible but tangible figure seemed to grow weary of opposition.

"Do not dispute," it repeated, "but obey and turn back!"

Jeremiah, however, stood firm and demanded rebelliously:

"And if Thy servant does not turn back?"

"Then he will have disobeyed me."

"And if he disobeys Thee?"

"Then even the last of my people will have broken faith with me, as all the others have done."

"So let it be!" cried the recalcitrant prophet, and he took a step towards the impassable abyss. Now a change took place in the luminous figure. Hesitantly it replied:

"But I do not wish that the last of my faithful servants should become unfaithful. . . ."

The dreamer rejoiced inwardly and already believed that he had won the battle. Shrugging his shoulders he cried:

"How canst Thou prevent me, Lord? All too strong is the longing in the heart of Thy servant."

The luminous figure seemed to recede still further. Its deliberate words came from another sphere, and not without a faint touch of regret:

"If thou canst not change the longing of thy heart, then must I change my plan."

Jeremiah was shaken to his very depths at these words. The gaping abyss had closed and the road lay before him smoother and broader than before.

"The Lord must change His plan?" he stammered.

"Since thou wilt not turn back," came the voice, "then I will turn back. For my plan had been to journey with the blinded King and the prisoners of Zion to Babylon, and to take up my dwelling place among them. But now that *thou* art journeying with them, *I* will turn back."

"No, Lord, no; do not do this thing," cried the defeated Jeremiah in despair, "but go with them, and I will obey and turn back. . . ."

He awoke with the enduring impression of having been embraced by two strong, compassionate arms.

A day or two later Jeremiah set out with the grief-stricken Maacha, accompanied by Baruch and Ebed-melech, to return home to the Remnant of Jacob in the unhappy land of Judah.

32

The Remnant

EVERYTHING came to pass as had been predicted. The almond blossoms of Jeremiah's first vision had changed to crackling flames. The seething pot in the north had spilled over and spurted glowing streams that scalded the whole land. When they returned home the prophet and his companions found on their way not a single hamlet or house that remained intact, only smoking ruins. In the fields lay those who had been massacred where they stood or whose bodies had been cast there that the roads might be clear. The air was tainted with a pestilential stench that grew more pervading the closer they approached to Jerusalem; and the clouds of birds that darkened the sky screeched their pleasure at the full table which Nergal had provided for them.

When Jeremiah raised his burning eyes to the familiar hills and mountains, it seemed to him as if the mountains swayed and the hills were in motion. Were the heights of Judah and the mountain ranges of Israel about to leave the land and wander with their children into exile? What was there left for them at home? Should they sing dirges for the empty pastures and the desolate orchards? There was no more reaping of corn or gathering of fruit; the pressing of the vine and shearing of sheep were at an end. The Lord had rolled up His land as a shepherd rolled up his woollen cloak. Or did Jeremiah's tortured eyes deceive him? Were the mountains and the hills rejoicing that they had been freed from this stubborn people who had dwelt upon them for countless generations? Once more they would see men like those who had lived there before Abraham, Isaac, and Jacob; men who were dull, silent, and pious, to whom God spoke but little and who spoke but little to God; men who lived easily and died easily and were such as the earth welcomed.

In terrible contrast to the emptiness of the countryside with its smoking ruins were the crowded roads and paths. Though several weeks had passed since the ninth day of Ab and the overwhelming of Jerusalem, there was still no end to the cruel processions of captives who were being driven to Babylon. Nergal Nebuzaradan was himself supervising the great migration. Unlike the earlier occasion when the Babylonians carried away their prisoners from Judah after the death of Jehoiakim and the fall of Coniah, the dignitaries had to leave their rank behind them and the wealthy their possessions. Everything of value, whether in money or chattels, fell into the hands of the victors; no distinction was made among princes, priests, and bondservants. All who came under the decree of expulsion were regarded as being in bondage. Marduk had no intention of burdening his land with a mob of distinguished idlers, with scribes, soothsayers, scholars, lazy dreamers, crafty money-changers, dealers in jewels, or other merchants. He had more than enough of that kind in Babylon already. But some ten myriads of slaves to bake bricks, cut weeds, drain swamps, irrigate steppes, and work at the hundreds of places where he was building under the sign of the Ram—these constituted a considerable enrichment of his country and a fitting payment for the war. Both high and low therefore had to become accustomed from the very start to the ruthless misery that awaited them, so that they might regard even the hardest labour at the end of their journey as pleasant and refreshing by comparison. Whoever found the effort beyond his strength could die by the wayside. What did it matter if a few thousand remained lying there? The exodus acted as an excellent sieve for the slaves. Marduk could use only strong arms in his work of construction. Nergal Nebuzaradan had prepared a central camp for the captives in the little town of Ramah in Benjamin; here were collected all those whom the Babylonian patrols managed to hunt out from the more remote villages, caverns, and mountain gorges after the great levies of the first days subsequent to the fall of Jerusalem. Only the old, the sick, the crippled, and the blind were allowed to remain in addition to the poorest of the peasants. The latter class is always unaffected by the course of historic events. Like cats who are attached to a house and not to the people who dwell in it, the poorer type of peasant belongs less to the nation than to the soil. Therefore, however numerous they are, they never constitute a danger for a conqueror. From his central camp in Ramah, Nebuzaradan sent the processions of exiles at suitable intervals to Babylon. And there was no end to them.

With unexpected generosity Marduk had permitted Maacha and her companions to obtain good riding-animals and to take with them an adequate number of attendants. Even so, they could proceed only step by step along the crowded roads. Every hour they encountered a new procession of wretched prisoners, consisting generally of a hundred men with their wives and children stumbling after them in little groups. The men were chained together either in pairs or in gangs, and in accordance with ancient military custom they bore heavy yokes on their bowed necks, so that they panted along under the burning sun with sweat pouring down their faces to mingle with their tears. The chafing yokes and chains soon wore through their thin garments, with the result that most of them had to journey into lifelong captivity in rags, and many of them were virtually naked. They were not allowed a moment's pause to breathe freely or any rest other than the regulation halts. The troop of horsemen who accompanied each of the processions struck at the men with their whips or the flats of their swords if there was any stoppage, if one of them refused or was unable to continue, or if anybody was overcome by the desire to lie down at the edge of the road to die. To increase their sufferings and lessen the opportunity to plan revolt, families and neighbours had been divided up and kept strictly apart, so that the men chained together all came from different parts of the country and were of various ages. The Lord was mingling His people like a mixed draught stirred in a cup.

The sight of the women was even more tragic than that of the men. The latter had to carry their yokes and chains, but they had no other burden. The women were loaded with all the immediate necessities of life that the Babylonians allowed them to take. Many a one was to be seen staggering along with an enormous sack on her back, a child on each arm, and a couple of older children wailing and stumbling at her side. In the pitiless rays of the sun the light skin of the young women, girls, and children blistered painfully, and their feet gradually turned to bleeding, shapeless lumps. If any of the women were good-looking and happened to stir the desire of their captors, then lots were cast to decide who should have them. When their piercing shrieks rang through the desolate countryside, the fettered men were unable to rush to their rescue and avenge them as the Law demanded. The Babylonians even took delight in giving their prisoners unclean food and filthy water at which they themselves shuddered in horror. On one occasion Jeremiah saw some Chaldean bowmen shoot down a number of carrion fowl and roast them. But the men and women of Judah refused to eat the forbidden flesh. Only one or two, beside themselves with despair or overcome by hunger, stretched out their hands to receive the abomination. The others sat still as death, closed their eyes, and let their heads sink lower and lower till they touched their knees. Meanwhile their conquerors unstrapped the wine jars from their saddle-horses and passed them from hand to hand, drinking amid laughter and uproarious singing in front of their parched prisoners. Even the women were too proud to betray their suffering; they pressed their moaning children more firmly to their breasts that their tormentors might not hear the cries of the little ones and rejoice still more.

Of the ten thousand terrible scenes that met the eyes of Jeremiah and his companions on their return home, this was but one. Again and again the prophet took Maacha's hand to draw her attention to some heart-rending sight, that she might realize that she was truly not alone in her affliction. In spite of the scorching sun, her hand was as cold as ice. Her whole being seemed to have frozen. She sat erect on the ass she was riding as if she belonged to another world. Since the judgment of Riblah she had not spoken, even to ask Jeremiah about the blinded King and his last leave-taking. Baruch and Ebed-melech thought that grief had stricken her dumb. When the others felt as if they would perish from the heat, she was attacked by a violent fit of shivering and her teeth chattered. When they stopped to rest, or at night, she was unable to get warm. Heated stones and all the blankets they could provide were of no help. It was as if her grief had dried up her blood. She lay shuddering under the awning, and the two maids whom Marduk had permitted to accompany her took turns during the night in rubbing her little white feet. But though they never ceased their ministrations, her feet remained stiff and cold, like those of a dead person. Yet when Jeremiah wanted to order a longer rest than usual because of her condition, she shook her head vehemently and her face became distorted with an expression of anger.

The goal of their journey was the little city of Mizpah, which lay not far from Anathoth on the borders of Judah and Benjamin. This was where the Remnant of Jacob had gathered, consisting of all the men of rank and wealth, together with their households, who had been allowed for various reasons and by favour of the King of Babylon to remain in their native land. Among them were the deserters and their families, the landowners and priests who had been hostile to Zedekiah and had openly gone over to the Babylonians during the war, but also some men who were pure of heart and, like the sons of Shaphan, had tried until the eleventh hour to avert the complete downfall of Jerusalem. Gedaliah had been appointed governor over the Remnant by Nebuchadnezzar and he ruled over them in Mizpah. His reputation had spread throughout the devastated land. People came even from Ephraim and Manasseh, from Issachar and Zebulun, tribes which had long been estranged from Judah, to gather round him. He had several thousands of families under his charge, and the number of souls was by no means insignificant. Wise preparations were being made to divide the country afresh, and Baruch did not conceal from Jeremiah his hopes that even the total destruction of Jerusalem and other cities was a wound that might be healed within a few generations. Jeremiah did not throw cold water on his optimism, for which, indeed, grounds were not lacking. Gedaliah was vigorous and energetic, and he was working day and night at the sacred task that had been entrusted to him. His less sturdy brother had already succumbed to his strenuous exertions. With iron resolution and courage the Governor overcame every obstacle; he had even succeeded in ensuring the partial preservation of the vintage and the olive harvest despite fire, massacre, and expulsion. In obedience to the wish of their dying father the sons of Ahikam had prepared the fold, and it was to this fold that Jeremiah and his companions were journeying. It was the duty of the new ruler of the people to take the wife of Zedekiah under his care.

One evening, while they were still on their way, they came to an ancient burial place not far from Ramah. Twelve great stones rose above a weather-worn tomb that had sunk deep into the earth, and there was no inscription to show which of the notable figures of antiquity was interred there. The travellers rested in the open, for their hearts were too heavy to enter Ramah, the headquarters of Nergal Nebuzaradan where he had established his camp for those who were being carried into captivity. Maacha, however, suddenly stood up, walked with solemn step towards the tomb, and seated herself on one of the grey stones. For the first time since the judgment of Riblah she opened her mouth to speak.

"This is the grave of Rachel, our ancestress," she said to Jeremiah, and there was a strangely stubborn note in her voice as if she expected him to contradict her.

"The Queen is mistaken," he corrected her gently. "This is not the grave of Rachel who bore Joseph and Benjamin.

Rachel lies buried in the Valley of Rephaim, near Bethlehem."

Maacha surveyed him contemptuously from head to foot. "What words are these, impious man! Surely I may know my own grave, to which I am returning after so much affliction?"

Jeremiah looked at her wide-eyed, whereupon she turned from him with a haughty gesture of rebuke. After a while she began to speak again, this time to herself:

"They have slain my two sons . . . Joseph and Benjamin. . . . They have slain all my children. . . . Yet it was not easy for me to bear my sons. . . . The wailing women are carrying my dead children in their arms to Babylon, my Adajah and Ichiel. . . . Lord, why hast Thou done this thing to Rachel's sons? . . . Thou who hast made it so difficult for mothers to bear children, why hast Thou done this thing? . . ."

She ceased to speak. Tears streamed down her sorrowful face, which might have been that of Rachel for whom Jacob served fourteen years. But there was no healing power in her tears and they brought her no relief. Jeremiah tried tenderly to persuade her to rise from the tomb, but she would not. She protested that her place was there, where she would at last be able to sleep again and be warm in death, as she had been for so long. He had to let her have her way and she spent the night sitting motionless on the stone like a statue of Rachel. Towards morning she slipped to the ground and fell asleep. Jeremiah took Ebed-melech aside and said to him:

"You must never oppose your mistress, but always do what she wishes so far as lies within your power. Be gentle and humour her. Perhaps the Lord will heal her, perhaps He will not; but stay with her wherever she may be and for as long as she wishes. You are well protected. When she is prepared to go on, then go with her to Mizpah, whither Baruch and I will precede you."

"My teacher may go with a tranquil mind," nodded the Ethiopian, "for my mistress is now my master."

Jeremiah bade the tall Ebed-melech bend his curly head, and he stretched out his hand to bless him.

"The Lord of hosts," he murmured, "who has given so many of the King's servants into the hand of death, all of them sons of Jacob, has spared you, a man from a strange land. And even more. Because of your faithfulness, you have been received among those who are most faithful."

"Received?" asked the Ethiopian sadly, as if he could not believe Jeremiah's words. "If I had children they would not be children of Jacob, but strangers, dark-skinned, unmarked by the hand of God."

Before he went, Jeremiah comforted him with the promise:

"The deeds of our hearts too, Ebed-melech, are not without their progeny."

As soon as they passed through the gate of Mizpah they heard the dreadful news of what had happened during the previous night. The house of the Governor was besieged by a wailing, cursing throng, but as Jeremiah and Baruch were recognized by the guards they were allowed to enter the court of the palace. In the centre of a muttering group of men they saw a body, wrapped in a bloodstained sheet, lying on the stone pavement. It was Gedaliah, whom the prophet had seen in his vision pierced by four swords. In reality it was not four, but ten swords that had lacerated the back and breast of Gedaliah. The worst aspect of this unutterable crime was the fact that it had been committed at a time when Marduk had decided to show favour to Judah and had sent special orders to Nergal Nebuzaradan putting an end to further expulsions. The central camp at Ramah was to be broken up without delay and the prisoners released without regard to rank or past conduct. At the same time an amnesty had been decreed throughout the country which affected all the fugitives who had gone into hiding either within or beyond the frontiers. There were no exceptions mentioned in the amnesty, not even the old warrior Elnathan or Prince Ishmael. Thus it had been possible for Ishmael, in whose veins flowed some drops of David's blood, to appear unexpectedly and unpunished in Mizpah a few days before. Accompanied by a number of his closest friends, he had come to pay homage to Gedaliah.

Among the grief-stricken mourners who surrounded the bloody corpse was a young man whom Jeremiah and Baruch had seen once or twice in Shaphan's room in the Temple. His name was Johanan, son of Kareah. In the confusion he seemed to have become the spokesman and leader. From him Jeremiah learned how the crime had been perpetrated that had destroyed the hope of the last Remnant.

It was less than three days before, said Johanan, that Gedaliah had gathered the people and the men of rank (including Ishmael and his friends) around him and had exhorted them to take no heed of the soldiers of Babylon, but to live quietly in the land and gird their hearts with patience. He himself would stay to govern them and further their cause with careful planning until the crushed nation should rise up again. Meanwhile they should all go in peace, fill their vessels with wine and oil and fruit, and resume the cultivation of their fields. Gedaliah had proffered this wise advice and the people had listened to him. But he intended to do more than persuade his enemies with prudent words. He wanted to bind them to his side with firm bonds, and to this end he had prepared a festive banquet to take place two days later. To this banquet he had invited Ishmael and nine of his companions, the Tartan whom Nebuzaradan had put in authority over the town of Mizpah, and some of his own chief collaborators. Though Johanan had warned the Governor of his danger, the latter had persisted in his plan. The young man repeated to Jeremiah the words he had spoken in Gedaliah's ear:

"I beseech you to forgo this banquet! Are you not aware that these men are plotting against you? Ishmael hates you and will try to take his revenge. He cannot forget that you deserted to the Babylonians and have been raised up by the enemy. His new master, Baalis, King of Ammon, has spurred him on to do you evil."

But Gedaliah had only laughed and replied scoffingly that he would have to abandon his belief in the supreme gifts of God, in reason and logical deduction, before he could believe that such a thing was possible. What grounds could Ishmael have for hating the man who had enabled him to return home unpunished and offered him the hope of again entering into possession of his estates? In any case he knew from Ishmael's own lips how strongly the prince approved of his present activities. Johanan recapitulated every argument that he had employed to persuade Gedaliah, who had brought the interview to an end by forbidding him to appear at the banquet lest his malice should envenom the joyous feast of reconciliation. When the night of the banquet arrived, everything happened as he had foreseen. After the wine had apparently warmed their hearts towards each other, Ishmael and his companions had suddenly drawn their swords and fallen upon Gedaliah like wild beasts. The other guests, too, had been slain, including the Babylonian Tartan.

Jeremiah gazed silently at the shrouded body in its blood-stained sheet. The last prop that supported the house had fallen. The noble mind and loyal friend had been overtaken by his end when he thought he was making a new beginning, just as he was hoping to ward off from the Remnant some of the evil effects of God's judgment. In his mind's eye Jeremiah saw the astute twins as they defended him with their shrewd arguments before Meshullam and the tribunal. Suddenly he was wrenched from his thoughts by an hubbub of agitated voices. The men assembled in the courtyard were shouting to him. He did not yet know the whole extent of Ishmael's crime. This dreadful murder had been only the beginning. Before the night was over, Ishmael, together with a band of ruthless fanatics like himself who had remained in concealment, had engaged in a savage massacre of unarmed men. Not only a number of the most important leaders among the Remnant had fallen victims to his vengeance, but also a company of innocent pilgrims from Ephraim who had been journeying on a pilgrimage to the ruins of the Temple. Towards morning they had been able to collect sufficient men and weapons to resist Ishmael's onslaught and drive the murderous crew towards the city of Gibeon. A message had just arrived to say that the Remnant of Judah were now in the throes of a bloody battle before the jeering eyes of Babylon. Johanan interrupted the incoherent cries and laments with the proud gesture of a newly appointed leader.

"We have now," he said to Jeremiah, "told you, though with much confusion, the whole terror which has befallen us and from which we are not yet free. What will be the outcome? Are we to flee? Or are we to stay? One of the Tartans and several others of the men of Babylon have been slain. The King of Babylon will not let this go unavenged, but will kill us all. Of that there can be no doubt. It is therefore my advice that we should go to Egypt without waiting until Nebuzaradan has reported this matter to Babylon. But as others among us have put forward different suggestions, we beseech you to let our supplication be accepted before you." The son of Kareah spoke with an affectation of subservience. "Pray for us unto the Lord your God for all this Remnant, for we are left but a few of many, as your eyes do behold us, that the Lord your God may show us the way wherein we may walk and the thing that we may do."

Through half-closed eyes Jeremiah observed the agitated men as they ran to and fro, plucked at their beards, beat their bodies, and argued angrily with one another. There was a bitter taste in his mouth as he thought of the blinded King and the processions of miserable captives on their way to Babylon, whither he himself had been forbidden by the Lord to journey. Yet it was in a very calm voice that he spoke to Johanan and the other men assembled in the courtyard where the murdered Gedaliah was lying.

"I have heard you; behold, I will pray unto the Lord your God, according to your words, and it shall come to pass that whatsoever thing the Lord shall answer you, I will declare it unto you. I will keep nothing back from you."

After having spoken thus he looked down once more at the bloody form of the man whom all his wisdom and generosity and hopefulness had not helped to rule a stiff-necked people. Giving loud voice to their praise and gratitude the men escorted him into Gedaliah's house, where he was to lodge with his disciple. That evening, while the lamp was still burning, Baruch seated himself beside Jeremiah's couch and tempted him.

"Of what use is it to pray so much," he asked, "and beseech the Lord with your pleading, since we both know what is best and what alone is to the advantage of this Remnant? Let them abide in the land, that this people may not wholly disappear. The King of Babylon will not change his mind because of Gedaliah. He has had enough of us and more than enough, and he wants but one thing—to hear no more of us. Let Jeremiah go to them in the morning and say: 'Abide in the land!' "

Jeremiah had sat up and was regarding Baruch with an intense look, half in anger and half in mockery.

"O shrewd Baruch!" he said. "You still have much to learn. How vividly you remind me now of the day when you stood among the sons of Ahikam in the Temple and were ashamed of my yoke, being so vain of your own wisdom! That is what distinguished me from you, from you and the sons of Shaphan. You always knew what would befall on the morrow. Only I, the prophet, did not know. If I were to send you with a message, would you announce something that I had not said? . . . I see that you understand! . . . Shall I then pretend to these unhappy men that word has come to me, only because I think I know the right way and wish with all my heart that it may be taken? Go to your couch and sleep! But because you have tempted me I will remain awake and entreat advice of the Lord."

For ten days and ten nights Jeremiah took little food and almost completely conquered sleep. He lay on the bare floor and prayed to the Lord as he had promised, beseeching an answer. The Lord held aloof and refused to listen to his supplication, seeming even to take pleasure in probing to the depths the sincerity of the one man on earth who was faithful to Him. Only on the tenth evening, when Jeremiah was at the point of collapse, did he hear the clear voice speaking to him.

When the sun rose again Jeremiah went out to Johanan and the rest of the people in order to communicate to them the words of God. But first he asked them:

"Did you not swear to me that you would obey the voice of the Lord, whether it be good or whether it be evil?"

"We swore it to you and called upon the Lord to be a witness between us!" some of them cried out. Jeremiah looked far over the heads of the crowd as he began to prophesy:

"Thus saith the Lord, the God of Israel! . . . If ye will still abide in this land, then will I build you, and not pull you down, and I will plant you, and not pluck you up. . . . Be not afraid of the King of Babylon, of whom ye are afraid. . . . But if ye say, We will not dwell in this land, but we will go into the land of Egypt, where we shall see no war, nor hear the sound of the trumpet, nor have hunger of bread, and there will we dwell: now therefore hear the word of the Lord, O ye Remnant of Judah, go ye not into Egypt! . . . But know that ye dissemble in your hearts if ye first demand to hear the voice of the Lord and then do not obey. . . ."

After these clear words there was an embarrassed silence, which soon changed to an agitated tumult, for during the past ten days the scales had been turned in favour of their journeying to Egypt, the most eager advocate of this course being Johanan. The latter spoke harshly to the prophet, just as the Kings of Judah had done in their time.

"Your ways are difficult, Jeremiah," he reproached him,

"for never to this day have you spoken that which you should have spoken. The Lord your God seems to delight in opposing everything which seems to our judgment good to do. What pledge have we that Babylon will give us peace and will not seek vengeance? The word of the Lord your God? It is a word formed by your own lips. If Babylon should seek vengeance, then you have only to plead that you did not hear aright. But in the pleasant House of Bondage we shall be certain of peace."

"You speak falsely!" cried a certain Azariah, another of the spokesmen. "The Lord our God has not sent you to say, Go not into Egypt, to sojourn there. But Baruch, the son of Neriah, sets you on against us, for to deliver us into the hand of the Chaldeans, that they might put us to death, and carry us away captives into Babylon."

Jeremiah stood silent among them as they argued and disputed, as if all this was no concern of his. When the men's wrath had exhausted itself, he said with a strange indifference:

"Remnant of Judah, I will not contend with you, for you do not err against me, but against your own souls. You have decided. Do as seems fitting unto you and prepare for your journey."

Johanan, however, seized Jeremiah firmly with both hands as if he intended to take him prisoner.

"Yes, we shall quickly prepare for our journey," he cried, "but we shall take you with us into the House of Bondage . . . as a pledge of the Lord your God!"

Jeremiah shook him off contemptuously and said very wearily:

"No need is there for you to compel me, since I go with you of my own accord and will lead you. For this is my task.

Where you are, there too must I be. But when you are down there in Tahpanhes and in Noph, you will melt away and become shades of the underworld, never to return."

With these words he turned away and left them in their bewilderment. In his heart he felt an unfamiliar and terrifying satisfaction because the Remnant had rejected the Lord's last offer.

Jeremiah and Baruch sat at the place where they had often rested or taken leave of each other. Their former farewells had been for only short periods of separation, but their parting now was to be for ever. Behind them stretched the hills of Anathoth. Little more remained of Hilkiah's estate than the ancient wall by which it had been surrounded. That morning Jeremiah had been unable to turn his eyes away from the breach in the wall as though he longed to climb over it as he had so often done, that he might wander through his devastated property. Then he had hurried past as if it were forbidden him, without visiting the grave of his parents or seeking to discover the dwelling place of Hanameel.

The warm gold of a mild autumnal day enveloped the resting travellers. The sun was climbing to its zenith and all the shadows in the lost land were tinged with a melancholy purple. Baruch knew that their parting was inevitable. Long since, his master had revealed to him that he, Jeremiah, had been commanded to abide with the Remnant, with the lees and the dregs, who would soon be journeying to the House of Bondage, where they would be submerged for ever. In view of what had been done and said at Mizpah, neither Jeremiah nor Baruch doubted any longer. The Remnant were what they had always been and could not be changed; they were the dross that remained in the furnace. The purifying fire, the glowing, unalloyed metal, were in Babylon, for the Lord journeyed with the exiles. Jeremiah, however, had been cast among the dross. He shared the fate of the Remnant and was not allowed to enter the new place of sojourning, but had been thrust back from its frontiers. Yet though he had already been engulfed with the Remnant, was there any reason why Baruch too should be swallowed up in Egypt? Baruch had encountered no prohibition like that terrible "Turn back!" which, for one whose only desire was to go forward, was like a mortal blow. The captives in Babylon needed such men as Baruch, for as Jeremiah's disciple he was looked upon with favour by Marduk and would be able, like no other, to help and prepare the way. Therefore the prophet had decided to release his disciple from their lifelong covenant and to send him to Babylon, that he might turn his experience with Jeremiah to advantage and employ his knowledge in separating the noble metal from the dross. Baruch was horrified at Jeremiah's intention and till the last minute he protested with all his strength against leaving his master.

"It is true that I am your disciple," he argued, "but how many years do I still lack until I shall be as old as you? There are but six or seven. I am not fitted for this new task either. Let me journey quietly with the Remnant, Jeremiah, that we may remain together as we have always done."

Jeremiah wrinkled his brows:

"It cannot be, Baruch. Cease to torture me, for you hurt me deeply. I must go down to the land where we shall be submerged and effaced. But to you it is granted to complete my work."

"To complete your work!" Baruch burst into a laugh. "Who am I that I should complete your work, I who cannot even make a beginning? When you commanded, I obeyed.

When you taught, I listened. When you spoke, I wrote down your words. Whom shall I obey henceforth? To whom shall I listen? Whose words shall I write down?"

"Your ears are full of words and will be so to the end, Baruch!"

Baruch flushed and cried with a stifled voice:

"That is what I mean . . . without Jeremiah there can be no Baruch! . . ."

"And Jeremiah?" asked the other very softly, and he too grew red. Then they were both silent for a long time and did not look at each other, but gazed far out towards the hills of Jerusalem. Jeremiah was the first to break the silence. He asked a question which often comes to the lips of old married people:

"Of what are you thinking?"

Baruch began to rock his body as if he were praying.

"I am thinking of that Passover night," he murmured in a grief-stricken voice, "when I waited for you at the gate of the Temple. It was a long time before you came, for you had been chosen not only to serve at the King's table but also to be a witness in the sanctuary. I was very cold, for there was a cool night breeze. When you came out of the gate you hung your cloak round the boy's shoulders. How often have you wrapped me in the cloak of your solicitude since that time! I remember clearly that midnight ride. The star of Ashtaroth, the Queen of Heaven, was so large and bright! I spoke to you of what I had read and studied during the day, while I waited idly in the city. Of the boy Samuel and of Eli, your forefather, who lay on his couch in the Temple and slept. I still remember the words: 'And the word of the Lord was precious in those days, there was no open vision. . . .' This place, Jeremiah, is where your ass shied."

Jeremiah passed his hand thoughtfully over the grass.

"There is a particular reason why you should remember that night, Baruch. The boy who followed behind me was my forerunner. At that time you knew more about me, though you were only sixteen years old, than I knew myself. It was the Lord who set you to spur on your older friend. And thus, in your innocence, you became my first awakener and guiding spirit. But neither of us knew whither my awakening was to lead us."

Baruch beat his breast with both fists and cried aloud:

"Woe is me now, for the Lord hath added grief to my sorrow! I fainted in my sighing and I find no rest."

Jeremiah turned to his afflicted disciple and gazed at him intently. Then he said slowly:

"The Lord saith thus, 'Behold, that which I have built will I break down, and that which I have planted I will pluck up, even this whole land.' And seek you great things for yourself? Seek them not. The Lord who has brought such great evil upon all flesh will give you your life for a prey. For it has been promised to you that your life will be given unto you for a prey in all places whither you go."

"I do not want this prey!" cried Baruch, his anger overcoming his tears.

To this Jeremiah made no reply, but let his hand rest on Baruch's knee until the time of parting had come, then he rose slowly to make his last journey up to the desolate Daughter of Zion and the ruins of the Temple before going down into Egypt. Baruch's way led in the opposite direction, through Ramah into Babylon. The two men, now grey-haired, embraced briefly and laid their cheeks together. Their hearts were so deeply stirred that they were at a loss for words. So that his reserve might not break down, Jeremiah spoke as if he believed what he did not believe: "Who knows, perhaps it may please God that we shall meet again? . . ."

"Who knows?" whispered Baruch roughly, to hide his emotion. Then they parted and neither of them looked back.

33

In the Temple

WITH the exception of the outer rings of Ephraim and Benjamin, which had been demolished immediately after the fall of the city, the walls of Jerusalem were still standing. The Babylonians took their time in razing the fortifications and other buildings to the ground. First of all they were waiting for the flesh of those who had been slain in battle or had died of plague, and whose bodies were lying everywhere in the streets and houses, to rot from the bones so that the pestilence should not spread. Throughout the land the sky was alive with flocks of carrion fowl flying from one feast to another, but over Zion they were massed in one black, permanent cloud. The birds of the air had to share their prey with the ravening beasts of the field, and Marduk's idle army of occupation, which had pitched its camp at a cautious distance from the walls, welcomed the scavenging work of the lynx, the fox, and the wild dog; the wolf, the jackal, and the hyena. Only when nothing remained but skeletons, and the air was free from the taint of death, could the Babylonians begin their final task of destruction.

The army had been left under the command of a general, a morose, elderly man, who was greatly vexed at having been appointed to the not particularly honourable post of watching over this city of putrefaction. He and his warriors envied those of their comrades who were on duty in the plains or had already returned to Babylon. When Nergal had to undertake the work of Ninurtu, he regarded it as a blow to his pride and experienced a sense of disquiet. The ill-humoured commander had taken up his quarters in one of the pavilions of the royal gardens outside the walls, and everyone who for any reason whatsoever wished to enter the doomed city had first to see him and obtain his permission. He sat, helmeted and in full armour, in front of the pavilion and rejected every request without exception, even when a son begged to be allowed to seek his father's corpse. Jerusalem was a forbidden city. Its very stones were destined for destruction and belonged not to the exiled people, but to Babylon. Babylon, however, suspected that considerable treasure still lay hidden there, in spite of the fact that an unremitting search had been conducted for twenty-eight days after the end of the siege, for the God of Jacob and the citizens of Jerusalem had the reputation of being exceedingly wealthy. Every corner of the Temple Mount had been dug up and laid bare in the hope of finding gold and jewels there, and the same had been done with the other hills on which the foundations of Zion rested. It was only when the search was concluded that they had set the city on fire in seventy different places. But the city was large, and when the conflagration had quenched its first pangs of hunger its appetite seemed to diminish and it spread more slowly. Even after many days there were glowing embers everywhere. Here and there a flame would suddenly spring up, and over the site of the Temple hung a thick veil of smoke.

When Jeremiah came to the commander of the Babylonians with his request to be allowed to enter Jerusalem, he was not turned away. The general had spent three years with the besieging army and knew that Marduk had singled out the celebrated prophet of an alien god for special favour. He therefore even brought himself to reply to Jeremiah's greeting of peace with a surly growl, but despite the granting of this unique concession he was cautious enough to offer an escort of two armed soldiers—as a protection, he declared, against the wild beasts that prowled about in the evening. The escort, however, was intended less for the safety of the strange man of Judah than for that of any hidden treasures that might be known only to the priests. Jeremiah declined the offer of protection, but the commander made up his mind to have him secretly watched.

"Why have you come? What are you seeking in the Temple?" he inquired with ill-concealed suspicion.

"An answer!" returned Jeremiah calmly. The Babylonian was puzzled by this laconic reply, yet it removed his fears concerning the intentions of the prophet. He decided that Jeremiah was a dull-witted person who, like all people of his type, was more interested in words than in material things and was therefore unlikely to constitute a danger. He signed to the sentry to allow him to pass.

Jeremiah's first shock was when he saw the desecrated graves of the royal family. The Babylonians had assumed that the sons of David were buried with the ostentation due to their rank, but they had been deeply disappointed when they found no little gold chariots and thrones, none of the hundreds of precious and elegant trifles that they had expected to discover in the tombs of the Kings of Judah. Such lack of pomp, which they regarded as evidence either of miserliness or of contempt for the dead, filled the seekers after loot with rage, and they took their revenge by strewing the bones on the ground, though even in their eyes this was sacrilege. With his head covered Jeremiah quickly walked past the scene of desecration. The skulls and bones of the Kings who had ruled since the days of David, whether they had been wise or wicked, lay mingled in confusion. Jeremiah thought of the five Kings of Judah whom he had known. Four of them he had served faithfully. Only Coniah and Zedekiah still lived out their miserable lives, both of them in chains, one of them blinded. With beating heart Jeremiah passed through this place of judgment, where the earth had cast up the bones of the House of David.

At the first step he took through the gate to enter the city, he was met by the suffocating, pestilential odour of rotting flesh and charred ruins. Zion, joyful Zion on its height, had been transformed into a stinking pit of decay, into one vast Cistern of the King's Son, only a thousand times more abominable. "Yes," he thought, "Thou hast hurled down into the pit the Daughter of Zion in her purple robes who was like the young Hamutal, the gaily adorned, voluptuous Daughter of Zion with her painted eyebrows and gilded nails. What are the visions of night, however vivid, compared with this vision of horror that I see by the golden, serene light of day? I prophesied and cried out and painted for them a picture of what was to come, I warned them again and again, but the visions of fear that Thou didst awaken in me, O Lord, were but a pale shadow compared with this, compared with *this* fulfilment! I hastened through this very street and in my fear I cried amidst the jeers of the urchins who followed me: 'Consider ye, and call for the mourning women, that they may come, and send for cunning women, that they may come! And let them make haste, and take up a wailing for us, that our eyes may run down with tears, and our eyelids gush out with waters!' Yea, Thou hast sent them swiftly, the mourning women! With a flapping of wings, a croaking, and a screeching, they fly high above me. How faithfully dost Thou keep Thy promise! The carcasses of men have fallen like dung upon the open field, like sheaves of corn they lie behind the advancing reaper and there is none to gather them. Alas, not only hast Thou kept Thy word, but Thou hast fulfilled it tenfold! Until the eleventh hour I hoped that there was exaggeration in Thee as there is in the words of men. Verily, now is death come up into their windows and is entered into their palaces, to cut off the children from without and the young men from the streets. These delights of their mothers, sweet-smelling flesh of life, milk and blood without blemish, lovely hands and feet, little limbs full of grace, hast Thou planted them but to crush them again? I plead with Thee that Thou answer me, and this day I will not yield. For the last time I enter Thy dwelling place, which the enemy has destroyed and desecrated, that I may hear and see and know! With clenched teeth I force my way through this hell, that is no realm of dreams like the region of Aapep in Amenti, but a reality from which there is no awakening!"

Without pausing Jeremiah continued on his way. Of all the journeys he had taken this was the most difficult, difficult for his feet and difficult for his soul. He could move but slowly through the heaps of stones and crumbling ruins, which blocked every street and rendered it unfamiliar. Often he did not know whether he was walking along a road or through the houses themselves. It was as if the Babylonian general had barred every way but this out of deliberate malice, so that Jeremiah should be compelled to traverse the whole city from the south in order to reach the palace and the Temple. Everywhere was destruction, and he was not spared the sight of a single iota. His terrible journey led him up and down, for sometimes he had to climb to the first floor of a house or crawl through a gap in a fallen heap of masonry before he could proceed farther along a street that was no longer a street. At every step his foot stumbled or was caught in a crevice. Venomous green tendrils were already twining round the stones, as if they sprang from a foul bog. Now and then he trod on something soft and slippery, and his very soul shuddered at the realization that here amid the rubble lay the children of Rachel, twisted and misshapen, their black, swollen faces staring up to the heavens with white teeth that seemed to grin mockingly. Each of these dead children of Rachel was an implacable question addressed to the inscrutable Zebaoth, and Jeremiah included all the questions in his own. His step hardly disturbed the vultures with their long, reddish, scraggy necks and ruffled plumage. They merely hopped a little to one side and resumed their feasting. The low, sleek crupper of a gorged hyena slunk swiftly by from time to time like an obscene thought. Many houses showed signs of having been taken by surprise, for the tables were laid with cups and plates. Terror had come unawares to seize an intimate scene in its paralysing grip, and only the overturned chairs bore witness to the panic of their occupants as they tried in vain to flee.

At last Jeremiah had passed through the lower town, which was like the lower world, and stood in front of the south gate of the palace. Here the Babylonians had hastily brought up their ordnance and torn great breaches in the walls. The gate itself was in ruins, and on all sides could be seen traces of the final battle in which the royal bodyguard had offered desperate resistance to the victorious enemy. Spears, lances, arrows, and stones from catapults littered the ground; the white paving was dyed and patterned with black blood.

But Jeremiah was able to breathe more freely. The Babylonians had been cautious enough to fling the bodies of the slain down into the Valley of Kidron and burn them on a pyre, so that the treasure-seekers might not be disturbed at their work by the stench of decay and fear of pestilence. Jeremiah walked through the gateway and saw the thousand-year-old beams of cedar from the shattered House of the Forest of Lebanon still glimmering and smoking. The hall of judgment and the throne-room, the offices, the living quarters, the House of Pharaoh's Daughter, the annexes, stables, storehouses, guard-rooms, and towers were charred heaps of ruins and rubble, from which an occasional flame leapt up. In the court of the guard, where he had once lived as a prisoner, Jeremiah sat down to rest. Calmly he gazed around and thought how small in its hour of destruction was that which had seemed to him so great while it still stood. A house torn down, even though it was one of Marduk's palaces, was more frightening in its insignificance than the grave. It revealed how tiny was the space that man was able to cover with all his tumultuous activity and transient power.

Suddenly Jeremiah grew angry with himself for having promised Baruch, as the most precious gift that could be granted to him on this mortal earth, that he would have his life "for a prey." All at once he understood why his disciple had fiercely rejected the Lord's offer. It was a pitiful promise! To have nothing for a prey but this life, to be permitted for a few more days or years to drag out an existence amid the pervading stench of putrefaction after having served the Lord so arduously, after having undergone so much affliction and seen so much futility! As he sat there among the ruins of the palace, Jeremiah began to seek converse with God concerning his task:

"Verily Thou hast employed me in Thy service and hast not given me leave to abandon my work. When I renounced my task in the days when I dwelt at Noph, Thou didst refuse to release me. Lord, I bear Thee no grudge on that account, for I was Thy servant. I will not again fall into fruitless pleading as in days of old. I have withstood all temptations, and I accept and yield willingly that which Thou dost give and demand. I have conquered the strongest desire of my heart and go not to Babylon with the living, but to Egypt with the dead, since Thou hast commanded it. Yet there is one thing, Lord, which I do not understand concerning the love which is in Thee. Thou dost command us in Thy Law to deal justly with our bondservants, but with me hast Thou dealt as harshly as the law-breakers in Israel have dealt with their slaves. Forgive me, Lord, if I speak foolishly in my heart, for the words do not pass beyond my lips. I do not complain because Thou didst send me forth and did not spare me, saying: 'Go hither and go thither! Speak this and speak that!' I went forth and I spoke, and they put me in the stocks and the dungeons and the stinking pit. A thousand times more would I have been willing to do and endure if only it had borne but a little fruit. The body which Thou hast created cannot exist without food, and the soul which Thou hast created cannot exist if it does not receive its recompense. Thou hast nourished my soul with futility from the beginning, and now that the day of judgment has come Thou dost give me nothing but my bare life for a prey. Yet this cannot be my recompense, for it would be worse than no recompense. Every time Thou hast employed me in Thy service, Thou hast spoken with a clear and distinct voice. But when I pleaded with Thee, I, Jeremiah, who am but frail and poor, then didst Thou hold aloof from my love and hold no converse with me. Dost Thou hear me, Lord, crying to Thee silently from this destruction? I cry for an answer, for a sign of Thy love after all this evil that Thou hast brought upon the living who came into the world without their seeking! Now I will summon up my strength and enter Thy destroyed and desecrated House for the last time before I go down with the lost shades to the shadows of the western land. When I enter Thy dishonoured and desolated House and approach Thy Holy of Holies like the High Priest, then grant me my recompense, then reveal Thyself to me, I beseech Thee, O Lord!"

Jeremiah rose up from where he sat. The tremendous recompense that he had demanded was far more than a vision and far more than a prophecy. He did not dare even to imagine what it might be. Slowly he left the debris-strewn court and came to the Gate of the Bodyguard, which had suffered but little damage.

All the time the Temple had stood, no one had ever entered the sanctuary alone. Jeremiah was the first soul to approach the House of the Lord, now lying in ruins, unaccompanied by attendant priests. He was as completely alone as he had been in his vision of the Cup of Fury, when as High Priest he received and entertained his beast-shaped guests. Then the leaden twilight of the end of the world had lain over Mount Moriah, while now the sky was filling with an ever-deepening gold. Jeremiah, the last of a priestly race, was acutely conscious of every step he took as he passed solemnly through the Temple. In the outer courtyard the columns of the surrounding galleries were for the most part still standing, but the roof had collapsed. Everywhere he saw charred and smoking beams. In their search for treasure the men of Babylon had prised up the flagstones and wrecked the chambers of the priests and scribes. Even the pulpits of the prophets had been torn down in the hope of finding hidden gold. Jeremiah crossed the shattered gallery and then he took the shoes from his feet. He was standing in the inner court of the priests. He felt a constriction of the heart as he saw that the great altar of burnt offerings had been taken away. The sacred rock, on which Abraham had not hesitated to sacrifice his beloved son, rose up naked from the earth. The sight of the bare rock of sacrifice filled his soul with horror as if at the uncovering of dead men's bones. The Molten Sea with its twelve brazen oxen had vanished. It had presumably found favour in Marduk's appreciative eyes, as had Boaz and Jachin, the brass pillars with their pomegranate capitals that sparkled in the light of the sun and the moon. A faint, sluggish flame licked the roof of the central sanctuary itself. With pickaxes and crowbars the Babylonians had destroyed the two wings with their twice nine and ninety treasure chambers. Between high-piled heaps of rubble yawned deep cavities that had been fenced off and were surrounded by scaffolding. The walls of the sanctuary itself were intact. Marduk had ordered special precautions to be taken to avoid damaging the precious panelling within, the exquisite cedarwood carving, and the thin, finely wrought plates of gold. Even the flooring of sandalwood, which had been fitted without the use of nail or rivet, and the ceiling of oleaster, which never lost its fragrance, had been carefully removed. Only the roof timbers, massive beams of pine, still glowed and crackled high above Jeremiah's head.

The last priest to enter the House of the Lord had to summon up all his courage, for in the terrifying solitude of desolation that surrounded him he was stricken with awe. With violently beating heart Jeremiah set his foot upon the steps leading to the threshold of the chambers that enclosed the divine dwelling place. At that moment he was oblivious of everything. He had forgotten the desecration of the sanctuary. He had forgotten that for a long time the Temple had meant little to him. He had forgotten even his unyielding resolve to insist on an answer that should be more than a vision or a prophecy. He was again the youth of that Passover night, long ago, who had been singled out to be a witness and to look into the Holy of Holies. Once more he saw the sanctuary. Three lingering rays of the sun poured through the charred roof-beams and lit up a high, bleak chamber with bare walls and bare floor from which the pliant sandalwood surface had been detached. A cold, lofty barn of grey stone! Gone was the candelabrum, gone was the golden altar where the incense had smoked, gone was the table with the holy bread. Even the four-coloured curtain of fine tissue was no longer there. A hole in the wall showed where once had been the door that led to the Holy of Holies.

Jeremiah approached hesitantly. His hands twitched. He wanted to cover his head as custom had demanded, but he did not do so. Drawing a deep breath, he stepped over the broken threshold. The Holy of Holies was no longer wrapped in the darkness that had been before creation. Through the gaps in the glowing roof, high above his head, filtered the sullen light of the sinking sun. Yet the primal gloom that had so long enveloped the Holy of Holies was not entirely gone. It had changed to a deep and awe-inspiring twilight. In the heart of this twilight there was nothing. The supreme and only tangible sanctuary that Israel possessed, the Ark with the tablets of Sinai, had vanished without trace. The inmost chamber of the Lord's dwelling place was as empty as the hearts of the defeated people. Not even a fragment of charred wood lay on the ground. Jeremiah, walking backwards, was about to depart, when a thought flashed through his mind that rooted him to the spot. Was he not the High Priest in the midst of this destruction? Was he not standing here in the Holy of Holies in the interval between the two "terrible days," the Day of Judgment and the Day of Atonement, which the shattered people could no longer celebrate? Jeremiah slowly covered his head to do what the High Priest, with covered head and trembling voice, had done once every year in that place. He opened his mouth and called aloud the true and unutterable name of God, the name which men were forbidden to speak:

"JHVH!"

J: the creating hand! H: the light of the beginning, from which all things flowed! V: the binding arms of time and space! H: the light of the end, to which all things returned!

Jeremiah had uttered as an invocation the brief syllables which comprised within themselves the Creator and the whole sum of the universe. For the first time his lips had formed the name whose fearful truth no man could fathom. When he again uncovered his head, he was exhausted and breathless as if he had been running. The light had turned to a reddish purple and he could feel that the atmosphere of the chamber had changed. He looked about him in trepidation, not knowing the cause of the transformation. Suddenly something seemed to call to him with penetrating urgency from the ground. He saw a faint shimmer, no larger than the palm of his hand, and he bent down. It was a fragment of stone. At first he thought that he had picked up a piece of the broken wall, but when he perceived how strangely it burned his skin as he touched it, he knew what he was holding in his hand. The Babylonians had smashed the tablets of Sinai on which the Lord had engraved His commandments. He had sent a fragment of the lost tablets to Jeremiah as an answer!

Jeremiah left the Holy of Holies and the court of the priests as if he was in a trance. At the outer steps of the gallery he leaned against one of the columns while everything reeled before his eyes. He looked closely at the fragment of stone, but could not understand what he saw written there. The ancient symbols, carved deep in the basalt, could not readily be deciphered. The red tinge in the sky deepened. Curiously shaped letters, torn from their context, covered the divine fragment, but in their midst, clear and distinct, was revealed the answer that was more than a vision and more than a prophecy:

". . . That thy days may be long . . ."

Jeremiah felt a shock of disappointment. Was the Lord giving him the same answer that he himself had given to Baruch? Was he, too, to be fobbed off with the trumpery promise that his own life would be spared when all else was being destroyed? His fingers began to tighten round the fragment of stone. But the Lord did not let His sanctified prophet suffer any longer. He revealed the purport of His answer in a flash of illumination such as Jeremiah had never before experienced. "That thy days may be long!" This did not mean: "So that thou shalt live a few years longer!" It meant: "I have done this thing to thee so that thou shalt prevail over death. I have executed judgment on Israel, so that it may rise again. From my hand springs only life, therefore how couldst thou, who art sprung from my hand, die and thy life have been in vain? I have created judgment and death to be a sieve. For Israel shall become more and more alive through death, and more and more pure through my judgment. Thou hast called upon my name, and I have answered thee by causing to sink into thy heart the certainty that Israel will survive, for thy time is rooted in my time. Look not around upon all this horror! Look upon the sign that I have sent thee in the midst of all this horror: 'That thy days may be long!' Thou hast suffered so that thou couldst become mine, so that I could become thine. Each defeat makes the victory greater. That the days of Israel may be long! Thou canst not exhaust the abundance of this promise."

No voice gave utterance to this illumination of a divine strategy that spanned eternity. It was a sudden awareness, an inexpressible and pervading assurance of ultimate victory, which filled Jeremiah's mind with a confused exultation.

He concealed the fragment of stone near his heart. The inexhaustible promise would be carried down to Egypt: "That thy days may be long!" At his breast the stone burned like fire, but it imbued him with such a glorious sensation of well-being that he would gladly have been consumed by it. His eyes brimmed over with rapture at the certitude of salvation. In none of the ecstatic moments of his life had he really been able to "rejoice with the Lord." Dimly he realized that now, for the first and only time in his life, he was experiencing something of this joy. Once more the setting sun blazed up, and Jeremiah held his hand before his eyes to shield them from the excess of light in which everything was steeped. Round his wrist he still wore the leather band, enclosing the amulet, which his mother had given to him. How long ago? Had it been that morning? Had countless ages passed since then?

Epilogue

At the Site of the Temple *(Incipit vita nova)*

THE man who was holding his wrist-watch close to his eyes saw that it was still twenty-three minutes to six and not a minute later. The sun was setting and the dome of the Mosque of Omar was flooded with purple.

"Why do you keep staring at your watch, Reeves?" asked a woman's voice, not without a certain apprehension and solicitude. The near-sighted Clayton Reeves realized then for the first time that, fearing he might fall, he had taken off his spectacles and was still holding them in his hand. He put them on again, and the world seemed to change. Dignified Moslems were ascending the steps and pacing past the pillared arch in front of which he and Dorothy Cowell stood side by side. She was pale, but into his face a healthier colour was coming as the seconds passed.

It had grown cold; Dorothy shivered in her light dress. With a show of eager interest that concealed her uneasiness she repeated what he had been telling her before he tore off his spectacles and stared at his watch as if he were dazed:

"Up here, from west to east, stretched the Temple of Solomon and the Temple of Herod, in which Christ preached. Why did you break off? Go on, I am listening. . . ."

Reeves gazed for a while at his companion with an air of remote friendliness, then he took a deep breath and said: "No! Let us go now!"

Silently they crossed the spacious Haram esh Sherif. On the following day began the Moslem feast of Bairam and the sacred precincts presented a colourful picture. But Reeves hardly saw the brightly clad figures that thronged the place. He walked past them with his shoulders thrust forward, his step swift and elastic. The first thing that had become clear to him was that the attack, the anticipation of which had caused him so many hours of tortured anxiety, had not taken place. The "absence" which he had experienced a few minutes before had not been that terrible loss of his ego with which he was familiar, but something new and wonderful. Intuitively he felt that his malady had been conquered by what had happened to him, that by some unknown healing agency the chaos within him had been turned to order. He thought again how he had swooned when, as a child, he first saw the sea as a wall towering up to the sky. Now he felt assured that he would never again succumb to his infirmity, that in the months since Leonora's death he had developed the power to resist the dark forces which threatened him and to sublimate them in creative work. In the corners of his eyes he felt with surprise the frozen tears of the ecstasy which had possessed him as he looked so fixedly at his watch a little while before. For what seemed countless ages he had despaired of that which was now granted to him. The feeling of happiness that came from an overflowing mind! The joy of taut nerves! A hundred characters, incidents, and ideas had been conceived in a single flash. What no logic, industry, or insight could have achieved was now his inalienable possession. He began feverishly to marshal the thoughts that thronged to his mind.

They had passed through the arcades and the gateway, and were now at the steps that led down to the old city. Dorothy paused and touched Clayton's hand, which had lost its icy coldness. His face, too, had changed and become animated; he looked younger. She made up her mind to ask him the question that had been worrying her:

"I was quite frightened, Reeves. What was the matter with you a few minutes ago? Were you feeling ill?"

"I thought I was going to be, Dorothy." He took her by the arm and drew her along a little impatiently. "I was afraid of an attack while you were with me; that is to say, I was afraid that I might faint. . . ." He hesitated, searching for the right words. "It was nothing, thank God! I am not ill. I think your prediction is going to come true. I am going to write again. As we were standing up there, something flashed into my mind. . . ."

"When you looked at your watch?"

He nodded silently. She did not speak either, but swallowed the word "inspiration," which had been on the tip of her tongue. The joy and fullness of his mind did not grow less. What he had seen during a moment of time as he stood on the site of the Temple was inexplicably gathered within him, even though he was no longer conscious of the thousand details. His soul had produced a perfect fabric, which he felt as something tangible and almost physically existent. He had only to touch one thread and an inexhaustible sequence of pictures would begin to unwind. He was well aware that his months of laborious study of the Bible had had no small share in shaping that which had come into his mind. Yet something else, something that was not written down and could not be learned from books, had taken possession of him as he stood on the broad steps that led to the court of the priests in the ancient Temple. Was it Cartwright's *akâsha*, the all-embracing chronicle, the mysterious picture-ether which condensed like a cloud over places that were saturated with history? Or was it something deeper, something more personal, a warning voice, a calling home, an answer which concerned him alone? He could not yet tell. But his whole being glowed with a fruitful eagerness to hasten to his lodging, where he could sit at his table and with impetuous hand, so that nothing might be lost, fashion the work that was already complete within him. It was not only that the work he wanted to create was already complete within him, but he himself was steady and courageous as he had never been before. For the first time he had unflinchingly confronted the whole truth about himself, and it had endowed him with a certitude that filled him with a hitherto unknown power.

In the crowded bazaars they had to slacken their pace; nevertheless Reeves thrust his way ruthlessly through the throng, and Dorothy had difficulty in keeping by his side. She still carried her hat in her hand, and he looked at her dark hair with the grey streak which invested her youthful appearance with a touch both of authority and of sadness. Suddenly, with a sidelong glance and smiling uncertainly, he said:

"I am really very grateful to you, Dorothy, that we . . . that you stayed with me . . . a little while ago. . . ."

She answered him softly:

"From now on you are going to do great things, Clayton."

"I can hardly wait to get down to work," was all he said. Dorothy, however, knew that in those few minutes Leonora had ceased to have a part in Clayton's soul. The dead woman had withdrawn to the place where the departed tarry when earthly love has conquered its loss. Dorothy felt almost pity for the wan wraith. They did not speak again until they stood before the brilliantly lit King David Hotel. In the last rays of the setting sun the tall minaret of the Citadel of Zion shot blackly towards the sky. Hesitantly Dorothy began:

"You need not answer me, Clayton, if you do not want to . . . but I have been thinking that what came into your mind when we were at the site of the Temple must have had some connexion with the Bible. . . ."

He was silent and thought for a while before he admitted:

"Yes. It was Jeremiah the prophet!"

"I don't know much about him," said the journalist, with a dubious look in her eyes. "My religious education has been neglected. Tell me about him!"

Clayton Reeves lowered his eyes. He seemed to be struggling to control a strangely militant anger.

"Jeremiah was a sensitive man, who was implacably opposed to his world and his age. Though he was timid, even the evident and potent iniquities of this earth could not vanquish him. For he obeyed none other than the voice of God, which spoke to him and within him. . . ."

He knew that these words revealed but the barest fraction of his actual experience. It would, indeed, be one of his future tasks to show that greatness is consistent only with running counter to the world and never with acceptance of it; that the eternally defeated are the eternally victorious; and that the Voice is more real than the clamour that seeks to drown it. He was filled with a joy of the spirit, for he knew that the Voice speaks with its primal power unquenched. It spoke to him and within him. Only he must attune his inward ear more keenly that it might listen with incorruptible integrity to the unique Truth.

A chill wind rose suddenly. Dorothy shivered and felt ill at ease, though she herself could not have said why. Clayton Reeves seemed to become more of a stranger to her every minute. The plate-glass windows of the luxurious hotel shone brilliantly in the deepening night. Dorothy looked longingly towards the brightly lit interior.

"Shall we go in? The others are waiting. . . ."

"Good-bye, Dorothy," said Reeves, and he took her hand. "I am not going in to meet the others. . . . I have found myself and must make a new beginning. . . ."